DEC 10 '81

D0742281

TERTELING LIBRARY
THE COLLEGE OF IDAHO
CALDWELL, IDAHO

PS1303
E17

111707

The Works of Mark Twain

VOLUME 15

EARLY TALES & SKETCHES

VOLUME 2 (1864–1865)

Editorial work for this volume has been made possible by a generous grant from the Editing Program of the National Endowment for the Humanities, an independent federal agency.

TERTELING LIBRARY
THE COLLEGE OF IDAHO
CALDWELL, IDAHO

THE WORKS OF MARK TWAIN

The following volumes in this edition of Mark Twain's previously published works have been issued to date:

ROUGHING IT
edited by Franklin R. Rogers and Paul Baender

WHAT IS MAN? AND OTHER PHILOSOPHICAL WRITINGS
edited by Paul Baender

THE ADVENTURES OF TOM SAWYER
TOM SAWYER ABROAD
TOM SAWYER, DETECTIVE
edited by John C. Gerber, Paul Baender, and Terry Firkins

THE PRINCE AND THE PAUPER
edited by Victor Fischer and Lin Salamo,
with the assistance of Mary Jane Jones

A CONNECTICUT YANKEE IN KING ARTHUR'S COURT
edited by Bernard L. Stein
with an introduction by Henry Nash Smith

EARLY TALES & SKETCHES, VOLUME 1 (1851–1864)
EARLY TALES & SKETCHES, VOLUME 2 (1864–1865)
edited by Edgar M. Branch and Robert H. Hirst,
with the assistance of Harriet Elinor Smith

The Works of Mark Twain

Editorial Board

JOHN C. GERBER, *CHAIRMAN*

PAUL BAENDER

WALTER BLAIR

WILLIAM M. GIBSON

General Editor of
The Works of Mark Twain
and
The Mark Twain Papers

ROBERT H. HIRST

The Works of Mark Twain

EARLY TALES
& SKETCHES

VOLUME 2
1864-1865

Edited by
EDGAR MARQUESS BRANCH and ROBERT H. HIRST

With the Assistance of
HARRIET ELINOR SMITH

PUBLISHED FOR
THE IOWA CENTER FOR TEXTUAL STUDIES
BY THE
UNIVERSITY OF CALIFORNIA PRESS
BERKELEY, LOS ANGELES, LONDON
1981

PS1303
E17
v. 2

CENTER FOR EDITIONS OF
AMERICAN AUTHORS
AN APPROVED TEXT
MODERN LANGUAGE
ASSOCIATION OF AMERICA

UNIVERSITY OF CALIFORNIA PRESS
BERKELEY AND LOS ANGELES, CALIFORNIA

UNIVERSITY OF CALIFORNIA PRESS, LTD.
LONDON, ENGLAND

PREVIOUSLY UNPUBLISHED MATERIAL BY MARK TWAIN
© 1981 BY THE MARK TWAIN FOUNDATION, WHICH
RESERVES ALL REPRODUCTION OR DRAMATIZATION RIGHTS
IN EVERY MEDIUM. THE IOWA-CALIFORNIA EDITION OF
THE TEXT OF *EARLY TALES & SKETCHES, VOLUME 2*,
NOW CORRECTLY ESTABLISHED FROM THE AUTHORITATIVE
DOCUMENTS AND FIRST PUBLISHED IN THIS VOLUME,
© 1981 BY THE REGENTS OF THE UNIVERSITY OF CALIFORNIA.
EDITORIAL INTRODUCTIONS, NOTES, AND APPARATUS
© 1981 BY THE REGENTS OF THE UNIVERSITY OF CALIFORNIA.
ISBN: 0-520-04382-0
LIBRARY OF CONGRESS CATALOG
CARD NUMBER: 75-46045

SERIES DESIGN BY HARLEAN RICHARDSON
IN COLLABORATION WITH DAVE COMSTOCK

MANUFACTURED IN THE UNITED STATES OF AMERICA

111707

Editorial Associates

DAHLIA ARMON

ROBERT PACK BROWNING

RICHARD E. BUCCI

VICTOR FISCHER

JAY GILLETTE

PAUL MACHLIS

KATE MALLOY

ROBERT SCHILDGEN

BERNARD L. STEIN

TERTELING LIBRARY
THE COLLEGE OF IDAHO
CALDWELL, IDAHO

ACKNOWLEDGMENTS

Our FIRST thanks must again go to the American taxpayers for their willingness to finance this and other efforts to preserve our national heritage. Editorial work for this collection was largely supported by a generous grant from the Editing Program of the National Endowment for the Humanities, an independent federal agency. It was begun under a contract with the United States Office of Education, Department of Health, Education, and Welfare, under the provisions of the Cooperative Research Program.

Mr. Branch was assisted in his work on the collection by a grant-in-aid from the American Council of Learned Societies in 1969, by a senior fellowship from the National Endowment for the Humanities in 1971, and by the continued support of the administration and the Faculty Research Committee of Miami University. Mr. Hirst was assisted by generous support from the Faculty Research Committee of the University of California at Los Angeles. Financial assistance for production costs was provided by the Graduate College of the University of Iowa. Editorial work for this volume was also supported by grants from the Charles E. Merrill Trust and from the William Randolph Hearst Foundation, and by matching funds from the National Endowment for the Humanities. Without such generous support the volume could not have been completed.

The photograph on page 420 is reproduced with permission from the Alfred Doten Collection, Special Collections Department, University of Nevada, Reno.

Acknowledgments of our personal and intellectual debts may be found in the first volume of this collection: they are too extensive to bear repeating here. We wish, however, to add our thanks to Henry Nash Smith, Acting Editor of the Mark Twain Papers (1979); James D. Hart, Director of The Bancroft Library; and Joseph A. Rosenthal, University Librarian, for their continuing support and assistance of the Mark Twain Project. Members and

former members of the editorial staff who have made special contributions to this volume are listed as editorial associates. But we
would especially like to thank Richard Bucci for his independent
contribution to the textual apparatus, Victor Fischer for his indispensable advice on matters of form and substance, and Harriet
Smith, who joins us on the title page, for her invaluable contribution at every stage of the work.

E.M.B.
R.H.H.

CONTENTS

ABBREVIATIONS
AND SHORT TITLES

THE FOLLOWING location symbols, abbreviations (for works by or about Mark Twain), and short titles (for general reference works) have been used for citation in this volume.

AD   Autobiographical Dictation

Bancroft   The Bancroft Library, University of California, Berkeley

Berkeley   Charles Franklin Doe Memorial Library, University of California, Berkeley

CWB   Clifton Waller Barrett Library, University of Virginia, Charlottesville

Doheny   Estelle Doheny Collection, The Edward Laurence Doheny Memorial Library, St. John's Seminary, Camarillo, California

Iowa   University of Iowa Library, Iowa City

MS   Manuscript

MTP   Mark Twain Papers, The Bancroft Library, University of California, Berkeley

PH   Photocopy

Texas   Humanities Research Center Library, University of Texas, Austin

TS   Typescript

Vassar   Jean Webster McKinney Family Papers, Francis Fitz Randolph Rare Book Room, Vassar College Library, Poughkeepsie, New York

Yale   Collection of American Literature, Beinecke Rare
            Book and Manuscript Library, Yale University, New
            Haven, Connecticut

WORKS CITED BY AN ABBREVIATION

AMT   *The Autobiography of Mark Twain,* ed. Charles
            Neider (New York: Harper and Brothers, 1959)

BAL   Jacob Blanck, *Bibliography of American Literature*
            (New Haven: Yale University Press, 1957), vol. 2

CL1   *Mark Twain's Collected Letters, Volume I (1853–
            1869),* ed. Lin Salamo (Berkeley, Los Angeles, London:
            University of California Press, 1981)

CL2   *Mark Twain's Collected Letters, Volume II (1869–
            1870),* ed. Frederick Anderson and Hamlin Hill
            (Berkeley, Los Angeles, London: University of Cali-
            fornia Press, 1981)

CofC   *Clemens of the "Call": Mark Twain in San Francisco,*
            ed. Edgar M. Branch (Berkeley and Los Angeles: Uni-
            versity of California Press, 1969)

Lex   Robert L. Ramsay and Frances G. Emberson, *A Mark
            Twain Lexicon* (New York: Russell and Russell, 1963)

MTB   Albert Bigelow Paine, *Mark Twain: A Biography,* 3
            vols. (New York: Harper and Brothers, 1912) [*Volume
            numbers in citations are to this edition; page num-
            bers are the same in all editions.*]

MTCH   *Mark Twain: The Critical Heritage,* ed. Frederick An-
            derson (New York: Barnes and Noble, 1971)

MTCor   *Mark Twain: San Francisco Correspondent,* ed.
            Henry Nash Smith and Frederick Anderson (San
            Francisco: Book Club of California, 1957)

MTDW   Henry Nash Smith, *Mark Twain: The Development
            of a Writer* (Cambridge: Harvard University Press,
            Belknap Press, 1962)

MTE   *Mark Twain in Eruption,* ed. Bernard DeVoto (New
            York: Harper and Brothers, 1940)

MTEnt   *Mark Twain of the "Enterprise,"* ed. Henry Nash Smith (Berkeley and Los Angeles: University of California Press, 1957)

MTHL   *Mark Twain-Howells Letters,* ed. Henry Nash Smith and William M. Gibson, 2 vols. (Cambridge: Harvard University Press, 1960)

MTTB   *Mark Twain's Travels with Mr. Brown,* ed. Franklin Walker and G. Ezra Dane (New York: Alfred A. Knopf, 1940)

N&J1   *Mark Twain's Notebooks & Journals, Volume I (1855-1873),* ed. Frederick Anderson, Michael B. Frank, and Kenneth M. Sanderson (Berkeley, Los Angeles, London: University of California Press, 1975)

N&J2   *Mark Twain's Notebooks & Journals, Volume II (1877-1883),* ed. Frederick Anderson, Lin Salamo, and Bernard L. Stein (Berkeley, Los Angeles, London: University of California Press, 1975)

RI   *Roughing It,* ed. Franklin R. Rogers and Paul Baender (Berkeley, Los Angeles, London: University of California Press, 1972)

S&B   *Mark Twain's Satires & Burlesques,* ed. Franklin R. Rogers (Berkeley and Los Angeles: University of California Press, 1967)

TIA   *Traveling with the Innocents Abroad,* ed. D. M. McKeithan (Norman: University of Oklahoma Press, 1958)

WIM   *What Is Man? And Other Philosophical Writings,* ed. Paul Baender (Berkeley, Los Angeles, London: University of California Press, 1973)

YSC   Cyril Clemens, *Young Sam Clemens* (Portland, Maine: Leon Tibbetts Editions, 1942)

WORKS CITED BY A SHORT TITLE

Angel, Myron, ed. *History of Nevada.* Oakland: Thompson and West, 1881.

Brown, T. Allston. *History of the American Stage.* New York: Dick and Fitzgerald, 1870.

Estavan, Lawrence, ed. *San Francisco Theatre Research.* 18 vols. San Francisco: Work Projects Administration, 1938–1942.

Gagey, Edmond M. *The San Francisco Stage: A History.* New York: Columbia University Press, 1950.

Kelly, J. Wells. *Second Directory of Nevada Territory.* San Francisco: Valentine and Co., 1863.

Langley, Henry G., comp. *The San Francisco Directory for the Year Commencing October, 1864.* San Francisco: Towne and Bacon, 1864.

————. *The San Francisco Directory for the Year Commencing December, 1865.* San Francisco: Towne and Bacon, 1865.

Lloyd, B. E. *Lights and Shades in San Francisco.* San Francisco: A. L. Bancroft and Co., 1876.

Mack, Effie Mona. *Nevada: A History of the State from the Earliest Times through the Civil War.* Glendale, California: Arthur H. Clark Company, 1935.

Odell, George C. D. *Annals of the New York Stage.* 15 vols. New York: Columbia University Press, 1927–1949.

Phelps, Alonzo. *Contemporary Biography of California's Leading Men.* 2 vols. San Francisco: A. L. Bancroft and Co., 1882.

Ratay, Myra Sauer. *Pioneers of the Ponderosa.* Sparks, Nevada: Western Printing and Publishing Company, 1973.

INTRODUCTION

THE SECOND VOLUME of this collection follows Clemens from his first days as a resident journalist in California, late in May 1864, through the end of his first full year as a California resident, 1865. In this twenty-month period he wrote most of his work for the San Francisco *Golden Era,* the *Morning Call,* the *Dramatic Chronicle,* and the *Californian.* He began to publish somewhat more regularly in eastern journals, like the New York *Saturday Press* and the *Weekly Review,* and toward the end of the period he started a long assignment as the daily correspondent from San Francisco to the Virginia City *Territorial Enterprise.* In November 1865 he published "Jim Smiley and His Jumping Frog" (no. 119), and by the beginning of 1866 the news of its success with eastern readers had begun to filter back to California. He was on the verge of national and international fame as a humorist.

This period saw Clemens change his employment from daily reporter for the *Call* to weekly columnist for the *Californian* and back again to daily columnist for the *Enterprise.* Although the seventy-seven sketches collected here include some routine comic journalism and some minor masterpieces, there are also a number of false starts and experiments. The one recurrent problem that lends a rough coherence throughout is Clemens' apparent reluctance to accept his vocation as a humorist—a reluctance that he overcame gradually but emphatically with the "Jumping Frog" tale. His problem was not that he doubted his talent—the sketches themselves constitute an irrefutable body of evidence for that talent—but rather that he shared with many of his contemporaries, at least on some occasions, a low opinion of the humorist's calling. "Funny fellows are all right and good in their place," said one such journalist, but "the sole supreme taste of the

1

public ought not to be in that direction."[1] Condescension of this kind usually brought Clemens into a defensive posture, and there are several sketches reprinted here in which he simply rejects this common attitude. But his more important and enduring response was to write a body of comic journalism that explored the possibilities of his material and the limitations of his audience, and that answered the skeptics with a new kind of humor. The sketches included here contain, for example, his earliest experiments with the vernacular community and his relationship with it, and they document some of his earliest ventures into the rich vein of controlled incoherence that became his trademark.

The general circumstances of composition of the entire collection are described in the introduction in volume 1. The headnotes give more specific information of this kind, while the explanatory notes identify specific persons and events mentioned in the sketches. The textual introduction in volume 1 sets forth the history of revision and reprinting of all the texts; the headnotes briefly indicate how each individual piece fits into this broader history, which is recapitulated in the "Description of Texts" in the present volume. The individual textual commentaries give full details of revision and reprinting; the mechanics of their use are explained in the "Guide to the Textual Apparatus."

E.M.B.

R.H.H.

August 1979

---

[1]"A Glance at San Francisco Literature," Grass Valley (Calif.) *National*, reprinted in *Californian* 2 (11 February 1865): 5.

SECTION 3

California, Part 1

1864-1865

76. Parting Presentation

13 June 1864

This piece, Clemens' first signed publication following his move from Nevada to San Francisco at the end of May 1864, appeared on June 13 on the front page of the San Francisco *Alta California*. It was headed by the following preface, possibly also by Mark Twain:

A most interesting and affecting ceremony was performed on the stage of Maguire's Opera House, at 3 P. M. yesterday; a large number of gentlemen having assembled to witness the presentation of a cane to Major Perry, the beautiful and accomplished engineer, of Capt. Merritt's wrecking party, who leaves by the *Constitution* this morning, for the East. The cane weighs something less than twelve pounds, and might have been copied from Emperor Norton's. The presentation speech was written upon a parchment seven feet long, by three and a half feet in width, and magnificently illuminated, and while it was being read by Mark Twain, Esq., of Virginia City, the entire audience was dissolved in tears. We have, at an immense expense, secured a copy of this eloquent production, and give it to our readers verbatim.

It is reasonably certain that many prominent citizens took part in this "presentation affair"—the name usually given to those bibulous stag gatherings elaborately staged to honor a popular member of the tribe of good fellows. Although Clemens was identified in the *Alta* as "Mark Twain, Esq., of Virginia City," the former "Washoe Giant" had recently been hired as a local reporter for the San Francisco *Morning Call*. The selection of this newcomer to preside over the occasion speaks for the reputation he had already acquired by mid-1864. His first formal public lecture was still two years in the future, but he was known in San Francisco not only as a newspaper humorist but as a resourceful master of ceremonies and the witty "governor" of the Nevada Third House. His brief tribute to Major Perry exudes the self-confidence of one who knew his audience and how to win it over.

Major Edward C. Perry of New York City was a veteran of the Army of the Potomac who was trained in marine engineering. Presumably he made friends easily, for he was one of a salvage crew brought to San Francisco only a few months before to raise the steamship *Aquila,* which had sunk fully loaded at Hathaway's wharf during a heavy storm the night of 15 November 1863. The *Aquila's* cargo was the dismantled monitor *Camanche,* a mobile fortress assigned by the War Department to protect San Francisco against the possibility of raids by marauding Confederate warships. By late April the salvage crew had removed the *Camanche* piece by piece from the *Aquila's* hold, and soon the steamship itself was afloat. Exactly one year after the *Aquila* had gone down, the reassembled *Camanche* was launched with great fanfare. Acting as local reporter for the *Call* from June to October 1864, Clemens kept tabs on the rebuilding of the monitor.[1]

Clemens' speech served its occasion well. Possibly his memory of this debut as a speaker in San Francisco influenced his decision two years later to lecture about the Sandwich Islands in the same city.

---

[1]See *CofC,* pp. 250–254, and Edgar M. Branch, "Major Perry and the Monitor *Camanche:* An Early Mark Twain Speech," *American Literature* 39 (May 1967): 170–179.

Parting Presentation

MAJOR PERRY:—Permit me, sir, on the part of your countless friends, the noble sons of the forest—the Diggers, the Pi-Utes, the Washoes, the Shoshones, and the numberless and nameless tribes of aborigines that roam the deserts of the Great Basin to the eastward of the snowy mountains further north—to present you this costly and beautiful *cane,* reared under their own eyes, and fashioned by their own inspired hands. The red men whom I represent, although visibly black from the wear and tear of out door life, from contact with the impurities of the earth, and from the absence of soap and their natural indifference to water, admire the unblemished virtue and the spotless integrity which they find in you; albeit these dusty savages are arrayed in rabbit skins and their princely blood is food for the very vermin they cherish and protect, they still respect you, because your repugnance to graybacks—either in the way of food or society—and your antipathy to the skins of wild beasts as raiment, is bold, undisguised and honest; finally, although these dingy warriors see no blood upon your hands, no human bones about your neck, no scalps suspended from your belt, they behold in you a brave whom they delight to honor—for they see you, in fancy, on the war-path in the three fights on the Bull's Run field; again in the historic seven-days' struggle before Richmond; and again sweeping down the lines with McClellan, in the fire and smoke and thunder of battle at Antietam, with a wound in your leg and blood in your eye! and they honor you as they would a High-you-muck-a-muck of many tribes, with crimson blankets and a hundred squaws. I am charged to say to you, that if you will visit the campoodies of the nomads of the desert, you shall fare sumptuously upon crickets and grasshoppers and the fat of the land: the skin of the wild coyote shall be your bed, and the daughters of the chiefs shall serve you.

Receive the cane kindly—cherish it in memory of your savage friends in San Francisco, and bear in mind always the lesson it teaches: its head is formed of a human hand clasping a fish—the hand will cling to the fish through good or evil fortune, until one or the other is destroyed. And the moral it teaches is this: When you undertake a thing, stick to it through storm and sunshine; never flinch—never yield an inch—never give up—*hold your grip* till you bust!

You have been a citizen of San Francisco four months, Major Perry; you came to raise the Aquila, with Captain Merritt, and you did it, and did it well—she rides at anchor in the bay. You held your grip. The consciousness of your success will be half your reward—and the other half will be duly paid in greenbacks by the Government. Your labors finished, you are now about to leave us to-morrow for your old home across the seas, and we are here to bid you God speed and a safe voyage.

In the name of Winnemucca, War Chief of the Pi-Utes; Sioux-Sioux, Chief of the Washoes; Buckskin Joe, Chief of the Pitt Rivers; Buffalo Jim, Chief of the Bannocks; Washakee, Grand Chief of the Shoshones; and further, in the names of the lordly chiefs of all the swarthy tribes that breathe the free air of the hills and plains of the Pacific Coast, I salute you. Behold! they stand before you—thirsty.

MARK TWAIN,
High-you-muck-a-muck.

77. "Mark Twain" in the Metropolis

17–23 June 1864

Clemens became the local reporter for the San Francisco *Morning Call* soon after he arrived from Virginia City at the end of May 1864. This letter to his former newspaper, the Virginia City *Territorial Enterprise*, leaves no doubt that his new pleasurable surroundings had not abated his skeptical cast of mind.

The original printing in the *Enterprise* does not survive, but the text is preserved in the San Francisco *Golden Era* for 26 June 1864, which introduced the extract as follows: "The Sage-Brush Humorist from Silver-Land, 'Mark Twain,' has come to town, and stops at the Occidental. He discourses the *Territorial Enterprise.*" The date of the first printing is not known, but since Clemens says that Caroline Richings had been playing at Maguire's Opera House "during the past fortnight," and since she had opened there on May 30, the letter might have been composed about June 14 and, allowing three days' transit time, published as early as June 17. On the other hand, the "fortnight" reference may not be precise, and the letter might have been written and published somewhat later. Mark Twain's comment on the momentary upward trend in Gould and Curry stock establishes the latest possible date of composition as June 20 or 21, for on June 22 the stock resumed its downward plunge. But still assuming three days' transit time from Virginia to San Francisco, the *Era* could not have published the letter on June 26 if it had appeared later than June 23. We therefore conjecture publication as sometime between June 17 and 23.

"Mark Twain" in the Metropolis

To a Christian who has toiled months and months in Washoe; whose hair bristles from a bed of sand, and whose soul is caked with a cement of alkali dust; whose nostrils know no perfume but the rank odor of sage-brush—and whose eyes know no landscape but barren mountains and desolate plains; where the winds blow, and the sun blisters, and the broken spirit of the contrite heart finds joy and peace only in Limburger cheese and lager beer— unto such a Christian, verily the Occidental Hotel is Heaven on the half shell. He may even secretly consider it to be Heaven on the entire shell, but his religion teaches a sound Washoe Christian that it would be sacrilege to say it.

Here you are expected to breakfast on salmon, fried oysters and other substantials from 6 till half-past 12; you are required to lunch on cold fowl and so forth, from half-past 12 until 3; you are obliged to skirmish through a dinner comprising such edibles as the world produces, and keep it up, from 3 until half-past 7; you are then compelled to lay siege to the tea-table from half-past 7 until 9 o'clock, at which hour, if you refuse to move upon the supper works and destroy oysters gotten up in all kinds of seductive styles until 12 o'clock, the landlord will certainly be offended, and you might as well move your trunk to some other establishment. [It is a pleasure to me to observe, incidentally, that I am on good terms with the landlord yet.]

Why don't you send Dan down into the Gould & Curry mine, to see whether it has petered out or not, and if so, when it will be likely to peter in again. The extraordinary decline of that stock has given rise to the wildest surmises in the way of accounting for it, but among the lot there is harm in but one, which is the expressed belief on the part of a few that the bottom has fallen out of the mine. Gould & Curry is climbing again, however.

It has been many a day since San Francisco has seen livelier times in her theatrical department than at present. Large audiences are to be found nightly at the Opera House, the Metropolitan, the Academy of Music, the American, the New Idea, and even the Museum, which is not as good a one as Barnum's. The Circus company, also, played a lucrative engagement, but they are gone on their travels now. The graceful, charming, clipper-built Ella Zoyara was very popular.

Miss Caroline Richings has played during the past fortnight at Maguire's Opera House to large and fashionable audiences, and has delighted them beyond measure with her sweet singing. It sounds improbable, perhaps, but the statement is true, nevertheless.

You will hear of the Metropolitan, now, from every visitor to Washoe. It opened under the management of the new lessees, Miss Annette Ince and Julia Dean Hayne, with a company who are as nearly all stars as it was possible to make it. For instance —Annette Ince, Emily Jordan, Mrs. Judah, Julia Dean Hayne, James H. Taylor, Frank Lawlor, Harry Courtaine and Fred. Franks, (my favorite Washoe tragedian, whose name they have put in small letters in the programme, when it deserves to be in capitals—because, whatever part they give him to play, don't he always play it well? and does he not possess the first virtue of a comedian, which is to do humorous things with grave decorum and without seeming to know that they are funny?)

The birds, and the flowers, and the Chinamen, and the winds, and the sunshine, and all things that go to make life happy, are present in San Francisco to-day, just as they are all days in the year. Therefore, one would expect to hear these things spoken of, and gratefully, and disagreeable matters of little consequence allowed to pass without comment. I say, one would suppose that. But don't you deceive yourself—any one who supposes anything of the kind, supposes an absurdity. The multitude of pleasant things by which the people of San Francisco are surrounded are not talked of at all. No—they damn the wind, and they damn the dust, and they give all their attention to damning them well, and to all eternity. The blasted winds and the infernal dust—these alone form the eternal topics of conversation, and a mighty absurd topic it seems to one just out of Washoe. There isn't enough wind here to keep breath in my body, or dust enough to keep sand in my craw. But it is human nature to find fault—to overlook that which is pleasant to the eye, and seek after that which is distasteful to it. You take a stranger into the Bank Exchange and show him the magnificent picture of Sampson and Delilah, and what is the first object he notices?—Sampson's fine face and flaming eye? or the noble beauty of his form? or the lovely, half-nude Delilah? or the muscular Philistine behind Sampson, who is furtively admiring her charms? or the perfectly counterfeited folds of the rich drapery below her knees? or the symmetry and truth to nature of Sampson's left foot? No, sir, the first thing that catches his eye is the scissors on the floor at Delilah's feet, and the first thing he says, "Them scissors is too modern—there warn't no scissors like that in them days, by a d—d sight!"

MARK TWAIN.

78. *The Evidence in the Case of Smith* vs. *Jones*

26 June 1864

This mock report of trial proceedings was published in the San Francisco *Golden Era*. The sketch's emphasis on the unreliability of witnesses makes it similar to various reports that Clemens made of other trials in the San Francisco *Morning Call*, and it is doubtless based on what he had often heard in the local police court: false or obviously conflicting testimony.[1] Speaking to that situation, Clemens here ironically appeals to "the high court of The People" and invokes the sense of justice supposedly innate in "the masses," while he simultaneously demonstrates that these same masses are the inexhaustible source of contentious litigant and false witness alike.

The sketch rides its point hard. Its heavy reliance on dialogue and its use of virtual stage directions suggest that the author was experimenting with dramatic narrative, perhaps even with play writing, at this time. If so, such an interest may help to explain why faint outlines of Scotty Briggs (in chapter 47 of *Roughing It*) appear in Alfred Sowerby, and why Washington Billings' narrative of the fight catches some of the rhythm and dialect quality of Huck Finn's speech, even if it cannot match the reliability of Huck's report of experience. Moreover, the vernacular characters are not merely unreliable witnesses: their slang and their naive tendency to exaggerate are amusing in part because they disconcert the straight characters, the judge and prosecuting attorney.

---

[1]For several examples of Clemens' news reports on this subject, see *CofC*, pp. 209–215; see also Appendix A, volume 2.

The Evidence in the Case of Smith vs. Jones

REPORTED BY MARK TWAIN.

I REPORTED this trial simply for my own amusement, one idle day last week, and without expecting to publish any portion of it—but I have seen the facts in the case so distorted and misrepresented in the daily papers that I feel it my duty to come forward and do what I can to set the plaintiff and the defendant right before the public. This can best be done by submitting the plain, unembellished statements of the witnesses as given under oath before his Honor Judge Shepheard, in the Police Court, and leaving the people to form their own judgment of the matters involved, unbiased by argument or suggestion of any kind from me.

There is that nice sense of justice and that ability to discriminate between right and wrong, among the masses, which will enable them, after carefully reading the testimony I am about to set down here, to decide without hesitation which is the innocent party and which the guilty in the remarkable case of Smith vs. Jones, and I have every confidence that before this paper shall have been out of the printing-press twenty-four hours, the high court of The People, from whose decision there is no appeal, will have swept from the innocent man all taint of blame or suspicion, and cast upon the guilty one a deathless infamy.

To such as are not used to visiting the Police Court, I will observe that there is nothing inviting about the place, there being no rich carpets, no mirrors, no pictures, no elegant sofa or arm-chairs to lounge in, no free lunch—and in fact, nothing to make a man who has been there once desire to go again—except in cases where his bail is heavier than his fine is likely to be, under which circumstances he naturally has a tendency in that direction again, of course, in order to recover the difference.

There is a pulpit at the head of the hall, occupied by a handsome, gray-haired Judge, with a faculty of appearing pleasant and impartial to the disinterested spectator, and prejudiced and frosty to the last degree to the prisoner at the bar.

To the left of the pulpit is a long table for reporters; in front of the pulpit the clerks are stationed, and in the centre of the hall a nest of lawyers. On the left again are pine benches behind a railing, occupied by seedy white men, negroes, Chinamen, Kanakas—in a word, by the seedy and dejected of all nations—and in a corner is a box where more can be had when they are wanted.

On the right are more pine benches, for the use of prisoners, and their friends and witnesses.

An officer, in a gray uniform, and with a star upon his breast, guards the door.

A holy calm pervades the scene.

The case of Smith vs. Jones being called, each of these parties (stepping out from among the other seedy ones) gave the Court a particular and circumstantial account of how the whole thing occurred, and then sat down.

The two narratives differed from each other.

In reality, I was half persuaded that these men were talking about two separate and distinct affairs altogether, inasmuch as no single circumstance mentioned by one was even remotely hinted at by the other.

Mr. Alfred Sowerby was then called to the witness-stand, and testified as follows:

"I was in the saloon at the time, your Honor, and I see this man Smith come up all of a sudden to Jones, who warn't saying a word, and split him in the snoot—"

Lawyer. —"Did what, Sir?"

Witness. —"Busted him in the snoot."

Lawyer. —"What do you mean by such language as that? When you say that the plaintiff suddenly approached the defendant, who was silent at the time, and 'busted him in the snoot,' do you mean that the plaintiff *struck* the defendant?"

Witness. —"That's me—I'm swearing to that very circumstance—yes, your Honor, that was just the way of it. Now, for instance, as if you was Jones and I was Smith. Well, I comes up all of a sudden and says I to your Honor, says I, 'D—n your old tripe—'" [Suppressed laughter in the lobbies.]

The Court. —"Order in the court! Witness, you will confine yourself to a plain statement of the facts in this case, and refrain from the embellishments of metaphor and allegory as far as possible."

Witness. —(Considerably subdued.)—"I beg your Honor's pardon—I didn't mean to be so brash. Well, Smith comes up to Jones all of a sudden and mashed him in the bugle—"

Lawyer. —"Stop! Witness, this kind of language will not do. I will ask you a plain question, and I require you to answer it simply, yes or no. Did—the—plaintiff—*strike*—the defendant? Did he *strike* him?"

Witness. —"You bet your sweet life he did. Gad! he gave him a paster in the trumpet—"

Lawyer. —"Take the witness! take the witness! take the witness! I have no further use for him."

The lawyer on the other side said he would endeavor to worry along without more assistance from Mr. Sowerby, and the witness retired to a neighboring bench.

Mr. McWilliamson was next called, and deposed as follows:

"I was a standing as close to Mr. Smith as I am to this pulpit, a-chaffing with one of the lager beer girls—Sophronia by name, being from summers in Germany, so she says, but as to that, I—"

Lawyer. —"Well, now, never mind the nativity of the lager beer girl, but state, as concisely as possible, what you know of the assault and battery."

Witness. —"Certainly—certainly. Well, German or no German,—which I'll take my oath I don't believe she is, being of a red-headed disposition, with long, bony fingers, and no more hankering after Limburger cheese than—"

Lawyer.—"Stop that driveling nonsense and stick to the assault and battery. Go on with your story."

Witness.—"Well, Sir, she—that is, Jones—he sidled up and drawed his revolver and tried to shoot the top of Smith's head off, and Smith run, and Sophronia she whalloped herself down in the saw-dust and screamed twice, just as loud as she could yell. I never see a poor creature in such distress—and then she sung out: 'O, H—ll's fire! what are they up to now? Ah, my poor dear mother, I shall never see you more!'—saying which, she jerked another yell and fainted away as dead as a wax figger. Thinks I to myself, I'll be danged if this ain't gettin' rather dusty, and I'll—"

The Court.—"We have no desire to know what you *thought;* we only wish to know what you *saw.* Are you sure Mr. Jones endeavored to shoot the top of Mr. Smith's head off?"

Witness.—"Yes, your Honor."

The Court.—"How many times did he shoot?"

Witness.—"Well, Sir, I couldn't say exactly as to the number—but I should think—well, say seven or eight times—as many as that, anyway."

The Court.—"Be careful now, and remember you are under oath. What kind of a pistol was it?"

Witness.—"It was a Durringer, your Honor."

The Court.—"A Deringer! You must not trifle here, Sir. A Deringer only shoots once—how then could Jones have fired seven or eight times?" [The witness is evidently as stunned by that last proposition as if a brick had struck him.]

Witness.—"Well, your Honor—he—that is, she—Jones, I mean—Soph—"

The Court.—"Are you sure he fired more than one shot? Are you sure he fired at all?"

Witness.—"I—I—well, perhaps he didn't—and—and your Honor may be right. But you see, that girl, with her dratted yowling—altogether, it might be that he did only shoot once."

Lawyer.—"And about his attempting to shoot the top of Smith's head off—didn't he aim at his body, or his legs? Come now."

Witness.—(entirely confused)—"Yes, Sir—I think he did—I—I'm pretty certain of it. Yes, Sir, he must a fired at his legs."

[Nothing was elicited on the cross-examination, except that the weapon used by Mr. Jones was a bowie knife instead of a deringer, and that he made a number of desperate attempts to scalp the plaintiff instead of trying to shoot him. It also came out that Sophronia, of doubtful nativity, did not faint, and was not present during the affray, she having been discharged from her situation on the previous evening.]

Washington Billings, sworn, said:—"I see the row, and it warn't in no saloon—it was in the street. Both of 'em was drunk, and one was a comin' up the street, and 'tother was a goin down. Both of 'em was close to the houses when they fust see each other, and both of 'em made their calculations to miss each other, but the second time they tacked across the pavement—driftin', like diagonal—they come together, down by the curb—almighty soggy, they did—which staggered 'em a moment, and then, over they went, into the gutter. Smith was up fust, and he made a dive for a cobble and fell on Jones; Jones dug out and made a dive for a cobble, and slipped his hold and jammed his head into Smith's stomach. They each done that over again, twice more, just the same way. After that, neither of 'em could get up any more, and so they just laid there in the slush and clawed mud and cussed each other."

[On the cross-examination, the witness could not say whether the parties continued the fight afterwards in the saloon or not—he only knew they began it in the gutter, and to the best of his knowledge and belief they were too drunk to get into a saloon, and too drunk to stay in it after they got there if there were any orifice about it that they could fall out of again. As to weapons, he saw none used except the cobble-stones, and to the best of his knowledge and belief they missed fire every time while he was present.]

Jeremiah Driscoll came forward, was sworn, and testified as follows:—"I saw the fight, your Honor, and it wasn't in a saloon, nor in the street, nor in a hotel, nor in—"

The Court.—"Was it in the City and County of San Francisco?"

Witness.—"Yes, your Honor, I—I think it was."

The Court. —"Well, then, go on."

Witness. —"It was up in the Square. Jones meets Smith, and they both go at it—that is, blackguarding each other. One called the other a thief, and the other said he was a liar, and then they got to swearing backwards and forwards pretty generally, as you might say, and finally one struck the other over the head with a cane, and then they closed and fell, and after that they made such a dust and the gravel flew so thick that I couldn't rightly tell which was getting the best of it. When it cleared away, one of them was after the other with a pine bench, and the other was prospecting for rocks, and—"

Lawyer. —"There, there, there—that will do—that—will—do! How in the world is any one to make head or tail out of such a string of nonsense as that? Who struck the first blow?"

Witness. —"I cannot rightly say, sir, but I think—"

Lawyer. —"You *think!*—don't you *know?*"

Witness. —"No, sir, it was all so sudden, and—"

Lawyer. —"Well, then, state, if you can, who struck the last."

Witness. —"I can't, sir, because—"

Lawyer. —"Because what?"

Witness. —"Because, sir, you see toward the last, they clinched and went down, and got to kicking up the gravel again, and—"

Lawyer. —(resignedly)—"Take the witness—take the witness."

[The testimony on the cross-examination went to show that during the fight, one of the parties drew a slung-shot and cocked it, but to the best of the witness' knowledge and belief, he did not fire; and at the same time, the other discharged a hand-grenade at his antagonist, which missed him and did no damage, except blowing up a bonnet store on the other side of the street, and creating a momentary diversion among the milliners. He could not say, however, which drew the slung-shot or which threw the grenade. (It was generally remarked by those in the court room, that the evidence of the witness was obscure and unsatisfactory.) Upon questioning him further, and confronting him with the parties to the case before the court, it transpired that the faces of Jones and Smith were unknown to him, and that he had been talking about an entirely different fight all the time.]

Other witnesses were examined, some of whom swore that

Smith was the aggressor, and others that Jones began the row; some said they fought with their fists, others that they fought with knives, others tomahawks, others revolvers, others clubs, others axes, others beer mugs and chairs, and others swore there had been no fight at all. However, fight or no fight, the testimony was straightforward and uniform on one point, at any rate, and that was, that the fuss was about two dollars and forty cents, which one party owed the other, but after all, it was impossible to find out which was the debtor and which the creditor.

After the witnesses had all been heard, his Honor, Judge Shepheard, observed that the evidence in this case resembled, in a great many points, the evidence before him in some thirty-five cases every day, on an average. He then said he would continue the case, to afford the parties an opportunity of procuring more testimony.

[I have been keeping an eye on the Police Court for the last few days. Two friends of mine had business there, on account of assault and battery concerning Washoe stocks, and I felt interested, of course. I never knew their names were James Johnson and John Ward, though, until I heard them answer to them in that Court. When James Johnson was called, one of these young men said to the other: "That's you, my boy." "No," was the reply, "it's you—my name's John Ward—see, I've got it written here on a card." Consequently, the first speaker sung out, "Here!" and it was all right. As I was saying, I have been keeping an eye on that Court, and I have arrived at the conclusion that the office of Police Judge is a profitable and a comfortable thing to have, but then, as the English hunter said about fighting tigers in India under a shortness of ammunition, "it has its little drawbacks." Hearing testimony must be worrying to a Police Judge sometimes, when he is in his right mind. I would rather be Secretary to a wealthy mining company, and have nothing to do but advertise the assessments and collect them in carefully, and go along quiet and upright, and be one of the noblest works of God, and never gobble a dollar that didn't belong to me—all just as those fellows do, you know. (Oh, *I* have no talent for sarcasm, it isn't likely.) But I trespass.]

Now, with every confidence in the instinctive candor and fair

dealing of my race, I submit the testimony in the case of Smith
vs. Jones, to the People, without comment or argument, well
satisfied that after a perusal of it, their judgment will be as righ-
teous as it is final and impartial, and that whether Smith be cast
out and Jones exalted, or Jones cast out and Smith exalted, the
decision will be a holy and a just one.

I leave the accused and the accuser before the bar of the
world—let their fate be pronounced.

79. Early Rising, As Regards Excursions to the Cliff House

3 July 1864

This sketch appeared in the San Francisco *Golden Era* one week after the previous piece, "The Evidence in the Case of Smith *vs.* Jones" (no. 78). It too seems to have emerged from Clemens' work as a reporter on the San Francisco *Morning Call*, for on 25 June 1864 he had published a straight news story there urging his readers to visit the Cliff House before "the winds get too fresh."[1] "Early Rising" is manifestly an attempt to elaborate the experience of his own recent trip into a humorous, essentially literary sketch.

The Cliff House that Clemens knew in 1864 had been built near Point Lobos in 1863 by Captain Junius G. Foster, a well-known San Franciscan. An excellent bar, superior cuisine, comfortable overnight accommodations, and an attractive location overlooking the Pacific Ocean and Seal Rocks made the Cliff House a popular resort.[2] Clemens' recent article in the *Call* was, in fact, like many similar stories by other local reporters in the city. Just before "Early Rising" was published, spunky Lisle Lester had written a piece called "Morning Rides," which advocated exhilarating 5 A.M. excursions to the Cliff House, where one could see "the ocean waves laughing on the beach below, and sea-lions moaning on the rocks."[3] Clemens' sketch may be read as a response to this sort of lyricism in particular, and in general to those other early risers—the utilitarian partisans of Ben Franklin—who care less for "the sun in the dawn of his glory" than for catching "the worm." Although the sketch follows a

---

[1]*CofC*, p. 127, reprinted in Appendix A2, volume 2.
[2]Lloyd, *Lights and Shades*, pp. 69–70; Langley, *Directory for 1864*, pp. 163, 460.
[3]*Pacific Monthly* 11 (July 1864): 753–754.

predictable pattern, it brims over with Clemens' humorous skepticism about the wisdom and practical value of such time-honored clichés.

Clemens' ocean-bound route apparently followed the macadamized San Francisco and Point Lobos Road from Lone Mountain four miles west to the Cliff House. For the return Clemens first drove south along the beach to the Ocean House, James R. Dickey's hotel and restaurant near Lake Merced. He then took the Ocean House Road, which twisted down through the hills to Mission Dolores and the nearby Jewish cemeteries. East of the mission he boarded a steamer, probably in the navigable portion of Mission Creek, and returned to the city by way of Mission Bay and San Francisco Bay.[4]

---

[4]Lloyd, *Lights and Shades*, pp. 68–69; Langley, *Directory for 1864*, pp. 133, 163, 431; William Crittenden Sharpsteen, "Vanished Waters of Southeastern San Francisco," *California Historical Society Quarterly* 21 (June 1942): 115; A. B. Holcombe and W. C. Kewen, *Atlas of the City and County of San Francisco* (Philadelphia: Wm. P. Humphreys and Co., 1876), p. 6.

Early Rising, As Regards Excursions to the Cliff House

Early to bed, and early to rise,
Makes a man healthy, wealthy and wise.
—*Benjamin Franklin.*

I don't see it.
—*George Washington.*

Now both of these are high authorities—very high and re-spectable authorities—but I am with General Washington first, last, and all the time on this proposition.

Because I don't see it, either.

I have tried getting up early, and I have tried getting up late—and the latter agrees with me best. As for a man's growing any wiser, or any richer, or any healthier, by getting up early, I know it is not so; because I have got up early in the station-house many and many a time, and got poorer and poorer for the next half a day, in consequence, instead of richer and richer. And sometimes, on the same terms, I have seen the sun rise four times a week up there at Virginia, and so far from my growing healthier on account of it, I got to looking blue, and pulpy, and swelled, like a drowned man, and my relations grew alarmed and thought they were going to lose me. They entirely despaired of my recovery, at one time, and began to grieve for me as one whose days were numbered—

whose fate was sealed—who was soon to pass away from them forever, and from the glad sunshine, and the birds, and the odorous flowers, and murmuring brooks, and whispering winds, and all the cheerful scenes of life, and go down into the dark and silent tomb—and they went forth sorrowing, and jumped a lot in the graveyard, and made up their minds to grin and bear it with that fortitude which is the true Christian's brightest ornament.

You observe that I have put a stronger test on the matter than even Benjamin Franklin contemplated, and yet it would not work. Therefore, how is a man to grow healthier, and wealthier, and wiser by going to bed early and getting up early, when he fails to accomplish these things even when he does not go to bed at all? And as far as becoming wiser is concerned, you might put all the wisdom I acquired in these experiments in your eye, without obstructing your vision any to speak of.

As I said before, my voice is with George Washington's on this question.

Another philosopher encourages the world to get up at sunrise because "it is the early bird that catches the worm."

It is a seductive proposition, and well calculated to trap the unsuspecting. But its attractions are all wasted on me, because I have no use for the worm. If I had, I would adopt the Unreliable's plan. He was much interested in this quaint proverb, and directed the powers of his great mind to its consideration for three or four consecutive hours. He was supposing a case. He was supposing, for instance, that he really wanted the worm—that the possession of the worm was actually necessary to his happiness—that he yearned for it and hankered after it, therefore, as much as a man *could* yearn for and hanker after a worm under such circumstances—and he was supposing, further, that he was opposed to getting up early in order to catch it (which was much the more plausible of the two suppositions). Well, at the end of three or four hours' profound meditation upon the subject, the Unreliable rose up and said: "If he were so anxious about the worm, and he couldn't get along without him, and he didn't want to get up early in the morning to catch him—why then, by George, he would just lay for him the night before!" I never would have thought of that. I looked at the youth, and said to myself, he is

malicious, and dishonest, and unhandsome, and does not smell
good—yet how quickly do these trivial demerits disappear in the
shadow when the glare from his great intellect shines out above
them!

I have always heard that the only time in the day that a trip to
the Cliff House could be thoroughly enjoyed, was early in the
morning; (and I suppose it might be as well to withhold an ad-
verse impression while the flow-tide of public opinion continues
to set in that direction.)

I tried it the other morning with Harry, the stock-broker, rising
at 4 A. M., to delight in the following described things, to wit:

A road unencumbered by carriages, and free from wind and
dust; a bracing atmosphere; the gorgeous spectacle of the sun in
the dawn of his glory; the fresh perfume of flowers still damp with
dew; a solitary drive on the beach while its smoothness was yet
unmarred by wheel or hoof, and a vision of white sails glinting in
the morning light far out at sea.

These were the considerations, and they seemed worthy a sacrifice of seven or eight hours' sleep.

We sat in the stable, and yawned, and gaped, and stretched,
until the horse was hitched up, and then drove out into the bracing atmosphere. (When another early voyage is proposed to me, I
want it understood that there is to be no bracing atmosphere in
the programme. I can worry along without it.) In half an hour we
were so thoroughly braced up with it that it was just a scratch
that we were not frozen to death. Then the harness came un-
shipped, or got broken, or something, and I waxed colder and
drowsier while Harry fixed it. I am not fastidious about clothes,
but I am not used to wearing fragrant, sweaty horse-blankets, and
not partial to them, either; I am not proud, though, when I am
freezing, and I added the horse-blanket to my overcoats, and tried
to wake up and feel warm and cheerful. It was useless, however
—all my senses slumbered, and continued to slumber, save the
sense of smell.

When my friend drove past suburban gardens and said the flowers never exhaled so sweet an odor before, in his experience, I
dreamily but honestly endeavored to think so too, but in my
secret soul I was conscious that they only smelled like horse-

blankets. (When another early voyage is proposed to me, I want it understood that there is to be no "fresh perfume of flowers" in the programme, either. I do not enjoy it. My senses are not attuned to the flavor—there is too much horse about it and not enough eau de cologne.)

The wind was cold and benumbing, and blew with such force that we could hardly make headway against it. It came straight from the ocean, and I think there are ice-bergs out there somewhere. True, there was not much dust, because the gale blew it all to Oregon in two minutes; and by good fortune, it blew no gravel-stones, to speak of—only one, of any consequence, I believe—a three-cornered one—it struck me in the eye. I have it there yet. However, it does not matter—for the future I suppose I can manage to see tolerably well out of the other. (Still, when another early voyage is proposed to me, I want it understood that the dust is to be put in, and the gravel left out of the programme. I might want my other eye if I continue to hang on until my time comes; and besides, I shall not mind the dust much hereafter, because I have only got to shut one eye, now, when it is around.)

No, the road was not encumbered by carriages—we had it all to ourselves. I suppose the reason was, that most people do not like to enjoy themselves too much, and therefore they do not go out to the Cliff House in the cold and the fog, and the dread silence and solitude of four o'clock in the morning. They are right. The impressive solemnity of such a pleasure trip is only equalled by an excursion to Lone Mountain in a hearse. Whatever of advantage there may be in having that Cliff House road all to yourself, we had—but to my mind a greater advantage would lie in dividing it up in small sections among the entire community; because, in consequence of the repairs in progress on it just now, it is as rough as a corduroy bridge—(in a good many places,) and consequently the less you have of it, the happier you are likely to be, and the less shaken up and disarranged on the inside. (Wherefore, when another early voyage is proposed to me, I want it understood that the road is not to be unencumbered with carriages, but just the reverse—so that the balance of the people shall be made to stand their share of the jolting and the desperate lonesomeness of the thing.)

From the moment we left the stable, almost, the fog was so thick that we could scarcely see fifty yards behind or before, or overhead; and for a while, as we approached the Cliff House, we could not see the horse at all, and were obliged to steer by his ears, which stood up dimly out of the dense white mist that enveloped him. But for those friendly beacons, we must have been cast away and lost.

I have no opinion of a six-mile ride in the clouds; but if I ever have to take another, I want to leave the horse in the stable and go in a balloon. I shall prefer to go in the afternoon, also, when it is warm, so that I may gape, and yawn, and stretch, if I am drowsy, without disarranging my horse-blanket and letting in a blast of cold wind.

We could scarcely see the sportive seals out on the rocks, writhing and squirming like exaggerated maggots, and there was nothing soothing in their discordant barking, to a spirit so depressed as mine was.

Harry took a cocktail at the Cliff House, but I scorned such ineffectual stimulus; I yearned for fire, and there was none there; they were about to make one, but the bar-keeper looked altogether too cheerful for me—I could not bear his unnatural happiness in the midst of such a ghastly picture of fog, and damp, and frosty surf, and dreary solitude. I could not bear the sacrilegious presence of a pleasant face at such a time; it was too much like sprightliness at a funeral, and we fled from it down the smooth and vacant beach.

We had that all to ourselves, too, like the road—and I want it divided up, also, hereafter. We could not drive in the roaring surf and seem to float abroad on the foamy sea, as one is wont to do in the sunny afternoon, because the very thought of any of that icy-looking water splashing on you was enough to congeal your blood, almost. We saw no white-winged ships sailing away on the billowy ocean, with the pearly light of morning descending upon them like a benediction—"because the fog had the bulge on the pearly light," as the Unreliable observed when I mentioned it to him afterwards; and we saw not the sun in the dawn of his glory, for the same reason. Hill and beach, and sea and sun were all wrapped in a ghostly mantle of mist, and hidden from our mortal vision. [When another early voyage is proposed to me, I want it understood that the sun in his glory, and the morning light, and the ships at sea, and all that sort of thing are to be left out of the programme, so that when we fail to see them, we shall not be so infernally disappointed.]

We were human icicles when we got to the Ocean House, and there was no fire there, either. I banished all hope, then, and succumbed to despair; I went back on my religion, and sought surcease of sorrow in soothing blasphemy. I am sorry I did it, now, but it was a great comfort to me, then. We could have had breakfast at the Ocean House, but we did not want it; can statues of ice feel hunger? But we adjourned to a private room and ordered redhot coffee, and it was a sort of balm to my troubled mind to observe that the man who brought it was as cold, and as silent, and as solemn as the grave itself. His gravity was so impressive, and so appropriate and becoming to the melancholy surroundings, that it won upon me and thawed out some of the better instincts of my nature, and I told him he might ask a blessing if he thought it would lighten him up any—because he looked as if he wanted to, very bad—but he only shook his head resignedly and sighed.

That coffee did the business for us. It was made by a masterartist, and it had not a fault; and the cream that came with it was so rich and thick that you could hardly have strained it through a wire fence. As the generous beverage flowed down our frigid throats, our blood grew warm again, our muscles relaxed, our torpid bodies awoke to life and feeling, anger and uncharitableness departed from us and we were cheerful once more. We got good cigars, also, at the Ocean House, and drove into town over a smooth road, lighted by the sun and unclouded by fog.

Near the Jewish cemeteries we turned a corner too suddenly, and got upset, but sustained no damage, although the horse did what he honestly could to kick the buggy out of the State while we were grovelling in the sand. We went on down to the steamer, and while we were on board, the buggy was upset again by some outlaw, and an axle broken.

However, these little accidents, and all the deviltry and misfortune that preceded them, were only just and natural consequences of the absurd experiment of getting up at an hour in the

morning when all God-fearing Christians ought to be in bed. I
consider that the man who leaves his pillow, deliberately, at sunrise, is taking his life in his own hands, and he ought to feel proud
if he don't have to put it down again at the coroner's office
before dark.

Now, for that early trip, I am not any healthier or any wealthier
than I was before, and only wiser in that I know a good deal better
than to go and do it again. And as for all those notable advantages,
such as the sun in the dawn of his glory, and the ships, and the
perfume of the flowers, etc., etc., etc., I don't see them, any more
than myself and Washington see the soundness of Benjamin
Franklin's attractive little poem.

If you go to the Cliff House at any time after seven in the
morning, you cannot fail to enjoy it—but never start out there
before daylight, under the impression that you are going to have a
pleasant time and come back insufferably healthier and wealthier
and wiser than your betters on account of it. Because if you do you
will miss your calculation, and it will keep you swearing about it
right straight along for a week to get even again.

Put no trust in the benefits to accrue from early rising, as set
forth by the infatuated Franklin—but stake the last cent of your
substance on the judgment of old George Washington, the Father
of his Country, who said "he couldn't see it."

And you hear me endorsing that sentiment.

80. *Original Novelette*

4 July 1864

This piece is among the more imaginative stories that Clemens succeeded in publishing in the San Francisco *Morning Call* under the guise of local items. Although ostensibly a news story, Clemens' literary interest is clearly predominant: he is writing a burlesque, or "condensed," novel in the fashion made popular in the West by Charles Henry Webb and Bret Harte. In fact, Clemens knew that these two men were at this time laboring together on the newly founded *Californian,* which published nothing but literary material. On 4 September 1864, after Harte became the magazine's editor, Clemens said of him in the *Call:* "Some of the most exquisite productions which have appeared in its pages emanated from his pen, and are worthy to take rank among even Dickens' best sketches."[1] "Original Novelette" is a modest attempt to follow the fashion of literary burlesque made popular by these men, and it suggests that Clemens was not content with his role as a reporter on a daily journal like the *Call.*

---

[1]"The Californian," San Francisco *Morning Call,* 4 September 1864, p. 3, reprinted in Appendix A33, volume 2.

Original Novelette

THE ONLY drawback there is to the following original novelette, is, that it contains nothing but truth, and must, therefore, be void of interest for readers of sensational fiction. The gentleman who stated the case to us said there was a moral to it, but up to the present moment we have not been able to find it. There is nothing moral about it. Chapter I.—About a year ago, a German in the States sent his wife to California to prepare the way, and get things fixed up ready for him. Chapter II.—She did it. She fixed things up, considerably. She fell in with a German who had been sent out here by his wife to prepare the way for her. Chapter III.—These two fixed everything up in such a way for their partners at home, that they could not fail to find it interesting to them whenever they might choose to arrive. The man borrowed all the money the woman had, and went into business, and the two lived happily and sinfully together for a season. Chapter IV.—Grand Tableau. The man's wife arrived unexpectedly in the Golden Age, and busted out the whole arrangement. Chapter V.—Now at this day the fallen heroine of this history is stricken with grief and refuses to be comforted; she has been cruelly turned out of the house by the usurping, lawful wife, and set adrift upon the wide, wide world, without a rudder. But she doesn't mind that so much, because she never had any rudder, anyhow. The noble maiden does mind being adrift, though, rudder or no rudder, because she has never been used to it. And so, all the day sits she sadly in the highway, weeping and blowing her nose, and slinging the result on the startled passers-by, and careless whether she lives or dies, now that her bruised heart can never know aught but sorrow any more. Last Chapter.—She cannot go to law to get her property back, because her sensitive nature revolts at the thought of giving publicity to her melancholy story. Neither can she return to her old home and fall at the feet of the husband of her early love, praying him to forgive, and bless and board her again, as he was wont to do in happier days; because when her destroyer shook her, behold he shook her without a cent. Now what is she to do? She wants to know. We have stated the case, and the thrilling original novelette is finished, and is not to be continued. But as to the moral, a rare chance is here offered the public to sift around and find it. We failed, in consequence of the very immoral character of the whole proceeding. Perhaps the best moral would be for the woman to go to work with renewed energy, and fix things, and get ready over again for her husband.

81. What a Sky-Rocket Did

12 August 1864

This brief sketch appeared unsigned in the San Francisco *Morning Call*, but Clemens' authorship is established by a letter he wrote to Orion and Mollie Clemens shortly after the piece appeared: "I have got Dr Bellows stuck after my local items. He says he never fails to read them—said he went into 'convulsions of laughter' over the account of 'What a Sky-Rocket Did.' " Clemens went on to tell an anecdote about an "old fellow down at San José, who is perfectly impervious to humor" and "takes everything he finds in a newspaper in dead earnest." Someone showed this gentleman "What a Sky-Rocket Did":

He read the article . . . with oppressive solemnity until he came to where the neighbors were expecting the fellow that went up with the rocket, & moved their families out of his way, & then he slammed the paper on the floor & rose up & angrily confronted the man—& says he, with measureless scorn in his tones: "Was expect'n of him *down!* They druther he'd fall in the *alley!* Moved ther families out to give him a *show!* Now look-a-here, my friend, you may go on & believe that, if you think you can stand it, but you'll excuse ME. I just think it's a *God dam lie!*"[1]

Clemens' obvious delight in this reaction suggests that "What a Sky-Rocket Did" was written in very much the same spirit that produced "A Petrified Man" (no. 28) and "A Bloody Massacre near Carson" (no. 66). However, the exact point of this very much milder hoax—obviously based on the facts—is now somewhat obscure. It seems that Clemens

---

[1]Clemens to Orion and Mollie Clemens, 14 August 1864, *CL1*, letter 89. The Reverend Henry W. Bellows was founder and president of the United States Sanitary Commission, and filled the pulpit of the First Unitarian Church from March to September 1864 following the death of Thomas Starr King. For his friendship with Clemens, see *CofC*, pp. 61–62, 66–68, 256–258.

felt he had scored against Captain Hinckley, who is mentioned so casually that, like G. T. Sewall in "A Petrified Man," he may be the primary target of the satire. William Crawley Hinckley was a former sea captain who had grown wealthy through trade and real-estate investments in San Francisco. For the four years prior to July 1864 he had been a member of the San Francisco board of supervisors, whose weekly meetings Clemens covered for the *Call*. There the conservative-minded Hinckley seems to have looked after the interests of property owners, and this fact may explain Clemens' relish in this "stretcher," which surreptitiously mocks the wealthy owner of poorly constructed tenement property.[2]

---

[2]See *CofC*, pp. 129–130.

What a Sky-Rocket Did

Night before last, a stick six or seven feet long, attached to an exploded rocket of large size, came crashing down through the zinc roof of a tenement in Milton Place, Bush street, between Dupont and Kearny, passed through a cloth ceiling, and fetched up on the floor alongside of a gentleman's bed, with a smash like the disruption of a china shop. We have been told by a person with whom we are not acquainted, and of whose reliability we have now no opportunity of satisfying ourselves, as he has gone to his residence, which is situated on the San José road at some distance from the city, that when the rocket tore up the splinters around the bed, the gentleman got up. The person also said that he went out—adding after some deliberation, and with the air of a man who has made up his mind that what he is about to say can be substantiated if necessary, that "he went out quick." This person also said that after the gentleman went out quick, he ran—and then with a great show of disinterestedness, he ventured upon the conjecture that he was running yet. He hastened to modify this rash conjecture, however, by observing that he had no particular reason for suspecting that the gentleman was running yet—it was only a notion of his, and just flashed on him, like. He then hitched up his team, which he observed parenthetically that he wished they belonged to him, but they didn't, and immediately drove away in the direction of his country seat. The tenement is there yet, though, with the hole through the zinc roof. The tenement is

the property of ex-Supervisor Hinckley, and some of the best educated men in the city consider that the hole is also, because it is
on his premises. It is a very good hole. If it could be taken from the
roof just in the shape it is now, it would be a nice thing to show at
the Mechanics' Fair; any man who would make a pun under circumstances like these, and suggest that it be turned over to the
Christian Commission Fair on account of its holy nature, might
think himself smart, but would the people—the plodding, thinking, intelligent masses—would *they* respect him? Far be it.
Doubtless. What shadows we are, and what shadows we pursue.
The foregoing facts are written to prepare the reader for the an-
nouncement that the stick, with the same exploded rocket attached, may be seen at the hall of the Board of Supervisors. It has
remained there to this day. The man who set it off, and hung on to
it, and went up with it, has not come down yet. The people who
live in Milton Place are expecting him, all the time. They have
moved their families, and got out of the way, so as to give him a
good show when he drops. They have said, but without insisting
on it, that if it would be all the same to him, they would rather he
would fall in the alley. This would mash him up a good deal,
likely, and scatter him around some, but they think they could
scrape him up and hold an inquest on him, and inform his parents. The Board of Supervisors will probably pass an ordinance
directing that missiles of the dangerous nature of rockets shall
henceforth be fired in the direction of the Bay, so as to guard
against accidents to life and property.

§ 82. The New Chinese Temple

19 August 1864

§ 83. The Chinese Temple

21 August 1864

§ 84. The New Chinese Temple

23 August 1864

§ 85. Supernatural Impudence

24 August 1864

These four sketches appeared in the San Francisco *Morning Call* while Clemens was working as its local reporter. Although they are of course unsigned, Clemens' authorship is assured by the fact that all four are preserved as clippings in his scrapbooks, and by the fact that Albert S. Evans, who is ridiculed in the last two sketches, publicly acknowledged Clemens as the author.

The subject of the series is the opening of the San Francisco temple of the Ning Yeung Association, a social and quasi-judicial organization that was formed in 1854 and became the largest of the Chinese Six Companies.[1] Clemens may have culled some facts from his scrapbook clip-

---

[1]William Hay, *The Chinese Six Companies* (San Francisco: The Chinese Consolidated Benevolent Association, 1942), pp. 5, 16.

pings when he described the Ning Yeung Association in chapter 54 of *Roughing It.* There he explained:

On the Pacific coast the Chinamen all belong to one or another of several great companies or organizations, and these companies keep track of their members, register their names, and ship their bodies home when they die. . . . The Ning Yeong Company . . . numbers eighteen thousand members on the coast. Its headquarters are at San Francisco, where it has a costly temple. . . . In it I was shown a register of its members, with the dead and the date of their shipment to China duly marked.[2]

The careful but informal description in the opening sketch, with its subdued, friendly humor and casually inserted information, gives way in the second piece to broader comedy: a burlesque portrait of "the old original Josh." In the third sketch Clemens finds himself in danger of "becoming imbued with Buddhism" and losing his national identity, but is recalled by the prospect of a drink to his "noble American instincts." This in turn leads to his ridicule of Evans, his counterpart on the San Francisco *Alta California.*[3]

Comic feuding among reporters and editors was a standard feature of Nevada journalism which Clemens brought with him when he moved to San Francisco and started working for the *Call:* two months before he wrote these sketches on the Josh House, he had begun baiting Evans in his local items column. Evans, who returned the compliment, created a character whom he called Mr. Stiggers, or Armand Leonidas Stiggers, a rather pathetic and dandyish fellow who was apparently meant as a parody of bohemians like Clemens. Perhaps to annoy Evans, Clemens regularly identified Stiggers with his creator, as he does in the third sketch here, where he accuses him of having consumed the temple's entire liquor supply. In the fourth sketch he extends this attack by quoting from Evans' *Alta* article on the new temple[4] and predicting that "Mr. Stiggers, of the Alta" will reply to his ridicule. Of course Evans did precisely that, addressing his remarks to "the gentle aborigine from the land of sage brush and alkali, whose soubriquet was given him by his friends as indicative of his capacity for doing the drinking for two." Evans

---

[2]*RI*, pp. 352–353.

[3]For additional information about Evans and Mark Twain's continuing public feud with him, see "Mark Twain Improves 'Fitz Smythe' " (nos. 129–134), as well as Appendix B, volume 2, which reprints a number of attributed items about Fitz Smythe.

[4]"Opening of a New Temple," San Francisco *Alta California,* 23 August 1864, p. 1.

went on to explain why Clemens found the temple's liquor cabinet empty, saying that the Chinese barkeeper maintains

two liquor cases—one from which to treat gentlemen who look as if they were disposed to indulge moderately and keep out of the calaboose, and the other, an empty one, which he shows to those whose faces indicate unmistakably that they can't be trusted when liquor is free. . . . There was a time . . . when you might have wrung in and got a drink with the rest, but that happy time is past, long past—Mark that, my boy, and go on with your weeping.[5]

Clemens continued to bait Evans for the next two years, not only in his columns in the *Call,* but also in the Virginia City *Territorial Enterprise* and the San Francisco *Dramatic Chronicle.*

---

[5]"That's What's the Matter," San Francisco *Alta California,* 24 August 1864, p. 1.

The New Chinese Temple

To-day the Ning-Yong Company will finish furnishing and decorating the new Josh house, or place of worship, built by them in Broadway, between Dupont and Kearny streets, and to-morrow they will begin their unchristian devotions in it. The building is a handsome brick edifice, two stories high on Broadway, and three on the alley in the rear; both fronts are of pressed brick. A small army of workmen were busily engaged yesterday, in putting on the finishing touches of the embellishments. The throne of the immortal Josh is at the head of the hall in the third story, within a sort of alcove of elaborately carved and gilded woodwork, representing human figures and birds and beasts of all degrees of hideousness. Josh himself is as ugly a monster as can be found outside of China. He is in a sitting posture, is of about middle stature, but excessively fat; his garments are flowing and ample, garnished with a few small circlets of looking-glass, to represent jewels, and streaked and striped, daubed from head to foot, with paints of the liveliest colors. A long strand of black horsehair sprouts from each corner of his upper lip, another from the centre of his chin, and one from just forward of each ear. He wears an open-work crown, which gleams with gold leaf. His rotund face is painted a glaring red, and the general expression of this fat and happy god is as if he had eaten too much rice and rats for dinner, and would like his belt loosened if he only had the energy to do it. In front of the throne hangs a chandelier of Chinese manufacture, with a wilderness of glass drops and curved candle-supports about it; but it is not as elegant and graceful as the American article. Under it, in a heavy frame-work, a big church bell is hung, also of Chinese workmanship: it is carved and daubed with many-colored paint all over. In front of the bell, three long tables are ranged, the fronts of two of which display a perfect maze-work of carving. The principal one shows, behind a glass front, several hundred splendidly gilded figures of kings on thrones, and bowing and smirking attendants, and horses on the rampage. The figures in this huge carved picture stand out in bold relief from the background, but they are not stuck on. The whole concern is worked out of a single broad slab of timber, and only the cunning hand of a Chinaman could have wrought it. Over the forward table is suspended a sort of shield, of indescribable shape, whose face is marked in compartments like a coat of arms, and in each of these is another nightmare of burnished and distorted human figures. The ceiling of this room, and both sides of it, are adorned with great sign boards, (they look like that to a content Christian, at any rate,) bearing immense Chinese letters or characters, sometimes raised from the surface of the wood and sometimes cut into it, and sometimes these letters being painted a bright red or green, and the grand expanse of sign board blazing with gold-leaf, or *vice versa*. These signs are presents to the Church from other companies, and they bear the names of those corporations, and possibly some extravagant Chinese moral or other, though if the latter was the case we failed to prove it by Ah Wae, our urbane and intelligent interpreter. Up and down the room, on both sides, are ranged alternate chairs and tables, made of the same hard, close-grained black wood used in the carved tables abovementioned; devout pagans lean their elbows on these little side tables, and swill tea while they worship Josh. Now, humble and unpretending Christian as we are, there was something infinitely comfortable and touching to us in this gentle mingling together of piety and breakfast. They have a large painted drum, and a pig or two, in this temple. How would it strike you, now, to stand at one end of this room with ranks of repentant Chinamen extending down either side before you, sipping purifying tea, and all about and above them a gorgeous cloud of glaring colors and dazzling gold and tinsel, with the bell tolling, and the drums thundering, and the gongs clanging, and portly, blushing old Josh in the distance, smiling upon it all, in his imbecile way, from out his splendid canopy? Nice, perhaps? In the second story there are more painted emblems and symbols than we could describe in a week. In the first story are six long white slats (in a sort of vault) split into one hundred and fifty divisions, each like the keys of a piano, and this affair is the death-register of the Ning-Yong Company. When a man dies, his name, age, his native place in China, and the place of his death in this country, are inscribed on one of these keys, and the record is always preserved. Ah Wae tells us that the Ning-Yong Company numbers eighteen or twenty thousand persons on this coast, now, and has numbered as high as twenty-eight thousand. Ah Wae speaks good English, and is the outside business man of the tribe—that is, he transacts matters with us barbarians. He will occupy rooms and offices in the temple, as will also the great Wy Gah, the ineffable High Priest of the temple, and Sing Song, or President of the Ning-Yong Company. The names of the temple, inscribed over its doors, are, "Ning Yong Chu Oh," and "Ning Yong Wae Quong;" both mean the same thing, but one is more refined and elegant, and is suited to a higher and more cultivated class of Chinese than the other— though to our notion they appear pretty much the same thing, as far as facility of comprehending them is concerned. To-morrow the temple will be opened, and all save Chinese will be excluded from it until about the 5th of September, when white folks will be free to visit it, due notice having first been given in the newspapers, and a general invitation extended to the public.

The Chinese Temple

The new Chinese Temple in Broadway—the "Ning Yong Wae Quong" of the Ning Yong Company, was dedicated to the mighty Josh night before last, with a general looseness in the way of beating of drums, clanging of gongs and burning of yellow paper, commensurate with the high importance of the occasion. In the presence of the great idol, the other day, our cultivated friend, Ah Wae, informed us that the old original Josh (of whom the image was only an imitation, a substitute vested with power to act for the absent God, and bless Chinamen or damn them, according to the best of his judgment,) lived in ancient times on the Mountain of Wong Chu, was seventeen feet high, and wielded a club that weighed two tons; that he died two thousand five hundred years ago, but that he is all right yet in the Celestial Kingdom, and can come on earth, or appear anywhere he pleases, at a moment's notice, and that he could come down here and cave our head in with his club if he wanted to. We hope he don't want to. Ah Wae told us all that, and we deliver it to the public just as we got it, advising all to receive it with caution and not bet on its truthfulness until after mature reflection and deliberation. As far as we are concerned, we don't believe it, for all it sounds so plausible.

The New Chinese Temple

BEING DULY provided with passes, through the courtesy of our cultivated barbaric friend, Ah Wae, outside business-agent of the Ning-Yong Company, we visited the new Chinese Temple again yesterday, in company with several friends. After suffocating in the smoke of burning punk and josh lights, and the infernal odors of opium and all kinds of edibles cooked in an unchristian manner, until we were becoming imbued with Buddhism and beginning to lose our nationality, and imbibe, unasked, Chinese instincts, we finally found Ah Wae, who roused us from our lethargy and saved us to our religion and our country by merely breathing the old, touching words, so simple and yet so impressive, and withal so familiar to those whose blessed privilege it has been to be reared in the midst of a lofty and humanizing civilization: "How do, gentlemen—take a drink?" By the magic of that one phrase, our noble American instincts were spirited back to us again, in all their pristine beauty and glory. The polished cabinet of wines and liquors stood on a table in one of the gorgeous halls of the temple, and behold, an American, with those same noble instincts of his race, had been worshipping there before us—Mr. Stiggers, of the Alta. His photograph lay there, the countenance subdued by accustomed wine, and reposing upon it appeared that same old smile of serene and ineffable imbecility which has so endeared it to all whose happiness it has been to look upon it. That apparition filled us with forebodings. They proved to be well founded. A sad Chinaman—the sanctified bar-keeper of the temple—threw open the cabinet with a sigh, exposed the array of

45

empty decanters, sighed again, murmured, "Bymbye, Stiggins been here," and burst into tears. No one with any feeling would have tortured the poor pagan for further explanations when manifestly none were needed, and we turned away in silence, and dropped a sympathetic tear in a fragrant rat-pie which had just been brought in to be set before the great god Josh. The temple is thoroughly fitted up now, and is resplendent with tinsel and all descriptions of finery. The house and its embellishments cost about eighty thousand dollars. About the 5th of September it will be thrown open for public inspection, and will be well worth visiting. There is a band of tapestry extending around a council-room in the second story, which is beautifully embroidered in a variety of intricate designs wrought in bird's feathers, and gold and silver thread and silk fibres of all colors. It cost a hundred and fifty dollars a yard, and was made by hand. The temple was dedicated last Friday night, and since then priests and musicians have kept up the ceremonies with noisy and unflagging zeal. The priests march backward and forward, reciting prayers or something in a droning, sing-song way, varied by discordant screeches somewhat like the cawing of crows, and they kneel down, and get up and spin around, and march again, and still the infernal racket of gongs, drums and fiddles, goes on with its hideous accompaniment, and still the spectator grows more and more smothered and dizzy in the close atmosphere of punk-smoke and opium-fumes. On a divan in one hall, two priests, clad in royal robes of figured blue silk, and crimson skull-caps, lay smoking opium, and had kept it up until they looked as drunk and spongy as the photograph of the mild and beneficent Stiggers. One of them was a high aristocrat and a distinguished man among the Chinamen, being no less a personage than the chief priest of the temple, and "Sing-Song" or President of the great Ning-Yong Company. His finger-nails are actually longer than the fingers they adorn, and one of them is twisted in spirals like a cork-screw. There was one room half full of priests, all fine, dignified, intelligent looking men, like Ah Wae, and all dressed in long blue silk robes, and blue and red topped skull caps, with broad brims turned up all round like wash-basins. The new temple is ablaze with gilded ornamentation, and those who are fond of that sort of thing would do well to stand ready to accept the forthcoming public invitation.

Supernatural Impudence

ALL THAT Mr. Stiggers, of the Alta, has to say about his monstrous conduct in the Ning-Yong Temple, day before yesterday, in drinking up all the liquors in the establishment, and breaking the heart of the wretched Chinaman in whose charge they were placed—a crushing exposure of which we conceived it our duty to publish yesterday—is the following: "We found a general festival, a sort of Celestial free and easy, going on, on arrival, and were waited on in the most polite manner by Ah Wee, who although a very young man, is thoroughly well educated, very intelligent, and speaks English quite fluently. With him we took a glass of wine and a cigar before the high altar, and with a general shaking hands all around our part of the ceremonies was concluded." That is the coolest piece of effrontery we have met with in many a day. He "concluded his part of the ceremonies by taking a glass of wine and a cigar." We should think a man who had acted as Mr. Stiggers did upon that occasion, would feel like keeping perfectly quiet about it. Such flippant gayety of language ill becomes him, under the circumstances. We are prepared, now, to look upon the most flagrant departures from propriety, on the part of that misguided young creature, without astonishment. We would not even be surprised if his unnatural instincts were to prompt him to come back at us this morning, and attempt to exonerate himself, in his feeble way, from the damning charge we have fastened upon him of gobbling up all the sacred whiskey belonging to those poor uneducated Chinamen, and otherwise strewing his path with destruction and devastation, and leaving nothing but tears and lamentation, and starvation and misery, behind him. We should not even be surprised if he were to say hard things about us, and expect people to believe them. He may possibly tremble and be silent, but it would not be like him, if he did.

86. [Sarrozay Letter from "the Unreliable"]

16–22 August 1864

The text of this untitled sketch is taken from a holograph preserved in the Jean Webster McKinney Family Papers, now at Vassar. The sketch has not been published before.

The approximate date of composition is established by the close relationship between the present sketch and "Inexplicable News from San José" (no. 87), which Clemens published in the San Francisco *Morning Call* on 23 August 1864. It seems likely that the *Call* piece was a later, shorter, and better-proportioned version of the present sketch: a number of passages from "Sarrozay Letter" appear almost verbatim in "Inexplicable News"—usually somewhat shorter, but occasionally longer, than in the first version. Clemens must have composed both sketches sometime after August 14, when he took his bibulous trip to San José, and it seems most likely that the present sketch was abandoned before he published "Inexplicable News" on August 23. This conjecture is supported by Mark Twain's prefatory note to the earlier version, which addresses the editors of the San Francisco *Golden Era*, presumably because he originally planned to publish it there: the publication of the *Call* version would have made the longer one unacceptable to the *Era* or to any other local paper. Thus if we allow one day for Clemens to return from San José (and recover from his hangover), we can assume that the present sketch was probably drafted between August 16 and 22.

Clemens was one of a convivial group of men who visited San José and Harrisburgh (Warm Springs) on August 14, traveling on the recently completed San Francisco and San José Railroad. Eight newspapermen and Lewis Leland, proprietor of the Occidental Hotel, made up the party. Of these, Clemens mentioned by name only Leland, "Livingston" (probably

49

Henry B. Livingston, law reporter for the San Francisco *Alta California*),[1] and "Steve" (probably his friend Steve Gillis). Warm Springs was a popular resort about twelve miles from San José. According to the reporter on the *Alta*, the men spent three hours there "in sauntering through the grounds, bathing, dining, etc."—the last apparently a euphemism for drinking.[2] Clemens introduced his own form of euphemism in the present sketch by attributing the drunken letter to the Unreliable (Clement T. Rice of the Virginia City *Union*). The manuscript shows that he originally signed the letter "Mark Twain," but thought better of this, canceled the signature, substituted "The Unreliable," and finally added the prefatory letter, which he signed "Mark Twain."

---

[1]Langley, *Directory for 1864*, pp. 246, 251.
[2]"Now and Then," San Francisco *Alta California*, 15 August 1864, p. 1.

[Sarrozay Letter from "the Unreliable"]

EDS. GOLDEN ERA:—Going down to San José last Sunday, to write a letter to the newspaper with which I am connected, I was taken somewhat sick, and the "Unreliable" being along, I ventured to entrust him with my work. I send you the result, for I have no use for it myself. This is the twentieth time I have been deceived by that well-meaning but unstable young man, and it shall be the last. Every time he gets a commission of this kind, he calls himself an editor, and gets drunk—to prove it, perhaps, though I cannot conceive how he hopes to establish such a fact by such an argument.

Yours, sadly,

MARK TWAIN.

SARROZAY, Last Sunday.

Sarrozay's beauriful place. Flowers—or maybe it's me—smells delishs—like sp—sp—sp—(ic!)—irits turpentine. Now, I'll stop that h(ic!)iccups *again*. All right.

It's a beauriful place. I'll tell you all about it. All the newsper m-men in Saffercisco's here this morring—one editor from Alta, one from Flag, one from Bulletin, one from Sacramento Union, one from Carson Independent, two from Morring Call—besides me—or *with* me—or somehow; nev' mind, you unstand—and Leland of the Occidental Hotel—all the newsper men in Saffrancisco, in fac,—an *all drunk*—think of that! All drunk but me. By

Georshe, I'm stonished. (Hic!) Shamed of 'em, too. Because, you
know, such conduct reflects on *me*—an reflectn on me, reflects
on the f—f'ternity, unstand?

Been out to Warrum Springs in a horse an four buggies, with
Leland, an Livingston, an Steve. Splennid place. Many women
there f'm Saffercisco. Enjoying themselves. All drunk. Baths ex-
lent—but makes 'em stagger. Singlar effect, ain't it? I like the
Warrum Springs. Four nice houses—sometimes scarrered
around—sometimes all in a jumble—sometimes all in a row.
Owing to something or other, praps. Everything looks dizzy—an
mixed. Curus.

Sarrozay's lovely place. Shade trees all down both sides street,
an in the middle—an gardens. That's two streets back of Connental Hotel. With a new church, in a scaffolding. I don' see how they
got her in—I don' see how they goin' to get her out. But she's
corraled—for good, praps. Poor ch(ic!)urch! Drat them hiccups.
It's f'm s—sociating with drunken beasts. Beauriful girls here,
staggering up an down that street, looking uneasy, an trying to
keep f'm running over people. Riding around, also, in buggies—
dangerous, when they're in such a condition.

Came down in the cars—no, on the locomotive. Nolan—Mike
Nolan, conductor, most intelligent, most polite, most obliging
conductor in the world. It was me that asked him lemme ride on
the cow-catcher, because I could see there warn't room enough in
the cars for me to enjoy myself strong. He said it was just the
thing—said he wanted some r-reliable man—some person he was
acquainted with, unstand?—an could depend on—to get on the
tender an hold the locomotive on the track. She was shaky. I held
her, all the way down. I held her down to the earth. The engineer
was grateful. Said I was a nice boy—nice, clean boy—an if I
hadn't held her down, she'd a left the State; she'd a gone to sea; *he*
couldn't a held her. The engineer's a gentleman. The only sober
man *I* see on that train.

Country on both sides charming, but mixed. All on the move.
Trees an bushes by the road appear to whiz; look strung out—
hazy, like dust was blowing through 'em. Houses there waltz
around all the time; see one ahead steadying herself a while, taking aim at you, an here she comes, like a shot; you dodge, an she

don't miss you a yard, sometimes. Everything on the move—turning round an round; everything drunk, you might say. Dangerous country to live in, praps, where everything's on the move; an you can't keep out of the way 'thout you're watching all the time. Even on the train, much as a man can do to dodge those houses; makes his neck tired, too, an scares him considerable.

Redwood City an Santa Clara's nice. But the houses discontented, all the same. Always waltzing around. Aggravating. I see a man follow a house all around town; never caught up with it while *I* was there. Where would that locomotive been, if I hadn't held her down? In the Bay, likely. Or chasing cattle.

Sarrozay's healthy, but s-streets roll in waves before you—made some of those newsper men awful sea-sick. I'm sleepy. I'm coming back on the c-cow-catcher to-night.

> "The b—bawry stood on the burring d—dog,
> Whence all but him had f-flowed—f'floored—f'fled—
> The f'flumes that lit the rattle's back—
> Sh-shone round him o'er the shed—"

I dono what's the marrer withat song. Drunk, too, praps. But if it's got no sense in it, *I* ain't going to put sense in it, an fix it up—not 'thout I'm paid for it. *I* never wrote the ridicklus thing. But I like it; don't you know, I *always* liked that song. I think it's pretty.

> "The b-bawry stood on the burring d-drake"

It's no use—I can't recklect it. But it's beauriful. (Hic!)

So long,

THE UNRELIABLE.

87. *Inexplicable News from San José*

23 August 1864

This sketch was published in the San Francisco *Morning Call.* Although it was not signed, Clemens referred to himself as "Mark Twain" in the sketch. In addition, he was demonstrably the author of "Sarrozay Letter from 'the Unreliable' " (no. 86), which amounts to an early version of the present sketch, contains several passages taken nearly verbatim from it, and survives in the author's holograph.

Judging from the manuscript of the early version, Clemens may have offered it to the San Francisco *Golden Era* and, when it was refused, salvaged his material by printing the present version in the *Call.* On the other hand, he may have revised his manuscript for purely literary reasons. Perhaps he recognized the limitations of drunken humor, and decided that his material was suitable only for a short newspaper sketch and not for a longer one in the *Era.* After first composing the manuscript and signing it "Mark Twain," he changed his mind and added the prefatory letter in which he interposed some distance between himself and the drunken letter writer. In the present sketch, Clemens extended that impulse by quoting only snippets of the drunken material, and by striking a familiar pose: the genteel "Moral Phenomenon," who is "filled . . . with humiliation" by the letter he has received. The two versions provide an opportunity to observe the apprentice writer experimenting with drunken dialect, as well as with the proper scope of this humorous device. On the whole, the second sketch is superior in highlighting (without obscuring, through phonetic spelling) the drunken observer's maudlin and befuddled state of mind, in its controlled incoherence, and in its judgment about when to stop.

Inexplicable News from San José

WE HAVE before us a letter from an intelligent correspondent, dated "Sarrozay, (San José?) Last Sunday;" we had previously ordered this correspondent to drop us a line, in case anything unusual should happen in San José during the period of his sojourn there. Now that we have got his chatty letter, however, we prefer, for reasons of our own, to make extracts from it, instead of publishing it in full. Considering the expense we were at in sending a special correspondent so far, we are sorry to be obliged to entertain such a preference. The very first paragraph in this blurred and scrawling letter pictured our friend's condition, and filled us with humiliation. It was abhorrent to us to think that we, who had so well earned and so proudly borne the appellation of "M. T., The Moral Phenomenon," should live to have such a letter addressed to us. It begins thus:

"MR. MARK TWAIN—Sir: Sarrozay's beauriful place. Flowers—or maybe it's me—smells delishs—like sp-sp-sp(ic!)irits turpentine. Hiccups again. Don' mind *them*—had 'em three days."

As we remarked before, it is very humiliating. So is the next paragraph:

"Full of newsper men—re porters. One from Alta, one from Flag, one from Bulletin, two from MORRING CALL, one from Sacramento Union, one from Carson Independent. And all drunk— all drunk but me. By Georshe! I'm stonished."

55

The next paragraph is still worse:

"Been out to Leland of the Occidental, and Livingston in the Warrum Springs, and Steve, with four buggies and a horse, which is a sp-splennid place—splennid place."

Here follow compliments to Nolan, Conductor of the morning train, for his kindness in allowing the writer to ride on the engine, where he could have "room to enjoy himself strong, you know," and to the Engineer for his generosity in stopping at nearly every station to give people a "chance to come on board, you understand." Then his wandering thoughts turn again affectionately to "Sarrozay" and its wonders:

"Sarrozay's lovely place. Shade trees all down both sides street, and in the middle and elsewhere, and gardens—second street back of Connental Hotel. With a new church in a tall scaffolding—I watched her an hour, but can't understand it. I don' see how they got her in—I don' see how they goin' to get her out. Corralled for good, praps. Hic! Them hiccups again. Comes from s-sociating with drunken beasts."

Our special next indulges in some maudlin felicity over the prospect of riding back to the city in the night on the back of the fire-breathing locomotive, and this suggests to his mind a song which he remembers to have heard somewhere. That is all he remembers about it, though, for the finer details of its language appear to have caved into a sort of general chaos among his recollections.

"The bawr stood on the burring dock,
    Whence all but him had f-flowed—f-floored—f-fled—
The f'flumes that lit the rattle's back
    Sh-shone round him o'er the shed—"

"I dono what's the marrer withat song. It don't appear to have any sense in it, somehow—but she used to be abou the fines' f-fusion—"

Soothing slumber overtook the worn and weary pilgrim at this point, doubtless, and the world may never know what beautiful thought it met upon the threshold and drove back within the portals of his brain, to perish in forgetfulness. After this effort, we trust the public will bear with us if we allow our special correspondent to rest from his exhausting labors for a season—a long season—say a year or two.

88. *How to Cure Him of It*

27 August 1864

Albert Bigelow Paine's account of the howling dog that disturbed Clemens and Steve Gillis on Minna Street was presumably gleaned from conversation with Gillis himself. It establishes, at any rate, Clemens' authorship of "How to Cure Him of It," which was published in the San Francisco *Morning Call* for 27 August 1864.

Paine describes Clemens' initial delight with their quarters: " 'Just look at it, Steve,' he said, 'What a nice, quiet place. Not a thing to disturb us.' " The next morning, however, "a dog began to howl. Gillis woke this time, to find his room-mate standing in the door that opened out into a back garden, holding a big revolver, his hand shaking with cold and excitement." Unable to hit the animal with the gun, "Mark Twain then let go such a scorching, singeing blast that the brute's owner sold him next day for a Mexican hairless dog."[1] "How to Cure Him of It" must have been still further relief.

Two years later, also in the *Call*, Clemens published " 'Mark Twain' on the Dog Question" (no. 197), which returned to the subject of canine "medication." Advising citizens on how to keep the city policemen from shooting their pet dogs, he wrote: "The presence of the dog is often betrayed to the Policeman by his bark. Remove the bark from his system and your dog is safe. This may be done by mixing a spoonful of the soother called strychnine in his rations. It will be next to impossible to ever get that dog to bark any more."[2] Both sketches exploit the same device used in "Those Blasted Children" (no. 72), which speaks of permanent "cures" for childhood diseases.

---

[1]*MTB*, 1:256.
[2]San Francisco *Morning Call*, 9 December 1866, p. 3.

How to Cure Him of It

IN A COURT in Minna street, between First and Second, they keep a puppy tied up which is insignificant as to size, but formidable as to yelp. We are unable to sleep after nine o'clock in the morning on account of it. Sometimes the subject of these remarks begins at three in the morning and yowls straight ahead for a week. We have lain awake many mornings out of pure distress on account of that puppy—because we know that if he does not break himself of that habit it will kill him; it is bound to do it—we have known thousands and thousands of cases like it. But it is easily cured. Give the creature a double handful of strychnine, dissolved in a quart of Prussic acid, and it will soo—oothe him down and make him as quiet and docile as a dried herring. The remedy is not expensive, and is at least worthy of a trial, even for the novelty of the thing.

89. Due Warning

18 September 1864

The author of "Due Warning," which appeared in the San Francisco *Morning Call*, identified himself in the text as "Mark Twain." The sketch elaborates on the similar dire warnings that Clemens had issued in "Unfortunate Thief" (no. 36) twenty months earlier, when his hat was stolen in Gold Hill, Nevada. His statement that the hat was "made by Tiffany" indicates that it was purchased from Tiffany's Eagle Hat Store on Washington Street in San Francisco.[1]

---

[1]Langley, *Directory for 1864*, p. 388.

Due Warning

SOME ONE carried away a costly and beautiful hat from the Occidental Hotel, (where it was doing duty as security for a board bill,) some ten days ago, to the great and increasing unhappiness of its owner. Its return to the place from whence it was ravished, or to this office, will be a kindness which we shall be only too glad to reciprocate if we ever get a precisely similar opportunity, and the victim shall insist upon it. The hat in question was of the "plug" species, and was made by Tiffany; upon its inner surface the name of "J. Smith" had once been inscribed, but could not easily be deciphered, latterly, on account of "Mark Twain" having been written over it. We do not know J. Smith personally, but we remember meeting him at a social party some time ago, and at that time a misfortune similar to the one of which we are now complaining happened to him. He had several virulent cutaneous diseases, poor fellow, and we have somehow acquired them, also. We do not consider that the hat had anything to do with the matter, but we mention the circumstance as being a curious coincidence. However, we do not desire to see the coincidence extend to the whole community, notwithstanding the fact that the contemplation of its progress could not do otherwise than excite a lively and entertaining solicitude on the part of the people, and therefore we hasten, after ten days' careful deliberation, to warn the public against the calamity by which they are threatened. And we will not disguise a selfish hope, at the same time, that these remarks

may have the effect of weaning from our hat the spoiler's affections, and of inducing him to part with it with some degree of
cheerfulness. We do not really want it, but it is a comfort to us in
our sorrow to be able thus to make it (as a commodity of barter
and sale to other parties,) something of a drug on the market, as
it were.

90. *The Mysterious Chinaman*

October 1864–mid-1865

The text of this poem is taken from a photographic copy of the holograph, now in the Doheny collection. The location of the holograph itself is not known.

Clemens wrote at the top of the manuscript, "(Written for M. E. G.'s Album.)." Presumably "M. E. G." was Mary Elizabeth Gillis, the sister of Clemens' good friends Jim and Steve Gillis. She was the sixth child of Angus and Margaret Alston Gillis, and may be the "Maim" mentioned in the poem. Mary's younger sister, Francina, may be the "Fannie" also mentioned.

The date of composition is difficult to establish, but it was probably in late 1864 or early 1865. Clemens had, of course, known Steve Gillis in Virginia City, and the pair had come together to San Francisco in May 1864. On September 25 Clemens told his family that while he and Steve were *"very* comfortably fixed" in their present quarters (probably 32 Minna Street), Gillis was about to marry and Clemens was planning to move. On December 4 he went to stay with Steve's older brother Jim in Jackass Hill (Tuolumne County), and did not return to the city until 26 February 1865. The San Francisco directory for 1865 indicates that upon his return Clemens boarded with the Gillis family at 44 Minna Street.[1] Although it is possible that Clemens inscribed "The Mysterious Chinaman" in Mary's album in late 1864, before leaving for Jackass Hill, it seems somewhat more likely that he did so while living with the family in March 1865, or somewhat later.

---

[1]Clemens to Jane Clemens and Pamela Moffett, 25 September 1864, *CL1*, letter 91; Langley, *Directory for 1864*, p. 106; N&J1, pp. 68, 82; Langley, *Directory for 1865*, pp. 121, 195.

"The Mysterious Chinaman" is Clemens' earliest known parody of "The Raven," a poem he knew well. On 20 December 1867 he would include a prose parody of the same poem in his letter to the Virginia City *Territorial Enterprise*, which read in part:

[Colonel Parker] remembered nothing that occurred after that, save that he awoke out of a deep sleep, apparently in the middle of a dark night— he does not know which night it was—and by his bedside, never flitting, still was sitting, still was sitting, that ghastly, grim and ancient Indian from the night's Plutonian shore—only he, and nothing more. Quoth the Indian, Nevermore. Then this ebon bird beguiling the Colonel's sad soul into smiling, by the grave and stern decorum of the countenance it bore, "Bird or fiend," he cried, upstarting, (wrathful to his heart's hot core). "What's the time of night, I wonder?—tell me that thou son of thunder, from the night's Plutonian shore. How long have I in dreams been soaring?—how long been wheezing, gagging, snoring?—how long in savage nightmares roaring, since I lay down before?" Quoth the buck,

"An hour or more. You've been sick and may be sicker, because of late you've stopped your liquor, a thing you've never done before; here's some stuff the doctor sent ye—of your folly quick repent ye—take it, Chief, and seek nepenthe—rememb'ring grief no more."

"Bird," the Colonel cried, upstarting, "Bird or fiend," he cried, upstanding. "Bird or fiend!" as if his soul in that one phrase he did outpour: "Pass that stuff the Doctor sent me—move the frame thy God hath lent thee —take thy form from off my door. Take thy beak from out my jug— go on thy bust outside my door." Quoth the Choctaw, "Nevermore."[2]

---

[2]"Mark Twain's Letters from Washington. Number III," Virginia City *Territorial Enterprise*, 11 January 1868, p. 2. The letter is scheduled to appear in the collection of social and political writings in The Works of Mark Twain.

The Mysterious Chinaman

Once upon a morning dreary, while I pondered, weak and weary,
Over many a quaint and curious shirt that me and Steve has
wore,*
While I was stretching, yawning, gaping, suddenly there came a
tapping,
As of some one gently rapping, rapping at my chamber door—
"I guess it's Maim," I muttered, "tapping at the chamber door—
At least it's she, if nothing more."

Presently my soul grew stronger—hesitating then no longer,
"Maim," said I, "or Fannie, truly your forgiveness I implore;
But the fact is, I was washing, and so gently you came sloshing,
And so faintly you came sloshing, sloshing round my chamber
door,
That I scarce was sure I heard you"—here I opened wide the
door—
Chung was there—and nothing more!

Then this leathery wretch beguiling my sad fancy into smiling,
By the grave and stern decorum of the countenance he bore—
"Though thy crest be shorn and shaven, thou," I said, "art sure no
Raven,

---

*The sacrifice of grammar to rhyme, in the second line, is a "poetic license"
which was imperatively demanded by the exigences of the case.—M. T.

Ghastly, grim and long-tailed scullion, wand'ring from the
  kitchen floor—
Tell me what thy lordly will is, ere you leave my chamber
  door"—
             Quoth Ah Chung, "No shabby *'door.'* " *(hic!)*

Much I marveled this ungainly brute to hear discourse so
  plainly,
Though his answer little meaning, little relevancy bore;
For we cannot help agreeing that no living human being
Ever yet was blest with seeing Chinaman outside his door
             With message like *"No shabby door."*

91. A Notable Conundrum

1 October 1864

Like two earlier sketches published in 1864—"The Evidence in the Case of Smith vs. Jones" and "Early Rising, As Regards Excursions to the Cliff House" (nos. 78 and 79)—the present sketch grew out of Clemens' reporting for the San Francisco *Morning Call*. During the month of September 1864 he was on continuing assignment to cover the Fourth Industrial Fair of the Mechanics' Institute, an organization interested in promoting technology and industrial prosperity in California. The institute's fair, housed in a spacious pavilion erected in Union Square, was crammed with exhibits. There the *Call* "local" regularly found an item or two, usually about novel or ingenious exhibits—too often a lackluster chore that required making a lot from a little.[1]

"A Notable Conundrum" is a bold, although not wholly successful, miscellany of anecdotes and observations about the fair. Its initial incident looks back to the love notes and scrambled vocabularies of "Territorial Sweets" (no. 39) and "Ye Sentimental Law Student" (no. 44). The miscellaneous character of the sketch is deliberately countenanced by the title, which is of course a complete misnomer: Clemens gives his impossible conundrum only in the penultimate paragraph, and concludes by saying that the young man who posed the conundrum "did not state what the answer was." Clemens continued to exploit this device in the two sketches that follow (nos. 92 and 93).

The sketch, despite its faults, marks an important point in Clemens' literary career, for it is the first of some twenty contributions that he wrote in 1864 and 1865 for the *Californian*. This distinguished literary journal had been founded the preceding May by Charles Henry Webb. But

---

[1]See *CofC*, pp. 104–115.

it was Bret Harte, the *Californian's* editor between 10 September and 19 November 1864, who presumably accepted the first nine of Clemens' sketches (nos. 91–99). Harte's presence on the staff was probably one reason Clemens regarded the *Californian* as a step upward. One week before his first sketch appeared, he wrote his family:

I have engaged to write for the new literary paper—the "Californian"— same pay I used to receive on the "Golden Era"—one article a week, fifty dollars a month. I quit the "Era," long ago. It wasn't high-toned enough. I thought that whether I was a literary "jackleg" or not, I wouldn't class myself with that style of people, anyhow. The "Californian" circulates among the highest class of the community, & is the best weekly literary paper in the United States—& I suppose I ought to know.[2]

Consistent with this view, Clemens made his *Californian* sketches more ambitiously literary than those he had published in the San Francisco *Golden Era* in September and October 1863.

Clemens included a clipping of this sketch in the Yale Scrapbook, which contained most of the western sketches he thought "worth republishing."[3] But when he helped prepare the printer's copy for the *Jumping Frog* book in January and February 1867, he struck through this clipping. The sketch was not reprinted in his lifetime.

---

[2]Clemens to Jane Clemens and Pamela Moffett, 25 September 1864, *CL1*, letter 91.

[3]Clemens to Jane Clemens and Pamela Moffett, 20 January 1866, *CL1*, letter 97: "I burned up a small cart-load of [sketches] lately—so *they* are forever ruled out of any book—but they were not worth republishing."

A Notable Conundrum

THE FAIR continues, just the same. It is a nice place to hunt for
people in. I have hunted for a friend there for as much as two
hours of an evening, and at the end of that time found the hunting
just as good as it was when I commenced.

If the projectors of this noble Fair never receive a dollar or even
a kindly word of thanks for the labor of their hands, the sweat of
their brows and the wear and tear of brain it has cost them to plan
their work and perfect it, a consciousness of the incalculable good
they have conferred upon the community must still give them a
placid satisfaction more precious than money or sounding compliments. They have been the means of bringing many a pair of
loving hearts together that could not get together anywhere else
on account of parents and other obstructions. When you see a
young lady standing by the sanitary scarecrow which mutely appeals to the public for quarters and swallows them, you may
know by the expectant look upon her face that a young man is
going to happen along there presently; and, if you have my luck,
you will notice by that look still remaining upon her face that you
are not the young man she is expecting. They court a good deal at
the Fair, and the young fellows are always exchanging notes with
the girls. For this purpose the business cards scattered about the
place are found very convenient. I picked up one last night which
was printed on both sides, but had been interlined in pencil, by
somebody's Arabella, until one could not read it without feeling

dizzy. It ran about in this wise—though the interlineations were not in parentheses in the original:

"John Smith, (My Dearest and Sweetest:) Soap Boiler and Candle Factor; (If you love me, if you love) Bar Soap, Castile Soap and Soft Soap, peculiarly suitable for (your Arabella, fly to the) Pacific coast, because of its non-liability to be affected by the climate. Those who may have kitchen refuse to sell, can leave orders, and our soap-fat carts will visit the (Art Gallery. I will be in front of the big mirror in an hour from now, and will go with you to the) corner designated. For the very best Soap and Candles the market affords, apply at the (Academy of Music. And from there, O joy! how my heart thrills with rapture at the prospect! with souls sur-charged with bliss, we will wander forth to the) Soap Factory, or to the office, which is located on the (moon-lit beach,) corner of Jackson street, near the milk ranch. (From Arabella, who sends kisses to her darling) JOHN SMITH, Pioneer Soap Boiler and Candle Factor."

Sweethearts usually treasure up these little affectionate billets, and that this one was lost in the Pavilion, seemed proof to me that its contents were rather distracting to the mind of the young man who received it. He never would have lost it if he had not felt unsettled about something. I think it is likely he got mixed, so to speak, as to whether he was the lucky party, or whether it was the soap-boiler. However, I have possession of her extraordinary document now, and this is to inform Arabella that, in the hope that I may answer for the other young man, and do to fill a void or so in her aching heart, I am drifting about, in an unsettled way, on the look-out for her—sometimes on the Pacific Coast, sometimes at the Art Gallery, sometimes at the soap factory, and occasionally at the moonlit beach and the milk ranch. If she happen to visit either of those places shortly, and will have the goodness to wait a little while, she can calculate on my drifting around in the course of an hour or so.

I cannot say that all visitors to the Fair go there to make love, though I have my suspicions that a good many of them do. Numbers go there to look at the machinery and misunderstand it, and still greater numbers, perhaps, go to criticise the pictures. There is a handsome portrait in the Art Gallery of a pensive young girl.

Last night it fell under the critical eye of a connoisseur from Arkansas. She examined it in silence for many minutes, and then she blew her nose calmly, and, says she, "I like it—it is so sad and thinkful."

Somebody knocked Weller's bust down from its shelf at the Fair, the other night, and destroyed it. It was wrong to do it, but it gave rise to a very able pun by a young person who has had much experience in such things, and was only indifferently proud of it. He said it was Weller enough when it was a bust, but just the reverse when it was busted. Explanation: He meant that it looked like Weller in the first place, but it did not after it was smashed to pieces. He also meant that it was well enough to leave it alone and not destroy it. The Author of this fine joke is among us yet, and I can bring him around if you would like to look at him. One would expect him to be haughty and ostentatious, but you would be surprised to see how simple and unpretending he is and how willing to take a drink.

But I have been playing the noble game of "Muggins." In that game, if you make a mistake of any kind, however trivial it may be, you are pronounced a muggins by the whole company, with great unanimity and enthusiasm. If you play the right card in the wrong place, you are a muggins; no matter how you play, in nine cases out of ten you are a muggins. They inform you of it with a shout which has no expression in it of regret. I have played this fine game all the evening, and although I knew little about it at first, I got to be quite a muggins at last. I played it very success-fully on a policeman as I went home. I had forgotten my night-key and was climbing in at the window. When he clapped his hand on my shoulder, I smiled upon him and, says I, "Muggins!" with much vivacity. Says he, "How so?" and I said, "Because I live here, and you play the wrong card when you arrest me for entering my own house." I thought it was rather neat. But then there was nobody at home to identify me, and I had to go all the way to the station-house with him and give bail to appear and answer to a charge of burglary. As I turned to depart says he "Muggins!" I thought that was rather neat also.

But the conundrum I have alluded to in the heading of this article, was the best thing of the kind that has ever fallen under my notice. It was projected by a young man who has hardly any education at all, and whose opportunities have been very meagre, even from his childhood up. It was this: "Why was Napoleon when he crossed the Alps, like the Sanitary cheese at the Mechanics' Fair?"

It was very good for a young man just starting in life; don't you think so? He has gone away now to Sacramento. Probably we shall never see him more. He did not state what the answer was.

92. Concerning the Answer to That Conundrum

8 October 1864

In a letter to his mother and sister written on 25 September 1864 Clemens said, "I wrote two articles last night for the *Californian*, so that lets me out for two weeks."[1] The first of these articles was probably the previous sketch, "A Notable Conundrum" (no. 91), but the second cannot now be identified. It was not his third contribution, "Still Further Concerning That Conundrum" (no. 93), because that was based on a performance of *Crown Diamonds* which he witnessed on October 10. And it was not the present sketch, because the opening sentence—"I went out, several days ago, to see the whale"—points to a date of composition soon after October 1: Clemens' visit to Ocean Beach must have occurred in the last days of September, shortly after a whale came ashore south of the Cliff House on September 26. The whale proved a great attraction to San Franciscans. When a second whale was stranded nearby on October 1—an event also alluded to in Clemens' first sentence— Captain Foster of the Cliff House, surely hoping for a fresh spate of customers at his bar, at once notified the newspapers.[2]

Clemens' companion on the excursion was John William (Johnny) Skae, a friend from Nevada days who was widely known as a good fellow and a lavish host. A native of Canada, Skae used his position as telegraph operator in Virginia City to make a fortune in stock speculation. He eventually became president of the Sierra Nevada Mining Company and a director of various other corporations, including the Hale and Norcross

---

[1]Clemens to Jane Clemens and Pamela Moffett, 25 September 1864, *CL1*, letter 91.
[2]San Francisco *Morning Call*: "A Whale Beached," 27 September 1864, p. 1; "Visiting the Whale," 29 September 1864, p. 3; "Another Whale Ashore," 2 October 1864, p. 1.

Mining Company.[3] In November 1867, just back from his unhappy experience with the *Quaker City* passengers, Clemens said, "If I were going
to start on a pleasure excursion around the world and to the Holy Land,
and had the privilege of making out her passenger list, I think I could do
it right and yet not go out of California." He included Skae's name among
the thirty-four Californians he placed on this ideal list. Clemens seems
to have associated Skae with good times, harmless mischief, "inimitable"
puns, and the rambling incoherence produced by "the intoxicating bowl"
(see "A Full and Reliable Account" and "The Facts," nos. 98 and 116). In
chapter 46 of *Roughing It* he described him as a nineteen-year-old Virginia City telegraph operator "who, when he could not make out German
names in the list of San Francisco steamer arrivals, used to ingeniously
select and supply substitutes for them out of an old Berlin city directory."[4] Clemens' account of Skae's family in the present sketch is in that
rich vein of comic free association which informs "The Facts," and it
faintly anticipates Jim Blaine's rambling monologue in chapter 53 of
Roughing It. But the sketch as a whole depends heavily on such conventional comic devices as the simpleton pose, drunken camaraderie, and
outrageously bad puns. Like the previous sketch it takes a leisurely pace,
and its title is another deliberate misnomer that now suggests Clemens'
continuing connection with the *Californian*.

Clemens included a clipping of this sketch in the Yale Scrapbook, and
in January or February 1867 he revised it slightly, intending to include it
in the *Jumping Frog* book. Either he or Charles Henry Webb eventually
decided against it, and the sketch was not reprinted in Clemens' lifetime.

---

[3]"Death of 'Johnny' Skae," San Francisco *Morning Call*, 17 July 1885, p. 1; Ratay,
Pioneers, pp. 40–41.

[4]"Letter from 'Mark Twain,'" San Francisco *Alta California*, written 20
November 1867, published 8 January 1868, reprinted in *TIA*, pp. 309–313; *RI*, p.
291.

Concerning the Answer to
That Conundrum

I WENT OUT, several days ago, to see the whale—I speak in the singular number, because there was only one whale on the beach at that time. The day was excessively warm, and my comrade was an invalid: consequently we travelled slowly, and conversed about distressing diseases and such other matters as I thought would be likely to interest a sick man and make him feel cheerful. Instead of commenting on the mild scenery we found on the route, we spoke of the ravages of the cholera in the happy days of our boyhood; instead of talking about the warm weather, we revelled in bilious fever reminiscences; instead of boasting of the extraordinary swiftness of our horse, as most persons similarly situated would have done, we chatted gaily of consumption; and when we caught a glimpse of long white lines of waves rolling in silently upon the distant shore, our hearts were gladdened and our stomachs turned by fond memories of sea-sickness. It was a nice comfortable journey, and I could not have enjoyed it more if I had been sick myself.

When we got to the Cliff House we were disappointed. I had always heard there was such a grand view to be seen there of the majestic ocean, with its white billows stretching far away until it met and mingled with the bending sky; with here and there a stately ship upon its surface, ploughing through plains of sunshine and deserts of shadow cast from the clouds above; and, near at hand, piles of picturesque rocks, splashed with angry surf and garrisoned by drunken, sprawling sea-lions and elegant, long-legged pelicans.

It was a bitter disappointment. There was nothing in sight but an ordinary counter, and behind it a long row of bottles with Old Bourbon, and Old Rye, and Old Tom, and the old, old story of man's falter and woman's fall, in them. Nothing in the world to be seen but these things. We staid there an hour and a half, and took observations from different points of view, but the general result was the same—nothing but bottles and a bar. They keep a field-glass there, for the accommodation of those who wish to see the sights, and we looked at the bottles through that, but it did not help the matter any to speak of; we turned it end for end, but instead of increasing the view it diminished it. If it had not been fashionable, I would not have engaged in this trivial amusement; I say trivial, because, notwithstanding they said everybody used the glass, I still consider it trivial amusement, and very undignified, to sit staring at a row of gin-bottles through an opera-glass. Finally, we tried a common glass tumbler, and found that it answered just as well, on account of the close proximity of the scenery, and did not seem quite so stupid. We continued to use it, and the more we got accustomed to it, the better we liked it. Although tame enough at first, the effects eventually became really extraordinary. The single row of bottles doubled, and then trebled itself, and finally became a sort of dissolving view of inconceivable beauty and confusion. When Johnny first looked through the tumbler, he said: "It is rather a splendid display, isn't it?" and an hour afterwards he said: "Thas so—'s a sp-(ic!)-splennid 'splay!" and set his glass down with sufficient decision to break it.

We went out, then, and saw a sign marked "CHICKEN SHOOTING," and we sat down and waited a long time, but finally we got weary and discouraged, and my comrade said that perhaps it was no use—may be the chicken was not going to shoot that day. We did not mind the disappointment so much, but the hiccups were so distressing. I am subject to them when I go abroad.

We left the hotel, then, and drove along the level beach, drowsily admiring the terraced surf, and listening to the tidings it was bringing from other lands in the mysterious language of its ceaseless roar, until we hove in sight of the stranded whale. We thought it was a cliff, an isolated hill, an island—anything but a fish, capable of being cut up and stowed away in a ship. Its proportions were magnified a thousand-fold beyond any conception we had previously formed of them. We felt that we could not complain of a disappointment in regard to the whale, at any rate. But we were not prepared to see a magnified mastodon, also; yet there seemed to be one towering high above the beach not far from the whale. We drove a hundred yards further—it was nothing but a horse.

Then the light of inspiration dawned upon me, and I knew what I would do if I kept the hotel, and the whale belonged to me. I would not permit any one to approach nearer than six or eight hundred yards to the show, because at that distance the light mists, or the peculiar atmosphere, or something, exaggerates it into a monster of colossal size. It grows smaller as you go towards it. When we got pretty close to it, the island shrunk into a fish—a very large one for a sardine, it is true, but a very small one for a whale—and the mastodon dwindled down to a Cayuse pony. Distance had been lending immensity to the view. We were disappointed again somewhat; but see how things are regulated! The very source of our disappointment was a blessing to us: As it was, there was just as much smell as two of us could stand; and if the fish had been larger there would have been more, wouldn't there? and where could we have got assistance on that lonely beach to help us smell it? Ah! it was the great law of compensation—the great law that regulates Nature's heedless agents, and sees that when they make a mistake, they shall at the self-same moment prevent that mistake from working evil consequences. Behold, the same gust of wind that blows a lady's dress aside, and exposes her ancle, fills your eyes so full of sand that you can't see it. Marvellous are the works of Nature!

The whale was not a long one, physically speaking—say thirty-five feet—but he smelt much longer; he smelt as much as a mile and a half longer, I should say, for we travelled about that distance beyond him before we ceased to detect his fragrance in the atmosphere. My comrade said he did not admire to smell a whale; and I adopt his sentiments while I scorn his language. A whale does not smell like magnolia, nor yet like heliotrope or

"Balm of a Thousand Flowers;" I do not know, but I should judge that it smells more like a thousand pole-cats.

With these few remarks I will now proceed to unfold a conundrum which I consider one of the finest that has ever emanated from the human mind. My invalid comrade produced it while we were driving along slowly in the open country this side of the Ocean House. I think it was just where we crossed the aqueduct of the Spring Valley Water Company, though I will not be certain; it might have been a little to the east of it, or maybe a little to the west, but at any rate it was in the immediate vicinity of it. I remember the time, though, very distinctly, for I was looking at my watch at the moment he commenced speaking, and it was a quarter of a minute after 3 o'clock—I made a memorandum of it afterward in my note-book which I will show you if you will remind me of it when I visit the CALIFORNIAN office. The sun was shining very brightly, but a light breeze was blowing from the sea, which rendered the weather pleasanter than it had been for several hours previously, and as it blew the dust in the same direction in which we were travelling, we experienced no inconvenience from it, although, as a general thing, I do not enjoy dust. It was under these circumstances that my invalid comrade, young John William Skae, who is in the quartz-milling business in Virginia City, now, but was born in the State of Pennsylvania, where his parents, and in fact most of his relatives, still reside, except one of his brothers, who is in the army, and his aunt, who married a minister of the gospel and is living out West, sometimes having an improving season in the vineyard and sometimes chased around considerable by the bushwhackers, who cannot abide preachers, and who stir them up impartially, just the same as they do those who have not yet got religion; and also except his first cousin, James Peterson, who is a skirmisher and is with the parson—he goes through the camp-meetings and skirmishes for raw converts, whom he brings to the front and puts them in the corral, or the mourner's bench, as they call it in that section, so that the parson can exhort them more handy—it was under these circumstances, as I was saying, that young Skae, who had been ruminating in dead silence for a long time, turned toward me with an unwholesome glare in his eye, at a quarter of a minute after 3

o'clock, while we were in the vicinity of the aqueduct of the
Spring Valley Water Company, and notwithstanding the light
breeze that was blowing and the filmy dust that was drifting
about us, says he: "Why is a whale like a certain bird which has
blue feathers and is mostly found in the West, where he is considered a good bird though not remarkable? It is, because he is the
Kingfisher—(the king fish, sir.)"

There was no house near by, except an old shed that had been
used by some workmen, but I took him to that and did what I
could for him; his whole nervous system seemed prostrated; he
only raised his head once, and asked in a feeble voice, but with an
expression of ineffable satisfaction in it—"How's that?" I knew
he did not want medicine—if anything could save him, it would
be rest and quiet. Therefore, I removed the horses to a distance,
and then went down the road, and by representing the case fairly
and openly to all passengers, I got them to drive by him slowly so
that they would make no noise to excite him. My efforts were
successful; his pulse was at two hundred and ninety when I put
him in the shed, and only forty-two when I took him out.

Now I thought that conundrum would have done honor to the
finest mind among us, and I think it especially good for an invalid
from Pennsylvania. How does it strike you? It is circumscribed in
its action, though, and is applicable only to men; you could not
say "Because it is the king fish, madam," without marring the
effect of the joke by rendering the point in a manner obscure.

Some friends of mine of great powers and high intellectual culture, and who naturally take an interest in conundrums, besought
me to procure the answer to that one about Napoleon and the
Sanitary cheese, and publish it. I have written to the Author of it,
and he informs me that he and his mother, who is a woman of
extraordinary sagacity and a profound thinker, are cyphering at it
night and day, and they confidently expect to have the answer
ready in time for your next week's issue. From what I can understand, they are making very encouraging progress; they have already found out why Napoleon was like the cheese, but thus far
they have not been able to ascertain in what respect the cheese
resembles Napoleon.

93. Still Further Concerning That Conundrum

15 October 1864

This sketch was Clemens' third consecutive weekly contribution to the *Californian*, and it continued (at least in the title) his rather lame joke about an unanswerable conundrum. Like the previous two sketches, its real subject was Mark Twain himself—here in the role of stuffed shirt, ostensibly showing the *Californian* editors how to write an opera review. His sketch is really a nonreview that concentrates on the fictional stagehand Signor Bellindo Alphonso Cellini—an "accomplished basso-relievo furniture-scout and sofa-shifter"—to the virtual exclusion of the real cast of *Crown Diamonds*, the members of Richings' Opera Troupe, who opened at Maguire's Academy of Music on 10 October 1864, the night Clemens attended.

By the time this sketch appeared in the *Californian* Clemens had left his post on the San Francisco *Morning Call*, for which he had earlier written several theater and opera notices. The basic joke in the present sketch may have been suggested by an item he had written for the *Call* in August 1864, a report on a recital at the fair of the Christian Commission:

The tableaux the other evening were gotten up in fine taste and gave great satisfaction, albeit while the one representing The Queen of Sheba at the Court of King Solomon, was before the house, the effect was unduly heightened by an assistant in citizen's dress rushing bald headed into Court, before he discovered that the curtain was still up. The Court betrayed surprise; and so would the original Solomon, if the same man, in the same modern costume, had ever appeared so unexpectedly before him. The intrusion was not premeditated; the gentleman was very deaf—so deaf, indeed, that he could not see that the curtain had not yet been lowered.[1]

---

[1]"The Fair," San Francisco *Morning Call*, 27 August 1864, p. 1, reprinted in *CofC*, pp. 102–103.

Both in the *Call* item and in the present sketch Clemens commented indirectly on the dilemma of the local reporter, who was bound in duty to cover theatrical events. In 1906 he remembered that as a *Call* reporter he and his colleagues regularly

visited the six theaters, one after the other: seven nights in the week, three hundred and sixty-five nights in the year. We remained in each of those places five minutes, got the merest passing glimpse of play and opera, and with that for a text we "wrote up" those plays and operas, as the phrase goes, torturing our souls every night from the beginning of the year to the end of it in the effort to find something to say about those performances which we had not said a couple of hundred times before.[2]

Clemens' disquisition on the imaginary stagehand was, in some sense, a solution to this problem, and a better form of entertainment (if not of criticism) than what he called the "boshy criticisms on the opera" usually published in the *Californian*. Signor Bellindo Alphonso Cellini also anticipated, in obvious ways, Basil Stockmar, the book-agent character Clemens added to the plot of *Hamlet*, an idea that probably came to him in November 1873.[3]

---

[2]AD, 13 June 1906, *MTE*, p. 255.
[3]*S&B*, p. 50.

Still Further Concerning
That Conundrum

In accordance with your desire, I went to the Academy of
Music on Monday evening, to take notes and prepare myself to
write a careful critique upon the opera of the *Crown Diamonds.*
That you considered me able to acquit myself creditably in this
exalted sphere of literary labor, was gratifying to me, and I should
even have felt flattered by it had I not known that I was so competent to perform the task well, that to set it for me could not be
regarded as a flattering concession, but, on the contrary, only a
just and deserved recognition of merit.

Now, to throw disguise aside and speak openly, I have long
yearned for an opportunity to write an operatic diagnostical and
analytical dissertation for you. I feel the importance of carefully-
digested newspaper criticism in matters of this kind—for I am
aware that by it the dramatic and musical tastes of a community
are moulded, cultivated and irrevocably fixed—that by it these
tastes are vitiated and debased, or elevated and ennobled, according to the refinement or vulgarity, and the competency or incom-
petency of the writers to whom this department of the public
training is entrusted. If you would see around you a people who
are filled with the keenest appreciation of perfection in musical
execution and dramatic delineation, and painfully sensitive to the
slightest departures from the true standard of art in these things,
you must employ upon your newspapers critics capable of discriminating between merit and demerit, and alike fearless in

praising the one and condemning the other. Such a person—
although it may be in some degree immodest in me to say so—
I claim to be. You will not be surprised, then, to know that I
read your boshy criticisms on the opera with the most exquisite
anguish—and not only yours, but those which I find in every paper in San Francisco.

You do nothing but sing one everlasting song of praise; when an
artist, by diligence and talent, makes an effort of transcendent
excellence, behold, instead of receiving marked and cordial attention, both artist and effort sink from sight, and are lost in the
general slough of slimy praise in which it is your pleasure to cause
the whole company, good, bad and indifferent, to wallow once a
week. With this brief but very liberal and hearty expression of
sentiment, I will drop the subject and leave you alone for the
present, for it behooves me now to set you a model in criticism.

The opera of the *Crown Diamonds* was put upon the stage in
creditable shape on Monday evening, although I noticed that the
curtains of the "Queen of Portugal's" drawing-room were not as
gorgeous as they might have been, and that the furniture had a
second-hand air about it, of having seen service in the preceding
reign. The acting and the vocalization, however, were, in the
main, good. I was particularly charmed by the able manner in
which Signor Bellindo Alphonso Cellini, the accomplished basso-relievo furniture-scout and sofa-shifter performed his part. I
have before observed that this rising young artist gave evidence of
the rarest genius in his peculiar department of operatic business,
and have been annoyed at noticing with what studied care a ven-
omous and profligate press have suppressed his name and suffered
his sublimest efforts to pass unnoticed and unglorified. Shame
upon such grovelling envy and malice! But, with all your neglect,
you have failed to crush the spirit of the gifted furniture-scout,
or seduce from him the affectionate encouragement and appreciation of the people. The moment he stepped upon the stage on
Monday evening, to carry out the bandit chieftain's valise, the
upper circles, with one accord, shouted, "Supe! supe!" and greeted
him with warm and generous applause. It was a princely triumph
for Bellindo; he told me afterwards it was the proudest moment of
his life.

I watched Alphonso during the entire performance and was never so well pleased with him before, although I have admired him from the first. In the second act, when the eyes of the whole audience were upon him—when his every movement was the subject of anxiety and suspense—when everything depended upon his nerve and self-possession, and the slightest symptom of hesitation or lack of confidence would have been fatal—he stood erect in front of the cave, looking calmly and unflinchingly down upon the camp-stool for several moments, as one who has made up his mind to do his great work or perish in the attempt, and then seized it and bore it in triumph to the foot-lights! It was a sublime spectacle. There was not a dry eye in the house. In that moment, not even the most envious and uncharitable among the noble youth's detractors would have had the hardihood to say he was not endowed with a lofty genius.

Again, in the scene where the Prime Minister's nephew is imploring the female bandit to fly to the carriage and escape impending wrath, and when dismay and confusion ruled the hour, how quiet, how unmoved, how grandly indifferent was Bellindo in the midst of it all!—what stolidity of expression lay upon his countenance! While all save himself were unnerved by despair, he serenely put forth his finger and mashed to a shapeless pulp a mosquito that loitered upon the wall, yet betrayed no sign of agitation the while. Was there nothing in this lofty contempt for the dangers which surrounded him that marked the actor destined hereafter to imperishable renown?

Possibly upon that occasion when it was necessary for Alphonso to remove two chairs and a table during the shifting of the scenes, he performed his part with undue precipitation; with the table upside down upon his head, and grasping the corners with hands burdened with the chairs, he appeared to some extent undignified when he galloped across the stage. Generally his conception of his part is excellent, but in this case I am satisfied he threw into it an enthusiasm not required and also not warranted by the circumstances. I think that careful study and reflection will convince him that I am right, and that the author of the opera intended that in this particular instance the furniture should be carried out with impressive solemnity. That he had this in view is evidenced by the slow and stately measure of the music played by the orchestra at that juncture.

But the crowning glory of Cellini's performance that evening was the placing of a chair for the Queen of Portugal to sit down in after she had become fatigued by earnestly and elaborately abusing the Prime Minister for losing the Crown Diamonds. He did not grab the chair by the hind leg and shove it awkwardly at her Majesty; he did not seize it by the seat and thrust it ungracefully toward her; he did not handle it as though he was undecided about the strict line of his duty or ignorant of the proper manner of performing it. He did none of these things. With a coolness and confidence that evinced the most perfect conception and the most consummate knowledge of his part, he came gently forward and laid hold of that chair from behind, set it in its proper place with a movement replete with grace, and then leaned upon the back of it, resting his chin upon his hand, and in this position smiled a smile of transfigured sweetness upon the audience over the Queen of Portugal's head. There shone the inspired actor! and the people saw and acknowledged him; they waited respectfully for Miss Richings to finish her song, and then with one impulse they poured forth upon him a sweeping tempest of applause.

At the end of the piece the idolized furniture-scout and sofa-skirmisher was called before the curtain by an enthusiastic shouting and clapping of hands, but he was thrust aside, as usual, and other artists, (who chose to consider the compliment as intended for themselves,) swept bowing and smirking along the footlights and received it. I swelled with indignation, but I summoned my fortitude and resisted the pressure successfully. I am still intact.

Take it altogether, the *Crown Diamonds* was really a creditable performance. I feel that I would not be doing my whole duty if I closed this critique without speaking of Miss Caroline Richings, Miss Jenny Kempton, Mr. Hill, Mr. Seguin and Mr. Peakes, all of whom did fair justice to their several parts, and deserve a passing notice. With study, perseverance and attention, I have no doubt these vocalists will in time achieve a gratifying success in their profession.

I believe I have nothing further to say. I will call around, to-morrow, after you have had time to read, digest and pass your judgment upon my criticism, and, if agreeable, I will hire out to you for some years in that line.

MARK TWAIN.

P. S.—No answer to that conundrum this week. On account of over-exertion on it the old woman has got to having fits here lately. However, it will be forthcoming yet, when she runs out of them, if she don't die in the meantime, and I trust she will not. We may as well prepare ourselves for the worst, though, for it is not to be disguised that they are shaking her up mighty lively.

94. *Whereas*

22 October 1864

This sketch was Clemens' most ambitious effort for the *Californian* to date, and in a manner that was both self-consciously literary and somewhat mechanical it combined humor with satire. The unusual first half of the sketch appears to be good-natured mimicry of the polite personal essay, as practiced by such masters as Goldsmith, Lamb, Irving, and Hawthorne. Like some of those writers, Mark Twain meditates, falls into reveries, and holds colloquies with himself in a gentle exclamatory manner, emitting such uncharacteristic appeals as "God bless my soul" while he spins out the conceit of Love's Bakery, the modern "Palace of Cupid" that he pretends to approach with all the naive and reverential awe that Goldsmith's Lien Chi Altangi feels for Westminster Abbey. This humorous essay serves as "a peculiarly fitting introductory to a story of love and misfortune"—comprising the second half of the sketch—in which Clemens takes aim at the concept of love-faithful-unto-death, the common stock of sentimental romance, and also burlesques a popular journalistic form, the column of advice offered to correspondents. (In June and July 1865 Clemens would again experiment with this type of burlesque in a weekly feature for the *Californian;* see "Answers to Correspondents," nos. 105–110.) In the genteel musings about Love's Bakery, love is seen as the shaper of destinies and the undiminishing master passion, albeit comically treated in Mark Twain's elaborate image of lovers "well kneaded together, baked to a turn, and ready for matrimony." By contrast, the tale of Breckinridge Caruthers' gruesome fate is a sadistic fantasy. Aurelia and her fiancé, with his "infernal propensity" for piecemeal disintegration, serve to ridicule the notion of extraordinary faithfulness taken to its extreme: Caruthers is a kind of concrete *reductio ad absurdum.*

The author thought well enough of his sketch to revise it in January or February 1867 for reprinting in the *Jumping Frog* book. But it was probably his editor, Charles Henry Webb, who decided to omit the introductory passage about Love's Bakery and to retitle the remainder "Aurelia's Unfortunate Young Man" (see the textual commentary). Clemens continued to revise and reprint the piece in 1872, 1874, and 1875, the last revision appearing in *Sketches, New and Old.* Less than a year later, however, he told William Dean Howells that he had "heard of readers convulsing audiences" with the sketch, but that if there was "anything really funny in the piece, the author is not aware of it."[1] The text reprinted here gives the full *Californian* version, not the one edited by Mark Twain and Webb in early 1867.

---

[1]Clemens to William Dean Howells, 23 August 1876, *MTHL,* 1:147.

Whereas

LOVE'S BAKERY! I am satisfied I have found the place now that I
have been looking for all this time. I cannot describe to you the
sensation of mingled astonishment, gladness, hope, doubt, anxiety, and balmy, blissful emotion that suffused my being and quiv-
ered in a succession of streaky thrills down my backbone, as I
stood on the corner of Third and Minna streets, last Tuesday, and
stared, spell-bound, at those extraordinary words, painted in large,
plain letters on a neighboring window-curtain—"LOVE'S BAK-
ERY." "God bless my soul!" said I, "will wonders never cease?—
are there to be no limits to man's spirit of invention?—is he to
invade the very realms of the immortal, and presume to guide and
control the great passions, the impalpable essences, that have
hitherto dwelt in the secret chambers of the soul, sacred from all
save divine intrusion?"

I read and re-read that remarkable sign with constantly-
increasing wonder and interest. There was nothing extraordinary
in the appearance of the establishment, and even if it had possessed anything of a supernatural air, it must necessarily have
been neutralized by the worldly and substantial look of a pyramid
of excellent bread that stood in the window—a sign very incon-
sistent, it seemed to me, with the character of a place devoted to
the high and holy employment of instilling the passion of love
into the human heart, although it was certainly in keeping with
the atrocious taste which was capable of conferring upon a vice-

royalty of heaven itself such an execrable name as "Love's Bakery." Why not Love's Bower, or the Temple of Love, or the Palace of Cupid?—anything—anything in the world would have been less repulsive than such hideous vulgarity of nomenclature as "Love's *Bakery.*"

The place seemed very complete, and well supplied with every facility for carrying on the business of creating love successfully. In a window of the second story was a large tin cage with a parrot in it, and near it was a sign bearing the inscription, "Preparatory School for Young Ladies"—that is, of course, a school where they are taught certain things necessary to prepare them for the bakery down below. Not far off is also a "Preparatory School for Young Gentlemen," which is doubtless connected with Love's Bakery too. I saw none of the pupils of either of the schools, but my imagination dwelt upon them with a deep and friendly interest. How irksome, I thought, must this course of instruction be to these tender hearts, so impatient to be baked into a state of perfect love!

Greatly moved by the singular circumstances which surrounded me, I fell into a profound and pleasing reverie. Here, I thought, they take a couple of hopeful hearts in the rough, and work them up, with spices and shortening and sweetening enough to last for a lifetime, and turn them out well kneaded together, baked to a turn, and ready for matrimony, and without having been obliged to undergo a long and harrowing courtship, with the desperate chances attendant thereon, of persevering rivals, unwilling parents, inevitable love-quarrels, and all that sort of thing.

Here, I thought, they will bake you up a couple in moderate circumstances, at short notice and at a cheap rate, and turn them out in good enough shape for the money, perhaps, but nevertheless burnt with the fire of jealousy on one side, and flabby and "duffy" with lukewarmness and indifference on the other, and spotted all over with the salæratus stains of a predisposition to make the conjugal cake bitter and unpalatable for all time to come.

Or they will take an excessively patrician pair, charge them a dozen prices, and deliver them to order in a week, all plastered over with the ghostly vines and flowers of blighted fancies, hopes and yearnings, wrought in chilly ice-work.

Or, perhaps, they will take a brace of youthful, tender hearts, and dish them up in no time, into crisp, delicate "lady-fingers," tempting to contemplate, and suggestive of that serene after-dinner happiness and sociability that come when the gross substantials have been swept from the board and are forgotten in soft dalliance with pastry and ices and sparkling Moselle.

Or maybe they will take two flinty old hearts that have harbored selfishness, envy and all uncharitableness in solitude for half a century, and after a fortnight's roasting, turn them out the hardest kind of hard-tack, invulnerable to all softening influences for evermore.

Here was a revolution far more extended, and destined to be attended by more momentous consequences to the nations of the earth, than any ever projected or accomplished by the greatest of the world's military heroes! Love, the master passion of the human heart, which, since the morning of the creation had shaped the destinies of emperors and beggars alike, and had ruled all men as with a rod of iron, was to be hurled from the seat of power in a single instant, as it were, and brought into subjection to the will of an inspired, a sublimely-gifted baker! By some mysterious magic, by some strange and awful invention, the divine emotion was to be confined within set bounds and limits, controlled, weighed, measured, and doled out to God's creatures in quantities and qualities to suit the purchaser, like vulgar beer and candles!

And in times to come, I thought, the afflicted lover, instead of reading Heuston & Hastings' omnipresent sign and gathering no comfort from it, will read "Go to Love's Bakery!" on the dead-walls and telegraph poles, and be saved.

Now I might never have published to the world my discovery of this manufactory of the human affections in a populous thoroughfare of San Francisco, if it had not occurred to me that some account of it would serve as a peculiarly fitting introductory to a story of love and misfortune, which it falls to my lot to relate. And yet even Love's Bakery could afford no help to the sufferers of whom I shall speak, for they do not lack affection for each other, but are the victims of an accumulation of distressing circumstances against which the efforts of that august agent would be powerless.

The facts in the case come to me by letter from a young lady who lives in the beautiful city of San José; she is personally unknown to me, and simply signs herself "Aurelia Maria," which may possibly be a fictitious name. But no matter, the poor girl is almost heart-broken by the misfortunes she has undergone, and so confused by the conflicting counsels of misguided friends and insidious enemies, that she does not know what course to pursue in order to extricate herself from the web of difficulties in which she seems almost hopelessly involved. In this dilemma she turns to me for help, and supplicates for my guidance and instruction with a moving eloquence that would touch the heart of a statue. Hear her sad story:

She says that when she was sixteen years old she met and loved with all the devotion of a passionate nature a young man from New Jersey, named Williamson Breckinridge Caruthers, who was some six years her senior. They were engaged, with the free consent of their friends and relatives, and for a time it seemed as if their career was destined to be characterized by an immunity from sorrow beyond the usual lot of humanity. But at last the tide of fortune turned; young Caruthers became infected with small-pox of the most virulent type, and when he recovered from his illness, his face was pitted like a waffle-mould and his comeliness gone forever. Aurelia thought to break off the engagement at first, but pity for her unfortunate lover caused her to postpone the marriage-day for a season, and give him another trial. The very day before the wedding was to have taken place, Breckinridge, while absorbed in watching the flight of a balloon, walked into a well and fractured one of his legs, and it had to be taken off above the knee. Again Aurelia was moved to break the engagement, but again love triumphed, and she set the day forward and gave him another chance to reform. And again misfortune overtook the unhappy youth. He lost one arm by the premature discharge of a Fourth-of-July cannon, and within three months he got the other pulled out by a carding-machine. Aurelia's heart was almost crushed by these latter calamities. She could not but be deeply grieved to see her lover passing from her by piecemeal, feeling, as she did, that he could not last forever under this disastrous process of reduction, yet knowing of no way to stop its dreadful career, and in her tearful despair she almost regretted, like brokers who hold on and lose, that she had not taken him at first, before he had suffered such an alarming depreciation. Still, her brave soul bore her up, and she resolved to bear with her friend's unnatural disposition yet a little longer. Again the wedding-day approached, and again disappointment overshadowed it: Caruthers fell ill with the erysipelas, and lost the use of one of his eyes entirely. The friends and relatives of the bride, considering that she had already put up with more than could reasonably be expected of her, now came forward and insisted that the match should be broken off; but after wavering awhile, Aurelia, with a generous spirit which did her credit, said she had reflected calmly upon the matter and could not discover that Breckinridge was to blame. So she extended the time once more, and he broke his other leg. It was a sad day for the poor girl when she saw the surgeons reverently bearing away the sack whose uses she had learned by previous experience, and her heart told her the bitter truth that some more of her lover was gone. She felt that the field of her affections was growing more and more circumscribed every day, but once more she frowned down her relatives and renewed her betrothal. Shortly before the time set for the nuptials another disaster occurred. There was but one man scalped by the Owens River Indians last year. That man was Williamson Breckinridge Caruthers, of New Jersey. He was hurrying home with happiness in his heart, when he lost his hair forever, and in that hour of bitterness he almost cursed the mistaken mercy that had spared his head.

At last Aurelia is in serious perplexity as to what she ought to do. She still loves her Breckinridge, she writes, with true womanly feeling—she still loves what is left of him—but her parents are bitterly opposed to the match, because he has no property and is disabled from working, and she has not sufficient means to support both comfortably. "Now, what should she do?" she asks with painful and anxious solicitude.

It is a delicate question; it is one which involves the life-long happiness of a woman, and that of nearly two-thirds of a man, and

I feel that it would be assuming too great a responsibility to do more than make a mere suggestion in the case. How would it do to build to him? If Aurelia can afford the expense, let her furnish her mutilated lover with wooden arms and wooden legs, and a glass eye and a wig, and give him another show; give him ninety days, without grace, and if he does not break his neck in the meantime, marry him and take the chances. It does not seem to me that there is much risk, any way, because if he sticks to his infernal propensity for damaging himself every time he sees a good opportunity, his next experiment is bound to finish him, and then you are all right, you know, married or single. If married, the wooden legs and such other valuables as he may possess, revert to the widow, and you see you sustain no actual loss save the cherished fragment of a noble but most unfortunate husband, who honestly strove to do right, but whose extraordinary instincts were against him. Try it, Maria! I have thought the matter over carefully and well, and it is the only chance I see for you. It would have been a happy conceit on the part of Caruthers if he had started with his neck and broken that first, but since he has seen fit to choose a different policy and string himself out as long as possible, I do not think we ought to upbraid him for it if he has enjoyed it. We must do the best we can under the circumstances, and try not to feel exasperated at him.

95. A Touching Story of George Washington's Boyhood

29 October 1864

Mark Twain seemed determined to provoke a laugh by giving deceptive titles to his *Californian* sketches. "Whereas" (no. 94) was an odd combination of humor and satire which had nothing whatever to do with its title. And in the present sketch, his fifth consecutive weekly contribution, he never got around to telling the story of "Little George Washington, who could Not Lie, and the Cherry Tree"—the classic American fable glorifying truth telling. His failure to make good on his title here was, perhaps, an oblique way of commenting on the minimal veracity of the sketch that he did write—as if any comment were really needed. The sketch records the narrator's passage from savage retribution and outrage to understanding, compassion, and peacemaking—a virtual burlesque on a story of Christian conversion.

On the whole, the strain of a weekly contribution to the *Californian* appears to be showing in this sketch: it is not in Mark Twain's best manner. Nevertheless, either he or Charles Henry Webb decided to include the sketch in the 1867 *Jumping Frog* book. And although Clemens omitted it from the collection of sketches that he prepared for the Routledges in 1872, he did not remove it from Hotten's *Choice Humorous Works* in 1873, but tried instead to revise it. The same temptation came upon him in 1875 while preparing copy for *Sketches, New and Old,* and he considered including the sketch there, but decided against it.

A Touching Story of
George Washington's Boyhood

I F IT PLEASE your neighbor to break the sacred calm of night with
the snorting of an unholy trombone, it is your duty to put up with
his wretched music and your privilege to pity him for the unhappy instinct that moves him to delight in such discordant
sounds. I did not always think thus; this consideration for musical amateurs was born of certain disagreeable personal experiences that once followed the development of a like instinct in
myself. Now this infidel over the way, who is learning to play on
the trombone, and the slowness of whose progress is almost
miraculous, goes on with his harrowing work every night, un-
cursed by me, but tenderly pitied. Ten years ago, for the same
offence, I would have set fire to his house. At that time I was a
prey to an amateur violinist for two or three weeks, and the suf-
ferings I endured at his hands are inconceivable. He played "Old
Dan Tucker," and he never played anything else—but he performed that so badly that he could throw me into fits with it if I
were awake, or into a nightmare if I were asleep. As long as he
confined himself to "Dan Tucker," though, I bore with him and
abstained from violence; but when he projected a fresh outrage,
and tried to do "Sweet Home," I went over and burnt him out. My
next assailant was a wretch who felt a call to play the clarionet.
He only played the scale, however, with his distressing instrument, and I let him run the length of his tether, also; but finally,
when he branched out into a ghastly tune, I felt my reason desert-

ing me under the exquisite torture, and I sallied forth and burnt
him out likewise. During the next two years I burned out an
amateur cornet-player, a bugler, a bassoon-sharp, and a barbarian
whose talents ran in the bass-drum line. I would certainly have
scorched this trombone man if he had moved into my neighborhood in those days. But as I said before, I leave him to his own
destruction now, because I have had experience as an amateur
myself, and I feel nothing but compassion for that kind of people.
Besides, I have learned that there lies dormant in the souls of all
men a penchant for some particular musical instrument, and an
unsuspected yearning to learn to play on it, that are bound to
wake up and demand attention some day. Therefore, you who rail
at such as disturb your slumbers with unsuccessful and demoralizing attempts to subjugate a fiddle, beware! for sooner or
later your own time will come. It is customary and popular to
curse these amateurs when they wrench you out of a pleasant
dream at night with a peculiarly diabolical note, but seeing that
we are all made alike, and must all develop a distorted talent for
music in the fullness of time, it is not right. I am charitable to my
trombone maniac; in a moment of inspiration he fetches a snort,
sometimes, that brings me to a sitting posture in bed, broad
awake and weltering in a cold perspiration. Perhaps my first
thought is that there has been an earthquake; perhaps I hear the
trombone, and my next thought is that suicide and the silence of
the grave would be a happy release from this nightly agony;
perhaps the old instinct comes strong upon me to go after my
matches; but my first cool, collected thought is that the trombone man's destiny is upon him, and he is working it out in
suffering and tribulation; and I banish from me the unworthy
instinct that would prompt me to burn him out.

    After a long immunity from the dreadful insanity that moves a
man to become a musician in defiance of the will of God that he
should confine himself to sawing wood, I finally fell a victim to
the instrument they call the Accordeon. At this day I hate that
contrivance as fervently as any man can, but at the time I speak of
I suddenly acquired a disgusting and idolatrous affection for it. I
got one of powerful capacity and learned to play "Auld Lang
Syne" on it. It seems to me, now, that I must have been gifted

with a sort of inspiration to be enabled, in the state of ignorance in which I then was, to select out of the whole range of musical composition the one solitary tune that sounds vilest and most distressing on the accordeon. I do not suppose there is another tune in the world with which I could have inflicted so much anguish upon my race as I did with that one during my short musical career.

After I had been playing "Lang Syne" about a week, I had the vanity to think I could improve the original melody, and I set about adding some little flourishes and variations to it, but with rather indifferent success, I suppose, as it brought my landlady into my presence with an expression about her of being opposed to such desperate enterprises. Said she, "Do you know any other tune but that, Mr. Twain?" I told her, meekly, that I did not. "Well, then," said she, "stick to it just as it is; don't put any variations to it, because it's rough enough on the boarders the way it is now."

The fact is, it was something more than simply "rough enough" on them; it was altogether too rough; half of them left, and the other half would have followed, but Mrs. Jones saved them by discharging me from the premises.

I only stayed one night at my next lodging-house. Mrs. Smith was after me early in the morning. She said, "You can go, sir; I don't want you here; I have had one of your kind before—a poor lunatic, that played the banjo and danced breakdowns, and jarred the glass all out of the windows; you kept me awake all night, and if you was to do it again I'd take and mash that thing over your head!" I could see that this woman took no delight in music, and I moved to Mrs. Brown's.

For three nights in succession I gave my new neighbors "Auld Lang Syne," plain and unadulterated, save by a few discords that rather improved the general effect than otherwise. But the very first time I tried the variations the boarders mutinied. I never did find anybody that would stand those variations. I was very well satisfied with my efforts in that house, however, and I left it without any regrets; I drove one boarder as mad as a March hare, and another one tried to scalp his mother. I reflected, though, that if I could only have been allowed to give this latter just one more touch of the variations, he would have finished the old woman.

I went to board at Mrs. Murphy's, an Italian lady of many excellent qualities. The very first time I struck up the variations, a haggard, care-worn, cadaverous old man walked into my room and stood beaming upon me a smile of ineffable happiness. Then he placed his hand upon my head, and looking devoutly aloft, he said with feeling unction, and in a voice trembling with emotion, "God bless you, young man! God bless you! for you have done that for me which is beyond all praise. For years I have suffered from an incurable disease, and knowing my doom was sealed and that I must die, I have striven with all my power to resign myself to my fate, but in vain—the love of life was too strong within me. But Heaven bless you, my benefactor! for since I heard you play that tune and those variations, I do not want to live any longer—I am entirely resigned—I am willing to die—I am anxious to die." And then the old man fell upon my neck and wept a flood of happy tears. I was surprised at these things, but I could not help feeling a little proud at what I had done, nor could I help giving the old gentleman a parting blast in the way of some peculiarly lacerating variations as he went out at the door. They doubled him up like a jack-knife, and the next time he left his bed of pain and suffering, he was all right, in a metallic coffin.

My passion for the accordeon finally spent itself and died out, and I was glad when I found myself free from its unwholesome influence. While the fever was upon me, I was a living, breathing calamity wherever I went, and desolation and disaster followed in my wake. I bred discord in families, I crushed the spirits of the light-hearted, I drove the melancholy to despair, I hurried invalids to premature dissolution, and I fear me I disturbed the very dead in their graves. I did incalculable harm and inflicted untold suffering upon my race with my execrable music, and yet to atone for it all, I did but one single blessed act, in making that weary old man willing to go to his long home.

Still, I derived some little benefit from that accordeon, for while I continued to practice on it, I never had to pay any board—landlords were always willing to compromise, on my leaving before the month was up.

Now, I had two objects in view, in writing the foregoing, one of which, was to try and reconcile people to those poor unfortunates who feel that they have a genius for music, and who drive their neighbors crazy every night in trying to develop and cultivate it, and the other was to introduce an admirable story about Little George Washington, who could Not Lie, and the Cherry Tree—or the Apple Tree, I have forgotten now, which, although it was told me only yesterday. And writing such a long and elaborate introductory has caused me to forget the story itself; but it was very touching.

96. *Daniel in the Lion's Den*
— *and Out Again All Right*

5 November 1864

"Daniel in the Lion's Den" appeared in the *Californian* on 5 November 1864 as Clemens' sixth consecutive weekly contribution. To judge by the prices that Clemens quoted for Burning Moscow and Gould and Curry stock, his sketch probably drew on a visit to the stock exchange made either on the afternoon of October 31 or on the morning of November 1.

The San Francisco Stock and Exchange Board was the city's leading organization of brokers. Its hall was at the corner of Montgomery and Washington streets, and its "portly President" was J. B. E. Cavallier, who presided over eighty members.[1] When Clemens came to San Francisco, he was already somewhat familiar with the operations of stock boards. But the Washoe Stock and Exchange Board had fewer members and transacted less business than its San Francisco counterpart. As a stockholder himself and as one who usually liked to associate with wealthy, influential men, Clemens no doubt enjoyed his visits to the board. Clearly he was among friends.

To be sure, by linking the brokers with thieves (Barabbas, the forty thieves), with dangerous animals (lions, as well as the standard bears and bulls), and with lost souls whose salvation would require a miracle as sensational as some of the Bible's best, Clemens acknowledged various conventional views of brokers as parasites, predators, or sinners. Still, they were men of the world essential to an economy based on mineral wealth—expert operators of an intricate social mechanism as intriguing to Clemens as a complex amalgamator or a typesetter. And if St. Peter barred their way through the Pearly Gates, the gold-paved streets of Paradise were, after all, dull by comparison with the activity at the board.

---

[1]Langley, *Directory for 1864*, p. 579.

Daniel in the Lion's Den
—and Out Again All Right

SOME PEOPLE are not particular about what sort of company they keep. I am one of that kind. Now for several days I have been visiting the Board of Brokers, and associating with brokers, and drinking with them, and swapping lies with them, and being as familiar and sociable with them as I would with the most respectable people in the world. I do this because I consider that a broker goes according to the instincts that are in him, and means no harm, and fulfils his mission according to his lights, and has a right to live, and be happy in a general way, and be protected by the law to some extent, just the same as a better man. I consider that brokers come into the world with souls—I am satisfied they do; and if they wear them out in the course of a long career of stock-jobbing, have they not a right to come in at the eleventh hour and get themselves half-soled, like old boots, and be saved at last? Certainly—the father of the tribe did that, and do we say anything against Barabbas for it to-day? No! we concede his right to do it; we admire his mature judgment in selling out of a worked-out mine of iniquity and investing in righteousness, and no man denies, or even doubts, the validity of the transaction. Other people may think as they please, and I suppose I am entitled to the same privilege; therefore, notwithstanding what others may believe, I am of the opinion that a broker can be saved. Mind, I do not say that a broker *will* be saved, or even that it is uncommon likely that such a thing will happen—I only say that Lazarus was raised from the dead, the five thousand were fed with twelve loaves of bread, the water was turned into wine, the Israelites crossed the Red Sea dry-shod, and a broker *can* be saved. True, the angel that accomplishes the task may require all eternity to rest himself in, but has that got anything to do with the establishment of the proposition? Does it invalidate it? does it detract from it? I think not. I am aware that this enthusiastic and may-be highly-colored vindication of the brokers may lay me open to suspicion of bribery, but I care not; I am a native of Washoe, and I will stand by anybody that stands by Washoe.

The place where stocks are daily bought and sold is called by interested parties the Hall of the San Francisco Board of Brokers, but by the impartial and disinterested the Den of the Forty Thieves; the latter name is regarded as the most poetic, but the former is considered the most polite. The large room is well stocked with small desks, arranged in semi-circular ranks like the seats of an amphitheatre, and behind these sit the th—the brokers. The portly President, with his gavel of office in his hand, an abundance of whiskers and moustaches on his face, spectacles on nose, an expression of energy and decision on his countenance and an open plaza on his head, sits, with his three clerks, in a pulpit at the head of the hall, flanked on either hand by two large cases, with glass doors, containing mineralogical specimens from Washoe and California mines—the emblems of the traffic. Facing the President, at the opposite end of the hall, is a blackboard, whereon is written in accusing capitals, "John Smith delinquent to John Jones, $1,550; William Brown delinquent to Jonas White, $475!" You might think brokers wouldn't mind that, maybe, but they do; a delinquent loses caste, and that touches his fine moral sensibilities—and he is suspended from active membership for the time being, and even expelled if his delinquency savors of blundering and ungraceful rascality—a thing which the Board cannot abide—and this inflicts exquisite pain upon the delicate nerves and tissues of his pocket, now when a seat in the Den is worth twelve or fifteen hundred dollars, and in brisker times even three thousand.

The session of the Board being duly opened, the roll is rapidly called, the members present responding, and the absentees being noted by the clerks for fines:

"Ackerman, (Here!) Adams, Atchison, (Here!) Babcock, Bocock,

(Here!) Badger, Blitzen, Bulger, Buncombe, (Here!) Caxton, (Here!) Cobbler, Crowder, Clutterback, (Here!) Dashaway, Dilson, Dodson, Dummy (Here!)"—and so on, the place becoming lively and animated, and the members sharpening their pencils, disposing their printed stock-lists before them, and getting ready for a sowing of unrighteousness and a harvest of sin.

In a few moments the roll-call was finished, the pencils all sharpened, and the brokers prepared for business—some with a leg thrown negligently over the arms of their chairs, some tilted back comfortably with their knees against their desks, some sitting half upright and glaring at the President, hungry for the contention to begin—but not a rascal of them tapping his teeth with his pencil—only dreamy, absent-minded people do that.

Then the President called "Ophir!" and after some bidding and counter-bidding, "Gould and Curry!" and a Babel arose—an infernal din and clatter of all kinds and tones of voices, inextricably jumbled together like original chaos, and above it all the following observation by the President pealed out clearly and distinctly, and with a rapidity of enunciation that was amazing:

"Fift'naitassfrwahn fift'nseftfive bifferwahn fift'naitfive botherty!"

I said I believed I would go home. My broker friend who had procured my admission to the Board asked why I wanted to go so soon, and I was obliged to acknowledge to him that I was very unfamiliar with the Kanaka language, and could not understand it at all unless a man spoke it exceedingly slow and deliberately.

"Oh," said he, "sit still; that isn't Kanaka; it's English, but he talks fast and runs one word into another; it is easy SOLD! to understand when you GIVE FIFTEEN-NINETY BUYER TEN NO DEPOSIT! come to get used to it. He always talks so, and sometimes he says THAT'S MINE! JIGGERS SOLD ON SLADDERY'S BID! his words so fast that even some of the members cannot comprehend them readily. Now what he said then was NO SIR! I DIDN'T SAY BUYER THIRTY, I SAID REGULAR WAY! 'Fifteen-eighty, (meaning fifteen hundred and eighty dollars,) asked for one, (one foot,) fifteen-seventy-five bid for one, fifteen-eighty-five buyer thirty, (thirty days' time on the payment,)' 'TWASN'T MY BID, IT WAS SWIGGINS TO BABCOCK! and he was repeating the bids and offers of the members after them as fast as they were made. I'll TAKE IT, CASH!"

I felt relieved, but not enlightened. My broker's explanation had got so many strange and incomprehensible interpolations sandwiched into it that I began to look around for a suitable person to translate that for me also, when it occurred to me that those interpolations were bids, offers, etc., which he had been throwing out to the assembled brokers while he was talking to me. It was all clear, then, so I have put his side-remarks in small capitals so that they may be clear to the reader likewise, and show that they have no connection with the subject matter of my friend's discourse.

And all this time, the clatter of voices had been going on. And while the storm of ejaculations hurtled about their heads, these brokers sat calmly in their several easy attitudes, but when a sale was made—when, in answer to some particularly liberal bid, somebody sung out "SOLD!" down came legs from the arms of chairs, down came knees propped against desks, forward shot the heads of the whole tribe with one accord, and away went the long ranks of pencils dancing over the paper! The sale duly recorded by all, the heads, the legs and the knees came up again, and the negligent attitudes were resumed once more.

The din moderated now, somewhat, and for awhile only a random and desultory fire was kept up as the President drifted down the stock-list, calling at intervals, "Savage!" "Uncle Sam!" "Chollar!" "Potosi!" "Hale and Norcross!" "Imperial!" "Sierra Nevada!" "Daney!" the monotony being broken and the uncomfortable attitudes demolished, now and then, by a lucky chance-shot that went to the mark and made a sale. But when the old gentleman called "Burning Moscow!" you should have seen the fiends wake up! you should have heard the racket! you should have been there to behold the metaphorical bull in the China shop! The President's voice and his mallet went into active service, then, and mingled their noise with the clamors of the mob. The members thus:

"Sell ten forty-five cash!" "Give forty-three for ten, regular way!" "Give forty-one cash for any part fifty!" "Twenty thirty-eight seller sixty!" "Give forty-four for ten buyer thirty!" "SOLD!"

(Down with your legs again, forward with your heads, and out with your pencils!) "Sell ten forty-three cash!" "Sold!" Then from every part of the house a din like this: "Ten more!" "Sold!" "Ten more!" "Sold!" "Ten more!" "Sold!" "Ten more!" "Sold!" "Ten—"

President (rap with his gavel)—"Silence! Orfuplease, (order if you please,) gentlemen! Higgins ten to Smithers—Dodson ten to Snodgrass—"

Billson—"No, sir! Billson ten to Snodgrass! It was me that sold 'em, sir!"

Dodson—"I didn't sell, sir, I bought—Jiggers ten to Dodson!"

President—"Billson ten to Snodgrass—Jiggers ten to Dodson—Slushbuster ten to Bladders—Simpson ten to Blivens—Guttersnipe ten to Hogwash—aw-right! go on!"

And they did go on, hotter and heavier than ever. And as they yelled their terms, the President repeated after them—the words flowing in a continuous stream from his mouth with inconceivable rapidity, and melting and mingling together like bottle-glass and cinders after a conflagration:

"Fortwahnasscash fortray bidbortenn fortsix botherty fortsevnoffsetherty fortfourbiffertenn—(smash! with the gavel) whasthat?—aw-right! fortfive offranparfortbotherty nodeposit fortfivenaf botherty bid fortsix biglerway!"

Which, translated, means: "Forty-one asked, cash; forty-three bid, buyer ten; forty-six, buyer thirty; forty-seven offered, seller thirty; forty-four bid for ten—(pause)—What's that? All right—forty-five offered for any part of forty, buyer thirty, no deposit; forty-five and a half, buyer thirty, bid; forty-six bid, regular way!"

And I found out that a "Bull" is a broker who raises the market-price of a stock by every means in his power, and a "Bear" is one who depresses it; that "cash" means that the stock must be delivered and paid for immediately—that is, before the banks close; that "regular way" means that delivery of the stock and payment must be made within two days; that it is the seller who "offers" stock, and the buyer who "bids" for it; that "buyer ten, thirty," or whatever the specified number may be, signifies the number of days the purchaser is allowed in which to call for the stock, receive it and pay for it, and it implies also that he must deposit in somebody's hands a fifth part of the price of the stock purchased, to be forfeited to the seller in case the full payment is not made within the time set—full payment must be made, though, notwithstanding the forfeit, or the broker loses his seat if the seller makes complaint to the Board within forty-eight hours after the occurrence of the delinquency; that when the words "no deposit" are added to "buyer thirty," they imply that the twenty per cent. deposit is not to be made, of course; that "seller thirty" means that any time the seller chooses, during the thirty days, he can present the stock to the buyer and demand payment—the seller generally selling at a figure below the market rate, in the hope that before his time is up a depression may occur that will enable him to pick up the stock at half price and deliver it—and the buyer taking chances on a great advance, within the month, that will accrue to his profit. Think of one of these adventurous "seller thirty's" "selling short," at thirty dollars a foot, several feet of a stock that was all corralled and withdrawn from the market within a fortnight and went to about fifteen hundred! It is not worth while to mention names—I suppose you remember the circumstance.

But I digress. Sometimes on the "second call" of stocks—that is, after the list has been gone through with in regular order, and the members are privileged to call up any stock they please—strategy is driven to the utmost limit by the friends of some pet wildcat or other, to effect sales of it to disinterested parties. The seller "offers" at a high figure, and the "bidder" responds with a low one; then the former comes warily down a dollar at a time, and the latter approaches him from below at about the same rate; they come nearer and nearer, skirmish a little in close proximity, get to a point where another bid or another offer would commit the parties to a sale, and then in the imminence of the impending event, the seller hesitates a second and is silent. But behold! as has been said of Woman, "The Broker that hesitates is lost!" The nervous and impatient President can brook no silence, no delay, and calls out: "Awstock?" (Any other stock?) Somebody yells "Burning Moscow!" and the tender wildcat, almost born, miscarries. Or perhaps the skirmishers fight shyly up to each other, counter and cross-counter, feint and parry, back and fill, and finally clinch a sale in the centre—the bidder is bitten, a smile flits from face to face, down come the legs, forward the ranks of heads, the pencils charge on the stock-lists, and the neat transaction is recorded with a rare gusto.

But twelve pages of foolscap are warning me to cut this thrilling sketch short, notwithstanding it is only half finished. However, I cannot leave the subject without saying I was agreeably disappointed in those brokers; I expected to see a set of villains with the signs of total depravity hung out all over them, but now I am satisfied there is some good in them; that they are not entirely and irredeemably bad; and I have been told by a friend, whose judgment I respect, that they are not any more unprincipled than they look. This was said by a man who would scorn to stoop to flattery. At the same time, though, as I scanned the faces assembled in that hall, I could not help imagining I could see old St. Peter admitting that band of Bulls and Bears into Paradise—see him standing by the half-open gate with his ponderous key pressed thoughtfully against his nose, and his head canted critically to one side, as he looks after them tramping down the gold-paved avenue, and mutters to himself: "Well, *you're* a nice lot, any way! Humph! I think you'll find it sort of lonesome in heaven, for if my judgment is sound, you'll not find a good many of *your* stripe in there!"

97 The Killing of Julius Cæsar "Localized"

12 November 1864

This sketch, the seventh of Clemens' weekly contributions to the *Californian*, appeared a month after he "resigned" his position as local reporter for the San Francisco *Morning Call*. It is an elaborate travesty of what Clemens himself referred to as "sensation items," those long and minutely detailed accounts of the latest bloody murder, usually found on page one. Despite the implicit scorn with which he treats this feature of contemporary journalism, Clemens was himself thoroughly experienced in the form. For example, "Daring Attempt to Assassinate a Pawnbroker in Broad Daylight!" appeared on the first page of the *Morning Call* for 18 August 1864: Clemens almost certainly wrote it.[1]

Needless to say, this "only true and reliable account" of Caesar's assassination is not taken from the *"Daily Evening Fasces,"* but from Shakespeare—in particular, act 3 of *Julius Caesar*, which is quoted and modernized throughout the "local" report. But Clemens is of course bolder than Shakespeare in his use of anachronism. The sketch contains an onslaught of humorous anachronism ranging from the "second edition" of the *Fasces* to the invocation of "the Coroner's inquest" and the "Chief of Police." With this device Clemens strikes glancing blows not only at the practice of "localizing" itself, but at the social and political mores of San Francisco.

Clemens reprinted the sketch, virtually without revision, in the 1867 *Jumping Frog* book. In reviewing that book the Boston *Evening Transcript* called this sketch a "capital rendering" of Caesar's assassination "after the fashion of modern newspaper reporters." The Sacramento

---

[1]It is reprinted in full in *CofC*, pp. 199–202. For additional "sensation items" attributed to Clemens at this time, see *CofC*, pp. 194–205.

Union suggested only that it was among the sketches "suggestive of [John] Phœnix."[2] Clemens continued to reprint the piece in 1872, 1873, and 1875.

---

[2]"New Publications," Boston *Evening Transcript*, 4 May 1867, p. 1; "The Celebrated Jumping Frog of Calaveras County," Sacramento *Union*, 6 June 1867, p. 1.

The Killing of
Julius Cæsar "Localized"

[BEING THE ONLY TRUE AND RELIABLE ACCOUNT
EVER PUBLISHED, AND TAKEN FROM THE ROMAN
"DAILY EVENING FASCES," OF THE DATE OF THAT
TREMENDOUS OCCURRENCE.]

NOTHING IN the world affords a newspaper reporter so much
satisfaction as gathering up the details of a bloody and mysterious
murder, and writing them up with aggravated circumstantiality.
He takes a living delight in this labor of love—for such it is to
him—especially if he knows that all the other papers have gone
to press and his will be the only one that will contain the dreadful
intelligence. A feeling of regret has often come over me that I was
not reporting in Rome when Cæsar was killed—reporting on an
evening paper and the only one in the city, and getting at least
twelve hours ahead of the morning paper boys with this most
magnificent "item" that ever fell to the lot of the craft. Other
events have happened as startling as this, but none that possessed
so peculiarly all the characteristics of the favorite "item" of the
present day, magnified into grandeur and sublimity by the high
rank, fame, and social and political standing of the actors in it. In
imagination I have seen myself skirmishing around old Rome,
button-holing soldiers, senators and citizens by turns, and trans-
ferring "all the particulars" from them to my note-book; and,

better still, arriving "at the base of Pompey's statue" in time to say persuasively to the dying Cæsar: "O, come now, you ain't so far gone, you know, but what you could stir yourself up a little and tell a fellow just how this thing happened, if you was a mind to, couldn't you—now do!" and get the "straight of it" from his own lips. And be envied by the morning paper hounds!

Ah! if I had lived in those days I would have written up that item gloatingly, and spiced it with a little moralizing here and plenty of blood there; and some dark, shuddering mystery; and praise and pity for some, and misrepresentation and abuse for others, (who didn't patronize the paper,) and gory gashes, and notes of warning as to the tendency of the times, and extravagant descriptions of the excitement in the Senate-house and the street, and all that sort of thing.

However, as I was not permitted to report Cæsar's assassination in the regular way, it has at least afforded me rare satisfaction to translate the following able account of it from the original Latin of the *Roman Daily Evening Fasces* of that date—second edition:

Our usually quiet city of Rome was thrown into a state of wild excitement, yesterday, by the occurrence of one of those bloody affrays which sicken the heart and fill the soul with fear, while they inspire all thinking men with forebodings for the future of a city where human life is held so cheaply, and the gravest laws are so openly set at defiance. As the result of that affray, it is our painful duty, as public journalists, to record the death of one of our most esteemed citizens—a man whose name is known wherever this paper circulates, and whose fame it has been our pleasure and our privilege to extend, and also to protect from the tongue of slander and falsehood, to the best of our poor ability. We refer to Mr. J. Cæsar, the Emperor elect.

The facts of the case, as nearly as our reporter could determine them from the conflicting statements of eye-witnesses, were about as follows: The affair was an election row, of course. Nine-tenths of the ghastly butcheries that disgrace the city now-a-days, grow out of the bickerings and jealousies and animosities engendered by these accursed elections. Rome would be the gainer by it if her very constables were elected to serve a century, for in our experience we have never even been able to choose a dog-pelter without celebrating the event with a dozen knock-downs and a general cramming of the station-house with drunken vagabonds over night. It is said that when the immense majority for Cæsar at the polls in the market was declared the other day, and the crown was offered to that gentleman, even his amazing unselfishness in refusing it three times, was not sufficient to save him from the whispered insults of such men as Casca, of the Tenth Ward, and other hirelings of the disappointed candidate, hailing mostly from the Eleventh and Thirteenth, and other outside districts, who were overheard speaking ironically and contemptuously of Mr. Cæsar's conduct upon that occasion.

We are further informed that there are many among us who think they are justified in believing that the assassination of Julius Cæsar was a put-up thing—a cut-and-dried arrangement, hatched by Marcus Brutus and a lot of his hired roughs, and carried out only too faithfully according to the programme. Whether there be good grounds for this suspicion or not, we leave to the people to judge for themselves, only asking that they will read the following account of the sad occurrence carefully and dispassionately before they render that judgment:

The Senate was already in session, and Cæsar was coming down the street toward the capitol, conversing with some personal friends, and followed, as usual, by a large number of citizens. Just as he was passing in front of Demosthenes and Thucydides' drug-store, he was observing casually to a gentleman who, our informant thinks, is a fortune-teller, that the Ides of March were come. The reply was, Yes, they were come, but not gone yet. At this moment Artemidorus stepped up and passed the time of day, and asked Cæsar to read a schedule or a tract, or something of the kind, which he had brought for his perusal. Mr. Decius Brutus also said something about an "humble suit" which *he* wanted read. Artemidorus begged that attention might be paid to his first, because it was of personal consequence to Cæsar. The latter replied that what concerned himself should be read last, or words to that effect. Artemidorus begged and beseeched him to read the paper instantly. [Mark that; it is hinted by William Shakspeare, who saw the beginning and the end of the unfortunate affray, that this "schedule" was simply a note discovering to Cæsar that a plot was brewing to take his life.] However, Cæsar shook him off, and refused to read any petition in the street. He then entered the capitol, and the crowd followed him.

About this time, the following conversation was overheard, and we consider that, taken in connection with the events which succeeded it, it bears an appalling significance: Mr. Popilius Lena remarked to George W. Cassius (commonly known as the "Nobby Boy of the Third Ward,"] a bruiser in the pay of the Opposition, that he hoped his enterprise to-day might thrive; and when Cassius asked, "What enterprise?" he only closed his left eye temporarily, and said with simulated indifference, "Fare you well," and sauntered toward Cæsar. Marcus Brutus, who is suspected of being the ringleader of the band that killed Cæsar, asked what it was that Lena had said; Cassius told him, and added in a low tone, *"I fear our purpose is discovered."*

Brutus told his wretched accomplice to keep an eye on Lena, and a moment after, Cassius urged that lean and hungry vagrant, Casca, whose reputation here is none of the best, to be sudden, for *he feared prevention.* He then turned to Brutus, apparently much excited, and asked what should be done, and swore that either he or Cæsar *should never turn back* — he would kill himself first. At this time, Cæsar was talking to some of the back-country members about the approaching fall elections, and paying little attention to what was going on around him. Billy Trebonius got into conversation with the people's friend and Cæsar's—Mark Antony—and under some pretence or other, got him away, and Brutus, Decius, Casca, Cinna, Metellus Cimber, and others of the gang of infamous desperadoes that infest Rome at present, closed around the doomed Cæsar. Then Metellus Cimber knelt down and begged that his brother might be recalled from banishment, but Cæsar rebuked him for his fawning, sneaking conduct, and refused to grant his petition. Immediately, at Cimber's request, first Brutus and then Cassius begged for the return of the banished Publius; but Cæsar still refused. He said he could not be moved; that he was as fixed as the North Star, and proceeded to speak in the most complimentary terms of the firmness of that star, and its steady character. Then he said he was like it, and he believed he was the only man in the country that was; therefore, since he was "constant" that Cimber should be banished, he was also "constant" that he should stay banished, and he'd be d—d if he didn't keep him so!

Instantly seizing upon this shallow pretext for a fight, Casca sprang at Cæsar and struck him with a dirk, Cæsar grabbing him by the arm with his right hand, and launching a blow straight from the shoulder with his left, that sent the reptile bleeding to the earth. He then backed up against Pompey's statue, and squared himself to receive his assailants. Cassius and Cimber and Cinna rushed upon him with their daggers drawn, and the former succeeded in inflicting a wound upon his body, but before he could strike again, and before either of the others could strike at all, Cæsar stretched the three miscreants at his feet with as many blows of his powerful fist. By this time the Senate was in an indescribable uproar; the throng of citizens in the lobbies had blockaded the doors in their frantic efforts to escape from the building, the Sergeant-at-Arms and his assistants were struggling with the assassins, venerable Senators had cast aside their encumbering robes and were leaping over benches and flying down the aisles in wild confusion toward the shelter of the Committee-rooms, and a thousand voices were shouting "PO-LICE! PO-LICE!" in discordant tones that rose above the frightful din like shrieking winds above the roaring of a tempest. And amid it all, great Cæsar stood with his back against the statue, like a lion at bay, and fought his assailants weaponless and hand-to-hand, with the defiant bearing and the unwavering courage which he had shown before on many a bloody field. Billy Trebonius and Caius Ligarius struck him with their daggers and fell, as their brother-conspirators before them had fallen. But at last, when Cæsar saw his old friend Brutus step forward, armed with a murderous knife, it is said he seemed utterly overpowered with grief and amazement, and dropping his invincible left arm by his side, he hid his face in the folds of his mantle and received the treacherous blow without an effort to stay the hand that gave it. He only said *"Et tu, Brute!"* and fell lifeless on the marble pavement.

We learn that the coat deceased had on when he was killed was the same he wore in his tent on the afternoon of the day he overcame the Nervii, and that when it was removed from the corpse it was found to be cut and gashed in no less than seven different places. There was nothing in the pockets. It will be exhibited at the Coroner's inquest, and will be damning proof of the fact of the killing. These latter facts may be relied on, as we get them from Mark Antony, whose position enables him to learn every item of news connected with the one subject of absorbing interest of to-day.

LATER.—While the Coroner was summoning a jury, Mark Antony and other friends of the late Cæsar got hold of the body and lugged it off to the Forum, and at last accounts Antony and Brutus were making speeches over it and raising such a row among the people that, as we go to press, the Chief of Police is satisfied there is going to be a riot, and is taking measures accordingly.

98 A Full and Reliable Account of the Extraordinary Meteoric Shower of Last Saturday Night

19 November 1864

Meteorites lit San Francisco skies on Saturday night, 12 November 1864, one week before this sketch appeared in the *Californian*. The "November Star-Shower," as the *American Journal of Science* called it, was predicted in the San Francisco press by the telegram from Professor Silliman with which Clemens began his sketch: the *Morning Call*, the *Alta California*, and the *Evening Bulletin* all printed it on November 11.[1] As he had promised in this telegram, Professor Silliman later published the statements of several sky watchers, none of whom observed as many striking phenomena as did Clemens.

The name "Silliman" was well known both to the scientific community and to ordinary nineteenth-century Americans. Benjamin Silliman, Sr., had founded the *American Journal of Science* in 1818 and had edited it until his death in November 1864, when his son, Professor Benjamin Silliman, Jr., became one of its editors. The son was a chemist who taught at Yale and the University of Louisville, a prolific writer on scientific subjects, and a consultant to mining and oil companies, which brought him to San Francisco in April 1864. After inspecting mining districts in California and interior regions for several months, he returned to San Francisco and the Occidental Hotel on August 31. Ten days later he left for Nevada again, this time accompanied by Clemens' old antagonist, Judge G. T. Sewall.[2] The newspapers followed Silliman's

---

[1]"Meteoric Showers and Things," San Francisco *Alta California*, 15 November 1864, p. 1; *American Journal of Science* n.s. 37 (May 1864): 377, and n.s. 38 (November 1864): 53. See the textual commentary.

[2]"From the Colorado," San Francisco *Alta California*, 1 September 1864, p. 1; "Arrivals at the Occidental Hotel," San Francisco *Morning Call*, 1 September 1864, p. 2; "Over the Mountains," San Francisco *Alta California*, 10 September 1864, p. 1. For more information on Sewall, see "Petrified Man" (no. 28).

movements and obviously respected his judgments about the mining potential of the areas he visited.

High spirits, alcoholic and otherwise, informed Clemens' latest sketch for the *Californian*, the eighth in the series, which bears no animus against Silliman or against science. The humor has some satiric bite, however, when it ridicules the pedantry behind studying "what materials a butterfly's wing is made of" or "whether the extraordinary bird called the Phœnix ever really existed or not." But most of the humor arises from Mark Twain's extravagantly unsober methods of assembling "evidence" for "the good of Science"—evidence that is as unreliable as the testimony Clemens observed in the police court.[3] The overall effect is that of an extravaganza, not a satire. Just as "City Marshal Perry" (no. 49) constructed a campaign biography from a wild mélange of punning references to "Perry," so this sketch whirls around the words "star" and "meteor," on which Clemens puns mercilessly. The resulting comedy may seem rather thin because it is so heavily dependent not only on these puns, but on the humor of drunken befuddlement.

Clemens included a clipping of this sketch in the Yale Scrapbook, and in January or February 1867 he revised it slightly, intending to include it in the *Jumping Frog* book. Either he or Charles Henry Webb decided against it, however, perhaps because it emphasized the humor of intoxication too relentlessly to permit easy modification for an eastern audience.

---

[3]See "The Evidence in the Case of Smith *vs.* Jones" (no. 78).

A Full and Reliable Account of the Extraordinary Meteoric Shower of Last Saturday Night

I FOUND the following paragraph in the morning papers of the 11th inst.:

VIRGINIA, November 10.—Astronomers anticipate a recurrence this year of the November meteoric shower of 1833. The mornings from the 11th to the 15th, are all likely to show an unusual number of meteors, especially from the 12th to the 14th. The best time of observation is from half-past one o'clock, A. M., onward. The radiant point is in the constellation Leo. Observers in California, Nevada and the Pacific Coast generally are requested to report their observations to Professor Silliman, Jr., San Francisco, for the American Journal of Science, where they will be published for the good of science.

B. SILLIMAN, JR.

PROF. B. SILLIMAN, JR.—*Dear Sir:* In accordance with the above request, which you so politely extended to all "observers," I took copious notes of the amazing meteoric phenomena of last Saturday night, and I now hasten to make my report to you for publication in the *American Journal of Science* "for the good of science."

I began my observations early in the evening, previously providing myself with the very best apparatus I could find wherewith to facilitate my labors. I got a telescopic glass tumbler, and two costly decanters, (containing *eau de vie* and Veuve Clicquot to wash out the instrument with whenever it should become clouded,) and seated myself in my window, very nearly under the constellation Leo. I then poured about a gill of liquid from each decanter into the telescopic tumbler and slowly elevated it to an angle of about ninety degrees. I did not see anything. The second trial was also a failure, but I had faith in that wash, and I washed out the instrument again. And just here let me suggest to you, Professor, that you can always depend on that mixture; rightly compounded, I expect it is the most powerful aid to human eyesight ever invented; assisted by it I have known a man to see two drinks on the counter before him when in reality there was but one—and so strong was the deception that I have known that man to get drunk on thirteen of these duplicate drinks when he was naturally gauged for twenty-six.

Very well; after I had washed out my glass the third time, three or four stars, of about the nineteenth magnitude I should judge, shot from the zenith and fell in the general direction of Oakland. During the fourth wash, and while I had one eye sighted on Venus and the other one closed in blissful repose, that planet fell upon the roof of the Russ House and bounced off into Bush street; immediately afterward, Jupiter fell and knocked a watchman's eye out—at least I think it was that star, because I saw the watchman clap his hand to his eye and say "By Jupiter!" The assertion was positive, and made without hesitation, as if he had the most perfect confidence in the accuracy of his judgment; but at the same time it is possible that he might have been mistaken, and that the damage was not done by Jupiter after all. I maintain, though, that the chances are all in favor of his being correct, because I have noticed that policemen usually know as much about stars as anybody, and take more interest in them than most people.

Up to this time the wind had been north by northeast half west, and I noticed an uncommon dryness in the atmosphere, but it was less marked after I applied the fifth wash. My barometer never having had any experience in falling stars, got hopelessly tangled in trying to get the run of things, and after waltzing frantically between "stormy" and "falling weather" for awhile without being able to make up its mind, it finally became thoroughly demoralized and threw up its commission. My thermometer did not indicate anything; I noted this extraordinary phenomenon, of course, but at the same time I reasoned—and, I think, with considerable sagacity—that it was less owing to the singular condition of the atmosphere than to the fact that there was no quicksilver in the instrument. About this time a magnificent spectacle dazzled my vision—the whole constellation of the Great Menken came flaming out of the heavens like a vast spray of gas-jets, and shed a glory abroad over the universe as it fell! [N. B. I have used the term "Great Menken" because I regard it as a more modest expression than the Great Bear, and consequently better suited to the columns of THE CALIFORNIAN, which goes among families, you understand—but when you come to transfer my report to the *Journal of Science,* Professor, you are at liberty to change it if you like.]

I applied the sixth wash. A sprinkle of sparkling fragments ensued—fragments of some beautiful world that had been broken up and cast out of the blue firmament—and then a radiance as of noonday flared out of the zenith, and Mercury, the winged symbol of Progress, came sweeping down like a banished sun, and catching in the folds of the flag that floats from the tall staff in the Plaza, remained blazing in the centre of its dim constellation of stars! "Lo, a miracle! the thirty-sixth star furnished from the imperial diadem of heaven! while yet no welcome comes from the old home in the Orient, behold the STATE OF NEVADA is recognized by God!" says I, and seized my telescope, filled her to the brim and washed her out again! The divinity student in the next room came in at this juncture and protested against my swearing with so much spirit, and I had some difficulty in making him understand that I had only made use of a gorgeous metaphor, and that there was really no profanity intended in it.

About this time the wind changed and quite a shower of stars fell, lasting about twenty minutes; a lull ensued, and then came several terrific discharges of thunder and lightning, and how it poured! you couldn't see the other side of the street for the hurtling tempest of stars! I got my umbrella—which I had previously provided along with my other apparatus—and started down the street. Of course there was plenty of light, although the street lamps were not lit—(you let that sagacious gas company alone,

Professor, to make a good thing out of it when the almanac adver-
tises anything of this kind. I put in these parentheses to signify a
complicated wink—you understand?) I met Charles Kean, and I
expect he was drunk; I drifted down the pavement, tacking from
one side of it to the other, and trying to give him a wide berth, but
it was no use; he would run into me, and he did—he brought up
square against me and fell. "Down goes another star," I observed,
and stopped a moment to make a note of it.

The meteoric storm abated gradually, and finally ceased, but by
that time the stars had cut my umbrella nearly all to pieces, and
there were a dozen or more sticking in it when I lowered it. It was
the most furious deluge I ever saw, while it lasted. Pretty soon I
heard a great huzzaing in the distance, and immediately afterward
I noticed a brilliant meteor streaming athwart the heavens with a
train of fire of incredible length appended to it. It swept the sky in
a graceful curve, and after I had watched its splendid career a few
seconds and was in the act of making the proper entry in my
note-book, it descended and struck me such a stunning thump in
the pit of the stomach that I was groveling in the dust before I
rightly knew what the matter was. When I recovered consciousness, I remarked "Down went a couple of us then," and made a
note of it. I saved the remains of this most remarkable meteor,
and I transmit them to you with this report, to be preserved in the
National Astronomical Museum. They consist of a fragment of a
torn and jagged cylinder the size of your wrist, composed of a
substance strongly resembling the pasteboard of this world; to
this is attached a slender stick some six feet long, which has
something of the appearance of the pine wood so well known to
the commerce of this earth, but of such a supernatural fineness of
texture, of course, as to enable one to detect its celestial origin at
once. There is food here for philosophic contemplation, and a
series of interesting volumes might be written upon a question
which I conceive to be of the utmost importance to Science, viz.:
Do they cultivate pines in Paradise? And if it be satisfactorily
demonstrated that they *do* cultivate pines in Paradise, may we
not reasonably surmise that they cultivate cabbages there also? O,
sublime thought! O, beautiful dream! The scientific world may
well stand speechless and awe-stricken in the presence of these

tremendous questions! But may we not hope that the learned German who has devoted half his valuable life to determining what materials a butterfly's wing is made of, and to writing unstinted books upon the subject, will devote the balance of it to profound investigation of the celestial cabbage question? And is it too much to hope that that other benefactor of our race who has proven in his thirteen inspired volumes that it is exceedingly mixed as to whether the extraordinary bird called the Phœnix ever really existed or not, will lend his assistance to the important work and turn out a few tomes upon the subject, wherewith to enrich our scientific literature? My dear sir, this matter is worthy of the noblest effort; for we know by the past experience of learned men, that whosoever shall either definitely settle this cabbage question, or indefinitely unsettle it with arguments and reasonings and deductions freighted with that odor of stately and incomprehensible wisdom which is so overpowering to the aspiring student and so dazzling and bewildering to the world at large, will be clothed with titles of dignity by our colleges, and receive medals of gold from the Kings and Presidents of the earth.

As I was meandering down the street, pondering over the matters treated of in the preceding paragraph, I ran against another man, and he squared off for a fight. I squared off, also, and dashed out with my left, but he dodged and "cross-countered." [I have since learned that he was educated at the Olympic Club.] That is to say, he ducked his head to one side and avoided my blow, and at the same time he let go with his right and caved the side of my head in. At this moment I beheld the most magnificent discharge of stars that had occurred during the whole evening. I estimated the number to be in the neighborhood of fifteen hundred thousand. I beg that you will state it at that figure in the *Journal of Science*, Professor, and throw in a compliment about my wasting no opportunity that seemed to promise anything for the good of the cause. It might help me along with your kind of men if I should conclude to tackle science for a regular business, you know. You see they have elected a new Governor over there in Nevada, and consequently I am not as much Governor of the Third House there as I was. It was a very comfortable berth; I had a salary of $60,000 a year when I could collect it.

While my stranger and myself were staggering under the two terrific blows which we had exchanged—and especially myself, on account of the peculiar nature of the "cross-counter" as above described—a singular star dropped in our midst which I would have liked well to possess, because of its quaint appearance, and because I had never seen anything like it mentioned in Mr. Dick's astronomy. It emitted a mild silvery lustre, and bore upon its face some characters which, in the fervor of my astronomical enthusiasm, I imagined spelt "Police—18," but of course this was an absurd delusion. I only mention it to show to what lengths scientific zeal will sometimes carry a novice. This marvellous meteor was already in the possession of another enthusiast, and he would not part with it.

On my way home, I met young John William Skae—the inimitable punster of Virginia City, and formerly of Pennsylvania, perhaps you know him?—and I knew from his distraught and pensive air that he was building a joke. I was anxious not to intrude any excitement upon him, which might have the effect of bringing the half-finished edifice down about my ears, but my very caution precipitated the catastrophe I was trying to avert. Said I, "Are you out looking for meteors, too?" His eye instantly lighted with a devilish satisfaction, and says he: "Well, sorter; I'm looking for my Susan—going to meteor by moonlight alone; O Heavens! why this sudden pang, this bursting brain! save me, save me or I perish!"

But I didn't save him—I let him drop; and I deserted him and left him moaning there in the gutter. A man cannot serve me that way twice and expect me to stand by him and chafe his temples and blow his nose and sand-paper his legs and fetch him round again. I would let him perish like an outcast first, and deny him Christian burial afterwards. That Skae has always been following me around trying to make me low-spirited with his dismal jokes, but since that time he caught me out in the lonely moor on the Cliff House road, and intimidated me into listening to that execrable pun on the Kingfisher, I have avoided him as I would a pestilence.

I will now close my report, Professor. If you had not just happened to print that assurance in your little notice that these things should be published in the *American Journal of Science,* "for the good of Science," I expect it never would have occurred to me to make any meteorological observations at all; but you see that remark corralled me. It has been the dearest wish of my life to do something for the good of Science and see it in print in such a paper as the one you mention, and when I saw this excellent opportunity presented, I thought it was now or never with me. It is a pity that the astonishing drawings which accompany this report cannot be published in the CALIFORNIAN; it could not be helped, though: the artist who was to have engraved them was not healthy, and he only took one look at them and then went out in the back yard and destroyed himself. But you can print them in the *Journal of Science,* anyhow, just the same; get an artist whose sensibilities have been toned down by chiseling melancholy devices on tombstones all his life, and let him do them up for you. He would probably survive the job.

MARK TWAIN.

99. *Lucretia Smith's Soldier*

3 December 1864

Clemens published "Lucretia Smith's Soldier" in the *Californian* almost exactly five months after his "Original Novelette" (no. 80) had appeared in the San Francisco *Morning Call*. Both are burlesque or "condensed" novels after the fashion introduced by Thackeray and practiced most influentially in the United States by Charles Henry Webb and Bret Harte.[1] In his preface to the present sketch Clemens implies that his target was not a specific novel or novelist, but the entire corpus of "those nice, sickly war stories in *Harper's Weekly.*" Examples are not difficult to find. "An Exchange of Prisoners," which appeared in the 3 January 1863 issue, comes remarkably close to his burlesque plot. It is a sentimental tale of a young girl so eager to make a sacrifice for her country that she promises to marry a man she does not love if he will become a soldier. When he returns from battle, he unites the girl with her true lover and then quietly disappears.[2]

Clemens was thoroughly familiar with the satiric possibilities of the condensed novel. The tale he tells here is a warning to all sentimentalists to get their facts straight, and its ending argues that the sentimental mask cannot really endure a serious misreading of the facts. The "novel" moves swiftly through four miniature chapters, each provided with a melodramatic climax, and all leading inexorably to his quite unsentimental conclusion. But while "Lucretia Smith's Soldier" burlesques the plot of those "sickly war stories," it also ridicules the platitudinous sentiment of novels like Pierce Egan's *Such Is Life*, to which Clemens al-

---

[1]Franklin R. Rogers, *Mark Twain's Burlesque Patterns* (Dallas: Southern Methodist University Press, 1960), pp. 16–25.

[2]*Harper's Weekly* 7 (3 January 1863): 7.

ludes in the last paragraph of his sketch: "Such is life, and the trail of the serpent is over us all." *Such Is Life* was being serialized in the San Francisco *Golden Era* for much of 1864, and the passage to which Clemens alludes appeared on August 14. (He says in his preface that he has been working on the burlesque "for the last three months.") Ormsby's closing remarks to Viola in Egan's novel are as follows:

"My love," he said, tenderly to her, "may your wishes be responded to by a kind Heaven! But toil, trial, vicissitudes, burdens of all kinds, are our inheritance; we have but to meet them boldly, for from them none of us are exempt; to endure them bravely, for the longest lane has its turning, the greatest sorrow has its consolation. Our sojourn here is made up of chances and changes, joys and griefs, splendors and miseries; let us, with equanimity, therefore, take the good with the evil, and bear all patiently, keeping in mind that "SUCH IS LIFE."[3]

Clemens' mocking conclusion to his own "melancholy history" draws upon the reader's familiarity with this mountain of platitudes, as well as on another novel about extraordinary trials and tribulations. Mary Elizabeth Braddon's *The Trail of the Serpent* had been serialized in the *Era* from December 1863 to February 1864, and its title in turn alluded to Thomas Moore's lines in *Lalla Rookh:* "Some flow'rets of Eden ye still inherit, / But the trail of the Serpent is over them all!"[4]

This brand of sentimental self-indulgence would always arouse Mark Twain's satiric impulses, but perhaps it is worth remembering that the present sketch was published at the very end of the period in his life described in chapter 59 of *Roughing It* as the time when he became "a very adept at 'slinking.' " It was a time when he "felt meaner, and lowlier and more despicable than the worms," and clung to a single coin "lest the consciousness coming strong upon me that I was *entirely* penniless, might suggest suicide."[5] Although Clemens probably exaggerated his situation in retrospect, he was still not likely to take much consolation from Ormsby's spectacularly banal advice to bear in mind that "Such is Life!"

"Lucretia Smith's Soldier" was immediately popular on both coasts. On 15 January 1865 the editor of the *California Sunday Mercury* reprinted it and said, "Speaking of funny things, just read 'The Course of True Love,' etc., on the third page of to-day's *Mercury*." Webb in turn quoted this comment and remarked rather sourly that it was "a funny thing, indeed; written by Mark Twain, and paid for and published in THE

---

[3]San Francisco *Golden Era* 12 (14 August 1864): 2.
[4]Lines 206–207 from "Paradise and the Peri," *Lalla Rookh* (1817).
[5]*RI,* pp. 380–381.

CALIFORNIAN, the article, after going the rounds of the Eastern press is republished here without a word of credit to either." Such unauthorized reprinting had become a general problem in Webb's eyes. In an article called "To the Eastern Press," published the same day, Webb claimed that Emilie Lawson, Ina Coolbrith, and Mark Twain had "been frequently sufferers by this practice," and he singled out the New York *Leader* as the worst offender.[6] Still later, on February 4, he was more explicit: " 'Mark Twain's' comical story of 'Lucretia Smith's Soldier,' fares better at the hands of the [New York] *Atlas,* being copied into that paper of December 3d, with credit to both author and THE CALIFORNIAN. But other journals Eastward were not as honest, and thus it was that the *Mercury* the other week came to republish the article, under the impression that it was new to this coast, calling attention to it as particularly 'funny.' "[7] It seems likely that Webb was secretly pleased by the attention his writers and his journal were receiving, but he did want explicit recognition for both. Clemens was certainly happy to be reprinted, for he had joined the *Californian* staff in part because it was "liberally copied from by papers like the Home Journal."[8]

Clemens and Webb decided to reprint this sketch in the 1867 *Jumping Frog* book, and it proved its popularity this time with reviewers. The Sacramento *Union* reprinted the entire sketch in its review, and said that it "risibly hits off the sentimental yarns of which the late war was prolific." And when the Routledges reprinted the little book in September 1867, one British reviewer singled out "Lucretia Smith's Soldier" as "an admirable burlesque upon the over-wrought tales of emotion which filled the American periodicals during the war. The style and feeling of those gushing narratives are both parodied with great slyness and apparent simplicity."[9] Clemens continued to reprint the sketch in 1872 and 1874, but even though he considered reprinting it in *Sketches, New and Old* (1875), it did not finally appear there.

---

[6]"Too Funny" and "To the Eastern Press," *Californian* 2 (21 January 1865): 5.
[7]"A Complaint of Friends," *Californian* 2 (4 February 1865): 8–9.
[8]Clemens to Orion and Mollie Clemens, 28 September 1864, *CL1*, letter 92.
[9]"The Celebrated Jumping Frog," Sacramento *Union,* 6 June 1867, p. 1; "Californian Humour," *London Review of Politics, Society, Literature, Art & Science* 15 (21 September 1867): 331.

Lucretia Smith's Soldier

[NOTE FROM THE AUTHOR.—*Mr. Editor:* I am an ardent admirer of those nice, sickly war stories in *Harper's Weekly,* and for the last three months I have been at work upon one of that character, which I now forward to you for publication. It can be relied upon as true in every particular, inasmuch as the facts it contains were compiled from the official records in the War Department at Washington. The credit of this part of the labor is due to the Hon. T. G. Phelps, who has so long and ably represented this State in Congress. It is but just, also, that I should make honorable mention of the obliging publishing firms Roman & Co. and Bancroft & Co., of this city, who loaned me *Jomini's Art of War,* the *Message of the President and Accompanying Documents,* and sundry maps and military works, so necessary for reference in building a novel like this. To the accommodating Directors of the Overland Telegraph Company I take pleasure in returning my thanks for tendering me the use of their wires at the customary rates. The inspiration which enabled me in this production to soar so happily into the realms of sentiment and soft emotion, was obtained from the excellent beer manufactured at the New York Brewery, in Sutter street, between Montgomery and Kearny. And finally, to all those kind friends who have, by good deeds or encouraging words, assisted me in my labors upon this story of "Lucretia Smith's Soldier," during the past three months, and whose names are too numerous for special mention, I take this method of tendering my sincerest gratitude.

M. T.]

CHAPTER I.

On a balmy May morning in 1861, the little village of Bluemass, in Massachusetts, lay wrapped in the splendor of the newly-risen sun. Reginald de Whittaker, confidential and only clerk in the house of Bushrod & Ferguson, general dry goods and grocery dealers, and keepers of the Post-office, rose from his bunk under the counter and shook himself. After yawning and stretching comfortably, he sprinkled the floor and proceeded to sweep it. He had only half finished his task, however, when he sat down on a keg of nails and fell into a reverie. "This is my last day in this shanty," said he. "How it will surprise Lucretia when she hears I am going for a soldier! How proud she will be—the little darling!" He pictured himself in all manner of warlike situations; the hero of a thousand extraordinary adventures; the man of rising fame; the pet of Fortune at last; and beheld himself, finally, returning to his old home, a bronzed and scarred Brigadier-General, to cast his honors and his matured and perfect love at the feet of his Lucretia Borgia Smith.

At this point a thrill of joy and pride suffused his system—but he looked down and saw his broom, and blushed. He came toppling down from the clouds he had been soaring among, and was an obscure clerk again, on a salary of two dollars and a half a week.

CHAPTER II.

At 8 o'clock that evening, with a heart palpitating with the proud news he had brought for his beloved, Reginald sat in Mr. Smith's parlor awaiting Lucretia's appearance. The moment she entered he sprang to meet her, his face lighted by the torch of love that was blazing in his head somewhere and shining through, and ejaculated "Mine own!" as he opened his arms to receive her.

"Sir!" said she, and drew herself up like an offended queen.

Poor Reginald was stricken dumb with astonishment. This chilling demeanor, this angry rebuff where he had expected the old, tender welcome, banished the gladness from his heart as the cheerful brightness is swept from the landscape when a dark cloud drifts athwart the face of the sun. He stood bewildered a moment, with a sense of goneness on him like one who finds himself suddenly overboard upon a midnight sea and beholds the ship pass into shrouding gloom, while the dreadful conviction falls upon his soul that he has not been missed. He tried to speak, but his pallid lips refused their office. At last he murmured:

"O, Lucretia, what have I done—what is the matter—why this cruel coldness? Don't you love your Reginald any more?"

Her lips curled in bitter scorn, and she replied, in mocking tones:

"Don't I love my Reginald any more? No, I *don't* love my Reginald any more! Go back to your pitiful junk shop and grab your pitiful yard-stick, and stuff cotton in your ears so that you can't hear your country shout to you to fall in and shoulder arms! Go!" And then, unheeding the new light that flashed from his eyes, she fled from the room and slammed the door behind her.

Only a moment more! Only a single moment more, he thought, and he could have told her how he had already answered the summons and signed his name to the muster-roll, and all would have been well—his lost bride would have come back to his arms with words of praise and thanksgiving upon her lips. He made a step forward, once, to recall her, but he remembered that he was no longer an effeminate dry-goods student, and his warrior soul scorned to sue for quarter. He strode from the place with martial firmness, and never looked behind him.

CHAPTER III.

When Lucretia awoke the next morning, the faint music of a fife and the roll of a distant drum came floating upon the soft spring breeze, and as she listened the sounds grew more subdued and finally passed out of hearing. She lay absorbed in thought for many minutes, and then she sighed and said, "Oh, if he were only with that band of fellows, how I could love him!"

In the course of the day a neighbor dropped in, and when the conversation turned upon the soldiers, the visitor said:

"Reginald de Whittaker looked rather down-hearted, and didn't shout when he marched along with the other boys this morning.

I expect it's owing to you, Miss Loo, though when I met him coming here yesterday evening to tell you he'd enlisted, he thought you'd like it and be proud of——Mercy! what in the nation's the matter with the girl?"

Nothing, only a sudden misery had fallen like a blight upon her heart, and a deadly pallor telegraphed it to her countenance. She rose up without a word and walked with a firm step out of the room, but once within the sacred seclusion of her own chamber, her strong will gave way and she burst into a flood of passionate tears. Bitterly she upbraided herself for her foolish haste of the night before, and her harsh treatment of her lover at the very moment that he had come to anticipate the proudest wish of her heart, and to tell her that he had enrolled himself under the battle-flag and was going forth to fight as *her* soldier. Alas! other maidens would have soldiers in those glorious fields, and be entitled to the sweet pain of feeling a tender solicitude for them, but she would be unrepresented. No soldier in all the vast armies would breathe her name as he breasted the crimson tide of war! She wept again—or, rather, she went on weeping where she left off a moment before. In her bitterness of spirit, she almost cursed the precipitancy that had brought all this sorrow upon her young life. "Drat it!" The words were in her bosom, but she locked them there, and closed her lips against their utterance.

For weeks and weeks she nursed her grief in silence while the roses faded from her cheeks. And through it all she clung to the hope that some day the old love would bloom again in Reginald's heart, and he would write to her—but the long summer days dragged wearily along, and still no letter came. The newspapers teemed with stories of battle and carnage, and eagerly she read them, but always with the same result: the tears welled up and blurred the closing lines—the name she sought was looked for in vain, and the dull aching returned to her sinking heart. Letters to the other girls sometimes contained brief mention of him, and presented always the same picture of him—a morose, unsmiling, desperate man, always in the thickest of the fight, begrimed with powder, and moving calm and unscathed through tempests of shot and shell, as if he bore a charmed life.

But at last, in a long list of maimed and killed, poor Lucretia read these terrible words, and fell fainting to the floor: "R. D. Whittaker, private soldier, desperately wounded!"

CHAPTER IV.

ON a couch in one of the wards of a hospital at Washington lay a wounded soldier; his head was so profusely bandaged that his features were not visible, but there was no mistaking the happy face of the young girl who sat beside him—it was Lucretia Borgia Smith's. She had hunted him out several weeks before, and since that time she had patiently watched by him and nursed him, coming in the morning as soon as the surgeons had finished dressing his wounds, and never leaving him until relieved at nightfall. A ball had shattered his lower jaw, and he could not utter a syllable; through all her weary vigils, she had never once been blessed with a grateful word from his dear lips; yet she stood to her post bravely and without a murmur, feeling that when he did get well again she would hear that which would more than reward her for all her devotion.

At the hour we have chosen for the opening of this chapter, Lucretia was in a tumult of happy excitement, for the surgeon had told her that at last her Whittaker had recovered sufficiently to admit of the removal of the bandages from his head, and she was now waiting with feverish impatience for the doctor to come and disclose the loved features to her view. At last he came, and Lucretia, with beaming eyes and a fluttering heart, bent over the couch with anxious expectancy. One bandage was removed, then another, and another, and lo! the poor wounded face was revealed to the light of day.

"O my own dar——"

What have we here! What is the matter! Alas! it was the face of a stranger!

Poor Lucretia! With one hand covering her upturned eyes, she staggered back with a moan of anguish. Then a spasm of fury distorted her countenance as she brought her fist down with a crash that made the medicine bottles on the table dance again, and exclaimed:

"O confound my cats if I haven't gone and fooled away three

mortal weeks here, snuffling and slobbering over the wrong soldier!"

It was a sad, sad truth. The wretched, but innocent and unwitting impostor was R. D., or Richard Dilworthy Whittaker, of Wisconsin, the soldier of dear little Eugenie Le Mulligan, of that State, and utterly unknown to our unhappy Lucretia B. Smith.

Such is life, and the trail of the serpent is over us all. Let us draw the curtain over this melancholy history—for melancholy it must still remain, during a season at least, for the real Reginald de Whittaker has not turned up yet.

100 *An Unbiased Criticism*

18 March 1865

A gap of some three and one-half months intervenes between this sketch and the previous one. On 4 December 1864 Clemens deserted San Francisco for a three-month stay in the mining camps of Calaveras and Tuolumne counties—an important moratorium that followed what he called his "slinking" days in chapter 59 of *Roughing It*. He spent most of his time at Angel's Camp and Jackass Hill, usually with Jim Gillis and Jim's fellow pocket miner Dick Stoker. This visit to the southern mining camps on the Mother Lode eventually produced Mark Twain's most famous sketch, "Jim Smiley and His Jumping Frog" (no. 119), but it also provided the raw material for "An Unbiased Criticism," which was Clemens' first publication after his return to San Francisco and which resumed his series of sketches in the *Californian*. The present sketch anticipates the more famous "Jumping Frog" story in its setting at Angel's Camp, and especially in its vivid monologue by Coon—a distinct forebear of Simon Wheeler.[1]

Like most of Clemens' earlier work for the *Californian*, this sketch takes its rise in part from a topical event reported in the newspapers. And like "A Touching Story of George Washington's Boyhood" (no. 95), it is an elaborate digression from the announced topic: paintings on exhibit in the new California Art Union. The prestigious Art Union, which Clemens mentions only in the opening and closing passages of his sketch, had Governor Frederick F. Low for its president and William C.

---

[1]Gladys C. Bellamy, *Mark Twain as a Literary Artist* (Norman: University of Oklahoma Press, 1950), pp. 145–146; Edgar M. Branch, " 'My Voice Is Still for Setchell': A Background Study of 'Jim Smiley and His Jumping Frog,' " *PMLA* 82 (December 1967): 591–593.

Ralston for its treasurer. Since the opening of its doors on 12 January 1865, the gallery had occupied the second-floor rooms at 312 Montgomery Street, where, for twenty-five cents, one could see a collection of about one hundred and thirty paintings by such artists as Charles Nahl, Frederick Butman, Thomas Hill, and Virgil Williams. A five-dollar annual fee entitled members to free admission at all times as well as to complimentary prints or engravings once a year.[2]

In response to the opening of the gallery, the city newspapers blossomed with art criticism—often ponderously moral or literary—which was evidently written by local art lovers who wished to remain anonymous, like the *Evening Bulletin's* Kuzzilbash or the *Morning Call's* Magilp. Magilp's review of Thomas Hill's recently completed "Scene from the Merchant of Venice," the only painting Clemens mentions in his sketch, discoursed fulsomely on Shylock's moral and intellectual features as revealed by his gesture and expression.[3] Sometimes readers responded to the critics, and sometimes the critics themselves warred. Out of this minor furor came the framework of Clemens' sketch. By carefully avoiding any hint of art criticism, Clemens declined to parody Magilp or any other critic, but the sustained irrelevance of what he did write constitutes a clever comment on the mediocre quality of the newspaper reviews.

Clemens explained his long digression—the main body of the sketch—by saying he wanted to demonstrate "that we were in the habit of reading everything thoroughly that fell in our way at Angel's, and that consequently we were familiar with all that had appeared in print about the new Art Union rooms." Coon's memorable description of the miners' reading habits bears this out, but it soon leads into the narrator's burlesque account of a local election in which the miners' most trivial reading defines the election issues. The men divide into political factions: modern counterparts of Swift's Big Endians and Little Endians. They argue over the relative merits of rival sewing machines and iron safes, or the propriety of the Christian Commission's having refused a cash contribution because the money was raised by an amateur "parlor theatrical." The leaders of these factions are bitter enemies on the hustings but cronies in the evenings. They are masters of political invective and patriotic propaganda.

---

[2]"Opening of the California Art Union—Its Plan and Objects," San Francisco *Evening Bulletin,* 12 January 1865, p. 2; "Opening of the Art Union," *Californian* 2 (14 January 1865): 8.

[3]"The California Art-Union," San Francisco *Morning Call,* 21 February 1865, p. 1.

The sketch ultimately descends from one of Clemens' lost Josh letters, in which he parodied a Fourth of July oration given in Esmeralda, as well as from his long Third House address of 1863.[4] It also reflects Clemens' recent reporting of the Lincoln and McClellan presidential campaigns. Mark Twain's rousing speech at the Union Hotel in Angel's Camp is perhaps no more hollow nor more fraudulently manipulative than some of the real speeches Clemens had summarized for the *Call* a few months before. It catches the rhythms, the clichés, and the appeals to prejudice of contemporary political oratory. Yet the satire is neither sharp nor bitter. Clemens takes an obvious delight in his miners, who occupy the realm of conscious fantasy. The portrait of Coon and his fellows is sympathetic, for beneath their bickering—which even they do not take seriously— lies a sound combination of decency, rugged individualism, shrewdness, and mutual respect. They are members of what Henry Nash Smith has called the vernacular community, and it is the narrator—a visiting outsider, after all—who is the chief demagogue.[5]

Clemens revised "An Unbiased Criticism" only once, in the Yale Scrapbook. But he, or more probably Webb, decided to reprint only Coon's memorable speech about the "mighty responsible old Webster-Unabridged" in the 1867 *Jumping Frog*. There it was called "Literature in the Dry Diggings," and Clemens reprinted it again in 1872 and 1874, although he declined to include it in *Sketches, New and Old* in 1875.

---

[4]See the introduction, volume 1, pp. 16–17, and *MTEnt*, pp. 102–109.

[5]See *MTDW*, pp. 1–21 and *passim*. Paul Schmidt has argued that the tale embodies a detailed burlesque of the characteristic features of republicanism, but it should be noted that Schmidt mistakenly attributes many of the narrator's comments to Ben Coon ("Mark Twain's Satire on Republicanism," *American Quarterly* 5 [Winter 1952]: 344–356).

An Unbiased Criticism

THE CALIFORNIA ART UNION—ITS MORAL EFFECTS UPON
THE YOUTH OF BOTH SEXES CAREFULLY CONSIDERED AND
CANDIDLY COMMENTED UPON.

The Editor of The Californian ordered me to go to the rooms
of the California Art Union and write an elaborate criticism upon
the pictures upon exhibition there, and I beg leave to report that
the result is hereunto appended, together with bill for same.

I do not know anything about Art and very little about music or
anatomy, but nevertheless I enjoy looking at pictures and listening to operas, and gazing at handsome young girls, about the same
as people do who are better qualified by education to judge of
merit in these matters.

After writing the above rather neat heading and preamble on
my foolscap, I proceeded to the new Art Union rooms last week,
to see the paintings, about which I had read so much in the papers
during my recent three months' stay in the Big Tree region of
Calaveras county; [up there, you know, they read *everything*, because in most of those little camps they have no libraries, and no
books to speak of, except now and then a patent-office report, or a
prayer-book, or literature of that kind, in a general way, that will
hang on and last a good while when people are careful with it, like
miners; but as for novels, they pass them around and wear them

out in a week or two. Now there was Coon, a nice bald-headed
man at the hotel in Angel's Camp. I asked him to lend me a book,
one rainy day: he was silent a moment, and a shade of melancholy
flitted across his fine face, and then he said: "Well, I've got a
mighty responsible old Webster-Unabridged, what there is left of
it, but they started her sloshing around, and sloshing around, and
sloshing around the camp before I ever got a chance to read her
myself, and next she went to Murphy's, and from there she went
to Jackass, and now, by G—d, she's gone to San Andreas, and I
don't expect I'll ever see that book again; but what makes me
mad, is that for all they're so handy about keeping her sashshay-
ing around from shanty to shanty and from camp to camp, none of
'em's ever got a good word for her. Now Coddington had her a
week, and she was too many for *him*—he couldn't spell the
words; he tackled some of them regular busters, tow'rd the middle, you know, and they throwed him; next, Dyer, *he* tried her
a jolt, but he couldn't *pronounce* 'em—Dyer can hunt quail or
play seven-up as well as any man, understand me, but he can't
pronounce worth a d—n; he used to worry along well enough,
though, till he'd flush one of them rattlers with a clatter of syllables as long as a string of sluice-boxes, and then he'd lose his grip
and throw up his hand; and so, finally, Dick Stoker harnessed her,
up there at his cabin, and sweated over her, and cussed over her,
and rastled with her for as much as three weeks, night and day, till
he got as far as R, and then passed her over to 'Lige Pickerell, and
said she was the all-firedest dryest reading that ever *he* struck;
well, well, if she's come back from San Andreas, you can get her
and prospect her, but I don't reckon there's a good deal left of her
by this time; though time was when she was as likely a book as
any in the State, and as hefty, and had an amount of general
information in her that was astonishing, if any of these cattle had
known enough to get it out of her;" and ex-corporal Coon proceeded cheerlessly to scout with his brush after the straggling
hairs on the rear of his head and drum them to the front for
inspection and roll-call, as was his usual custom before turning in
for his regular afternoon nap:] but as I was saying, they read everything, up there, and consequently all the Art criticisms, and the
"Parlor Theatricals *vs.* Christian Commission" controversy, and

even the quarrels in the advertising columns between rival fire-
proof safe and sewing-machine companies were devoured with
avidity. Why, they eventually became divided on these questions,
and discussed them with a spirit of obstinacy and acrimony that I
have seldom seen equalled in the most important religious and
political controversies. I have known a Grover & Baker fanatic
to cut his own brother dead because he went for the Florence. As
you have already guessed, perhaps, the county and township elections were carried on these issues alone, almost. I took sides, of
course—every man had to—there was no shirking the responsibility; a man must be one thing or the other, either Florence or
Grover & Baker, unless, of course, he chose to side with some
outside machine faction, strong enough to be somewhat formidable. I was a bitter Florence man, and I think my great speech in
the bar-room of the Union Hotel, at Angel's, on the night of the
13th of February, will long be remembered as the deadliest blow
the unprincipled Grover & Baker cabal ever got in that camp, and
as having done more to thwart their hellish designs upon the
liberties of our beloved country than any single effort of any one
man that was ever made in that county. And in that same speech I
administered a scathing rebuke to the *"Lillie Union and Constitution Fire and Burglar Proof Safe Party,"* (for I was a malignant
Tilton & McFarland man and would break bread and eat salt with
none other,) that made even the most brazen among them blush
for the infamous and damnable designs they had hatched and
were still hatching against the Palladium of Freedom in Calaveras
county. The concluding passage of my speech was considered to
have been the finest display of eloquence and power ever heard in
that part of the country, from Rawhide Ranch to Deadhorse Flat. I
said:

"FELLOW-CITIZENS: A word more, and I am done. Men of Calaveras—men of Cuyoté Flat—men of Jackass —BEWARE OF COD-
DINGTON! [Cheers.] Beware of this atrocious ditch-owner—this
vile water-rat—this execrable dry-land shrimp—this bold and
unprincipled mud-turtle, who sells water to Digger, Chinaman,
Greaser and American alike, and at the self-same prices—who
would sell you, who would sell me, who would sell us ALL,
to carry out the destructive schemes of the '*Enlightened* [Bah!]

Freedom & Union Grover & Baker Loop-Stitch Sewing Machine Party' [groans] of which wretched conglomeration of the ruff-scruff and rag-tag-and-bob-tail of noble old Calaveras he is the appropriate leader—BEWAR-R-E of him! [Tremendous applause.] Again I charge you as men whom future generations will hold to a fearful responsibility, to BEWARE OF CODDINGTON! [Tempests of applause.] Beware of this unsavory remnant of a once pure and high-minded man!* [Renewed applause.] Beware of this faithless modern Esau, who would sell his birthright of freedom and ours, for a mess of pottage!—for a mess of tripe!—for a mess of sauer-kraut and garlic!—for a mess of anything under the sun that a Christian Florence patriot would scorn and a Digger Indian turn from with loathing and disgust!† [Thunders of applause.] Remember Coddington on election day! and remember him but to damn him! I appeal to you, sovereign and enlightened Calaver-asses, and my heart tells me that I do not appeal in vain! I have done. [Earthquakes of applause that made the welkin tremble for many minutes, and finally died away in hoarse demands for the villain Coddington, and threats to lynch him.]

I felt exhausted, and in need of rest after my great effort, and so I tore myself from my enthusiastic friends and went home with Coddington to his hospitable mansion, where we partook of an excellent supper and then retired to bed, after playing several games of seven-up for beer and booking some heavy election bets.

The contest on election day was bitter, and to the last degree exciting, but principles triumphed over party jugglery and chica-nery, and we carried everything but the Constable, (Unconditional Button-Hole Stitch and Anti-Parlor Theatrical candidate,) and Tax Collector, (Moderate Lillie Fire-Proof and Fusion Grover & Button-Hole Stitch Machines,) and County Assessor, (Radical Christian Commission and Independent Sewing Machine can-didate,) and we could have carried these, also, but at the last moment fraudulent handbills were suddenly scattered abroad containing sworn affidavits that a Tilton & McFarland safe,

---

*He used to belong to the Florence at first.   M. T.
†I grant you that that last part was a sort of a strong figure, seeing that that tribe are not over-particular in the matter of diet, and don't usually go back on anything that they can chaw.   M. T.

on its way from New York, had melted in the tropical sunshine after fifteen minutes' exposure on the Isthmus; also, that the lock stitch, back-stitch, fore-and-aft, forward-and-back, down-the-middle, double-and-twist, and the other admirable stitches and things upon which the splendid reputation of the Florence rests, had all been cabbaged from the traduced and reviled Button-Hole Stitch and Grover & Baker machines; also, that so far from the Parlor-Theatrical-Christian-Commission controversy being finished, it had sprung up again in San Francisco, and by latest advices the Opposition was ahead. What men could do, we did, but although we checked the demoralization that had broken out in our ranks, we failed to carry all our candidates. We sent express to San Andreas and Columbia, and had strong affidavits—sworn to by myself and our candidates—printed, denouncing the other publications as low and disreputable falsehoods and calumnies, whose shameless authors ought to be driven beyond the pale of civilized society, and winding up with the withering revelation that the rain had recently soaked through one of Lillie's Fire and Burglar-Proof safes in San Francisco, and badly damaged the books and papers in it; and that, in the process of drying, the safe warped so that the door would not swing on its hinges, and had to be "prized" open with a butter-knife. O, but that was a rough shot! It blocked the game and saved the day for us—and just at the critical moment our reserve (whom we had sent for and drummed up in Tuolumne and the adjoining counties, and had kept out of sight and full of chain-lightning, sudden death and scorpion-bile all day in Tom Deer's back-yard,) came filing down the street as drunk as loons, with a drum and fife and lighted transparencies, (daylight and dark were all the same to *them* in *their* condition,) bearing such stirring devices as:

> *"The Florence is bound to rip, therefore,* LET HER RIP!*"*
> *"Grover & Baker, how are you* NOW?*"*
> *"Nothing can keep the Opposition cool in the other world but Tilton & McFarland's Chilled Iron Safes!"* etc., etc.

A vast Florence machine on wheels led the van, and a sick Chinaman bearing a crippled Grover & Baker brought up the rear. The procession reeled up to the polls with deafening cheers for

the Florence and curses for the "loop stitch scoun'rels," and de-
posited their votes like men for freedom of speech, freedom of
the press and freedom of conscience in the matter of sewing
machines, provided they are Florences.

I had a very comfortable time in Calaveras county, in spite of
the rain, and if I had my way I would go back there, and argue the
sewing machine question around Coon's bar-room stove again
with the boys on rainy evenings. Calaveras possesses some of the
grandest natural features that have ever fallen under the contemplation of the human mind—such as the Big Trees, the famous
Morgan gold mine which is the richest in the world at the present
time, perhaps, and "straight" whisky that will throw a man a
double somerset and limber him up like boiled maccaroni before
he can set his glass down. Marvelous and incomprehensible is the
straight whisky of Angel's Camp!

But I digress to some extent, for maybe it was not really necessary to be quite so elaborate as I have been in order to enable the
reader to understand that we were in the habit of reading everything thoroughly that fell in our way at Angel's, and that consequently we were familiar with all that had appeared in print
about the new Art Union rooms. They get all the papers regularly
every evening there, 24 hours out from San Francisco.

However, now that I have got my little preliminary point established to my satisfaction, I will proceed with my Art criticism.

The rooms of the California Art Union are pleasantly situated
over the picture store in Montgomery street near the Eureka
Theatre, and the first thing that attracts your attention when you
enter is a beautiful and animated picture representing the Trial
Scene in the *Merchant of Venice.* They did not charge me anything for going in there, because the Superintendent was not noticing at the time, but it is likely he would charge you or another
man twenty-five cents—I think he would, because when I tried to
get a dollar and a half out of a fellow I took for a stranger, the
new-comer said the usual price was only two bits, and besides he
was a heavy life-member and not obliged to pay anything at
all—so I had to let him in for a quarter, but I had the satisfaction
of telling him we were not letting life-members in free, now, as
much as we *were.* It touched him on the raw. I let another fellow

in for nothing, because I had cabined with him a few nights in Esmeralda several years ago, and I thought it only fair to be hospitable with him now that I had a chance. He introduced me to a friend of his named Brown, (I was hospitable to Brown also,) and me and Brown sat down on a bench and had a long talk about Washoe and other things, and I found him very entertaining for a stranger. He said his mother was a hundred and thirteen years old, and he had an aunt who died in her infancy, who, if she had lived, would have been older than his mother, now. He judged so because, originally, his aunt was born before his mother was. That was the first thing he told me, and then we were friends in a moment. It could not but be flattering to me, a stranger, to be made the recipient of information of so private and sacred a nature as the age of his mother and the early decease of his aunt, and I naturally felt drawn towards him and bound to him by a stronger and a warmer tie than the cold, formal introduction that had previously passed between us. I shall cherish the memory of the ensuing two hours as being among the purest and happiest of my checkered life. I told him frankly who I was, and where I came from, and where I was going to, and when I calculated to start, and all about my uncle Ambrose, who was an Admiral, and was for a long time in command of a large fleet of canal boats, and about my gifted aunt Martha, who was a powerful poetess, and a dead shot with a brickbat at forty yards, and about myself and how I was employed at good pay by the publishers of THE CALIFORNIAN to come up there and write an able criticism upon the pictures in the Art Union—indeed I concealed nothing from Brown, and in return he concealed nothing from me, but told me everything he could recollect about his rum old mother, and his grandmother, and all his relations, in fact. And so we talked, and talked, and exchanged these tender heart-reminiscences until the sun drooped far in the West, and then Brown said "Let's go down and take a drink."

101. Important Correspondence

6 May 1865

When Charles Henry Webb resumed editorial control of the *Californian* on 26 November 1864, Clemens had almost completed his first nine contributions: "Lucretia Smith's Soldier" (no. 99) was published on December 3, just before he left San Francisco. Webb published his tenth, "An Unbiased Criticism" (no. 100), after his return in March 1865. And on April 8 he facetiously assured his readers that Mark Twain would *not* become a contributor to the newly founded *Journal of the Trades and Workingmen.* That journal had evidently announced that Mark Twain was "going over the mountains in quest of petroleum, and will stop on the way at several places to furnish it with characteristic articles." Webb said: "In both instances we fear the *Journal* is wrong, as Mark tells us that he wouldn't even cross over to Oakland for all the oil that town could hold; and as for the other thing we know that he is engaged to write for THE CALIFORNIAN for a longer period of years than the chances are that he will live, and at a greater salary than the proprietors can possibly pay."[1] But Webb resigned as editor of the magazine the following week. Although a new editor was not formally announced until December, all indications are that Bret Harte was both a heavy contributor and the acting editor at this time.[2] Clemens did not again contribute until May 6, when he published "Important Correspondence."

---

[1]"Two New Journals," *Californian* 2 (8 April 1865): 8.
[2]*Californian* 2 (15 April 1865): 8. Although Harte was not named as editor until December 9, three weeks before he again resigned in favor of Webb, several facts suggest he had been acting in that capacity since Webb resigned on April 15. On December 2, for instance, when the magazine announced that Webb would be contributing a column called "Inigoings," replacing the "Mouse-Trap" by "Trem," it also said that the "editorship remains unchanged," implying some continuity

In writing this sketch Clemens again took his cue from an event of current local interest. In mid-January 1865 the Right Reverend William Ingraham Kip resigned the pastorate of Grace Cathedral in San Francisco while remaining bishop of California, a position he had held since 1857 and would retain until his death in 1893. The efforts by the vestry to obtain his pastoral replacement from among the "first-class clergymen of the East" and their repeated failure to do so were described on April 29 by Frank W. Gross, a friend of Clemens' and the local editor of the San Francisco *Evening Bulletin:*

PROCURING A CLERGYMAN FROM THE EAST UNDER DIFFICULTIES.—The vestry of Grace Cathedral have for some time been trying to procure one of the first-class clergymen of the East. They have successively extended invitations to the Rev. Phillips Brooks of Philadelphia, the Rev. Dr. Cummings of Chicago, and the Rev. Dr. Hawks of Baltimore—all of whom have respectfully declined. The last invitation was extended to Dr. Hawks, and some hopes were indulged, until recently, that he would come; but the attractions East were too strong for him. The Doctor has resigned his parish in Baltimore, and has recently been preaching once each Sunday in the Church of the Annunciation, New York, into which he has succeeded in infusing a new life. A number of gentlemen there have clubbed together and offered Dr. Hawks a high salary and a new church, or, if he likes, the purchase of the Church of St. George the Martyr, up town. The vestry of Grace Cathedral offered Dr. Hawks a salary of $7,000, but it is understood that he is to receive $10,000 in New York, which, according to the present price of legal tenders, is quite as good, while the expenses of living there are less than in California. Grace Church will have to try again, and either be content to pay a larger salary, or take up with a lower order of clerical talent. This is not the first time church-goers at the East have outbid the same class here, as three or four of the churches in this city can testify. There seems to be quite as lively an appreciation of able and eloquent preachers at the East as in San Francisco, but they only show it when a call reaches their pastors from the Pacific coast. Several of the divines there have lately been directly indebted to San Francisco for an increase in their salary, and other perquisites.[3]

Extracts from correspondence concerning calls to the Fifth Street Baptist Church and the Howard Street Presbyterian Church had been published

---

(*Californian* 4 [2 December 1865]: 9). And when Clemens recalled this period in 1906, he said that "Harte was doing a good deal of writing for the *Californian*—contributing 'Condensed Novels' and sketches to it and also acting as editor, I think" (*AMT,* p. 123). The "Condensed Novels" began with the issue of July 1.

[3]San Francisco *Evening Bulletin,* 29 April 1865, p. 5. Gross is identified as the "local editor" of the *Bulletin* in Langley, *Directory for 1865,* p. 205. Clemens implied that Gross was an "intimate" friend in a letter to Jervis Langdon, 29 December 1868, *CL1,* letter 256.

in the *Bulletin* only two weeks before this article appeared.[4] Clemens seized upon the form of the first and the facts of the second *Bulletin* articles to produce "Important Correspondence" and "Further of Mr. Mark Twain's Important Correspondence" (no. 102), two of his finest early satires on clerical hypocrisy.

Bishop Kip was well known to Clemens and to other Californians as an orthodox High Church Episcopalian of remarkable energy and ambition. He had written several books on church history and doctrine, and had almost single-handedly organized the Episcopal church in California. When he came West from New York in 1854 as missionary bishop, his pastorate included the entire state, in which only two congregations were functioning. Eleven years later the church's strength statewide attested to his tireless travels and effective administration. For many of these early years Kip also filled the pulpit of San Francisco's Grace Church. In 1860 he laid the cornerstone of Grace Cathedral at California and Stockton streets, and two years later he formally dedicated the building, thus fulfilling his ambition of establishing the first cathedral of the Episcopal church in America.

Not all San Franciscans approved Kip's success in converting modest Grace Church into the costly, debt-ridden Grace Cathedral. Two months after "Important Correspondence" appeared, for instance, one San Francisco editor said of the bishop:

During the eleven years of his labors among us, his soul yearned for "a Cathedral" and a "Parish School." Blissful visions of a "Dean and Chapter" also floated airily in his imagination. His great soul meantime overlooked such petty trifles as struggling parishes unable to support pastors, and threadbare parsons, in distant parts of the State. . . . What is a starving parson, or a country flock without a shepherd, when weighed against the splendors of a Cathedral, with "responding choirs," and an intoned service?[5]

The writer further noted with pleasure that the parsons of the bishop's diocese had recently voted, in his absence and against his will, to officially substitute the name "Grace Church" for "Grace Cathedral." The vestry did not succeed in replacing Kip until more than a year later when, in September 1866, the Reverend H. Goodwin, assistant minister under Kip, became rector of the cathedral.

To what degree Clemens was aware of these hostile feelings within the

---

[4]"New Clergymen for Our City Pulpits," San Francisco *Evening Bulletin,* 15 April 1865, p. 3.
[5]"The Cathedral Question," *News Letter and Pacific Mining Journal* 15 (8 July 1865): 9.

vestry is uncertain, although his initial allusion to the "noble edifice known as Grace Cathedral" seems tinged with irony and a hint of disapproval. In fact, it is safe to say that Clemens showed a persistent prejudice against High Church orthodoxy at least as late as June 1866, when he attacked Bishop Thomas N. Staley in the Hawaiian Islands.[6] The ministers most severely ridiculed in these two sketches were, of course, Episcopalians. (He gave the Reverend Charles Wadsworth, a Presbyterian, and the Reverend Horatio Stebbins, a Unitarian, much less harsh treatment.) Clemens' characterization of the Right Reverend Francis Lister Hawks emphasizes his desire for money and prestige—without greatly exaggerating the facts as solemnly reported by Frank Gross in the *Bulletin*—but Clemens thereby strikes indirectly at Bishop Kip as well. Against Hawks's genteel hypocrisy and eye to the main chance, the author sympathizes with the ungodly, the vulgar, and the deprived—the latter so aptly symbolized by the little boy who missed out on the biscuits.

The main structural device of the sketch—Mark Twain's offering to assist the embarrassed minister—amounts to a major discovery for the apprentice writer. He here exploits the role of the somewhat vulgar adviser to the ministry whose efforts to help, because they are ostensibly prompted "by a spirit of enlarged charity," cannot be ignored, and yet because they are vulgar, cannot be wholly welcomed either. Mark Twain here assumes the role vis-à-vis the Reverend Hawks that "Mr. Brown" customarily assumes vis-à-vis "Mr. Mark Twain" in the Sandwich Islands letters. Mark Twain frankly admits that he is "not of the elect, so to speak," even though he is "a sort of a Presbyterian in a general way, and a brevet member of one of the principal churches of that denomination." We sympathize with this "sinner at large" who, like Tom Sawyer, cannot keep his mind from straying during church service. Speaking throughout in somewhat exaggerated western slang, Mark Twain momentarily transforms himself into a member of the vernacular community, while he ridicules the Reverend Hawks for his mercenary interests, his hypocrisy about slang, and his poor sense of humor. But perhaps the strongest attack comes on the denominational preoccupations of the church. Mark Twain undercuts these doctrinal differences like a true Freemason,[7] suggesting that he can write sermons for all the San Fran-

---

[6]Clemens to the Sacramento *Union*, written 30 June, published 30 July 1866, reprinted in Walter Francis Frear, *Mark Twain and Hawaii* (Chicago: Lakeside Press, 1947), pp. 352–355.

[7]Clemens was an active Mason at this time, having served as a junior deacon at a meeting of the Angel's Camp lodge as recently as 8 February 1865 (*N&J1*, p. 278

cisco ministers merely by tinkering with the "doctrinal points" and making the same "old sermon" available successively to an Episcopalian, a Methodist, a Unitarian, and finally a Presbyterian. But he reserves his strongest censure for the practice of praying first for the congregation, and then for "other denominations," "near relations," and so on, until the "sinners at large" are reached. "How would it do," he asks in the penultimate paragraph, "to be less diffuse? . . . How would it answer to adopt the simplicity and the beauty and the brevity and the comprehensiveness of the Lord's Prayer as a model? But perhaps I am wandering out of my jurisdiction." The ultimate point of this comic strategy was, after all, to suggest that he and the other vulgar sinners at large were, despite their bad manners, more genuinely Christian—Christian in the "truest sense of the term" as he said of Henry W. Bellows[8]—than the genteel ministers to whom he pretends to pay homage. Clemens had discovered a device that would serve him well in many later sketches and in *The Innocents Abroad*.

---

n. 45; the precise date is taken from a PH of the lodge records in MTP). Alexander E. Jones has pointed out that one of the tenets of Freemasonry which must have appealed to Clemens was that "religious creeds are of human origin, and their differences reflect differences in environment and custom" ("Mark Twain and Freemasonry," *American Literature* 26 [November 1954]: 370).

[8]Clemens to Jane Clemens et al., 4 December 1866, *CL1*, letter 115.

Important Correspondence

BETWEEN MR. MARK TWAIN OF SAN FRANCISCO,
AND REV. BISHOP HAWKS, D. D., OF NEW YORK,
REV. PHILLIPS BROOKS OF PHILADELPHIA, AND
REV. DR. CUMMINS OF CHICAGO, CONCERNING
THE OCCUPANCY OF GRACE CATHEDRAL.

For a long time I have taken a deep interest in the efforts being made to induce the above-named distinguished clergymen—or, rather, some one of them—to come out here and occupy the pulpit of the noble edifice known as Grace Cathedral. And when I saw that the vestry were uniformly unsuccessful, although doing all that they possibly could to attain their object, I felt it my duty to come forward and throw the weight of my influence—such as it might be—in favor of the laudable undertaking. That by so doing I was not seeking to curry favor with the vestry—and that my actions were prompted by no selfish motive of any kind whatever—is sufficiently evidenced by the fact that I am not a member of Grace Church, and never had any conversation with the vestry upon the subject in hand, and never even hinted to them that I was going to write to the clergymen. What I have done in the matter I did of my own free will and accord, without any solicitation from anybody, and my actions were dictated solely by

a spirit of enlarged charity and good feeling toward the congregation of Grace Cathedral. I seek no reward for my services; I desire
none but the approval of my own conscience and the satisfaction
of knowing I have done that which I conceived to be my duty, to
the best of my ability.

M. T.

The correspondence which passed between myself and the Rev.
Dr. Hawks was as follows:

LETTER FROM MYSELF TO BISHOP HAWKS.

SAN FRANCISCO, March, 1865.
REV. DR. HAWKS—*Dear Doctor.*—Since I heard that you have
telegraphed the vestry of Grace Cathedral here, that you cannot
come out to San Francisco and carry on a church at the terms
offered you, viz: $7,000 a year, I have concluded to write you on
the subject myself. A word in your ear: say nothing to anybody
—keep dark—but just pack up your traps and come along out
here—I will see that it is all right. That $7,000 dodge was only
a *bid*—nothing more. They never expected you to clinch a bar-
gain like that. I will go to work and get up a little competition
among the cloth, and the result of it will be that you will make
more money in six months here than you would in New York
in a year. I can do it. I have a great deal of influence with the
clergy here, and especially with the Rev. Dr. Wadsworth and the
Rev. Mr. Stebbins—I write their sermons for them. [This latter
fact is not generally known, however, and maybe you had as well
not mention it.] I can get them to strike for higher wages any time.

You would like this berth. It has a greater number of attractive
features than any I know of. It is such a magnificent field, for one
thing,—why, sinners are so thick that you can't throw out your
line without hooking several of them; you'd be surprised—the
flattest old sermon a man can grind out is bound to corral half a
dozen. You see, you can do such a land-office business on such a
small capital. Why, I wrote the most rambling, incomprehensible
harangue of a sermon you ever heard in your life for one of the
Episcopalian ministers here, and he landed seventeen with it at
the first dash; then I trimmed it up to suit Methodist doctrine,
and the Rev. Mr. Thomas got eleven more; I tinkered the doctrinal
points again, and Stebbins made a lot of Unitarian converts with
it; I worked it over once more, and Dr. Wadsworth did almost as
well with it as he usually does with my ablest compositions. It
was passed around, after that, from church to church, undergoing

changes of dress as before, to suit the vicissitudes of doctrinal climate, until it went the entire rounds. During its career we took in, altogether, a hundred and eighteen of the most abject reprobates that ever traveled on the broad road to destruction.

You would find this a remarkably easy berth—one man to give out the hymns, another to do the praying, another to read the chapter from the Testament—you would have nothing in the world to do but read the litany and preach—no, not *read* the litany, but sing it. They sing the litany here, in the Pontifical Grand Mass style, which is pleasanter and more attractive than to read it. You need not mind that, though; the tune is not difficult, and requires no more musical taste or education than is required to sell "Twenty-four—self-sealing—envelopes—for f-o-u-r cents," in your city. I like to hear the litany sung. Perhaps there is hardly enough variety in the music, but still the effect is very fine. Bishop Kip never could sing worth a cent, though. However, he has gone to Europe now to learn. Yes, as I said before, you would have nothing in the world to do but preach and sing that litany; and, between you and me, Doc, as regards the music, if you could manage to ring in a few of the popular and familiar old tunes that the people love so well you would be almost certain to create a sensation. I think I can safely promise you that. I am satisfied that you could do many a thing that would attract less attention than would result from adding a spirited variety to the music of the litany.

Your preaching will be easy. Bring along a barrel of your old obsolete sermons; the people here will never know the difference.

Drop me a line, Hawks; I don't know you, except by reputation, but I like you all the same. And don't you fret about the salary. I'll make *that* all right, you know. You need not mention to the vestry of Grace Cathedral, though, that I have been communicating with you on this subject. You see, I do not belong to their church, and they might think I was taking too much trouble on their account—though I assure you, upon my honor, it is no trouble in the world to me; I don't mind it; I am not busy now, and I would rather do it than not. All I want is to have a sure thing that you get your rights. You can depend upon me. I'll see you through this business as straight as a shingle; I haven't been drifting around all my life for nothing. I know a good deal more than a boiled carrot, though I may not appear to. And although I am not of the elect, so to speak, I take a strong interest in these things, nevertheless, and I am not going to stand by and see them come any seven-thousand-dollar arrangement over you. I have sent them word in your name that you won't take less than $18,000,

and that you can get $25,000 in greenbacks at home. I also inti-
mated that I was going to write your sermons—I thought it might
have a good effect, and every little helps, you know. So you can
just pack up and come along—it will be all right—I am satisfied
of that. You needn't bring any shirts, I have got enough for us
both. You will find there is nothing mean about *me*—I'll wear
your clothes, and you can wear mine, just the same as so many
twin brothers. When I like a man, I *like* him, and I go my death for
him. My friends will all be fond of you, and will take to you as
naturally as if they had known you a century. I will introduce you,
and you will be all right. You can always depend on them. If you
were to point out a man and say you did not like him, they would
carve him in a minute.

Hurry along, Bishop. I shall be on the lookout for you, and will
take you right to my house and you can stay there as long as you
like, and it shan't cost you a cent.

Very truly, yours,

MARK TWAIN.

REPLY OF BISHOP HAWKS.

NEW YORK, April, 1865.

MY DEAR MARK.—I had never heard of you before I received
your kind letter, but I feel as well acquainted with you now as if I
had known you for years. I see that you understand how it is with
us poor laborers in the vineyard, and feel for us in our struggles to
gain a livelihood. You will be blessed for this—you will have your
reward for the deeds done in the flesh—you will get your deserts
hereafter. I am really sorry I cannot visit San Francisco, for I can
see now that it must be a pleasant field for the earnest worker to
toil in; but it was ordered otherwise, and I submit with becoming
humility. My refusal of the position at $7,000 a year was not
precisely meant to be final, but was intended for what the ungodly term a "flyer"—the object being, of course, to bring about
an increase of the amount. That object was legitimate and proper,
since it so nearly affects the interests not only of myself but of
those who depend upon me for sustenance and support. Perhaps
you remember a remark I made once to a vestry who had been
solicited to increase my salary, my family being a pretty large one:
they declined, and said it was promised that Providence would
take care of the young ravens. I immediately retorted, in my happiest vein, that there was no similar promise concerning the
young Hawks, though! I thought it was very good, at the time.
The recollection of it has solaced many a weary hour since then,

when all the world around me seemed dark and cheerless, and it is a source of tranquil satisfaction to me to think of it even at this day.

No; I hardly meant my decision to be final, as I said before, but subsequent events have compelled that result in spite of me. I threw up my parish in Baltimore, although it was paying me very handsomely, and came to New York to see how things were going in our line. I have prospered beyond my highest expectations. I selected a lot of my best sermons—old ones that had been forgotten by everybody—and once a week I let one of them off in the Church of the Annunciation here. The spirit of the ancient sermons bubbled forth with a bead on it and permeated the hearts of the congregation with a new life, such as the worn body feels when it is refreshed with rare old wine. It was a great hit. The timely arrival of the "call" from San Francisco insured success to me. The people appreciated my merits at once. A number of gentlemen immediately clubbed together and offered me $10,000 a year, and agreed to purchase for me the Church of St. George the Martyr, up town, or to build a new house of worship for me if I preferred it. I closed with them on these terms, my dear Mark, for I feel that so long as not even the little sparrows are suffered to fall to the ground unnoted, I shall be mercifully cared for; and besides, I know that come what may, I can always eke out an existence so long as the cotton trade holds out as good as it is now. I am in cotton to some extent, you understand, and that is one reason why I cannot venture to leave here just at present to accept the position offered me in San Francisco. You see I have some small investments in that line which are as yet in an undecided state, and must be looked after.

But time flies, Mark, time flies; and I must bring this screed to a close and say farewell—and if forever, then forever fare thee well. But I shall never forget you, Mark—never!

Your generous solicitude in my behalf—your splendid inventive ability in conceiving of messages to the vestry calculated to make them offer me a higher salary—your sublime intrepidity in tendering those messages as having come from me—your profound sagacity in chaining and riveting the infatuation of the vestry with the intimation that you were going to write my sermons for me—your gorgeous liberality in offering to divide your shirts with me and to make common property of all other wearing apparel belonging to both parties—your cordial tender of your friends' affections and their very extraordinary services—your noble hospitality in providing a home for me in your palatial mansion—all these things call for my highest admiration and gratitude, and call not in vain, my dearest Mark. I shall never cease to pray for you and hold you in kindly and tearful remembrance. Once more, my gifted friend, accept the fervent thanks and the best wishes of

Your obliged servant,
Rev. Dr. Hawks.

Writes a beautiful letter, don't he?

But when the Bishop uses a tabooed expression, and talks glibly about doing a certain thing "just for a flyer," don't he shoulder the responsibility of it on to "the ungodly," with a rare grace?

And what a solid comfort that execrable joke has been to his declining years, hasn't it? If he goes on thinking about it and swelling himself up on account of it, he will be wanting a salary after a while that will break any church that hires him. However, if he enjoys it, and really thinks it *was* a good joke, I am very sure I don't want to dilute his pleasure in the least by dispelling the illusion. It reminds me, though, of a neat remark which the editor of *Harper's Magazine* made three years ago, in an article wherein he was pleading for charity for the harmless vanity of poor devil scribblers who imagine they are gifted with genius. He said *they* didn't know but what their writing was fine—and then he says: "Don't poor Martin Farquhar Tupper fondle his platitudes and think they are poems?" That's it. Let the Bishop fondle his little joke—no doubt it is just as good to him as if it were the very soul of humor.

But I wonder who in the mischief *is* "St.-George-the-Martyr-Up-Town?" However, no matter—the Bishop is not going to take his chances altogether with St.-George-the-Martyr-Up-Town, or with the little sparrows that are subject to accidents, either—he has a judicious eye on cotton. And he is right, too. Nobody deserves to be helped who don't try to help himself, and "faith without works" is a risky doctrine.

Now, what is your idea about his last paragraph? Don't you think he is spreading it on rather thick?—as "the ungodly" would term it. Do you really think there is any rain behind all that thunder and lightening? Do you suppose he really means it? They are mighty powerful adjectives—uncommonly powerful adjectives—and sometimes I seem to smell a faint odor of irony about them. But that could hardly be. He evidently loves me. Why, if I could be brought to believe that that reverend old humorist was discharging any sarcasm at me, I would never write to him again as long as I live. Thinks I will "get my deserts hereafter"—I don't hardly like the ring of that, altogether.

He says he will pray for me, though. Well, he couldn't do anything that would fit my case better, and he couldn't find a subject who would thank him more kindly for it than I would. I suppose I shall come in under the head of "sinners at large"—but I don't mind that; I am no better than any other sinner and I am not entitled to especial consideration. They pray for the congregation first, you know—and with considerable vim; then they pray mildly for other denominations; then for the near relations of the congregation; then for their distant relatives; then for the surrounding community; then for the State; then for the Government officers; then for the United States; then for North America; then for the whole Continent; then for England, Ireland and Scotland; France, Germany and Italy; Russia, Prussia and Austria; then for the inhabitants of Norway, Sweden and Timbuctoo; and those of Saturn, Jupiter and New Jersey; and then they give the niggers a lift, and the Hindoos a lift, and the Turks a lift, and the Chinese a lift; and then, after they have got the fountain of mercy baled out as dry as an ash-hopper, they bespeak the sediment left in the bottom of it for us poor "sinners at large."

It ain't just exactly fair, is it? Sometimes, (being a sort of a Presbyterian in a general way, and a brevet member of one of the principal churches of that denomination,) I stand up in devout attitude, with downcast eyes, and hands clasped upon the back of the pew before me, and listen attentively and expectantly for awhile; and then rest upon one foot for a season; and then upon the other; and then insert my hands under my coat-tails and stand erect and look solemn; and then fold my arms and droop forward and look dejected; and then cast my eye furtively at the minister; and then at the congregation; and then grow absent-minded, and catch myself counting the lace bonnets; and marking the drowsy members; and noting the wide-awake ones; and averaging the bald heads; and afterwards descend to indolent conjectures as to whether the buzzing fly that keeps stumbling up the window-pane and sliding down backwards again will ever accomplish his object to his satisfaction; and, finally, I give up and relapse into a dreary reverie—and about this time the minister reaches my department, and brings me back to hope and consciousness with a kind word for the poor "sinners at large."

Sometimes we are even forgotten altogether and left out in the cold—and then I call to mind the vulgar little boy who was fond of hot biscuits, and whose mother promised him that he should have all that were left if he would stay away and keep quiet and be a good little boy while the strange guest ate his breakfast; and who watched that voracious guest till the growing apprehension in his young bosom gave place to demonstrated ruin, and then sung out: "There! I know'd how it was goin' to be—I know'd how it was goin' to be, from the start! Blamed if he hain't gobbled the last biscuit!"

I do not complain, though, because it is very seldom that the Hindoos and the Turks and the Chinese get all the atoning biscuits and leave us sinners at large to go hungry. They *do* remain at the board a long time, though, and we often get a little tired waiting for our turn. How would it do to be less diffuse? How would it do to ask a blessing upon the specialities—I mean the congregation and the immediate community—and then include the whole broad universe in one glowing, fervent appeal? How would it answer to adopt the simplicity and the beauty and the brevity and the comprehensiveness of the Lord's Prayer as a model? But perhaps I am wandering out of my jurisdiction.

The letters I wrote to the Rev. Phillips Brooks of Philadelphia, and the Rev. Dr. Cummins of Chicago, urging them to come here and take charge of Grace Cathedral, and offering them my countenance and support, will be published next week, together with their replies to the same.

102. *Further of Mr. Mark Twain's Important Correspondence*

13 May 1865

This sketch, published in the *Californian* on 13 May 1865, continues the record of "Mr. Mark Twain's" involvement with efforts to fill the vacancy in Grace Cathedral. But this time his satire covers the whole spectrum of clerical hypocrites, from Phillips Brooks and George Cummins—whose letters Mark Twain declines to publish because they might awaken "a diseased curiosity in the public mind concerning the private matters of ministers of the gospel"—to the Reverend "T. St. Matthew Brown"—one of forty-eight applicants who "are all willing to sacrifice their dearest worldly interests and break the tenderest ties that bind them to their rural homes, to come and fight the good fight in our stately church."

Phillips Brooks—an Episcopalian, a Bostonian, and a Harvard man—was descended from a long line of Congregational clergymen. Ordained in 1859, he held pastorates for ten years in Philadelphia. In 1869 he became the rector of Trinity Church, Boston. An influential preacher who published many collections of sermons and religious essays after 1877, he was eventually elected bishop of Massachusetts in 1891. At the time of this sketch, Brooks had already achieved a reputation for piety and patriotism.

The "Rev. Dr. Cummins" was probably George David Cummins, ordained in the Episcopal church in 1845 and rector of churches in Virginia, Washington, D.C., and Maryland before his call to Trinity Church, Chicago, in 1863. He was elected assistant bishop of Kentucky in 1866. Seven years later he withdrew from the Protestant Episcopal church to found the Reformed Episcopal church, of which he was named presiding bishop.

The range of Mark Twain's powers of impersonation is strikingly evident in this sketch. The telegrams from Brooks and Cummins are, perhaps, slight compared to his earlier imaginary letter from Hawks, but he conjures up a remarkably worldly image in very few lines: "Don't be a fool, Mike. Draw on me for five or six hundred." The "foreign correspondence" from T. St. Matthew Brown, however, anticipates some of Mark Twain's burlesque characters in the unfinished *Quaker City* play (October–November 1867) and, more importantly, the king and the duke in *Huckleberry Finn.*

Clemens preserved both sketches (nos. 101 and 102) in the Yale Scrapbook, and seems to have considered including part of the second one in the 1867 *Jumping Frog* book. But neither sketch was reprinted in his lifetime.

Further of Mr. Mark Twain's Important Correspondence

I PROMISED, last week, that I would publish in the present number of THE CALIFORNIAN the correspondence held between myself and Rev. Phillips Brooks of Philadelphia, and Rev. Dr. Cummins of Chicago, but I must now beg you to release me from that promise. I have just received telegrams from these distinguished clergymen suggesting the impolicy of printing their letters; the suggestion is accompanied by arguments so able, so pointed and so conclusive that, although I saw no impropriety in it before, I am forced now to concede that it *would* be very impolitic to publish their letters. It could do but little good, perhaps, and might really do harm, in awakening a diseased curiosity in the public mind concerning the private matters of ministers of the gospel. The telegrams and accompanying arguments are as follows:

FROM REV. PHILLIPS BROOKS.

PHILADELPHIA, Friday, May 12.
MR. MICK TWINE:* Am told you have published Bishop Hawks' letter. You'll ruin the clergy! Don't—*don't* publish mine. Listen to reason—come, now, don't make an ass of yourself. Draw on me for five hundred dollars.

REV. PHILLIPS BROOKS.

[Although I feel it my duty to suppress his letter, it is proper to state for the information of the public, that Phil. gets a higher salary where he is, and consequently he cannot come out here and

159

take charge of Grace Cathedral. *Mem.* —He is in petroleum to some extent, also.—M. T.]

FROM REV. DR. CUMMINS.

CHICAGO, Thursday, May 11.

MR. MACSWAIN:* Have you really been stupid enough to publish Bishop Hawks' letter? Ge-whillikins! don't publish mine. Don't be a fool, Mike.* Draw on me for five or six hundred.

REV. DR. CUMMINS.

[I am conscious that it would be improper to print the Doctor's letter, but it may be as well to observe that *he* also gets a higher salary where he is, and consequently he cannot come out here and take charge of Grace Cathedral. *Mem.* —He is speculating a little in grain.—M. T.]

I am afraid I was rather hasty in publishing Bishop Hawks' letter. I am sorry I did it. I suppose there is no chance now to get an Argument out of him, this late in the day.

FOREIGN CORRESPONDENCE.

I am a suffering victim of my infernal disposition to be always trying to oblige somebody without being asked to do it. Nobody asked me to help the vestry of Grace Cathedral to hire a minister; I dashed into it on my own hook, in a spirit of absurd enthusiasm, and a nice mess I have made of it. I have not succeeded in securing either of the three clergymen I wanted, but that is not the worst of it—I have brought such a swarm of low-priced back-country preachers about my ears that I begin to be a little appalled at the work of my own hands. I am afraid I have evoked a spirit that I cannot lay. A single specimen of the forty-eight letters addressed to me from the interior will suffice to show the interest my late publication has excited:

FROM REV. MR. BROWN.

GRASSHOPPER CHATEAU, 1865.

BRO. TWAIN: I feel that the opportunity has arrived at last for me to make a return somewhat in kind for the countless blessings

---

*Excuse the unhappy telegraph—it never spells names right.—M. T.

which have been poured—poured, as it were—upon my unworthy head. If you get the vacancy in Grace Cathedral for me, I
will accept of it at once, and at any price, notwithstanding I
should sacrifice so much here in a worldly point of view, and
entail so much unhappiness upon my loving flock by so doing—
for I feel that I am "called," and it is not for me, an humble
instrument, to disobey. [The splotch you observe here is a tear.] It
stirs the deepest emotions in my breast to think that I shall soon
leave my beloved flock; bear with this seeming childishness, my
friend, for I have reared this dear flock, and tended it for years, and
I fed it with spiritual food, and sheared it—ah, me, and sheared
it—I cannot go on—the subject is too harrowing. But I'll take
that berth for less than any man on the continent, if you'll get it
for me. I send you specimen sermons—some original and some
selected and worked over.   * * *

Your humble and obedient servant,
T. St. Matthew Brown.

They all want the berth at Grace Cathedral. They would all be
perfectly satisfied with $7,000 a year. They are all willing to sac-
rifice their dearest worldly interests and break the tenderest ties
that bind them to their rural homes, to come and fight the good
fight in our stately church. They all feel that they could do more
good and serve their master better in a wider sphere of action.
They all feel stirring within them souls too vast for confinement
in narrow flats and gulches. And they all want to come here and
spread. And worse than all, they all devil *me* with their bosh, and
send *me* their sermons to read, and come and dump their baggage
in *my* hall, and take possession of *my* bed-rooms by assault, and
carry *my* dinner-table by storm, instead of inflicting these miseries upon the vestry of Grace Cathedral, who are the proper
victims, by virtue of their office. Why in thunder do they come
harrassing *me?* What have *I* got to do with the matter? Why, I do
not even belong to the church, and have got no more to do with
hiring pastors for it than the Dey of Algiers has. I wish they would
ease up a little on me; I mixed into this business a little too
brashly—so to speak—and without due reflection; but if I get out
of it once all right, I'll not mix in any more—never any more;
now that's honest—I never will.

I have numerous servants, but they are all worked down. My

housekeeper is on the verge of open rebellion. Yesterday she said: "I lay I'll take and hyste some of them preachers out of this mighty soon, now." And she'll do it. I shall regret it. I could entertain no sentiment but that of regret to see a clergyman "hysted" out of my establishment, but what am I to do? I cannot help it. If I were to interfere I should get "hysted" myself.

My clerical guests are healthy. Their appetites are good. They are not particular as to food. They worry along very well on spring chickens. I don't feel safe with them, though, because if it is considered that a steamboat on the Mississippi is inviting disaster when she ventures to carry more than two ministers at a time, isn't it likely that the dozen I have got in my house will eventually produce an earthquake? The tradition goes that three clergymen on a steamboat will ground her, four will sink her, and five and a gray mare added will blow her up. If I had a gray mare in my stable, I would leave this city before night.

103. How I Went to the Great Race between Lodi and Norfolk

27 May 1865

This sketch appeared in the *Californian* four days after San Francisco's foremost sports event of the spring season: the two-mile race between the Kentucky-bred horses Lodi and Norfolk, which took place on 23 May 1865 at Ocean Race Course, located on a one-hundred-acre plot northeast of Ocean House. Construction of the course had been completed only three days earlier. A superior track, forty-two stables, and a grandstand able to seat about twelve hundred persons, with bar, apartments, and a club room below, awaited the San Franciscans who swarmed over the grounds on the day of the race.[1]

In San José just one year before the race, Lodi had soundly beaten Theodore Winters' horse Margarita and won a reputation as California's fastest racer. Later that year Winters purchased Norfolk, offspring of the famous Kentucky horse Lexington and recent winner of the Jersey Derby at Patterson, for a record price of $15,001. Following Norfolk's arrival in San Francisco, Judge Charles H. Bryan, Lodi's owner, issued his challenge: Lodi would meet Norfolk on any California track, each owner putting up a stake of $5,000 or $10,000. In January 1865 Winters accepted the challenge. On May 23 Norfolk earned Winters the rich purse by a decisive victory: although the first race was a dead heat, Norfolk handily won the second and third. Twice more during 1865 Norfolk beat Lodi, the last time setting the fastest three-mile time on record.[2]

---

[1]"The Turf at San Francisco," San Francisco *Evening Bulletin*, 20 May 1865, p. 5.
[2]"The Two-Mile Race at San José Yesterday," San Francisco *Morning Call*, 6 May 1864, p. 1; "Arrival of Norfolk," San Francisco *Alta California*, 10 August 1864, p. 1; "Lodi and Norfolk," Sacramento *Union*, 23 January 1865, p. 3; "'The Great Running Match," San Francisco *Evening Bulletin*, 24 May 1865, p. 5; Lloyd, *Lights and Shades*, p. 479.

Benjamin W. Homestead of the "Incidental Hotel" was a "fictitious" name for John C. Olmstead, a clerk at the Occidental Hotel: we may be sure that it did not prevent readers from "finding out who it is I refer to, and where his place of business is." The walk Homestead proposed to his victims was a seven-mile trek over the Ocean House Road. According to the San Francisco *Evening Bulletin* of May 24, all transportation to the racetrack by coach, barouche, rockaway, and buggy had been hired days before the race. Even distant Oakland had been stripped of vehicles. Eventually express wagons, grocery wagons, vegetable carts, and saddle horses were pressed into service. Between 10 A.M. and 2 P.M. eight thousand persons flowed over the roads leading to the great race, and although some of them doubtless walked, Clemens almost certainly did not. His failure to report the race, however, may have been due to his friendship for Judge Bryan, Lodi's owner. Although Clemens also knew Winters, it may be that, as Effie Mona Mack reported, Bryan persuaded Clemens to sit up with him all night in Lodi's stall, in order to prevent foul play, and that the next day Clemens was too exhausted to attend the race.[3] Still, this was not his first *Californian* sketch to promise something in the title that he had no intention of delivering in the text.

Clemens included a clipping of this sketch in the Yale Scrapbook, and in January or February 1867 he revised it slightly, intending to include it in the *Jumping Frog* book. Apparently he or Charles Henry Webb decided against it, however, perhaps because local revisions could not overcome its topical nature.

---

[3]Ratay, *Pioneers*, p. 326 n. 25.

How I Went to the Great Race between Lodi and Norfolk

THERE CAN be no use in my writing any account whatever of the great race, because that matter has already been attended to in the daily papers. Therefore, I will simply describe to you *how* I went to the race. But before I begin, I would like to tell you about Homestead—Benj. W. Homestead, of the Incidental Hotel. [I do not wish to be too severe, though, and so I use fictitious names, to prevent your finding out who it is I refer to, and where his place of business is.]

It will ease my mind to tell you about him. You know Homestead, clerk at the Incidental Hotel, and you know he has the reputation of being chatty, and sociable, and accommodating—a man, in fact, eminently fitted to make a guest feel more at home in the hotel than in his own house with his own wife, and his own mother, and his wife's mother, and her various friends and relatives, and all the other little comforts that go to make married life a blessing, and create what is known as "Sweet Home," and which is so deservedly popular—I mean among people who have not tried it. You know Homestead as that kind of a man. Therefore, you would not suppose that attractive exterior of his, and that smiling visage, and that seductive tongue capable of dark and mysterious crimes.

Very well, I will ask you to listen to a plain, unprejudiced statement of facts:

On or about the 21st of the present month, it became apparent to me that the forthcoming race between *Norfolk* and *Lodi* was awakening extraordinary attention all over the Pacific coast, and even far away in the Atlantic States. I saw that if I failed to see this race I might live a century, perhaps, without ever having an opportunity to see its equal. I went at once to a livery stable—the man said his teams had all been engaged a week before I called. I got the same answer at all the other livery stables, except one. They told me there that they had a nice dray, almost-new, and a part of a horse—they said part of a horse because a good deal of him was gone, in the way of a tail, and one ear and a portion of the other, and his upper lip, and one eye; and, inasmuch as his teeth were exposed, and he had a villainous cast in his remaining eye, these defects, added to his damaged ears and departed tail, gave him an extremely "gallus" and unprepossessing aspect—but they only asked two hundred and forty dollars for the turn-out for the day.

I resisted the yearning I felt to hire this unique establishment.

Then they said they had a capacious riding-horse left, but all the seats on him except one had been engaged; they said he was an unusually long horse, and he could seat seven very comfortably; and that he was very gentle, and would not kick up behind; and that one of the choicest places on him for observation was still vacant, and I could have it for nineteen dollars—and so on and so on; and while the passenger agent was talking, he was busy measuring off a space of nine inches for me pretty high up on the commodious animal's neck.

It seemed to me that the prospect of going to the races was beginning to assume a very "neck-or-nothing" condition, but nevertheless I steadfastly refused the supercargo's offer, and he sold the vacancy to a politician who was used to being on the fence and would naturally consider a seat astride a horse's neck in the light of a pleasant variety.

I then walked thoughtfully down to the Incidental, turning over in my mind various impossible expedients for getting out to the Ocean Race-Course. I thought of the horse-cars and the steam-cars, but without relief, for neither of these conveyances could carry me within four miles of the place. At the hotel I met the abandoned Homestead, and as nearly as I can recollect, the following conversation ensued:

"Ah, Mark, you're the very man I was looking for. Take a drink?"

I cannot be positive, but it is my impression that I either stated that I would, or else signified assent by a scarcely perceptible eagerness of manner common to me under circumstances of this nature.

While we were drinking, Homestead remarked, with considerable vivacity:

"Yes, I was just looking for you. I am going out to the great race on Tuesday, and I've a vacancy and want company. I'd like to have you go along with me if you will."

I set my glass down with a suddenness and decision unusual with me on such occasions, and seizing his hand, I wrung it with heartfelt warmth and cordiality. It is humiliating to me to reflect, now, that at that moment I even shed some tears of gratitude, and felt them coursing down the backbone of my nose and dripping from the end of it.

Never mind the remainder of the conversation—suffice it that I was charged to be at the Incidental punctually at ten o'clock on Tuesday morning, and that I promised to do so.

Well, at the appointed time, I *was* there. That is, I was as near as I could get—I was on the outskirts of a crowd that occupied all the pavement outside and filled the office inside. Young Smith, of Buncombe and Brimstone, approached me with an air of superiority, and remarked languidly that he guessed he would go to the races. He dropped his airs, though, very suddenly, and came down to my level when I told him *I* was going to the races also. He said he thought all the conveyances in town had been secured a week ago. I assumed a crushing demeanor of wealthy indifference, and remarked, rather patronizingly, that I had seen greater races—in Europe and other places—and did not care about seeing this one, but then Homestead had insisted so on my going with him that—

"The very devil!" says young Smith, "give us your hand! we're *compangyongs dew vo-yaj!*" (he affects the French, does young Smith,)—"*I'm* going with Homestead, too, my boy!"

We grew cordial in a moment, and went around, arm-in-arm, patronizing the balance of the crowd. But somehow, every man we accosted silenced our batteries as I had silenced young Smith's in the first place—they were all going with Homestead. I tell you candidly, and in all seriousness, that when I came to find out that there were a hundred and fifty men there, all going to the races, and all going with Homestead, I began to think it was—was— singular, at the very least, not to say exceedingly strange.

But I am tired of this infamous subject—I am tired of this disgraceful narrative, and I shall not finish it.

However, as I have gone this far, I *will* quote from a conversation that occurred in front of the hotel at ten o'clock. The degraded Homestead stepped out at the door, and bowed, and smiled his hated smile, and said, blandly:

"Ah, you are all here, I see. I am glad you are so punctual, for there is nothing that worries me so much when I am going on a little trip like this for recreation, as to be delayed. Well, boys, time presses—let's make a start."

"I guess we're all ready, Mr. Homestead," said one gentleman, "but—but how are you going?"

The depraved Homestead smiled, as if he were going to say something very smart, and then, "Oh," says he, "I'M GOING TO WALK!"

I have made a plain, simple statement of the facts connected with this outrage, and they can be substantiated by every man who was present upon that occasion. I will now drop this subject forever.

104 . *A Voice for Setchell*

27 May 1865

"A Voice for Setchell" appeared in the *Californian* immediately adjacent to the previous sketch, "How I Went to the Great Race between Lodi and Norfolk" (no. 103). It was probably Bret Harte who introduced it by saying that "a correspondent of THE CALIFORNIAN, whose style its readers will probably recognize, sends us the following." Although the sketch was signed merely "X," the familiar style and the presence of a clipping of it in the Yale Scrapbook are sufficient to establish that Clemens was its author.[1]

The sketch is an enthusiastic encomium of Dan Setchell, a comedian and monologuist of exceptional ability. Setchell had begun acting in 1853 on the New York stage. He made a name in such plays as H. J. Conway's adaptation of *Uncle Tom's Cabin*, and *The Winter's Tale*, in which he played the clown. Opening the summer season of 1863 at the Winter Garden in John Maddison Morton's farce *A Regular Fix*, he played the lead role of Hugh De Brass and was an immediate hit. Another great success that season was Frank Wood's burlesque *Leah, the Forsook*, in which Setchell played the shrewish maiden Leah. Setchell arrived in San Francisco on 27 April 1865. He drew crowded houses and won almost universal approval there and in the interior during the remainder of the year. He excelled as Van Dunder in John Poole's comedy *The Old Dutch Governor*, as Mr. Beetle in Tom Taylor's *The Babes in the Woods*, and as

---

[1]The Yale Scrapbook contains clippings of Clemens' work exclusively. He probably began to compile it in February or March 1866, shortly after telling his family that he intended to "take the scissors & slash my old sketches out of the Enterprise & the Californian" (Clemens to Jane Clemens and Pamela Moffett, 20 January 1866, *CL1*, letter 97). For further details, see the textual introduction, volume 1, and the textual commentary for this sketch.

Madam Vanderpants in *Wanted, One Thousand Milliners.* On June 19 he would appear as the title character in the first stage production of *Artemus, Showman,* a play written expressly for Setchell by Frederick G. Maeder and Thomas B. MacDonough. Perhaps his most appreciated role was one made famous by William Burton: Captain Ned Cuttle in John Brougham's dramatization of *Dombey and Son,* a play Clemens knew well. Late in January 1866, at the age of thirty-five, Setchell sailed for New Zealand and was lost at sea.[2]

Setchell was a good friend of Artemus Ward's (who also died young, at thirty-three, in 1867) and may have influenced his platform style. Joseph T. Goodman in 1892 repeated the rumor that "Dan Setchell, the prince of comedians . . . had schooled [Artemus Ward] in his art," but said that he preferred "to believe that the style of Artemus was native to himself, as were his airy flights of fancy." In any case, both Setchell and Ward were comedians, masters of the technique Clemens himself had defined as early as June 1864 when he wrote that the "first virtue of a comedian . . . is to do humorous things with grave decorum and without seeming to know that they are funny."[3]

"A Voice for Setchell" arose from the same impulse that prompted Clemens to write "Enthusiastic Eloquence" (no. 111), published in the San Francisco *Dramatic Chronicle* less than a month later. Clemens there defends another "low" art, the banjo music of Tommy Bree and Sam Pride, calling it *"genuine music*—music that will . . . break out on your hide like the pin-feather pimples on a picked goose," just as in the present sketch he defends Setchell's comic acting and, by implication, the genuine importance of humor and humorists. In fact, ever since his "slinking" period in San Francisco the previous winter, Clemens had been struggling with his own vocation as a humorist. Five months after this sketch appeared he was depressed, in debt, and still rebellious toward what he described for Orion as his " 'call' to literature, of a low order—*i.e.* humorous."[4] Clemens' defense of Setchell, and his feelings about their common vocation, give this slight sketch its importance.

Significantly, the piece is a direct answer to Albert S. Evans' denigration of Setchell's comic acting. Writing as "Amigo" in the Gold Hill

---

[2]Laurence Hutton, *Plays and Players* (New York: Hurd and Houghton, 1875), pp. 249–251; Odell, *New York Stage,* 6: 317, 437, 7: 481; Brown, *American Stage,* p. 333; theatrical notices and reviews in San Francisco and interior newspapers from April 1865 through January 1866.

[3]Joseph T. Goodman, "Artemus Ward," San Francisco *Chronicle,* 10 January 1892, p. 1; " 'Mark Twain' in the Metropolis" (no. 77).

[4]Clemens to Orion and Mollie Clemens, 19–20 October 1865, *CL1,* letter 95.

News, Evans had, just two weeks earlier, called Setchell a "low comedian" whose style suited "the class which usually seeks amusement in entertainments not frequented to any great extent by ladies." Evans' attitude softened somewhat a week later, but he still insisted that Setchell was "not to Burton's standard by a long ways," a remark to which Clemens alludes in his penultimate paragraph. These criticisms came uncomfortably close to Clemens' own low opinion of his calling, but such an attack seems always to have called up his greatest powers in defense. When the Reverend Mr. Sabine refused to bury George Holland, the actor, in 1871, Clemens attacked him too for failing to see that "actors were made for a high and good purpose, and that they *accomplish the object of their creation* and accomplish it well."[5] He was now engaged in a struggle to believe that about himself, and his defense of Setchell therefore illuminates the most famous creation of this period, "Jim Smiley and His Jumping Frog" (no. 119), written in October 1865.[6]

---

[5]"Our San Francisco Correspondence," Gold Hill *News,* 13 May 1865, p. 2; ibid., 20 May 1865; "The Indignity Put upon the Remains of George Holland by the Rev. Mr. Sabine," *Galaxy* 11 (February 1871): 320–321, reprinted in *WIM,* pp. 51–55.

[6]See Edgar M. Branch, " 'My Voice Is Still for Setchell': A Background Study of 'Jim Smiley and His Jumping Frog,' " *PMLA* 82 (1967): 591–601.

A Voice for Setchell

M Y VOICE is for Setchell. What with a long season of sensational, snuffling dramatic bosh, and tragedy bosh, and electioneering bosh, and a painful depression in stocks that was anything but bosh, the people were settling down into a fatal melancholy, and growing prematurely old—succumbing to imaginary miseries and learning to wear the habit of unhappiness like a garment— when Captain Cuttle Setchell appeared in the midst of the gloom, and broke the deadly charm with a wave of his enchanted hook and the spell of his talismanic words, *"Awahst! awahst! awahst!"* And since that night all the powers of dreariness combined have not been able to expel the spirit of cheerfulness he invoked. Therefore, my voice is still for Setchell. I have experienced more real pleasure, and more physical benefit, from laughing naturally and unconfinedly at his funny personations and extempore speeches than I have from all the operas and tragedies I have endured, and all the blue mass pills I have swallowed in six months. As a comedian, this man is the best the coast has seen, and is above criticism; and therefore one feels at liberty to laugh at any effort of his which seems funny, without stopping to undergo that demoralizing process of first considering whether some other great comedian, somewhere else, hasn't done the same thing a shade funnier, some time or other, years ago.

Mr. Setchell has established his reputation here, and a powerful verdict has been rendered in his favor. All who have seen good acting, and know what they are doing, endorse this verdict. True, I have heard one man say he was not as good as Burton in "Captain Cuttle," and another that he had seen better actors in *A Regular Fix*, but then I attached no great importance to the opinions of these critics, because the first named (judging by the date of Burton's death) could not have been above thirteen years of age when that renowned actor appeared for the last time upon any earthly stage, and the other was reared and educated in Little Rock, Arkansas, and therefore has not had as good an opportunity of forming a correct dramatic taste as if he had resided in London all his life. At least, such is my opinion, though I do not insist upon it.

One reason why I do not weaken before these two critics, is because every time Mr. Setchell plays, crowds flock to hear him, and no matter what he plays those crowds invariably laugh and applaud extravagantly. That kind of criticism can always be relied upon as sound, and not only sound but honest.

§ 105 *Answers to Correspondents*

3 June 1865

Without preliminary fanfare the *Californian* of 3 June 1865 announced that all letters to its new department, "Answers to Correspondents," should be "addressed to Mr. MARK TWAIN, who has been detailed from the editorial staff to conduct it. Courting Etiquette, Distressed Lovers, of either sex, and Struggling Young Authors, as yet 'unbeknown' to Fame, will receive especial attention."[1] The first of six weekly columns that Clemens contributed to the *Californian* followed immediately.

It is not known whether Webb, Harte, or Clemens himself initiated the idea of a *Californian* column for correspondents, but the editorial staff was certainly well aware of the popularity of such columns, which were a standard feature of literary papers throughout the country. Webb had quoted with approval two "Answers to Correspondents" written by Josh Billings for the New York *Mercury*,[2] and Clemens had recently shown a disposition to burlesque the form in "Whereas" (no. 94), which concludes with Mark Twain's ostensible answer to a letter from the troubled Aurelia. Nevertheless, it seems likely that the founders of the *Californian* regarded such columns, at least at first, as a concession to popular taste. On May 27 the editor (probably Harte at this time) said that the *Californian* had survived its first year of publication "without having to abandon any of its claims to literary superiority, or without forfeiting its self-respect." But the journal had in fact made some minor concessions: when Webb had retaken the editor's chair the previous November, he added several "new features," including "a complete record of home news" and a "digest of the telegraphic news of each week."[3] The addition

---

[1]*Californian* 3 (3 June 1865): 4. This rubric, or a shortened form of it, preceded all of the six columns in the *Californian*.

[2]"Answers to Correspondents," *Californian* 2 (25 February 1865): 3.

[3]Untitled editorial, *Californian* 3 (27 May 1865): 8; "The Californian," *Californian* 1 (26 November 1864): 8.

of a correspondents' column was a similar move away from the purely literary plan with which Webb had begun.

In the standard correspondents' column readers were permitted to make inquiries, air their opinions, and even publish their own verse, while the editor provided answers, comments, and criticisms of his readers' contributions. Editorial response ranged from the prosaically solemn to the vivacious and witty, since few editors could wholly resist the opportunity to show their superior wit or literary expertise at the expense of the contributors. Some columns seem to have been straightforwardly serious, such as "To Correspondents" in the *California Sunday Mercury:* "PROPRIETY.—We must decline the publication of your communication, still we agree with you that it is rude and in bad taste for people to laugh or talk loudly and boisterously at the theatre or in other public places."[4] But the comparable column in the San Francisco *Golden Era* included a wide range of contributions (from readers signing themselves as "A Poor Drayman," "Ecce Homo," "Osage," "Bold Soldier Boy," "Holy Moses," etc.) and a mixture of serious and flippant comments from the editor. Thus "Postal" inquired seriously about how to apply for a contract to carry the mail, and "An Inquirer" wondered why the Emancipation Proclamation had not been read during the Fourth of July celebration—and both were treated straightforwardly. On the other hand, "Jessie," seeking a cure for a broken heart, was told: "Well, let it break. We are not in the medical or surgical line. Does your heart owe anybody? If the debts exceed the assets it would be as well to put your heart through insolvency." "Classique" asked about the word "bilque" and was told, "It is not an elegant addition to a refined lingual entertainment"; "Smarty" from Mud Springs was told that "drawers of water" made "rather inefficient raiment." And every week "struggling" authors were mildly encouraged or verbally decapitated. Occasionally answers verged on the realm of literary burlesque, as when the editor published rules of etiquette: gentlemen were advised, for instance, that "it is quite an elegant accomplishment to sharpen your pen-knife in company on your boot, having first moistened the leather by expectorating on it." Brief, cryptic replies of a line or two were typically added to the end of such columns. In fact, some editors, like the one who wrote "Answers to Correspondents" for the San Francisco *News Letter and Pacific Mining Journal,* tended to favor this form of one-liner exclusively: "Anxious

---

[4] *California Sunday Mercury: A Journal of American Literature* 7 (11 June 1865): 4.

Inquirer" was told, for example, "Corns may be removed with a cold chisel. Afterwards bathe the part with turpentine."[5]

The comic version of "Answers to Correspondents" was, therefore, no innovation, and probably did not meet Harte's and Webb's standards for the *Californian*. But in turning their column over to Mark Twain, the editors rightly assumed that he would take a more adventuresome tack. Mark Twain's six columns are actually burlesques of the form itself. He ridiculed silly or unnecessary questions as well as specious, overly intricate, or archly self-satisfied answers. He satirized various nuisances, show-offs, hypocrites, and superpatriots, as well as sentimentalists of all kinds. He conjured up a range of imaginary characters and attitudes, and supplied appropriately varied responses. While the comic columnists in the *Era* and the *Mercury* manifestly relied on real persons for their letters, it is clear that Clemens set out to work with his own creations—or at most, creations based remotely on the facts. Presumably he continued to do so, even after being deluged with real letters following publication of his first column: "I always had an idea that most of the letters written to editors were written by the editors themselves," he said in his second contribution (no. 106), "but I find, now, that I was mistaken." It was the distinctively burlesque form of Clemens' work that made it sufficiently literary for the *Californian*. Significantly, when he discontinued the column in July, it was carried on for only a few weeks by "Trem" in the "Mouse-Trap."[6] Without Mark Twain's imaginative skill, such a column necessarily reverted to the merely comic and descended below the *Californian's* announced standard of "literary superiority."

---

[5]*Golden Era* 13 (8 January 1865): 4; 13 (9 July 1865): 4; 13 (18 December 1864): 4; 13 (5 March 1865): 4; 13 (18 December 1864): 4; 13 (15 January 1865): 4; "Answers to Correspondents," *News Letter and Pacific Mining Journal* 14 (29 October 1864): 13.

[6]"The Mouse-Trap," *Californian* 3 (19 August 1865): 1; 3 (26 August 1865): 1. In his last column, "Trem" gave the following item: "FLORA.—Mark Twain, though it may appear paradoxical, is single. Yes; very good-looking."

Answers to Correspondents

DISCARDED LOVER.—"I loved and still love, the beautiful Edwitha Howard, and intended to marry her. Yet during my temporary absence at Benicia, last week, alas! she married Jones. Is my happiness to be thus blasted for life? Have I no redress?"

Of course you have. All the law, written and unwritten, is on your side. The *intention* and not the *act* constitutes crime—in other words, constitutes the *deed*. If you call your bosom friend a fool, and *intend* it for an insult, it *is* an insult; but if you do it playfully, and meaning no insult, it is *not* an insult. If you discharge a pistol *accidentally*, and kill a man, you can go free, for you have done no murder—but if you try to kill a man, and manifestly *intend* to kill him, but fail utterly to do it, the law still holds that the *intention* constituted the crime, and you are guilty of murder. Ergo, if you had married Edwitha *accidentally*, and without really *intending* to do it, you would not actually be married to her at all, because the *act* of marriage could not be complete without the *intention*. And, ergo, in the strict spirit of the law, since you deliberately *intended* to marry Edwitha, and didn't do it, you *are* married to her all the same—because, as I said before, the *intention* constitutes the crime. It is as clear as day that Edwitha is your wife, and your redress lies in taking a club and mutilating Jones with it as much as you can. Any man has a right to protect his own wife from the advances of other men. But you have another alternative—you were married to Edwitha *first*, because of your deliberate intention, and now you can prosecute her for bigamy, in subsequently marrying Jones. But there is another phase in this complicated case: You *intended* to marry Edwitha, and consequently, according to law, she is your wife— there is no getting around that—but she didn't marry you, and if she *never intended* to marry you *you are not her husband,* of course. Ergo, in marrying Jones, she was guilty of bigamy, because she was the wife of another man at the time—which is all very well as far as it goes—but then, don't you see, she had no other *husband* when she married Jones, and consequently she was *not* guilty of bigamy. Now according to this view of the case, Jones married a *spinster,* who was a *widow* at the same time and another man's *wife* at the same time, and yet who had no *husband* and *never had one,* and never had any *intention* of getting married, and therefore, of course, *never had* been married; and by the same reasoning you are a *bachelor,* because you have never been any one's *husband,* and a *married man* because you have a wife living, and to all intents and purposes a *widower,* because you have been deprived of that wife, and a consummate *ass* for going off to Benicia in the first place, while things were so mixed. And by this time I have got myself so tangled up in the intricacies of this extraordinary case that I shall have to give up any further attempt to advise you—I might get confused and fail to make myself understood. I think I could take up the argument where I left off, and by following it closely awhile, perhaps I could prove to your satisfaction, either that you never existed at all, or that you are dead, now, and consequently don't need the faithless Edwitha—I think I could do that, if it would afford you any comfort.

MR. MARK TWAIN—Sir: I wish to call your attention to a matter which has come to my notice frequently, but before doing so, I may remark, *en passant,* that I don't see why your parents should have called you Mark Twain; had they known your *ardent* nature, they would doubtless have named you Water-less Twain. However, *Mark* what I am about to call your attention to, and I do so knowing you to be "capable and honest" in your inquiries after truth, and that you can fathom the mysteries of Love. Now I want to know why, (and this is the object of my enquiry,) a man should proclaim his love in large gilt letters over his door and in his windows. Why does he do so? You may have noticed in the Russ House Block, one door south of the hotel entrance an inscription thus: "I Love Land." Now if this refers to real estate he should not say "love;" he should say "like." Very true, in speaking of one's native soil, we say, "Yes, my native land I love thee," but I am satisfied that even if you could suppose this inscription had any remote reference to a birthplace, it does not mean a ranch or eligibly-situated town site. Why does he do it? why does he?

Yours, without prejudice,
NOMME DE PLUME.

Now, did it never strike this sprightly Frenchman that he could have gone in there and asked the man himself "why he does it," as easily as he could write to me on the subject? But no matter—this is just about the weight of the important questions usually asked of editors and answered in the "Correspondents' Column;" sometimes a man asks how to spell a difficult word—when he might as well have looked in the dictionary; or he asks who discovered America—when he might have consulted history; or he asks who in the mischief Cain's wife was—when a moment's reflection would have satisfied him that nobody knows and nobody cares —at least, except himself. The Frenchman's little joke is good, though, for doubtless "Quarter-less twain," *would* sound like "Water-less twain," if uttered between two powerful brandy punches. But as to why the man in question loves land—I cannot imagine, unless his constitution resembles mine, and he don't love water.

ARABELLA.—No, neither Mr. Dan Setchell nor Mr. Gottschalk are married. Perhaps it will interest you to know that they are both uncommonly anxious to marry, however. And perhaps it will interest you still more to know that in case they do marry, they will doubtless wed females; I hazard this, because, in discussing the question of marrying, they have uniformly expressed a preference for your sex. I answer your inquiries concerning Miss Adelaide Phillips in the order in which they occur, by number, as follows: I. No.   II. Yes.   III. Perhaps.   IV. "Scasely."

PERSECUTED UNFORTUNATE.—You say you owe six months' board, and you have no money to pay it with, and your landlord keeps harassing you about it, and you have made all the excuses and explanations possible, and now you are at a loss what to say to him in future. Well, it is a delicate matter to offer advice in a case like this, but your distress impels me to make a suggestion, at least, since I cannot venture to do more. When he next importunes you, how would it do to take him impressively by the hand and ask, with simulated emotion, *"Monsieur Jean, votre chien, comme se porte-il?"* Doubtless that is very bad French, but you'll find that it will answer just as well as the unadulterated article.

ARTHUR AUGUSTUS.—No, you are wrong; that is the proper way to throw a brickbat or a tomahawk, but it doesn't answer so well for a boquet—you will hurt somebody if you keep it up. Turn your nosegay upside down, take it by the stems, and toss it with an upward sweep—did you ever pitch quoits?—that is the idea. The practice of recklessly heaving immense solid boquets, of the general size and weight of prize cabbages, from the dizzy altitude of the galleries, is dangerous and very reprehensible. Now, night before last, at the Academy of Music, just after Signorina Sconcia had finished that exquisite melody, "The Last Rose of Summer," one of these floral pile-drivers came cleaving down through the atmosphere of applause, and if she hadn't deployed suddenly to the right, it would have driven her into the floor like a shingle-nail. Of course that boquet was well-meant, but how would you have liked to have been the target? A sincere compliment is always grateful to a lady, so long as you don't try to knock her down with it.

§ 106. Answers to Correspondents

10 June 1865

The second of Clemens' columns for the *Californian* contained an item—the communication from "MELTON MOWBRAY, *Dutch Flat*"— which would haunt him in much the same way that a more outrageous hoax, "A Bloody Massacre near Carson" (no. 66), had done in 1863. Imitating a typical occurrence in correspondents' columns, he had Melton Mowbray submit "a lot of doggerel" ostensibly written in Dutch Flat. The verse came, of course, from Byron's "Destruction of Sennacherib," a poem Clemens and many of his readers had memorized as schoolchildren. He went on to ridicule the unconscious snobbery of the typical editor by pronouncing it "very good Dutch Flat poetry," but not up to the standards of the "metropolis. It is too smooth and blubbery; it reads like buttermilk gurgling from a jug." To Clemens' amazement, and delight, the same paper that had been so badly fooled by his "Bloody Massacre" hoax, the Gold Hill *News,* was again taken in. And as he observed in his next column (no. 107), the San Francisco *American Flag* also "got sold by the same rather glaring burlesque." The ensuing newspaper controversy supplied him with material for at least three further columns: nos. 107, 108, and 109.

Clemens selected and revised portions of his second column to help make up a composite "Answers to Correspondents" sketch for the 1867 *Jumping Frog* book. For the "Melton Mowbray" section he supplied an explanatory footnote in the Yale Scrapbook: "This absurd squib was received in perfect good faith by several editors on the Pacific Coast, & they rated the author unsparingly for not knowing that the 'Destruction of the Sennacherib['] was not originally composed in Dutch Flat!" The composite sketch, with the new title Clemens gave it in January or February 1867, is reprinted in the present collection as "Burlesque 'Answers to Correspondents' " (no. 201).

Answers to Correspondents

AMATEUR SERENADER.—Yes, I will give you some advice, and do it with a good deal of pleasure. I live in a neighborhood which is well stocked with young ladies, and consequently I am excruciatingly sensitive upon the subject of serenading. Sometimes I suffer. In the first place, always tune your instruments before you get within three hundred yards of your destination—this will enable you to take your adored unawares, and create a pleasant surprise by launching out at once upon your music; it astonishes the dogs and cats out of their presence of mind, too, so that if you hurry you can get through before they have a chance to recover and interrupt you; besides, there is nothing captivating in the sounds produced in tuning a lot of melancholy guitars and fiddles, and neither does a group of able-bodied, sentimental young men so engaged look at all dignified. Secondly, clear your throats and do all the coughing you have got to do before you arrive at the seat of war—I have known a young lady to be ruthlessly startled out of her slumbers by such a sudden and direful blowing of noses and "h'm-h'm-ing" and coughing, that she imagined the house was beleaguered by victims of consumption from the neighboring hospital; do you suppose the music was able to make her happy after that? Thirdly, don't stand right under the porch and howl, but get out in the middle of the street, or better still, on the other side of it—distance lends enchantment to the sound; if you have previously transmitted a hint to the lady that she is going to be serenaded, she will understand who the music is for; besides, if you occupy a neutral position in the middle of the street, may be all the neighbors round will take stock in your serenade and invite you in to take wine with them. Fourthly, don't sing a whole opera through—enough of a thing's enough. Fifthly, don't sing "Lilly Dale"—the profound satisfaction that most of us derive from the reflection that the girl treated of in that song is dead, is constantly marred by the resurrection of the lugubrious ditty itself by your kind of people. Sixthly, don't let your screaming tenor soar an octave above all the balance of the chorus, and remain there setting everybody's teeth on edge for four blocks around; and, above all, don't let him sing a solo; probably there is nothing in the world so suggestive of serene contentment and perfect bliss as the spectacle of a calf chewing a dish-rag, but the nearest approach to it is your reedy tenor, standing apart, in sickly attitude, with head thrown back and eyes uplifted to the moon, piping his distressing solo: now do not pass lightly over this matter, friend, but ponder it with that seriousness which its importance entitles it to. Seventhly, after you have run all the chickens and dogs and cats in the vicinity distracted, and roused them into a frenzy of crowing, and cackling, and yowling, and caterwauling, put up your dreadful instruments and go home. Eighthly, as soon as you start, gag your tenor—otherwise he will be letting off a screech every now and then to let the people know he is around; your amateur tenor singer is notoriously the most self-conceited of all God's creatures. Tenthly, don't go serenading at all—it is a wicked, unhappy and seditious practice, and a calamity to all souls that are weary and desire to slumber and be at rest. Eleventhly and lastly, the father of the young lady in the next block says that if you come prowling around his neighborhood again with your infamous scraping and tooting and yelling, he will sally forth and deliver you into the hands of the police. As far as I am concerned myself, I would like to have you come, and come often, but as long as the old man is so prejudiced, perhaps you had better serenade mostly in Oakland, or San José, or around there somewhere.

ST. CLAIR HIGGINS, *Los Angeles.* —"My life is a failure; I have adored, wildly, madly, and she whom I love has turned coldly from me and shed her affections upon another; what would you advise me to do?" You should shed your affections on another, also—or on several, if there are enough to go round. Also, do everything you can to make your former flame unhappy. There is an absurd idea disseminated in novels, that the happier a girl is with another man, the happier it makes the old lover she has blighted. Don't you allow yourself to believe any such nonsense as that. The more cause that girl finds to regret that she did not marry you, the more comfortable you will feel over it. It isn't poetical, but it is mighty sound doctrine.

ARITHMETICUS, *Virginia, Nevada.*—"If it would take a cannon-ball $3\frac{1}{3}$ seconds to travel four miles, and $3\frac{3}{8}$ seconds to travel the next four, and $3\frac{5}{8}$ seconds to travel the next four, and if its rate of progress continued to diminish in the same ratio, how long would it take it to go fifteen hundred millions of miles?" I don't know.

AMBITIOUS LEARNER, *Oakland.*—Yes, you are right—America was not discovered by Alexander Selkirk.

JULIA MARIA.—Fashions? It is out of my line, Maria. How am I to know anything about such mysteries—I that languish alone? Sometimes I am startled into a passing interest in such things, but not often. Now, a few nights ago, I was reading the *Dramatic Chronicle* at the opera, between the acts—reading a poem in it, and reading it after my usual style of ciphering out the merits of poetry, which is to read a line or two near the top, a verse near the bottom and then strike an average, (even professional critics do that)—when—well, it had a curious effect, read as I happened to read it:

" 'What shall I wear?' asked Addie St. Clair,
    As she stood by her mirror so young and fair"—

and then I skipped a line or so, while I returned the bow of a strange young lady, who, I observed too late, had intended that courtesy for a ruffian behind me, instead of for myself, and read:

"The *modiste* replied, 'It were wicked to hide
    Such peerless perfection that should be your pride' "—

and then I skipped to the climax, to get my average, and read—

" 'My beautiful bride!' a low voice replied,
  As handsome Will Vernon appeared at her side,
  'If you wish from all others my heart to beguile,
  Wear a smile to-night, darling—your own sunny smile.' "

Now there's an airy costume for you! a "sunny smile!" There's
a costume, which, for simplicity and picturesqueness, grand-dis-
counts a Georgia major's uniform, which is a shirt-collar and a
pair of spurs. But when I came to read the remainder of the poem,
it appeared that my new Lady Godiva had other clothes beside her
sunny smile, and so—it is not necessary to pursue a subject further which no longer possesses any startling interest. Ask me no
questions about fashions, Julia, but use your individual judgment
in the matter—"wear your own sunny smile," and such millinery
traps and trimmings as may be handy and will be likely to set it
off to best advantage.

NOM DE PLUME.—Behold! the Frenchman cometh again, as
follows:

"Your courteous attention to my last enquiry induces this
acknowledgment of your kindness. I availed myself of your
suggestions and made the enquiry of the gentleman, and he told
me very frankly that it was—none of my business. So you see we
do sometimes have to apply to your correspondence column for
correct information, after all. I read in the papers a few days since
some remarks upon the grammatical construction of the sentences—'Sic semper traditoris' and 'Sic semper traditoribus,'
and I procured a Latin grammar in order to satisfy myself as to the
genative, dative and ablative cases of traitors—and while wend-
ing my weary way homewards at a late hour of the night, thinking
over the matter, and not knowing what moment some cut-throat
would knock me over, and, as he escaped, flourishing my watch
and portmonaie, exclaim, 'Sic semper tyranis,' I stumbled over an
individual lying on the sidewalk, with a postage stamp pasted on
his hat in lieu of a car ticket, and evidently in the *objective case*
to the phrase 'how come you so?' As I felt in his pockets to see if
his friends had taken care of his money, lest he might be robbed,
he exclaimed, tragically, '*Si*(hic) *semper tarantula-juice!*' Not
finding the phrase in my grammar, which I examined at once, I
thought of your advice and *asked* him what he meant, said he 'I
mean jis what I say, and I intend to sti-hic to it.' He was *quarter-*
less, Twain; when I *sounded* him he hadn't a cent, although he
smelled strong of a 5-scent shop."

Melton Mowbray, *Dutch Flat.*—This correspondent sends a lot of doggerel, and says it has been regarded as very good in Dutch Flat. I give a specimen verse:

"The Assyrian came down, like a wolf on the fold,
And his cohorts were gleaming in purple and gold;
And the sheen of his spears shone like stars on the sea,
When the blue wave rolls nightly on deep Galilee."

There, that will do. That may be very good Dutch Flat poetry, but it won't do in the metropolis. It is too smooth and blubbery; it reads like buttermilk gurgling from a jug. What the people ought to have, is something spirited—something like "Johnny comes marching home." However, keep on practicing, and you may succeed yet. There is genius in you, but too much blubber.

Laura Matilda.—No, Mr. Dan Setchell has never been in the House of Correction. That is to say he never went there by compulsion; he remembers going there once to visit a very dear friend —one of his boyhood's friends—but the visit was merely temporary, and he only staid five or six weeks.

Professional Beggar.—No, you are not obliged to take green-backs at par.

Note.—Several letters, chiefly from young ladies and young bachelors, remain over, to be answered next week, want of space precluding the possibility of attending to them at present. I always had an idea that most of the letters written to editors were written by the editors themselves. But I find, now, that I was mistaken.

§ 107 *Answers to Correspondents*
17 June 1865

The third column that Clemens contributed to the *Californian* was his most spirited and appealing. He combined a choice selection of his own personal grievances, literary and otherwise, with some astute self-advertising. He praised his earlier sketch "Whereas" (no. 94) and continued the joke about Dutch Flat poetry, quoting the Gold Hill *News* at length (see no. 106). But perhaps the most significant passage contains the work of a character who would soon reappear in a larger role, Simon Wheeler. Wheeler sends a poem from Sonora, a "rich gold-mining region" east of San Francisco. It is about a gambling parson, "among the whitest men I ever see," who has gone broke by playing poker and has returned home to Arkansas: "He Done His Level Best."

Clemens was quite proud of this poem, which of course exploits the other side of the Dutch Flat poetry joke. When Bret Harte's 1865 anthology of California verse, *Outcroppings*, was accused of omitting all but poetry written in the cities, Harte said in the *Californian* that "Phœnix's 'He Was Accidentally Shot,' and Mark Twain's 'He Done His Level Best,' are fair instances of the poetical tendencies of 'inland domesticity ignorant of the cosmopolitan sea,'" a phrase rashly used by the irate Sacramento *Union* reviewer of *Outcroppings*. Harte further admitted, not without humor, that both of these poems "certainly have been wrongfully overlooked in the volume." Clemens wrote to Charles Warren Stoddard in April 1867: "I wrote a sublime poem — 'He Done His Level Best' — & what credit did I ever get for it? — None. Bret left it out of the Outcroppings. I never will write another poem. I am not appreciated."[1]

---

[1]"A Shelf of Criticism," *Californian* 4 (23 December 1865): 8; Clemens to Charles Warren Stoddard, 23 April 1867, *CL1*, letter 127.

This proved a hollow threat, of course, as readers of chapter 17 of *Huckleberry Finn* will recall. There Clemens exploits the same burlesque device of an endlessly repeated but distinctly unmusical rhyme in his incomparable "Ode to Stephen Dowling Bots, Dec'd."

Clemens used only the first half of this column in the composite "Answers to Correspondents" sketch for the 1867 *Jumping Frog* book, probably because the second half was not preserved in the Yale Scrapbook, which nevertheless does preserve his revisions of the early portion.

Answers to Correspondents

MORAL STATISTICIAN.—I don't want any of your statistics. I took your whole batch and lit my pipe with it. I hate your kind of people. You are always ciphering out how much a man's health is injured, and how much his intellect is impaired, and how many pitiful dollars and cents he wastes in the course of ninety-two years' indulgence in the fatal practice of smoking; and in the equally fatal practice of drinking coffee; and in playing billiards occasionally; and in taking a glass of wine at dinner, etc., etc., etc. And you are always figuring out how many women have been burned to death because of the dangerous fashion of wearing expansive hoops, etc., etc., etc. You never see but one side of the question. You are blind to the fact that most old men in America smoke and drink coffee, although, according to your theory, they ought to have died young; and that hearty old Englishmen drink wine and survive it, and portly old Dutchmen both drink and smoke freely, and yet grow older and fatter all the time. And you never try to find out how much solid comfort, relaxation and enjoyment a man derives from smoking in the course of a lifetime, (and which is worth ten times the money he would save by letting it alone,) nor the appalling aggregate of happiness lost in a lifetime by your kind of people from *not* smoking. Of course you can save money by denying yourself all these little vicious enjoyments for fifty years, but then what can you do with it?—what use can you put it to? Money can't save your infinitesimal soul; all the use that money can be put to is to purchase comfort and enjoyment in this life—therefore, as you are an enemy to comfort and enjoyment, where is the use in accumulating cash? It won't do for you to say that you can use it to better purpose in furnishing a good table, and in charities, and in supporting tract societies, because you know yourself that you people who have no petty vices are never known to give away a cent, and that you stint yourselves so in the matter of food that you are always feeble and hungry. And you never dare to laugh in the daytime for fear some poor wretch, seeing you in a good humor, will try to borrow a dollar of you; and in church you are always down on your knees when the contribution box comes around; and you always pay your debts in greenbacks, and never give the revenue officers a true statement of your income. Now you know all these things yourself, don't you? Very well, then, what is the use of your stringing out your miserable lives to a lean and withered old age? What is the use of your saving money that is so utterly worthless to you? In a word, why don't you go off somewhere and die, and not be always trying to seduce people into becoming as "ornery" and unloveable as you are yourselves, by your ceaseless and villainous "moral statistics?" Now I don't approve of dissipation, and I don't indulge in it, either, but I haven't a particle of confidence in a man who has no redeeming petty vices whatever, and so I don't want to hear from you any more. I think you are the very same man who read me a long lecture, last week, about the degrading vice of smoking cigars, and then came back, in my absence, with your vile, reprehensible fire-proof gloves on, and carried off my beautiful parlor stove.

SIMON WHEELER, *Sonora.* —The following simple and touching remarks and accompanying poem have just come to hand from the rich gold-mining region of Sonora:

To Mr. Mark Twain: The within parson, which I have sot to poettry under the name and style of "He Done His Level Best," was one among the whitest men I ever see, and it ain't every man that knowed him that can find it in his heart to say he's glad the pore cuss is busted and gone home to the States. He was here in an early day, and he was the handyest man about takin holt of anything that come along you most ever see, I judge; he was a cheerful, stirrin cretur, always doin something, and no man can say he ever see him do anything by halvers. Preachin was his nateral gait, but he warn't a man to lay back and twidle his thums because there didn't happen to be nothing doin in his own espeshial line—no sir, he was a man who would meander forth and stir up something for hisself. His last acts was to go his pile on "kings-*and*," (calklatin to fiil, but which he didn't fill,) when there was a "flush" out agin him, and naterally, you see, he went under. And so, he was cleaned out, as you may say, and he struck the home-trail, cheerful but flat broke. I knowed this talonted man in Arkansaw, and if you would print this humbly tribute to his gorgis abillities, you would greatly obleege his onhappy friend.

SONORA, Southern Mines, June, 1865.

HE DONE HIS LEVEL BEST.

Was he a mining on the flat—
  He done it with a zest;
Was he a leading of the choir—
  He done his level best.

If he'd a reglar task to do,
  He never took no rest;
Or if twas off-and-on—the same—
  He done his level best.

If he was preachin on his beat,
  He'd tramp from east to west,
And north to south—in cold and heat
  He done his level best.

He'd yank a sinner outen (Hades*)
  And land him with the blest—
Then snatch a prayer 'n waltz in again,
  And do his level best.

He'd cuss and sing and howl and pray,
  And dance and drink and jest,
And lie and steal—all one to him—
  He done his level best.

Whate'er this man was sot to do,
  He done it with a zest:
No matter *what* his contract was,
  HE'D DO HIS LEVEL BEST.

---

*You observe that I have taken the liberty to alter a word for you, Simon—to tone you down a little, as it were. Your language was unnecessarily powerful.   M. T.

Verily, this man *was* gifted with "gorgis abillities," and it is a happiness to me to embalm the memory of their lustre in these columns. If it were not that the poet crop is unusually large and rank in California this year, I would encourage you to continue writing, Simon—but as it is, perhaps it might be too risky in you to enter against so much opposition.

INQUIRER wishes to know which is the best brand of smoking tobacco, and how it is manufactured. The most popular—mind I do not feel at liberty to give an opinion as to the best, and so I simply say the most popular—smoking tobacco is the miraculous conglomerate they call "Killickinick." It is composed of equal parts of tobacco stems, chopped straw, "old soldiers," fine shavings, oak leaves, dog-fennel, corn-shucks, sun-flower petals, outside leaves of the cabbage plant, and any refuse of any description whatever that costs nothing and will burn. After the ingredients are thoroughly mixed together, they are run through a chopping-machine. The mass is then sprinkled with fragrant Scotch snuff, packed into various seductive shapes, labelled "Genuine Killickinick, from the old original manufactory at Richmond," and sold to consumers at a dollar a pound. The choicest brands contain a double portion of "old soldiers," and sell at a dollar and a half. "Genuine Turkish" tobacco contains a treble quantity of old soldiers, and is worth two or three dollars, according to the amount of service the said "old soldiers" have previously seen. N. B. This article is preferred by the Sultan of Turkey; his picture and autograph are on the label. Take a handful of "Killickinick," crush it as fine as you can, and examine it closely, and you will find that you can make as good an analysis of it as I have done; you must not expect to discover any particles of genuine tobacco by this rough method, however—to do that, it will be necessary to take your specimen to the mint and subject it to a fire-assay. A good article of cheap tobacco is now made of chopped pine-straw and Spanish moss; it contains one "old soldier" to the ton, and is called "Fine Old German Tobacco."

ANNA MARIA says as follows: "We have got such a nice literary society, O! you can't think! It is made up of members of our church, and we meet and read poetry and sketches and essays, and such things—mostly original—in fact, we have got talent enough among ourselves, without having to borrow reading matter from books and newspapers. We met a few evenings since at a dwelling on Howard, between Seventh and Eighth, and ever so many things were read. It was a little dull, though, until a young gentleman, (who is a member of our church, and oh, so gifted!) unrolled a bundle of manuscript and read *such* a funny thing about "Love's Bakery," where they prepare young people for matrimony, and about a young man who was engaged to be married, and who had the small-pox, and the erysipelas, and lost one eye and got both legs broken, and one arm, and got the other arm pulled out by a carding-machine, and finally got so damaged that there was scarcely anything of him left for the young lady to marry. You ought to have been there to hear how well he read it, and how they all laughed. We went right to work and nominated him for the Presidency of the Society, and he only lost it by two votes."

Yes, dear, I remember that "*such* a funny thing" which he read—I wrote it myself, for THE CALIFORNIAN, last October. But as he read it well, I forgive him—I can't bear to hear a good thing read badly. You had better keep an eye on that gifted young man, though, or he will be treating you to Washington's Farewell Address in manuscript the first thing you know—and if *that* should pass unchallenged, nothing in the world could save him from the Presidency.

CHARMING SIMPLICITY.

I once read the following paragraph in a newspaper:

"*Powerful Metaphor.*—A Western editor, speaking of a quill-driving cotemporary, says 'his intellect is so dense that it would take the auger of common sense longer to bore into it than it would to bore through Mont Blanc with a boiled carrot!'"

I have found that man. And I have found him—not in Stockton—not in Congress—not even in the Board of Education—but in the editorial sanctum of the Gold Hill *News.* Hear him:

"BYRON BUSTED.—The most fearful exhibition of literary ignorance—to say nothing of literary judgment—that we have had occasion to notice in many a year, is presented by the San Francisco CALIFORNIAN, a professedly literary journal. It is among the 'Answers to Correspondents.' Lord Byron's magnificent and universally admired verses on the Destruction of Sennacherib, are sent from Dutch Flat to the Californian, and are there not recognized, but denounced as a 'lot of doggerel.' Ye Gods! Perhaps the editor will try to get out of his 'fix' by saying it was all in fun— that it is a Dutch Nix joke! Read the comments:

" 'Melton Mowbray, *Dutch Flat.*—This correspondent sends us a lot of doggerel, and says it has been regarded as very good in Dutch Flat. I give a specimen verse:

'The Assyrian came down, like a wolf on the fold,
And his cohorts were gleaming in purple and gold;
And the sheen of his spears shone like stars on the sea,
When the blue wave rolls nightly on deep Galilee.'

" 'There, that will do. That may be very good Dutch Flat poetry, but it won't do in the metropolis. It is too smooth and blubbery; it reads like buttermilk gurgling from a jug. What the people should have, is something spirited—something like 'Johnny comes marching home.' However, keep on practicing, and you may succeed yet. There is genius in you, but too much blubber.' "

Come, now, friend, about what style of joke *would* suit your capacity?—because we are anxious to come within the comprehension of all. Try a good old one; for instance: "Jones meets Smith; says Smith, 'I'm glad it's raining, Jones, because it'll start everything out of the ground.' 'Oh, Lord, I hope not,' says Jones, 'because then it would start my first wife out!' " How's that? Does that "bore through?"

Since writing the above, I perceive that the *Flag* has fallen into the wake of the *News,* and got sold by the same rather glaring burlesque that disposed of its illustrious predecessor at such an exceedingly cheap rate.

Literary Connoisseur asks "Who is the author of these fine lines?

'Let dogs delight to bark and bite,
For God hath made them so!' "

Here is a man gone into ecstasies of admiration over a nursery rhyme! Truly, the wonders of this new position of mine do never cease. The longer I hold it the more I am astonished, and every new applicant for information, who comes to me, leaves me more helplessly stunned than the one who went before him. No, I *don't* know who wrote those "fine lines," but I expect old Wat's-'is-name, who wrote old Watt's hymns, is the heavy gun you are after. However, it may be a bad guess, and if you find it isn't him, why then lay it on Tupper. That is my usual method. It is awkward to betray ignorance. Therefore, when I come across anything in the poetry line, which is particularly mild and aggravating, I always consider it pretty safe to lay it on Tupper. The policy is subject to accidents, of course, but then it works pretty well, and I hit oftener than I miss. A "connoisseur" should never be in doubt about anything. It is ruinous. I will give you a few hints. Attribute all the royal blank verse, with a martial ring to it, to Shakspeare; all the grand ponderous ditto, with a solemn lustre as of holiness about it, to Milton; all the ardent love poetry, tricked out in affluent imagery, to Byron; all the scouring, dashing, descriptive warrior rhymes to Scott; all the sleepy, tiresome, rural stuff, to Thomson and his eternal *Seasons*; all the genial, warm-hearted jolly Scotch poetry, to Burns; all the tender, broken-hearted song-verses to Moore; all the broken-English poetry to Chaucer or Spenser—whichever occurs to you first; all the heroic poetry, about the impossible deeds done before Troy, to Homer; all the nauseating rebellion mush-and-milk about young fellows who have come home to die—just before the battle, mother—to George F. Root and kindred spirits; all the poetry that everybody admires and appreciates, but nobody ever reads or quotes from, to Dryden, Cowper and Shelley; all the grave-yard poetry to Elegy Gray or Wolfe, indiscriminately; all the poetry that you can't understand, to Emerson; all the harmless old platitudes, delivered with a stately and oppressive pretense of originality, to Tupper, and all the "Anonymous" poetry to yourself. Bear these rules in mind, and you will pass muster as a connoisseur; as long as you can talk glibly about the "styles" of authors, you will get as much credit as if you were really acquainted with their works. Throw out a mangled French phrase occasionally, and you will pass for an accomplished man, and a Latin phrase dropped now and then will gain you the reputation of being a learned one. Many a distinguished "connoisseur" in *belles lettres* and classic erudition travels on the same capital I have advanced you in this rather

lengthy paragraph. Make a note of that "Anonymous" suggestion—never let a false modesty deter you from "cabbaging"
anything you find drifting about without an owner. I shall publish a volume of poems, shortly, over my signature, which became the "children of my fancy" in this unique way.

ETIQUETTICUS, *Monitor Silver Mines.*—"If a lady and gentleman are riding on a mountain trail, should the lady precede the
gentleman, or the gentleman precede the lady?" It is not a matter
of politeness at all—it is a matter of the heaviest mule. The heavy
mule should keep the lower side, so as to brace himself and stop
the light one should he lose his footing. But to my notion you are
worrying yourself a good deal more than necessary about
etiquette, up there in the snow belt. You had better be skirmishing for bunch-grass to feed your mule on, now that the snowy
season is nearly ready to set in.

§ 108. *Answers to Correspondents*

24 June 1865

Clemens' fourth column for the *Californian* attacked boorish ostentation and sentimental notions of children. It continued his response to the Dutch Flat poetry hoax, begun in no. 106, and it ridiculed the practice of making accusations of disloyalty to the Union on scant grounds: Clemens' former editor, Charles Henry Webb, had recently suffered from such a charge at the hands of the press, and Clemens, as a son of Missouri, was always in danger of experiencing it in person.

Clemens worked his way around to this touchy subject by referring, in "TRUE SON OF THE UNION," to a political wrangle that had been resolved six weeks earlier, but had been alluded to by the San Francisco *Morning Call* just one week before his column appeared.[1] Briefly, the appointment of the San Francisco collector of customs from August 1863 until November 1865, Charles James, had been widely regarded as political patronage and attributed to the influence of Senator John Conness. Sometime in early 1865, James became involved in a controversy over his discharge of Samuel Pillsbury, a customs employee. Pillsbury had alleged, in protesting his dismissal to the secretary of the treasury, that he was fired when he voted for a slate of unpledged delegates to the Union State Convention rather than support the delegates pledged to Senator Conness. Because the delegates to this convention nominated candidates for the state legislature, which in turn selected senatorial candidates, James was open to the charge of "Senator-making." This accusation was supported by the fact that the secretary of the treasury had reinstated Pillsbury in early May 1865.[2]

---

[1]"Battle of Bunker Hill," San Francisco *Morning Call*, 18 June 1865, p. 1.

[2]"No Yoke in the Custom House," San Francisco *Evening Bulletin*, 8 May 1865, p. 2; "Candidates for United States Senator," ibid., 17 June 1865, p. 2.

Clemens began his piece by quoting the letter from "A New England Mechanic" to the *Call*, which criticized the "worthy Collector." He then dismissed it with bemused contempt, noting "how quibbling and fault-finding breed in a land of newspapers," and went on to print an obviously fictional complaint that he had "intercepted" on its way to the office of another local paper, the *"Flaming Loyalist."* This document explicitly transforms failure to observe the anniversary of the battle of Bunker Hill into an act of treason—an absurdity that Clemens finally answers with a rhetorical question: "If the oriental artisan and the sentinel agriculturalist held the offices of these men, would they ever *attend to anything else* but the flag-flying and gin-soaking outward forms of patriotism and official industry?"

This invented case must have seemed familiar to readers of the *Californian*, for on March 18, Webb had publicly answered a charge of disloyalty from the Marysville (Calif.) *Appeal* of March 12, which had said: "The editor of the *Californian* is as bitter a Copperhead as ever went unhung. . . . The editor of the *Californian*, like the editor of the *Express*, is loyal to the Southern Conthieveracy, loyal to the rebellion, and loyal to anything in opposition to our Government." Webb's answer, published in the editorial columns of his magazine, said in part:

A better illustration of the reckless journalism we have so often taken occasion to deprecate and denounce could not be desired. We do not know the editor of the *Appeal*, even by name; have never seen him to our knowledge, and certainly have never interchanged political views with him. Yet he, without the slightest warrant, takes occasion to denounce "THE EDITOR OF THE CALIFORNIAN" as "AS BITTER A COPPERHEAD AS EVER WENT UNHUNG!" This is scarcely courteous; we would characterize the assertion as untruthful by the only English word which befits it, were it not that we are opposed to bandying those words in print which men very seldom speak to each other, and never except to inflict a brand which is more disgraceful than a blow. Our friends in this city are well acquainted with our political sentiments, and we do not care to explain them to every stranger who chooses to arraign us. THE CALIFORNIAN in its course has always been consistently and unequivocally loyal. . . . The present editor . . . has never uttered or written a treasonable word in his life, and all his friends and associates know him to be utterly and thoroughly Union in feeling and expression; he can point with equal pride to the fact that he never has stood in the market place, vaunting his own loyalty while causelessly questioning that of his neighbor, and clamoring to be rewarded for the simple performance of his duty in giving all his efforts and energies to the preservation of the Nation's integrity.[3]

---

[3]"A Good 'Goak,' " Marysville (Calif.) *Appeal*, 15 March 1865, p. 2; "Representative Reckless Journalism," *Californian* 2 (18 March 1865): 1.

The editors of the *Call* promptly came to Webb's assistance, stating that the *Appeal* editor was "entirely mistaken," that Webb's "record, not only in this State but the Atlantic States, forbids such a conclusion," and that "the falsehood was first sent abroad by a city reporter, and has been copied with relentless fidelity by the interior press."[4] The San Francisco *Dramatic Chronicle* teased Webb about his angry reaction, saying that he encroached "upon the province of omnipotence, by insane attempts to manufacture 'Things' out of 'nothings,' " a reference to Webb's column ("Things") in the *Californian*. On March 25 Webb alluded to this joke in his column, but the matter was obviously quite serious for him.[5] The situation was certainly not improved by what followed: Lincoln was assassinated on April 14, and Webb retired from the editorship of the *Californian* the next day. None of this, we may be sure, was lost on Clemens, who nevertheless waited until late June to make his own comments on the matter, contained here in "TRUE SON OF THE UNION."

Clemens used only three sections of this column—"SOCRATES MURPHY," "ARITHMETICUS," and "YOUNG MOTHER"—to help make up the composite "Answers to Correspondents" sketch for the 1867 *Jumping Frog* book, revising them in the Yale Scrapbook. "TRUE SON OF THE UNION" was omitted, probably because it seemed both dated and topical in January or February 1867.

---

[4]Quoted in "A Good 'Goak,' " Marysville (Calif.) *Appeal,* 19 March 1865, p. 2.

[5]"Not So," San Francisco *Dramatic Chronicle,* 20 March 1865, p. 2; "Things," *Californian* 2 (25 March 1865): 1. Webb had been suspected of disloyalty before, as Franklin Walker points out (*San Francisco's Literary Frontier* [Seattle and London: University of Washington Press, 1939], pp. 183–184). His immediate problems probably stemmed from some irreverent remarks about Lincoln in recent *Californian* editorials like "The President's Message" and "The President's Inaugural" (*Californian* 2 [10 December 1864]: 8; 2 [11 March 1865]: 8). In the latter he had said: "Coming from the pen of one who is certainly more noted for puns than for piety, it [the inaugural address] suggests the idea of burlesque." On April 8 and 15, after the capture of Richmond, he published two editorials that show his concern over the *Appeal's* charge of disloyalty. See "Victory! Victory!" and "The Uses of Victory," *Californian* 2 (8 April 1865): 8; 2 (15 April 1865): 8.

Answers to Correspondents

TRUE SON OF THE UNION.—Very well, I will publish the following extract from one of the dailies, since you seem to consider it necessary to your happiness, and since your trembling soul has found in it evidence of lukewarm loyalty on the part of the Collector—but candidly, now, don't you think you are in rather small business? I do, anyhow, though I do not wish to flatter you:

"BATTLE OF BUNKER HILL.

SAN FRANCISCO, June 17, 1865.
Messrs. Editors: Why is it that on this day, the greatest of all in the annals of the rights of man—viz: the Glorious Anniversary of the Battle of Bunker Hill—*our Great Ensign of Freedom does not appear on the Custom House?* Perhaps our worthy Collector is so busy Senator-making that it might have escaped his notice. You will be pleased to assign an excuse for the above official delinquency, and oblige

A NEW ENGLAND MECHANIC."

Why was that published? I think it was simply to gratify a taste for literary pursuits which has suddenly broken out in the system of the artisan from New England; or perhaps he has an idea, somehow or other, in a general way, that it would be a showing of neat and yet not gaudy international politeness for Collectors of ports to hoist their flags in commemoration of British victories, (for the physical triumph was theirs, although we claim all the moral effect of a victory;) or perhaps it struck him that "this day, the greatest of all *in the annals of the rights of man,"* (whatever that may mean, for it is a little too deep for me,) was a fine, high-sounding expression, and yearned to get it off in print; or perhaps it occurred to him that "the Glorious Anniversary," and "our Great Ensign of Freedom," being new and startling figures of speech, would probably create something of a sensation if properly marshalled under the leadership of stunning capitals, and so he couldn't resist the temptation to trot them out in grand dress parade before the reading public; or perhaps, finally, he really *did* think the Collector's atrocious conduct partook of the character of a devilish "official delinquency," and imperatively called for explanation or "excuse." And still, after all this elaborate analysis, I am considerably "mixed" as to the actual motive for publishing that thing.

But observe how quibbling and fault-finding breed in a land of newspapers. Yesterday I had the good fortune to intercept the following bitter communication on its way to the office of a cotemporary, and I am happy in being able to afford to the readers of THE CALIFORNIAN the first perusal of it:

Editors of the Flaming Loyalist: What does it mean? The extraordinary conduct of Mr. John Doe, one of the highest Government officials among us, upon the anniversary of the battle of Bunker Hill—that day so inexpressibly dear to every loyal American heart because our patriot forefathers got worsted upon that occasion—is matter of grave suspicion. It was observed (by those who have closely watched Mr. Doe's actions ever since he has been in office, and who have thought his professions of loyalty lacked the genuine ring,) that this man, *who has uniformly got drunk, heretofore, upon all the nation's great historical days, remained thoroughly sober upon the hallowed 17th of June.* Is not this significant? Was this the pardonable forgetfulness of a loyal officer, or rather, was it not the deliberate act of a malignant and a traitorous heart? You will be pleased to assign an excuse for the above official delinquency, and oblige

> A SENTINEL AGRICULTURIST UPON THE
> NATIONAL WATCHTOWER.

Now isn't that enough to disgust any man with being an officeholder? Here is a drudging public servant who has always served his masters patiently and faithfully, and although there was nothing in his instructions requiring him to get drunk on national holidays, yet with an unselfishness, and an enlarged public spirit, and a gushing patriotism that did him infinite credit, he *did* always get as drunk as a loon on these occasions—ay, and even upon any occasion of minor importance when an humble effort on his part could shed additional lustre upon his country's greatness, never did he hesitate a moment to go and fill himself full of gin. Now observe how his splendid services have been appreciated—behold how quickly the remembrance of them hath passed away—mark how the tried servant has been rewarded. This grateful officer—this pure patriot—has been known to get drunk five hundred times in a year for the honor and glory of his country and his country's flag, and no man cried "Well done, thou good and faithful servant"—yet the very first time he ventures to remain sober on a battle anniversary (exhausted by the wear and tear of previous efforts, no doubt,) this spying "Agriculturist," who has deserted his onion-patch to perch himself upon the National Watch-Tower at the risk of breaking his meddlesome neck, discovers the damning fact that he is firm on his legs, and sings out: "He don't keep up his lick!—he's DISLOYAL!"

Oh, stuff! a public officer has a hard enough time of it, at best, without being constantly hauled over the coals for inconsequential and insignificant trifles. If you *must* find fault, go and ferret out something worth while to find fault with—if John Doe or the Collector neglect the actual business they are required by the Government to transact, impeach them. But pray allow them a little poetical license in the choice of occasions for getting drunk and hoisting the National flag. If the oriental artisan and the sentinel agriculturalist held the offices of these men, would they ever *attend to anything else* but the flag-flying and gin-soaking outward forms of patriotism and official industry?

SOCRATES MURPHY.—You speak of having given offense to a gentleman at the Opera by *unconsciously* humming an air which the tenor was singing at the time. Now, part of that is a deliberate falsehood. You were not doing it "unconsciously;" no man does such a mean, vulgar, egotistical thing as that unconsciously. You were doing it to "show off;" you wanted the people around you to know you had been to operas before, and to think you were not such an ignorant, self-conceited, supercilious ass as you looked; I can tell you Arizona opera-sharps, any time; you prowl around beer-cellars and listen to some howling-dervish of a Dutchman exterminating an Italian air, and then you come into the Academy and prop yourself up against the wall with the stuffy aspect and the imbecile leer of a clothing-store dummy, and go to droning along about half an octave below the tenor, and disgusting everybody in your neighborhood with your beery strains. [N. B. If this rough-shod eloquence of mine touches you on a raw spot occasionally, recollect that I am talking for your good, Murphy, and that I am simplifying my language so as to bring it clearly within the margin of your comprehension; it might be gratifying to you to be addressed as if you were an Oxford graduate, but then you wouldn't understand it, you know.] You have got another abominable habit, my sage-brush amateur. When one of those Italian footmen in British uniform comes in and sings "O tol de rol!—O, Signo-o-o-ra!—loango—congo—Venezue-e-e-la! whack fol de rol!" (which means "Oh, noble madame, here's one of them dukes from the palace, out here, come to borrow a dollar and a half,") you always stand with expanded eyes and mouth, and one pile-driver uplifted, and your ample hands held apart in front of your face, like a couple of canvas-covered hams, and when he gets almost through, how you do uncork your pent-up enthusiasm and applaud with hoof and palm! You have it pretty much to yourself, and then you look sheepish when you find everybody staring at you. But how very idiotic you do look when something really fine is sung—you generally keep quiet, then. Never mind, though, Murphy, entire audiences do things at the Opera that they have no business to do; for instance, they never let one of those thousand-dollar singers finish—they always break in with their ill-timed applause just as he or she, as the case may be, is preparing to throw all his or her concentrated sweetness into the final strain, and so all that sweetness is lost. Write me again, Murphy—I shall always be happy to hear from you.

ARITHMETICUS, *Virginia, Nevada.* —"I am an enthusiastic student of mathematics, and it is so vexatious to me to find my progress constantly impeded by these mysterious arithmetical technicalities. Now do tell me what the difference is between Geometry and Conchology?"

Here *you* come again, with your diabolical arithmetical conundrums, when I am suffering death with a cold in the head. If you could have seen the expression of ineffable scorn that darkened my countenance a moment ago and was instantly split from the centre in every direction like a fractured looking-glass by my last sneeze, you never would have written that disgraceful question. Conchology is a science which has nothing to do with mathematics; it relates only to shells. At the same time, however, a man who opens oysters for a hotel, or shells a fortified town, or sucks eggs, is not, strictly speaking, a conchologist—a fine stroke of sarcasm, that, but it will be lost on such an intellectual clam as you. Now compare conchology and geometry together, and you will see what the difference is, and your question will be answered. But don't torture me with any more of your ghastly arithmetical horrors (for I do detest figures anyhow,) until you know I am rid of my cold. I feel the bitterest animosity toward you at this moment—bothering me in this way, when I can do nothing but sneeze and quote poetry and snort pocket-handkerchiefs to atoms. If I had you in range of my nose, now, I would blow your brains out.

YOUNG MOTHER.—And so you think a baby is a thing of beauty and a joy forever? Well, the idea is pleasing, but not original— every cow thinks the same of its own calf. Perhaps the cow may not think it so elegantly, but still she thinks it, nevertheless. I honor the cow for it. We all honor this touching maternal instinct wherever we find it, be it in the home of luxury or in the humble cow-shed. But really, madam, when I come to examine the matter in all its bearings, I find that the correctness of your assertion does not manifest itself in all cases. A sore-faced baby with a neglected nose cannot be conscientiously regarded as a thing of beauty, and inasmuch as babyhood spans but three short years, no baby is competent to be a joy "forever." It pains me thus to demolish two-thirds of your pretty sentiment in a single sentence, but the position I hold in this chair requires that I shall not permit you to deceive and mislead the public with your plausible figures of speech. I know a female baby aged eighteen months, in this city, which cannot hold out as a "joy" twenty-four hours on a stretch, let alone "forever." And it possesses some of the most remarkable eccentricities of character and appetite that have ever fallen under my notice. I will set down here a statement of this infant's operations, (conceived, planned and carried out by itself, and without suggestion or assistance from its mother or any one else,) during a single day—and what I shall say can be substantiated by the sworn testimony of witnesses. It commenced by eating one dozen large blue-mass pills, box and all; then it fell down a flight of stairs, and arose with a bruised and purple knot on its forehead, after which it proceeded in quest of further refreshment and amusement. It found a glass trinket ornamented with brasswork—mashed up and ate the glass, and then swallowed the brass. Then it drank about twenty or thirty drops of laudanum, and more than a dozen table-spoonsful of strong spirits of camphor. The reason why it took no more laudanum was, because there was no more to take. After this it lay down on its back, and shoved five or six inches of a silver-headed whalebone cane down its throat; got it fast there, and it was all its mother could do to pull the cane out again, without pulling out some of the child with it. Then, being hungry for glass again, it broke up several wine glasses, and fell to eating and swallowing the fragments, not minding a cut or two. Then it ate a quantity of butter, pepper, salt and California matches, actually taking a spoonful of butter, a spoonful of salt, a spoonful of pepper, and three or four lucifer matches, at each mouthful. (I will remark here that this thing of beauty likes painted German lucifers, and eats all she can get of them; but she infinitely prefers California matches—which I regard as a compliment to our home manufactures of more than ordinary value, coming, as it does, from one who is too young to flatter.) Then she washed her head with soap and water, and afterwards ate what soap was left, and drank as much of the suds as she had room for, after which she sallied forth and took the cow familiarly by the tail, and got kicked heels over head. At odd times during the day, when this joy forever happened to have nothing particular on hand, she put in the time by climbing up on

places and falling down off them, uniformly damaging herself in
the operation. As young as she is, she speaks many words tolerably distinctly, and being plain-spoken in other respects, blunt and
to the point, she opens conversation with all strangers, male or
female, with the same formula—"How do, Jim?" Not being
familiar with the ways of children, it is possible that I have been
magnifying into matter of surprise things which may not strike
any one who is familiar with infancy as being at all astonishing.
However, I cannot believe that such is the case, and so I repeat
that my report of this baby's performances is strictly true—and if
any one doubts it, I can produce the child. I will further engage
that she shall devour anything that is given her, (reserving to
myself only the right to exclude anvils,) and fall down from any
place to which she may be elevated, (merely stipulating that her
preference for alighting on her head shall be respected, and, therefore, that the elevation chosen shall be high enough to enable her
to accomplish this to her satisfaction.) But I find I have wandered
from my subject—so, without further argument, I will reiterate
my conviction that not *all* babies are things of beauty and joys
forever.

BLUE-STOCKING, *San Francisco.*—Do I think the writer in the
Golden Era quoted Burns correctly when he attributed this language to him?

"O, wad the power the gift tae gie us."

No, I don't. I think the proper reading is—

"O, wad some power the giftie gie us."

But how do you know it is Burns? Why don't you wait till you
hear from the *Gold Hill News?* Why do you want to rush in ahead
of the splendid intellect that discovered as by inspiration that the
"Destruction of the Sennacherib" was not written in Dutch Flat?

AGNES ST. CLAIR SMITH.—This correspondent writes as fol-
lows: "I suppose you have seen the large oil painting (entitled 'St.
Patrick preaching at Tara, A. D. 432,') by J. Harrington, of San
Francisco, in the window of the picture store adjoining the Eureka
Theatre, on Montgomery street. What do you think of it?"

Yes, I have seen it. I think it is a petrified nightmare. I have not time to elaborate my opinion.

DISCOURAGING.

The fate of Mark Twain's exquisite bit of humor, in which he treats Byron's "Sennacherib" as a communication from a Dutch Flat poet, will teach a lesson to our wits. The next time that Mark gets off a good thing in the same fine vein, he will probably append "a key" to the joke.—*Dramatic Chronicle.*

Ah! but you forget the Gold Hill *News* and the *Flag.* Would they understand the "key" do you think?

§ 109 *Answers to Correspondents*

1 July 1865

Clemens' fifth column for the *Californian* contained some further comments about his contemporary journalists on the San Francisco *American Flag*, the *Golden Era*, and the Gold Hill *News*. It also contained a charming essay on one of his favorite euphemisms, "Geewhillikins." But the main preoccupation of the column, taking up more than half its length, was his critique of San Francisco theatrical criticism as practiced by the local papers and literary journals.

Theatrical criticism as described by "Young Actor" was, as Clemens had good reason to know, common—not to say universal. Newspaper critics combined an inclination to be capricious and arbitrary with a taste for rivalry and quarreling: witness the longstanding public disagreement between Thomas Maguire and the de Young brothers, publishers of the newly founded San Francisco *Dramatic Chronicle*. When Clemens worked for the San Francisco *Call* he, like other reporters, "wrote up" the city's plays and operas without having time to witness the whole performance, much less think of anything intelligent to say about it.[1] The combination of the critics' temperament and such circumstances was, as he well knew, deadly.

Four months after this column appeared in the *Californian*, Clemens went to work once again as a critic, this time for the *Dramatic Chronicle*, but his opinion of his colleagues' work was never lower. It was probably he who published " 'Call' Style of Criticism" in the *Chronicle* on 4 November 1865. This was a severe attack on the "critical honesty of the *Morning Call*" because "its estimates of histrionic talent are susceptible of change under a change of circumstances." He went on to point

---

[1]AD, 13 June 1906, *MTE*, p. 255.

out that the *Call's* criticism of Felicita Vestvali during September did not "jibe" with its comments on her in October, after she had brought "suit against the manager [Thomas Maguire] for money she thinks justly due her." While the earlier comments amounted to strong praise, and characterized her as a "star" and "in almost the 'first rank of leading artistes,' " later criticisms reversed this trend:

Her enthusiastic admirer—the *Call* man—throws off on her instantly—sweeps all his former praise to the winds and stultifies himself with a single telling expression of irony. He opens his account of the suit in this way: "Mademoiselle starts in by declaring herself a star *(extraordinary conceit!)*" etc., etc., etc. O, what a falling off was there, my countrymen! He first went to work and convinced her that she was a star by argument and illustration, and now turns round and makes fun of her for believing him! We cannot put any confidence in such oscillating criticism as that. If she wasn't a star, what did you go and pretend to the public that she was one for?[2]

Somewhat later the same year, on December 13, Clemens reiterated this sardonic view of theater critics—this time in connection with the projected visit of Edwin Forrest to San Francisco in May 1866. In a letter to the Virginia City *Territorial Enterprise* he anticipated their response as follows:

These mosquitoes would swarm around him and bleed dramatic imperfections from him by the column. With their accustomed shameless presumption, they would tear the fabric of his well earned reputation to rags, and call him a poor, cheap humbug and an over[r]ated concentration of mediocrity. . . . They would always wind up their long-winded "critiques"—these promoted newsboys and shoemakers would—with the caustic, the cutting, the withering old stand-by which they have used with such blighting effect on so many similar occasions, to wit: "If Mr. Forrest calls that sort of thing *acting*—very well; but we must inform him, that although it may answer in other places, it will not do here." . . . Their grand final shot is always a six-hundred pounder, and always comes in the same elegant phraseology: they would pronounce Mr. Forrest a *"bilk!"* You cannot tell me anything about these ignorant asses who do up what is called "criticism" hereabouts—I know them "by the back."[3]

Clemens did not think that bad drama criticism was necessarily provincial criticism—as his allusion in the sketch to the New York *Herald's*

---

[2] " 'Call' Style of Criticism," San Francisco *Dramatic Chronicle,* 4 November 1865, p. 2.

[3] "San Francisco Letter," written 13 December, published 16–17 December 1865, Virginia City *Territorial Enterprise,* clipping in the Yale Scrapbook, p. 37. Mark Twain tentatively revised this item, a subsection called "Managerial," for inclusion in the 1867 *Jumping Frog* book. It was not reprinted. "Managerial" is scheduled to appear in the collection of criticism in The Works of Mark Twain.

earlier abuse of Forrest shows. In the long invented letter from "YOUNG ACTOR" he was giving a fictional rendering based upon his own experience as a newspaper critic, and reader. That experience led him, as his answer to "YOUNG ACTOR" shows, to some genuine wisdom: "Pay no attention to the papers, but watch the audience."

Clemens and Webb considered including the section on "Geewhillikins" in the composite sketch "Burlesque 'Answers to Correspondents' " (no. 201), published in the 1867 *Jumping Frog* book. But perhaps because they had already found ample material for a long sketch in the four previous columns, no part of this one or the final one (no. 110) was reprinted.

Answers to Correspondents

Young Actor.—This gentleman writes as follows: "I am desperate. *Will* you tell me how I can possibly please the newspaper critics? I have labored conscientiously to achieve this, ever since I made my *début* upon the stage, and I have never yet entirely succeeded in a single instance. Listen: The first night I played after I came among you, I judged by the hearty applause that was frequently showered upon me, that I had made a 'hit'—that my audience were satisfied with me—and I was happy accordingly. I only longed to know if I had been as successful with the critics. The first thing I did in the morning was to send for the papers. I read this: 'Mr. King Lear Macbeth made his first appearance last night, before a large and fashionable audience, as "Lord Blucher," in Bilgewater's great tragedy of *Blood, Hair and the Ground Tore Up.* In the main, his effort may be set down as a success—a very gratifying success. His voice is good, his manner easy and graceful, and his enunciation clear and distinct; his conception of the character he personated was good, and his rendition of it almost perfect. This talented young actor will infallibly climb to a dizzy elevation upon the ladder of histrionic fame, but it rests with himself to say whether this shall be accomplished at an early day or years hence. If the former, then he must at once correct his one great fault—we refer to his habit of throwing extraordinary spirit into passages which do not require it—his habit of *ranting,* to speak plainly. It was this same unfortunate habit which caused him to spoil the noble scene between "Lord Blucher" and "Viscount Cranberry," last night, in that portion of the third act where the latter unjustly accuses the former of attempting to seduce his pure and honored grandmother. His rendition of "Lord Blucher's" observation—

"Speak but another syllable, vile, hell-spawned miscreant, and thou diest the death of a ter-r-raitor!"

was uttered with undue excitement and unseemly asperity—there was too much rant about it. We trust Mr. Macbeth will consider the hint we have given him.' That extract, Mr. Twain, was from the *Morning Thunderbolt*. The *Daily Battering-Ram* gave me many compliments, but said that in the great scene referred to above, I gesticulated too wildly and too much—and advised me to be more circumspect in future, in these matters. I played the same piece that night, and toned myself down considerably in the matter of ranting and gesticulation. The next morning neither the *Thunderbolt* or the *Battering-Ram* gave me credit for it, but the one said my 'Lord Blucher' overdid the pathetic in the scene where his sister died, and the other said I laughed too boisterously in the one where my servant fell in the dyer's vat and came out as green as a meadow in Spring-time. The *Daily American Earthquake* said I was too *tame* in the great scene with the 'Viscount.' I felt a little discouraged, but I made a note of these suggestions and fell to studying harder than ever. That night I toned down my grief and my mirth, and worked up my passionate anger and my gesticulation just the least in the world. I may remark here that I began to perceive a moderation, both in quantity and quality, of the applause vouchsafed me by the audience. The next morning the papers gave me no credit for my efforts at improvement, but the *Thunderbolt* said I was too loving in the scene with my new bride, the *Battering-Ram* said I was not loving enough, and the *Earthquake* said it was a masterly performance and never surpassed upon these boards. I was check-mated. I sat down and considered how I was going to engineer that love-scene to suit all the critics, until at last I became stupefied with perplexity. I then went down town, much dejected, and got drunk. The next day the *Battering-Ram* said I was too spiritless in the scene with the 'Viscount,' and remarked sarcastically that I threatened the 'Viscount's' life with a subdued voice and manner eminently suited to conversation in a funeral procession. The *Thunderbolt* said my mirth was too mild in the dyer's vat scene, and observed that instead of laughing heartily, as it was my place to do, I smiled as blandly—and as guardedly, apparently—as an undertaker in the cholera season. These mortuary comparisons had a very depressing effect upon my spirits, and I turned to the *Earthquake* for comfort. That authority said 'Lord Blucher' seemed to take the death of his idolized sister uncommonly easy, and suggested with exquisite irony that if I would use a toothpick, or pretend to pare my nails, in the death-bed scene, my attractive indifference would be the perfection of acting. I was almost desperate, but I went to work earnestly again to apply the newspaper hints to my 'Lord Blucher.' I ranted in the 'Viscount' scene (this at home in my private apartments) to suit the *Battering-Ram,* and then toned down considerably, to approach the *Earthquake's* standard; I worked my grief up strong in the death-bed scene to suit the latter paper, and then modified it a good deal to comply with the *Thunderbolt's* hint; I laughed boisterously in the dyer's vat scene, in accordance with the suggestion of the *Thunderbolt,* and then toned down toward the *Battering-Ram's* notion of excellence. That night my audience did not seem to know whether to applaud or not, and the result was that they came as near doing neither one thing nor the other as was possible. The next morning the *Semi-Monthly Literary Bosh* said my rendition of the character of 'Lord Blucher' was faultless—that it was stamped with the seal of inspiration; the *Thunderbolt* said I was an industrious, earnest and aspiring young dramatic student, but I was possessed of only ordinary merit, and could not hope to achieve more than a very moderate degree of success in my profession—and added that my engagement was at an end for the present; the *Battering-Ram* said I was a tolerably good stock-actor, but that the practice of managers in imposing such people as me upon the public as stars, was very reprehensible—and added that my engagement was at an end for the present; the *Earthquake* critic said he had seen worse actors, but not *much* worse—and added that my engagement was at an end for the present. So much for newspapers. The *Monthly Magazine of Literature and Art* (high authority,) remarked as follows: 'Mr. King Lear Macbeth commenced well, but the longer he played, the worse he played. His first performance of "Lord Blucher" in *Blood, Hair and the Ground Tore Up,* may be entered upon the record as a remarkably fine piece of acting—but toward the last he got to making it the most extraordinary exhibition of theatrical lunacy we ever witnessed. In the scene with the "Viscount," which calls for sustained, vigorous, fiery declamation, his manner was an incomprehensible mixture of "fever-heat" and "zero"—to borrow the terms of the thermometer; in the dyer's vat scene he was alternately torn by spasms of mirth and oppressed by melancholy; in the death-bed scene his countenance exhibited profound grief one moment and blank vacancy in the next; in the love scene with his bride—but why particularize? throughout the play he was a mixture—a conglomeration—a miracle of indecision—an aimless, purposeless dramatic lunatic. In a word, his concluding performances of the part of "Lord Blucher" were execrable. We simply assert this, but do not attempt to account for it—we know his first performance was excellence itself, but how that excellence so soon degenerated into the pitiable exhibition of last night, is beyond our ability to determine.' Now, Mr. Twain, you have the facts in this melancholy case—and any suggestion from you as to how I can please these critics will be gratefully received."

I can offer no suggestion, "Young Actor," except that the ordinary run of newspaper criticism will not do to depend upon. If you keep on trying to shape yourself by such models, you will go mad, eventually. Several of the critics you mention probably never saw you play an entire act through in their lives, and it is possible that the balance were no more competent to decide upon the merits of a dramatic performance than of a sermon. Do you note how unconcernedly and how pitilessly they lash you as soon as your engagement is ended? Sometimes those "criticisms" are written and in type before the curtain rises. Don't you remember that the New York *Herald* once came out with a column of criticism upon Edwin Forrest's "Hamlet," when unfortunately the bill had been changed at the last moment, and Mr. Forrest played "Othello"

instead of the play criticised? And only lately didn't the same
paper publish an elaborate imaginary description of the funeral
ceremonies of the late Jacob Little, unaware that the obsequies
had been postponed for twenty-four hours? It is vastly funny, your
"working yourself up" to suit the *Thunderbolt*, and "toning yourself down" to suit the *Battering-Ram*, and doing all sorts of similarly absurd things to please a lot of "critics" who had probably
never seen you play at all, but who threw in a pinch of instruction
or censure among their praise merely to give their "notices" a
candid, impartial air. Don't bother yourself any more in that way.
Pay no attention to the papers, but watch the audience. A silent
crowd is damning censure—good, hearty, enthusiastic applause is
a sure sign of able acting. It seems you played well at first—I
think you had better go back and start over again at the point
where you began to instruct yourself from the newspapers. I have
often wondered, myself, when reading critiques in the papers,
what would become of an actor if he tried to follow all the fearfully conflicting advice they contained.

MARY, *Rincon School.*—Sends a dainty little note, the contents
whereof I take pleasure in printing, as follows, (suppressing, of
course, certain expressions of kindness and encouragement which
she intended for my eye alone): "Please spell and define *gewhili-
kins* for me."

Geewhillikins is an ejaculation or exclamation, and expresses
surprise, astonishment, amazement, delight, admiration, disappointment, deprecation, disgust, sudden conviction, incredulity,
joy, sorrow—well, it is capable of expressing pretty nearly any
abrupt emotion that flashes through one's heart. For instance, I
say to Jones, "Old Grimes is dead!" Jones knowing old Grimes
was in good health the last time he heard from him, is surprised,
and he naturally exclaims, "Geewhillikins! is that so?" In this
case the word simply expresses surprise, mixed with neither joy
nor sorrow, Grimes' affairs being nothing to Jones. I meet Morgan,
and I say, "Well, I saw Johnson, and he refuses to pay that bill."
Johnson exclaims, "Geewhillikins! is that so?" In this case the
word expresses astonishment and disappointment, together with
a considerable degree of irritation. I meet young Yank, and I ob-

serve, "The country is safe now—peace is declared!" Yank swings
his hat and shouts, "Geewhillikins! is that so?"—which expresses surprise and extreme delight. I stumble on Thompson,
and remark, "There was a tornado in Washoe yesterday which
picked up a church in Virginia and blew it to Reed's Station, on
the Carson river, eighteen miles away!" Thompson says, "Gee-
e-e-*whillikins!*" with a falling inflection and strong emphasis on
that portion of the word which I have italicized—thus, with discriminating judgment, imbuing the phrase with the nicest shades
of amazement, wonder, and mild incredulity. Stephens, who is
carrying home some eggs in his "hind-coat pocket," sits down on
them and mashes them—exclaiming, as he rises, gingerly explor-
ing the mucilaginous locality of his misfortune with his hand,
"*Gee*-whillikins!"—with strong emphasis and falling inflection
on the first syllable, and falling inflection on the last syllable
also—thus expressing an extremity of grief and unmitigated disgust which no other word in our whole language is capable of
conveying. That will do, I suppose—you cannot help understanding my definition, now, and neither will you fail to appreciate the
extraordinary comprehensiveness of the word. We will now consider its orthography. You perceive that I spell it with two e's and
two l's, which I think is the proper method, though I confess the
matter is open to argument. Different people spell it in different
ways. Let us give a few examples:

> "The horse 'raired' up with a furious neigh,
> And over the hills he scoured away!
> Mazeppa closed his despairing eye,
> And murmured, 'Alas! and must I die!
> 'GEE-WHILIKINS!' "

[*Byron's Mazeppa.*

> "Sir Hilary charged at Agincourt—
> Sooth 'twas an awful day!
> And though in that old age of sport
> The rufflers of the camp and court
> Had little time to pray,
> 'Tis said Sir Hilary muttered there
> Four syllables by way of prayer:
> 'GEE-WHILLIKINS!' "

[*Winthrop Mackworth Praed.*

If the Gold Hill *News* or the *American Flag* say the above excerpts are misquotations, pay no attention to them—they are anything but good authority in matters of this kind. The *Flag* does not spell the word we are speaking of properly, either, in my opinion. I have in my mind a communication which I remember having seen in that paper the morning the result of the presidential election was made known. It possessed something of an exulting tone, and was addressed to a heavy gun among the Copperheads—the editor of the late *Democratic Press*, I think—and read as follows:

"BERIAH BROWN, ESQ.—*Dear Sir:* How are you *now?*
            "Yours, truly,
                                  G. WHILLIKINS."

You will have to accept my definition, Mary, for want of a better. As far as the spelling is concerned, you must choose between Mr. Praed and myself on the one hand, and Lord Byron and the *American Flag* on the other, bearing in mind that the two last named authorities disagree, and that neither of them ever knew much about the matter in dispute, anyhow.

ANXIETY.—*S. F.*—Need have no fear of General Halleck. There is no truth in the report that he will compel approaching maternity to take the oath of allegiance.—*Golden Era.*

Another impenetrable conundrum—or, to speak more properly, another fathomless riddle. I shall have to refer to Webster:

"APPROACHING, *ppr.* Drawing nearer; advancing toward."
"MATERNITY, *n.* The character or relation of a mother."

Consequently, "approaching maternity" means the *condition* of being about to become a mother. And according to the profound, the deep, the bottomless expounder who instructs "Anxiety" in my text, General Halleck "will not compel" that *condition* to "take the oath of allegiance." Any numscull could have told that—because how can an insensible, impalpable, invisible *condition* take an oath? That expounder comes as near being a "condition" as anybody, no doubt, but still he cannot take an oath in his character *as* a "condition;" he must take it simply in his character as a man. None but human beings can take the oath of allegiance under our constitution. But didn't you mean that women in the said condition would not be required to take the oath merely *because* they happened to be in that condition?—or didn't you mean that the woman wouldn't have to take it on behalf of her forthcoming progeny?—or didn't you mean that the forthcoming progeny wouldn't be required to take it itself, either before or immediately after it was born? Or, what in the very mischief *did* you mean?—what were you driving at?—what were you trying to ferry across the trackless ocean of your intellect? Now you had better stop this sort of thing, because it is becoming a very serious matter. If you keep it up, you will eventually get some of your subscribers so tangled up that they will seek relief from their troubles and perplexities in the grave of the suicide.

MARK TWAIN.—'Twas a burning shame to misquote Burns. The wretch who deliberately substituted *italic* for the original would, we verily believe, enjoy martyrdom. Previous thereto his eyes should be stuck full of exclamation points!—*Golden Era.*

Are you wool-gathering, or is it I? I have read that paragraph fourteen or fifteen times, very slowly and carefully, but I can't see that it means anything. Does the point lie in a darkly suggested pun upon "original would" (original *wood?*)—or in the "exclamation *points?*"—or in the bad grammar of the last sentence?—or in— Come, now—explain your ingenious little riddle, and don't go on badgering and bullyragging people in this mysterious way.

GOLD HILL NEWS.—This old scoundrel calls me an "old humbug from Dutch Nick's." Now this is not fair. It is highly improper for gentlemen of the press to descend to personalities, and I never permit myself to do it. However, as this abandoned outcast evidently meant his remark as complimentary, I take pleasure in so receiving it, in consideration of the fact that the fervent cordiality of his language fully makes up for its want of elegance.

§ 110. *Answers to Correspondents*

8 July 1865

Clemens' sixth and final column of answers to correspondents appeared in the *Californian* shortly after he had begun writing occasional, perhaps even daily, letters to the Virginia City *Territorial Enterprise* in late June. Although this column was his longest, it expressed, both directly and indirectly, his impatience to be done with the weekly obligation. In his reply to "STUDENT OF ETIQUETTE" he said that even though he declined to answer it, the question was "no more absurd than a dozen I can find any day gravely asked and as gravely answered in the 'Correspondents' Column' of literary papers throughout the country." This was a sign that he had tired of his original purpose—to burlesque such columns: "If these editors choose to go on answering foolish questions in the grandiloquent, oracular style that seems to afford them so much satisfaction, I suppose it is no business of mine."

The long first section of the column was, in fact, only an ostensible burlesque answer. The Fourth of July festivities for 1865 followed the surrender at Appomattox by only three months, and they were, therefore, more enthusiastic than usual. In his long answer to "INQUIRER, *Sacramento,*" Clemens cast a critical eye not only on the details of these festivities in San Francisco, but on the quality of the journalism that chronicled them. Late in May the board of supervisors had appointed a network of committees to plan and build such new features as the gaudy "Triumphal Arch," a structure that to Clemens suggested a "colossal bird-cage" or a "grand metropolitan barber-shop" in execrable taste. The program itself remained much the same as in former years: early morning gun salutes; a grand procession of civic and military groups winding through the city; an oration at the Metropolitan Theatre, this year by John

219

W. Dwinelle; and in the evening, fireworks followed by a festive ball. There was one innovation, however, which Clemens did not comment on in his column for the *Californian:* in most of the major cities of the state black citizens had been invited to participate in the parade, and at least in San Francisco the blacks did march, despite the opposition of many whites. In a letter to the *Enterprise* published sometime in mid-July, Clemens took up the subject with characteristic good humor (see "Mark Twain on the Colored Man," no. 115).

Answers to Correspondents

INQUIRER, *Sacramento.* — At your request I have been down and walked under and around and about the grand, gaudy and peculiar

INDEPENDENCE ARCH

which rears its awful form at the conjunction of Montgomery and California streets, and have taken such notes as may enable me to describe it to you and tell you what I think of it. [N. B. I am writing this on Monday, the day preceding the Glorious Fourth.] My friend, I have seen arch-traitors and arch-deacons and architects, and archæologists, and archetypes, and arch-bishops, and, in fact, nearly all kinds of arches, but I give you the word of an honest man that I never saw an arch like this before. I desire to see one more like it and then die. I am the more anxious in this respect because it is not likely that I shall ever get a chance to see one like it in the next world, for something tells me that there is not such an arch as this in any of the seven heavens, and there certainly cannot be anything half as gay in the other place.

I am calling this *one* arch all the time, but in reality it is a cluster of four arches; when you pass up Montgomery street you pass under two of them, and when you pass up California street you pass under the other two. These arches spring from the tops of four huge square wooden pillars which are about fifteen or twenty feet high and painted with dull, dead, blue mud or blue-mass, or something of that kind. Projecting from each face of these sombre columns are bunches of cheap flags adorned with tin spear-heads. The contrast between the dark melancholy blue of the pillars and the gorgeous dyes of the flags is striking and picturesque. The arches reach as high as the eaves of an ordinary three-story house, and they are wide in proportion, the pillars standing nearly the width of the street apart. A flagstaff surmounts each of the pillars. The Montgomery street arches are faced with white canvas, upon which is inscribed the names of the several States in strong black paint; as there is a "slather" of gory red and a "slather" of ghostly white on each side of these black names, a cheerful barber-pole contrast is here presented. The broad tops of the arches are covered (in the barber-pole style, also, which seems to have been the groundwork of this fine conception,) with alternate patches of white and sickly pink cotton, and these patches having a wrinkled and disorderly appearance, remind me unpleasantly of a shirt I "done up" once in the Humboldt country, beyond the Sierras. The general effect of this open, airy, summer-house combination of arches, with its splashes and dashes of blue and red and pink and white, is intensely streaky and stripy; and altogether, if the colossal bird-cage were only "weatherboarded" it would just come up to one's notion of what a grand metropolitan barber-shop ought to be. Or if it were glazed it would be a neat thing in the way of a show-lamp to set up before a Brobdignag theatre. Surmounting the centres of two of the arches—those facing up and down Montgomery street—are large medallion portraits of Lincoln and Washington—daubs—apparently executed in whitewash, mud and brick-dust, with a mop. In these, also, the barber-shop ground-plan is still adhered to with a discriminating and sensitive regard to consistency; Washington is clean-shaved, but he is not done getting shampooed yet; his white hair is foamy with lather, and his countenance bears the expectant aspect of a man who knows that the cleansing shower-bath is about to fall. Good old Father Abe, whose pictured face, heretofore, was always serious, but never unhappy, looks positively worn and dejected and tired out, in the medallion—has exactly the expression of one who has been waiting a long time to get shaved and there are thirteen ahead of him yet. I cannot help admiring how the eternal fitness of things has been preserved in the execution of these portraits. To one who delights in "the unities" of art, could anything be more ravishing than the appropriate appearance and expression of the two countenances, overtopped as they are by sheaves of striped flags and surrounded on all sides by the glaring, tinted bars that symbol the barber's profession? I believe I have nothing left to describe in connection with the two arches which span Montgomery street. However, upon second thought, I forgot to mention that over each of the two sets of portraits stoops a monstrous painted eagle, with wings uplifted over his back, neck stretched forward, beak parted, and eager eye, as if he were on the very point of grabbing a savory morsel of some kind—an imaginary customer of the barber-shop, maybe.

The arch which fronts up California street is faced with white canvas, prominently sewed together in squares, and upon this broad white streak is inscribed in large, plain, black, "horse-type," this inscription:

"HONOR TO THE FOUNDERS AND SAVIOURS OF THE REPUBLIC."

For some unexplained reason, the "Founders" of the Republic are aggrandized with a capital "F," and the equally meritorious Saviors of it snubbed with a small "s." True, they gave the Saviors a "u"—a letter more than is recommended by Webster's dictionary—but I consider that a lame apology and an illiberal and inadequate compensation for "nipping" their capital S. The centre-piece of this arch consists of an exceedingly happy caricature of the coat-of-arms of California, done in rude imitation of fresco. The female figure is a placid, portly, straight-haired squaw in complete armor, sitting on a recumbent hog, and so absorbed in contemplation of the cobble-stones that she does not observe that she has got her sack of turnips by the wrong end, and that dozens of them are rolling out at the other; neither does she observe that the hog has seized the largest turnip and has got it in his mouth; neither does she observe that her great weight is making it mighty uncomfortable for the hog; she does not notice that she is mashing the breath out of him and making his eyes bulge out with a most agonized expression—nor that it is as much as he can do to hold on to his turnip. There is nothing magnanimous in this picture. Any true-hearted American woman, with the kindly charity and the tenderness that are inseparable from the character, would get up for a minute and give the hog a chance to eat his turnip in peace.

The centre-piece of the opposite arch is a copy of the one just described, except that the woman is a trifle heavier, and of course the distress of the hog is aggravated in a corresponding degree. The motto is—

"MINE EYES HAVE SEEN THE GLORY OF THE COMING OF THE LORD."

This is an entirely abstract proposition, and does not refer to the surrounding splendors of the situation.

I have now described the arch of which you have heard such glowing accounts (set afloat in the first place by incendiary daily prints, no doubt,) and have thus satisfied your first request. Your second—that I would tell you what I think of it, can be done in a few words. It cost $3,000, and I think it cost a great deal too much, considering the unhappy result attained. I think the taste displayed was very bad—I might even say barbarous, only the tone of some of my preceding paragraphs might lead people to think I was making a pun. If you will notice me you will observe that I never make a pun intentionally—I never do anything like that in cold blood. To proceed—I think the same money expended with better judgment would have procured a set of handsome, graceful arches which could be re-trimmed and used again, perhaps; but I think these can't, as we have no ferry slips now that require gateways resplendent with cheap magnificence; I think the whole affair was gotten up in too great a hurry to be done well—the committee was appointed too late in the day; I suppose the appointing power did not know sooner that the Fourth of July was coming this year; I think the committee did as well as they could under the circumstances, because a member of it told me so, and he could have no object in deceiving me; I think many people considered the cluster of arches, with their Sunday-school-picnic style of ornamentation, pretty, and took a good deal of pride in the same, and therefore I am glad that this article will not be published until the Fourth has come and gone, for I would be sorry that any remarks of mine should mar the pleasure any individual might otherwise take in that truly extraordinary work of art.

Now you have the arches as they looked before the Fourth—the time when the above paragraphs were written. But I must confess—and I don't do it *very* reluctantly—that on the morning of the Fourth they were greatly improved in appearance. One cause was that innumerable small flags had been mounted on the arches, and hid the broad red and pink patchwork covering of the latter from sight, and another that the fiery colors so prevalent about the structure had been pleasantly relieved by the addition of garlands and festoons of evergreens to the embellishments, and the suspension of a champagne basket of other greens and flowers from the centre of it, chandelier fashion. Also, as by this time all Montgomery street was a quivering rainbow of flags, one could not help seeing that the decorations of the arches had to be pretty strong in coloring to keep up any sort of competition with the brilliant surroundings.

As I have disparaged this work of art before it had a chance to put on its best looks, and as I still don't think a great deal of it, I will act fairly by it, and print the other side of the question, so that you can form a just estimate of its merits and demerits by comparing the arguments of the prosecution and defence together. I will re-publish here the opinion entertained of it by the reporter of the *Alta,* one of its most fanatical, and I may even say, rabid admirers. I will go further and endorse a portion of what he says, but not all, by a good deal. I don't endorse the painting "in the highest style of the decorative art," (although it sounds fine—I may say eloquent,) nor the "magnificent basket," either:

"The most noticeable feature of the display on this street was the

GRAND TRIUMPHAL ARCH,

at the intersection of California and Montgomery streets, designed by M. F. Butler, Esq., the architect; erected by A. Snyder; painted, in the highest style of the decorative art, by Hopps & Son; and draped and adorned with flags and flowers by Chas. M. Plum, upholsterer, and A. Barbier, under the management and supervision of a Committee, consisting of John Sime, W. W. Dodge and M. E. Hughes. This arch was one of the chief attractions throughout the day and evening. On Montgomery street, distributed on both north and south sides, were the names of the thirty-six sovereign States of the Union, to each one a separate shield, and the names of the leading Generals of the Revolution, side by side with those of the War for the Union, and on the California street side the names of officers of the Army and Navy, past and present, the face of the arch on the east side bearing the words:

'Mine eyes have seen the glory of the coming of the Lord,'

And on the west side—

'Honor to the Founders and Saviors of our Republic.'

The centre of both the arches on Montgomery street were ornamented with portraits of Washington and Lincoln, and surmounted with flags beautifully and tastefully grouped. The flags of various nations were also grouped under the base of the arches at the four corners, and the whole structure was hung with evergreen wreaths and flowers, while a magnificent floral basket hung suspended under the centre of the structure by wreaths depending from the arches. As the procession passed under this arch, the petals of the roses and other flowers were constantly falling upon it in showers as the wreaths swung to and fro in the summer breeze."

Now for my side again. The following blast is from the *Morning Call.* The general felicity of the thing is to be ascribed to the fact that the reporter listened to some remarks of mine used in the course of a private conversation with another man, and turned them to account as a "local item." He is excusable for taking things from me, though, because I used to take little things from him occasionally when I reported with him on the *Call:*

STRAIGHTENING UP.—The likenesses of "Pater Patriæ," and "Salvator Patriæ," on the ornamental (!) barber-shop at the corner of Montgomery and California streets, have been straightened up, and now wear a closer similarity to what might be supposed to represent men of steady habits. While we hold in the most profound veneration the memory of those illustrious men, as well as the day we propose to celebrate, yet we defy any person to look at that triumphal structure, its *blue* pillars and tawdry arches, utterly ignoring architecture and taste—and not laugh.

Now for the other side. The following highly-flavored compliment is also from the *Morning Call*, (same issue as the above extract,) but was written by the chief editor—and editors and reporters will differ in opinion occasionally:

A FINE DISPLAY.—All things promise a fine display to-day, the finest probably that has ever been witnessed in this city. The splendid triumphal arches at the intersection of Montgomery and California streets, will be especial objects of admiration. They were designed by M. F. Butler, Esq., the architect, have been erected under his supervision, and are at once splendid specimens of his artistic skill as well as of the taste of the Committee who chose his designs over all others presented for the occasion. Mr. B. is the pioneer, as well as among the best architects of this State, and this last work, though of a somewhat ephemeral nature, is worthy of the artist who designed and superintended it, and was properly entrusted to one of our oldest citizens as well as one of the most loyal men of the State.

Now for my side. The following is also from the *Call*, (same issue as both the above extracts:)

THAT ARCH.—The following bit of satire, from a correspondent, is pretty severe on the anomalous structure our Committee have dignified with the name of triumphal arch:
"The grand Patriotic or Union Arch erected at the corner of Montgomery and California streets, is a magnificent affair. I presume it will be retained there for a number of weeks. But is n't there a very important omission about the structure? Erected in commemoration of the Nation's birthday and all its subsequent glories, should not the portrait of the author of the Declaration of Independence crown one of its beautiful arches?

'76."

Now for the other side once more. The following is from the *Bulletin*. The concluding portion of the first sentence is time-worn and stereotyped, though, and I don't consider that it ought to count against me. It is always used on such occasions and is never intended to mean anything:

"The triumphal arch which is now being completed under the direction of M. F. Butler, architect, at the junction of Montgomery and California streets, is the most imposing structure of its kind that has ever been erected on this coast. [Here follows a description of it in dry detail.] The arches are beautifully trimmed with evergreen, and the whole structure is to be adorned with a profusion of flags representing all nations, with appropriate mottoes and names of popular Generals scattered here and there among the Stars and Stripes."

And, finally, for my side again. Having this thing all my own way I have decided that I am entitled to the closing argument. The following is from the *American Flag:*

TRIUMPHAL ARCH.—A triumphal arch had been erected at the intersection of California and Montgomery streets, at a cost of $3,000. It consisted of four arches, one fronting and spanning each street, and resting upon four large pillars, thirty feet in height, painted a dingy blue, festooned with flags of various nations, and exhibiting upon each side, painted upon shields, the names, two upon each shield of the heroes of 1776 and 1865,—Grant, Greene; Sheridan, Montgomery; Dahlgren, Decatur; Dupont, Porter, &c. Near the center of each of the arches fronting on Montgomery street, were rather poorly painted portraits, also painted upon a shield, of Washington and Lincoln, surrounded by large spread eagles, and bearing beneath, the initials "W. L;" upon these arches were inscribed upon red and white shields, the names of all the States; the arch facing California street, west, bore the inscription "Honor to the Founders and to the Saviors of the Republic;" and that opposite, "Mine eyes have seen the glory of the coming of the Lord;" and near the center of both was a picture of a female of rather a lugubrious countenance, seated upon a lion couchant, bearing in her left hand a staff, and upon her head something bearing a striking resemblance to the metalic caps worn by the mail-clad warriors of ancient Greece, all of which, we presume, was intended to represent the "Goddess of Liberty victorious over the British Lion," but as we were unable to read the name of the damsel upon the shield which she held in her right hand, we will not be positive on that point. The whole affair was finely decorated with evergreens, flowers, wreaths, flags, etc., and would have been creditably ornamented, had more taste and skill been displayed in the paintings.

The prosecution "rests" here. And the defense will naturally have to "rest" also, because I have given them all the space I intend to. The case may now go to the jury, and while they are out I will give judgment in favor of the plaintiff. I learned that trick from the Washoe judges, long ago. But it stands to reason that when a thing is so frightfully tawdry and devoid of taste that the

Flag can't stand it, and when a painting is so diabolical that the *Flag* can't admire it, they must be wretched indeed. Such evidence as this is absolutely damning.

Student of Etiquette.—Asks: "If I step upon one end of a narrow bridge just at the moment that a mad bull rushes upon the other, which of us is entitled to precedence—which should give way and yield the road to the other?"

I decline to answer—leave it to the bull to decide. I am shrouded in doubts upon the subject, but the bull's mind will probably be perfectly clear. At a first glance it would seem that this "Student of Etiquette" is asking a foolish and unnecessary question, inasmuch as it is one which naturally answers itself— yet his inquiry is no more absurd than a dozen I can find any day gravely asked and as gravely answered in the "Correspondents' Column" of literary papers throughout the country. John Smith meets a beautiful girl on the street and falls in love with her, but as he don't know her name, nor her position in society, nor where she lives, nor in fact anything whatever about her, he sits down and writes these particulars to the *Weekly Literary Bushwhacker,* and gravely asks what steps he ought first to take in laying siege to that girl's affections—and is as gravely answered that he must not waylay her when she is out walking alone, nor write her anonymous notes, nor call upon her unendorsed by her friends, but his first move should be to *procure an introduction in due form.* That editor, with a grand flourish of wisdom, would have said: "Give way to the bull!" I, with greater wisdom, scorn to reply at all. If I were in a sarcastic vein, though, I might decide that it was Smith's privilege to butt the bull off the bridge—if he could. Again—John Jones finds a young lady stuck fast in the mud, but never having been introduced to her, he feels a delicacy about pulling her out, and so he goes off, with many misgivings, and writes to the *Diluted Literary Sangaree* about it, craving advice: he is seriously informed that it was not only his privilege, but his duty, to pull the young lady out of the mud, without the formality of an introduction. Inspired wisdom! He too, would have said: "Back down, and let the bull cross first." William Brown writes to the *Weekly Whangdoodle of Literature and Art* that he is madly in love with the divinest of her sex, but unhappily her affections and her hand are already pledged to another— how must he proceed? With supernatural sagacity the editor arrives at the conclusion that it is Brown's duty, as a Christian and gentleman, to go away and let her alone. Marvelous! He, too, would have said: "Waive etiquette, and let the bull have the bridge." However, we will drop the subject for the present. If these editors choose to go on answering foolish questions in the grandiloquent, oracular style that seems to afford them so much satisfaction, I suppose it is no business of mine.

MARY, *Rincon School.*—No, you are mistaken—*bilk* is a good dictionary word. True, the newspapers generally enclose it in quotation marks, (thus: "bilk,") which is the usual sign made use of to denote an illegitimate or slang phrase, but as I said before, the dictionaries recognize the word as good, pure English, nevertheless. I perfectly agree with you, however, that there is not an uglier or more inelegant word in any language, and I appreciate the good taste that ignores its use in polite conversation. For your accommodation and instruction, I have been looking up authorities in the Mercantile Library, and beg leave to offer the result of my labors, as follows:

From Webster's Dictionary, edition of 1828.
BILK, *v. t.* [Goth. *bilaikan,* to mock or deride. This Gothic word appears to be compound, *bi* and *laikan,* to leap or exult.]
To frustrate or disappoint; to deceive or defraud, by nonfulfilment of engagement; as, to *bilk* a creditor.   *Dryden.*
BILKED, *pp.* Disappointed; deceived; defrauded.

From Walker's Dictionary.
BILK, *v. a.* To cheat; to deceive.

From Wright's Universal Pronouncing Dictionary.
BILK. To deceive; to defraud.

From Worcester's Dictionary.
BILK, *v. a.* [Goth. *bi-laikan,* to scoff, to deride.] To cheat; to defraud; to deceive; to elude.
But be sure, says he, don't you *bilk* me.   *Spectator.*

From Spiers and Surenne's French Pronouncing Dictionary.
BILK, v. a. 1. *frustrer;* 2. (argot) *flouer* (escroquer, duper).

From Adler's German and English Dictionary.

To BILK, *v. a.* schnellen, prellen, betrügen, im Stiche lassen, (besonders um die [mit der] Bezahlung); *joc.* einen Husaren machen.

From Seoane's Spanish Dictionary.

To BILK. *va.* Engañar, defraudar, pegarla, chasquear, no pagar lo que se debe.

From Johnson's Dictionary.

To BILK. *v. a.* [derived by Mr. *Lye* from the Gothick *bilaican.*] To cheat; to defraud, by running in debt, and avoiding payment.

Bilk'd stationers for yeomen stood prepared.   *Dryd.*

> What comedy, what farce can more delight,
> Than grinning hunger, and the pleasing sight
> Of your *bilk'd* hopes?   *Dryden.*

From Richardson's Dictionary.

BILK. Mr. Gifford says, "Bilk seems to have become a cant word about this (Ben Jonson's) time, for the use of it is ridiculed by others, as well as Jonson. It is thus *explained* in Cole's *English Dictionary*, 'Bilk, nothing; also to deceive.' " Lye, from the Goth. *Bilaikan,* which properly signifies *insultando illudere.*
To cheat, to defraud, to elude.

Tub. Hee will ha' the last word, though he take *bilke* for't.
Hugh. Bilke! what's that?
Tub. Why nothing, a word signifying nothing; and borrow'd here to express nothing.   *B. Jonson. Tale of a Tub,* Act i. sc. 1.

[He] was then ordered to get into the coach, or behind it, for that he wanted no instructors; but be sure you dog you, says he, don't you *bilk* me.—*Spectator,* No. 498.

> Patrons in days of yore, like patrons now,
> Expected that the bard should make his bow
> At coming in, and ev'ry now and then
> Hint to the world that they were more than men;
> But, like the patrons of the present day,
> They never *bilk'd* the poet of his pay.
>   *Churchill. Independence.*

The tabooed word "bilk," then, is more than two hundred years old, for Jonson wrote the "Tale of a Tub" in his old age—say about the year 1630—and you observe that Mr. Gifford says it "seems to have become a cant word in Jonson's time." It must have risen above its vulgar position and become a legitimate phrase afterwards, though, else it would not have been uniformly printed in dictionaries without protest or explanation, almost from Jonson's time down to our own—for I find it thus printed in the very latest edition of Webster's Unabridged. Still, two centuries of toleration have not been able to make it popular, and I think you had better reflect awhile before you decide to write to Augustus that he is a bilk.

111. Enthusiastic Eloquence

23 June 1865

This appreciation of the banjo music played by Tommy Bree, Charley Rhoades, and Sam Pride appeared in the San Francisco *Dramatic Chronicle* on 23 June 1865. The *Chronicle* editors introduced it with these words: "Mark Twain, who occasionally condescends to drop in at the Academy of Music, though as a general thing he prefers negro minstrelsy to Italian opera, thus puts on record his sentiments with reference to the comparative merits of the banjo and the piano." But the article, brief as it is, was more than that: it was a reiteration of Clemens' preference for the "spirit of cheerfulness" over the "powers of dreariness," which he had expressed in "A Voice for Setchell" (no. 104) just one month before.

Tommy Bree, the popular ballad singer whom Clemens praised in the sketch, had opened at the Olympic Theatre only two days earlier. Charley Rhoades, another Pacific Coast banjo player (whose musical career had begun in the California mining camps), had been featured at the same theater for three months prior to Bree's appearance. Sam Pride, who was black (unlike most performers in "negro minstrelsy"), had been known to Clemens at least since April 1863, when the author mentioned him in his local column for the Virginia City *Territorial Enterprise*, saying that he had just "heard Sam. Pride's banjo make a very excellent speech in English to the audience" at La Plata Hall.[1] Louis Moreau Gottschalk, a distinguished concert pianist who had opened in San Francisco on 10 May 1865, was, in Clemens' eyes, no match for these experts on "the glory-beaming banjo!"

"Enthusiastic Eloquence" is the first acknowledged sketch that

---

[1]"The Minstrels," Virginia City *Territorial Enterprise*, 3 April 1863, reprinted in Appendix B12, volume 1.

Clemens published in the *Chronicle*. The paper referred to the article, in a mysteriously facetious postscript, as "the foregoing extract," and the word "extract" might imply that the *Chronicle* had reprinted only one item from a longer letter in the *Enterprise*. But on balance, it seems probable that "Enthusiastic Eloquence" had not been previously published: Bree had opened at the Olympic only two days before the sketch appeared in the *Chronicle*—insufficient time for it to travel to Virginia City and return in the *Enterprise*. The likelihood is strong that the sketch was either lifted from a manuscript destined for the *Enterprise*, or else written casually, as part of an article on San Francisco entertainments, for the *Chronicle*. Michael H. de Young, cofounder of the paper, recalled that Clemens was one of "those Bohemians" who "hung around" the office and wrote for the newspaper, "though paid no regular salaries." De Young said that Clemens even had "desk room with us . . . and made his headquarters in our office."[2] This recollection probably applies to the circumstances under which the present sketch was written and published, for in October 1865 Clemens would join the *Chronicle* on a more formal basis, earning $40 a month for dramatic criticisms.

---

[2]Michael H. de Young, "History of the *San Francisco Chronicle*," TS in Bancroft.

Enthusiastic Eloquence

I HAVE modified my musical creed a little since I have enjoyed the opportunity of comparing Tommy Bree, the banjoist of the Olympic, with Gottschalk. I like Gottschalk well enough. He probably gets as much out of the piano as there is in it. But the frozen fact is, that all that he *does* get out of it is "tum, tum." He gets "tum, tum," out of the instrument thicker and faster than my landlady's daughter, Mary Ann; but, after all, it simply amounts to "tum, tum." As between Gottschalk and Mary Ann, it is only a question of quantity; and so far as quantity is concerned, he beats her three to one. The piano may do for love-sick girls who lace themselves to skeletons, and lunch on chalk, pickles, and slate pencils. But give me the banjo. Gottschalk compared to Sam Pride or Charley Rhoades, is as a Dashaway cocktail to a hot whisky punch. When you want *genuine music*—music that will come right home to you like a bad quarter, suffuse your system like strychnine whisky, go right through you like Brandreth's pills, ramify your whole constitution like the measles, and break out on your hide like the pin-feather pimples on a picked goose,—when you want all this, just smash your piano, and invoke the glory-beaming banjo!

112. Just "One More Unfortunate"

27–30 June 1865

This sketch is one of the earliest extant items from a series of letters Clemens wrote, eventually on a daily basis, for the Virginia City *Territorial Enterprise* in 1865 and 1866. The *Enterprise* printing, which probably appeared in late June 1865, does not survive. The sketch is preserved in the Downieville (Calif.) *Mountain Messenger* for July 1, which attributed it to "Mark Twain, a correspondent of the Virginia Enterprise."

Clemens' title alludes to a popular poem by Thomas Hood, "The Bridge of Sighs," the first line of which ("One more Unfortunate") had become a cliché for a "wronged innocent"—often a young woman who commits suicide to escape disappointment or dishonor. For example, on July 13 the San Francisco *Morning Call* published "One More Unfortunate," a story of a girl in New Jersey who is rescued while trying to drown herself because her parents have thwarted her love affair.[1] Clemens' treatment of the subject is, of course, ironic, although it is difficult to be sure whether he is more interested in ridiculing the gullibility of the "stern policemen" who have tears in their eyes for "just 'one more unfortunate,' " or in excoriating the "scallawag whom it would be base flattery to call a prostitute!" Certainly his usual sympathy with the vernacular community seems in the background here, perhaps because the subject—a young white girl "living with a strapping young nigger"—touched his Victorian and southern sensibilities rather more closely than did the harmless maunderings of Ben Coon. But Clemens' harshness toward the "victim" is partly a pose adopted for directing ridicule at the sentimentalists, and it is partly mitigated by his almost involuntary de-

---

[1] "One More Unfortunate," San Francisco *Morning Call*, 13 July 1865, p. 1.

light with the young woman's verbal dexterity—her catalog of "quaint and suggestive names," and her talent for "ornamental swearing, and fancy embroidered filagree slang" which he acknowledges, somewhat begrudgingly, make her "a shade superior to any artist I ever listened to."

Just "One More Unfortunate"

IMMORALITY IS not decreasing in San Francisco. I saw a girl in the city prison last night who looked as much out of place there as I did myself—possibly more so. She was petite and diffident, and only sixteen years and one month old. To judge by her looks, one would say she was as sinless as a child. But such was not the case. She had been living with a strapping young nigger for six months! She told her story as artlessly as a school-girl, and it did not occur to her for a moment that she had been doing anything unbecoming; and I never listened to a narrative which seemed more simple and straightforward, or more free from ostentation and vain-glory. She told her name, and her age, to a day; she said she was born in Holborn, City of London; father living, but gone back to England; was not married to the negro, but she was left without any one to take care of her, and he had taken charge of that department and had conducted it since she was fifteen and a half years old very satisfactorily. All listeners pitied her, and said feelingly: "Poor heifer! poor devil!" and said she was an ignorant, erring child, and had not done wrong wilfully and knowingly, and they hoped she would pass her examination for the Industrial School and be removed from the temptation and the opportunity to sin. Tears —and it was a credit to their manliness and their good feeling —tears stood in the eyes of some of those stern policemen.

O, woman, thy name is humbug! Afterwards, while I sat taking some notes, and not in sight from the women's cell, some of the old blisters fell to gossiping, and lo! young Simplicity chipped in and clattered away as lively as the vilest of them! It came out in the conversation that she was hail fellow well met with all the old female rapscallions in the city, and had had business relations with their several establishments for a long time past. She spoke affectionately of some of them, and the reverse of others; and dwelt with a toothsome relish upon numberless reminiscences of her social and commercial intercourse with them. She knew all manner of men, too—men with quaint and suggestive names, for the most part—and liked "Oyster-eyed Bill," and "Bloody Mike," and "The Screamer," but cherished a spirit of animosity toward "Foxy McDonald" for cutting her with a bowie-knife at a strumpet ball one night. *She* a poor innocent kitten! Oh! She was a scallawag whom it would be base flattery to call a prostitute! She a candidate for the Industrial School! Bless you, she has graduated long ago. She is competent to take charge of a University of Vice. In the ordinary branches she is equal to the best; and in the higher ones, such as ornamental swearing, and fancy embroidered filagree slang, she is a shade superior to any artist I ever listened to.

113. *Advice for Good Little Boys*

1 July 1865

This sketch was published in the San Francisco *Youths' Companion*, probably on 1 July 1865. Since the second volume of the newspaper, covering May to December 1865, is no longer extant, the first printing does not survive. The text is preserved in the Yreka City (Calif.) *Weekly Union* for July 8, which explained: "Mark Twain (Sam Clemens) is writing occasionally for the San Francisco *Youths' Companion*, a very interesting little paper and published by Frank Smith. 'Sam' lately 'chipped in' with the following." Since both the *Companion* and the *Union* were published only on Saturdays, it seems reasonable to suppose that the piece appeared in San Francisco exactly one week before it was reprinted in Yreka City, although an earlier date is possible.

On 10 December 1864 Charles Henry Webb had noted in the *Californian* the appearance of "the first number of the *California Youths' Companion*" on December 3. "It is a non-sectarian family journal, devoted to the advancement of the youth of our city, and is to be published weekly, by Messrs. Smith & Edgar."[1] The nonsectarian nature of this journal probably suggested Clemens' theme in this sketch. His nuggets of advice to good little boys preached a harmlessly cynical wisdom that was a refreshing departure from the standard advice of Sunday school books, Isaac Watts's poems, and McGuffey's maxims. He had probably read comparably subversive stories, like the one in the *Golden Era* that told of young Samuel, who found a gold watch and "knew that virtue is its own reward, and therefore rewarded himself for his virtue, by keeping the watch. The owner might not have given him more than half the value of

---

[1]"Local Matters of the Week," *Californian* 2 (10 December 1864): 12.

it. Samuel is still making money."[2] But the present sketch does not attempt such a coherent story. It is a faint but intriguing anticipation of Clemens' lifelong interest in satirizing "Sunday school fiction." Within six months he would return to the subject, publishing "The Christmas Fireside" (no. 148) in the *Californian*, a sketch that he often reprinted under its subtitle, "The Story of the Bad Little Boy Who Didn't Come to Grief."

[2]"Stories for Good Little Boys and Girls," *Golden Era* 12 (15 May 1864): 6.

Advice for Good Little Boys

You ought never to take anything that don't belong to you—if you can not carry it off.

If you unthinkingly set up a tack in another boy's seat, you ought never to laugh when he sits down on it—unless you can't "hold in."

Good little boys must never tell lies when the truth will answer just as well. In fact, real good little boys will never tell lies at all—not at all—except in case of the most urgent necessity.

It is wrong to put a sheepskin under your shirt when you know that you are going to get a licking. It is better to retire swiftly to a secret place and weep over your bad conduct until the storm blows over.

You should never do anything wicked and then lay it on your brother, when it is just as convenient to lay it on another boy.

You ought never to call your aged grandpapa a "rum old file"—except when you want to be unusually funny.

You ought never to knock your little sisters down with a club. It is better to use a cat, which is soft. In doing this you must be careful to take the cat by the tail in such a manner that she cannot scratch you.

114. *Advice for Good Little Girls*

1 or 8 July 1865

This sketch was probably published in the San Francisco *Youths' Companion*, either in the same issue as the previous sketch, "Advice for Good Little Boys" (no. 113), or in the issue of the week immediately following. It is clear that the two sketches are companion pieces for which the formula was identical: conventional advice for children's good behavior is subverted by a refined appreciation of those "peculiarly aggravating circumstances" that justify exceptions to the rules. Although the precise date and sequence remains in doubt, it seems likely that Clemens followed the conventional formulation "boys and girls" and published the present sketch simultaneously with, or later than, "Advice for Good Little Boys." If the latter, it seems unlikely that he delayed longer than one week before completing the sequel, and we therefore conjecture a date of 1 or 8 July 1865, although it might easily have been somewhat earlier or later.

The first printing in the *Youths' Companion* is not extant. Our text is taken from the 1867 *Jumping Frog* book, which presumably reprinted it from a clipping supplied by Clemens. The text may, therefore, contain errors as well as revisions introduced either by the author or by his editor, Charles Henry Webb. Clemens revised the sketch and reprinted it in 1872 and 1874, but even though he considered including it in *Sketches, New and Old* (1875), it was not ultimately reprinted there.

Advice for Good Little Girls

Good little girls ought not to make mouths at their teachers for every trifling offense. This kind of retaliation should only be resorted to under peculiarly aggravating circumstances.

If you have nothing but a rag doll stuffed with saw-dust, while one of your more fortunate little playmates has a costly china one, you should treat her with a show of kindness, nevertheless. And you ought not to attempt to make a forcible swap with her unless your conscience would justify you in it, and you know you are able to do it.

You ought never to take your little brother's "chawing-gum" away from him by main force; it is better to rope him in with the promise of the first two dollars and a half you find floating down the river on a grindstone. In the artless simplicity natural to his time of life, he will regard it as a perfectly fair transaction. In all ages of the world this eminently plausible fiction has lured the obtuse infant to financial ruin and disaster.

If at any time you find it necessary to correct your brother, do not correct him with mud—never on any account throw mud at him, because it will soil his clothes. It is better to scald him a little; for then you attain two desirable results—you secure his immediate attention to the lesson you are inculcating, and, at the same time, your hot water will have a tendency to remove impurities from his person—and possibly the skin also, in spots.

If your mother tells you to do a thing, it is wrong to reply that you won't. It is better and more becoming to intimate that you will do as she bids you, and then afterward act quietly in the matter according to the dictates of your better judgment.

You should ever bear in mind that it is to your kind parents that you are indebted for your food and your nice bed and your beautiful clothes, and for the privilege of staying home from school when you let on that you are sick. Therefore you ought to respect their little prejudices and humor their little whims and put up with their little foibles, until they get to crowding you too much.

Good little girls should always show marked deference for the aged. You ought never to "sass" old people—unless they "sass" you first.

115. Mark Twain on the Colored Man

7–19 July 1865

This account of the black marchers in San Francisco's Fourth of July celebration is only a portion of Clemens' letter describing the day's festivities for the Virginia City *Territorial Enterprise*. The original letter has been lost. The text of this sketch is preserved in the San Francisco *Golden Era* for 23 July 1865. If Clemens wrote his account immediately after the event, it could have been published as early as July 7. But there is a possibility that he delayed somewhat: at least as late as July 6 he was also working hard on the longest of his "Answers to Correspondents" (no. 110). Moreover, the *Golden Era* did not reprint the present item until Sunday, July 23. On the other hand, the *Enterprise* must have published the letter no later than July 19 in order for that paper to reach San Francisco in time for Sunday's issue of the *Era*.

In Sacramento, Stockton, Sonora, and indeed throughout California, blacks had been officially invited for the first time to march in the traditional Fourth of July parades. But in most of the cities the invitation caused resentment and open displays of bigotry. In Sacramento the fire companies refused to take part if blacks joined in—and separate parades were therefore held. Blacks in Placerville and Stockton eventually declined the invitation in order to keep the peace. But in San Francisco they accepted and did not back down.

The order of march placed blacks in the ninth and last division of the parade. Despite this symbolic segregation, many whites objected to their inclusion. On June 30 a meeting of some two hundred persons, mostly Irishmen and butchers according to one reporter, was held to protest even this slight recognition.[1] The city press, however, was nearly unanimous

---

[1] "Prejudice," San Francisco *News Letter and Pacific Mining Journal* 15 (1 July 1865): 9.

246

in condemning this protest. Bret Harte's *Californian* said that the surly whites were saying, in effect, "No . . . you may fight with us, serve as a shield for white men, ward off the deadly bullets which would else reach [our] hearts. You may mourn with us but you shall have no part in our rejoicings." And the *Evening Bulletin* scathingly advised all objecting whites to stay home—advice which hundreds followed. But the blacks turned out in full force, elaborately dressed. The newspapers reported that onlookers gave them a lion's share of the applause along the parade route, and that when they alone of all the marching groups doffed their hats to the portraits of Lincoln and Washington on the Triumphal Arch they received an ovation.[2]

Given this background, it should be clear that Clemens' somewhat gruff handling of the subject—his use of the word "niggers" and the phrase "them damned niggers"—did not imply his agreement with the white protesters, but just the reverse. Clemens' admiration for Sam Pride, and his open friendship with the black editor of the San Francisco *Elevator*, as well as this sketch, show that his attitude toward blacks was not that of a typical southerner or even a typical San Franciscan.[3]

---

[2]*Californian* 3 (8 July 1865): 1; "Feeble Demonstration of Expiring Prejudice," San Francisco *Evening Bulletin*, 1 July 1865, p. 2; "Independence Day," ibid., 5 July 1865, p. 5.

[3]For a different view of Clemens' attitude toward blacks, see Arthur G. Pettit, *Mark Twain & the South* (Lexington: University Press of Kentucky, 1974), p. 34. "Mark Twain on the Colored Man" was not known to Pettit.

Mark Twain on the Colored Man

AND AT THE fag-end of the procession was a long double file of the proudest, happiest scoundrels I saw yesterday—niggers. Or perhaps I should say "them damned niggers," which is the other name they go by now. They did all it was in their power to do, poor devils, to modify the prominence of the contrast between black and white faces which seems so hateful to their white fellow-creatures, by putting their lightest colored darkies in the front rank, then glooming down by some unaggravating and nicely graduated shades of darkness to the fell and dismal blackness of undefiled and unalloyed niggerdom in the remote extremity of the procession. It was a fine stroke of strategy—the day was dusty and no man could tell where the white folks left off and the niggers began. The "damned naygurs"—this is another descriptive title which has been conferred upon them by a class of our fellow-citizens who persist, in the most short-sighted manner, in being on bad terms with them in the face of the fact that they have got to sing with them in heaven or scorch with them in hell some day in the most familiar and sociable way, and on a footing of most perfect equality—the "damned naygurs," I say, smiled one broad, extravagant, powerful smile of grateful thankfulness and profound and perfect happiness from the beginning of the march to the end; and through this vast, black, drifting cloud of smiles their white teeth glimmered fitfully like heat-lightning on a summer's night. If a white man honored them with a smile in return, they were utterly overcome, and fell to bowing like Oriental devotees, and attempting the most extravagant and impossible smiles, reckless of lock-jaw. They might as well have left their hats at home, for they never put them on. I was rather irritated at the idea of letting these fellows march in the procession myself, at first, but I would have scorned to harbor so small a thought if I had known the privilege was going to do them so much good. There seemed to be a religious-benevolent society among them with a banner—the only one in the colored ranks, I believe—and all hands seemed to take boundless pride in it. The banner had a picture on it, but I could not exactly get the hang of its significance. It presented a very black and uncommonly sick-looking nigger, in bed, attended by two other niggers—one reading the Bible to him and the other one handing him a plate of oysters; but what the very mischief this blending of contraband dissolution, raw oysters and Christian consolation, could possibly be symbolical of, was more than I could make out.

116. *The Facts*

26 August 1865

Clemens published this long sketch in the *Californian* seven weeks after his last contribution, the final installment of "Answers to Correspondents" (no. 110). By now he was earning his living not as a weekly contributor to the *Californian,* but as a journalist writing a daily letter to the Virginia City *Territorial Enterprise*—a task so grueling that he had little energy left over for the literary weeklies. Between late June and the end of December 1865 Clemens published only eight original items in the *Californian*—roughly one a month—while continuing to send a daily letter (most of them now lost) to the *Enterprise.* This change in the pattern of his work may suggest why he returned to the subject of contemporary journalism in the present sketch, "The Facts."

In October 1870 Clemens recalled that the sketch "was written in San Francisco . . . six or seven years ago, to burlesque a painfully incoherent style of local itemizing which prevailed in the papers there at that day."[1] Posing as the innocent subeditor of the *Californian,* Clemens pretends to print a note received from his friend John William Skae[2]—a note that unravels into pure incoherence. When the item draws fire from the "boss-editor" (Bret Harte at this time) and the "chief hair-splitter" (unidentified), Clemens undertakes a mock defense of local journalism. It is the overly finicky *Californian* editors, he deadpans, who fail to appreciate "Stiggers' jokes" (Albert S. Evans' jokes in the *Alta California,* that is), the *American Flag's* "poetry," the *Morning Call's* "grammar," and the *Evening Bulletin's* "country correspondents." "Now who but

---

[1]"Favors from Correspondents," *Galaxy* 10 (October 1870): 575–576.
[2]For details of Clemens' friendship with Skae, see the headnote to "Concerning the Answer to That Conundrum" (no. 92).

THE CALIFORNIAN would ever have found fault with Johnny Skae's item. No daily paper in town would, anyhow. It is after the same style, and is just as good, and as interesting and as luminous as the articles published every day in the city papers." Just so.

The *Californian* had, in fact, made it a practice to attack the quality of local journalism, both in its weekly column "The Mouse-Trap" (by "Trem") and through editorial articles. On July 15, for instance, Trem published a long paragraph about the "local reporter of the *Alta*":

What sparkling witticisms do we find in his column. In Thursday's paper, in his Police Court report, he says, "Mary Kane was again convicted on the charge of getting drunk and raising her namesake." Ha, ha, ha, he, he, he. Don't you see? Raising Cain. True he has made that joke every time Mary Kane has appeared in the Police Court, but it is a good joke, a very good joke, and bright things can never die. Then he tells us that "John Odor, a soldier who is in bad odor with the police, was convicted." Isn't that funny? Couldn't do that sort of thing, you know, for a penny a line. . . . The *Alta* is quite proud of him, and they say in the office that it's real nice to have a funny man who can write interesting items to make the paper sell while the wires are down.[3]

On August 26, in the same issue that contained "The Facts," Trem took up the subject of the *Flag's* poetry. "WE have always admired the poetry published in the *Flag*. If an editorial paragraph calls attention to 'a beautiful poem on our fourth page,' we turn with avidity to the fourth page. The poets whose productions the *Flag* enshrines are not like those of whom Horace said: '*Parturiunt montes; nascetur ridiculus mus.*' " He then reprinted one stanza as an example, maliciously reproducing the numerous typographical errors:

BYE-ANDY-EB.

Was the parting very bitter? t?
Was the hand-clasp very tigh
Is a storm of tear-drops falling
From a ace all sad and white?
Think not of it, in the future
Calmer, fairer days are nigh;
Gaze not backward, but look onward
For a sunny "bye-and-bye."

This was, according to Trem, "peculiar, but very pretty."[4] His ridicule of the *Flag's* poetry was typical of the *Californian* and marked a general distinction between the bohemians and more commercially minded and

---

[3]"The Mouse-Trap," *Californian* 3 (15 July 1865): 1.
[4]"The Mouse-Trap," *Californian* 3 (26 August 1865): 1.

literarily naive journalists. One week after this paragraph appeared the *Californian* reprinted part of a *Flag* poem that suggests a continuing feud: "Critics and Rhymers" was ostensibly "inscribed to those critical geniuses of the *'purely literary press'* who would, if they could, emulate the excellence of 'THE FLAG's Poets.' "[5]

Trem likewise attacked the bad grammar and poor diction in the *Call.* "SOME people appear to take delight in disfiguring the English language by coining hideous words," he said on July 8. "The dramatic critic of the *Call* deserves to be talked to death by Chinook Indians for making use of the expression *'embracive of* the entire strength of the company,' in speaking of the cast of a play."[6]

Harte himself had attacked the "country correspondents" in the *Bulletin* as recently as June 10. Citing several excruciatingly banal and self-preoccupied comments from "C.," who was giving his "notes of a trip to Clear Lake," and from "Diaphragm," who offered his "Notes of a Trip to the Big Trees," he remarked with his patented arch sneer:

Of such stuff are *amateur* correspondents made. We have devoted some space to pointing out their peculiarities, with no further intention except that of correcting what we conceive to be a growing evil. We do not blame people for writing such things. They are necessary and excellent safety-valves for the pent-up sentiments or prejudices which permeate mankind, and they yield an excitement to the writer which is certainly the cheapest and most innocuous form of dissipation. . . . It is only the *publication* of such articles that makes them objectionable, and brings them within the sphere of legitimate criticism. Everything that tends to deteriorate or enervate the literary standard should be excluded from the columns of a respectable journal. . . . Literary men and editors have to serve a severe apprenticeship; and we do not see why the rules which govern their ideas of excellence should be suspended for the benefit of these Bucolic amateurs who waste their time and ink in imitation.[7]

Clemens' attack on the "painfully incoherent style of local itemizing" therefore came in two parts. The first was Johnny Skae's item itself: an example bearing strong resemblances to Simon Wheeler's rambling account in "Jim Smiley and His Jumping Frog" (no. 119) and Jim Blaine's narrative in chapter 53 of *Roughing It.* The second was of course the

---

[5]"The Mouse-Trap," *Californian* 3 (2 September 1865): 1

[6]"The Mouse-Trap," *Californian* 3 (8 July 1865): 1.

[7]"Amateur Correspondents," *Californian* 3 (10 June 1865): 8. The relationship between Harte's sketch and Clemens' was pointed out recently by Jeffrey F. Thomas, "The World of Bret Harte's Fiction" (Ph.D. diss., University of California, Berkeley, 1975), p. 77.

mock defense of all the "virtues that distinguish [local] articles and render them so acceptable to the public." Clemens and his editor, Charles Henry Webb, decided to reprint only the first part of the sketch in the 1867 *Jumping Frog* book, perhaps because the second by then seemed too parochial. But Mark Twain continued to revise and reprint the first part in 1872, 1874, and 1875.

The Facts

CONCERNING THE RECENT TROUBLE BETWEEN MR.
MARK TWAIN AND MR. JOHN WILLIAM SKAE, OF
VIRGINIA CITY—WHEREIN IT IS ATTEMPTED TO BE
PROVED THAT THE FORMER WAS NOT TO BLAME
IN THE MATTER.

Mysterious.—Our esteemed friend, Mr. John William Skae, of Virginia City, walked into our office at a late hour last night with an expression of profound and heartfelt suffering upon his countenance, and sighing heavily, laid the following item reverently upon the desk and walked slowly out again. He paused a moment at the door and seemed struggling to command his feelings sufficiently to enable him to speak, and then, nodding his head toward his manuscript, ejaculated in a broken voice, "Friend of mine—Oh how sad!" and burst into tears. We were so moved at his distress that we did not think to call him back and endeavor to comfort him until he was gone and it was too late. Our paper had already gone to press, but knowing that our friend would consider the publication of this item important, and cherishing the hope that to print it would afford a melancholy satisfaction to his sorrowing heart, we stopped the press at once and inserted it in our columns:

Distressing Accident.—Last evening about 6 o'clock, as Mr. William Schuyler, an old and respectable citizen of South Park, was leaving his residence to go down town, as has been his usual custom for many years, with the exception only of a short interval in the Spring of 1850 during which he was confined to his bed by injuries received in attempting to stop a runaway horse by thoughtlessly placing himself directly in its wake and throwing up his hands and shouting, which, if he had done so even a single moment sooner must inevitably have frightened the animal still more instead of checking its speed, although disastrous enough to himself as it was, and rendered more melancholy and distressing by reason of the presence of his wife's mother, who was there and saw the sad occurrence, notwithstanding it is at least likely, though not necessarily so, that she should be reconnoitering in another direction when incidents occur, not being vivacious and on the lookout, as a general thing, but even the reverse, as her own mother is said to have stated, who is no more, but died in the full hope of a glorious resurrection, upwards of three years ago, aged 86, being a Christian woman and without guile, as it were, or property, in consequence of the fire of 1849, which destroyed every blasted thing she had in the world. But such is life. Let us all take warning by this solemn occurrence, and let us endeavor so to conduct ourselves that when we come to die we can do it. Let us place our hands upon our hearts and say with earnestness and sincerity that from this day forth we will beware of the intoxicating bowl.—*First Edition of the Californian.*

[SECOND EDITION OF THE CALIFORNIAN.]

THE boss-editor has been in here raising the very mischief, and tearing his hair and kicking the furniture about, and abusing me like a pick-pocket. He says that every time he leaves me in charge of the paper for half an hour I get imposed upon by the first infant or the first idiot that comes along. And he says that distressing item of Johnny Skae's is nothing but a lot of distressing bosh, and has got no point to it, and no sense in it, and no information in it, and that there was no earthly necessity for stopping the press to publish it. He says every man he meets has insinuated that somebody about THE CALIFORNIAN office has gone crazy.

Now all this comes of being good-hearted. If I had been as unaccommodating and unsympathetic as some people, I would have told Johnny Skae that I wouldn't receive his communication at such a late hour, and to go to blazes with it—but no, his snuffling distress touched my heart, and I jumped at the chance of doing something to modify his misery. I never read his item to see whether there was anything wrong about it, but hastily wrote the few lines which preceded it and sent it to the printers. And what has my kindness done for me? It has done nothing but bring down upon me a storm of abuse and ornamental blasphemy.

Now I will just read that item myself, and see if there is any foundation for all this fuss. And if there is, the author of it shall hear from me.

    *   *   *   *   *   *   *

I have read it, and I am bound to admit that it seems a little mixed at a first glance. However, I will peruse it once more.

    *   *   *   *   *   *   *

I have read it again, and it does really seem a good deal more mixed than ever.

    *   *   *   *   *   *   *

I have read it over five times, but if I can get at the meaning of it, I wish I may get my just deserts. It won't bear analysis. There are things about it which I cannot understand at all. It don't say what ever became of William Schuyler. It just says enough about him to get one interested in his career, and then drops him. Who is William Schuyler, anyhow, and what part of South Park did he live in? and if he started down town at six o'clock, did he ever get there? and if he did, did anything happen to him? is *he* the individual that met with the "distressing accident?" Considering the elaborate circumstantiality of detail observable in the item, it seems to me that it ought to contain more information than it does. On the contrary, it is obscure—and not only obscure but utterly incomprehensible. Was the breaking of Mr. Schuyler's leg fifteen years ago the "distressing accident" that plunged Mr. Skae into unspeakable grief, and caused him to come up here at dead of night and stop our press to acquaint the world with the unfortunate circumstance? Or did the "distressing accident" consist in the destruction of Schuyler's mother-in-law's property in early times? or did it consist in the death of that person herself 3 years ago, (albeit it does not appear that she died by accident?) In a word, what *did* that "distressing accident" consist in? What did that driveling ass of a Schuyler stand *in the wake* of a runaway horse for, with his shouting and gesticulating, if he wanted to stop him? And how the mischief could he get run over by a horse that had already passed beyond him? And what are we to "take warning" by? and how is this extraordinary chapter of incomprehensibilities going to be a "lesson" to us? And above all, what has the "intoxicating bowl" got to do with it, anyhow? It is not stated that Schuyler drank, or that his wife drank, or that his mother-in-law drank, or that the horse drank—wherefore, then, the reference to the intoxicating bowl? It does seem to me that if Mr. Skae had let the intoxicating bowl alone himself, he never would have got into so much trouble about this infernal imaginary distressing accident. I have read his absurd item over and over again, with all its insinuating plausibility, until my head swims, but I can make neither head nor tail of it. There certainly seems to have been an accident of some kind or other, but it is impossible to determine what the nature of it was, or who was the sufferer by it. I do not like to do it, but I feel compelled to request that the next time anything happens to one of Mr. Skae's friends, he will append such explanatory notes to his account of it as will enable me to find out what sort of an accident it was and who it happened to. I had rather all his friends should die than that I should be driven to the verge of lunacy again in trying to cipher out the meaning of another such production as the above.

But now, after all this fuss that has been made by the chief cook about this item, I do not see that it is any more obscure than the general run of local items in the daily papers after all. You don't usually find out much by reading local items, and you don't in the case of Johnny Skae's item. But it is just THE CALIFORNIAN's style to be so disgustingly particular and so distressingly hypercritical. If Stiggers throws off one of his graceful little jokes, ten to one THE CALIFORNIAN will come out the very next Saturday and find fault with it, because there ain't any point to it—find fault with it because there is no place in it where you can laugh—find fault with it because a man feels humiliated after reading it. They don't appear to know how to discriminate. They don't appear to understand that there are different kinds of jokes, and that Stiggers' jokes may be of that kind. No; they give a man no credit for originality—for striking out into new paths and opening up new domains of humor; they overlook all that, and just cramp an *Alta* joke down to their own narrow and illiberal notion of what a joke ought to be, and then if they find it hasn't got any point to it, they turn up their noses and say it isn't any joke at all. I do despise such meanness.

And they are just the same way with the *Flag's* poetry. They never stop to reflect that the author may be striking out into new fields of poetry—no; they simply say, "Stuff! this poem's got no sense in it; and it hasn't got any rhyme to it to speak of; and there is no more rhythm about it than there is to a Chinese oration"— and then, just on this evidence alone, they presume to say it's not poetry at all.

And so with the *Call's* grammar. If the local of the *Call* gets to branching out into new and aggravating combinations of words and phrases, they don't stop to think that maybe he is humbly trying to start something fresh in English composition and thus make his productions more curious and entertaining—not they; they just bite into him at once, and say he isn't writing grammar. And why? We repeat: And why? Why, merely because he don't choose to be the slave of their notions and Murray's.

And just so with the *Bulletin's* country correspondents. Because one of those mild and unoffending dry-goods clerks with his hair parted in the middle writes down to the *Bulletin* in a column and a half how he took the stage for Calistoga; and paid his fare; and got his change; stating the amount of the same; and that he had thought it would be more; but unpretentiously intimates that it could be a matter of no consequence to him one way or the other; and then goes on to tell about who he found at the Springs; and who he treated; and who treated him; and proceeds to give the initials of all the ladies of quality sojourning there; and does it in such a way as to conceal, as far as possible, how much they dote on his society; and then tells how he took a bath; and how the soap escaped from his fingers; and describes with infinite

humor the splashing and scrambling he had to go through with
before he got it again; and tells how he took a breezy gallop in the
early morning at 9 A. M. with Gen. E. B. G.'s charming and accomplished daughter, and how the two, with souls o'ercharged
with emotions too deep for utterance, beheld the glorious sun
bathing the eastern hills with the brilliant magnificence of his
truly gorgeous splendor, thus recalling to them tearful reminiscences of other scenes and other climes, when their hearts were
young and as yet unseared by the cold clammy hand of the vain,
heartless world—dreaming thus, in blissful unconsciousness, he
of the stream of ants travelling up his body and down the back of
his neck, and she of the gallinipper sucking the tip-end of her
nose—because one of these inoffensive pleasure-going correspondents writes all this to the *Bulletin*, I say, THE CALIFORNIAN
gets irritated and acrimonious in a moment, and says it is the
vilest bosh in the world; and says there is nothing important
about it, and wonders who in the nation cares if that fellow *did*
ride in the stage, and pay his fare, and take a bath, and see the sun
rise up and slobber over the eastern hills four hours after daylight;
and asks with withering scorn, "Well, what does it all amount
to?" and wants to know who is any wiser now than he was before
he read the long winded correspondence; and intimates that the
Bulletin had better be minding the commercial interests of the
land than afflicting the public with such wishy-washy trash. That
is just the style of THE CALIFORNIAN. No correspondence is good
enough for its hypercritical notions unless it has got something in
it. The CALIFORNIAN sharps don't stop to consider that maybe
that disbanded clerk was up to something—that maybe he was
sifting around after some new realm or other in literature—that
maybe perhaps he was trying to get something through his
head—well, they don't stop to consider anything; they just say,
because it is trivial, and awkwardly written, and stupid, and devoid of information, that it is Bosh, and that is the end of it! THE
CALIFORNIAN hates originality—that is the whole thing in a nut-
shell. *They* know it all. They are the *only* authority—and if *they*
don't like a thing, why of course it won't do. Certainly not. Now
who but THE CALIFORNIAN would ever have found fault with
Johnny Skae's item. No daily paper in town would, anyhow. It is

after the same style, and is just as good, and as interesting and as luminous as the articles published every day in the city papers. It has got all the virtues that distinguish those articles and render them so acceptable to the public. It is not obtrusively pointed, and in this it resembles the jokes of Stiggers; it warbles smoothly and easily along, without rhyme or rhythm or reason, like the *Flag's* poetry; the eccentricity of its construction is appalling to the grammatical student, and in this it rivals the happiest achievements of the *Call*; it furnishes the most laborious and elaborate details to the eye without transmitting any information whatever to the understanding, and in this respect it will bear comparison with the most notable specimens of the *Bulletin's* country correspondence; and finally, the mysterious obscurity that curtains its general intent and meaning could not be surpassed by all the newspapers in town put together.

(THIRD EDITION OF THE CALIFORNIAN.)

More trouble. The chief hair-splitter has been in here again raising a dust. It appears that Skae's item has disseminated the conviction that there has been a distressing accident somewhere, of some kind or other, and the people are exasperated at the agonizing uncertainty of the thing. Some have it that the accident happened to Schuyler; others say that inasmuch as Schuyler disappeared in the first clause of the item, it must have been the horse; again, others say that inasmuch as the horse disappeared in the second clause without having up to that time sustained any damage, it must have been Schuyler's wife; but others say that inasmuch as she disappeared in the third clause all right and was never mentioned again, it must have been the old woman, Schuyler's mother-in-law; still others say that inasmuch as the old woman died three years ago, and not necessarily by accident, it is too late in the day to mention it now, and so it must have been the house; but others sneer at the latter idea, and say if the burning of the house sixteen years ago was so "distressing" to Schuyler, why didn't he wait fifty years longer before publishing the incident, and then maybe he could bear it easier. But there is trouble abroad, at any rate. People are satisfied that there has been

an accident, and they are furious because they cannot find out
who it has happened to. They are ridiculously unreasonable. They
say they don't know who Schuyler is, but that's neither here nor
there—if anything has happened to him they are going to know
all about it or somebody has got to suffer.

That is just what it has come to—personal violence. And it is
all bred out of that snivelling lunatic's coming in here at midnight, and enlisting my sympathies with his infamous imaginary
misfortune, and making me publish his wool-gathering nonsense.
But this is throwing away time. Something has got to be done.
There has got to be an accident in the Schuyler family, and that
without any unnecessary delay. Nothing else will satisfy the public. I don't know any man by the name of Schuyler, but I will go
out and hunt for one. All I want now is a Schuyler. And I am
bound to have a Schuyler if I have to take Schuyler Colfax. If I can
only get hold of a Schuyler, I will take care of the balance of the
programme—I will see that an accident happens to him as soon
as possible. And failing this, I will try and furnish a disaster to the
stricken Skae.

§ 117. *The Only Reliable Account of the Celebrated Jumping Frog of Calaveras County*

1 September–16 October 1865

§ 118. *Angel's Camp Constable*

1 September–16 October 1865

§ 119. *Jim Smiley and His Jumping Frog*

18 November 1865

In 1896 Clemens' close friend Joseph Hopkins Twichell said that the "celebrated 'Jumping Frog of Calaveras County' . . . was a story (it had some basis of fact) with which [Clemens] had long been wont on occasion to entertain private circles. When at some one's urgency he at length wrote it out, it appeared to him so poor and flat that he pigeonholed it in contempt, and it required further urgency to persuade him to let it be printed."[1] This statement is almost certainly based on a conversation with Clemens, and as a capsule history of the jumping frog story it seems about right, for it is corroborated by other collateral accounts and by the three sketches grouped together here. "The Only Reliable Account" (no. 117) and "Angel's Camp Constable" (no. 118) are taken from two of the author's holographs preserved by his sister, Pamela, and now in the Jean Webster McKinney Family Papers at Vassar. They have not been published before. The third is taken from the New York *Saturday Press* of

---

[1]"Mark Twain," *Harper's New Monthly Magazine* 92 (May 1896): 818.

18 November 1865, where Clemens first published his most famous tale. The evidence of the manuscripts—paper, ink color, style of handwriting, and content—is that Clemens wrote both late in 1865, probably soon before he wrote "Jim Smiley and His Jumping Frog." Both manuscripts were abandoned: they are complete, but obviously unfinished, since their last pages remain only partly filled. We conjecture that they were among the "poor and flat" versions that Clemens reportedly pigeonholed in contempt, and that they were written in September or during the first two weeks of October 1865. And we further conjecture that "Jim Smiley and His Jumping Frog" (no. 119) was composed rapidly, between October 16 and 18, although it was not published in New York until a month later.

Clemens had left San Francisco in early December 1864 to visit Jim Gillis and Dick Stoker at Jackass Hill, California. The purpose of this retreat from the pressures of the city to the calm of backwoods mining towns is not certainly known, but Clemens appears to have been in a somber mood. While at Jackass Hill and nearby Angel's Camp he and his companions were confined indoors by the continuous winter rain, and so they listened to the miners and residents tell a variety of anecdotes from the local collection of folklore. Clemens recorded a number of stories in his notebooks. "New Years night—dream of Jim Townsend—'I could take this x x x book & x x x every x x x in California, from San Francisco to the mountains,' " he wrote. On about January 25 he added, "Met Ben Coon, Ill river pilot here." And then on about February 6 he wrote, "Coleman with his jumping frog—bet stranger $50—stranger had no frog, & C got him one—in the meantime stranger filled C's frog full of shot & he couldn't jump—the stranger's frog won."[2]

Writing to Jim Gillis five years later, Clemens said in part:

You remember the one gleam of jollity that shot across our dismal sojourn in the rain & mud of Angel's Camp—I mean that day we sat around the tavern stove & heard that chap tell about the frog & how they filled him with shot. And you remember how we quoted from the yarn & laughed over it, out there on the hillside while you & dear old Stoker panned & washed. I jotted the story down in my note-book that day, & would have been glad to get ten or fifteen dollars for it—I was just that blind. But then we were *so* hard up.[3]

And in 1894 Clemens again recalled the occasion, this time in somewhat greater detail:

I heard the story told by a man who was not telling it to his hearers as a thing new to them, but as a thing which *they had witnessed and would*

---

[2]*N&J1*, pp. 69, 75, 80. The reference to Townsend is explained below.
[3]Clemens to James N. Gillis, 26 January 1870, *CL2*, letter 154.

remember. He was a dull person, and ignorant; he had no gift as a story-teller, and no invention; in his mouth this episode was merely history —history and statistics; and the gravest sort of history, too; he was entirely serious, for he was dealing with what to him were austere facts, and they interested him solely because they *were* facts; he was drawing on his memory, not his mind; he saw no humor in his tale, neither did his listeners; neither he nor they ever smiled or laughed; in my time I have not attended a more solemn conference. To him and to his fellow gold-miners there were just two things in the story that were worth considering. One was, the smartness of the stranger in taking in its hero, Jim Smiley, with a loaded frog; and the other was the stranger's deep knowledge of a frog's nature—for he knew (as the narrator asserted and the listeners conceded) that a frog *likes shot* and is always ready to eat it. Those men discussed those two points, and those only. They were hearty in their admiration of them, and none of the party was aware that a first rate story had been told, in a first rate way, and that it was brimful of a quality whose presence they never suspected—humor.[4]

Clemens did not here specify who the "chap" was who told this story. But the anecdote itself had been current in oral and written folklore for years, and one version, probably written by James W. E. Townsend (the same Townsend whose dream Clemens recorded on New Year's night), had appeared in the Sonora *Herald* in 1853.[5]

On 26 February 1865 Clemens returned from his three-and-one-half-month stay in the mining camps. "Home again," he recorded in his notebook for that day, "home again at the Occidental Hotel, San Francisco—find letters from 'Artemus Ward' asking me to write a sketch for his new book of Nevada Territory travels which is soon to come out. Too late—ought to have got the letters 3 months ago. They are dated early in November."[6] Presumably Clemens wrote as much to Ward on or about March 1, also mentioning some of his recent experiences in Angel's

---

[4]"Private History of the 'Jumping Frog' Story" (no. 365), first published in the *North American Review* 158 (April 1894): 446–453. Clemens corrected this version when he reprinted the story in the "authorized Uniform Edition" of *How to Tell a Story and Other Essays* (1899). That correction is adopted here.

[5]Oscar Lewis, *The Origin of the Celebrated Jumping Frog of Calaveras County* (San Francisco: Book Club of California, 1931); *N&J1*, p. 69. Clemens' use of the words "Only Reliable Account" and "Celebrated" in his title indicates that he claimed no originality for the story itself, even though it was doubtless he who created Smiley's many "pet heroes." As late as September 1867, however, critics in California were carping at his assimilation of folklore. The San Francisco *Times* said on September 6: "We must confess to experiencing some doubt as to his originality when we are told that his famous story 'The Jumping Frog of Calaveras,' was really written by Sam Seabough, now of the Sacramento *Union*, and by 'Mark' appropriated for his own" ("Not Exactly the Correct Thing," quoted in "A Literary Piracy," *Californian* 7 [7 September 1867]: 8).

[6]*N&J1*, p. 82.

Camp—perhaps including the jumping frog story. In a letter (now lost) that could not have reached Clemens before the first of May, Ward apparently said, "Write it. . . . There is still time to get it into my volume of sketches. Send it to Carleton, my publisher in New York." Albert Bigelow Paine, who recorded this phrase as Clemens remembered it, said that the author "promised to do this, but delayed fulfillment somewhat."[7]

Indeed, it seems likely that Clemens did delay for several months. On March 18, however, he published his first experiment with the narrator Coon—almost certainly based on the Illinois river pilot he had met, Ben Coon—in "An Unbiased Criticism" (no. 100). On June 17 he introduced the narrator Simon Wheeler, who was clearly derived from Coon, and to whom Clemens now attributed "He Done His Level Best" ("Answers to Correspondents," no. 107). For most of June he was kept busy writing a weekly column of answers to correspondents for Bret Harte's *Californian*, but it must have been about this time that he was accustomed "to entertain private circles" with the frog story. Bret Harte recalled hearing it shortly after Clemens returned from "the mining districts."

In the course of conversation he remarked that the unearthly laziness that prevailed in the town he had been visiting was beyond anything in his previous experience. He said the men did nothing all day long but sit around the bar-room stove, spit, and "swop lies." He spoke in a slow, rather satirical drawl, which was in itself irresistible. He went on to tell one of those extravagant stories, and half unconsciously dropped into the lazy tone and manner of the original narrator. . . . The story was "The Jumping Frog of Calaveras."[8]

While in London in March 1897, Clemens gave the following further account of the story's genesis to James Ross Clemens:

The idea of writing the Jumping Frog Story only very slowly took shape in my mind . . . and was discarded time and time again as being too far-fetched. In fact I had actually written out a delightful story which James Townsend, the prototype of Harte's "Truthful James," had told one day in Lundie Diggings about a tame fox who used to sweep his master's cabin and dust off the furniture with his unusually bushy tail—but for some reason or other I simply couldn't get the thing just to my liking.

---

[7]*MTB*, 1:277. The quotation from Artemus Ward was not from a letter, but "in accordance with Mr. Clemens's recollection of the matter." Since Paine knew that Ward was not on the Pacific Coast at this time it seemed likely "that the telling of the frog story and his approval of it were accomplished by exchange of letters."

[8]Twichell, "Mark Twain," p. 818; T. Edgar Pemberton, *The Life of Bret Harte* (New York: Dodd, Mead and Co., 1903), p. 74. See also " 'The Jumping Frog of Calaveras' by Mark Twain with an Introductory and Explanatory Note by J. G. H.," *Overland Monthly* 40 (September 1902): 287–288.

Each time I rewrote it, it seemed less humorous than when originally told by the inimitable Townsend.

Then one dismal afternoon as I lay on my hotel bed, completely nonplussed and about determined to inform Artemus that I had nothing appropriate for his collection, a still small voice began to make itself heard.

"Try me! Try me! Oh, please try me! Please do!"

It was the poor little jumping frog, "Henry Clay," that old Ben Coon had described! Because of the insistence of its pleading and for want of a better subject, I immediately got up and wrote out the tale for my friend who had followed up his first letter with several more requests. But if it hadn't been for the little fellow's apparition in this strange fashion, I never would have written about him—at least not at that time.[9]

It seems unlikely that Clemens' frog "Daniel Webster" was ever called "Henry Clay," but the confusion of orators (if not of politics) is understandable and may be due to James Ross Clemens' faulty memory. The other facts ring true: the suggestion that Jim Townsend's story about a domestic fox preceded the frog story as the subject of Wheeler's monologue, the indication that the final story "only very slowly took shape," the attribution of the original narration to Ben Coon, and the statement that Artemus Ward had written "several more" letters urging Clemens to send a contribution. Twichell had said in 1896, less than a year earlier, that Clemens first pigeonholed his manuscript and returned to it only after "further urgency" had been applied. These later letters from Ward could hardly have reached Clemens much before the beginning of September 1865.

The two manuscripts published here, as well as the earlier experiments with Ben Coon and Simon Wheeler published in the *Californian*, suggest that Clemens saw the humorous possibilities of his narrator more clearly than he saw how to bring that narrator and his frog story into conjunction. At least two closely related problems seem to have been troubling him: precisely what stance to adopt toward his vernacular narrator (how much or how little condescension), and how to simulate the effect he could achieve so easily in oral narration when, as Harte remarked, he "half unconsciously dropped into the lazy tone and manner of the original narrator." In "The Only Reliable Account" Clemens addressed Ar-

---

[9]Quoted in *YSC*, pp. 216–217. Cyril Clemens introduced the document in the following words: "Back in the bustling city again, at the Occidental Hotel, he found among a batch of mail a letter from Artemus Ward begging a contribution for a new anthology of humor. At first he did not know what to send, and he gave the author's father, James Ross Clemens, a very interesting account (now for the first time published) of how he solved the problem." The nature of this account is not known, but it was probably a transcription of a conversation, not a holograph by the author.

temus Ward much as he would in the third version, offering him the sketch for "the history of your travels," and characterizing Wheeler as a "venerable rural historian" living in "unostentatious privacy," from whom he had obtained a "just and true account" of the jumping frog. But Clemens then spent almost as many words as the finished tale would require simply sketching the "decaying city of Boomerang." He never got around to letting Wheeler speak at all, much less tell the frog story.

"Angel's Camp Constable," on the other hand, seems to be an effort to correct this tendency to overemphasize the frame story. It begins: "I was told that if I would mention any of the venerable Simon Wheeler's pet heroes casually, he would be sure to tell me all about them, but that I must not laugh during the recital, as he would think I was making fun of them, and it would give him mortal offense." After this we are plunged almost immediately into Wheeler's monologue. The introductory sentences suggest, however, that Constable Bilgewater—a name Clemens had also recorded in his notebook at Angel's Camp[10]—was only the first of Wheeler's "pet heroes" to be treated in the story. These sentences also warn us rather too directly that his "recital" is supposed to be humorous, and they cast the author as clearly condescending toward "the old gentleman [who] oozed gratified vanity at every pore." Like the first version, however, this one never gets around to telling the story of the jumping frog: the manuscript is another false start, and Clemens did not mention his grandiose constable again until sometime in August 1878.[11]

These technical difficulties were tied up with Clemens' conception of himself, particularly his doubts about pursuing the "low" calling of a humorist. Partly because of when they were written, and partly because Simon Wheeler's monologues are a kind of literary free association, we find a number of circumstances in these stories that mirror the conflict between ambition and self-doubt that Clemens appears to have experienced. In the lingering description of the backwater community of Boomerang, for instance, Clemens conveys something of the nostalgia he would feel for the Quarles Farm. But the nostalgia is complicated here by the fact that Boomerang sits unwittingly on immense mineral

---

[10]About January 30, just a few days before hearing the frog story, he wrote: "W Bilgewater, says she, Good God what a name" (*N&J1*, p. 76). For a list of other occurrences of the name in Clemens' work, see the explanatory note on it for "Answers to Correspondents" (no. 109).

[11]In his notebook for that time he wrote: "The Angel's Camp constable who always saw everything largely. Two men walking tandem was a procession; <2> 3 men fighting was a riot; 5 <a riot; 15> an insurrection, & <25> 15 a revolution" (*N&J2*, p. 136). It is not known whether Clemens in fact wrote anything further about the constable.

wealth—wealth that has been quietly bought up by a "New York company" from the residents, who fail to recognize the value of what they own. Passive retirement is no solution. On the other hand, Constable Bilgewater has foolishly resigned his post in Angel's Camp because "they'd heard of him in New York, I reckon, and I s'pose they wanted him there, and so he went. And he was right. There warn't business enough here for a man of his talents, though what there was he made the most of." Bilgewater's view of his own vocation, like Simon Wheeler's respect for him, are comic precisely because both are so contrary to the facts. But even here it is not quite clear how Mark Twain judges Bilgewater, "who attained to considerable eminence, and whom I have frequently heard of in various parts of the world."

Clemens, too, had begun to be heard of in New York. His *Californian* sketches were being reprinted there, as Webb had noted in January and February 1865. And probably on October 17, the day before he finished the manuscript of "Jim Smiley and His Jumping Frog," Clemens saw an article in the New York *Round Table* that placed him among the "foremost" of the "merry gentlemen of the California press." On October 19 he confided to Orion that he would now pursue his fame as a humorist, "unworthy & evanescent though it must of necessity be," despite the fact that his talent had been deprived of the "steam of *education.*" He explained that it was "only now, when editors of standard literary papers in the distant east give me high praise . . . that I really begin to believe there must be something in it."[12] Clemens' self-doubts, particularly about his education, also appear in the third, published version of the tale. As Henry Nash Smith pointed out in 1962, the "elegiac theme of mute inglorious Miltons" applies to all of Simon Wheeler's "pet

---

[12]"American Humor and Humorists," New York *Round Table*, 9 September 1865, p. 2; Clemens to Orion and Mollie Clemens, 19–20 October 1865, *CL1*, letter 95. Clemens wrote Orion the day after this extract from the *Round Table* had appeared in "Recognized," San Francisco *Dramatic Chronicle*, 18 October 1865, p. 3. Since Clemens was contributing to the *Chronicle* on a casual basis (see the headnote to "Enthusiastic Eloquence," no. 111) and had just joined the paper's staff on a slightly more formal basis (*CL1*, letter 95), it seems likely that he saw the *Round Table* article before the *Chronicle* quoted from it. He certainly saw it before the *Californian* quoted from it on Saturday, October 23 (p. 5). It should be noted that Bret Harte was well aware of the significance of such recognition and what it implied about the local audience. On 11 November 1865 he criticized California's taste and said in part: "A California humorist, whose crude, but original sketches have been a feature of our local press, is handsomely recognised by a critical Eastern authority, and the criticism read here by a class who never before heard of the humorist" ("Home Culture," *Californian* 3 [11 November 1865]: 8).

heroes," including Daniel Webster: "Smiley said all a frog wanted was education, and he could do most anything—and I believe him."[13] Both the fear of being forgotten and unjustly obscure, like Boomerang, and the fear of being ridiculed for his presumption, like Bilgewater, appear indirectly in the basic fantasies of these three stories. "I wonder what they think of him in New York," says Wheeler about his hero. It is a comic question precisely because of its childlike assumption that fame cannot have failed to attend Bilgewater "in New York."

An abundance of evidence suggested in 1967 that Clemens wrote the third version of his sketch in the week of 16 to 23 October 1865.[14] It now seems likely, although not certain, that Clemens actually composed it between 16 and 18 October, presumably having reached the point of near despair he described for James Ross Clemens. He probably did not send his manuscript to New York by overland mail, which took about one month and remained an uncertain means at best. Because he doubtless knew Ward's book was nearing publication, and because transit time by Pacific Mail Steamship could be as brief as twenty-one days between San Francisco and New York,[15] it seems likely that Clemens chose this method instead. The only steamer to leave San Francisco in the week of 16 to 23 October was the *Golden City,* which departed at 11:20 A.M. "with 72 packages United States mails" on October 18; its cargo was transferred by rail across the Isthmus of Panama to the *Ocean Queen,* which arrived in New York on November 10. (The next steamer to leave San Francisco was the *Colorado* on October 30, and its cargo did not arrive in New York until December 4.)[16] If Clemens did as we suppose, then one week must have elapsed between the arrival of the mails in New York on November 10 and publication in the *Saturday Press* on

---

[13]*MTDW,* p. 11.

[14]Edgar M. Branch, " 'My Voice Is Still for Setchell': A Background Study of 'Jim Smiley and His Jumping Frog,' " *PMLA* 82 (December 1967): 591–601.

[15]The steamship *Colorado* arrived in San Francisco on October 24, for instance, "bringing the passengers and mails that left New York October 2d, and making the trip in the very quick time of 21 days" ("Arrival of the Steamship 'Colorado,' " San Francisco *Evening Bulletin,* 24 October 1865, p. 3). The *Bulletin* of November 24, however, could publish New York news only to October 26—a typical time lag for overland mail.

[16]"Arrival of the Steamship 'Golden City,' " San Francisco *Evening Bulletin,* 24 November 1865, p. 3; "Shipping Intelligence . . . Arrived," New York *Tribune,* 11 November 1865, p. 7; "Arrival of the Steamship 'Colorado,' " San Francisco *Evening Bulletin,* 4 December 1865, p. 5; "Shipping Intelligence . . . Arrived," New York *Tribune,* 5 December 1865, p. 7. Clemens might have made use of other steamers from the opposition lines, but none left within the period during which he completed his sketch.

November 18. On November 11 George W. Carleton advertised *Artemus Ward: His Travels* as ready "this morning" in the New York *Tribune,* although the book was probably published even earlier than that (piracies appeared in England by November 18 at the latest). In any case, Carleton would have been unable to include Clemens' sketch in Ward's book and could easily have turned the manuscript over to the editor of the *Press,* Henry Clapp, saying, as Clemens recalled in 1897, "Here, Clapp, here's something you can use!"[17] Clemens himself noted in January 1866 that his sketch was "a squib which would never have been written but to please Artemus Ward, & then it reached New York too late to appear in his book." And one year later he said, while preparing the sketch for his *Jumping Frog* book, that it was "originally written, by request, for Artemus Ward's last book, but arrived in New York after that work had gone to press."[18]

In mid-September the *Californian* had noted a general revival in periodical literature in the East, following the end of the war. It particularly mentioned "the smart *Saturday Press,*"

whilom a "brief abstract and chronicle" of "Pfaff's," snappy with absinthian wit, and dying of its own Bohemian excesses and dissipations, [which] has been revived under apparently more moral auspices, and in respectable quarto form. Let us hope that this corruption has put on incorruption. Artemus Ward is a contributor to its first number in a not over-bright theatrical criticism.[19]

This may explain why Clemens thought, as he said years later, that the *Press* was close to collapse. Certainly its editor was quite genuinely happy to publish "Jim Smiley and His Jumping Frog" and to promise—accurately, but on what authority is not known—future contributions from the same pen.

We give up the principal portion of our editorial space, to-day, to an exquisitely humorous sketch—"Jim Smiley and his Jumping Frog"—by Mark Twain, who will shortly become a regular contributor to our columns. Mark Twain is the assumed name of a writer in California who has long been a favorite contributor to the San Francisco press, from

---

[17]New York *Tribune,* 11 November 1865, p. 2; "Literary Items," New York *Tribune,* 18 November 1865, p. 9; quoted in *YSC,* p. 217. Paine gave the line as "Here, Clapp, here's something you can use in your paper" (*MTB,* 1:277–278).

[18]Clemens to Jane Clemens and Pamela Moffett, 20 January 1866, *CL1,* letter 97; page 23A of the Yale Scrapbook, reproduced in photofacsimile on p. 528 of the textual introduction in volume 1. The latter inscription must have been written in mid-January or February 1867.

[19]"Revival in the Eastern Literary Press," *Californian* 3 (16 September 1865): 8.

which his articles have been so extensively copied as to make him nearly as well known as Artemus Ward.[20]

Within three weeks of publication the sketch had, like its less distinguished predecessors, been widely reprinted. The New York correspondent of the San Francisco *Alta California*, Richard Ogden (["Podgers"], wrote on December 10 to say that it had "set all New York in a roar. . . . I have been asked fifty times about it and its author, and the papers are copying it far and near. It is voted the best thing of the day." He added a question that may have touched Bret Harte on a tender place: "Cannot the *Californian* afford to keep Mark all to itself? It should not let him scintillate so widely without first being filtered through the California press."[21] Even before this report arrived, however, Bret Harte had acknowledged the value of Clemens' latest work by reprinting it, on December 16, in the *Californian*—incorporating a few changes that Clemens himself may have authorized. But the full nature and extent of the eastern storm of praise did not reach California until Podgers' letter was published on 10 January 1866. Three days later Charles Henry Webb said in his column "Inigoings" in the *Californian:* "I should have expressed my pleasure at the hit which 'Podgers' says Mark Twain has made at the East in 'Jim Smiley and his Jumping Frog.' But he deserves it all. For he's a good fellow, and his sketch 'is good' . . . better than any of their funny fellows can do."[22]

Clemens' own reaction to this success was mixed. The day after Podgers' remarks were published he told the local reporter of the San Francisco *Examiner* about an old ambition, recently revived. The *Examiner* said, in part, "That rare humorist, 'Mark Twain,' whose fame is rapidly extending all over the country, informs us that he has commenced the work of writing a book."[23] To his family on January 20 he confided that

[20]*Saturday Press,* 18 November 1865, p. 248. Clemens said in 1906 that "Clapp used it to help out the funeral of his dying literary journal, *The Saturday Press*" (AD, 21 May 1906, *MTE,* p. 144). And in an entry made at an unknown time, commenting on his original notebook entry for the frog story, he wrote: "Wrote this story for Artemus—his idiot publisher, Carleton gave it to Clapp's Saturday Press" (N&J1, p. 80).

[21]"Letter from New York," written 10 December 1865, published in the *Alta California,* 10 January 1866, p. 1.

[22]"Inigoings," *Californian* 4 (13 January 1866): 1. For the details of Clemens' possible alteration of the text for the *Californian* and his subsequent revisions of the text, see the textual commentary.

[23]" 'Mark Twain' Is Writing a Book," San Francisco *Examiner,* 12 January 1866, p. 3. Clemens included a reprinting of this item, probably taken from the steamer edition of the *Alta California,* in his 20 January 1866 letter to this family (CL1, letter 97).

he was actually thinking of three books, and he enclosed a clipping of Podgers' comments in the *Alta*, adding a note of self-deprecation: "To think that after writing many an article a man might be excused for thinking tolerably good, those New York people should single out a villainous backwoods sketch to compliment me on!—'Jim Smiley & His Jumping Frog.' " This low opinion of his sketch would soon change. In June 1866 he proudly reported the approval of Anson Burlingame and his son; in April 1867 he said that James Russell Lowell had pronounced "the Jumping Frog . . . the finest piece of humorous writing ever produced in America"; and in December 1869 he endorsed this view in a letter to Olivia Langdon, saying he thought it "the best humorous sketch America has produced, yet."[24] In 1867 Clemens gave the sketch pride of place in the *Jumping Frog* book, but even though he continued to reprint it, he seemed to convey his low opinion of it by planning to use it in the various cheap pamphlets that so obsessed him from 1870 until 1874. The original version is reprinted here. It was revised by both Clemens and his editor, Webb, for the 1867 *Jumping Frog* book, and revised again in 1872 and 1874.[25] But whatever the author's later opinion of it, "Jim Smiley and His Jumping Frog" was an impeccably shaped yarn that took extraordinary delight in someone's saying humorous things without being aware of it.[26] And it both expressed and to some extent resolved the personal dilemma Clemens was feeling about his calling as a humorist.

---

[24]Clemens to Jane Clemens and Pamela Moffett, 20 January 1866, *CL1*, letter 97; Clemens to Jane Clemens and Pamela Moffett, 21 June 1866, *CL1*, letter 105; Clemens to Jane Clemens et al., 19 April 1867, *CL1*, letter 125; Clemens to Olivia Langdon, 14 December 1869, *CL2*, letter 129.

[25]See the textual introduction in volume 1, pp. 527–535, 557, 613.

[26]For an excellent analysis of the way this tale exemplifies Clemens' theory of humor, see Paul Baender, "The 'Jumping Frog' as a Comedian's First Virtue," *Modern Philology* 60 (February 1963): 192–200.

The Only Reliable Account of the Celebrated Jumping Frog of Calaveras County

TOGETHER WITH SOME REFERENCE TO THE DECAYING
CITY OF BOOMERANG, AND A FEW GENERAL REMARKS
CONCERNING MR. SIMON WHEELER, A RESIDENT OF THE
SAID CITY IN THE DAY OF ITS GRANDEUR.

MR. A. WARD—*Dear Sir:*
In accordance with your request I herewith furnish you with a
report of the present condition and appearance of the once flourishing mining town of Boomerang, to supply a vacancy which
must necessarily occur in the history of your travels in consequence of your having neglected to travel in that direction.

Also, in accordance with your instructions, I made the acquaintance of Simon Wheeler, the venerable rural historian, who
resided at Boomerang in early times, (though for years past he has
lived in unostentatious privacy on the picturesque borders of
Lake Tulare,) and obtained from him a just and true account of the
celebrated Jumping Frog of Calaveras County for your pages.

EN ROUTE FOR BOOMERANG.

I traveled from here toward Boomerang by steamboat a part of
the way, and took the stage early the next morning. All day long
we slopped through the mud, over a monotonous plain, with eyes
fixed on the gleaming snows of the distant Sierras, and dreary

enough the journey was. About every five miles we encountered a
rickety weather-beaten farm-house, and then sketched and re-
sketched its dismal outlines in imagination until we came to the
next one—which was always a more dilapidated one the further
we proceeded inland—and finally when the tedious sun went
down, my mind's eye presented no panorama of the day's travel
but two long lines of staggering fences, interrupted at stated
intervals by desolate cabins, with here and there a melancholy
dog or a broken-hearted cow. I was glad to see the day close in. I
was glad there was no Joshua there to command the sun to stand
still.

BOOMERANG—PAST.

I staid in Boomerang five or six days. In it there are probably
twenty crazy houses occupied and thirty still crazier ones tenant-
less. The stream that flows through the middle of the town winds
its tortuous course through symmetrical piles of pebbles and
boulders that had passed through the gold miner's sluice-boxes
years ago and were dumped into the positions they now occupy.
In those days this stream swarmed with men of every nationality
under the sun, and some took out a thousand dollars a day and
none less than thirty or forty. At night they collected in splendid
saloons, in their savage-looking costumes, and gambled away
moderate fortunes, and got drunk on costly foreign liquors, and
dissected each other with eighteen-inch bowie-knives in their
frank, off-hand way, and all were gay and happy.

They rolled ten-pins; they played billiards; they indulged in
expensive balls; they ordered elegant suppers, and ate them and
paid for them; they turned out on great occasions in grand dress
parade—firemen, soldiers, benevolent societies—and had silken
banners, and walked under gorgeous triumphal arches and fulminated their sentiments from thundering cannon. They had a
newspaper and a telegraph, and talked of a railroad. They never
quite reached to the dignity of supporting a Board of Aldermen,
but they had a sort of semi-responsible body of Trustees and a
Mayor. And also an entirely responsible but inefficient police
force consisting of a constable. Their streets were crowded with

stores and shops, and the stores and shops were thronged with hurrying, excited customers.

BOOMERANG — PRESENT.

Behold the Boomerang of to-day! Where the stream formerly swarmed with bearded miners, five skinny, long-tailed Chinamen shovel and sluice starvation wages out of the poverty-stricken banks of pebbles. Where splendid saloons once collected the cheerful multitudes to gamble and drink and carve each other, a solitary, dilapidated gin-mill gapes hungrily for customers and finds them not. There are no banquets, no ten-pins, no balls, in Boomerang to-day. Dejected stragglers mope where grand processions marched before; and they invoke the ghost of their departed splendor in inexpensive gin, and pop their patriotism from an anvil on the Fourth of July. They have no newspaper and no telegraph, and the railroad is a forgotten dream. The Board of Trustees have wandered to distant lands, and the inefficient constable is dead. The streets that were crowded with stores and shops are desolate, and the throngs that bought and sold in them have gone away toward the rising sun. Lo! thy pride is humbled, thy hopes are blighted, the day of thy glory hath departed, and thy history is even as the history of a human life, O Boomerang!

Well, you can hardly realize such extraordinary changes. Yonder is a dwelling house that was new and rather handsome ten years ago, and cost five thousand dollars unfurnished. The owner would take two hundred and fifty for it to-day. Here is a house that once had a piano in it, and also a young lady. A piano and a young lady where now is nought but a wide-spread epidemic of unpainted old tenements, surrounded by discouraged gardens reveling in weeds!

Town-lots in Boomerang were once sold by the front foot and at extravagant prices, but now they are offered by the acre and not sold at all.

At the very same restaurant in Boomerang where men once feasted on costly imported delicacies and stimulated their appetites with rich foreign wines, you must put up with beans and bacon, now, and wash them down with muddy coffee.

The sole remaining saloon is kept by a man who tries honestly to make a living out of his own custom, because he has no other to speak of. True, Calvin Smith used to come down from Horsefly once a month and get drunk, but here lately he has grown so irregular that there is no dependence to be placed in him. The saloon-keeper awoke to this fact too late and couldn't sell out, because Smith's custom constituted the "good-will" of the concern, and who would buy a gin-mill whose good-will was so manifestly irregular as this?

The single billiard table in that saloon is a relic of former times. The "counters" are so fly-blown that you cannot tell the white string from the black one; the table-cover is faded, and threadbare, and is patched in a dozen places; one of the pockets is bottomless; the cues are warped like willow fishing-rods and the leathers on them are worn as hard and smooth as trunk-nails; if you get the "warp" of your cue right, you stand some chance of getting your "English" on the side you want it on—but if you don't you can depend on accomplishing the reverse; none but old citizens who have stuck to the town and "kept the hang" of those cues from the first can hit the balls with them at all, I think—or at any rate do it every time without fail. Concerning the balls I may say that to an outsider there is no perceptible difference between them as to color; true, there *is* a bare suspicion of red on two of them, but if you look fixedly at the other two you will infallibly imagine there is a suspicion of red on them also, and so when strangers play the ruined and melancholy bar-keeper will come forward from time to time, as necessity requires, and decide with unspeakable solemnity which is the "dark red," and which the "pale," and which is the "spot" ball and which isn't, and then retire slowly behind his bar with the air of a man who considers human knowledge as vain and little worth when the proud soul is borne down by a royal despair. And if you recklessly hint that the "dark red" of his decision is really the "pale," how his watery eye withers you with its lofty compassion!—as who should say, "I have handled them for fifteen years, poor ignorant worm!" These remarkable balls are chipped and scarred and cracked and blistered beyond all power of conception, and when they are under way they bounce and scamper and clatter as if they had cogs on

them. I never saw a man make a "shot" on that table that he tried
to make, but I did see shots made which Phelan and Kavanaugh
would unhesitatingly pronounce impossible. You might drive
one of those balls against another, for instance; your ball bounds
to the left we will say; it glances from a rough seam in the cloth
and flies back to the right; it staggers against a patch and goes off
to the left again; it gets into a rut in the table and rolls ten inches
in a straight line in defiance of all rules of philosophy to the
contrary; it strikes the angle of a patch and returns to the right
once more, and closes its extraordinary career within half an inch
of the "dark red;" very well, you think you haven't "counted"—
but just as the thought crosses your mind, your ball, which has
only balanced for an instant on one of the warts on its surface,
"keels over" in consequence of a gouged place on its under side,
and touches the "dark red!" There are no miracles like that laid
down in Mr. Phelan's hand-book of billiards.

I seem to have wandered from my subject somewhat. However,
no matter—if your readers can't tell by intuition what a town
looks like which not only tolerates but is perfectly satisfied with
a billiard table like that, it would be a waste of labor on my part to
try to describe it to them intelligibly; and if they can't form a
correct estimate of the enterprise of a community where only
liquor enough is drank to support one barkeeper and that bar-
keeper has to drink that liquor himself, it would be presumption
in me to try to furnish an estimate they could hope to understand.
I am not inspired—let me pass on to

BOOMERANG—FUTURE.

The real wealth of Boomerang is still in the bowels of the earth.
The town is surrounded by a network of the richest gold-bearing
lodes in California—lodes which, when thoroughly opened, will
produce more bullion in six months than the Boomerangers
washed from the gulches in fifteen years. The ancient magnificence of Boomerang will yet return to her with a doubled and
redoubled lustre she dreams not of to-day. But will the disconso-
late barkeeper profit by these things? will the 5 skinny Chinamen
become Mandarins of two tails and inexhaustible cash? will the
seedy stragglers—the gin-soaking, anvil-bursting dreamers—be

exalted and arrayed in the purple and fine linen of the new em-
pire? No—they have sold their birthright for a mess of pottage
and a New York company has bought it. Alas! poor Boomerangers! in the fulness of time you will wake up some day and be
astonished!

Angel's Camp Constable

I WAS TOLD that if I would mention any of the venerable Simon Wheeler's pet heroes casually, he would be sure to tell me all about them, but that I must not laugh during the recital, as he would think I was making fun of them, and it would give him mortal offense. I was fortified with the names of some of these admired personages.

So, after some little unimportant conversation, I said:

"There was formerly a constable here by the name of Bilge-water, who attained to considerable eminence, and whom I have frequently heard of in various parts of the world—did you know him?"

The old gentleman oozed gratified vanity at every pore, but its expression took no more enthusiastic form. Nothing could seduce him from his unsmiling mien or force any enthusiasm into the smooth monotony of his voice.

"Yes, I knew that feller," said he; "I knew him as well as I know my own wife. Him and me was always friends, and very particular friends, too, as I may say. He was constable here for as much as three years, and I think he could have been constable yet, but they'd heard of him in New York, I reckon, and I s'pose they wanted him there, and so he went. And he was right. There warn't business enough here for a man of his talents, though what there was he made the most of. He always liked to have people pay him a good deal of respect, and he liked to have them call things belonging to his line by big names, and there he was right again—because to be a constable, and the only constable in the deestrict besides, is a position that most any man would be proud of, there's no getting around that. So he made the most of what business there was. He would come down in the morning and knock around here all day long for a week, laying for a riot, or an insurrection—because that was what he called it when fellers would get to fighting—he never called fights rows, or fracases, or such names. There warn't anything small about him—names nor anything. Well, may be about the end of the week a couple of the boys would get at it, and he'd wade in and break it up—he always broke it up rough. And always when any thing like that happened, he'd swear his boots was new and that he wore 'em out on that occasion.

"I see him one day with his eye on a nigger and an Irishman that was quarreling, though he didn't appear to be noticing of 'em. By-and-bye they got at it and Bilgewater sung out angry-like, 'Hell, here's another riot,' run out and says, 'In the name of the constable of this deestrict, I command the peace'—and he give the Irishman a terrible kick with his right foot and the nigger another with his left and then knocked 'em endways with his fist as they fell. That was the end of that business, you know.

"Then Bilgewater looked at his boots and they was ripped open, and he says "Nother pair of boots busted; dang my cats if I ever put down an insurrection but what I've got to lose a pair of boots by it.' And so he took them two fellers before the Squire and charged them with being engaged in a riot, and made a speech and showed his boots to the court and got them fined forty dollars apiece.

"Well, when he'd got through with one of them cases, he'd come down to the horse-trough here in front of the hotel to wash his face, and everybody'd crowd around, and one would dip out some water for him and another'd hold the towel, and a dozen would ask him what was up. Bilgewater would look sour and seem to be disgusted, and say, 'O damn such a place as this—keeps a man on the go, all the time—and what thanks does he get for it, I'd like to know? Riots—hell, there ain't a day that there ain't a riot. What have I been doing now? What do you s'pose I've been doing but putting down another d—d insurrection? But I reckon it ain't no work to do that?—Oh, no—certainly not—an insurrection ain't anything to put down—Oh, I'm surprised at myself for thinking so, for a minute—humph! why bless you, it's play—certainly, that's what it is, it's play. Well, it may be play for some, but as for me, play or no play, if this rioting is going to go on this way much longer, *I'm* not going to be constable, that's all.' But you see, he always talked that way because I s'pose he knowed he was the quickest and the handiest man about busting up a riot that had ever been in the camp. I wonder what they think of him in New York. There's one thing certain—if they see him snatch a riot once they'll conclude pretty quick that he's no slouch.'

Jim Smiley and His Jumping Frog

Mr. A. Ward,

Dear Sir:—Well, I called on good-natured, garrulous old Simon
Wheeler, and I inquired after your friend Leonidas W. Smiley, as
you requested me to do, and I hereunto append the result. If you
can get any information out of it you are cordially welcome to it. I
have a lurking suspicion that your Leonidas W. Smiley is a
myth—that you never knew such a personage, and that you only
conjectured that if I asked old Wheeler about him it would remind
him of his infamous *Jim* Smiley, and he would go to work and
bore me nearly to death with some infernal reminiscence of him
as long and tedious as it should be useless to me. If that was your
design, Mr. Ward, it will gratify you to know that it succeeded.

I found Simon Wheeler dozing comfortably by the bar-room
stove of the little old dilapidated tavern in the ancient mining
camp of Boomerang, and I noticed that he was fat and bald-
headed, and had an expression of winning gentleness and simplicity upon his tranquil countenance. He roused up and gave me
good-day. I told him a friend of mine had commissioned me to
make some inquiries about a cherished companion of his boyhood
named Leonidas W. Smiley—Rev. Leonidas W. Smiley—a young
minister of the gospel, who he had heard was at one time a resident of this village of Boomerang. I added that if Mr. Wheeler
could tell me anything about this Rev. Leonidas W. Smiley, I
would feel under many obligations to him.

Simon Wheeler backed me into a corner and blockaded me there with his chair—and then sat down and reeled off the monotonous narrative which follows this paragraph. He never smiled, he never frowned, he never changed his voice from the quiet, gently-flowing key to which he turned the initial sentence, he never betrayed the slightest suspicion of enthusiasm—but all through the interminable narrative there ran a vein of impressive earnestness and sincerity, which showed me plainly that so far from his imagining that there was anything ridiculous or funny about his story, he regarded it as a really important matter, and admired its two heroes as men of transcendent genius in finesse. To me, the spectacle of a man drifting serenely along through such a queer yarn without ever smiling was exquisitely absurd. As I said before, I asked him to tell me what he knew of Rev. Leonidas W. Smiley, and he replied as follows. I let him go on in his own way, and never interrupted him once:

There was a feller here once by the name of *Jim* Smiley, in the winter of '49—or maybe it was the spring of '50—I don't recollect exactly, some how, though what makes me think it was one or the other is because I remember the big flume wasn't finished when he first come to the camp; but anyway, he was the curiosest man about always betting on anything that turned up you ever see, if he could get anybody to bet on the other side, and if he couldn't he'd change sides—any way that suited the other man would suit *him*—any way just so's he got a bet, *he* was satisfied. But still, he was lucky—uncommon lucky; he most always come out winner. He was always ready and laying for a chance; there couldn't be no solitry thing mentioned but what that feller'd offer to bet on it—and take any side you please, as I was just telling you: if there was a horse race, you'd find him flush or you find him busted at the end of it; if there was a dog-fight, he'd bet on it; if there was a cat-fight, he'd bet on it; if there was a chicken-fight, he'd bet on it; why if there was two birds setting on a fence, he would bet you which one would fly first—or if there was a camp-meeting he would be there reglar to bet on parson Walker, which he judged to be the best exhorter about here, and so he was, too, and a good man; if he even see a straddle-bug start to go any wheres, he would bet you how long it would take him to get wherever he was going to, and if you took him up he would foller that straddle-bug to Mexico but what he would find out where he was bound for and how long he was on the road. Lots of the boys here has seen that Smiley and can tell you about him. Why, it never made no difference to *him*—he would bet on *anything*—the dangdest feller. Parson Walker's wife laid very sick, once, for a good while, and it seemed as if they warn't going to save her; but one morning he come in and Smiley asked him how she was, and he said she was considerable better—thank the Lord for his inf'nit mercy—and coming on so smart that with the blessing of Providence she'd get well yet—and Smiley, before he thought, says, "Well, I'll resk two-and-a-half that she don't, anyway."

Thish-yer Smiley had a mare—the boys called her the fifteen-minute nag, but that was only in fun, you know, because, of course, she was faster than that—and he used to win money on that horse, for all she was so slow and always had the asthma, or the distemper, or the consumption, or something of that kind. They used to give her two or three hundred yards' start, and then pass her under way; but always at the fag-end of the race she'd get excited and desperate-like, and come cavorting and spraddling up, and scattering her legs around limber, sometimes in the air, and sometimes out to one side amongst the fences, and kicking up m-o-r-e dust, and raising m-o-r-e racket with her coughing and sneezing and blowing her nose—and always fetch up at the stand just about a neck ahead, as near as you could cipher it down.

And he had a little small bull-pup, that to look at him you'd think he warn't worth a cent, but to set around and look ornery, and lay for a chance to steal something. But as soon as money was up on him he was a different dog—his under-jaw'd begin to stick out like the for'castle of a steamboat, and his teeth would un-cover, and shine savage like the furnaces. And a dog might tackle him, and bully-rag him, and bite him, and throw him over his shoulder two or three times, and Andrew Jackson—which was the name of the pup—Andrew Jackson would never let on but what he was satisfied, and hadn't expected nothing else—and the bets being doubled and doubled on the other side all the time, till the money was all up—and then all of a sudden he would grab that other dog just by the joint of his hind legs and freeze to it—not chaw, you understand, but only just grip and hang on till they throwed up the sponge, if it was a year. Smiley always came out winner on that pup till he harnessed a dog once that didn't have no hind legs, because they'd been sawed off in a circular saw, and when the thing had gone along far enough, and the money was all up, and he came to make a snatch for his pet holt, he saw in a minute how he'd been imposed on, and how the other dog had him in the door, so to speak, and he 'peared surprised, and then he looked sorter discouraged like, and didn't try no more to win the fight, and so he got shucked out bad. He gave Smiley a look as much as to say his heart was broke, and it was *his* fault, for putting up a dog that hadn't no hind legs for him to take holt of, which was his main dependence in a fight, and then he limped off a piece, and laid down and died. It was a good pup, was that Andrew Jackson, and would have made a name for hisself if he'd lived, for the stuff was in him, and he had genius—I know it, because he hadn't had no opportunities to speak of, and it don't stand to reason that a dog could make such a fight as he could under them circumstances, if he hadn't no talent. It always makes me feel sorry when I think of that last fight of his'on, and the way it turned out.

Well, thish-yer Smiley had rat-terriers and chicken cocks, and tom-cats, and all them kind of things, till you couldn't rest, and you couldn't fetch nothing for him to bet on but he'd match you. He ketched a frog one day and took him home and said he cal'lated to educate him; and so he never done nothing for three months but set in his back yard and learn that frog to jump. And you bet you he *did* learn him, too. He'd give him a little hunch behind, and the next minute you'd see that frog whirling in the air like a doughnut—see him turn one summerset, or maybe a couple, if he got a good start, and come down flat-footed and all right, like a cat. He got him up so in the matter of ketching flies, and kept him in practice so constant, that he'd nail a fly every time as far as he could see him. Smiley said all a frog wanted was education, and he could do most anything—and I believe him. Why, I've seen him set Dan'l Webster down here on this floor— Dan'l Webster was the name of the frog—and sing out, "Flies! Dan'l, flies," and quicker'n you could wink, he'd spring straight up, and snake a fly off'n the counter there, and flop down on the floor again as solid as a gob of mud, and fall to scratching the side of his head with his hind foot as indifferent as if he hadn't no idea he'd done any more'n any frog might do. You never see a frog so modest and straightfor'ard as he was, for all he was so gifted. And when it come to fair-and-square jumping on a dead level, he could get over more ground at one straddle than any animal of his breed you ever see. Jumping on a dead level was his strong suit, you understand, and when it come to that, Smiley would ante up money on him as long as he had a red. Smiley was monstrous proud of his frog, and well he might be, for fellers that had travelled and ben everywheres all said he laid over any frog that ever *they* see.

Well, Smiley kept the beast in a little lattice box, and he used to fetch him down town sometimes and lay for a bet. One day a feller—a stranger in the camp, he was—come across him with his box, and says:

"What might it be that you've got in the box?"

And Smiley says, sorter indifferent like, "It might be a parrot, or it might be a canary, maybe, but it ain't—it's only just a frog."

And the feller took it, and looked at it careful, and turned it round this way and that, and says, "H'm—so 'tis. Well, what's *he* good for?"

"Well," Smiley says, easy and careless, "He's good enough for *one* thing I should judge—he can out-jump ary frog in Calaveras county."

The feller took the box again, and took another long, particular look, and give it back to Smiley and says, very deliberate, "Well —I don't see no points about that frog that's any better'n any other frog."

"Maybe you don't," Smiley says. "Maybe you understand frogs, and maybe you don't understand 'em; maybe you've had experience, and maybe you ain't only a amature, as it were. Anyways, I've got *my* opinion, and I'll resk forty dollars that he can outjump ary frog in Calaveras county."

And the feller studied a minute, and then says, kinder sad, like, "Well—I'm only a stranger here, and I ain't got no frog—but if I had a frog I'd bet you."

And then Smiley says, "That's all right—that's all right—if you'll hold my box a minute I'll go and get you a frog;" and so the feller took the box, and put up his forty dollars along with Smiley's, and set down to wait.

So he set there a good while thinking and thinking to hisself, and then he got the frog out and prized his mouth open and took a teaspoon and filled him full of quail-shot—filled him pretty near up to his chin—and set him on the floor. Smiley he went out to the swamp and slopped around in the mud for a long time, and finally he ketched a frog and fetched him in and give him to this feller and says:

"Now if you're ready, set him alongside of Dan'l, with his fore-paws just even with Dan'l's, and I'll give the word." Then he says, "one—two—three—jump!" and him and the feller touched up the frogs from behind, and the new frog hopped off lively, but Dan'l give a heave, and hysted up his shoulders—so—like a Frenchman, but it wasn't no use—he couldn't budge; he was planted as solid as a anvil, and he couldn't no more stir than if he was anchored out. Smiley was a good deal surprised, and he was disgusted too, but he didn't have no idea what the matter was, of course.

The feller took the money and started away, and when he was going out at the door he sorter jerked his thumb over his shoulder—this way—at Dan'l, and says again, very deliberate, "Well—*I* don't see no points about that frog that's any better'n any other frog."

Smiley he stood scratching his head and looking down at Dan'l a long time, and at last he says, "I do wonder what in the nation that frog throwed off for—I wonder if there ain't something the matter with him—he 'pears to look mighty baggy, somehow"—and he ketched Dan'l by the nap of the neck, and lifted him up and says, "Why blame my cats if he don't weigh five pound"—and turned him upside down, and he belched out about a double-handful of shot. And then he see how it was, and he was the maddest man—he set the frog down and took out after that feller, but he never ketched him. And——

[Here Simon Wheeler heard his name called from the front-yard, and got up to go and see what was wanted.] And turning to me as he moved away, he said: "Just sit where you are, stranger, and rest easy—I ain't going to be gone a second."

But by your leave, I did not think that a continuation of the history of the enterprising vagabond Jim Smiley would be likely to afford me much information concerning the Rev. Leonidas W. Smiley, and so I started away.

At the door I met the sociable Wheeler returning, and he buttonholed me and recommenced:

"Well, thish-yer Smiley had a yaller one-eyed cow that didn't have no tail only just a short stump like a bannanner, and——"

"O, curse Smiley and his afflicted cow!" I muttered, good-naturedly, and bidding the old gentleman good-day, I departed.

Yours, truly,

MARK TWAIN.

§ 120   The Cruel Earthquake

10–11 October 1865

Clemens published four sketches about the San Francisco earthquake that took place on 8 October 1865: two of these survive in fragments reprinted by the western press, and two survive in their original printings. "The Cruel Earthquake" originally appeared in the Virginia City *Territorial Enterprise* on about October 10 or 11. It survives only in the Gold Hill *News*, which reprinted it on October 13, introducing the extract as follows: "That funny cuss, Mark Twain, who, when his last hour shall arrive, will probably laugh grim Death out of countenance, writes to the *Enterprise* the following funny incidents which occurred in San Francisco last Sunday."

In the fuller account preserved in "The Great Earthquake in San Francisco" (no. 123), Clemens timed the first shock at 12:48 P.M. The tremor rocked buildings and shattered windows and walls, not only in San Francisco but in Santa Cruz, San José, and other towns along the California coast. For several days afterward newspapers carried statistic-laden accounts of the damage as well as anecdotes like those that Clemens recorded for the *Enterprise.* The distinction of his accounts was, as the Gold Hill *News* observed, their remarkable ability to inspire laughter even in the face of "grim Death." Clemens had, in fact, been exploiting the comic possibilities of earthquakes ever since 1864, when he regularly reported on them for the San Francisco *Morning Call.*[1] Earthquakes and the damage they caused were, on the one hand, a "luxury . . . for the morning papers" (as he said in "The Great Earthquake"). On the other hand, they were a natural opportunity for a comic journalist. By personifying earthquakes, or simply by treating them as an expression of supernatural intelligence, Clemens playfully mocked those who ordinarily claimed to speak for that intelligence, like the Reverend Horatio

---

[1]See "The Supernatural Boot-Jack" section in *CofC,* pp. 39–42, and Appendix A, volume 2.

Stebbins and the Reverend Mr. Harmon. And by a sustained use of the reporter's deadpan manner, he made fun of ordinary people—including himself—whose presence of mind and pretensions to courage were severely tested by this natural premonition of ultimate doom.

The Cruel Earthquake

SINGULAR EFFECTS OF THE SHOCK
ON THE REV. MR. STEBBINS.

Now THE Rev. Mr. Stebbins acted like a sensible man—a man with his presence of mind about him—he did precisely what I thought of doing myself at the time of the earthquake, but had no opportunity—he came down out of his pulpit and embraced a woman. Some say it was his wife. Well, and so it might have been his wife—I'm not saying it wasn't, am I? I am not going to intimate anything of that kind—because how do *I* know but what it *was* his wife? I say it might have been his wife—and so it might—I was not there, and I do not consider that I have any right to say it was not his wife. In reality I am satisfied it *was* his wife—but I am sorry, though, because it would have been so much better presence of mind to have embraced some other woman. I was in Third street. I looked around for some woman to embrace, but there was none in sight. I could have expected no better fortune, though, so I said, "O certainly—just my luck."

A SINGULAR ILLUSTRATION.

When the earthquake arrived in Oakland, the commanding officer of the Congregational Sabbath School was reading these words, by way of text: "And the earth shook and trembled!" In an instant the earthquake seized the text and preached a powerful sermon on it. I do not know whether the commanding officer resumed the subject again where the earthquake left off or not, but if he did I am satisfied that he has got a good deal of "cheek." I do not consider that any modest man would try to improve on a topic that had already been treated by an earthquake.

A MODEL ARTIST STRIKES AN ATTITUDE.

A young gentleman who lives in Sacramento street, rushed down stairs and appeared in public with no raiment on save a knit undershirt, which concealed his person about as much as its tin-foil cap conceals a champagne bottle. He struck an attitude such as a man assumes when he is looking up, expecting danger from above, and bends his arm and holds it aloft to ward off possible missiles—and standing thus he glared fiercely up at the fire-wall of a tall building opposite, from which a few bricks had fallen. Men shouted at him to go in the house, people seized him by the arm and tried to drag him away—even tender-hearted women, (O, Woman!—O ever noble, unselfish, angelic woman!—O, Woman, in our hours of ease uncertain, coy, and hard to please—when anything happens to go wrong with our harness, a ministering angel thou), women, I say, averted their faces, and nudging the paralyzed and impassible statue in the ribs with their elbows beseeched him to take their aprons—to take their shawls—to take their hoop-skirts—anything, anything, so that he would not stand there longer in such a plight and distract people's attention from the earthquake. But he wouldn't budge—he stood there in his naked majesty till the last tremor died away from the earth, and then looked around on the multitude—and stupidly enough, too, until his dull eye fell upon himself. He went back up stairs, then. He went up lively.

WHAT HAPPENED TO A FEW VIRGINIANS—
CHARLEY BRYAN CLIMBS A TELEGRAPH POLE.

But where is the use in dwelling on these incidents? There are enough of them to make a book. Joe Noques, of your city, was playing billiards in the Cosmopolitan Hotel. He went through a window into the court and then jumped over an iron gate eighteen feet high, and took his billiard cue with him. Sam Witgenstein took refuge in a church—probably the first time he was ever in one in his life. Judge Bryan climbed a telegraph pole. Pete Hopkins narrowly escaped injury. He was shaken abruptly from the summit of Telegraph Hill and fell on a three-story brick house ten feet below. I see that the morning papers (always ready to smooth over things), attribute the destruction of the house to the earthquake. That is newspaper magnanimity—but an earthquake has no friends. Extraordinary things happened to everybody except me. No one even spoke to me—at least only one man did, I believe —a man named Robinson—from Salt Lake, I think—who asked me to take a drink. I refused.

§ 121. *Popper Defieth Ye Earthquake*

15–31 October 1865

This sketch survives in a damaged clipping from an unidentified newspaper in the Yale Scrapbook. The last line of the clipping reads "my last shake.—MARK TWAIN, in the E," indicating that the sketch originally appeared in one of Clemens' daily letters to the Virginia City *Territorial Enterprise,* and that the clipping itself is a reprinting of the *Enterprise,* which is lost. The letter was written long enough after the earthquake of 8 October 1865 for Popper to have begun reconstruction of his building, but probably before the end of the month: on October 29 the San Francisco *Alta California* noted that the front of Popper's building had been repaired to the top of the second story and that "in a week or two, nothing will be left there to show the effects of the earthquake"; [1] and one of Clemens' remarks ("Popper is rebuilding it again just as thin as it was before") suggests that restoration was not yet complete when he made his observations. The original letter could therefore have appeared in the *Enterprise* at any time between October 15 and 31, or even somewhat later.

L. Popper's four-story brick building, under construction at Third and Mission streets, became the "greatest wreck" resulting from the earthquake. On October 14 the San Francisco *News Letter and Pacific Mining Journal* published a dramatic drawing of the structure at the moment of its collapse. [2] Clemens himself said he witnessed its destruction in "The Great Earthquake in San Francisco" (no. 123), noting there that "the walls were only three bricks thick, a fact which, taking into account

---

[1] "Popper's Building," San Francisco *Alta California,* 29 October 1865, p. 1.
[2] "The Earthquake of Sunday," San Francisco *Morning Call,* 10 October 1865, p. 1; San Francisco *News Letter and Pacific Mining Journal* 15 (14 October 1865): 12.

the earthquakiness of the country, evinces an unquestioning trust in Providence, on the part of the proprietor, which is as gratifying as it is impolitic and reckless." Despite Clemens' skepticism, however, a committee of architects selected to examine the damaged building and approve plans for its reconstruction observed that "the injury was confined solely to the front" and that the "reconstruction of the front, and interior work in connection therewith, will render the structure secure and reliable."[3] It is not known whether Clemens or the architects proved more correct in their predictions.

The present text must be treated with caution: the last two sentences have been editorially conjectured on the basis of fragments too small to guarantee accuracy. Discovery of another reprinting or of the *Enterprise* itself would almost certainly correct the text provided here.[4]

---

[3]"Popper's Building," San Francisco *Morning Call*, 5 November 1865, p. 1.
[4]For details, see the textual commentary.

Popper Defieth Ye Earthquake

Where's Ajax now, with his boasted defiance of the lightning? Who is Ajax to Popper, and what is lightning to an earthquake? It is taking no chances to speak of to defy the lightning, for it might pelt away at you for a year and miss you every time—but I don't care what corner you hide in, if the earthquake comes it will shake you; and if you will build your house weak enough to give it a fair show, it will melt it down like butter. Therefore, I exalt Popper above Ajax, for Popper defieth the earthquake. The famous shake of the 8th of October snatched the front out of Popper's great four-story shell of a house on the corner of Third and Mission as easily as if it had been mere pastime; yet I notice that the reckless Popper is rebuilding it again just as thin as it was before, and using the same old bricks. Is this paying proper respect to earthquakes? I think not. If I were an earthquake, I would never stand for such insolence from Popper. I am confident that I would shake that shell down, even if it took my last shake.

§ 122. Earthquake Almanac

17 October 1865

This sketch was published in the San Francisco *Dramatic Chronicle* on 17 October 1865, two days before Clemens wrote to Orion: "The Dramatic Chronicle pays me—or rather *will* begin to pay me, next week—$40 a month for dramatic criticisms." Unlike "Enthusiastic Eloquence" (no. 111), which Clemens had published there in late June, the present sketch was probably written as part of a concerted effort to get out of debt.[1]

Drawing on the obvious public interest in the earthquake of October 8, Clemens spoofed the sententious weather forecasts to be found in almanacs, medical or otherwise. Patent medicine almanacs had begun to appear in about the mid-1840s and were soon commonplace, usually being given away free by drugstores in the months before Christmas. While Clemens was a local reporter in Virginia City, for instance, Morrill's Drug Store advertised its large supply of medical almanacs free for the asking. In addition to astrological forecasts, phases of the moon and positions of the planets, and miscellaneous advice and remedies, these almanacs often included pithy notes about the expected weather for each day of the month. Clemens' burlesque effectively caught their gnomic, all-wise tone, while adding a touch of the doomsday atmosphere he liked to project onto the San Francisco earthquakes.

Either Clemens or Charles Henry Webb decided to reprint this sketch as "A Page from a Californian Almanac" in the 1867 *Jumping Frog* book. But even though Clemens revised and again reprinted the piece in 1872, in 1873 he declined to reprint it, telling Andrew Chatto to "leave out this puling imbecility."[2] It was not subsequently reprinted.

---

[1]Clemens to Orion and Mollie Clemens, 19–20 October 1865, *CL1*, letter 95. As the letter to Orion shows, his reason for assuming the added burden of the *Chronicle* job was to get out of debt. For a sampling of the work he contributed to the *Chronicle* in this period, see Appendix B, volume 2.

[2]See the textual commentary.

Earthquake Almanac

EDS. CHRONICLE:—At the instance of several friends who feel a boding anxiety to know beforehand what sort of phenomena we may expect the elements to exhibit during the next month or two, and who have lost all confidence in the various patent medicine almanacs, because of the unaccountable reticence of those works concerning the extraordinary event of the 8th inst., I have compiled the following almanac expressly for this latitude:

Oct. 17.—Weather hazy; atmosphere murky and dense. An expression of profound melancholy will be observable upon most countenances.

Oct. 18.—Slight earthquake. Countenances grow more melancholy.

Oct. 19.—Look out for rain. It would be absurd to look in for it. The general depression of spirits increased.

Oct. 20.—More weather.

Oct. 21.—Same.

Oct. 22.—Light winds, perhaps. If they blow, it will be from the "east'ard, or the nor'ard, or the west'ard, or the suth'ard," or from some general direction approximating more or less to these points of the compass or otherwise. Winds are uncertain—more especially when they blow from whence they cometh and whither they listeth. N. B.—Such is the nature of winds.

Oct. 23.—Mild, balmy earthquakes.

Oct. 24.—Shaky.

Oct. 25.—Occasional shakes, followed by light showers of bricks and plastering. N. B.—Stand from under.

Oct. 26.—Considerable phenomenal atmospheric foolishness. About this time expect more earthquakes, but do not look out for them, on account of the bricks.

Oct. 27.—Universal despondency, indicative of approaching disaster. Abstain from smiling, or indulgence in humorous conversation, or exasperating jokes.

Oct. 28.—Misery, dismal forebodings and despair. Beware of all light discourse—a joke uttered at this time would produce a popular outbreak.

Oct. 29.—Beware!

Oct. 30.—Keep dark!

Oct. 31.—Go slow!

Nov. 1.—Terrific earthquake. This is the great earthquake month. More stars fall and more worlds are slathered around carelessly and destroyed in November than in any other month of the twelve.

Nov. 2.—Spasmodic but exhilarating earthquakes, accompanied by occasional showers of rain, and churches and things.

Nov. 3.—Make your will.

Nov. 4.—Sell out.

Nov. 5.—Select your "last words." Those of John Quincy Adams will do, with the addition of a syllable, thus: "This is the last of earth-quakes."

Nov. 6.—Prepare to shed this mortal coil.

Nov. 7.—Shed!

Nov. 8.—The sun will rise as usual, perhaps; but if he does he will doubtless be staggered some to find nothing but a large round hole eight thousand miles in diameter in the place where he saw this world serenely spinning the day before.

MARK TWAIN.

§123. *The Great Earthquake in San Francisco*

25 November 1865

On 20 January 1866, two months after this sketch appeared in the New York *Weekly Review* and three weeks after Bret Harte stepped down as editor of the *Californian,* Clemens wrote his family that both he and Harte had "quit the 'Californian.' He will write for a Boston paper hereafter, and I for the 'New York Weekly Review'—and possibly for the 'Saturday Press' sometimes. I am too lazy to write oftener than once a month, though."[1] This was an optimistic estimate of his future contributions to the *Review.* Only two further original contributions appeared there in 1866: "An Open Letter to the American People" (no. 181) on February 17, and "How, for Instance?" (no. 192) on September 29. In addition, however, the editors of the *Review* reprinted five sketches from the *Californian.*

It is not clear by what means Clemens gained access to the columns of the relatively distinguished *Review.* Nevertheless, it is probably significant that on 25 February 1865 the *Californian* had reported a change in the *Review's* editorial staff:

We see it stated that Henry Clapp, Jr., "Figaro," formerly of the *Leader,* Edward H. House, of the *Tribune,* and William Winter ("Mercutio," of the *Albion,*) three of the ablest dramatic critics in the country, are all writers for Mr. C. B. Seymour's new weekly paper, entitled the New York *Review.*[2]

---

[1]Clemens to Jane Clemens and Pamela Moffett, 20 January 1866, *CL1,* letter 97.
[2]*Californian* 2 (25 February 1865): 5. The editor at this time was Charles Henry Webb.

And in the same issue of the *Californian* the New York correspondent reported that "the *Leader* (weekly newspaper) has lately split in half, and one party, under Henry Clapp, has gone over to the *Weekly Review,* taking 'Figaro' and 'McArone' along with them."[3] In view of Henry Clapp's position as editor of the New York *Saturday Press* and his role in publishing the "Jumping Frog" sketch, his connection with the *Review* suggests that he may also have been instrumental in arranging the publication of "The Great Earthquake in San Francisco." Both sketches must have been sent to New York in the same steamer, for on November 18 (the day the "Jumping Frog" appeared) the *Review* announced that its next issue would carry "a contribution from the sprightly pen of MARK TWAIN, one of the cleverest of the San Francisco writers."[4] Paul J. Carter, who first identified this sketch, has pointed out that the *Review* had quite serious pretensions to literary merit.[5] It seems possible that Clapp, who was evidently pleased with the "Jumping Frog," now helped Clemens to reach a larger and more highbrow audience through the columns of that journal.

"The Great Earthquake" is Clemens' fullest account of the 8 October 1865 earthquake, although it is possible that his *Enterprise* letters (nos. 120 and 121) were originally as full or fuller. Recognizing the appeal of the extraordinary but true story, especially for eastern readers, Clemens dated his sketch October 8, the day of the earthquake, in order to help create the illusion of on-the-spot reporting. But it is clear that several days had passed before he wrote the sketch. It is ambitious and carefully composed, and it manifestly builds upon details that he used in his *Enterprise* letters as well. Moreover, it draws on anecdotes and facts gleaned from other newspaper accounts, and probably gathers in some of the "toothsome gossip" (as Clemens called it in *Roughing It*)[6] which amused San Franciscans for days after the event. When the earth shook, Clemens was in fact close to the center of the greatest damage—at Mission and Third streets—and observed the partial collapse of Popper's building there. It was a stroke of reporter's luck which he turned to good advantage: his report succeeded in conveying a sense of immediate presence and authenticity, more than any other contemporary account we have

---

[3]"Atlantic Gossip," a letter from New York dated 18 January 1865 and signed "Desultory," *Californian* 2 (25 February 1865): 8–9.

[4]New York *Weekly Review,* 18 November 1865, p. 5; see the headnote to "Three Versions of the Jumping Frog" (nos. 117–119).

[5]Paul J. Carter, "Mark Twain Describes a San Francisco Earthquake," *PMLA* 72 (December 1957): 997–1004.

[6]*RI,* p. 376.

seen. He strung his anecdotes and detailed observations on the story line of his personal progress through the city streets, convincingly projecting the voice of someone who had been there. This piece constitutes some of the best comic journalism Clemens ever published, and was one of the sources he would eventually use in his account of the earthquake in chapter 58 of *Roughing It*.

The Great Earthquake in San Francisco

SAN FRANCISCO, Oct. 8, 1865.
EDITORS REVIEW.

Long before this reaches your city, the telegraph will have mentioned to you, casually, that San Francisco was visited by an earthquake to-day, and the daily prints will have conveyed the news to their readers with the same air of indifference with which it was clothed by the unimpassioned lightning, and five minutes afterward the world will have forgotten the circumstance, under the impression that just such earthquakes are every-day occurrences here, and therefore not worth remembering. But if you had been here you would have conceived very different notions from these. To-day's earthquake was no ordinary affair. It is likely that future earthquakes in this vicinity, for years to come, will suffer by comparison with it.

I have tried a good many of them here, and of several varieties—some that came in the form of a universal shiver; others that gave us two or three sudden upward heaves from below; others that swayed grandly and deliberately from side to side; and still others that came rolling and undulating beneath our feet like a great wave of the sea. But to-day's specimen belonged to a new, and, I hope, a very rare, breed of earthquakes. First, there was a quick, heavy shock; three or four seconds elapsed, and then the city and county of San Francisco darted violently from north-west to south-east, and from south-east to north-west five times with extraordinary energy and rapidity. I say "darted," because that word comes nearest to describing the movement.

I was walking along Third street, and facing north, when the first shock came; I was walking fast, and it "broke up my gait" pretty completely—checked me—just as a strong wind will do when you turn a corner and face it suddenly. That shock was coming from the north-west, and I met it half-way. I took about six or seven steps (went back and measured the distance afterwards to decide a bet about the interval of time between the first and second shocks), and was just turning the corner into Howard street when those five angry "darts" came. I suppose the first of them proceeded from the south-east, because it moved my feet toward the opposite point of the compass—to the left—and made me stagger against the corner house on my right. The noise accompanying the shocks was a tremendous rasping sound, like the violent shaking and grinding together of a block of brick houses. It was about the most disagreeable sound you can imagine.

I will set it down here as a maxim that the operations of the human intellect are much accelerated by an earthquake. Usually I do not think rapidly—but I did upon this occasion. I thought rapidly, vividly, and distinctly. With the first shock of the five, I thought—"I recognize that motion—this is an earthquake." With the second, I thought, "What a luxury this will be for the morning papers." With the third shock, I thought, "Well, my boy, you had better be getting out of this." Each of these thoughts was only the hundredth part of a second in passing through my mind. There is no incentive to rapid reasoning like an earthquake. I then sidled out toward the middle of the street—and I may say that I sidled out with some degree of activity, too. There is nothing like an earthquake to hurry a man up when he starts to go anywhere. As I went I glanced down to my left and saw the whole front of a large four-story brick building spew out and "splatter" abroad over the street in front of it. Another thought steamed through my brain. I thought this was going to be the greatest earthquake of the century, and that the city was going to be destroyed entirely, and I took out my watch and timed the event. It was twelve minutes to one o'clock, P. M. This showed great coolness and presence of mind on my part—most people would have been hunting for something to climb, instead of looking out for the best interests of history.

As I walked down the street—down the middle of the street— frequently glancing up with a sagacious eye at the houses on either side to see which way they were going to fall, I felt the earth shivering gently under me, and grew moderately sea-sick (and remained so for nearly an hour; others became excessively sleepy as well as sea-sick, and were obliged to go to bed, and refresh themselves with a sound nap.) A minute before the earthquake I had three or four streets pretty much to myself, as far as I could see down them (for we are a Sunday-respecting community, and go out of town to break the Sabbath) but five seconds after it I was lost in a swarm of crying children, and coatless, hatless men and shrieking women. They were all in motion, too, and no two of them trying to run in the same direction. They charged simultaneously from opposite rows of houses, like opposing regiments from ambuscades, and came together with a crash and a yell in the centre of the street. Then came chaos and confusion, and a general digging out for somewhere else, they didn't know where, and didn't care.

Everything that *was* done, was done in the twinkling of an eye—there was no apathy visible anywhere. A street car stopped close at hand, and disgorged its passengers so suddenly that they all seemed to flash out at the self-same instant of time.

The crowd was in danger from outside influences for a while. A horse was coming down Third street, with a buggy attached to him, and following after him—either by accident or design—and the horse was either frightened at the earthquake or a good deal surprised—I cannot say which, because I do not know how horses are usually affected by such things—but at any rate he must have been opposed to earthquakes, because he started to leave there, and took the buggy and his master with him, and scattered them over a piece of ground as large as an ordinary park, and finally fetched up against a lamp-post with nothing hanging to him but a few strips of harness suitable for fiddle-strings. However he might have been affected previously, the expression upon his countenance at this time was one of unqualified surprise. The driver of the buggy was found intact and unhurt, but to the last degree dusty and blasphemous. As the crowds along the street had fortunately taken chances on the earthquake and opened out to let the horse pass, no one was injured by his stampede.

When I got to the locality of the shipwrecked four-story building before spoken of, I found that the front of it, from eaves to pavement, had fallen out, and lay in ruins on the ground. The roof and floors were broken down and dilapidated. It was a new structure and unoccupied, and by rare good luck it damaged itself alone by its fall. The walls were only three bricks thick, a fact which, taking into account the earthquakiness of the country, evinces an unquestioning trust in Providence, on the part of the proprietor, which is as gratifying as it is impolitic and reckless.

I turned into Mission street and walked down to Second without finding any evidences of the great ague, but in Second street itself I traveled half a block on shattered window glass. The large hotels, farther down town, were all standing, but the boarders were all in the street. The plastering had fallen in many of the rooms, and a gentleman who was in an attic chamber of the Cosmopolitan at the time of the quake, told me the water "sloshed" out of the great tanks on the roof, and fell in sheets of spray to the court below. He said the huge building rocked like a cradle after the first grand spasms; the walls seemed to "belly" inward like a sail; and flakes of plastering began to drop on him. He then went out and slid, feet foremost down one or two hundred feet of banisters—partly for amusement, but chiefly with an eye to expedition. He said he flashed by the frantic crowds in each succeeding story like a telegraphic dispatch.

Several ladies felt a faintness and dizziness in the head, and one, (incredible as it may seem) weighing over two hundred and fifty pounds, fainted all over. They hauled her out of her room, and deluged her with water, but for nearly half an hour all efforts to resuscitate her were fruitless. It is said that the noise of the earthquake on the ground floor of the hotel, which is paved with marble, was as if forty freight trains were thundering over it. The large billiard saloon in the rear of the office was full of people at the time, but a moment afterward numbers of them were seen flying up the street with their billiard-cues in their hands, like a squad of routed lancers. Three jumped out of a back window into the central court, and found themselves imprisoned—for the tall, spike-armed iron gate which bars the passage-way for coal and provision wagons was locked.

"What did you do then?" I asked.

"Well, Conrad, from Humboldt—you know him—Conrad said, 'let's climb over, boys, and be devilish quick about it, too'—and he made a dash for it—but Smith and me started in last and were first over—because the seat of Conrad's pants caught on the spikes at the top, and we left him hanging there and yelling like an Injun."

And then my friend called my attention to the gate and said: "There's the gate—ten foot high, I should think, and nothing to catch hold of to climb by—but don't you know I went over that gate like a shot out of a shovel, and took my billiard-cue along with me?—I did it, as certain as I am standing here—but if I could do it again for fifteen hundred thousand dollars, I'll be d—d—not unless there was another earthquake, anyway."

From the fashionable barber-shops in the vicinity gentlemen rushed into the thronged streets in their shirt-sleeves, with towels round their necks, and with one side of their faces smoothly shaved, and the other side foamy with lather.

One gentleman was having his corns cut by a barber, when the premonitory shock came. The barber's under-jaw dropped, and he stared aghast at the dancing furniture. The gentleman winked complacently at the by-standers, and said with fine humor, "Oh, go on with your surgery, John—it's nothing but an earthquake; no use to run, you know, because if you're going to the devil anyhow, you might as well start from here as outside." Just then the earth commenced its hideous grinding and surging movement, and the gentleman retreated toward the door, remarking, "However, John, if we've *got* to go, perhaps we'd as well start from the street, after all."

On North Beach, men ran out of the bathing houses attired like the Greek slave, and mingled desperately with ladies and gentlemen who were as badly frightened as themselves, but more elaborately dressed.

The City Hall which is a large building, was so dismembered, and its walls sprung apart from each other, that the structure will doubtless have to be pulled down. The earthquake rang a merry peal on the City Hall bell, the "clapper" of which weighs seventy-eight pounds. It is said that several engine companies turned out, under the impression that the alarm was struck by the fire-telegraph.

Bells of all sorts and sizes were rung by the shake throughout the city, and from what I can learn the earthquake formally announced its visit on every door-bell in town. One gentleman said: "My door-bell fell to ringing violently, but I said to myself, 'I know *you*—you are an Earthquake; and you appear to be in a hurry; but you'll jingle that bell considerably before *I* let you in—on the contrary, I'll crawl under this sofa and get out of the way of the plastering.' "

I went down toward the city front and found a brick warehouse mashed in as if some foreigner from Brobdignag had sat down on it.

All down Battery street the large brick wholesale houses were pretty universally shaken up, and some of them badly damaged, the roof of one being crushed in, and the fire-walls of one or two being ripped off even with the tops of the upper windows, and dumped into the street below.

The tall shot tower in First street weathered the storm, but persons who watched it respectfully from a distance said it swayed to and fro like a drunken giant.

I saw three chimneys which were broken in two about three feet from the top, and the upper sections slewed around until they sat corner-wise on the lower ones.

The damage done to houses by this earthquake is estimated at over half a million of dollars.

But I had rather talk about the "incidents." The Rev. Mr. Harmon, Principal of the Pacific Female Seminary, at Oakland, just across the Bay from here, had his entire flock of young ladies at church—and also his wife and children—and was watching and protecting them jealously, like one of those infernal scaly monsters with a pestilential breath that were employed to stand guard over imprisoned heroines in the days of chivalry, and who always proved inefficient in the hour of danger—he was watching them, I say, when the earthquake came, and what do you imagine he did, then? Why that confiding trust in Providence which had sustained him through a long ministerial career all at once deserted him, and he got up and ran like a quarter-horse. But that was not the misfortune of it. The exasperating feature of it was that his wife and children and all the school-girls remained bravely in their seats and sat the earthquake through without flinching. Oakland talks and laughs again at the Pacific Female Seminary.

The Superintendent of the Congregational Sunday School in Oakland had just given out the text, "And the earth shook and trembled," when the earthquake came along and took up the text and preached the sermon for him.

The Pastor of Starr King's church, the Rev. Mr. Stebbins, came down out of his pulpit after the first shock and embraced a woman. It was an instance of great presence of mind. Some say the woman was his wife, but I regard the remark as envious and malicious. Upon occasions like this, people who are too much scared to seize upon an offered advantage, are always ready to depreciate the superior judgment and sagacity of those who profited by the opportunity they lost themselves.

In a certain aristocratic locality up-town, the wife of a foreign dignitary is the acknowledged leader of fashion, and whenever she emerges from her house all the ladies in the vicinity fly to the windows to see what she has "got on," so that they may make immediate arrangements to procure similar costumes for themselves. Well, in the midst of the earthquake, the beautiful foreign woman (who had just indulged in a bath) appeared in the street *with a towel around her neck.* It was all the raiment she had on. Consequently, in that vicinity, a towel around the neck is considered the only orthodox "earthquake costume." Well, and why not? It is elegant, and airy, and simple, and graceful, and pretty, and are not these the chief requisites in female dress? If it were generally adopted it would go far toward reconciling some people to these dreaded earthquakes.

An enterprising barkeeper down town who is generally up with the times, has already invented a sensation drink to meet the requirements of our present peculiar circumstances. A friend in whom I have confidence, thus describes it to me: "A tall ale-glass is nearly filled with California brandy and Angelica wine—one part of the former to two of the latter; fill to the brim with champagne; charge the drink with electricity from a powerful galvanic battery, and swallow it before the lightning cools. Then march forth—and before you have gone a hundred yards you will think you are occupying the whole street; a parlor clock will look as big as a church; to blow your nose will astonish you like the explosion of a mine, and the most trivial abstract matter will seem as important as the Day of Judgment. When you want this extraordinary drink, disburse your twenty-five cents, and call for an 'EARTHQUAKE.' "

MARK TWAIN.

124. Bob Roach's Plan for Circumventing a Democrat

21–24 October 1865

This sketch was part of Clemens' daily letter to the Virginia City *Territorial Enterprise*. The *Enterprise* printing is lost, and the sketch is preserved only in the San Francisco *Examiner* for 30 November 1865, which attributed it to the *"S. F. Cor. Virginia Enterprise."* Clemens' allusion to the San Francisco city and county elections "yesterday" shows that he wrote the letter on October 19. It was probably published in the *Enterprise* shortly thereafter, between October 21 and 24.

Like "Captain Montgomery" (no. 161), published in the *Enterprise* three months later, this sketch draws upon Clemens' memories of piloting days. Although it cannot now be demonstrated, it seems very likely that Clemens knew Robert Roach, carpenter of the *Aleck Scott* and the alleged author of this grotesque means of "circumventing" Democrats. Clemens' own account in *Life on the Mississippi*, especially chapters 13 through 15, leaves little doubt that he was a cub pilot on the *Aleck Scott*. And certainly he was familiar, by report and by direct experience, with river-bank burials. On 5 June 1851 Orion Clemens' newspaper, the Hannibal *Journal*, reported that steamboats were "burying their passengers at every wood yard, both from cabin and deck," as a result of deaths from cholera. Hannibal itself was especially hard hit by yellow fever during the winter of 1849–1850, and it seems inevitable that Clemens therefore saw this practice.[1]

What Clemens made of these memories and yarns is, of course, something quite unique. It is particularly striking to find him drawing on his recollections of piloting days at this time, for on the day he wrote this

---

[1]Dixon Wecter, *Sam Clemens of Hannibal* (Boston: Houghton Mifflin Co., 1952), p. 214.

letter to the *Enterprise* he also wrote his brother Orion, saying in part that he "never had but two *powerful* ambitions" in life. "One was to be a pilot, & the other a preacher of the gospel."[2] Now that he had at last resolved to give these two ambitions up, he was already turning over the possibility of writing about the first of them.

[2]Clemens to Orion and Mollie Clemens, 19–20 October 1865, *CL1*, letter 95.

Bob Roach's Plan for
Circumventing a Democrat

WHERE DID all these Democrats come from? They grow thicker
and thicker and act more and more outrageously at each succes-
sive election. Now yesterday they had the presumption to elect
S. H. Dwinelle to the Judgeship of the Fifteenth District Court,
and not content with this, they were depraved enough to elect
four out of the six Justices of the Peace! Oh, 'Enery Villiam, where
is thy blush! Oh, Timothy Hooligan, where is thy shame! It's out.
Democrats haven't got any. But Union men staid away from the
election—they either did that or else they came to the election
and voted Democratic tickets—I think it was the latter, though
the *Flag* will doubtless say it was the former. But these Democrats
didn't stay away—you never catch a Democrat staying away from
an election. The grand end and aim of his life is to vote or be voted
for, and he accommodates to circumstances and does one just as
cheerfully as he does the other. The Democracy of America left
their native wilds in England and Connaught to come here and
vote—and when a man, and especially a foreigner, who don't
have any voting at home any more than an Arkansas man has
ice-cream for dinner, comes three or four thousand miles to
luxuriate in occasional voting, he isn't going to stay away from an
election any more than the Arkansas man will leave the hotel
table in "Orleans" until he has destroyed most of the ice cream.
The only man I ever knew who could counteract this passion on
the part of Democrats for voting, was Robert Roach, carpenter of

the steamer Aleck Scott, "plying to and from St. Louis to New Orleans and back," as her advertisement sometimes read. The Democrats generally came up as deck passengers from New Orleans, and the yellow fever used to snatch them right and left— eight or nine a day for the first six or eight hundred miles; consequently Roach would have a lot on hand to "plant" every time the boat landed to wood—"plant" was Roach's word. One day as Roach was superintending a burial the Captain came up and said:

"God bless my soul, Roach, what do you mean by shoving a corpse into a hole in the hill-side in this barbarous way, face down and its feet sticking out?"

"I always plant them foreign Democrats in that manner, sir, because, damn their souls, if you plant 'em any other way they'll dig out and vote the first time there's an election—but look at that fellow, now—you put 'em in head first and face down and the more they dig the deeper they'll go into the hill."

In my opinion, if we do not get Roach to superintend our cemeteries, enough Democrats will dig out at the next election to carry their entire ticket. It begins to look that way.

125. [San Francisco Letter]

26-28 October 1865

Clemens wrote this letter on 24 October 1865, and it was probably published in the Virginia City *Territorial Enterprise* two or three days later. The first section is preserved in the San Francisco *Evening Bulletin*, which reprinted it from the *Enterprise* on October 30, whereas the last two sections are preserved in an undated clipping in the Yale Scrapbook. The scrapbook clipping has been paired with the *Bulletin* extract on the basis of the subheading of the last section, "MORE FASHIONS—EXIT 'WATERFALL,'" which resumes the theme of fashions and hairstyles begun in the first part of the letter. The allusion in the middle section to the meeting of the San Francisco board of supervisors "last night" establishes the date of composition as October 24.[1] The partial sentence at the end of the first section shows that not all of the letter has been recovered: editorial ellipses indicate possible or demonstrable omissions in the present text.

"RE-OPENING OF THE PLAZA," the middle section of the letter, scarcely qualifies as a coherent sketch, but it touches on an important and recurring interest of Clemens'—his distaste for bureaucratic regulation of the simple pleasures of life. Having refurbished Portsmouth Square with green lawn, the supervisors proceeded to regulate its use by dogs as well as people—and Clemens here registers his "vulgar" protest. He would embody much the same rebellious feelings in "Colloquy between a Slum Child and a Moral Mentor" (no. 219) early in 1868.

---

[1]Under the heading "Reopening of the Plaza," the *Alta California* reported: "Order prohibiting persons from walking on the grass plats of Portsmouth Square, shutting out dogs, and opening the Plaza at seven A.M. and closing the same at sunset, each day in the year, was finally passed" ("Board of Supervisors," San Francisco *Alta California*, 24 October 1865, p. 1).

But perhaps the central interest of this letter (or at least of what has been preserved) lies in Clemens' return to the familiar role of a struggling, concerned expert in ladies' fashions—one who is, nevertheless, well over his head. "Fashions are mighty tanglesome things to write," he observes in the first section, and true to his word he wanders away from his subject in the middle section, only to return to it, somewhat more angrily, in the last. The basic form of the joke is commonplace in Clemens' early work: "Mark Twain—More of Him" (no. 64) and "The Lick House Ball" (no. 65), both written in 1863, are good examples. Within a month of the present letter he would return to the theme with "The Pioneers' Ball" (no. 137), published in the *Enterprise*. And his interest would persist, at least as late as January 1868, when he wrote "Fashions" (no. 221) as part of a letter to the Chicago *Republican*.

Clemens struck through the portion of the letter which is now in the Yale Scrapbook, probably in January or February 1867, while preparing material for his *Jumping Frog* book. The clipping itself follows a page stub, which may indicate that the earlier section was considered a potential sketch for the book. None of the letter was, however, reprinted.

[San Francisco Letter]

. . . .

A LOVE OF A BONNET DESCRIBED.

WELL, YOU ought to see the new style of bonnets, and then die.
You see, everybody has discarded ringlets and bunches of curls,
and taken to the clod of compact hair on the "after-guard," which
they call a "waterfall," though why they name it so I cannot make
out, for it looks no more like one's general notion of a waterfall
than a cabbage looks like a cataract. Yes, they have thrown aside
the bunches of curls which necessitated the wearing of a bonnet
with a back-door to it, or rather, a bonnet without any back to it at
all, so that the curls bulged out from under an overhanging spray
of slender feathers, sprigs of grass, etc. You know the kind of bonnet I mean; it was as if a lady spread a diaper on her head, with
two of the corners brought down over her ears, and the other
trimmed with a bunch of graceful flummery and allowed to hang
over her waterfall—fashions are mighty tanglesome things to
write—but I am coming to it directly. The diaper was the only
beautiful bonnet women have worn within my recollection—
but as they have taken exclusively to the waterfalls, now, they
have thrown it aside and adopted, ah me, the infernalest, old-
fashionedest, ruralest atrocity in its stead you ever saw. It is perfectly plain and hasn't a ribbon, or a flower, or any ornament
whatever about it; it is severely shaped like the half of a lady's

thimble split in two lengthwise—or would be if that thimble had a perfectly square end instead of a rounded one—just imagine it—glance at it in your mind's eye—and recollect, no ribbons, no flowers, no filagree—only the plainest kind of plain straw or plain black stuff. It don't come forward as far as the hair, and it fits to the head as tightly as a thimble fits, folded in a square mass against the back of the head, and the square end of the bonnet half covers it and fits as square and tightly against it as if somebody had hit the woman in the back of the head with a tombstone or some other heavy and excessively flat projectile. And a woman looks as distressed in it as a cat with her head fast in a tea-cup. It is infamous.

. . . .

mustered out of service.

RE-OPENING OF THE PLAZA.

The Plaza, or Portsmouth Square, is "done," at last, and by a resolution passed by the Board of Supervisors last night, is to be thrown open to the public henceforth at 7 o'clock A. M. and closed again at 7 o'clock P. M. every day. The same resolution prohibits the visits of dogs to this holy ground, and denies to the public the privilege of rolling on its grass. If I could bring myself to speak vulgarly, I should say that the latter clause is rough—very rough on the people. To be forced to idle in gravel walks when there is soft green grass close at hand, is tantalizing; it is as uncomfortable as to lie disabled and thirsty in sight of a fountain; or to look at a feast without permission to participate in it, when you are hungry; and almost as exasperating as to have to smack your chops over the hugging and kissing going on between a couple of sweethearts without any reasonable excuse for inserting your own metaphorical shovel. And yet there is one consolation about it on Nature's eternal equity of "compensation." No matter how degraded and worthless you may become here, you cannot go to grass in the Plaza, at any rate. The Plaza is a different thing from what it used to be; it used to be a text from a desert—it was not large enough for a whole chapter; but now it is traversed here and there by walks of precise width, and which are graded to a degree of rigid accuracy which is constantly suggestive of the spirit level; and the grass plots are as strictly shaped as a dandy's side-whiskers, and their surfaces clipped and smoothed with the same mathematical exactness. In a word, the Plaza looks like the intensely brown and green perspectiveless diagram of stripes and patches which an architect furnishes to his client as a plan for a projected city garden or cemetery. And its glaring greenness in the midst of so much sombreness is startling and yet piercingly pleasant to the eye. It reminds one of old John Dehle's vegetable garden in Virginia, which, after a rain, used to burn like a square of green fire in the midst of the dull, gray desolation around it.

MORE FASHIONS — EXIT "WATERFALL."

I am told that the Empress Eugenie is growing bald on the top of her head, and that to hide this defect she now combs her "back-hair" forward in such a way as to make her look all right. I am also told that this mode of dressing the hair is already fashionable in all the great civilized cities of the world, and that it will shortly be adopted here. Therefore let your ladies "stand-by" and prepare to drum their ringlets to the front when I give the word. I shall keep a weather eye out for this fashion, for I am an uncompromising enemy of the popular "waterfall," and I yearn to see it in disgrace. Just think of the disgusting shape and appearance of the thing. The hair is drawn to a slender neck at the back, and then commences a great fat, oblong ball, like a kidney covered with a net; and sometimes this net is so thickly bespangled with white beads that the ball looks soft, and fuzzy, and filmy and gray at a little distance — so that it vividly reminds you of those nauseating garden spiders in the States that go about dragging a pulpy, grayish bag-full of young spiders slung to them behind; and when I look at these suggestive waterfalls and remember how sea-sick it used to make me to mash one of those spider-bags, I feel sea-sick again, as a general thing. Its shape alone is enough to turn one's stomach. Let's have the back-hair brought forward as soon as convenient. N. B.—I shall feel much obliged to you if you can aid me in getting up this panic. I have no wife of my own and therefore as long as I have to make the most of other people's it is a matter of vital importance to me that they should dress with some degree of taste.

126. *Steamer Departures*

31 October–2 November 1865

This comically petulant explosion of temper is preserved in the Yale Scrapbook, where it is found in a clipping from an unidentified newspaper. The clipping begins: " 'Mark Twain,' in a late San Francisco letter to the Virginia *Enterprise*, gets off the following production of a sour temper." The sketch makes use of a passenger list for the Pacific Mail Steamship Company's *Colorado*, which sailed for Panama on 30 October 1865 with six hundred passengers. Clemens probably wrote the letter containing this item on October 29, the day the passenger list was published in most of the San Francisco papers.[1] If so, it must have appeared in the Virginia City *Territorial Enterprise* two or three days later.

Among the passengers who departed with the *Colorado* were General William S. Rosecrans and Senator John Conness. But the name on which Clemens dwells at greatest length did not appear there. His "J. Schmeltzer" is probably a deliberate misreading of "J. Schweitzer," a name which does appear on the list. It seems unlikely, at any rate, that the *Enterprise* or the unidentified newspaper reprinting the *Enterprise* had mistaken the name, for Clemens returned to the subject briefly in "More California Notables Gone," which he published in the San Francisco *Dramatic Chronicle* on November 1. Ribbing his newspaper foe Fitz Smythe (Albert S. Evans) for making much of the passenger list, he said in part: "And, above all, why did he let J. Schmeltzer go away without a parting dose of adulation? Oh, unhappy Schmeltzer, you didn't make your 'pile,' perhaps!"[2]

---

[1]"Sailing of the 'Colorado,' " San Francisco *Morning Call*, 29 October 1865, p. 3; "The Departing Steamer," San Francisco *Alta California*, 29 October 1865, p. 1.
[2]Reprinted in Appendix B3, volume 2.

Steamer Departures

I FEEL savage this morning. And as usual, when one wants to growl, it is almost impossible to find things to growl about with any degree of satisfaction. I cannot find anything in the steamer departures to get mad at. Only, I wonder who "J. Schmeltzer" is?—and what does he have such an atrocious name for?—and what business has he got in the States?—who is there in the States who cares whether Schmeltzer comes or not? The conduct of this unknown Schmeltzer is exasperating to the last degree.

And off goes General Rosecrans, without ever doing anything to give a paper a chance to abuse him. He has behaved himself, and kept quiet, and avoided scandalous meddling with the Oakland Seminaries, and paid his board in the most aggravating manner. Let him go.

And Conness is gone. Oh, d—n Conness!

127. Exit "Bummer"

8 November 1865

The text of Clemens' obituary of the dog Bummer is found in the *Californian* of 11 November 1865, where Bret Harte introduced it as follows:

As we have devoted but little space to an event which has filled our local contemporaries with as much sorrow (judging from the columns of lamentation it has called forth) as would the decease of the best biped in the city, we give "Mark Twain's" view of the occurrence, as recorded in the ENTERPRISE of the 8th. Strangely enough, Mark, who can't stand the "ballad infliction," seems to think there has not been quite enough "Bummer."[1]

For almost two years in the early 1860s the masterless dog Bummer and his faithful protégé Lazarus were the town's pets, as well known to San Franciscans as Emperor Norton and Freddy Coombs, the eccentric phrenologist who was called Washington II. Famous as rat catchers and well versed in the art of cadging food, both dogs were given the freedom of the city by special ordinance. Lazarus had died, evidently by poison, on 3 October 1863, and was much mourned. He was eventually replaced, as Clemens indicates, by another "obsequious vassal," a fact that Clemens had reported for the San Francisco *Morning Call* in July 1864.[2]

A few days after Bummer's death on November 2 Clemens also reported on Edward Jump's lithograph showing the deceased Bummer lying in state amidst funeral candles, feasting with the spirit of Lazarus at a

---

[1] *Californian* 3 (11 November 1865): 12. The allusion in the final sentence is to " 'Mark Twain' on the Ballad Infliction," reprinted from the *Enterprise* in the *Californian* 3 (4 November 1865): 7. This item is scheduled to appear in the collection of criticism in The Works of Mark Twain.

[2] "Another Lazarus," reprinted in *CofC*, pp. 49–50.

free lunch table in the background, and a brigade of rats approaching to view "the dead king, and rejoice over his downfall."[3]

---

[3]"San Francisco Correspondence," *Napa County Reporter,* 11 November 1865, p. 2; see also Robert E. Cowan, Anne Bancroft, and Addie L. Ballou, *The Forgotten Characters of Old San Francisco* (Los Angeles: Ward Ritchie Press, 1964), pp. 61–89, and *CofC,* pp. 49–50, 308.

Exit "Bummer"

THE OLD vagrant "Bummer" is really dead at last; and although he was always more respected than his obsequious vassal, the dog "Lazarus," his exit has not made half as much stir in the newspaper world as signalised the departure of the latter. I think it is because he died a natural death: died with friends around him to smooth his pillow and wipe the death-damps from his brow, and receive his last words of love and resignation; because he died full of years, and honor, and disease, and fleas. *He* was permitted to die a natural death, as I have said, but poor Lazarus "died with his boots on"—which is to say, he lost his life by violence; he gave up the ghost mysteriously, at dead of night, with none to cheer his last moments or soothe his dying pains. So the murdered dog was canonized in the newspapers, his shortcomings excused, and his virtues heralded to the world; but his superior, parting with his life in the fullness of time, and in the due course of nature, sinks as quietly as might the mangiest cur among us. Well, let him go. In earlier days he was courted and caressed; but latterly he had lost his comeliness—his dignity had given place to a want of self-respect, which allowed him to practice mean deceptions to regain for a moment that sympathy and notice which had become necessary to his very existence, and it was evident to all that the dog had had his day: his great popularity was gone forever. In fact, Bummer should have died sooner: there was a time when his death would have left a lasting legacy of fame to his name. Now, however, he will be forgotten in a few days. Bummer's skin is to be stuffed and placed with that of Lazarus.

128. *Pleasure Excursion*

9–12 November 1865

On the afternoon of 7 November 1865 the new tugboat *Rescue* made its trial trip in San Francisco Bay. Probably on that day or the next Clemens wrote about the bibulous event in his daily letter to the Virginia City *Territorial Enterprise*, which published it probably two or three days later. The *Enterprise* printing has been lost. The present text has been reconstructed from two independent reprintings, one in the San Francisco *Golden Era* of November 19, and the other in the San Francisco *Examiner* of December 2.[1]

A group of merchants and underwriters interested in San Francisco shipping and commerce had commissioned the building of the *Rescue* at North Point. On November 8 it towed its first ship, the *Nonpareil*, to sea. But the day before, loaded with baskets of champagne and with flags flying and calliope playing, it left North Point carrying a select company of "high-toned newspaper reporters, numerous military officers, and gentlemen of note." The *Rescue* sailed a course around the Bay, touching at all major points before docking at Pacific Street wharf late in the afternoon. Clemens' evident delight in being "at sea," not to mention in convivial company, probably led him to exaggerate the *Rescue's* average speed. City newspapers agreed that she averaged ten, not "fifteen miles an hour."[2]

---

[1]For details, see the textual commentary.

[2]" 'Mark Twain's' Trial Trip," San Francisco *Golden Era* 13 (19 November 1865): 5; "Trial Trip of the 'Rescue,' " San Francisco *Alta California*, 8 November 1865, p. 1; "Trial Trip," San Francisco *Evening Bulletin*, 8 November 1865, p. 3; "Excursion of the 'Rescue,' " San Francisco *Morning Call*, 8 November 1865, p. 3.

Pleasure Excursion

W<small>E LUNCHED</small>, then, and shortly began to drink champagne—
by the basket. I saw the tremendous guns frowning from the fort; I
saw San Francisco spread out over the sand-hills like a picture; I
saw the huge fortress at Black Point looming hazily in the distance; I saw tall ships sweeping in from the sea through the
Golden Gate; I saw that it was time to take another drink, and
after that I saw no more. All hands fell to singing "When we were
Marching Through Georgia," and the remainder of the trip was
fought out on that line. We landed at the steamboat wharf at 5
o'clock, safe and sound. Some of those reporters I spoke of said we
had been to Benicia, and the others said we had been to the Cliff
House, but, poor devils, they had been drinking, and they did not
really know where we had been. I know, but I do not choose to
tell. I enjoyed that trip first-rate. I am rather fond of a trip on a fast
boat with a jolly crowd. That was a jolly crowd. Sometimes they
were all out forward standing on their heads, and then the boat
wouldn't steer because her rudder was sticking up in the air like a
sail of a wind-mill; and sometimes they were all aft turning hand-
springs and playing "mumble peg," and then the boat wouldn't
steer because she stood so straight up in the water that her head
caught all the wind that was blowing; and sometimes they were
all on the starboard side eating and drinking and singing, and then
she wouldn't steer because she was listed worse than any soldier

that ever listed since the war began. Still, even under these trying circumstances, the boat made fifteen miles an hour, and so I suppose that on an even keel she can make a hundred, or thereabouts. I enjoyed that excursion.

§ 129. *[Editorial " Puffing"]*

15–18 November 1865

Under the heading "Good for Mark" the San Francisco *Examiner* noted on 20 November 1865: "The San Francisco correspondent of the *Territorial Enterprise* in one of his last letters to that paper, in speaking of the disgusting disposition to puff individuals, manifested by the press of the Bay City, is thus expressive." It followed this with the brief extract here assigned the title "Editorial 'Puffing,' " obviously only a portion of Clemens' latest *Enterprise* letter. We conjecture that it appeared in the *Enterprise* sometime between 15 and 18 November 1865.

Clemens' principal targets in this comment were the local editor of the *Alta California*, Albert S. Evans (whom he usually called "Fitz Smythe"), and the local reporter on the *Morning Call* who, as Clemens had reason to know, was under strict orders not to offend the paper's Irish clientele. "Editorial 'Puffing' " is, in fact, the first of seven sketches grouped together here because they all deal satirically with Fitz Smythe during a period when Clemens seemed particularly interested in pursuing him.

Albert S. Evans of New Hampshire made his slow and circuitous way to California during the 1840s and 1850s by way of Indiana, Illinois, and Texas. In San Francisco he became a journalist, reporting for the *Morning Call* before serving as city editor for the *Alta California* and correspondent for the Gold Hill *News*, Chicago *Tribune*, and New York *Tribune*. Evans was an industrious and moralistic man with a pedestrian skill as a writer and a stillborn sense of humor—in short, an ideal target for Clemens, who was a veteran of newspaper controversies by the time he settled in San Francisco in May 1864. Within a month of his arrival in the city, Clemens and Evans were trading insults through their local columns. The feud continued, not without some genuine bitterness, through the latter part of 1865 and early months of 1866.

Clemens' immediate target in the present sketch was Evans' article "Banquet to a Departing Merchant." There Evans unctuously reported a farewell banquet for Moses Ellis, "one of our principal, and, we are pleased to say, prosperous pioneer merchants," who he added, "leaves us to-day on a visit to the home of his nativity."[1] Clemens' sketch mocked these phrases, very much in the spirit which informed his earlier piece in the San Francisco *Dramatic Chronicle*, "More California Notables Gone."[2]

---

[1]San Francisco Alta California, 30 October 1865, p. 1.
[2]Reprinted in Appendix B3, volume 2.

[Editorial "Puffing"]

LET "JOHN Wychecombe Smith, Esq., one of our pioneer merchants, and one among our wealthiest and most respected citizens," leave in the steamer "to revisit the home of his nativity," and one of these papers will give you half a column of sorrow and distress about it, and wind up with the eternal "but we are happy to say that not many months will elapse ere he will be with us again"—and forget to mention that a distinguished and war-bronzed Major-General went in the same steamer with the wealthy and successful Smith. The other paper would let John Wychecombe Smith go to the States, or to the devil, either, a dozen times over, and always maintain an insolent silence about it: but let Moike Mulrooney, or Tim Murphy, or Judy O'Flaherty, receive a present of raal Irish whisky from the ould country, and it will never let you hear the last of it.

§ 130. The Old Thing

18 November 1865

This sketch was originally part of Clemens' letter to the Virginia City *Territorial Enterprise* published on 18 November 1865. The *Enterprise* printing does not survive, but the text is preserved in the *Californian* of November 25, which introduced it as follows: " 'MARK TWAIN,' in summing up the facts and theories of the What Cheer House robbery, says (correspondence Virginia *Enterprise*, Nov. 18th:)."

Robert B. Woodward's What Cheer House on Sacramento Street was a restaurant and hotel with homey attractions like an excellent library and a large fireplace. On the night of November 13 the hotel safe was robbed of about $25,000—most of it belonging to guests—by an unknown intruder who struck the night watchman. Three months later, on 17 February 1866, William Welch was indicted for the crime, but ultimately acquitted. In the meantime, verdicts for the recovery of many thousands of dollars were given against Woodward for not having kept his guests' money safe. And for many of the intervening weeks the city's reporters, with Albert Evans in the vanguard, agitated both the mysterious crime and its attendant lawsuits in their columns. Evans was particularly fertile in suggesting dark and melodramatic theories about the identity of the culprit, and he began his theorizing on November 14 with an article that said in part: "The similarity of the details of this robbery to those of that which came so near proving fatal to young Meyers, in the Commercial street pawnbroker's shop, over a year since, will strike our readers at once."[1] It was this article that prompted "The Old Thing," which

---

[1] "Robbery at the What Cheer House," San Francisco *Morning Call*, 14 November 1865, p. 2; "The What Cheer House Robbery," San Francisco *Evening Bulletin*, 19 February 1866, p. 3; "Conclusion of the What Cheer House Trial," ibid., 12 May 1866, p. 5; "The What Cheer House Cases," ibid., 23 February 1866, p. 5; "Daring Hotel Robbery," San Francisco *Alta California*, 14 November 1865, p. 1.

Clemens probably wrote on November 14 or 15. All of the crimes that Clemens alludes to here had occurred in 1864, while he was reporting on the *Morning Call,* and although he somewhat exaggerated Evans' propensity for theorizing, his charges are for the most part true.[2]

---

[2]For details, see the explanatory notes. Clemens continued this feud with Evans in his San Francisco *Dramatic Chronicle* column; see Appendixes B12, B15, and B17, volume 2.

The Old Thing

As USUAL, the *Alta* reporter fastens the mysterious What Cheer robbery on the same horrible person who knocked young Meyers in the head with a slung-shot a year ago and robbed his father's pawnbroker shop of some brass jewelry and crippled revolvers, in broad daylight; and he laid that exploit on the horrible wretch who robbed the Mayor's Clerk, who half-murdered detective officer Rose in a lonely spot below Santa Clara; and he proved that this same monster killed the lone woman in a secluded house up a dark alley with a carpenter's chisel, months before; and he demonstrated by inspired argument that the same villain who chiselled the woman tomahawked a couple of defenceless women in the most mysterious manner up another dark alley a few months before that. Now, the perpetrator of these veiled crimes has never been discovered, yet this wicked reporter has taken the whole batch and piled them coolly and relentlessly upon the shoulders of one imaginary scoundrel, with a comfortable, "Here, these are yours," and with an air that says plainly that no denial, and no argument in the case, will be entertained. And every time anything happens that is unlawful and dreadful, and has a spice of mystery about it, this reporter, without waiting to see if maybe somebody else didn't do it, goes off at once and jams it on top of the old pile, as much as to say, "Here—here's some more of your work." Now this isn't right, you know. It is all well enough for Mr. Smythe to divert suspicion from himself—nobody objects to that—but it is not right for him to lay every solitary thing on this mysterious stranger, whoever he is—it is not right, you know. He ought to give the poor devil a show. The idea of accusing "The Mysterious" of the What Cheer burglary, considering who was the last boarder to bed and the first one up!

Smythe is endeavoring to get on the detective police force. I think it will be wronging the community to give this man such a position as that—now you know that yourself, don't you? He would settle down on some particular fellow, and every time there was a rape committed, or a steamship stolen, or an oyster cellar rifled, or a church burned down, or a family massacred, or a black-and-tan pup stolen, he would march off with portentous mien and snatch that fellow and say, "Here, you are at it again, you know," and snake him off to the Station House.

§ 131. San Francisco Letter

24 or 26 December 1865

This installment of Clemens' daily correspondence to the Virginia City *Territorial Enterprise* is not a sustained comic attack on Albert Evans and the *Alta California*, but his ridicule of them is scattered so promiscuously throughout the rambling and rather diffuse letter that it has seemed best to reproduce virtually all of it here.[1] The letter was written on 22 December 1865 and probably appeared in the *Enterprise* shortly thereafter, on December 24 or 26 (December 25 was a Monday, the day on which the *Enterprise* did not publish). The full text was preserved by Clemens in the Yale Scrapbook, where he later struck through the clipping—presumably in January or February 1867, while preparing copy for his *Jumping Frog* book.

Although both "Editorial Poem" and "More Wisdom!" needle the *Alta* for its banality, the central element in the letter is Clemens' attack in "Facetious," where he pounces on Evans' most glaring weakness as a reporter: his painfully labored efforts at humor. Like other local reporters, Evans strove to inject at least incidental humor into the budget of daily items. To this end he had invented, in 1864, the character Armand Leonidas Stiggers—a dandified bohemian who loafed about the *Alta* office, where he was not wanted. Stiggers (whose surname Evans later changed to "Fitz Smythe") was portrayed as a bungler whose awkward predicaments regularly found their way into Evans' column of city news. Clemens, no doubt deliberately mistaking Evans' intention, soon identified Fitz Smythe with his creator and the two became one, not only for Clemens, but for his fellow journalists on the San Francisco *Dramatic Chronicle* and the *Californian* as well.

---

[1] The opening section—"How Long, O Lord, How Long!"—about recent problems with the local police judge is scheduled to appear in the collection of social and political writings in The Works of Mark Twain.

San Francisco Letter

. . . .

EDITORIAL POEM.

THE FOLLOWING fine Christmas poem appears in the *Alta* of this morning, in the unostentatious garb of an editorial. This manner of "setting it" robs it of half its beauty. I will arrange it as blank verse, and then it will read much more charmingly:

"CHRISTMAS COMES BUT ONCE A YEAR."

"The Holidays are approaching. We hear
Of them and see their signs every day.
The children tell you every morn
How long it is until the glad New Year.
The pavements all are covered o'er
With boxes, which have arrived
Per steamer and are being unpacked
In anticipation sweet, of an unusual demand.
The windows of the shops
Montgomery street along,
Do brilliant shine
With articles of ornament and luxury;
The more substantial goods,
Which eleven months now gone
The place have occupied,
Having been put aside for a few revolving weeks,
Silks, satins, laces, articles of gold and silver,

337

Jewels, porcelains from Sevres,
And from Dresden;
Bohemian and Venetian glass,
Pictures, engravings,
Bronzes of the finest workmanship
And price extravagant, attract
The eye at every step
Along the promenades of fashion.
The hotels
With visitors are crowded, who have come
From the ultimate interior to enjoy
Amusements metropolitan, or to find
A more extensive market, and prices lower
For purchases, than country towns afford.
Abundant early rains a prosperous year
Have promised—and the dry
And sunny weather which prevailed hath
For two weeks past, doth offer
Facilities profound for coming to the city,
And for enjoyment after getting here.
The ocean beach throughout the day,
And theatres, in shades of evening, show
A throng of strangers glad residents as well.
All appearances do indicate
That this blithe time of holiday
In San Francisco will
Be one of liveliness unusual, and brilliancy withal!"
[Exit Chief Editor, bowing low—impressive music.]

I cannot admire the overstrong modesty which impels a man to
compose a stately anthem like that and run it together in the solid
unattractiveness of a leading editorial.

FACETIOUS.

This morning's *Alta* is brilliant. The fine poem I have quoted is
coppered by a scintillation of Fitz Smythe's in the same column.
He calls the thieving scalliwags of the Fourteenth Infantry "nip-
tomaniacs." That is not bad considering that it much more intel-
ligently describes their chief proclivity than "kleptomaniac"
describes the weakness of another kind of thieves. The merit of this
effort ranks so high that it is a mercy it is only a smart remark
instead of a joke—otherwise Fitz Smythe must have perished,

and instantly. For fear that this remark may be obscure to some persons I will explain by informing the public that the sooth-sayers were called in at the time of Fitz Smythe's birth, and they read the stars and prophecied that he was destined to lead a long and eventful life, and to arrive to great distinction for his untiring industry in endeavoring, for the period of near half a century, to get off a joke. They said that many times during his life the grand end and aim of his existence would seem to be in his reach, and his mission on earth on the point of being fulfilled; but again and again bitter disappointment would overtake him; what promised so fairly to be a joke would come forth still-born; but he would rise superior to despair and make new and more frantic efforts. And these wise men said that in the evening of his life, when hope was well nigh dead with him, he would some day, all unexpect-edly to himself, and likewise to the world, produce a genuine joke, and one of marvelous humor—and then his head would cave in, and his bowels be rent asunder, and his arms and his legs would drop off and he would fall down and die in dreadful agony. "Niptomaniac" is a felicitous expression, but God be thanked it is not a joke. If it had been, it would have killed him—the mission of Armand Leonidas Fitz Smythe would have been accomplished.

MAYO AND ALDRICH.

The last news from Frank Mayo will be gratifying to his host of friends and admirers in California and Nevada. His rank is "Stock Star," and he plays the leading characters in heavy pieces, and, the Boston papers say, plays them as well as is done by any great actor in America, and make no exceptions. He traveled through the chief cities with the Keans, starring by himself in afterpieces, and playing with the Keans when there was no afterpiece—taking such parts as "Henry VIII." The Philadelphia papers said the Keans were very well, but Mr. Mayo was the best actor in the lot!

Louis Aldrich, in his new Boston engagement, will take high rank also, and play "first old man" and such characters. He will do well in the East. You never saw a man make such striding advances in professional excellence as Aldrich has done since he first played in Virginia. He "holds over" Mayo in one respect—he will study, and study hard, too—and Mayo won't.

FINANCIAL.

In an editorial setting forth the palpable fact that California and Nevada are cutting their own throats by their mistaken sagacity in hanging on to their double-eagle circulating medium, instead of smoothing the way for the adoption of greenbacks as our currency, the *Flag* touches upon several matters of immediate interest to Washoe, and I make an extract:

In the large city of Virginia, the San Francisco system of moneyed exclusiveness prevails completely. Two or three usurers have taken advantage of the necessities of the community and, upon loans at exorbitant interest, obtained some sort of possession of nearly all of the real estate and house property in the city. The Bank of California through its various connections, has worked itself into the proprietorship of the most valuable mines, and this has been accomplished by first depreciating the stock and then buying it under the stress of "a stock panic." Men who cannot sustain the depreciation, maintain their credit and transact their business independent of a high value of their mining stock, must yield in order to ease their fall, and then, as they become ruined, they witness the outrage of their ruin, and retire in despair from enterprise and competition. The stock market has lately been unusually depressed. The California speculators and Specific Contract fellows of the two States have caused the depression, and now, having absorbed nearly all of the mining property, they are preparing to create a "revival" of stock speculation whereby they will again deceive the public, realize enormous sums and effect new ruin in every direction but their own.

PERSONAL.

I do not know why I should head these two items from the *Call* "personal," but I do:

THE "TERRITORIAL ENTERPRISE."—This admirably conducted paper has entered on its eighth year of existence.

CHANGED.—The Virginia *Union* has changed from a morning to an evening paper. It manifests a restlessness which may precede speedy dissolution.

MOCK DUEL—ALMOST.

A French broker on Montgomery street quarreled with his rival in a tender affair, the other day, and a challenge passed, and was accepted. The seconds determined to merely load the pistols with blank cartridges, and have some fun out of the matter; but they got to drinking rather freely, ran all night, and when the party arrived on the dueling ground, at early dawn, the seconds were not sober enough to act their part with sufficient gravity to carry their plan through successfully. The principals discovered that they were being trifled with, and indignantly left the ground. I could get no names. All I could find out was that the seconds were two well-known "sports," that the challenge was sent and accepted in good faith, and that one of the principals was a broker.

"MORE WISDOM!"

The *Alta* is most unusually and astonishingly brilliant this morning. I cannot do better than give it space and let it illumine your columns. It lets off a level column of editorial to prove that bees eat clover; mice eat bees; cats eat mice; cats bask in the sun; the spots on the sun derange the electric currents; that derangement produces earthquakes; earthquakes make cold weather; and the bees, and the mice, and the cats, and the spots on the sun, and the electric currents, and the earthquakes, and the cold weather, mingling together in one grand fatal combination, produce cholera! Listen to the *Alta:*

We know that we have sometimes to go a long way around to trace an effect to its cause. Darwin, in "The Origin of Species," states a fact which may be used with advantage in illustration, viz.: The presence of a large number of cats in a village is favorable to the spread of red clover. The reader will at once exclaim—what on earth can cats have to do with that species of the genus *trifolium?* The answer is—the humble-bee, by a peculiarity of its organization, can alone extract the nectar from the flower of the red clover. In passing from flower to flower it conveys the pollen necessary for the fertilization and consequent spread of the plant. The field mice prey upon the humble-bee, break up its nests, and eat its stores of honey, while the cats destroy the mice; hence it follows that in the natural propagation of the plant in question, the feline tribe perform an important part.

Bearing such curious revelations as these in mind, it is easy enough to present a theory to cover the case of mother earth at this time, namely: that the spots on the face of the sun derange the electric currents of the earth; that the derangement of the

electric currents produces earthquakes; that earthquakes contribute to cold weather, by permitting the escape of some of the
caloric of the interior of the globe, and that all these changes, in
some way, are the cause of the rinder-pest and cholera.

Solomon's wisdom was foolishness to this.

MARK TWAIN.

§132. *Fitz Smythe's Horse*

16–18 January 1866

This sketch was one of two items extracted by the San Francisco *Golden Era* from the recent "*S. F. Correspondence of the Territorial Enterprise*" and reprinted on 21 January 1866 under the heading "Mark Twain."[1] The *Enterprise* printing is lost, but since the *Era* published weekly, and since it required about three days' travel time for the *Enterprise* to reach San Francisco, we have estimated that the sketch first appeared in that paper sometime between January 16 and 18, although a slightly earlier date is possible.

Albert Evans had served in the Mexican War and was a man generally disposed to favor policemen and soldiers, so long as they upheld the law and maintained order. He was tall and lean, sported a long pointed moustache and a heavy beard, and often rode his horse. In this sketch Clemens seized upon these characteristics, not in a direct attack, but using a strategy of indirection that would serve him well in the future. The innocent monologue of Clemens' little boy is at once a vernacular tall tale—the youngster noticeably warms to his subject—and an ingenious satire on Fitz Smythe, who is frankly portrayed by the boy as both stiffly ridiculous in his person and too tightfisted to feed his horse anything but old newspapers. The horse bears a family resemblance to many other personified animals in Clemens' work, including the horse Bunker (described in a January 1862 letter),[2] and the horse who served him in the

---

[1] The other sketch was "What Have the Police Been Doing?"—which is scheduled to appear in the collection of social and political writings in The Works of Mark Twain.

[2] Clemens to Jane Clemens, 30 January 1862, *CL1*, letter 38.

Sandwich Islands (see "The Steed 'Oahu,' " no. 188). The little boy himself, despite some uncertain touches by his creator, is a genuine forebear of Huckleberry Finn.

The satire in this sketch was sufficiently memorable to be reprinted, against Clemens' will, in *Beadle's Dime Book of Fun No. 3* in 1866.[3] And in April 1867 the editor of "The Lion's Mouth" column in the *Californian* publicly recalled reading it after Evans, no longer the local editor of the *Alta California,* had written that paper from Arizona that his "bay mare, which [he] brought from San Francisco, and always prized so highly," had been stolen by Indians. Harking back to " 'Mark Twain's' amusing and truthful description of the habits of Fitz-Smythe's horse," the editor said that Clemens had "made public many interesting particulars concerning the bay mare, which may explain why she left Fitz-Smythe. We do not believe that she was stolen; she strayed away in search of food. The horse—or mare—was, during the period of Fitz-Smythe's residence in this city, fed entirely on newspapers—so Mark Twain says—and used to devour on an average five hundred old exchanges a day." According to this facetious reporter, the mare had obviously wandered off in search of a newspaper office.[4]

---

[3]"If I were in the east, now, I could stop the publication of a piratical book which has stolen some of my sketches" (Clemens to Mollie Clemens, 22 May 1866, *CL1,* letter 104). See the textual commentary.

[4]"The Unhappy Fitz-Smythe," *Californian* 6 (6 April 1867): 1.

Fitz Smythe's Horse

Yesterday, as I was coming along through a back alley, I glanced over a fence, and there was Fitz Smythe's horse. I can easily understand, now, why that horse always looks so dejected and indifferent to the things of this world. They feed him on old newspapers. I had often seen Smythe carrying "dead loads" of old exchanges up town, but I never suspected that they were to be put to such a use as this. A boy came up while I stood there, and said, "That hoss belongs to Mr. Fitz Smythe, and the old man —that's my father, you know—the old man's going to kill him."

"Who, Fitz Smythe?"

"No, the hoss—because he et up a litter of pups that the old man wouldn't a taken forty dol—"

"Who, Fitz Smythe?"

"No, the hoss—and he eats fences and everything—took our gate off and carried it home and et up every dam splinter of it; you wait till he gets done with them old *Altas* and *Bulletins* he's a chawin' on now, and you'll see him branch out and tackle a-n-y-thing he can shet his mouth on. Why, he nipped a little boy, Sunday, which was going home from Sunday school; well, the boy got loose, you know, but that old hoss got his bible and some tracts, and them's as good a thing as *he* wants, being so used to papers, you see. You put anything to eat anywheres, and that old hoss'll shin out and get it—and he'll eat anything he can bite, and he don't care a dam. He'd climb a tree, he would, if you was to put

anything up there for him—cats, for instance—he likes cats—
he's et up every cat there was here in four blocks—he'll take
more chances—why, he'll bust in anywheres for one of them
fellers; I see him snake a old tom cat out of that there flower-pot
over yonder, where she was a sunning of herself, and take her
down, and she a hanging on and a grabbling for a holt on something, and you could hear her yowl and kick up and tear around
after she was inside of him. You see Mr. Fitz Smythe don't give
him nothing to eat but them old newspapers and sometimes a
basket of shavings, and so you know, he's got to prospect or
starve, and a hoss ain't going to starve, it ain't likely, on account
of not wanting to be rough on cats and sich things. Not that hoss,
anyway, you bet you. Because *he* don't care a dam. You turn him
loose once on this town, and don't you know he'd eat up m-o-r-e
goods-boxes, and fences, and clothing-store things, and animals,
and all them kind of valuables? Oh, you bet he would. Because
that's his style, you know, and he don't care a dam. But you ought
to see Mr. Fitz Smythe ride him around, prospecting for them
items—you ought to see him with his soldier coat on, and his
mustashers sticking out strong like a cat-fish's horns, and them
long laigs of his'n standing out so, like them two prongs they prop
up a step-ladder with, and a jolting down street at four mile a
week—oh, what a guy!—sets up stiff like a close pin, you know,
and thinks he looks like old General Macdowl. But the old man's
a going to hornisswoggle that hoss on account of his goblin up
them pups. Oh, you bet your life the old man's *down* on him. Yes,
sir, coming!" and the entertaining boy departed to see what the
"old man" was calling him for. But I am glad that I met the boy,
and I am glad I saw the horse taking his literary breakfast, because
I know now why the animal looks so discouraged when I see
Fitz Smythe rambling down Montgomery street on him—he has
altogether too rough a time getting a living to be cheerful and
frivolous or anyways frisky.

§ 133. *Closed Out*

30–31 January 1866

This sketch was included in Clemens' "San Francisco Letter" to the Virginia City *Territorial Enterprise* written on 28 January 1866. It seems likely that it appeared in that paper two or three days later. A clipping of the entire letter is preserved in the Yale Scrapbook.[1]

Clemens here returned to a technique he had often used in Nevada: the imputation of a ravenously destructive appetite to his comic enemy. The Unreliable is given this trait, for example, in "Letter from Carson City," "Letter from Carson," and "The Unreliable" (nos. 40, 42, and 46). Clemens' immediate purpose, however, was to turn the tables on Albert Evans, who had accused him of stripping San Francisco of "all the available material" that Adair Wilson had planned to use for writing a book to be called *"The Free Lunch Table."*[2]

---

[1]Two further selections from this letter, "Bearding the Fenian in His Lair" (no. 170) and "Neodamode" (no. 171), appear in their chronological position in this collection.

[2]"Our San Francisco Correspondence," Gold Hill *News*, 4 November 1865, p. 2.

Closed Out

The fine restaurant between Clay and Commercial, on Montgomery street, has been sold at auction. It was fitted up three months ago at a cost of thirty-six hundred dollars, and brought only fourteen hundred yesterday under the hammer. At first it did a prosperous business—made money fast. Everybody was glad of it, for the proprietor was an estimable man, and was struggling to gather together by honest industry a small independence, so that he might go back to the Fatherland of his daily dreams, and clasp once more to his breast the wife who has waited and watched for him through weary years, kiss once more his little ones, and hear their innocent prattle, and their childish glee, and the music of their restless little feet. But about that time Fitz Smythe went there to board, and that let him out, you know. But such is human life. Here to-day and gone to-morrow. A dream—a shadow—a ripple on the water—a thing for invisible gods to sport with for a season and then toss idly by—idly by. It is rough.

§ 134. Take the Stand, Fitz Smythe

6-7 February 1866

This highly personal attack on Albert Evans is part of Clemens' "San Francisco Letter" written on 3 February 1866 and probably published in the Virginia City *Territorial Enterprise* on February 6 or 7 (February 5 was a Monday). A clipping of the entire letter is preserved in the Yale Scrapbook.[1]

Evans' local reports in the *Alta California* and his letters to the Gold Hill *News* provide ample evidence that he was biased in favor of the San Francisco police. Clemens, on the other hand, had been carrying out a series of attacks, through his letters in the *Enterprise*, on corruption in the city government and especially in the police department.[2] This difference in point of view was exaggerated by Clemens' superior powers as a humorist, which unfailingly dwarfed the "prairie wisdom" of his opponent. In short, Clemens' charges in this sketch may be overstated somewhat, but they capture the spirit if not the letter of the truth, and his genuine outrage lends bite and depth to his *ad hominem* attack.

---

[1]Another selection from the same letter, "More Cemeterial Ghastliness" (no. 172), appears in its chronological position in this collection.

[2]Clemens' attacks on the police are scheduled to appear in the collection of social and political writings in The Works of Mark Twain.

Take the Stand, Fitz Smythe

Fitz Smythe ("Amigo," of the Gold Hill *News*) is the champion of the police, and is always in a sweat because I find fault with them. Now I don't find fault with them often, and when I do I sometimes do it honestly; even Fitz Smythe will not have cheek to say he expresses his honest opinions when he invariably and eternally slobbers them over with his slimy praise and can never find them otherwise than pure and sinless in every case. No man is always blameless—Fitz Smythe ought to recollect that and bestow his praise with more judgment. Fitz knows he would abuse them like pirates if they were all to die suddenly. I know it, because he always abuses dead people. He was a firm, unswerving friend of poor Barney Olwell until the man was hanged and buried, and then look what hard names he called him in the last *News*. Fitz can ruin the reputation of any man with a paragraph or two of his praise. I don't say it in a spirit of anger, but I am telling it for a plain truth. I have only stirred the police up and irritated them a little with my cheerful abuse, but Fitz Smythe has utterly ruined their character with his disastrous praise. I don't ask any man to take my evidence alone in this matter—I refer doubters to the police themselves. But for Fitz Smythe's kindly meant but calamitous compliments, the police of San Francisco would stand as high to-day as any similar body of men in the world. But you know yourself that you soon cease to attach weight to the compliments of a man whose mouth is an eternally-flowing fountain of flattery. Fitz Smythe praises all alike—makes no distinction. There is that man Ansbro—I don't know him—never saw him, that I know of—but I know, and so does Fitz Smythe, that he does twice as much work as any other detective on the force—but does Fitz Smythe praise him any more than he praises those pets who never do anything at all? Not he—he makes no discrimination. And Chappell? but why argue the case? When those officers do anything Fitz impartially rings in all the balance of the force to share the credit, sometimes. Fitz, you won't do. I have told you so fifty times, and I tell you again, that you won't do. I can warm you up with ten sentences, and make you dance like a hen on a hot griddle, any time, Fitz Smythe. I know your weak spot. I can touch you on the raw whenever I please, make you lose your temper and write the most spiteful, undignified things. You see you will always be a little awkward with a pen, Fitz, because your head isn't sound—isn't well balanced; you have good points, you know, but they are kept down and crowded out by bad ones. You don't know that when a man is in a controversy he is at a great disadvantage when he loses his temper. It leaves him too open to ridicule, you know. And you can't stand ridicule, Fitz; it cuts you to the quick; it just makes you howl; I know that as well as you do, Fitz, and I am saying these things for your own good; you are young, and you are apt to let the fire of youth drive you into exceedingly unhappy performances. I do not mean that you are so young in years, you know, but young in experience of the world. You ought to be modest; the same wisdom which was so potent in Illinois and the wilds of Texas does not overpower the people of a great city like it used to do there, you know. Ah, no—they read you, attentively—because you write with a certain attractiveness Fitz Smythe—but they say "Oh, this prairie wisdom is too wide—too flat; and this swamp wisdom's too deep altogether."

And they don't attach any weight to your praise of the police. They say, "Oh, this fellow don't know—he ain't used to police—they don't have 'em in the wilds of Texas where this Ranger come from."

But you are certainly the most interesting subject to write about, Fitzy—I never get hold of you but I want to stay with you and hang on to you just as if you were a jug. I didn't intend to write two lines this time, Fitz; I only wanted to get you, as Excuser and Explainer-in-Chief to the Police, to go on the witness stand and inform me when it is possible for a man to lug a prisoner about a mile through the thickest settled portion of this city—clear to the station-house—and never come across a policeman. Read this communication from the *Morning Call*, Fitz—and it is a true version—and then go on and explain it, Fitz—try it, you long-legged rip!

WHERE ARE THE POLICE?

EDITORS MORNING CALL:—On Thursday night a terrible onslaught was made on the house of a peaceable citizen on Larkin street by a band of soldiers. The man, awakened by this attempt to enter his dwelling, called on his neighbors for help. One came to his aid, the soldiers threatened to fire on the families, but, after a severe fight and long chase, the citizen and his neighbor captured two of the rascals near the Spring Valley School House. They have been held over to appear before the County Court. The citizen, with his prisoner, came from the Presidio Road, along Larkin, down Union, along Stockton, down Broadway to Kearny street, before he met an officer. The neighbor, with his prisoner, came from the same place, down Union to Powell, along that street to Washington, and down to the lower side of the Plaza, before he met an officer. This was between three and four, A. M. What I wish to know is, where were the Police, and cannot we, in the remote parts, be protected by at least one officer?

§ 135. *Remarkable Dream*

8–10 February 1866

"Remarkable Dream" is part of Clemens' "San Francisco Letter" written on 6 February 1866 and probably published in the Virginia City *Territorial Enterprise* sometime between February 8 and 10. A clipping of the entire letter is preserved in the Yale Scrapbook.[1]

Some care and much evident pleasure went into this fanciful satire on Albert Evans. Clemens had good reason to suggest, as this sketch does at elaborate length, that Fitz Smythe was a liar. Evans' column in the January 29 issue of the Gold Hill *News* implied not only that Clemens had been locked up for drunkenness, but that he had associated with thieves and resisted arrest. Under the guise of giving advice Evans had said, "When you have been searched, and your tobacco and toothpick safely locked up, go quietly into the cell and lay down on your blankets, instead of standing at the grating, cursing and indulging in obscene language until they lock you up." On February 9, perhaps having read "Remarkable Dream," Evans said in another letter to the Gold Hill *News:* "I am pained beyond measure, friend of my heart, to learn that Mark Twain insists on regarding as *personal* that friendly advice I gave in my letter of two weeks since. . . . I beg leave to assure you that nothing personal was intended. Having due regard for my reputation for veracity, I cannot, of course, take it upon myself to deny that Twain might not at one time have profited by the advice."[2] Considering the snide tone of both Evans' letters, the restraint and good humor of Clemens' reply are notable.

---

[1]Another selection from the same letter, "Ministerial Change" (no. 174), appears in its chronological position in this collection.

[2]"Our San Francisco Correspondence," Gold Hill *News*, 29 January 1866, p. 2; ibid., 12 February 1866, p. 2. For a fuller account of the quarrel, see *MTCor*, pp. 38–40.

Clemens' knowledge of Cervantes, whom he had read as early as 1860, probably helped shape his portrait of Fitz Smythe astride his steed—a kind of debased, timeserving Don Quixote or, as Tom Pepper expresses it in the sketch, one of "those noble knights whose nature it is to war against truth wherever they find it." The sketch was, at any rate, sufficiently successful for Clemens to revise it extensively in the Yale Scrapbook, and to consider reprinting it in the 1867 *Jumping Frog* book. Although it was not ultimately included there, it was memorable enough to the editor of the *Californian's* "Lion's Mouth" column for him to mention it late in August 1867, while Mark Twain was in the Holy Land:

Mark will first direct his steps to the spot rendered to him sacred by association with Ananias, an individual whose regard for veracity was fully equal to that of Mark himself. It is not unlikely that Ananias' shade will accompany Mark throughout his wanderings, a mutual, beautiful, and natural sympathy being established between them, more particularly arising from Mark's efforts to repopularize Ananias about a year and a half ago, when he introduced him to the San Francisco public, as engaged in the business of swapping lies with Fitz-Smythe, on the outskirts of hell.[3]

---

[3]"Mark Twain," *Californian* 7 (31 August 1867): 1. The item appeared under "City Gossip" in "The Lion's Mouth."

Remarkable Dream

I DREAMED last night that I was sitting in my room smoking my pipe and looking into the dying embers on the hearth, conjuring up old faces in their changing shapes, and listening to old voices in the moaning winds outside, when there was a knock at the door and a man entered—bowed—walked deliberately forward and sat down opposite me. He was dressed in a queer old garb of I don't know how many centuries ago. He said, with a perceptible show of vanity:

"My name's Ananias—may have heard of me, perhaps?"

I said, reflectively, "No—no—I think not, Mr. Anan——"

"Never heard of me! Bismillah! Och hone! gewhil——. But you couldn't have read the Scriptures!"

I rose to my feet in great surprise: "Ah—is it possible?—I remember now—I remember your history. Yes, yes, yes, I remember you made a little statement that wouldn't wash, so to speak, and they took your life for it. They—they bounced a thunderbolt on your head, or something of that sort, didn't they?"

"Yes, but drop these matters and let's to business. The thief sympathizes with the thief, the murderer with the murderer, the vagabond with the vagabond: I, too, feel for *my* kind—I want to do something for this Fitz Smythe——"

"Give me your hand!—this sentiment does you honor, sir, it does you honor! And this solicitude of the Prince of Liars for the humble disciple Fitz Smythe is well merited, it is indeed—for although, Sire, his efforts may not be brilliant, they make up for that defect in bulk and quantity; such steady persistence as his, such unwearying devotion to his art, are deserving of the highest encomium."

"You know the man—I see that—and he is worthy of your admiration. As you say, his lies are not brilliant, but they never slack up—they are always on time. Some of them are awkward—very stupid and awkward—but that is to be expected, of course, where a man is at it so constantly and exhaustively as Fitz Smythe—or as we call him in hell, 'Brother Smythe'—we all take the *Alta*. But they are strong!—they are awkward and stupid, but they are powerful free from truth! You take his mildest lie—take those he tells about Mark Twain, for instance (who is the only newspaper man I have ever come across who wouldn't lie and couldn't lie, shame to him,)—take those lies—take even the very mildest of them, and don't you know they'd let a man out mighty quick in my time? Why there'd have been more thunder and lightning after him in two seconds! If Fitz Smythe had lived in my time and told that little lie he told about you last—just that little one, even—he'd have been knocked from Jericho to Jacksonville quick as winking! Lord bless you but they were mighty particular in those days! Notice how they hazed me!"

"So they did, sir, so they did—they snatched you very lively indeed, sir."

"But we'll come to business, now. No man's productions are more admired in the regions of the damned than Fitz Smythe's. We have watched his career with pride and satisfaction, and at a meeting held in Perdition last night a committee of the most distinguished liars the world has ever produced was appointed to visit the earth and confer upon our gifted disciple certain marks of distinction to which we consider him entitled—orders of merit, they are—honors which he has laboriously earned. We wish to confer these compliments upon him through you, his bosom friend. Now, therefore, I, Ananias Chief of Liars by Seniority, do hereby create our worthy disciple Armand Leonidas Fitz Smythe Amigo Stiggers, a Knight of the Grand Order of the Liars of St. Ananias, and confer upon him the freedom of hell. And the symbol of this order being a horse, I do hereby present him this noble animal, which manifests its preference for falsehood over truth by devouring daily newspapers in preference to any other food."

I looked at the horse, as he stood there chewing up my last *Bulletin,* and recognized him as the beast Fitz Smythe rides every day. Ananias now bade me good evening, and said his wife, another member of the Committee, would now call upon me.

The door opened, and the ancient Sapphira, who was stricken with death for telling a lie, ages ago, stood before me. She said:

"I have heard my husband; he has spoken well; it is sufficient. I do hereby create Armand Leonidas Fitz Smythe Amigo Stiggers a Knight of the Order of the Liars of St. Sapphira, and clothe him with the regalia pertaining to the same—this pair of gray pantaloons—a sign and symbol of the matrimonial supremacy which I have enjoyed in my household from time immemorial."

And she left the gray pantaloons and departed, saying the next member of the Committee who would appear would be the most noble the Baron de Munchausen. The door opened and the world-famed liar entered:

"I come to do honor to my son, the inspired Armand Leonidas Fitz Smythe Amigo Stiggers. It ill beseemeth a father to boast at length of his own offspring, wherefore I shall say no more in that respect, but proceed to create him a Knight of the Noble Order of the Liars of St. Munchausen, and invest him with the regalia pertaining to the same—this gray frock coat—which hath been a symbol of depravity in all ages of the world." And the great Baron shed a few tears of paternal pride and murmured, "Kiss him for his father," and went away. As he disappeared he remarked that the next and last member of the committee would now wait upon me, in the person of Thomas Pepper. And in a moment the re-nowned Tom Pepper, who was such a preposterous liar that he couldn't get to heaven and they wouldn't have him in hell, was present! He said:

"I have watched the great Armand Leonidas Fitz Smythe Amigo Stiggers with extraordinary interest. So we all have—but how heedless we are! Those who were with you within this hour praised him without stint and mentioned his excellencies—yet not one of them has discovered his crowning grace—his highest gift. It is this—he always tells the truth with such windy, wordy, blundering awkwardness that nobody ever believes it, and so his truths usually pass for his most splendid falsehoods! [I could not help acknowledging to myself that this was so.] A man with such a talent as that is bound to achieve high distinction and do great service in our ranks; and for this talent of his more than for his wonderful abilities in distorting facts, I do hereby confer upon him the Sublime Order of the Knights of the Liars of St. Pepper, and present him with the symbol pertaining to the same—this grim, twisted, sharply-projecting, sunburned mustache, whose fashion and pattern are only permitted to be used by those noble knights whose nature it is to war against truth wherever they find it, and to go a long, long way out of their road to prospect for chances to lie. I am the only man the world ever produced who was so wonderful a romancer that he could neither get a show in heaven nor hell, and Fitz Smythe will be the second one. It will be jolly. It is lonesome now, but when Smythe comes we two will loaf around on the outside of damnation and swap lies and be p-e-r-fectly happy. Good day, old Petrified Facts, good day." And Tom Pepper, the most splendid liar the world ever gave birth to, was gone!

That was my dream. And don't you know that for as much as six hours afterwards I fully believed it was nothing *but* a dream? But just before three o'clock to-day I thought my hair would turn white with amazement when I saw Amigo Fitz Smythe issue from that alley near the *Alta* office riding the very horse Ananias gave him, and that horse eating a file of the Gold Hill *News*; and wearing the same gray pantaloons Mrs. Sapphira Ananias gave him; and the gray coat that Baron Munchausen gave him, and with his pensive nose overhanging those two skewers—that absurd sunburned mustache, I mean—which Tom Pepper gave him. So it was reality. It was no dream after all! This lets me out with Fitz Smythe, you know. I cannot associate with that kind of stock. I don't want the worst characters in hell to be running after me with friendly messages and little testimonials of admiration for Smythe, and blowing about his talents, and bragging on him, and belching their villainous fire and brimstone all through the atmosphere and making my place smell worse than a menagerie. I have too much regard for my good name and my personal comfort, and so this lets me out with Fitz Smythe.

136. "Mark Twain" on the Launch of the Steamer "Capital"

18 November 1865

Clemens published this sketch in the *Californian* on 18 November 1865, the same day that the New York *Saturday Press* published "Jim Smiley and His Jumping Frog" (no. 119). He did not contribute to the *Californian* again until "The Christmas Fireside" (no. 148) was published on December 23.

On November 4 the California Steam Navigation Company launched its new steamboat, the *Capital*, which had been built to replace the old *Antelope* in the San Francisco–Sacramento trade and represented the latest in riverboat architecture and fittings. The San Francisco *Evening Bulletin* reported that the launch had been successfully completed "at the Potrero this morning, in the presence of several thousand spectators."

The ferry-boat *San Antonio* took out a large party of ladies and gentlemen to witness the launch, and the waters of the bay in the vicinity of the Potrero were thickly spotted with yachts, sail-boats and row boats filled with pleasure parties, while the hill-sides in the neighborhood of the yard were covered with spectators of both sexes. . . . At precisely 11½ oclock, the time advertised for the launch, the last of the stays was knocked away, the signal gun was fired, and the steamer glided slowly down the ways into the water amid the cheers of the spectators, mingled with the strains of music from the band on board the *San Antonio*, which struck up the appropriate air of *Life on the Ocean Wave*. The gradual descent from the ways gave an impetus sufficient only to send the boat a hundred yards or less into the water, but the swan-like gracefulness with which she rode the waves and the beauty and symmetry of her model won the admiration of all beholders.

Similar accounts appeared in the *Morning Call* and the *Alta California*.[1]

---

[1]"The Launch of the New Steamer," San Francisco *Evening Bulletin*, 4 November 1865, p. 5; "Launch of the 'Capital,' " San Francisco *Morning Call*, 5 November 1865, p. 1.

Scorning all such "inevitable old platitudinal trash," Clemens here set out to deliver an account of the launch "which should astonish and delight the whole intellectual world—which should dissect, analyze, and utterly exhaust the subject—which should serve for a model in this species of literature for all time to come." In fact, he returned to his time-worn ploy of promising to deliver what he never intended to write. The drinking session with Muff Nickerson and various gentlemen from Reese River, Excelsior, and Mud Springs is only a frame for the inset story of the scriptural panoramist, told, as Clemens says, "in Mr. Nickerson's own language." Nickerson does not affect Simon Wheeler's deadpan manner, but his narrative is thoroughly vernacular both in language and in the familiar antithesis between the "moral religious show" conceived by the panoramist and the "old mud-dobber" pianist, whose perfectly good intentions lead him to play unabashedly secular songs for a solemn occasion—"Life on the Ocean Wave" for Christ's walk on the Sea of Galilee, for instance.

Clemens and Webb decided to reprint the sketch in the 1867 *Jumping Frog* book, and it was probably Webb who made several cuts in the frame story. When the book was reprinted by the Routledges in England, Tom Hood reviewed it favorably in *Fun* and said in part: "In several of the sketches we get a charming insight into American usages. We are told, for instance, that young 'bucks and heifers' always come it strong on panoramas because it 'gives them a chance of tasting one another's mugs in the dark.' Our readers will hardly recognise the seductive process of osculation in this expression."[2] Unaware of this praise, Clemens proceeded to revise out the passage referred to when he reprinted the sketch in England in 1872. And he continued to tone down the slang and the colorful language of the original, saying at one point that it was "too vigorous for repetition, and is better left out." The sketch that he ultimately reprinted in *Sketches, New and Old* as "The Scriptural Panoramist" had lost not only much of its original language, but the whole of the frame story. The original version is, of course, reprinted here: the author's revisions of his text are described in the textual commentary.

---

[2]"Our Library Table," *Fun* 6 (19 October 1867): 65.

"Mark Twain" on the Launch of the Steamer "Capital"

I GET MR. MUFF NICKERSON TO GO WITH ME
AND ASSIST IN REPORTING THE GREAT STEAM-
BOAT LAUNCH. HE RELATES THE INTERESTING
HISTORY OF THE TRAVELLING PANORAMIST.

I WAS JUST starting off to see the launch of the great steamboat *Capital*, on Saturday week, when I came across Mulph, Mulff, Muff, Mumph, Murph, Mumf, Murf, Mumford, Mulford, Murphy Nickerson—(he is well known to the public by all these names, and I cannot say which is the right one)—bound on the same errand. He said that if there was one thing he took more delight in than another, it was a steamboat launch; he would walk miles to see one, any day; he had seen a hundred thousand steamboat launches in his time, and hoped he might live to see a hundred thousand more; he knew all about them; knew everything—*every*thing connected with them—said he "had it all down to a scratch;" he could explain the whole process in minute detail; to the uncultivated eye a steamboat-launch presented nothing grand, nothing startling, nothing beautiful, nothing romantic, or awe-inspiring or sublime—but to an optic like his (which saw not the dull outer coating, but the radiant gem it hid from other eyes,) it presented all these—and behold, he had power to lift the veil and display the vision even unto the uninspired. He could do this by word of mouth—by explanation and illustration. Let a man stand by his side, and to him that launch should seem arrayed in the beauty and the glory of enchantment!

This was the man I wanted. I could see that plainly enough. There would be many reporters present at the launch, and the papers would teem with the inevitable old platitudinal trash which this sort of people have compelled to do duty on every occasion like this since Noah launched his ark—but I aspired to higher things. I wanted to write a report which should astonish and delight the whole intellectual world—which should dissect, analyze, and utterly exhaust the subject—which should serve for a model in this species of literature for all time to come. I dropped alongside of Mr. M. M. M. M. M. M. M. M. M. Nickerson, and we went to the launch together.

We set out in a steamer whose decks were crowded with persons of all ages, who were happy in their nervous anxiety to behold the novelty of a steamboat launch. I tried not to pity them, but I could not help whispering to myself, "These poor devils will see nothing but some stupid boards and timbers nailed together—a mere soulless hulk—sliding into the water!"

As we approached the spot where the launch was to take place, a gentleman from Reese River, by the name of Thompson, came up, with several friends, and said he had been prospecting on the main deck, and had found an object of interest—a bar. This was all very well, and showed him to be a man of parts—but like many another man who produces a favorable impression by an introductory remark replete with wisdom, he followed it up with a vain and unnecessary question—Would we take a drink? This to me!—This to M. M. M., etc., Nickerson!

We proceeded, two-by-two, arm-in-arm, down to the bar in the nether regions, chatting pleasantly and elbowing the restless multitude. We took pure, cold, health-giving water, with some other things in it, and clinked our glasses together, and were about to drink, when Smith, of Excelsior, drew forth his handkerchief and wiped away a tear; and then, noticing that the action had excited some attention, he explained it by recounting a most affecting incident in the history of a venerated aunt of his—now deceased—and said that, although long years had passed since the

touching event he had narrated, he could never take a drink without thinking of the kind-hearted old lady.

Mr. Nickerson blew his nose, and said with deep emotion that
it gave him a better opinion of human nature to see a man who
had had a good aunt, eternally and forever thinking about her.

This episode reminded Jones, of Mud Springs, of a circumstance
which happened many years ago in the home of his childhood,
and we held our glasses untouched and rested our elbows on the
counter, while we listened with rapt attention to his story.

There was something in it about a good natured, stupid man,
and this reminded Thompson of Reese River of a person of the
same kind whom he had once fallen in with while travelling
through the back-settlements of one of the Atlantic States, and
we postponed drinking until he should give us the facts in the
case. The hero of the tale had unintentionally created some con-
sternation at a camp-meeting by one of his innocent asinine
freaks, and this reminded Mr. M. Nickerson of a reminiscence
of his temporary sojourn in the interior of Connecticut some
months ago, and again our uplifted glasses were stayed on their
way to our lips, and we listened attentively to

THE ENTERTAINING HISTORY
OF THE SCRIPTURAL PANORAMIST.

[I give the story in Mr. Nickerson's own language.]

There was a fellow travelling around, in that country, (said
Mr. Nickerson,) with a moral religious show—a sort of a scriptural panorama—and he hired a wooden-headed old slab to play
the piano for him. After the first night's performance, the showman says:

"My friend, you seem to know pretty much all the tunes there
are, and you worry along first-rate. But then didn't you notice that
sometimes last night the piece you happened to be playing was a
little rough on the proprieties so to speak—didn't seem to jibe
with the general gait of the picture that was passing at the time,
as it were—was a little foreign to the subject, you know—as if
you didn't either trump or follow suit, you understand?"

"Well, no," the fellow said; he hadn't noticed, but it might be;
he had played along just as it came handy.

So they put it up that the simple old dummy was to keep his eye on the panorama after that, and as soon as a stunning picture was reeled out, he was to fit it to a dot with a piece of music that would help the audience get the idea of the subject, and warm them up like a camp-meeting revival. That sort of thing would corral their sympathies, the showman said.

There was a big audience that night—mostly middle-aged and old people who belonged to the church and took a strong interest in Bible matters, and the balance were pretty much young bucks and heifers—*they* always come out strong on panoramas, you know, because it gives them a chance to taste one another's mugs in the dark.

Well, the showman began to swell himself up for his lecture, and the old mud-dobber tackled the piano and run his fingers up and down once or twice to see that she was all right, and the fellows behind the curtain commenced to grind out the panorama. The showman balanced his weight on his right foot, and propped his hands on his hips, and flung his eye over his shoulder at the scenery, and says:

"Ladies and gentlemen, the painting now before you illustrates the beautiful and touching parable of the Prodigal Son. Observe the happy expression just breaking over the features of the poor suffering youth—so worn and weary with his long march: note also the ecstasy beaming from the uplifted countenance of the aged father, and the joy that sparkles in the eyes of the excited group of youths and maidens and seems ready to burst in a welcoming chorus from their lips. The lesson, my friends, is as solemn and instructive as the story is tender and beautiful."

The mud-dobber was all ready, and the second the speech was finished he struck up:

> "Oh, we'll all get blind drunk
> When Johnny comes marching home!"

Some of the people giggled, and some groaned a little. The showman couldn't say a word. He looked at the piano sharp, but he was all lovely and serene—*he* didn't know there was anything out of gear.

The panorama moved on, and the showman drummed up his grit and started in fresh:

"Ladies and gentlemen, the fine picture now unfolding itself to your gaze exhibits one of the most notable events in Bible History—our Savior and his disciples upon the Sea of Galilee. How grand, how awe inspiring are the reflections which the subject invokes! What sublimity of faith is revealed to us in this lesson from the sacred writings! The Savior rebukes the angry waves, and walks securely upon the bosom of the deep!"

All around the house they were whispering: "Oh, how lovely! how beautiful!" and the orchestra let himself out again:

> "Oh, a life on the ocean wave,
> And a home on the rolling deep!"

There was a good deal of honest snickering turned on this time, and considerable groaning, and one or two old deacons got up and went out. The showman gritted his teeth and cursed the piano man to himself, but the fellow sat there like a knot on a log, and seemed to think he was doing first-rate.

After things got quiet, the showman thought he would make one more stagger at it, any how, though his confidence was beginning to get mighty shaky. The supes started the panorama to grinding along again, and he says:

"Ladies and gentlemen, this exquisite painting illustrates the raising of Lazarus from the dead by our Savior. The subject has been handled with rare ability by the artist, and such touching sweetness and tenderness of expression has he thrown into it, that I have known peculiarly sensitive persons to be even affected to tears by looking at it. Observe the half-confused, half-inquiring look, upon the countenance of the awakening Lazarus. Observe, also, the attitude and expression of the Savior, who takes him gently by the sleeve of his shroud with one hand, while he points with the other toward the distant city."

Before anybody could get off an opinion in the case, the innocent old ass at the piano struck up:

> "Come rise up, William Ri-i-ley,
> And go along with me!"

It was rough on the audience, you bet you. All the solemn old flats got up in a huff to go, and everybody else laughed till the windows rattled.

The showman went down and grabbed the orchestra, and shook him up, and says:

"That lets you out, you know, you chowder-headed old clam! Go to the door-keeper and get your money, and cut your stick!— vamose the ranch! Ladies and gentlemen, circumstances over which I have no control compel me prematurely to dismiss—"

"By George! it was splendid!—come! all hands! let's take a drink!"

It was Phelim O'Flannigan, of San Luis Obispo, who interrupted. I had not seen him before. "What was splendid?" I inquired.

"The launch!"

Our party clinked glasses once more, and drank in respectful silence.

MARK TWAIN.

P. S.—You will excuse me from making a model report of the great launch. I was with Mulf Nickerson, who was going to "explain the whole thing to me as clear as glass," but, you see, they launched the boat with such indecent haste, that we never got a chance to see it. It was a great pity, because Mulph Nickerson understands launches as well as any man.

137. The Pioneers' Ball

19 or 21 November 1865

Clemens' burlesque report of the fashions at the ball of the Society of California Pioneers was probably written shortly after it took place on 16 November 1865: the savage bluntness of his final paragraph, and his repeated allusions to female nudity, suggest temporarily relaxed inhibitions. The sketch was published in the Virginia City *Territorial Enterprise* several days later, probably on November 19 or 21 (November 20 was a Monday). Although the original *Enterprise* printing has been lost, the sketch was reprinted by the *Californian* on November 25, and by the *Golden Era* (and the *California Weekly Mercury*) on November 26. The present text is reconstructed from two of these reprintings.[1]

The Society of California Pioneers—an exclusive group founded in 1850—claimed approximately eight hundred members in 1865. Its purpose was to collect and preserve the memory of the pioneers, defined as those who were in California before 1 January 1850. They held their ball at the Occidental Hotel. It was the first given by the society in almost three years and was intended to inaugurate a series of social events planned for the new Pioneer Hall on Montgomery Street. For Lewis and Jerome Leland, the proprietors of the Occidental and Clemens' good friends, it was the climax of a busy fall season that had included an elegant reception for Schuyler Colfax and his party of visiting eastern nabobs.[2]

---

[1]The reprinting in the *California Weekly Mercury* has not been found. The San Francisco *Dramatic Chronicle* said on November 29, however, that the *Mercury* had reprinted the sketch without giving credit: "This is not the fair thing. The *Enterprise* pays its contributors, and we suspect that 'Mark Twain' is one of the 'high-priced' Bohemians who decline to write for six bits per column" ("Say There, Now!" San Francisco *Dramatic Chronicle*, 29 November 1865, p. 2).

[2]"The Pioneers' Ball," San Francisco *Golden Era* 13 (19 November 1865): 8.

Clemens' sketch is less elaborate than "The Lick House Ball" and "Mark Twain—More of Him" (nos. 65 and 64), but it follows in the somewhat bolder tone set by his recent "San Francisco Letter" (no. 125). Bret Harte called it a "characteristic description of 'noticeable costumes'" and a "clever satire on Jenkins."[3] ("Jenkins" was the generalized name for any platitudinous journalist who placed conventional respectabilities above honest reporting. To "Jenkins," for example, went the credit for initiating the "style of initials only" in society reports.)[4]

Clemens and Webb reprinted part of this sketch in the 1867 *Jumping Frog* book, and Clemens continued to revise (chiefly to shorten) and reprint it in 1872, 1874, and 1875. The version that appeared in the last year in *Sketches, New and Old* was probably edited by Elisha Bliss for use as filler on page 256 of that book. The original text, as reconstructed here from two independent reprintings of the *Enterprise*, has not been reprinted before.

---

[3]"The Pioneer Ball," *Californian* 3 (25 November 1865): 12.
[4]" 'Jenkins' at the Reception," *Californian* 2 (22 April 1865): 4.

The Pioneers' Ball

Iт wаs estimated that four hundred persons were present at the ball. The gentlemen wore the orthodox costume for such occasions, and the ladies were dressed the best they knew how. N. B.—Most of these ladies were pretty, and some of them absolutely beautiful. Four out of every five ladies present were pretty. The ratio at the Colfax party was two out of every five. I always keep the run of these things. While upon this department of the subject, I may as well tarry a moment and furnish you with descriptions of some of the most noticeable costumes.

Mrs. W. M. was attired in an elegant *pate de foi gras,* made expressly for her, and was greatly admired.

Miss S. had her hair done up. She was the centre of attraction for the gentlemen, and the envy of all the ladies.

Miss G. W. was tastefully dressed in a *tout ensemble,* and was greeted with deafening applause wherever she went.

Mrs. C. N. was superbly arrayed in white kid gloves. Her modest and engaging manner accorded well with the unpretending simplicity of her costume, and caused her to be regarded with absorbing interest by every one.

The charming Miss M. M. B. appeared in a thrilling waterfall, whose exceeding grace and volume compelled the homage of pioneers and emigrants alike. How beautiful she was!

The queenly Mrs. L. R. was attractively attired in her new and beautiful false teeth, and the *bon jour* effect they naturally produced was heightened by her enchanting and well-sustained smile. The manner of this lady is charmingly pensive and melancholy, and her troops of admirers desired no greater happiness than to get on the scent of her sozodont-sweetened sighs and track her through her sinuous course among the gay and restless multitude.

Miss R. P., with that repugnance to ostentation in dress which is so peculiar to her, was attired in a simple white lace collar, fastened with a neat pearl-button solitaire. The fine contrast between the sparkling vivacity of her natural optic and the steadfast attentiveness of her placid glass eye was the subject of general and enthusiastic remark.

The radiant and sylph-like Mrs. T., late of your State, wore hoops. She showed to good advantage, and created a sensation wherever she appeared. She was the gayest of the gay.

Miss C. L. B. had her fine nose elegantly enameled, and the easy grace with which she blew it from time to time, marked her as a cultivated and accomplished woman of the world; its exquisitely modulated tone excited the admiration of all who had the happiness to hear it.

Being offended with Miss X., and our acquaintance having ceased permanently, I will take this opportunity of observing to her that it is of no use for her to be slopping off to every ball that takes place, and flourishing around with a brass oyster-knife skewered through her waterfall, and smiling her sickly smile through her decayed teeth, with her dismal pug nose in the air. There is no use in it—she don't fool anybody. Everybody knows she is old; everybody knows she is repaired (you might almost say built) with artificial bones and hair and muscles and things, from the ground up—put together scrap by scrap—and everybody knows, also, that all one would have to do would be to pull out her key-pin and she would go to pieces like a Chinese puzzle. There, now, my faded flower, take that paragraph home with you and amuse yourself with it; and if ever you turn your wart of a nose up at me again I will sit down and write something that will just make you rise up and howl.

138. The Guard on a Bender

25 November 1865

Perhaps as part of his effort to get out of debt,[1] Clemens wrote three letters to the *Napa County Reporter* while he was also contributing a daily letter to the Virginia City *Territorial Enterprise* and frequent squibs to the San Francisco *Dramatic Chronicle*.[2] They appeared on 11 and 25 November and 2 December 1865. The present sketch and the next one, "Benkert Cometh!" (no. 139), comprised most of his second letter, published in Napa City on November 25. According to the dateline it was written in San Francisco on November 23.

Clemens' account of the "valiant corporal" and his men may have exaggerated the befogged wanderings of the provost guard through an area of some twenty-one square blocks. But he wrote with precision about places and streets that he had come to know thoroughly from his days as a *Morning Call* reporter in 1864.[3]

---

[1]See Clemens to Orion and Mollie Clemens, 19–20 October 1865, *CL1*, letter 95: "If I do not get out of debt in 3 months,—pistols or poison for one—exit *me*."
[2]See Appendix B, volume 2.
[3]For details, see the explanatory notes.

The Guard on a Bender

At 2 O'CLOCK yesterday morning, a corporal and five men belonging to the Provost Guard started up from headquarters to relieve the sentries in front of the mint. They were as drunk as lords when they started, and the further they went the drunker they got. They brought up at the "Blue Wing" saloon in the course of their wanderings, and took a drink or so and set out to complete their mission. They went in the wrong direction. The Corporal marched in front down Montgomery street, and kept a sharp lookout for the mint building, and finally thought he had found it. He examined the "Bank Exchange" with a critical eye for a while, and then placed a guard over it and started for home. He did not go far, however, before it occurred to his foggy mind that something was wrong—he was alone, and he ought to have the relieved guard with him. So he went back, took another look, and decided that the Bank Exchange was not the mint, and ordered his men to take up the line of march again. The party stopped at the "Old Corner" a few moments; the corporal put the men through the manual of arms on the pavement—and it was a remarkably loose performance—and then took them in and treated them.

By this time a squad of late idlers had got interested in the expedition, and were bent on seeing it out. The valiant corporal marched up to Wells, Fargo & Co's building and left a guard over it, and reeled down street again. And again he could not account for his being alone. He went back and formed his troop into line of battle, and demanded of them what had become of "that other d—d guard." One man touched his hat and ventured to suggest, in language carefully framed to give as little offense as possible, that they were taking care of some other place instead of the mint.

"Silence!" thundered the corporal, and gave the man to understand that he must not arrogate to himself more wisdom than his officer. Then he drifted around at large for an hour or so, putting his army through a drunken drill at intervals, when his perplexity became too burdensome for him, and successively placing under military guard the Lick House, the Occidental Market, and St. Mary's Cathedral and other buildings which resembled the mint about as much as the mint resembles a top sail schooner. Toward daylight the weary troop marched down Washington street, and turned into Kearny, and the corporal set them to watch the City Hall. He then went in and ordered the lights in Chief Burke's office to be put out, and was informed that the regulations required them to be kept burning in the police department. The corporal was glad to find he was at the police station; he said his guard at the mint had deserted their post, and he had placed the relief guard in possession of it some twenty times since two o'clock, but he couldn't go to headquarters without the retiring squad, and so he had been obliged every time to start out cruising after them afresh. He said of course they had got drunk and got into the station house. He did not want them if that was the case, but promised to come "in the morning" and get them out. So he gave the order "Double file—left wheel—march!" or something to that effect, and shortly disappeared down the street in the fog. He continued to "cruise" after the lost men and the lost mint all day, maybe, for at nine o'clock the guard in front of that building had not yet been relieved.

139 *Benkert Cometh!*

25 November 1865

This sketch formed the second section of Clemens' 25 November 1865 letter from San Francisco to the *Napa County Reporter.*[1] The pianist who provides Clemens with this slight joke, George Felix Benkert, is remembered today chiefly as the composer of several songs and as a teacher of John Philip Sousa. According to a report published two days before Clemens wrote his letter, Benkert had sailed for San Francisco on November 16. He would give his first San Francisco concert on 7 June 1866 at the Academy of Music.[2] As Clemens doubtless knew, mining boots manufactured by L. and C. Benkert Company of Philadelphia were distributed through the company's agent, another George F. Benkert, at 210 Pine Street in San Francisco. The boots were widely advertised, and used, in California and Washoe mining camps.

---

[1] See the headnote to "The Guard on a Bender" (no. 138).

[2] "Musician Coming," San Francisco *Evening Bulletin,* 21 November 1865, p. 3; "Mr. Benkert's Concert," ibid., 8 June 1866, p. 3.

Benkert Cometh!

THE PAPERS announce that Geo. F. Benkert, an eminent pianist of Philadelphia, is on his way out here to give us some concerts. Now, don't you know that fellow will be mighty popular in California? Certainly he will. That is, if he is the same man who makes the boots. The boys all like those Benkert boots, and they will patronize their manufacturer's concerts liberally. Up in the mining towns they will just take it for granted that it is the boot-making Benkert, unless they are specially notified that it is not, and they will go to the concerts reflecting thus: "Dang this feller, I like his boots, and so I'll give him a hyste with his music." And I think it will astonish this Benkert some, in the mining camps, to look across the top of his piano, and see the feet of his male patrons, propped on the backs of the benches, and long gleaming rows of bran-new hob-nailed Benkert boots staring him in the face! The boys will naturally hit upon this method of paying him a delicate and appreciative compliment.

140 Uncle Lige

28–30 November 1865

This sketch is preserved in the *Californian*, which reprinted it on 2 December 1865, probably within a few days of its appearance in the Virginia City *Territorial Enterprise*. Under the heading " 'Mark Twain' Overpowered" Bret Harte supplied a preface explaining that the *Enterprise* "having recently published one of those 'affecting incidents,' which are occasionally met with by 'localitems,' when there is a dearth of fires, runaways, etc., 'Mark Twain' issues the following as a companion-piece."

In the first sentence of the sketch Clemens says that he is relating "a companion novelette to the one published by Dan the other day, entitled 'Uncle Henry.' " Dan De Quille's "Uncle Henry" is not extant, but preserved among his papers is another, undoubtedly similar, sketch, from which we may infer what it was like. This other novelette, called "The Home 'Under the Star,' " was published in the *Enterprise* on an unknown date; it displays the same kind of sentimentality that Clemens mocks in his "Uncle Lige." It speaks of the tender attachment between "Uncle Will from Washoe" and his niece, "little Wilhemina," who always "clasped her arms about his neck and refused to be separated from him." Wilhemina is entranced by her uncle's description of his home under the star in the West, and even years after his return to Nevada she yearns to join him there. When she is fatally scalded, she speaks her final words gazing at the western sky: "Oh, there it is. Now I can find my way to Uncle Will—I can see his star." On top of this sentiment-laden death scene Dan piles a thick layer of blatant moralizing.[1]

Clemens may have been thinking, as Howard Baetzhold has argued, of Dickens' sentimentality (Little Nell and her grandfather in *The Old*

---

[1]Carton 1, folder 145, William Wright Papers, Bancroft.

Curiosity Shop, for example).[2] But Clemens' undoubted familiarity with Dan De Quille's style, and also with his predilection for writing about his Quaker uncles,[3] probably suggested as a more immediate target Dan's novelette, which Clemens urges Joe Goodman to publish with his own in "book form" to send out "to destroy such of our fellow citizens as are spared by the cholera." "Uncle Lige" bears comparison with two earlier examples of the "condensed" novel in the present volume, "Original Novelette" (no. 80) and "Lucretia Smith's Soldier" (no. 99).

---

[2]Howard G. Baetzhold, *Mark Twain and John Bull* (Bloomington: Indiana University Press, 1970), p. 307.

[3]See "How My Quaker Uncle Fixed a Fighting Ram," San Francisco *Golden Era* 12 (31 July 1864): 5.

Uncle Lige

I WILL NOW relate an affecting incident of my meeting with Uncle Lige, as a companion novelette to the one published by Dan the other day, entitled "Uncle Henry."

A day or two since—before the late stormy weather—I was taking a quiet stroll in the western suburbs of the city. The day was sunny and pleasant. In front of a small but neat "bit house," seated upon a bank—a worn out and discarded faro bank—I saw a man and a little girl. The sight was too much for me, and I burst into tears. Oh, God! I cried, this is too rough! After the violence of my emotion had in a manner spent itself, I ventured to look once more upon that touching picture. The left hand of the girl (how well I recollect which hand it was! by the warts on it)—a fair-haired, sweet-faced child of about eight years of age—rested upon the right shoulder (how perfectly I remember it was his right shoulder, because his left shoulder had been sawed off in a saw-mill) of the man by whose side she was seated. She was gazing toward the summit of Lone Mountain, and prating of the grave-stones on the top of it and of the sunshine and Diggers resting on its tomb-clad slopes. The head of the man drooped forward till his face almost rested upon his breast, and he seemed intently listening. It was only a pleasing pretence, though, for there was nothing for him to hear save the rattling of the carriages on the gravel road beside him, and he could have straightened himself up and heard that easy enough, poor fellow. As I approached, the child observed me, notwithstanding her extreme youth, and ceasing to talk, smilingly looked at me, strange as it may seem. I stopped, again almost overpowered, but after a struggle I mastered my feelings sufficiently to proceed. I gave her a smile—or rather, I swapped her one in return for the one I had just received, and she said:

"This is Uncle Lige—poor blind-drunk Uncle Lige."

This burst of confidence from an entire stranger, and one so young withal, caused my subjugated emotions to surge up in my breast once more, but again, with a strong effort, I controlled them. I looked at the wine-bred cauliflower on the poor man's nose and saw how it had all happened.

"Yes," said he, noticing by my eloquent countenance that I *had* seen how it had all happened, notwithstanding nothing had been said yet about anything having happened, "Yes, it happened in Reeseriv' a year ago; since tha(ic)at time been living here with broth—Robert'n lill Addie *(e-ick!)*."

"Oh, he's the best uncle, and tells me such stories!" cried the little girl.

"At's aw-ri, you know (ick!)—at's aw ri," said the kind-hearted, gentle old man, spitting on his shirt bosom and slurring it off with his hand.

The child leaned quickly forward and kissed his poor blossomy face. We beheld two great tears start from the man's sightless eyes, but when they saw what sort of country they had got to travel over, they went back again. Kissing the child again and again and once more and then several times, and afterwards repeating it, he said:

"H(o-ook!)—oorah for Melical eagle star-spalgle baller! At's aw-ri, you know—(ick!)—at's aw-ri"—and he stroked her sunny curls and spit on his shirt bosom again.

This affecting scene was too much for my already over-charged feelings, and I burst into a flood of tears and hurried from the spot.

Such is the touching story of Uncle Lige. It may not be quite as sick as Dan's, but there is every bit as much reasonable material in it for a big calf like either of us to cry over. Cannot you publish the two novelettes in book form and send them forth to destroy such of our fellow citizens as are spared by the cholera?

141. *Webb's Benefit*

2 December 1865

This brief sketch was part of Clemens' third and last letter to the *Napa County Reporter*. It was written in San Francisco on 30 November 1865 and published two days later in Napa City.

Dion Boucicault's second Irish drama, the popular *Arrah-na-Pogue,* ran for almost two months at San Francisco's Metropolitan Theatre during the fall of 1865. First produced in Dublin late in 1864, the play was revised by Boucicault for the London and New York productions the following year. In San Francisco it regularly drew large audiences and was enthusiastically reviewed in the local press. *Arrah-no-Poke,* Charles Henry Webb's clever but superficial parody of Boucicault's work, opened on November 15 at the Academy of Music. It was blessed with an excellent cast, including Dan Setchell and Harry Wall, who, according to Webb himself, joined with Bret Harte in contributing ideas for the parody. To some critics *Arrah-no-Poke* augured well for a future school of California playwrights, and its financial success doubtless stimulated Clemens' interest in writing for the stage.[1] The benefit performance for Webb, alluded to in Clemens' sketch, occurred on Monday night, November 27, three days before he wrote his letter to the *Reporter.*

Charles Henry Webb, the founder and first editor of the *Californian,* had been a friend of Clemens' for almost two years. Experienced as a whaler, a journalist for the New York *Times,* and a war correspondent, he had arrived in San Francisco in April 1863. He became the city editor for the San Francisco *Evening Bulletin,* where Clemens first knew him, be-

---

[1]"Letter from San Francisco," Sacramento *Union,* 24 November 1865, p. 2; "Theatrical Record," San Francisco *Morning Call,* 26 November 1865, p. 1; *CofC,* pp. 27–28.

fore founding the *Californian* in May 1864. He returned to New York in 1866, leaving San Francisco on the steamer *Sacramento* on April 18. During the three years that he remained in the West he contributed regularly to the *Golden Era* and the Sacramento *Union* using the pen names "Inigo" and "John Paul" respectively. He also contributed to and edited the *Californian* in three separate stints: from 29 May through 3 September 1864, from 26 November 1864 through 15 April 1865, and from 6 January 1866 until his departure in April.[2] In addition to *Arrah-no-Poke* he also wrote the stage comedy *Our Friend from Victoria.*

Although it was Bret Harte who first solicited Clemens' work for the *Californian,* Webb did publish several of Clemens' sketches in late 1864 and early 1865, and he publicly supported his friend's talents on a number of occasions. When the New York *Round Table* praised Mark Twain as the "foremost among the merry gentlemen of the California press," Webb greeted the notice as one who had long known what New Yorkers had only just discovered:

To my thinking Shakspeare had no more idea that he was writing for posterity than Mark Twain has at the present time, and it sometimes amuses me to think how future Mark Twain scholars will puzzle over that gentleman's present hieroglyphics and occasionally eccentric expressions. Apropos, of Twain, who is a man of Mark, I am glad to see that his humor has met with recognition at the East, and that mention is made of him in that critical journal, the *Round Table.* They may talk of coarse humor, if they please, but in his case it is simply the strength of the soil—the germ is there and it sprouts good and strong. To my mind Mark Twain and Dan Setchell are the Wild Humorists of the Pacific.[3]

This comment was written on November 1, just one month before Clemens returned the compliment—somewhat less emphatically—in "Webb's Benefit."

Webb continued to foster Clemens' interests in 1866 and 1867, partly by republishing selections from his letters to the Sacramento *Union* in the *Californian,* but most importantly by serving as editor and publisher of the 1867 *Jumping Frog* book. Webb had already published *Liffith Lank* in book form on 3 January 1867 when Clemens arrived in New York nine days later. Webb recalled the situation this way:

My friend Mark Twain coming East while I was publishing my own works, and being desirous of getting before the public, I undertook to publish a book for him—moved to a belief in its success from the fact

---

[2]AD, 21 May 1906, *MTE,* p. 143; "Inigoings," *Californian* 4 (5 May 1866): 8–9; 1 (3 September 1864): 8; 1 (26 November 1864): 8; 2 (15 April 1865): 8; 4 (6 January 1866): 8.

[3]"Letter from San Francisco," Sacramento *Union,* 3 November 1865, p. 2.

that nearly all the principal publishers in the United States had refused it. This selection from his miscellaneous writings was given to the world as The Jumping Frog of Calaveras and Other Sketches, by Mark Twain, a book of some 220 pages. It made an immediate success, and the copyright to-day would be worth to any publisher $5000 a year. At the request of the author, who wished to use some of the sketches in another form, and suppress others entirely, the stereotype plates were melted down about a year since, and The Jumping Frog has disappeared as a book from the trade forever.[4]

Webb published St. Twel'mo a few days after the Jumping Frog book, and he later published two collections of his own work, John Paul's Book (1874) and Parodies, Prose and Verse (1876).

---

[4]Charles Henry Webb, "An Autobiography, by John Paul," A Manual of American Literature: A Text-Book for Schools and Colleges, ed. John S. Hart (Philadelphia: Eldredge and Brother, 1873), pp. 443–444. For a fuller discussion of the Jumping Frog book, see the textual introduction in volume 1, pp. 503–546.

Webb's Benefit

THE ACADEMY of Music was well filled on Monday night, the occasion being the benefit of C. H. Webb, author of the new burlesque, "Arrah-no-Poke." I believe no play written on the Coast has paid the author as much coin as Mr. Webb has made out of this. During the interval between the pieces, Mr. Setchell read a humorous letter from Webb, which was received with hearty laughter, and then followed it up with a speech which was kindly received, until the orator ventured to branch out into a fine flight of eloquence; the audience would not stand that. The venerable expression, "through storm and sunshine," delivered with some little elocutionary flourish, evoked a burst of laughter which swept the house like a tornado. Now isn't it infamous that a professed humorist can never attempt anything fine, but people will at once imagine there is a joke about it somewhere, and laugh accordingly. I *did* once see an audience fooled by a humorist, though, or at least badly perplexed. An actress at the Opera House was playing the part of a houseless, friendless, persecuted and heart-broken young girl, and had so wrought upon the audience with her distress, that many were in tears. To heighten the effect, the playwright had put into the mouth of an humble character, the words, — "Poor thing, how she sighs!" Mr. Barry delivered these with touching pathos—so far so good—but he could not resist the temptation to add, in an undertone, "Ah me, how she sighs!—if she keeps on increasing her size this way, she'll oversize her grief eventually and die, poor creature!" The sorrowing maiden let her sad face droop gently behind her hand, and Mr. Barry assumed an air of severe and inflexible gravity, and so the audience dared venture upon nothing further than to look exceedingly uncertain. One irreverent man in the corner, did ejaculate "Oh, geewhillikens!" in a subdued tone of dissent, but he received no encouragement from the perplexed audience, and he pushed the matter no further.

142. *A Rich Epigram*

8–10 December 1865

This verse about Thomas Maguire, San Francisco's leading theater manager and impresario for three decades, was probably written shortly after the event to which it refers, and therefore published in the Virginia City *Territorial Enterprise* sometime between 8 and 10 December 1865. The original printing is not extant. The verse survives in the San Francisco *American Flag* for 20 December 1865, which introduced it with these words: " 'Mark Twain' has constructed the following extremely funny thing, at the expense of the enlightened and war-like 'Napoleon of the Stage.' "

Thomas Maguire came to California from New York in 1849. He began his theatrical career by opening the first Jenny Lind Theatre in 1850. Plucky, enterprising, hot-tempered, and constantly embroiled in courtroom controversy, Maguire did more than anyone else to bring novelty and talent to the San Francisco stage. In 1865, as proprietor of the Academy of Music and the Opera House, he completely dominated the city's theater. But in November and December of that year he made news with two highly personal disagreements: one with the composer and pianist W. J. Macdougall, the other with the Polish actress and opera singer Felicita Vestvali.[1]

On December 5, while in Kohler's music store, Maguire attacked Macdougall, strangling and pummeling him from behind. The day before, Macdougall had scheduled Miss Emily Thorne, a popular English comedienne and vocalist, to appear with him in a benefit concert for the

---

[1]Lois Foster Rodecape, "Tom Maguire, Napoleon of the Stage," *California Historical Society Quarterly* 20 (December 1941): 289–314; 21 (March 1942): 39–74; 21 (June 1942): 141–182; 21 (September 1942): 129–175.

British Benevolent Society of California. She had been prevented from appearing, however, by other arrangements made by her manager, Tom Maguire. Macdougall reacted to this slight by distributing a news release charging Maguire with broken promises, and the enraged Irishman responded with his attack. Maguire was ultimately fined fifty dollars for assault and battery.[2]

Maguire's earlier controversy was with Felicita Vestvali over her contract with him. Vestvali arrived in San Francisco on August 25 to play one hundred engagements within one hundred and thirty days. In October she charged Maguire with willful violation of her contract because he refused to schedule her performances with reasonable regularity. When Maguire learned that she meant to enforce her contract, he threatened to break every bone in her body. On October 31 her charges against Maguire for threatening bodily harm were dismissed in police court on his promise to refrain from violence. But the same day Vestvali entered a $30,000 breach of contract suit.[3]

Clemens' verse touches on both of these very public quarrels. His allusion to her as a "gentle Jew gal" refers to her popular role as the Jewish mother Gamea in the play *Gamea, the Fortune Teller*. Vestvali was an accomplished actress, known especially for her excellent impersonations of men.

---

[2]"Amusements," San Francisco *Dramatic Chronicle*, 4 December 1865, p. 2; ibid., 5 December 1865, p. 3; "Still Another Opera House Row," ibid., 6 December 1865, p. 3; "Maguire's Fine," San Francisco *Evening Bulletin*, 14 December 1865, p. 3.

[3]"Theatrical Record," San Francisco *Morning Call*, 27 August 1865, p. 1; "Starring under Difficulties," ibid., 1 November 1865, p. 1; "The Vestvali-Maguire Case. Examination in the Police Court," San Francisco *Evening Bulletin*, 1 November 1865, p. 3; "Magnificent Suit," San Francisco *Dramatic Chronicle*, 1 November 1865, p. 3; "The Star Chamber—Vestvali the Magnificent—The Threatened Smash among the Dramatic Planets," San Francisco *Golden Era* 13 (5 November 1865): 4.

A Rich Epigram

Tom Maguire,
Torn with ire,
Lighted on Macdougall,
Grabbed his throat,
Tore his coat,
And split him in the bugle.

Shame! Oh, fie!
Maguire, why
Will you thus skyugle?
Why bang and claw,
And gouge and chaw
The unprepared Macdougall?

Of bones bereft,
See how you've left,
Vestvali, gentle Jew gal—
And now you've slashed,
And almost hashed,
The form of poor Macdougall.

143. *A Graceful Compliment*

10–31 December 1865

This sketch was probably part of Clemens' regular San Francisco letter to the Virginia City *Territorial Enterprise*. An incomplete clipping of it survives in the Yale Scrapbook. The clipping bears an advertisement for the Bank of America on the back dated "de 10 tf," meaning December 10 until further notice. This suggests that the letter was not published before December 10, but it could have been published on that day or anytime after in December 1865, or perhaps even a little later.

Clemens' uneasy joking about his bohemian lack of money and property must be understood in the context of his resolution, less than two months before, to go "to work in dead earnest" to get out of debt. He said then that if he did "not get out of debt in 3 months," he would commit suicide. On December 13 he told Orion that he had made a proposition to Herman Camp to sell the family's 30,000 acres of Tennessee land. "Now I don't want that Tenn land to go for taxes, & I don't want any 'slouch' to take charge of the sale of it. I am tired being a beggar—tired being chained to this accursed homeless desert,—I want to go back to a Christian land once more." When this plan failed to meet Orion's approval, Clemens was again thrown back on his own resources. He did not get out of debt until sometime in 1868: in January of that year he told his family "I am gradually getting out of debt," while in December he told Jervis Langdon that he did not "owe a cent" to anyone.[1]

Although there is an obvious hazard in taking the figures in this sketch literally, if we do assume that Clemens did not much alter the facts, it is

---

[1]Clemens to Orion and Mollie Clemens, 19–20 October 1865, *CL1*, letter 95; Clemens to Orion Clemens, 13 December 1865, *CL1*, letter 96; Clemens to Jane Clemens and Pamela Moffett, 24 January 1868, *CL1*, letter 181; Clemens to Jervis Langdon, 29 December 1868, *CL1*, letter 256.

possible to estimate his income for 1864. The tax laws applying to that year indicate that Clemens' income over and above the $600 general exemption was taxed at the rate of five percent. Depending on whether or not he took an additional $200 exemption permitted renters, his income for 1864 was somewhere between $1,225 and $1,425.[2]

Clemens evidently considered using this sketch in his 1867 *Jumping Frog* book, for he slightly revised the clipping and listed it in the back of the Yale Scrapbook as among the seven sketches that he said did not "run average." It was not ultimately reprinted.

---

[2]Harry Edwin Smith, *The United States Federal Internal Tax History from 1861 to 1871* (Boston: Houghton, Mifflin Co., 1914), pp. 45–66; *MTCor*, p. 72.

A Graceful Compliment

ONE WOULD hardly expect to receive a neat, voluntary compliment from so grave an institution as the United States Revenue Office, but such has been my good fortune. I have not been so agreeably surprised in many a day. The Revenue officers, in a communication addressed to me, fondle the flattering fiction that I am a man of means, and have got "goods, chattels and effects" —and even "real estate!" Gentlemen, you couldn't have paid such a compliment as that to any man who would appreciate it higher, or be more grateful for it than myself. We will drink together, if you object not.

I am taxed on my income! This is perfectly gorgeous! I never felt so important in my life before. To be treated in this splendid way, just like another William B. Astor! Gentlemen, we *must* drink.

Yes, I am taxed on my income. And the printed paper which bears this compliment—all slathered over with fierce-looking written figures—looks as grand as a steamboat's manifest. It reads thus:

"COLLECTOR'S OFFICE,   ⎱
U. S. INTERNAL REVENUE, FIRST DIS'T. CAL. ⎰

Name . . . . .M. Twain
Residence . . . . .At Large
List and amount of tax $31 25
Penalty 3 12

Warrant 2 45
    Total amount $36 82
Date................................November 20, 1865.
                             C. ST GG,
                          Deputy Collector.
☞ Please present this at the Collector's office."

Now I consider that really handsome. I have got it framed beautifully, and I take more pride in it than any of my other furniture. I trust it will become an heirloom and serve to show many generations of my posterity that I was a man of consequence in the land—that I was also the recipient of compliments of the most extraordinary nature from high officers of the national government.

On the other side of this complimentary document I find some happy blank verse headed "Warrant," and signed by the poet "Frank Soulé, Collector of Internal Revenue." Some of the flights of fancy in this Ode are really sublime, and show with what facility the poetic fire can render beautiful the most unpromising subject. For instance: "You are hereby commanded to distrain upon so much of the goods, chattels and effects of the within named person, *if any such can be found, etc.*" However, that is not so much a flight of fancy as a flight of humor. It is a fine flight, though, anyway. But this one is equal to anything in Shakspeare: "But in case sufficient goods, chattels and effects cannot be found, then you are hereby commanded to seize so much of the real estate of said person as may be necessary to satisfy the tax." There's poetry for you! They are going to commence on my real estate. This is very rough. But then the officer is expressly instructed to find it first. That is the saving clause for me. I will get them to take it all out in real estate. And then I will give them all the time they want to find it in.

But I can tell them of a way whereby they can ultimately enrich the Government of the United States by a judicious manipulation of this little bill against me—a way in which even the enormous national debt may be eventually paid off! Think of it! Imperishable fame will be the reward of the man who finds a way to pay off the national debt without impoverishing the land; I offer to furnish that method and crown these gentlemen with that fadeless glory. It is so simple and plain that a child may understand it. It is thus: I perceive that by neglecting to pay my income tax within ten days after it was due, I have brought upon myself a "penalty" of three dollars and twelve cents extra tax for that ten days. Don't you see?—let her run! Every ten days, $3 12; every month of 31 days, $10; every year, $120; every century, $12,000; at the end of a hundred thousand years, $1,200,000,000 will be the interest that has accumulated. . . .

144. *"Christian Spectator"*

13–15 December 1865

This sketch is taken from Clemens' "San Francisco Letter" to the Virginia City *Territorial Enterprise* written on 11 December 1865 and published two or three days later. A clipping of the entire letter is preserved in the Yale Scrapbook.

Although "Christian Spectator" is ostensibly a review of the "second number" of the Reverend O. P. Fitzgerald's *Christian Spectator,* Clemens takes the occasion to comment indirectly on the "incendiary religious matter about hell-fire, and brimstone, and wicked young men knocked endways by a streak of lightning while in the act of going fishing on Sunday." Within a few days he would publish "The Christmas Fireside" (no. 148), subtitled "The Story of the Bad Little Boy That Bore a Charmed Life," which takes up the notion of divine punishment and ridicules the hypocritical piety of the Sunday school movement. Henry Nash Smith noted in 1954 that this theme "later acquired major importance when Mark Twain began *Tom Sawyer* as an attack on the conception of the Good Boy set forth in 'the Sunday-school books.' "[1]

The "review" is surprisingly good-natured, probably because Clemens found the editor of the *Spectator* much less "hide-bound" than he expected. Amid a flurry of slight jokes and puns, Clemens comments indirectly on the San Francisco police (with whom he would clash more seriously in a few weeks), and his paratactic style at times approximates the less self-conscious ramblings of Simon Wheeler. The justice of his remarks cannot now be tested, however. The 1865 *Christian Spectator,* which was published in San Francisco, is no longer extant.

---

[1]*MTCor,* p. 76.

"Christian Spectator"

Rᴇᴠ. O. P. Fɪᴛᴢɢᴇʀᴀʟᴅ, of the Minna street Methodist Church South, is fairly under way, now, with his new *Christian Spectator.* The second number is before me. I believe I can venture to recommend it to the people of Nevada, of both Northern and Southern proclivities. It is not jammed full of incendiary religious matter about hell-fire, and brimstone, and wicked young men knocked endways by a streak of lightning while in the act of going fishing on Sunday. Its contents are not exciting or calculated to make people set up all night to read them. I like the *Spectator* a great deal better than I expected to, and I think you ought to cheerfully spare room for a short review of it. The leading editorial says: "A journal of the character of the *Spectator* is always to a great extent the reflex of the editor's individuality." Then follows a pleasant moral homily entitled "That Nubbin;" then puffs of a religious college and a Presbyterian church; then some poetical reflections on the happy fact "The War is Over;" then a "hyste" of some old slow coach of a preacher for not getting subscribers for the *Spectator* fast enough; then a confidential hint to the reader that he turn out and gather subscriptions—and forward the money; then a puff of the Oakland Female Seminary; then a remark that the *Spectator's* terms are cash; then a suggestion that the paper would make a gorgeous Christmas present—the only joke in the whole paper, and even this one is written with a fine show of seriousness; then a complimentary blast for Bishop Pierce; then a column of "Personal Items" concerning distinguished Confederates, chiefly; then something about "Our New Dress"—not one of Ward's shirts for the editor, but the paper's new dress; then a word about "our publishing house at Nashville, Tenn.;" then a repetition of the fact that "our terms are cash;" then something concerning "our head"—not the editor's, which is "level," but the paper's; then follow two columns of religious news not of a nature to drive one into a frenzy of excitement. On the outside is one of those entertaining novelettes, so popular among credulous Sabbath-school children, about a lone woman silently praying a desperate and blood-thirsty robber out of his boots—he looking on and fingering his clasp-knife and wiping it on his hand, and she calmly praying, till at last he "blanched beneath her fixed gaze, a panic appeared to seize him, and he closed his knife and went out." Oh, that won't do, you know. That is rather too steep. I guess she must have scalded him a little. There is also a column about a "remarkable police officer," and praising him up to the skies, and showing, by facts, sufficient to convince me that if he belonged to our force, Mr. Fitzgerald was drawing it rather strong. I read it with avidity, because I wished to know whether it was Chief Burke, or Blitz, or Lees, the parson was trying to curry favor with. But it was only an allegory, after all; the impossible policeman was "Conscience." It was one of those fine moral humbugs, like some advertisements which seduce you down a column of stuff about General Washington and wind up with a recommendation to "try Peterson's aromatic soap."

Subscribe for the vivacious *Christian Spectator;* C. A. Klose is financial agent.

145. *More Romance*

13–15 December 1865

This sketch, like "Christian Spectator" (no. 144), is taken from Clemens'
"San Francisco Letter" written on 11 December 1865 and published a
few days later in the Virginia City *Territorial Enterprise*. Rather slight
in its overall dimensions, the sketch affords an interesting insight into
Clemens' deeply ingrained habit of creating a miniature narrative from
the facts. It is apparent that his story depends as much on his imaginative reconstruction of events as it does on hearsay, rumor, and contemporary witnesses. And his mock indignation at this case of wronged love,
in which Vernon, "an ass of a lover from the wilds of Arizona," confronts
"French Mary" of the "Thunderboldt Saloon" and "very properly [tries]
to blow her brains out," manages to evoke a sardonic smile more than a
hundred years later.

More Romance

THE PRETTY waiter girls are always getting people into trouble. But I beg pardon—I should say "ladies," not "girls." I learned this lesson "in the days when I went gypsying," which was a long time ago. I said to one of these self-important hags, "Mary, or Julia, or whatever your name may be, who is that old slab singing at the piano—the girl with the 'bile' on her nose?" Her eyes snapped. "You call her *girl!*—you shall find out yourself—she is a *lady,* if you please!" They are all "ladies," and they take it as an insult when they are called anything else. It was one of these charming ladies who got shot, by an ass of a lover from the wilds of Arizona, yesterday in the Thunderboldt Saloon, but unhappily not killed. The fellow had enjoyed so long the society of ill-favored squaws who have to be scraped before one can tell the color of their complexions, that he was easily carried away with the well sea-soned charms of "French Mary" of the Thunderboldt Saloon, and got so "spooney" in his attentions that he hung around her night after night, and breathed her garlicky sighs with ecstasy. But no man can be honored with a beer girl's society without paying for it. French Mary made this man Vernon buy basket after basket of cheap champagne and got a heavy commission, which is usually their privilege; in the saloon her company always cost him five or ten dollars an hour, and she was doubtless a still more expensive luxury out of it.

It is said that he was always insisting upon her marrying him, and threatening to leave and go back to Arizona if she did not. She could not afford to let the goose go until he was completely plucked, and so she would consent, and set the day, and then the poor devil, in a burst of generosity, would celebrate the happy event with a heavy outlay of cash. This ruse was played until it was worn out, until Vernon's patience was worn out, until Vernon's purse was worn out also. Then there was no use in humbugging the poor numscull any longer, of course; and so French Mary deserted him, to wait on customers who had cash—the unfeeling practice always observed by lager beer ladies under similar circumstances. She told him she would not marry him or have anything more to do with him, and he very properly tried to blow her brains out. But he was awkward, and only wounded her dangerously. He killed himself, though, effectually, and let us hope that it was the wisest thing he could have done, and that he is better off now, poor fellow.

146. *Grand Fete-Day at the Cliff House*

19–21 December 1865

This sketch survives in the San Francisco *Examiner* for 23 December 1865, which reprinted it with this preface: "INTERESTING DISPLAY.— Mark Twain in a late letter to the *Territorial Enterprise* furnishes the following bill of festivities to be indulged in at the Cliff House on Christmas day." The sketch must have appeared in the Virginia City *Territorial Enterprise* sometime between December 19 and 21; the *Enterprise* printing has been lost.

Since the city's newspapers give no evidence of a Christmas day program at the Cliff House, Clemens' "bill of festivities" must have been designed to satirize special Christmas programs at the local theaters. For instance, the Metropolitan Theatre featured actors and artists presenting ballets, songs, pantomimes, the great "Niagara Leap" (by the acrobatic team of the Buislay Brothers), and tableaux such as "The Queen of the Flowers" and "The Shower of Gold."[1] Clemens' various "artistes" were well known to him and to the public: most were prominent turfmen and stable owners like Jim Eoff and Harris Covey or town characters like Michael Reese and Emperor Norton.

---

[1]"Amusements," San Francisco *Alta California*, 24 December 1865, p. 4.

Grand Fete-Day at the Cliff House

PERFORMANCE TO COMMENCE PRECISELY AT HIGH NOON.

THE FOLLOWING celebrated artistes have been engaged at a ruinous expense, and will perform the following truly marvelous feats:

PETE HOPKINS, the renowned Spectre of the Mountains, will walk a tight rope—the artist himself being tighter than the rope at the time—from the Cliff House to Seal Rock, and will ride back on the Seal known as Ben Butler, or the Seal will ride back on him, as circumstances shall determine.

JIM EOFF will exhibit the horse Patchen, and explain why he did not win the last race.

HARRIS COVEY will exhibit Lodi and Jim Barton, and BILLY WILLIAMSON will favor the audience with their pedigree and sketches of their history. N.B.—This will be very entertaining.

JEROME LELAND will exhibit the famous cow, in a circus ring prepared for the occasion, and perform several feats of perilous cowmanship on her back.

COMMODORE PERRY CHILDS will take a drink—the weather permitting. This was to have been done by another acrobat, but he is out of practice, and Mr. Childs has kindly volunteered in his place.

MICHAEL REESE will dance the Stock Gallopade, in which fine exhibition he will be assisted by several prominent brokers.

After which JUDGE BRYAN will sing two verses of "Neapolitaine"—by request.

The whole to conclude with the grand tableau of the "Children in the Wood"—Children in the Wood: Emperor Norton and the Spectre of the Mountains.

147. *Macdougall vs. Maguire*

22–23 December 1865

This sketch is taken from Clemens' "San Francisco Letter" to the Virginia City *Territorial Enterprise*. It was written on 20 December 1865 and probably published two or three days later. A complete clipping of the letter is preserved in the Yale Scrapbook.

Clemens here returned to the subject, and the form, he had used two weeks earlier in "A Rich Epigram" (no. 142). On December 18 W. J. Macdougall sued Thomas Maguire for $5,000 compensation for injuries sustained on December 5.[1] Maguire retaliated with a countersuit charging libel. The verdict was not returned until September the following year: Macdougall was awarded $310, while Maguire was given $300.[2] Although Clemens advised Macdougall to "pitch in and whale Maguire" instead of suing him, he was not unsympathetic with the pianist's injuries. In an earlier section of the letter, not reprinted here, he said that Macdougall was "banged to a pulp by Tom Maguire," and yet was "modest enough to demand only five thousand dollars by way of damages."[3]

---

[1]See the headnote to "A Rich Epigram" (no. 142).

[2]"Maguire Sued for Assault and Battery," San Francisco *Evening Bulletin,* 19 December 1865, p. 3; "By Telegraph to the Union," Sacramento *Union,* 8 September 1866, p. 3.

[3]"Sam Brannan" in "San Francisco Letter," Virginia City *Territorial Enterprise,* written 20 December, published 22–23 December 1865, clipping in Yale Scrapbook, p. 47.

Macdougall vs. Maguire

THE TALK occasioned by Maguire's unseemly castigation of Macdougall, while the latter was engaged in conversation with a lady, was dying out, happily for both parties, but Mr. Macdougall has set it going again by bringing that suit of his for $5,000 for the assault and battery. If he can get the money, I suppose that is at least the most profitable method of settling the matter. But then, will he? Maybe so, and maybe not. But if he feels badly—feels hurt—feels disgraced at being chastised, will $5,000 entirely soothe him and put an end to the comments and criticisms of the public? It is questionable. If he would pitch in and whale Maguire, though, it would afford him real, genuine satisfaction, and would also furnish me with a great deal more pleasing material for a paragraph than I can get out of the regular routine of events that transpire in San Francisco—which is a matter of still greater importance. If the plaintiff in this suit of damages were to intimate that he would like to have a word from me on this subject, I would immediately sit down and pour out my soul to him in verse. I would tune up my muse and sing to him the following pretty

NURSERY RHYME.

Come, now, Macdougall!
Say—
Can lucre pay
For thy dismembered coat—
Thy strangulated throat—
Thy busted bugle?

Speak thou! poor W. J.!
    And say—
    I pray—
If gold can soothe your woes,
Or mend your tattered clothes,
Or heal your battered nose,
Oh bunged-up lump of clay!

        No!—arise!
        Be wise!
Macdougall, d—n your eyes!
Don't legal quips devise
To mend your reputation,
And efface the degradation
    Of a blow that's struck in ire!
But 'ware of execration,
Unless you take your station
In a strategic location,
In mood of desperation,
And "lam" like all creation
    This infernal Tom Maguire!

148. *The Christmas Fireside*

23 December 1865

Although Bret Harte reprinted "Jim Smiley and His Jumping Frog" in the *Californian* on 16 December 1865, and reprinted several items from the *Enterprise* on other days, "The Christmas Fireside" was the first of two original sketches by Clemens that Harte published on 23 December 1865. Clemens' story of the bad little boy Jim had been anticipated by "Advice for Good Little Boys" (no. 113), published the previous July in the San Francisco *Youths' Companion,* but the present sketch was his first fully developed attack on moralistic juvenile fiction: it was a germ for *Tom Sawyer,* and it was part of a large trend toward ridiculing such simpleminded fiction in nineteenth-century American literature.

Subtitled "The Story of the Bad Little Boy That Bore a Charmed Life," the sketch is a burlesque fable that subverts the moral world of sentimental tales about good and bad little boys who always meet properly deserved ends. Clemens and Webb reprinted it in the 1867 *Jumping Frog* book as "The Story of the Bad Little Boy," and the author returned to the theme several times before beginning *Tom Sawyer* in 1873. "The Story of Mamie Grant, the Child-Missionary" was written (but left unpublished) in July 1868.[1] And in the May 1870 *Galaxy* Clemens published "The Story of the Good Little Boy Who Did Not Prosper" (no. 294), which he introduced with these words: "The following has been written at the instance of several literary friends, who thought that if the history of 'The Bad Little Boy who Did not Come to Grief' (a moral sketch which I published five or six years ago) was worthy of preservation several weeks

---

[1]*N&J1*, pp. 499–506. See also *S&B*, pp. 31–32.

in print, a fair and unprejudiced companion-piece to it would deserve a similar immortality."[2]

---

[2]*Galaxy* 9 (May 1870): 724. For a consideration of "The Christmas Fireside" see Walter Blair, "On the Structure of *Tom Sawyer*," *Modern Philology* 37 (August 1939): 75–88, and *Mark Twain & Huck Finn* (Berkeley and Los Angeles: University of California Press, 1960), pp. 65–67.

The Christmas Fireside

FOR GOOD LITTLE BOYS AND GIRLS.

By Grandfather Twain.

THE STORY OF THE BAD LITTLE BOY
THAT BORE A CHARMED LIFE.

ONCE THERE was a bad little boy, whose name was Jim—though, if you will notice, you will find that bad little boys are nearly always called James in your Sunday-school books. It was very strange, but still it was true, that this one was called Jim.

He didn't have any sick mother, either—a sick mother who was pious and had the consumption, and would be glad to lie down in the grave and be at rest, but for the strong love she bore her boy, and the anxiety she felt that the world would be harsh and cold toward him when she was gone. Most bad boys in the Sunday books are named James, and have sick mothers who teach them to say, "Now, I lay me down," etc., and sing them to sleep with sweet plaintive voices, and then kiss them good-night, and kneel down by the bedside and weep. But it was different with this fellow. He was named Jim, and there wasn't anything the matter with his mother—no consumption, or anything of that kind. She was rather stout than otherwise, and she was not pious;

moreover, she was not anxious on Jim's account; she said if he were to break his neck, it wouldn't be much loss; she always spanked Jim to sleep, and she never kissed him good-night; on the contrary, she boxed his ears when she was ready to leave him.

Once, this little bad boy stole the key of the pantry and slipped in there and helped himself to some jam, and filled up the vessel with tar, so that his mother would never know the difference; but all at once a terrible feeling didn't come over him, and something didn't seem to whisper to him, "Is it right to disobey my mother? Isn't it sinful to do this? Where do bad little boys go who gobble up their good kind mother's jam?" and then he didn't kneel down all alone and promise never to be wicked any more, and rise up with a light, happy heart, and go and tell his mother all about it and beg her forgiveness, and be blessed by her with tears of pride and thankfulness in her eyes. No; that is the way with all other bad boys in the books, but it happened otherwise with this Jim, strangely enough. He ate that jam, and said it was bully, in his sinful, vulgar way; and he put in the tar, and said that was bully also, and laughed, and observed that "the old woman would get up and snort" when she found it out; and when she did find it out he denied knowing anything about it, and she whipped him severely, and he did the crying himself. Everything about this boy was curious—everything turned out differently with him from the way it does to the bad Jameses in the books.

Once he climbed up in Farmer Acorn's apple tree to steal apples, and the limb didn't break and he didn't fall and break his arm, and get torn by the farmer's great dog, and then languish on a sick bed for weeks and repent and become good. Oh, no—he stole as many apples as he wanted, and came down all right, and he was all ready for the dog, too, and knocked him endways with a rock when he came to tear him. It was very strange—nothing like it ever happened in those mild little books with marbled backs, and with pictures in them of men with swallow-tailed coats and bell-crowned hats and pantaloons that are short in the legs, and women with the waists of their dresses under their arms and no hoops on. Nothing like it in any of the Sunday-school books.

Once he stole the teacher's penknife, and when he was afraid it would be found out and he would get whipped, he slipped it into

George Wilson's cap—poor Widow Wilson's son, the moral boy, the good little boy of the village, who always obeyed his mother, and never told an untruth, and was fond of his lessons and infatuated with Sunday-school. And when the knife dropped from the cap and poor George hung his head and blushed, as if in conscious guilt, and the grieved teacher charged the theft upon him, and was just in the very act of bringing the switch down upon his trembling shoulders, a white-haired improbable justice of the peace did not suddenly appear in their midst and strike an attitude and say, "Spare this noble boy—there stands the cowering culprit! I was passing the school door at recess, and, unseen myself, I saw the theft committed!" And then Jim didn't get whaled, and the venerable justice didn't read the tearful school a homily, and take George by the hand and say such a boy deserved to be exalted, and then tell him to come and make his home with him, and sweep out the office, and make fires, and run errands, and chop wood, and study law, and help his wife to do household labors, and have all the balance of the time to play, and get forty cents a month, and be happy. No, it would have happened that way in the books, but it didn't happen that way to Jim. No meddling old clam of a justice dropped in to make trouble, and so the model boy George got threshed, and Jim was glad of it. Because, you know, Jim hated moral boys. Jim said he was "down on them milksops." Such was the coarse language of this bad, neglected boy.

But the strangest things that ever happened to Jim was the time he went boating on Sunday and didn't get drowned, and that other time that he got caught out in the storm when he was fishing on Sunday, and didn't get struck by lightning. Why, you might look, and look, and look through the Sunday-school books, from now till next Christmas, and you would never come across anything like this. Oh, no—you would find that all the bad boys who go boating on Sunday invariably get drowned, and all the bad boys who get caught out in storms, when they are fishing on Sunday, infallibly get struck by lightning. Boats with bad boys in them always upset on Sunday, and it always storms when bad boys go fishing on the Sabbath. How this Jim ever escaped is a mystery to me.

This Jim bore a charmed life—that must have been the way of it. Nothing could hurt him. He even gave the elephant in the menagerie a plug of tobacco, and the elephant didn't knock the top of his head off with his trunk. He browsed around the cupboard after essence of peppermint, and didn't make a mistake and drink aqua fortis. He stole his father's gun and went hunting on the Sabbath, and didn't shoot three or four of his fingers off. He struck his little sister on the temple with his fist when he was angry, and she didn't linger in pain through long summer days and die with sweet words of forgiveness upon her lips that redoubled the anguish of his breaking heart. No—she got over it. He ran off and went to sea at last, and didn't come back and find himself sad and alone in the world, his loved ones sleeping in the quiet church-yard, and the vine-embowered home of his boyhood tumbled down and gone to decay. Ah, no—he came home drunk as a piper, and got into the station house the first thing.

And he grew up, and married, and raised a large family, and brained them all with an axe one night, and got wealthy by all manner of cheating and rascality, and now he is the infernalest wickedest scoundrel in his native village, and is universally respected, and belongs to the Legislature.

So you see there never was a bad James in the Sunday-school books that had such a streak of luck as this sinful Jim with the charmed life.

149. Enigma

23 December 1865

This was the second sketch by Clemens that Bret Harte published in the *Californian* on 23 December 1865. It was, as Clemens himself said, his "first effort in the enigma line," but it was not his last. In the July 1870 *Galaxy* he published a second "Enigma" (no. 309), which, like this one, obviously had no answer. Clemens' burlesque had no specific target, so far as we know, but the practice of publishing such word puzzles was common to most family magazines, including the San Francisco *Youths' Companion*, which had published "Advice for Good Little Boys" (no. 113).

Enigma

I AM COMPOSED of sixteen or seventeen letters.

My 16, 14, 3, 4, 6, 9, 15, is something or other, in a general way.

My 2, 11, 7, 14, is something else.

My 9, 6, 4, 10, 15, 11, is the other thing.

My 6, 16, 8, 14, 9, 3, 2, 1, 11, is most anything.

My 5, 3, 9, 14, 7, 3, 1, 11, 5, 6, 16, 2, 13, is most anything else.

My 4, 2, 16, 9, is a good deal like some of the things referred to above, though in what respect it has baffled even me to determine.

My 9, 3, 8, 12, is—is—well, I suppose it *is*, although I cannot see why.

Now, if anybody can cipher out that enigma, he is an abler man than I am, notwithstanding I got it up myself. It would be a real favor if some one would try, however. I have figured at it, and worked at it, and sweated over it, until I am disgusted, and *I* can make neither head nor tail of it. I thought it was rather neat at first, but I do not like it so well, now that I can't find out the answer to it. It looks rather easy at a first glance, but you will notice that the further you get into it the more it widens out.

This is my first effort in the enigma line, and, to speak the plain truth, I am considerably stunned at my own success. I do not seem to have just got the hang of this sort of thing, somehow. But I offer the entertaining little trifle to your readers for what it is worth—it may serve to amuse an idle year—and it cannot do much harm—it cannot more than drive a man mad, and make him massacre his relations.

150. *Another Enterprise*

26–27 December 1865

"Another Enterprise" is taken from Clemens' "San Francisco Letter" written on 23 December 1865 and published probably three or four days later in the Virginia City *Territorial Enterprise*. Clemens preserved a clipping of the entire letter in the Yale Scrapbook.

On the same day Clemens wrote his letter the San Francisco *Morning Call* praised Peter M. Scoofy for his fine haul of fat oysters from the Gulf of California,[1] a matter that would not have escaped Clemens, who had grown fond of this shellfish while still in Virginia City. In the present sketch, however, his main interest lay in creating the monologue of George Marshall, who in his own way reminds us of Simon Wheeler and Jim Blaine. He is also a "crude counterpart of the Old Travellers in *The Innocents Abroad.*"[2] His real identity remains uncertain, but he may well have been the Virginia City *Union* reporter whom Clemens mentions in chapters 55 and 58 of *Roughing It* as having made a handsome profit on the sale of mining property in New York City in 1864.

---

[1] "Another Luxury," San Francisco *Morning Call*, 23 December 1865, p. 1.

[2] Edgar M. Branch, *The Literary Apprenticeship of Mark Twain* (Urbana: University of Illinois Press, 1950), p. 133.

Another Enterprise

A MR. P. M. SCOOFY, of this city, has been raising oysters for two years past, on the Mexican coast, and his first harvest—eight tons—arrived yesterday on the John L. Stephens. They arrived in admirable condition—finer and fatter than they were when they started; for oysters enjoy traveling, and thrive on it; and they learn a good deal more on a flying trip than George Marshall did, and nearly as much as some other Washoe European tourists I could mention, but they are dignified and do not gabble about it so much. I would rather have the society of a traveled oyster than that of George Marshall, because I would not hesitate to show my displeasure if that oyster were to suddenly become gay and talkative, and say: "I was in England, you know, by G—; I went up to Liverpool and there I took the cars and went to London, by —— ——; I been in Pall Mall, and Cheapside, and Whitefriars, and all them places—been in all of 'em: I been in the Tower of London, and seen all them d—d armors and things they used to wear in an early day; I hired a feller for a shil'n', and he took me all around there and showed me the whole hell-fired arrangement, you know, by G——; and I give him a glass of of'n-of, as they call it, and he jus' froze to me. You show one of them fellers the color of a bit, and he'll stay with you all day, by —— ——. And I went to Rome—that ain't no slouch of a town, you know—and old? —— ——! you bet your life. There ain't anything like it in this country—*you* can't put up any idea how it is; you can't tell a d——d thing about Rome 'thout you see it, by——. And I been to Paris—*Parree,* French call it—you never hear them say Par-*riss*—they would laugh if they was to hear any body call it Par-riss, you know. I was there three weeks. I was on the *Pong-Nuff,* and I been to the *Pal-lay Ro-yoll* and the *Tweeleree,* all them d——d places, and the *Boolyver* and the *Boys dee Bullone.* I stood there in the *Boys dee Bullone* and see old Loois Napoleon and his wife come by in his carriage—I was as close to him as from here to that counter there, by G—; I see him take his hat off and bow to them whoopin' French bilks by —— ——; I stood right there that close—as close as that counter when he went by; I was close enough to a spit in his face if I'd been a mind to, by ——. Hell, a feller might live *here* a million years, and what would he ever see, by G—d. Parree's the place—style, *there,* you know—people got money, *there,* by — —. Let's take a drink, by G—." I wouldn't let a traveled oyster inflict that sort of thing on me, you understand, and refer to the Deity, and to the Savior by his full name, to verify every other important statement. I would rather have the oyster's company than Marshall's when his reminiscences are big within him, but the moment I received the information that "I been to Europe, and all them places, by G—," I would start that oyster on a journey that would astonish it more than all the wonders of "Parree" and "all them d—d places" combined.

I have forgotten what I was going to say about Mr. Scoofy and his Mexican oyster farm, but it don't matter. The main thing is that he will hereafter endeavor to keep this market supplied with his delicious marine fruit; and another great point is that his Mexican oysters are as far superior to the poor little insipid things we are accustomed to here, as is the information furnished by Alexander Von Humboldt concerning foreign lands to that which one may glean from George Marshall in the course of a brief brandy-punch tournament.

151. Spirit of the Local Press

26–27 December 1865

Like the previous sketch, "Another Enterprise" (no. 150), this one is taken from Clemens' "San Francisco Letter" written on 23 December 1865 and published in the Virginia City *Territorial Enterprise* three or four days later.

Clemens' title deliberately echoes the standard heading used by the local papers for the column which recapitulated news from other cities, as in the Sacramento *Bee's* "Spirit of the San Francisco Press."[1] The satiric attack is based largely on the facts: Clemens' first five examples refer to items published in the local column of the San Francisco *Alta California*, which he had castigated somewhat more directly just the day before (see "San Francisco Letter," no. 131). The *Alta* also published items about a soldier stealing a washboard and the "unknown Chinaman dead on Sacramento steamer" referred to in Clemens' penultimate paragraph.[2] The other items listed by him did not appear in the San Francisco press for December 23, so far as can now be determined.

Although Clemens did not mention Fitz Smythe (Albert S. Evans), the sketch might be considered part of the sustained rivalry with him. But there is some sign that Clemens was criticizing the whole idea of reporting local news, not just Evans. He knew very well, from his experience on the *Enterprise*, on the *Call*, and most recently as a daily correspondent, that all city editors and newspaper reporters were obliged to report the trivial if true events of the day.[3]

---

[1]Sacramento *Bee*, 18 February 1865, p. 2.

[2]"A Sanitary Measure" and "Sudden Death," San Francisco *Alta California*, 23 December 1865, p. 1.

[3]See *CofC*, pp. 19–21, 209–213.

Spirit of the Local Press

San Francisco is a city of startling events. Happy is the man whose destiny it is to gather them up and record them in a daily newspaper! That sense of conferring benefit, profit and innocent pleasure upon one's fellow-creatures which is so cheering, so calmly blissful to the plodding pilgrim here below, is his, every day in the year. When he gets up in the morning he can do as old Franklin did, and say, "This day, and all days, shall be unselfishly devoted to the good of my fellow-creatures—to the amelioration of their condition—to the conferring of happiness upon them—to the storing of their minds with wisdom which shall fit them for their struggle with the hard world, here, and for the enjoyment of a glad eternity hereafter. And thus striving, so shall I be blessed!" And when he goes home at night, he can exult and say: "Through the labors of these hands and this brain, which God hath given me, blessed and wise are my fellow-creatures this day!

"I have told them of the wonder of the swindling of the friend of Bain, the unknown Bain from Petaluma Creek, by the obscure Catharine McCarthy, out of $300—and told it with entertaining verbosity in half a column.

"I have told them that Christmas is coming, and people go strangely about, buying things—I have said it in forty lines.

"I related how a vile burglar entered a house to rob, and actually went away again when he found he was discovered. I told it briefly, in thirty-five lines.

"In forty lines I told how a man swindled a Chinaman out of a couple of shirts, and for fear the matter might seem trivial, I made a pretense of only having mentioned it in order to base upon it a criticism upon a grave defect in our laws.

"I fulminated again, in a covert way, the singular conceit that Christmas is at hand, and said people were going about in the most unaccountable way buying stuff to eat, in the markets—52 lines.

"I glorified a fearful conflagration that came so near burning something, that I shudder even now to think of it. Three thousand dollars worth of goods destroyed by water—a man then went up and put out the fire with a bucket of water. I puffed our fine fire organization—64 lines.

"I printed some other extraordinary occurrences—runaway horse—28 lines; dog fight—30 lines; Chinaman captured by officer Rose for stealing chickens—90 lines; unknown Chinaman dead on Sacramento steamer—5 lines; several 'Fourteener' items, concerning people frightened and boots stolen—52 lines; case of soldier stealing a washboard worth fifty cents—three-quarters of a column. Much other wisdom I disseminated, and for these things let my reward come hereafter."

And his reward *will* come hereafter—and I am sorry enough to think it. But such startling things do happen every day in this strange city!—and how dangerously exciting must be the employment of writing them up for the daily papers!

152. *Convicts*

31 December 1865

"Convicts" is the last known sketch that Clemens published in 1865. It was part of a "San Francisco Letter" written on December 28 and published three days later in the Virginia City *Territorial Enterprise*. It survives in a unique clipping from the *Enterprise* reproduced in photofacsimile by Richard E. Lingenfelter.[1]

On December 10 a group of five Comstock reporters sat for their collective portrait (reproduced below) at Sutterly Brothers in Virginia City, and then celebrated the occasion by making the rounds of the saloons and ordering a lavish dinner at the International Hotel. The men were William Wright (Dan De Quille), William M. Gillespie, and Alfred Doten of the *Enterprise*, Robert E. Lowery of the Virginia City *Union*, and Charles A. Parker of the Gold Hill *News*—all of them Clemens' friends from Nevada days. Copies of the photograph were distributed to various western newspapers, and one reached Clemens on December 27. His response is reminiscent of his earlier good-natured ribbing of Clement T. Rice (the "Unreliable") and Dan De Quille.

---

[1]*The Newspapers of Nevada: A History and Bibliography* (San Francisco: John Howell Books, 1964), following p. 4.

THE COMSTOCK REPORTERS, 1865
WILLIAM M. GILLESPIE, CHARLES A. PARKER, "DAN DE QUILLE" WILLIAM WRIGHT,
ROBERT E. LOWERY, AND ALF DOTEN

Doten Collection, University of Nevada

Convicts

SOME ONE (I do not know who,) left me a card photograph, yesterday, which I do not know just what to do with. It has the names
of Dan De Quille, W. M. Gillespie, Alf. Doten, Robert Lowery and
Charles A. Parker on it, and appears to be a pictured group of
notorious convicts, or something of that kind. I only judge by the
countenances, for I am not acquainted with these people, and do
not usually associate with such characters. This is the worst lot of
human faces I have ever seen. That of the murderer Doten, (murderer, isn't he?) is sufficient to chill the strongest heart. The cool
self-possession of the burglar Parker marks the man capable of
performing deeds of daring confiscation at dead of night, unmoved
by surrounding perils. The face of the Thug, De Quille, with its
expression of pitiless malignity, is a study. Those of the light-
fingered gentry, Lowery and Gillespie, show that ineffable repose
and self-complacency so deftly assumed by such characters after
having nipped an overcoat or a pair of brass candlesticks and are
aware that officers have suspected and are watching them. I am
very glad to have this picture to keep in my room, as a hermit
keeps a skull, to remind me what I may some day become myself.
I have permitted the Chief of Police to take a copy of it, for
obvious reasons.

APPENDIXES

APPENDIX A

The following items appeared in the San Francisco *Morning Call* during Clemens' brief tenure as its local editor in mid-1864. The case for attributing them to Clemens is given in full by Edgar M. Branch in *Clemens of the "Call."*[1] The interested reader should consult that volume both for a fuller selection than the one given here, and for annotation of names and allusions in the local items.

---

[1]*CofC,* pp. 29–35.

A1. Another of Them

23 June 1864

AT FIVE MINUTES to nine o'clock last night, San Francisco was favored by another earthquake. There were three distinct shocks, two of which were very heavy, and appeared to have been done on purpose, but the third did not amount to much. Heretofore our earthquakes—as all old citizens experienced in this sort of thing will recollect—have been distinguished by a soothing kind of undulating motion, like the roll of waves on the sea, but we are happy to state that they are shaking her up from below now. The shocks last night came straight up from that direction; and it is sad to reflect, in these spiritual times, that they might possibly have been freighted with urgent messages from some of our departed friends. The suggestion is worthy a moment's serious reflection, at any rate.

A2. A Trip to the Cliff House

25 June 1864

IF ONE TIRE of the drudgeries and scenes of the city, and would breathe the fresh air of the sea, let him take the cars and omnibuses, or, better still, a buggy and pleasant steed, and, ere the sea breeze sets in, glide out to the Cliff House. We tried it a day or two since. Out along the railroad track, by the pleasant homes of our citizens, where architecture begins to put off its swaddling clothes, and assume form and style, grace and beauty, by the neat gardens with their green shrubbery and laughing flowers, out where were once sand hills and sand-valleys, now streets and homesteads. If you would doubly enjoy pure air, first pass along by Mission Street Bridge, the Golgotha of Butcherville, and wind along through the alleys where stand the whiskey mills and grunt the piggeries of "Uncle Jim." Breathe and inhale deeply ere you reach this castle of Udolpho, and then hold your breath as long as possible, for Arabia is a long way thence, and the balm of a thousand flowers is not for sale in that locality. Then away you go over paved, or planked, or Macadamized roads, out to the cities of the dead, pass between Lone Mountain and Calvary, and make a straight due west course for the ocean. Along the way are many things to please and entertain, especially if an intelligent chaperon accompany you. Your eye will travel over in every direction the vast territory which Swain, Weaver & Co. desire to fence in, the little homesteads by the way, Dr. Rowell's arena castle, and Zeke Wilson's Bleak House in the sand. Splendid road, ocean air that swells the lungs and strengthens the limbs. Then there's the Cliff House, perched on the very brink of the ocean, like a castle by the Rhine, with countless sea-lions rolling their unwieldy bulks on the rocks within rifle-shot, or plunging into and sculling about in the foaming waters. Steamers and sailing craft are passing, wild fowl scream, and sea-lions growl and bark, the waves roll into breakers, foam and spray, for five miles along the beach, beautiful and grand, and one feels as if at sea with no rolling motion nor sea-sickness, and the appetite is whetted by the drive and the breeze, the ocean's presence wins you into a happy frame, and you can eat one of the best dinners with the hungry relish of an ostrich. Go to the Cliff House. Go ere the winds get too fresh, and if you like, you may come back by Mountain Lake and the Presidio, overlook the Fort, and bow to the Stars and Stripes as you pass.

A3. Missionaries Wanted for San Francisco

28 June 1864

WE DO NOT like it, as far as we have got. We shall probably not fall so deeply in love with reporting for a San Francisco paper as to make it impossible ever to wean us from it. There is a powerful saving-clause for us in the fact that the conservators of public information—the persons whose positions afford them opportunities not enjoyed by others to keep themselves posted concerning the important events of the city's daily life—do not appear to know anything. At the offices and places of business we have visited in search of information, we have got it in just the same shape every time, with a promptness and uniformity which is startling, perhaps, but not gratifying. They all answer and say unto you, "I don't know." We do not mind that, so much, but we do object to a man's parading his ignorance with an air of overbearing egotism which shows you that he is proud of it. True merit is modest, and why should not true ignorance be? In most cases, the head of the concern is not at home; but then why not pay better wages and leave men at the counter who would not be above knowing something? Judging by the frills they put on—the sad but infallible accompaniment of forty dollars a year and found—these fellows are satisfied they are not paid enough to make it an object to know what is going on around them, or to state that their crop of information has failed, this century, without doing it with an exaggeration of dignity altogether disproportioned to the importance of the thing. In Washoe, if a man don't know anything, he will at least go on and tell you what he don't know, so that you can publish it in case you do not stumble upon something of more vital interest to the community, in the course of the day. If a similar course were pursued here, we might always have something to write about—and occasionally a column or so left over for next day's issue, perhaps.

A4. The Kahn of Tartary

29 June 1864

LENA KAHN, otherwise known as Mother Kahn, or the Kahn of Tartary, who is famous in this community for her infatuated partiality for the Police Court as a place of recreation, was on hand there again yesterday morning. She was mixed up in a triangular row, the sides of the triangle being Mr. Oppenheim, Mrs. Oppenheim, and herself. It appeared from the evidence that she formed the base of the triangle—which is to say, she was at the bottom of the row, and struck the first blow. Moses Levi, being sworn, said he was in the neighborhood, and heard Mrs. Oppenheim scream; knew it was her by the vicious expression she always threw into her screams; saw the defendant (her husband) go into the Tartar's house and gobble up the partner of his bosom and his business, and rescue her from the jaws of destruction (meaning Mrs. Kahn,) and bring her forth to sport once more amid the ——. At this point the lawyer turned off Mr. Levi's gas, which seemed to be degenerating into poetry, and asked him what his occupation was? The Levite said he drove an express wagon. The lawyer—with that sensitiveness to the slightest infringement of the truth, which is so becoming to the profession—inquired severely if he did not sometimes drive the horse also! The wretched witness, thus detected before the multitude in his deep-laid and subtle prevarication, hung his head in silence. His evidence could no longer be respected, and he moved away from the stand with the consciousness written upon his countenance of how fearful a thing it is to trifle with the scruples of a lawyer. Mrs. Oppenheim next came forward and gave a portion of her testimony in damaged English, and the balance in dark and mysterious German. In the English glimpses of her story it was discernible that she had innocently trespassed upon the domain of the Khan, and had been rudely seized upon in such a manner as to make her arm turn blue, (she turned up her sleeve and showed the Judge,) and the bruise had grown worse since that day, until at last it was tinged with a ghastly green, (she turned up her sleeve again for impartial judicial inspection,) and instantly after receiving this affront, so humiliating to one of gentle blood, she had been set upon without cause or provocation, and thrown upon the floor and "licked." This last expression possessed a charm for Mrs. Oppenheim, that no persuasion of Judge or lawyers could induce her to forego, even for the sake of bringing her wrongs into a stronger light, so long as those wrongs, in such an event, must be portrayed in language less pleasant to her ear. She said the Khan had licked her, and she stuck to it and reiterated with unflinching firmness. Becoming confused by repeated assaults from the lawyers in the way of badgering questions, which her wavering senses could no longer comprehend, she relapsed at last into hopeless German again, and retired within the lines. Mr. Oppenheim then came forward and remained under fire for fifteen minutes, during which time he made it as plain as the disabled condition of his English would permit him to do, that he was not in anywise to blame, at any rate; that his wife went out after a warrant for the arrest of the Kahn; that she stopped to "make it up" with the Kahn, and the redoubtable Kahn tackled her; that he was dry-nursing the baby at the time, and when he heard his wife scream, he suspected, with a sagacity which did him credit, that she wouldn't have "hollered 'dout dere vas someding de matter;" therefore he piled the child up in a corner remote from danger, and moved upon the works of the Tartar; she had waltzed into the wife and finished her, and was already on picket duty, waiting for the husband, and when he came she smacked him over the head a couple of times with the deadly bludgeon she uses to elevate linen to the clothes-line with; and then, stimulated by this encouragement, he started to the Police Office to get out a warrant for the arrest of the victorious army, but the victorious army, always on the alert, was there ahead of him, and he now stood in the presence of the Court in the humiliating position of a man who had aspired to be plaintiff, but overcome by strategy, had sunk to the grade of defendant. At this point his mind wandered, his vivacious tongue grew thick with mushy German syllables, and the last of the Oppenheims sank to rest at the feet of justice. We had done less than our duty had we allowed this most important trial—freighted, as it was, with matters of the last importance to every member of this community, and every conscientious, law-abiding man and woman upon whom the sun of civilization shines to-day—to be given to the world in the columns, with no more elaboration than the customary "Benjamin Oppenheim, assault and battery, dismissed; Lena Oppenheim and Fredrika Kahn, held to answer." We thought, at first, of starting in that way, under the head of "Police Court," but a second glance at the case showed us that it was one of a most serious and extraordinary nature, and ought to be put in such a shape that the public could give to it that grave and deliberate consideration which its magnitude entitled it to.

A5. House at Large

1 July 1864

AN OLD TWO-STORY, sheet-iron, pioneer, fire-proof house, got loose from her moorings last night, and drifted down Sutter street, toward Montgomery. We are not informed as to where she came from or where she was going to—she had halted near Montgomery street, and appeared to be studying about it. If one might judge from the expression that hung about her dilapidated front and desolate windows, she was thoroughly demoralized when she stopped there, and sorry she ever started. Is there no law against houses loafing around the public streets at midnight?

A6. Calaboose Theatricals

14 July 1864

ANNA JAKES, drunk and disorderly, but excessively cheerful, made her first appearance in the City Prison last night, and made the dreary vaults ring with music. It was of the distorted, hifalutin kind, and she evidently considered herself an opera sharp of some consequence. Her idea was that "Whee-heeping sad and lo hone-ly" was not calculated to bring this cruel war to a close shortly, and she delivered herself of that idea under many difficulties; because, in the first place, Mary Kane, an old offender, was cursing like a trooper in a neighboring cell; and secondly, a man in another apartment who wanted to sleep, and who did not admire anybody's music, and especially Anna Jakes', kept inquiring, "*Will* you dry up that infernal yowling, you heifer?"—swinging a hefty oath at her occasionally—and so the cruel war music was so fused and blended with blasphemy in a higher key, and discouraging comments in a lower, that the pleasurable effect of it was destroyed, and the argument and the moral utterly lost. Anna finally fell to singing and dancing, both, with a spirit that promised to last till morning, and Mary Kane and the weary man got disgusted and withdrew from the contest. Anna Jakes says she is a highly respectable young married lady, with a husband in the Boise country; that she has been sumptuously reared and expensively educated; that her impulses are good and her instincts refined; that she taught school a long time in the city of New York, and is an accomplished musician; and finally, that her sister got married last Sunday night, and she got drunk to do honor to the occasion—and with a persistency that is a credit to one of such small experience, she has been on a terrific bender ever since. She will probably let herself out on the cruel war for Judge Shepheard, in the Police Court, this morning.

A7 The "Coming Man" Has Arrived

16 July 1864

THE "COMING MAN" HAS ARRIVED—And he fetched his things with him. John Smith was brought into the city prison last night, by Officers Conway and Minson, so limbered up with whiskey that you might have hung him on a fence like a wet shirt. His battered slouch-hat was jammed down over his eyes like an extinguisher; his shirt-bosom (which was not clean, at all,) was spread open, displaying his hair trunk beneath; his coat was old, and short-waisted, and fringed at the edges, and exploded at the elbows like a blooming cotton-boll, and its collar was turned up, so that one could see by the darker color it exposed, that the garment had known better days, when it was not so yellow, and sunburnt, and freckled with grease-spots, as it was now; it might have hung about its owner symmetrically and gracefully, too, in those days, but now it had a general hitch upward, in the back, as if it were climbing him; his pantaloons were of coarse duck, very much soiled, and as full of wrinkles as if they had been made of pickled tripe; his boots were not blacked, and they probably never had been; the subject's face was that of a man of forty, with the sun of an invincible good nature shining dimly through the cloud of dirt that enveloped it. The officers held John up in a warped and tangled attitude, like a pair of tongs struck by lightning, and searched him, and the result was as follows: Two slabs of old cheese; a double handful of various kinds of crackers; seven peaches; a box of lip-salve, bearing marks of great age; an onion; two dollars and sixty-five cents, in two purses, (the odd money being considered as circumstantial evidence that the defendant had been drinking beer at a five-cent house;) a soiled handkerchief; a fine-tooth comb; also one of coarser pattern; a cucumber pickle, in an imperfect state of preservation; a leather string; an eye-glass, such as prospectors use; one buckskin glove; a printed ballad, "Call me pet names;" an apple; part of a dried herring; a copy of the Boston Weekly Journal, and copies of several San Francisco papers; and in each and every pocket he had two or

three chunks of tobacco, and also one in his mouth of such remarkable size as to render his articulation confused and uncertain. We have purposely given this prisoner a fictitious name, out
of the consideration we feel for him as a man of noble literary
instincts, suffering under temporary misfortune. He said he always read the papers before he got drunk; go thou and do likewise.
Our literary friend gathered up his grocery store and staggered
contentedly into a cell; but if there is any virtue in the boasted
power of the press, he shall stagger out again to-day, a free man.

A8. The County Prison

17 July 1864

A VISIT TO the County Prison, in Broadway above Kearny street, will satisfy almost any reasonable person that there are worse hardships in life than being immured in those walls. It is a substantial-looking place, but not a particularly dreary one, being as neat and clean as a parlor in its every department. There are two long rows of cells on the main floor—thirty-one, altogether —disposed on each side of an alley-way, built of the best quality of brick, imported from Boston, and laid in cement, which is so hard that a nail could not be driven into it; each cell has a thick iron door with a wicket in its centre for the admission of air and light, and a narrow aperture in the opposite wall for the same purpose; these cells are just about the size and have the general appearance of a gentleman's state-room on a steamboat, but are rather more comfortable than those dens are sometimes; a two-story bunk, a slop-bucket and a sort of table are the principal furniture; the walls inside are whitewashed, and the floors kept neat and clean by frequent scrubbing; on Wednesdays and Saturdays the prisoners are provided with buckets of water for general bathing and clothes-washing purposes, and they are required to keep themselves and their premises clean at all times; on Tuesdays and Fridays they clean up their cells and scrub the floors thereof. In one of these rows of cells it is pitch dark when the doors are shut, but in the other row it is very light when the wickets are open. From the number of books and newspapers lying on the bunks, it is easy to believe that a vast amount of reading is done in the County Prison; and smoking too, we presume, because, although the rules forbid the introduction of spirituous liquors, wine, or beer into the jail, nothing is said about tobacco. Most of the occupants of the light cells were lying on the bunks reading, and some of those in the dark ones were standing up at the wickets similarly employed. "Sick Jimmy," or James Rodgers, who was found guilty of manslaughter a day or two ago, in killing Foster, has been permitted by Sheriff Davis to occupy one of the light cells, on account of his ill health. He says his quarters would be immensely comfortable if one didn't mind the irksomeness of the confinement. We could hear the prisoners laughing and talking in the cells, but they are prohibited from making much noise or talking from one cell to another. There are three iron cells standing isolated in the yard, in which a batch of Chinamen wear the time away in smoking opium two hours a day and sleeping the other twenty-two. The kitchen department is roomy and neat, and the heavy tragedy work in it is done by "trusties," or prisoners detailed from time to time for that duty. Up stairs are the cells for the women; two of these are dark, iron cells, for females confined for high crimes. The others are simply well lighted and ventilated wooden rooms, such as the better class of citizens over in Washoe used to occupy a few years ago, when the common people lived in tents. There is nothing gorgeous about these wooden cells, but plenty of light and white-washing make them look altogether cheerful. Mesdames O'Keefe, McCarty, Mary Holt and "Gentle Julia," (Julia Jennings,) are the most noted ladies in this department. Prison-keeper Clark says the quiet, smiling, pious-looking Mrs. McCarty is just the boss thief of San Francisco, and the misnamed "Gentle Julia" is harder to manage, and gives him more trouble than all the balance of the tribe put together. She uses "awful" language, and a good deal of it, the same being against the rule. Mrs. McCarty dresses neatly, re-clines languidly on a striped mattress, smiles sweetly at vacancy, and labors at her "crochet-work" with the serene indifference of a princess. The four ladies we have mentioned are unquestionably stuck after the County Prison; they reside there most of the time, coming out occasionally for a week, to steal something, or get on a bender, and going back again as soon as they can prove that they have accomplished their mission. A lady warden will shortly be placed in charge of the women's department here, in accordance with an act of the last Legislature, and we feel able to predict that Gentle Julia will make it mighty warm for her. Most of the cells, above and below, are occupied, and it is proposed to put another story on the jail at no distant day. We have no suggestions to report concerning the County Jail. We are of the opinion that it is all right, and doing well.

A9. Assault

19 July 1864

MRS. CATHERINE MORAN was arraigned before Judge Cowles yesterday, on a charge of assault with an axe upon Mrs. Eliza Markee, with intent to do bodily injury. A physician testified that there were contused wounds on plaintiff's head, and also a cut through the scalp, which bled profusely. The fuss was all about a child, and that is the strangest part about it—as if, in a city so crowded with them as San Francisco, it were worth while to be particular as to the fate of a child or two. However, mothers appear to go more by instinct than political economy in matters of this kind. Mrs. Markee testified that she heard war going on among the children, and she rushed down into the yard and found her Johnny sitting on the stoop, building a toy wagon, and Mrs. Moran standing over him with an axe, threatening to split his head open. She asked the defendant not to split her Johnny. The defendant at once turned upon her, threatening to kill her, and struck her two or three times with the axe, when she, the plaintiff, grabbed the defendant by the arms and prevented her from scalping her entirely. Blood was flowing profusely. Mr. Killdig described the fight pretty much as the plaintiff had done, and said he parted, or tried to part the combatants, and that he called upon Mr. Moran to assist him, but that neutral power said the women had been sour a good while—let them fight it out. Another witness substantiated the main features of the foregoing testimony, and said the warriors were all covered with blood, and the children of both, to the number of many dozens, had fled in disorder and taken refuge under the house, crying, and saying their mothers were killing each other. Mrs. Murphy, for the defence, testified as follows: "I was coomun along, an' Misses Moran says to me, says she, this is the redwood stick she tried to take me life wid, or wan o' thim other sticks, Missis Murphy, dear, an' says I, Missis Moran, dairlin'," —— Here she was shut off, merely because the Court did not care about knowing what Mrs. Moran told her about the fight, and consequently we have nothing further of this important witness's testimony to offer. The case was continued. Seriously, instead of a mere ordinary she-fight, this is a fuss of some consequence, and should not be lightly dealt with. It was an earnest attempt at manslaughter—or woman-slaughter, at any rate, which is nearly as bad.

A10. The Boss Earthquake

22 July 1864

WHEN WE CONTRACTED to report for this newspaper, the important matter of two earthquakes a month was not considered in the salary. There shall be no mistake of that kind in the next contract, though. Last night, at twenty minutes to eleven, the regular semi monthly earthquake, due the night before, arrived twenty-four hours behind time, but it made up for the delay in uncommon and altogether unnecessary energy and enthusiasm. The first effort was so gentle as to move the inexperienced stranger to the expression of contempt and brave but very bad jokes; but the second was calculated to move him out of his boots, unless they fitted him neatly. Up in the third story of this building the sensation we experienced was as if we had been sent for and were mighty anxious to go. The house seemed to waltz from side to side with a quick motion, suggestive of sifting corn meal through a sieve; afterward it rocked grandly to and fro like a prodigious cradle, and in the meantime several persons started down stairs to see if there were anybody in the street so timid as to be frightened at a mere earthquake. The third shock was not important, as compared with the stunner that had just preceded it. That second shock drove people out of the theatres by dozens. At the Metropolitan, we are told that Franks, the comedian, had just come on the stage, (they were playing the "Ticket-of-Leave Man,") and was about to express the unbounded faith he had in May; he paused until the jarring had subsided, and then improved and added force to the text by exclaiming, "It will take more than an earthquake to shake my faith in that woman!" And in that, Franks achieved a sublime triumph over the elements, for he "brought the house down," and the earthquake could n't. From the time the shocks commenced last night, until the windows had stopped rattling, a minute and a half had elapsed.

An. Good Effects of a High Tariff

22 July 1864

WE ARE PLEASED to hear of the prosperous condition of the Dashaway Society. Their ranks, we are assured, are constantly filling up. The *draught* with them is working well, causing many to volunteer. The bounty they receive is sobriety, respect and health, and the blessings of families. We will not attribute all these new recruitings to the high tariff, and the difficulty of obtaining any decent whiskey. But some who join give this as their reason. They fear strychnine more than inebriation. They find it impossible to exhaust all the tarantula juice in the country, as they have been endeavoring to do for a long while, in hopes to get at some decent "rum" after all the tangle-leg should have been swallowed, and so conclude to save tariff on liquors and life by coming square up to the hydrant. Their return to original innocence and primitive bibations will be gladly welcomed. Water is a forgiving friend. After years of estrangement it meets the depraved taste with the same friendship as before. Water bears no enmity. But it must be a strange meeting—water pure and the tongues of some of our solid drinkers of Bourbon and its dishonest relations. Alkali water to the innocent mouths of cattle from the waters of the Mississippi could not seem stranger nor more disagreeable at first. But it will come around right at last. Success to the tariff and the Dashaways.

A12 A Scene at the Police Court — The Hostility of Color

22 July 1864

A LONG FILE of applicants, perhaps seventy-five or eighty, passed in review before the Police Commissioners yesterday afternoon, anxious to be employed by the city in snatching drunks, burglars, petty larceners, wife-whippers, and all offenders generally, under the authority of a star on the left breast. One of the candidates—a fine, burly specimen of an Emeralder—leaned negligently against the door-post, speculating on his chances of being "passed," and at the same time whiffing industriously at an old dhudeen, blackened by a thousand smokes. He was smoking thus thoughtfully when a contraband passed him, conveying a message to some official in the Court.

"There goes another applicant," said a wag at his elbow.

"What?" asked the smoker.

"A darkey looking for a sit on the Police," was the reply.

"An' do they give nagurs a chance on the Polis?"

"Of course."

"Then, be J—s," said Pat, knocking the ashes out of his pipe and stowing it away, "I'm out of the ring; I wouldn't demane mesilf padrowling o'nights with a nagur."

He gave one glance at the innocent and unsuspecting darkey, and left the place in disgust.

A13. Arrest of a Secesh Bishop

22 July 1864

REV. H. H. KAVANAUGH, represented as a Bishop of the M. E. Church South, whose home until quite recently has been in Georgia, but who for some weeks past has been traveling around in this part of the State organizing Churches and preaching the Gospel as the M. E. Church South understand it, to many Congregations of rebel sympathizers, was on Monday arrested by Captain Jackson, United States Marshal for the Southern District of this State. The arrest was made at Black's ranch, Salt Spring Valley, Calaveras county, whilst the Bishop was holding a camp meeting. By the Reverend gentleman's request, he was granted his parole until he could preach a sermon, on promise to report himself at this city yesterday for passage on the San Francisco steamer, which he did accordingly. We cannot state the precise charges on which he was arrested.

Getting military information is about the slowest business we ever undertook. We clipped the above paragraph from the Stockton Independent at eleven o'clock yesterday morning, and went skirmishing among the "chief captains," as the Bible modestly terms Brigadier-Generals, in search of further information, from that time until half-past seven o'clock in the evening, before we got it. We will engage to find out who wrote the "Junius Letters" in less time than that, if we have a mind to turn our attention to it. We started to the Provost Marshal's office, but met another reporter, who said: "I suppose I know where you're going, but it's no use—just come from there—military etiquette and all that, you know—those fellows are mum—won't tell anything about it—damn!" We sought General McDowell, but he had gone to Oakland. In the course of the afternoon we visited all kinds of headquarters and places, and called on General Mason, Colonel Drum, General Van Bokkelen, Leland of the Occidental, Chief Burke, Keating, Emperor Norton, and everybody else that would be likely to know the Government's business, and knowing it, be willing to impart the coveted information for a consideration such as the wealthy fraternity of reporters are always prepared to promise. We did finally get it, from a high official source, and without any charge whatever—but then the satisfaction of the thing was all sapped out of it by exquisite "touches on the raw"—which means, hints that military matters were not proper subjects to branch out on in the popular sensational way so palatable to the people, and mild but extremely forcible suggestions about the unhappy fate that has overtaken fellows who ventured to experiment on "contraband news." We shall not go beyond the proper limits, if we fully appreciate those suggestions, and we think we do. We were told that we might say the military authorities, hearing where the Bishop had come from, (and may be what he was about—we will just "chance" that notion for a "flyer,") did send Captain Jackson to simply ask the Bishop to come down to San Francisco; (he didn't arrest the Bishop, at all—but most anybody would have come on a nice little invitation like that, without waiting for the formal compliment of an arrest: another excessively smart suggestion of ours, and we *do hope* it isn't contraband;) the Captain only requested the Bishop to come down here and explain to the authorities what he was up to; and he did—he arrived here night before last—and explained it in writing, and that document and the Bishop have been taken under advisement, (and we think we were told a decision had been arrived at, and that it was not public property just yet—but we are not sure, and we had rather not take any chances on this part of the business.) We do know, however, that the Bishop and his document are still under advisement as far as the public are concerned, and we would further advise the public not to get in a sweat about it, but to hold their grip patiently until it is proper for them to know all about the matter. This is all we know concerning the Bishop and his explanation, and if we have branched out too much and shed something that trenches upon that infernal "contraband" rule, we want to go home.

A14. Trot Her Along

30 July 1864

FOR SEVERAL DAYS a vagrant two-story frame house has been wandering listlessly about Commercial street, above this office, and she has finally stopped in the middle of the thoroughfare, and is staring dejectedly towards Montgomery street, as if she would like to go down there, but really don't feel equal to the exertion. We wish they would trot her along and leave the street open; she is an impassable obstruction and an intolerable nuisance where she stands now. If they set her up there to be looked at, it is all right; but we have looked at her as much as we want to, and are anxious for her to move along; we are not stuck after her any.

A15. Disgusted and Gone

31 July 1864

THAT MELANCHOLY old frame house that has been loafing around Commercial street for the past week, got disgusted at the notice we gave her in the last issue of the CALL, and drifted off into some other part of the city yesterday. It is pleasing to our vanity to imagine that if it had not been for our sagacity in divining her hellish designs, and our fearless exposure of them, she would have been down on Montgomery street to-day, playing herself for a hotel. As it is, she has folded her tents like the Arabs, and quietly stolen away, behind several yoke of oxen.

A16. *Another Lazarus*

31 July 1864

THE LAMENTED Lazarus departed this life about a year ago, and from that time until recently poor Bummer has mourned the loss of his faithful friend in solitude, scorning the sympathy and companionship of his race with that stately reserve and exclusiveness which has always distinguished him since he became a citizen of San Francisco. But, for several weeks past, we have observed a vagrant black puppy has taken up with him, and attends him in his promenades, bums with him at the restaurants, and watches over his slumbers as unremittingly as did the sainted Lazarus of other days. Whether that puppy really feels an unselfish affection for Bummer, or whether he is actuated by unworthy motives, and goes with him merely to ring in on the eating houses through his popularity at such establishments, or whether he is one of those fawning sycophants that fasten upon the world's heroes in order that they may be glorified by the reflected light of greatness, we cannot yet determine. We only know that he hangs around Bummer, and snarls at intruders upon his repose, and looks proud and happy when the old dog condescends to notice him. He ventures upon no puppyish levity in the presence of his prince, and essays no unbecoming familiarity, but in all respects conducts himself with the respectful decorum which such a puppy so situated should display. Consequently, in time, he may grow into high favor.

A17. Sombre Festivities

2 August 1864

ALL DAY YESTERDAY the cars were carrying colored people of all shades and tints, and of all sizes and both sexes, out to Hayes' Park, to celebrate the anniversary of the emancipation of their race in England's West Indian possessions years ago. They rode the fiery untamed steeds that are kept for equestrian duty in the grounds; they practised pistol shooting, but abstained from destroying the targets; they swung; they promenaded among the shrubbery; they filled themselves up with beer and sandwiches —all just as the thing is done there by white folks—and they essayed to dance, but the effort was not a brilliant success. It was interesting to look at, though. For languid, slow-moving, pretentious, impressive, solemn, and excessively high-toned and aristocratic dancing, commend us to the disenthralled North American negro, when there is no restraint upon his natural propensity to put on airs. White folks of the upper stratum of society pretend to walk through quadrilles, in a stately way, but these saddle-colored young ladies can discount them in the slow-movement evidence of high gentility. They don't know much about dancing, but they "let on" magnificently, as if the mazes of a quadrille were their native element, and they move serenely through it and tangle it hopelessly and inextricably, with an unctuous satisfaction that is surpassingly pleasant to witness. By the middle of the afternoon about two hundred darkies were assembled at the Park; or rather, to be precise, there was not much "darky" about it, either; for if the prevailing lightness of tint was worth anything as evidence, the noble miscegenationist had been skirmishing considerably among them in days gone by. It was expected that the colored race would come out strong in the matter of numbers (and otherwise) in the evening, when a grand ball was to be given and last all night.

A18. *Attempted Suicide*

7 August 1864

YESTERDAY, AT eleven o'clock in the forenoon, Emanuel Lopus, barber, of room No. 23, Mead House, wrote to the idol of his soul that he loved her better than all else beside; that unto him the day was dark, the sun seemed swathed in shadows, when she was not by; that he was going to take the life that God had given him, and enclosed she would please find one lock of hair, the same being his. He then took a teaspoonful of laudanum in a gallon of gin, and lay down to die. That is one version of it. Another is, that he really took an honest dose of laudanum, and was really anxious to put his light out, so much so, indeed, that after Dr. Murphy had come, resolved to pump the poison from his stomach or pump his heart out in the attempt, and after he had comfortably succeeded in the first mentioned proposition, this desperate French barber rose up and tried to whip the surgeon for saving his life, and defeating his fearful purpose, and wasting his laudanum. Another version is, that he went to his friend Jullien, in the barber shop under the Mead House, and told him to smash into his trunk after he had breathed his last and shed his immortal soul, and take from it his professional soap, and his lather-brush and his razors, and keep them forever to remember him by, for he was going this time without reserve. This was a touching allusion to his re-peated assertions, made at divers and sundry times during the past few years, that he was going off immediately and commit suicide. Jullien paid no attention to him, thinking he was only drunk, as usual, and that his better judgment would prompt him to substitute his regular gin at the last moment, instead of the deadlier poison. But on going to No. 23 an hour afterwards, he found the wretched Lopus in a heavy stupor, and all unconscious of the things of earth, and the junk-bottle and the laudanum phial on the bureau. We have endeavored to move the sympathy of the public in behalf of this poor Lopus, and we have done it from no selfish motive, and in no hope of reward, but only out of the commiseration we feel for one who has been suffering in solitude while the careless world around him was absorbed in the pursuit of life's foolish pleasures, heedless whether he lived or died. If we have succeeded—if we have caused one sympathetic tear to flow from the tender eye of pity, we desire no richer recompense. They took Lopus to the station-house yesterday afternoon, and from thence he was transferred to the French Hospital. We learn that he is getting along first-rate, now.

A19. *Mysterious*

9 August 1864

IF YOU HAVE got a house, keep your eye on it, these times, for there is no knowing what moment it will go tramping around town. We meet these dissatisfied shanties every day marching boldly through the public streets on stilts and rollers, or standing thoughtfully in front of gin shops, or halting in quiet alleys and peering round corners, with a human curiosity, out of one eye, or one window if you please, upon the dizzy whirl and roar of commerce in the thoroughfare beyond. The houses have been taking something lately that is moving them a good deal. It is very mysterious, and past accounting for, but it cannot be helped. We have just been informed that an unknown house—two stories, with a kitchen—has stopped before Shark alley, in Merchant street, and seems to be calculating the chances of being able to scrouge through it into Washington street, and thus save the trouble of going around. We hardly think she can, and we had rather she would not try it; we should be sorry to see her get herself fast in that crevice, which is the newspaper reporter's shortest cut to the station-house and the courts. Without wishing to be meddlesome or officious, we would like to suggest that she would find it very comfortable and nice going round by Montgomery street, and plenty of room. Besides, there is nothing to be seen in Shark alley, if she is only on a little pleasure excursion.

A20. Assault by a House

9 August 1864

THE VAGRANT HOUSE we have elsewhere alluded to as prowling around Merchant street, near Shark alley—we mean Dunbar alley—finally started to go around by Montgomery street, but at the first move fell over and mashed in some windows and broke down a new awning attached to the house adjoining the "Ivy Green" saloon.

A21. What Goes with the Money?

19 August 1864

SINCE THE RECENT extraordinary exposé of the concerns of the Grass Valley Silver Mining Company, by which stockholders discovered, to their grief and dismay, that figures *could* lie as to what became of some of their assessments, and could also be ominously reticent as to what went with the balance, people have begun to discuss the possibility of inventing a plan by which they may be advised, from time to time, of the manner in which their money is being expended by officers of mining companies, to the end that they may seasonably check any tendency towards undue extravagance or dishonest expenditures that may manifest itself, instead of being compelled to wait a year or two in ignorance and suspense, to find at last that they have been bankrupted to no purpose. And it is time their creative talents were at work in this direction. The longer they sleep the dread sleep of the Grass Valley, the more terrible will be the awakening from it. Money is being squandered with a recklessness that knows no limit—that had a beginning, but seemingly hath no end, save in a beggarly minority of dividend-paying companies—and after these years of expectation and this waste of capital, what account of stewardship has been rendered unto the flayed stockholder? What does he know about the disposition that has been made of his money? What brighter promise has he now than in any by-gone time that he is not to go on hopelessly paying assessments and wondering what becomes of them, until Gabriel sounds his trumpet? The Hale & Norcross officers decide to sink a shaft. They levy forty thousand dollars. Next month they have a mighty good notion to go lower, and they levy a twenty thousand dollar assessment. Next month, the novelty of sinking the shaft has about worn off, and they think it would be nice to drift a while—twenty thousand dollars. The following month it occurs to them it would be so funny to pump a little—and they buy a forty thousand dollar pump. Thus it goes on for months and months, but the Hale & Norcross sends us no bullion, though most of the time there is an encouraging rumor afloat that they are "right in the casing!" Take the Chollar Company, for instance. It seems easy on its children just now, but who does not remember its regular old monotonous assessment anthem? "Sixty dollars a foot! sixty dollars a foot! sixty dollars a foot!" month in and month out, till the persecuted stockholder howled again. The same way with the Best & Belcher, and the same way with three-fourths of the mines on the main lead, from Cedar Hill to Silver City. We could scarcely name them all in a single article, but we have given a specimen or so by which the balance may be measured. And what has gone with the money? We pause (a year or two) for a reply. Now, in some of the States, all banks are compelled to publish a monthly statement of their affairs. Why not make the big mining companies do the same thing? It would make some of them fearfully sick at first, but they would feel all the better for it in the long-run. The Legislature is not in session, and a law to this effect cannot now be passed; but if one company dare voluntarily to set the example, the balance would follow by pressure of circumstances. But that first bold company does not exist, perhaps; if it does, a grateful community will be glad to hear from it. Where is it? Let it come forward and offer itself as the sacrificial scapegoat to bear the sins of its fellows into the wilderness.

A22. It Is the Daniel Webster

21 August 1864

MINING COMPANIES' ACCOUNTS.—The MORNING CALL of yesterday has a lively article on Mining Companies, suggesting that Mining Trustees should publish quarterly statements of Expenditures and Receipts, concluding with:

"The Legislature is not in session, and a law to this effect cannot now be passed; but if one company dare voluntarily to set the example, the balance would follow by pressure of circumstances. But that first bold company does not exist, perhaps; if it does, a grateful community will be glad to hear from it. Where is it? Let it come forward and offer itself as the sacrificial scape-goat to bear the sins of its fellows into the wilderness."

In answer to this the officers of the Daniel Webster Mining Company, located in Devil's Gate District, Nevada Territory, have requested us to inform the shareholders and others who have purchased stock in this Company at high prices, that a complete exhibit of the Company's affairs will be made public in the Argus on Saturday next. This Company, in consequence of a couple of shareholders in Nevada Territory, (legal gentlemen at that,) paying their previous assessments in green-backs, has been the first to levy an assessment payable in currency. We believe, however, they will be the first "who dare" to make public their accounts. We hope the Coso will be the next to follow suit, as a correspondent of ours, in Sacramento, (whose letter appears under the appropriate heading,) seems anxious to learn what has become of the forty-three thousand two hundred dollars collected by this Company for assessments the last year.—[S. F. Argus, Saturday.

So there *are* company officers who are bold enough, fair enough, true enough to the interests entrusted to their keeping, to let stockholders, as well as all who may chance to become so, know the character of their stewardship, and whose records are white enough to bear inspection. We had not believed it, and we are glad that a Mining Company worthy of the name of Daniel Webster existed to save to us the remnant of our faith in the uprightness of these dumb and inscrutable institutions. We have nothing to fear now; all that was wanting was some one to take the lead. Other Companies will see that this monthly or quarterly exhibit of their affairs is nothing but a simple act of justice to their stockholders and to others who may desire to become so. They will also see that it is *policy* to let the public know where invested money will be judiciously used and strictly accounted for; and, our word for it, Companies that *dare* to show their books, will soon fall into line and adopt the system of published periodical statements. In time it will become a *custom,* and custom is more binding, more impregnable, and more exacting than any law that was ever framed. In that day the Coso will be heard from; and so will Companies in Virginia, which sport vast and gorgeously-painted shaft and machinery houses, with costly and beautiful green chicken-cocks on the roof, which are able to tell how the wind blows, yet are savagely ignorant concerning dividends. So will other Companies come out and say what it cost to build their duck ponds; so will still others tell their stockholders why they paid sixty thousand dollars for machinery worth about half the money; another that we have in our eye will show what they did with an expensive lot of timbers, when they haven't got enough in their mine to shingle a chicken-coop with; and yet others will let us know if they are still "in the casing," and why they levy a forty-thousand-dollar assessment every six weeks to run a drift with. Secretaries, Superintendents, and Boards of Trustees, that don't like the prospect, had better resign. The public have got precious little confidence in the present lot, and the public will back this assertion we are making in its name. Stockholders are very tired of being at the mercy of omnipotent and invisible officers, and are ripe for the inauguration of a safer and more sensible state of things. And when it is inaugurated, mining property will thrive again, and not before. Confidence is the mainstay of every class of commercial enterprise.

A23. No Earthquake

23 August 1864

IN CONSEQUENCE OF the warm, close atmosphere which smothered the city at two o'clock yesterday afternoon, everybody expected to be shaken out of their boots by an earthquake before night, but up to the hour of our going to press the supernatural boot-jack had not arrived yet. That is just what makes it so unhealthy—the earthquakes are getting so irregular. When a community get used to a thing, they suffer when they have to go without it. However, the trouble cannot be remedied; we know of nothing that will answer as a substitute for one of those convulsions—to an unmarried man.

A24. Rain

23 August 1864

ONE OF THOSE singular freaks of Nature which, by reference to the dictionary, we find described as "the water or the descent of water that falls in drops from the clouds—a shower," occurred here yesterday, and kept the community in a state of pleasant astonishment for the space of several hours. They would not have been astonished at an earthquake, though. Thus it will be observed that nothing accustoms one to a thing so readily as getting used to it. You will always notice that, in America. We were thinking this refreshing rain would make everybody happy. Not so the cows. An agricultural sharp informs us that yesterday's rain was a misfortune to California—that it will kill the dry grass upon which the cattle now subsist, and also the young grass upon which they were calculating to subsist hereafter. We know nothing whatever about the matter, but we do know that if what this gentleman says is strictly true, the inevitable deduction is that the cattle are out of luck. We stand to that.

A25. A Dark Transaction

24 August 1864

A GLOOM PERVADED the Police Court, as the sable visages of Mary Wilkinson and Maria Brooks, with their cloud of witnesses, entered within its consecrated walls, each to prosecute and defend respectively in counter charges of assault and battery. The cases were consolidated, and crimination and recrimination ruled the hour. Mary said she was a meek-hearted Christian, who loved her enemies, including Maria, and had prayed for her on the very morning of the day when the latter threw a pail of water and a rock against her. Maria said she didn't throw; that she wasn't a Christian herself, and that Mary had the very devil in her. The case would always have remained in doubt, but Mrs. Hammond overshadowed the Court, and flashed defiance at counsel, from her eyes, while indignation and eloquence burst from her heaving bosom, like the long pent up fires of a volcano, whenever any one presumed to intimate that her statement might be improved in point of credibility, by a slight explanation. Even the gravity of the Court was somewhat disturbed when three hundred weight of black majesty, hauteur, and conscious virtue, rolled on to the witness stand, like the fore quarter of a sunburnt whale, a living embodiment of Desdemona, Othello, Jupiter, Josh, and Jewhilikens. She appeared as counsel for Maria Brooks, and scornfully repudiated the relationship, when citizen Sam Platt, Esq., prefaced his interrogation with the endearing, "Aunty." "I'm not your Aunty," she roared. "I'm Mrs. Hammond," upon which the citizen S. P., Esq., repeated his assurances of distinguished regard, and caved a little. Mrs. Hammond rolled off the stand; and out of the Court room, like the fragment of a thunder cloud, leaving the "congregation," as she called it, in convulsions. Mary Brooks and Maria Wilkinson were both convicted of assault and battery, and ordered to appear for sentence.

A26. Enthusiastic Hard Money Demonstration

30 August 1864

THE ERA OF our prosperity is about to dawn on us. If it don't it had orter. The jingle of coin will still be heard in our pockets and tills. It's all right. The Hard Money Association held an adjourned meeting at the Police Court room last night, for the express purpose of considering dollars. The meeting was an adjourned one. It staid adjourned. It wasn't anything else. The room was dimly lighted. It looked like the Hall of Eolis. Silently sat some ten or a dozen of the galvanized protectors of our prosperity. They looked for all the world like an infernal council in conclave. They were dumb; but what great plans for the suppression of the green backed dragon were born in that silence still remains hid in the arcana of the mysterious cabal. They said nothing, they did nothing. Like fixed statues they sat, all wrapped in contemplation of their mighty scheme. They didn't adjourn, for from the first it was an adjourned meeting, and it staid adjourned. Soon they all left —parted quietly, mysteriously, awfully. The lights were turned out, and—nothing more. Money is still hard.

A27. "Shiner No. 1"

31 August 1864

THAT INDUSTRIOUS wild "Shiner" with his heavy brass machine for testing the strength of human muscles, is around again, in his original swallow-tail gray coat. That same wanderer, coat and machine, have been ceaselessly on the move throughout California and Washoe, for a year or more, and still they look none the worse for wear. And still the generous proposition goeth up from the wanderer's lips, in the by-places and upon the corners of the street: "Wan pull for a bit, jintlemen, an' anny man that pulls eighteen hundher' pounds can thry it over agin widout expinse." And still the wanderer seeketh the eighteen-hundred pounder up and down in the earth, and findeth him not; and still the public strive for that gratis pull, and still they are disappointed—still do they fall short of the terms by a matter of half a ton or so. Go your ways, and give the ubiquitous "Shiner" a chance to find the man upon whom it is his mission upon earth to confer the blessing of a second pull "widout expinse."

A28. The Cosmopolitan Hotel Besieged

1 September 1864

As a proof that it is good policy to advertise, and that nothing that appears in a newspaper is left unread, we will state that the mere mention in yesterday's papers that the Cosmopolitan Hotel would be thrown open for public inspection, caused that place to be besieged at an early hour yesterday evening, by some thirty thousand men, women and children; and the chances are that more than as many more had read the invitation, but were obliged to forego the pleasure of accepting it. By eight o'clock, the broad halls and stairways of the building, from cellar to roof, were densely crowded, with people of all ages, sexes, characters, and conditions in life; and a similar army were collected in the street outside, unable to gain admission—there was no room for them. The lowest estimate we heard of the number of persons who passed into the Hotel was twenty thousand, and the highest sixty thousand; so we split the difference, and call it thirty thousand. And among this vast assemblage of refined gentlemen, elegant ladies, and tender children, was mixed a lot of thieves, ruffians, and vandals. They stole everything they could get their hands on—silverware from the dining-room, hankerchiefs from gentlemen, veils and victorines from ladies, and even gobbled up sheets, shirts and pillow-cases in the laundry, and made off with them. They wantonly destroyed costly parlor ornaments, and pulled down and trampled under foot the handsome lace curtains of some of the windows. They "went through" Mr. Henning's room, and left him not even a sock or a boot. (We observed, a day or two ago, that he had a bushel and a half of the latter article stacked up at the foot of his bed.) The masses, wedged together in the halls and on the staircases, grew hot and angry, and smashed each other over the head with canes, and punched each other in the face with their fists, and to stop the thieving and save loss to helpless visitors, and get rid of the pickpockets, the gas had to be turned off in some parts of the house. At ten o'clock, when we were there, there was a constant stream of people passing out of the hotel, and other streams pouring towards it from every direction, to be disappointed in their hopes of seeing the wonders within it, for the proprietors having already suffered to the extent of several thousands of dollars in thefts and damages to furniture, were unwilling to admit decent people any longer, for fear of another invasion of rascals among them. Another grand rush was expected to follow the letting out of the theatres. The Cosmopolitan still stands, however, and to-day it opens for good, and for the accommodation of all them that do eat and sleep, and have the wherewithal to pay for it.

A29. Rincon School Militia

1 September 1864

BEFORE DISBANDING for a fortnight's furlough, the boys connected with Rincon School had a grand dress parade, yesterday. They are classed into regular military companies, and officered as follows, by boys chosen from their own ranks: Company A, Captain John Welch; B, Captain John Warren; C, Captain Henry Tucker; D, Captain William Thompson; E, Captain Robinson; F, Captain Charles Redman; G, Captain Cyrus Myers; H, Captain Henry Tabor. Companies I and J have no regularly elected officers, we are told. The drummers of the regiment are two youngsters named Douglas Williams and John Seaborn, and their talent for making a noise amounts almost to inspiration. Both are first-class drummers. The Rincon boys have been carefully drilled in military exercises for a year, now, and have acquired a proficiency which is astonishing. They go through with the most elaborate manœuvres without hesitating and without making a mistake; to execute every order promptly and perfectly has become second nature to them, and requires no more reflection than it does to a practised boarder to go to dinner when he hears the gong ring. The word "drill" is the proper one—those boys' legs and arms have been drilled into a comprehension of those orders that they execute them mechanically, even though the restless mind may be thinking of anything else in the world at the moment. Professor Robinson has been the military instructor of the Rincon Regiment for several months past. The School exercises, earlier in the day, were very interesting, and consisted of dialogues, declamations, vocal and instrumental music, calisthenics, etc. "The Humors of the Draft," a sort of comedy, illustrative of the shifts to which unwarlike patriots are put in order to compass exemption, was well played by a number of the School boys, and was received with shouts of laughter. Douglas Williams played, on his drum, a solo which would have been a happy accompaniment to one of our choicest earthquakes. A young girl sang that lugubrious ditty, "Wrap the Flag around me, Boys," and the extraordinary purity and sweetness of her voice actually made pleasant music of it, impossible as such a thing might seem to any one acquainted with that marvellous piece of composition. The Principal's, Mr. Pelton's, heir, an American sovereign of eight Summers and no Winters at all, since his life has been passed here where it has pleased the Almighty to omit that season, gave a recitation in French, and one in German; and from the touching pathos and expression which he threw into the latter, and the liquid richness of his accent, we are satisfied the subject was a noble one and wrought in beautiful language, but we could not testify unqualifiedly, in this respect, without access to a translation. The Rincon School was mustered out of service, yesterday evening, for the term of two weeks.

A30. Fine Picture of Rev. Mr. King

1 September 1864

CALIFORNIA AND Nevada Territory are flooded with distressed-looking abortions done in oil, in water-colors, in crayon, in lithography, in photography, in sugar, in plaster, in marble, in wax, and in every substance that is malleable or chiselable, or that can be marked on, or scratched on, or painted on, or which by its nature can be compelled to lend itself to a relentless and unholy persecution and distortion of the features of the great and good man who is gone from our midst—Rev. Thomas Starr King. We do not believe these misguided artistic lunatics meant to confuse the lineaments, and finally destroy and drive out from our memories the cherished image of our lost orator, but just the contrary. We believe their motive was good, but we know their execution was atrocious. We look upon these blank, monotonous, over-fed and sleepy-looking pictures, and ask, with Dr. Bellows, "Where was the seat of this man's royalty?" But we ask in vain of these wretched counterfeits. There is no more life or expression in them than you may find in the soggy, upturned face of a pickled infant, dangling by the neck in a glass jar among the trophies of a doctor's back office, any day. But there is one perfect portrait of Mr. King extant, with all the tenderness and goodness of his nature, and all the power and grandeur of his intellect drawn to the surface, as it were, and stamped upon the features with matchless skill. This picture is in the possession of Dr. Bellows, and is the only one we have seen in which we could discover no substantial ground for fault finding. It is a life size outline photograph, elaborately wrought out and finished in crayon by Mrs. Frances Molineux Gibson, of this city, and has been presented by her to Rev. Dr. Bellows, to be sold for the benefit of the Sanitary Commission. It will probably be exhibited for a while at the Mechanics' Fair, after which it will be disposed of, as above mentioned. Dr. Bellows desires to keep it, and will do so if bids for it do not take altogether too high a flight.

A31. The Hurdle-Race Yesterday

4 September 1864

THE GRAND FEATURE at the Bay View Park yesterday, was the hurdle race. There were three competitors, and the winner was Wilson's circus horse, "Sam." Sam has lain quiet through all the pacings and trottings and runnings, and consented to be counted out, but this hurdle business was just his strong suit, and he stepped forward promptly when it was proposed. There was a much faster horse (Conflict) in the list, but what is natural talent to cultivation? Sam was educated in a circus, and understood his business; Conflict would pass him under way, trip and turn a double summerset over the next hurdle, and while he was picking himself up, the accomplished Sam would sail gracefully over the hurdle and slabber past his adversary with the easy indifference of conscious superiority. Conflict made the fastest time, but he fooled away too many summersets on the hurdles. The proverb saith that he that jumpeth fences with ye circus horse will aye come to grief.

A32. A Terrible Monster Caged

4 September 1864

A MOST WRETCHED criminal was brought into the Police Court yesterday morning, on a charge of petty larceny. He stands between three and four feet in his shoes, and has arrived at the age of ten years. His name does not appear on the register, so the world must remain in ignorance of that. He is an orphan who has been provided with a home in a respectable family of this city, and is charged with having taken some chips and sticks from about Dr. Toland's fine new building, which it is supposed he uses in kindling the fires for the family he lives with. The person whose vigilance discovered grounds for suspecting this fatherless and motherless boy of the horrible crime, is a carpenter who works at the building. The county is indebted to him. The little fellow came into Court under a strong guard. He was terrified almost out of his senses, and looked as if he expected the Judge to order his head to be chopped off at once. The matter, if entertained at all, will be heard on Monday, and in the meantime the little boy will anticipate worlds of misery. It is a matter of wonder to some that a deliberate attempt to send an indefinite number of souls to Davy Jones' locker, by one who occupies a prominent position, escapes Judicial scrutiny, while the whole force conservatorial is hot foot in the chase after some little ragged shaver, some fledgling of St. Giles, unkempt and uncared for, who flits from corner to corner, and from hole to hole, as if fleeing from his own shadow. But such persons don't understand conservatorial policy. Let the hoary headed sinners go, they can get no worse, and soon will die off, but look sharply after the young crop. The old trunk will decay after a while and fall before the tempest, but the sapling must be hewn down.

A33. The Californian

4 September 1864

THIS STERLING literary weekly has changed hands, both in the matter of proprietorship and editorial management. Mr. Webb has sold the paper to Captain Ogden, a gentleman of fine literary attainments, an able writer, and the possessor of a happy bank account—three qualifications which, in the lump, cannot fail to insure the continued success of the Californian. Mr. Frank Brett Harte will assume the editorship of the paper. Some of the most exquisite productions which have appeared in its pages emanated from his pen, and are worthy to take rank among even Dickens' best sketches. Taking all things in consideration, if the Californian dies now, it must be by the same process that resurrected Lazarus, which we are proud to be able to state was a miracle. After faithfully laboring night and day for about four months, and publishing fifteen numbers of the best paper in its particular department ever issued on this coast, Mr. Webb will now go and rest a while on the shores of Lake Tahoe. He has chosen to rest himself by fishing, and he is wise; for the fish in Lake Tahoe are not troublesome; they will let a man rest there till he rots, and never inflict upon him the fatigue of putting on a fresh bait. "Inigo" has our kindest wishes for his present and future happiness, though, rot or no rot.

A34. A Promising Artist

6 September 1864

THE LARGE OIL painting in the picture store under the Russ House, of the "Blind Fiddler," is the work of a very promising California artist, Mr. William Mulligan, of Healdsburg, formerly of St. Louis, Mo. In the main, both the conception and execution are good, but the latter is faulty in some of the minor details. Dr. Bellows has a smaller picture, however, by the same artist, which betrays the presence of genius of a high order in the hand that limned it. The subject is a dying drummer-boy, half sitting, half reclining, upon the battle field, with his body partly propped upon his broken drum, and his left arm hanging languidly over it. Near him lie his cap and his drum-sticks—unheeded, discarded, useless to him forever more. The dash of blood upon his shirt, the dreamy, away-at-home look upon the features, the careless, resigned expression of the nerveless arm, tell the story. The colors in the picture are not gaudy enough to suit the popular taste, perhaps, but they represent nature truthfully, which is better. Mr. Mulligan has demonstrated in every work his hands have wrought, that he is an artist of more than common ability, and he deserves a generous encouragement. One or two of his pictures will probably be exhibited at the Mechanics' Fair now being held in this city.

$A35.$ Earthquake

8 September 1864

THE REGULAR semi-monthly earthquake arrived at ten minutes to ten o'clock, yesterday morning. Thirty-six hours ahead of time. It is supposed it was sent earlier, to shake up the Democratic State Convention, but if this was the case, the calculation was awkwardly made, for it fell short by about two hours. The Convention did not meet until noon. Either the earthquake or the Convention, or both combined, made the atmosphere mighty dense and sulphurous all day. If it was the Democrats alone, they do not smell good, and it certainly cannot be healthy to have them around.

A 36. Cross Swearing

9 September 1864

THAT A THING cannot be all black and all white at the same time, is as self evident as that two objects cannot occupy the same space at the same time, and when a man makes a statement under the solemn sanction of an oath, the implication is that what he utters is a fact, the verity of which is not to be questioned. Notwithstanding witnesses are so often warned of the nature of an oath, and the consequences of perjury, yet it is a daily occurrence in the Police Court for men and women to mount the witness stand and swear to statements diametrically opposite. Swearing positively—leaving mere impressions out of the question—on the one hand that the horse was as black as night, and on the other that he was white as the driven snow. Two men have a fight, and a prosecution for assault and battery ensues. Each party comes up prepared to prove respectively and positively the guilt and innocence of the party accused. A swears point blank that B chased him a square and knocked him down, and exhibits wounds and blood to corroborate his statements. B brings a witness or two who saw the whole affair, from probably a distant stand point, and he testifies that nothing connected with the fight could have escaped his observation, and that it was A who chased B a square and knocked him down, and between these two solemn statements the Court has to decide. How can he do it? It is an impossibility, and thus many a culprit escapes punishment. There was a case in point Tuesday morning. A German named Rosenbaum prosecuted another German named Levy, for running into his wagon and breaking an axletree. He swore that he kept as far over to the right hand side of the street as a hole in the planking would permit, stopped his wagon when he saw the impending collision, and warned Levy off. Notwithstanding, Levy drove his vehicle against his wheel, breaking the axle, so as to require a new one which would cost twenty-five dollars. He stated also that Levy had been trying to injure him in that way for a long while. Levy brought a witness who swore that between Rosenbaum's wagon

473

and the hole in the street, there was room for a wagon or two to pass; that Rosenbaum challenged the collision, and that it was unavoidable on the part of Levy; that instead of stopping his wagon, the prosecuting witness drove ahead at a trot until the wagons became entangled, and that no damage whatever was done to Rosenbaum. On the whole, that instead of Levy running into Rosenbaum's wagon, Rosenbaum intentionally brought about the collision for the purpose of recovering damages off of Levy. The case was stronger than we have stated it, and the Judge could do nothing but dismiss the matter. That there was perjury on one side, was apparent. Yet this is but the history of one-half the cases that are adjudicated in the Police Court. There should be examples made of some of these reckless swearers. It would probably have a wholesome effect.

$\mathcal{A}$37. Interesting Litigation

15 September 1864

SAN FRANCISCO beats the world for novelties; but the inventive faculties of her people are exercised on a specialty. We don't care much about creating things other countries can supply us with. We have on hand a vast quantity of a certain kind of material and we must work it up, and we do work it up often to an alarming pitch. Controversy is our forte. Californians can raise more legal questions and do the wager of combat in more ways than have been eliminated from the arcana of civil and military jurisprudence since Justinian wrote or Agamemnon fought. Suits—why we haven't names for half of them. A man has a spite at his neighbor—and what man or man's wife hasn't—and he forthwith prosecutes him in the Police Court, for having onions for breakfast, under some ordinance or statutory provision having about as much relation to the case as the title page of Webster's Dictionary. And then, there's an array of witnesses who are well posted in everything else except the matter in controversy. And indefatigable attorneys enlighten the Court by drawing from the witnesses the whole detailed history of the last century. And then again we are in doubt about some little matter of personal or public convenience, and slap goes somebody into Court under duress of a warrant. If we want to determine the age of a child who has grown out of our knowledge, we commence a prosecution at once against some one else with children, and elicit from witnesses enough chronological information to fill a whole encyclopedia, to prove that our child of a doubtful age was cotemporary with the children of defendant, and thus approximate to the period of nativity sought for. A settlement of mutual accounts is arrived at by a prosecution for obtaining goods or money under false pretences. Partnership affairs are elucidated in a prosecution for grand larceny. A burglary simply indicates that a creditor called at the house of his debtor the night before market morning, to collect a small bill. We have nothing but a civil code. A portion of our laws are criminal in name only. We have no law for crime.

Cut, slosh around with pistols and dirk knives as you will, and the worst that comes of it is a petty charge of carrying concealed weapons; and murder is but an aggravated assault and battery. We go into litigation instinctively, like a young duck goes into the water. A man can't dig a shovel full of sand out of a drift that threatens to overwhelm his property, nor put a fence around his lot that some person has once driven a wagon across, but what he is dragged before some tribunal to answer to a misdemeanor. Personal revenge, or petty jealousies and animosities, or else the pursuit of information under difficulties, keep up a heavy calendar, and the Judge of the Court spends three-fourths of his time listening to old women's quarrels, and tales that ought, in many cases, to consign the witnesses themselves to the prison cell, and dismissing prosecutions that are brought without probable cause, nor the shadow of it. A prosecuting people we are, and we are getting no better every day. The census of the city can almost be taken now from the Police Court calendar; and a month's attendance on that institution will give one a familiar acquaintance with more than half of our domestic establishments.

A38. A Terrible Weapon

21 September 1864

A CHARGE OF assault with a deadly weapon, preferred in the Police Court yesterday, against Jacob Friedberg, was dismissed, at the request of all parties concerned, because of the scandal it would occasion to the Jewish Church to let the trial proceed, both the assaulted man and the man committing the assault being consecrated servants of that Church. The weapon used was a butcher-knife, with a blade more than two feet long, and as keen as a razor. The men were butchers, appointed by dignitaries of the Jewish Church to slaughter and inspect all beef intended for sale to their brethren, and in a dispute some time ago, one of them partly split the other's head open, from the top of the forehead to the end of his nose, with the sacred knife, and also slashed one of his hands. From these wounds the sufferer has only just recovered. The Jewish butcher is not appointed to his office in this country, but is chosen abroad by a college of Rabbis and sent hither. He kills beeves designed for consumption by Israelites, (or any one else, if they choose to buy,) and after careful examination, if he finds that the animal is in any way diseased, it is condemned and discarded; if the contrary, the seal of the Church is placed upon it, and it is permitted to be sent into the market—a custom that might be adopted with profit by all sects and creeds. It is said that the official butcher always assures himself that the sacred knife is perfectly sharp and without a wire edge, before he cuts a bullock's throat; he then draws it with a single lightning stroke (and at any rate not more than two strokes are admissible,) and if the knife is still without a wire edge after the killing, the job has been properly done; but if the contrary is the case, it is adjudged that a bone has been touched and pain inflicted upon the animal, and consequently the meat cannot receive the seal of approval and must be thrown aside. It is a quaint custom of an ancient Church, and sounds strangely enough to modern ears. Considering that the

dignity of the Church was in some sense involved in the miscon-
duct of its two servants, the dismissal of the case without a hearing was asked and granted.

*A*39. *Advice to Witnesses*

29 September 1864

WITNESSES IN THE Police Court, who expect to be questioned on
the part of the prosecution, should always come prepared to answer the following questions: "Was you there, at the time?" "Did
you see it done, and if you did, how do you know?" "City and
County of San Francisco?" "Is your mother living, and if so, is she
well?" "You say the defendant struck the plaintiff with a stick.
Please state to the Court what kind of a stick it was?" "Did it
have the bark on, and if so, what kind of bark did it have on?" "Do
you consider that such a stick would be just as good with the bark
on, as with it off, or vicy versy?" "Why?" "I think you said it
occurred in the City and County of San Francisco?" "You say your
mother has been dead seventeen years—native of what place, and
why?" "You don't know anything about this assault and battery,
do you?" "Did you ever study astronomy?—hard, isn't it?" "You
have seen this defendant before, haven't you?" "Did you ever
slide on a cellar door when you were a boy?" "Well—that's all."
"Stay: did this occur in the City and County of San Francisco?"
The Prosecuting Attorney may mean well enough, but meaning
well and doing well are two very different things. His abilities are
of the mildest description, and do not fit him for a position like
the one he holds, where energy, industry, tact, shrewdness, and
some little smattering of law, are indispensable to the proper
fulfilment of its duties. Criminals leak through his fingers every
day like water through a sieve. He does not even afford a cheerful
amount of competition in business to the sharp lawyers over
whose heads he was elected to be set up as an ornamental effigy in
the Police Court. He affords a great deal less than no assistance to
the Judge, who could convict sometimes if the District Attorney
would remain silent, or if the law had not hired him at a salary of
two hundred and fifty dollars a month to unearth the dark and
ominous fact that the "offence was committed in the City and
County of San Francisco." The man means well enough, but he

don't know how; he makes of the proceedings in behalf of a sacred right and justice in the Police Court, a drivelling farce, and he ought to show his regard for the public welfare by resigning.

APPENDIX B

On 19 October 1865 Clemens told his brother Orion: "The Dramatic Chronicle pays me—or rather *will* begin to pay me, next week—$40 a month for dramatic criticisms. Same wages I got on the *Call*, & more agreeable & less laborious work."[1] The sketches collected in this appendix are not the dramatic criticisms he wrote in the last months of 1865, but a variety of brief notes and squibs that he wrote and published in the San Francisco *Dramatic Chronicle* while he was also providing dramatic criticism for that journal.[2] These items, many of them closely tied with signed or clearly authorial sketches in the body of the collection, are reprinted here for the first time. The items are, however, only a selection from many more that could easily be by Clemens: we have tried to reprint only those that seem to be his beyond much doubt.

---

[1]Clemens to Orion and Mollie Clemens, 19–20 October 1865, *CL1*, letter 95.
[2]The drama reviews are scheduled to appear in the collection of criticism in The Works of Mark Twain.

B1. *Attention, Fitz Smythe!*

26 October 1865

This item appeared on 26 October 1865, one day after "Arrival of the 'Colorado,' " presumably written by Albert S. Evans (Fitz Smythe), was published in the San Francisco *Alta California.*[1] Clemens quotes (with some changes) from this article in his first sentence (see the textual commentary).

THE MATHEMATICAL Fitz Smythe, of the *Alta,* says in his paper that "the *Colorado* arrived from Panama after the quick passage of twelve days *and twenty-four hours.*" That mode of expressing oneself in a solemn, religious paper like the *Alta* is extremely reprehensible. It is dreadfully well calculated to deceive—for who notices the odd hours? and who don't notice the round numbers and give the steamer credit for a twelve-day trip? Fitz Smythe, you won't do! Fitz Smythe, the atmosphere of the Police Court is destroying your religious principles! Fitz Smythe, beware! You will be a moral Augean Stable the first thing you know, Fitz Smythe! And in that case, there will be no Hercules found in these days equal to the job of shoveling you out! First class in mathematics, stand up: Armand Leonidas Fitz Smythe, how many days do twelve days and twenty-four hours make?

---

[1]San Francisco *Alta California,* 25 October 1865, p. 1.

B2 Lisle Lester on Her Travels

30 October 1865

This item appeared on 30 October 1865, several weeks after Lisle Lester published her "Notes of the Insane" in the Marysville *Appeal*.[1] She was the editor of the *Pacific Monthly*, just under thirty years of age, and, according to one contemporary description, "a spunky little piece of femininity weighing about 95 lbs. avoirdupois, and as chock full of good natured impudence and wit as ninety-five pounds of woman can well be."[2] The italicized words in Clemens' quotation from her *Appeal* article were styled in this way by him (see the textual commentary). For her response, see Appendix B6.

LISLE LESTER, who is probably the worst writer in the world, though a good-hearted woman and a woman who means well, notwithstanding the distressing productions of her pen, has been visiting the Insane Asylum and favors the Marysville *Appeal* with some of her experiences. She is touched by the spectacle of mothers whose minds are so darkened by the clouds of insanity that "even the sight of an old child fails to recall the sweet relationship." "Old child" is a rather pleasing expression, but it has an odd sound, especially when it drops unexpectedly into the midst of a paragraph which is perfectly saturated with pathos — or bathos — which is the case in the present instance. She recounts the sad history of a German girl in the asylum, and flavors the fearful tale with some decidedly queer phrases — thus: "She, the betrothed, saw the heart of him she loved was with the younger sister, and, strange as it is for women, she gave him up, *handed him to the sister* with her blessing and good will, wrapt up her grief, *shut down* her hopes, and to be alone came to America." Wouldn't it have been more expressive to have said that "she shook him" and then wrapped up her grief, etc.? We cannot improve upon the steam-power of the phrase which informs us that she "shut down her hopes." Of another patient, she says: "Wheat

---

[1]Marysville *Appeal*, 12 September 1865, p. 1.
[2]"Lisle Lester and the 'Protective Union,'" San José *Mercury*, 28 July 1864, p. 2.

in Michigan, lands in Ohio, houses in California, fill up the crevices of her fancy." Isn't that rather crowding the "crevices?"
Wouldn't it be more roomy to say these houses and things fill up
the cañons of her fancy? As to Lisle Lester's grammar, we feel that
we are speaking tamely when we say that it is powerful.

B3. *More California Notables Gone*

1 November 1865

Clemens quotes from "Banquet to a Departing Merchant" in his third sentence.[1] This article, presumably one of Evans', gives a flattering account of Moses Ellis, a wealthy importer and dealer in groceries, who was honored at a lavish dinner attended by many fellow merchants before he sailed on the steamship *Colorado*. Senator John Conness, General William S. Rosecrans, and Angela Starr King, sister of the late Reverend Thomas Starr King, were also among the *Colorado's* passengers. For Clemens' other comments on the sailing of the *Colorado* see "Steamer Departures" and "Editorial 'Puffing' " (nos. 126 and 129).

THE STEAMER did not pan out well for Fitz Smythe on Monday. He only got one departing notability out of the whole list of passengers. Moses Ellis retired from business with a heavy income, was banquetted at the Occidental by the merchants of the city, "left us on a visit to the home of his nativity," and Fitz Smythe gloats over it to the extent of a "stickfull." But why did he neglect Conness? Why Rosecrans? Why Angela Starr King? And, above all, why did he let J. Schmeltzer go away without a parting dose of adulation? Oh, unhappy Schmeltzer, you didn't make your "pile," perhaps!

---

[1]San Francisco *Alta California*, 30 October 1865, p. 1.

B4. "Chrystal" on Theology

3 November 1865

Clemens here alludes to a series of letters by "Chrystal" from Searsville, San Mateo County, to the San Francisco *Alta California*. They appeared under the heading "How to Conduct a Newspaper" and discoursed on agriculture, poetry, and mining. Letter 6, the one to which Clemens specifically refers, was subtitled "Chrystal on Immortality" and said in part: "If persons cultevates nobel and refined thoughts and dus nobel actions, thay will imortalize thar spirits. but if persons alows thar minds to sink into digredation and depravity, thar spirits will sink away into mortality and ceas to exist."[1] Clemens' interest in this sort of natural eccentric is well documented; this item is clearly identified as his by the recurrent phrase "keep up his lick." Four days later, when another writer in the *Dramatic Chronicle* used the same phrase, he felt obliged to acknowledge its author: "As that irreverent wretch, Mark Twain would say, 'she didn't keep up her lick.' "[2]

THERE IS NO use in a man trying to maintain a particular tone of feeling—a certain mood—when circumstances and surroundings are against him. He may hold out for a while, but in the end he is bound to succumb to those circumstances and surroundings, and tune up afresh and in unison with their key-note. There is no use in a man trying to be a cynical, stoical humbug in the society of a lovely girl; and there is no use in his hoping to keep up a boisterous flow of spirits all through a Quaker meeting; and there is no use in his trying to remain cheerful and wide awake in a chloroform factory. It is no use for a man to attempt any of these things, because he can't "keep up his lick." "Chrystal," the San Mateo editorial correspondent of the *Alta*, who started out but one short week ago with a series of the liveliest and most enter-

---

[1]"How to Conduct a Newspaper. Chapter VI. Chrystal on Immortality," San Francisco *Alta California*, 1 November 1865, p. 1.

[2]"Amusements," San Francisco *Dramatic Chronicle*, 7 November 1865, p. 3. Clemens frequently used the phrase: see "Answers to Correspondents" (no. 108), "The Chapman Family" (no. 162), "A New Biography of Washington" (no. 183), and *MTTB*, p. 136.

taining articles (as contrasted with the general run of articles in that paper) has fallen! He has succumbed to the sleepy influences of that dreamy old chloroform factory. His sprightliness waned apace, and he has sunk down at last into a dreary homily on the immortality of the human soul—for the delectation of merchants and brokers, who are so partial to that sort of thing, and to teach the *Alta* editors "How to Conduct a Great Commercial Newspaper." Alas! poor "Chrystal!" His surroundings were too much for him. He couldn't "keep up his lick!"

B5. Oh, You Robinson!

6 November 1865

Early in November 1865 the San Francisco papers publicized the charge of bigamy brought against John R. Robinson, formerly a prosperous city banker. Pleading desertion, Robinson had sued Kate Anderson Robinson for divorce on 7 January 1861. He failed to win his suit in San Francisco, but was ultimately granted a divorce decree by a Salt Lake City court on 18 June 1864. He married Laura Hatch on October 29, and his first wife then brought suit. The case against him was dismissed.[1]

ONE OF Rev. Mr. Stebbins' deacons has been arrested for bigamy, and is to be examined in the Police Court. Mr. Robinson—John R. Robinson—is the culprit. It is charged that he married Kate R. Anderson in 1854, and afterward tried to get divorced from her in our courts. But he failed; and then he sent a statement of the case to Brigham Young's Probate Court, and that inspired body did the business for him—though the chances are that these proceedings were exceedingly irregular in all their details, and that Brigham's Probate had no jurisdiction in the matter anyhow. However, it suited Robinson, and he went and got Rev. Mr. Stebbins to marry him to Laura Hatch in 1864, and then sailed in to hatch some more trouble. This kind of thing isn't going to do, Robinson. You must put a stop to it, you know. You are putting things into people's heads that shouldn't be there. And, moreover, your example is calculated to divert business from the California courts. The "Robertsonian method of teaching French" is very good, but the Robinsonian method of getting divorces is rather too brash. You won't do, Robinson. Robinson, you ought to be ashamed of yourself!

---

[1]"Charge of Bigamy," San Francisco *Evening Bulletin*, 2 November 1865, p. 3; "A Questionable Divorce," San Francisco *Morning Call*, 3 November 1865, p. 2; "Our San Francisco Dispatch," Marysville *Appeal*, 3 November 1865, p. 3; "From San Francisco," Chicago *Times*, 19 December 1865, p. 1.

B6. A Word from Lisle Lester

7 November 1865

Clemens evidently received Lisle Lester's reply to his "Lisle Lester on Her Travels" (Appendix B2) shortly after publishing that irreverent squib, but he remained unimpressed. This item is in the genre of the apology that only makes matters worse—one of his most deadly.

It comes to us in the shape of a neat little note of two or three pages, and seems intended to convey some information of some kind or other, but it fails altogether if such be the object—for we can say, in all honesty and candor and without any disposition to be either facetious or severe, that we do not understand a solitary sentence in it. It might as well have been written in Sanscrit, for all that we can make out of it. She says: "The recent compliment paid me in your little sheet is *not* the cause of this address," etc. Very well, then, why write the "address" at all—for the article which she has the charity to call a "compliment" is the only one in which we ever recollect of mentioning her in the CHRONICLE. Then she goes on and talks incoherently about some mysterious personage who has been trying to "injure" her—but as we know nothing about this personage, and as we have made no attempt to injure her ourselves, we cannot see how we are interested in the matter. She winds up by saying she "feels *injured*, not *insulted*." In another place she seems to intimate that we are not "*gentlemen*" (the italics are hers). After that *we* feel injured, but not insulted, also. So neither party has any advantage; both are injured and neither insulted; this squares the account and makes a perfectly equitable "stand-off." Therefore, all things being serene and lovely, let the sanguinary hatchet be interred. Is it a "whack?"

B7. Explanation

7 November 1865

Clemens here quoted from Evans' *Alta California* article "A Palpable Sell," a story about two deadbeats who cheat a shoeshine boy out of his fee.[1]

THIS FITZ SMYTHIANISM in yesterday's *Alta*—"He thought he smelled a magnificent *rodent*"—is calculated to inflict painful suspense and distress upon the ignorant if left unexplained. It is merely a corruption of a familiar and harmless expression, and means: "He thought he smelt a rat." But this thing must be stopped. We cannot afford to be constantly fooling away time and space in translating the *Alta* for its patrons, and saving them from demoralizing panic or suicide every day.

---

[1]San Francisco *Alta California*, 6 November 1865, p. 1.

B8. *"Surplusage"*

8 November 1865

Clemens again quotes from "A Palpable Sell" in the *Alta* (see the previous item).

FITZ SMYTHE says: "On examination of their boots they discovered that they had more real estate than blacking on the outer surface, and an examination of their pockets showed conclusively that both parties were teetotally impecunious." How sparkling! What a fine flow of humor! And yet how low-spirited it makes a man feel to read it. Translated into simple English, and despoiled of its gorgeous panoply of funniness, the quotation becomes: "Their boots were soiled with dust and they had no money."

B9. *Stand Back!*

9 November 1865

The editorial to which Clemens refers here, "The Moses Frank Decision," appeared in the *Alta California* three days before this squib.
Criticizing the California Supreme Court's decision to uphold the conviction of Moses Frank for forgery, the editors said that the decision
reinforced the notion that "any number of separate acts may be charged
in the same count, provided they all amount to the same crime," and that
such a procedure unfairly favors the prosecution at the expense of the
defense.[1] In January 1864 Moses Frank, a wealthy San Francisco merchant, had been elected president of the Utah Mining Company of Esmeralda. He and F. J. Baum, his business partner, who became mine
superintendent, then systematically looted the company of $70,000
through a series of swindles and forgeries. After they were exposed, Baum
escaped to Mexico but Frank was captured while trying to flee. His first
trial ended in acquittal because, as it was later proved, his agent had
bribed the jurors. Frank was retried, convicted, and sentenced to six years
in prison. The Supreme Court upheld the decision.[2]

The style of this item is unmistakably Clemens', and the phrase
"blood, hair and the ground tore up" amounts to a signature: he used it
in "Answers to Correspondents" (no. 109) and in "Ministerial Change"
(no. 174).

LET THE Supreme Court stand back and give the *Alta* a chance.
The *Alta* knows more about these things than the Supreme Court
does. What does a man who is defeated in the Supreme Court stop
there for? Why don't he appeal his case to the *Alta?* All this
withering irony is called forth by a luminous editorial in Monday's issue of that paper in which the conduct of the Supreme
Court is sharply criticised, the Judges instructed, and one or two
of their decisions set aside with unspeakable gravity. Let all hands

---

[1] San Francisco *Alta California,* 6 November 1865, p. 1.
[2] "The Case of Moses Frank.—Is He a Fitting Subject for Public Sympathy?" San
Francisco *Evening Bulletin,* 9 November 1865, p. 3.

"take a fresh holt" on the earth, now, and look out for "blood, hair and the ground tore up"—for the *Alta* has hung an anvil on her safety valve, and is going to try the Moses Frank forgery case all over again!

B10. Cheerful Magnificence

11 November 1865

Clemens here attacks Evans' article "Magnificent Funeral Car," published in the *Alta California* the day before.[1] Atkins Massey was a prominent undertaker, and two months earlier Clemens had attacked him in "A Small Piece of Spite," making him "come to his milk, mighty quick," as the author wrote his family.[2]

OUR FRIEND, Fitz Smythe of the *Alta*, goes into raptures over a certain "magnificent funeral car" recently received by "Atkins Massey, the well-known undertaker." Fitz Smythe fairly "gloats" over this piece of sepulchral gorgeousness, summoning his choicest rhetoric to the task of describing its beauties and perfections. He dwells unctuously on its "elegance of design," its "beauty of finish," its "costly material and workmanship," which he avers, in an esctasy of admiration, quite "excel anything of the kind ever produced in America." Furthermore, he expresses the opinion that "the term, luxury of grief, may well be applied to this magnificent establishment." What delightful enthusiasm, considering the subject! It seems as if the fascinated youth really hankered after "the luxury" of being locomoted to Lone Mountain in that "gorgeous establishment."

---

[1]San Francisco *Alta California*, 10 November 1865, p. 1.
[2]San Francisco *Morning Call*, 6 September 1864, p. 1, reprinted in *CofC*, pp. 233–236; Clemens to Jane Clemens and Pamela Moffett, 25 September 1864, *CL1*, letter 91.

B11. In Ecstasies

13 November 1865

Clemens here continued the theme of "Cheerful Magnificence" (see Appendix B10).

FITZ SMYTHE has gone into spasms of delight over a magnificent hearse (our language is tame, compared to his,) which has just been imported here by one of our undertakers. This "genius of abnormal tastes" is generally gloating over a rape, or a case of incest, or a dismal and mysterious murder, or something of that kind; he is always going into raptures about something that other people shiver at. Now, he looks with a lecherous eye on this gorgeous star-spangled banner bone-wagon, and would become positively frantic with delight if he could only see it in its highest reach of splendor once with a five hundred dollar coffinful of decaying mortality in it. He could not contain his enthusiasm under such thrilling circumstances; he would swing his hat on the street corners and cheer the funeral procession. This fellow must be cramped down a little. He would burst with ecstasy if he could clasp a real, sure-enough body-snatcher to his bosom once, and be permitted to make an item of it. He must be gagged. Otherwise he will seduce some weak patron of the *Alta* into dying, for the sake of getting the first ride in the pretty hearse.

B12. Ye Ancient Mystery

16 November 1865

The resemblance of this item and Appendixes B15 and B17 to the extract from Clemens' letter to the Virginia City *Territorial Enterprise* published on 18 November 1865 ("The Old Thing," no. 130) is unmistakable. All four pieces refer to Evans' article "Daring Hotel Robbery," published in the *Alta California* on 14 November 1865,[1] and attack him for specious reasoning in connecting various crimes committed over a three-year period.

FITZ SMYTHE has got one mysterious goblin on whom he lays all the dark crimes done in the city for which a plausible perpetrator cannot be otherwise drummed up. The first effort of this goblin was the murder and chopping to pieces of several persons in an obscure alley two or three years ago—on which occasion he carried off some small articles of value. Next, a lonely woman, living in a lonely by-street, was attacked at dead of night and slashed to death with a carpenter's chisel. Fitz Smythe said the goblin did it, and called attention to the startling similarity of the two cases in proof of the theory—barring of course that the goblin stole something in the first case but did not in the second. After a long interval something else occurred in the mysterious line—Fitz Smythe laid it on the goblin, as usual—said it was just after his style of doing business. After another interval the Mayor's clerk was robbed of a large sum of money in the night. "The goblin again!" whispers Fitz Smythe, with a shudder, and goes to work and compares all the ghost's former exploits together and makes out a clear case against him. Then, after another interval, comes the Meyers case in Commercial street, where a youth is slung-shotted at noonday and his father's pawnbroker shop robbed of some jewelry and second-hand meerschaum pipes—Fitz Smythe instantly recognizes the "peculiar style" of the goblin, and falls down in an agony of distress. He says: "Look at his old original

[1]San Francisco *Alta California,* 14 November 1865, p. 1.

murders where he stole things; look how he chiseled that woman, where he didn't steal things; look how he went through the Mayor's clerk, but didn't touch him or mutilate him; look how he beat officer Rose nearly to death and cut his throat with a mysterious penknife, in the ancient Alameda; look how he knocked young Meyers endways with a dreadful slung shot, and took some second-hand pipes and old socks: look at these instances, look at them!—all out of the common order of things—all terrible and 'peculiar'—all so similar, and yet so little alike—all evidently done by the same cool, shrewd, calculating hand—Oh, God, it is the goblin!''—and Fitz Smythe shudders at the bare thought. Poor fellow, he has had a long respite—so long, indeed, that his fears have gradually become toned down until his items were beginning to lose their wildness and read somewhat coherently, when lo! the mysterious What Cheer robbery suddenly resurrects the terrible goblin again and turns Fitz Smythe's hair gray in a single night! He don't go back over all the goblin's exploits this time. He considers that he has firmly established the goblin's guilt in those things long ago; so he merely tacks the new burglary on to his last feat—the pawnbroker robbery—and makes the chain complete from the What Cheer to the mysterious murderers of three years ago. But he overestimates the facility of the public for being "struck at once" with his far-fetched and dissimilar similarities. Hear him; "The similarity of the details of this robbery to those of that which came so near proving fatal to young Meyers, in the Commercial street pawnbroker's shop, over a year since, will strike our readers at once." Fitz Smythe, you won't do. You never come across a pumpkin but you think you have found a mare's nest.

B13. *Ambiguous*

17 November 1865

Clemens here alludes to Evans' reports on the weekly meetings of the board of education—in particular, one published on 15 November 1865.[1] In that report Evans twice mentioned petitions that had been received and then "referred, with power"—short for "referred with power to act."

IN REPORTING the Board of Education the *Alta* says sometimes, "The petition was received and referred with power." That is too vague. Why don't you state how much power? Why can't you cipher it down a little closer? Couldn't you say the petition was referred with one-horse power, or four-horse power, or forty-horse power, or somehow that way, so that one could form a kind of definite idea of the degree of force employed in referring the petition! Now don't you go on keeping people in suspense in this sort of way. You are big enough to know what you are talking about, but you don't half the time.

---

[1]"Board of Education," San Francisco *Alta California,* 15 November 1865, p. 1.

B44. Improving

17 November 1865

Clemens here refers to several articles that appeared in the San Francisco *Alta California* between 7 and 11 November 1865. "Our London Letter" from "Bee" is a thoroughly dull report. "In the Humboldt—Notes of an Overland Trip to the Oil Regions" is the first of two letters from "Harry Palmer," who wrote in part: "From yonder eminence, as far as the eye can pierce through the distant blue horizon, it rests upon the waving scenery in the gentle breeze. The slight uprisings and descents undulate the gigantic forest and impose upon the view, while the tinted sunbeams paint the picturesque of the ivy-green, broad as the expanse of the deep." "Notes by the Way through Napa Valley" by "Charlie" does contain the passage that Clemens quotes. "The Policy of Louis Napoleon" is a fatuous editorial arguing that the world's nations "distinctly repudiate aggressive warfare" and that Louis Napoleon's government "is the gentlest despotism of history." Under "Financial and Commercial" the reporter, in speaking of the superintendent of the Green Yankee mine, quoted these lines:

> His rod an oak,
> His line a cable's length,
> His hook he baited with a dragon's tail,
> He sat upon a rock and bobbed for whale.[1]

Clemens would greatly expand on Fitz Smythe's effort "to make one joke before he dies" in "Facetious" (no. 131).

THERE IS such a confounded prejudice against the *Alta* that we don't suppose it will be a bit of use our saying that it is not as stupid as it used to be. It's a fact nevertheless. The *Alta* is improving. It has a good London correspondent; then look at those letters from "Harry Palmer in the Humboldt!" Don't they show genius? Read "Charlie's" "Notes by the Way through Napa Valley." His description of Calistoga is a sweet thing in descriptions. He talks of "the perfumed breezes that in the sweet springtide and summer

---

[1]San Francisco *Alta California:* 9 November 1865, p. 1; 7 November 1865, p. 1; 11 November 1865, p. 2; 11 November 1865, p. 4.

play and gambol there." Yes, and think of the perfumed "sports" that in the sweet spring and summer play and *gamble* there! You forgot to mention them in your description, Charlie. How many notes, by the way, did you get for that puff of Calistoga, Charlie? It doesn't signify; business is business. On Saturday the *Alta* had a leader on "The Policy of Louis Napoleon!" There's pluck for you! There's moral hardihood! People may laugh at the *Alta* writing on such a subject as the policy of Louis Napoleon, but that leader was not half bad; there was nothing very new in it, but it was written in tolerably good English. Then Fitz Smythe, though *he* never will learn to write the English language correctly, has almost given up his insane attempts to make one joke before he dies. Altogether, the *Alta* is certainly improving. Even the commercial reporter is getting lively and sportive, and to make up for the suppression of the "Poets' Corner," quotes little bits of poetry. We have hopes that the *Alta* will become a newspaper yet.

B15. No Verdict

17 November 1865

In this item Clemens continues his feud with Evans over the What Cheer House robbery (see Appendix B12). He alludes here to Evans' article "No Clue Yet," published two days before this squib, in which he discounted his earlier theory that the night clerk had been knocked unconscious by a sandbag. Evans now favored the theory that the robber choked the clerk, reasoning that a robber carrying a sandbag would have thrown it away and taken the coin that had been left in the safe.[1]

FITZ SMYTHE has not succeeded in making up his mind positively yet as to who robbed the What Cheer House, though he is still fulminating some stunning theories on the subject. It is a significant fact that on the morning of the burglary Fitz Smythe bundled up all the bills he owed the What Cheer House for board and put them into the hands of a constable for collection, and then packed up his alternate shirt and his other pair of socks, and went somewhere else to roost.

---

[1]San Francisco *Alta California*, 15 November 1865, p. 1.

B16. Bad Precedent

18 November 1865

Clemens again alludes to Evans' report on the board of education (see Appendix B13).

THE ALTA says: "A communication was received by the Board of Education from Mrs. Stout, requesting permission to have a Christmas tree in her school." This sort of thing should not be encouraged. We pay our teachers to teach, and for no other purpose; and it stands to reason that if they get to cultivating shrubbery, the interests of education are bound to suffer. Oh! this won't do. It would institute a pernicious precedent. Once you let these teachers get stuck after shrubbery, so to speak, and they will soon go to trying even more unseasonable and extraordinary experiments than attempting to raise Christmas trees in November. Let them raise trees in school, and they would shortly be wanting to have turnip patches and cabbage orchards under the benches— and then what would become of the pupils?—what then would become of the holy cause of education? Come, let up.

B17. *The Goblin Again!*

20 November 1865

Clemens here returns to the subject of the What Cheer House robbery and Fitz Smythe's theories about it (see Appendix B12).

A MR. JOHNSON inveigled a Mr. Nichols into a dark room the other night, knocked him in the head with a club in the most mysterious manner, and then decamped and has not since been heard of. Go after him, Fitz Smythe! He is your dreadful goblin, sure. Don't you notice the "strange similarity" between this affair and the robbing of the What Cheer House, and the braining of Meyers' clerk, and the robbing of the Mayor's secretary, and the mutilation of officer Rose, and the chiseling of the lone woman, and the murder of the unknown family up a dark alley? Scat! Sick him, Fitz Smythe!

B18. The Whangdoodle Mourneth

24 November 1865

Clemens here recapitulates his criticism of the flaws and foolishnesses of the local press. See, for example, his comments in the six "Answers to Correspondents" (nos. 105–110) and in "The Facts" (no. 116).

HAVE WE driven our best friends away from us? We are afraid we have actually done this foolish thing. We used to get the rarest material for squibs out of the *Flag's* execrable poetry; and out of the *Call's* hilarious romancing; and out of the *Examiner's* bottomless wisdom; and out of the *Alta's* dreary editorials; and out of the *Flag's* thunder-and-lightning-and-whisky ditto; and out of Fitz Smythe's dismal jokes; and out of the *Mercury's* French atrocities; and out of the Grass Valley *Union's* engaging simplicity—but behold! all these affluent leads are worked out—stripped to the bed-rock—and we are left poor and desolate in our old age. We have driven the *Flag's* villainous poetry from its columns, and it deals in sleepy poetical mediocrity now; we have broken the wing of the *Call's* soaring imagination and brought it down to earthy, unembellished facts; we have fished up the *Examiner* out of its vasty deeps of wisdom and made it "hug the shore" on soundings; we have galvanized the dead corpses of the *Alta's* leaders; we have banished the thunder, and the glare, and the gorgeous whisky-blossoms from the *Flag's* ditto; we have subjugated Fitz Smythe; we have stayed the *Mercury's* bloody French atrocities; we have hushed the sweet prattle of the innocent *Union!* All the papers have left the open plain of extremes and taken to the woods in the middle ground of non-committalism. We have improved the literature of the land to our own undoing. Come back, good friends, come back!

B19. Too Terse

30 November 1865

One week before Clemens wrote this squib, the *Dramatic Chronicle* reprinted a local item from the *Alta California* of 22 November 1865 about a runaway butcher's cart, heading it

Thrilling Original Tale.
The Wild Horse of the Sand-hills
or,
The Blighted Butcher's Cart
By Armand Leonidas Fitz Smythe.

There is little doubt that this heading was Clemens' work.[1] In the present column he alludes to this "runaway-horse item," and to a more recent one called "Public Spirited."[2]

FITZ SMYTHE had another fine runaway-horse item yesterday, but he only made nine lines of it. Come now, elaborate it and make it funny like you did that other one. Don't you know that your entertaining runaway horse literature is getting to be looked for eagerly in the *Alta* every morning? Give us a one-horse poem, can't you? Don't be mean, Fitz Smythe—don't be mean.

---

[1]San Francisco *Dramatic Chronicle*, 23 November 1865, p. 3.
[2]San Francisco *Alta California*, 28 November 1865, p. 1.

B20. *Shame!*

30 November 1865

Clemens alludes here to Evans' article "The Perfection of Art," published two days earlier in the *Alta California*—a particularly lame attempt at humor.[1]

FITZ SMYTHE brags on his beautiful new false teeth, and tells how closely they resemble nature, and how they defy the keenest scrutiny, and how they even impose upon the wearer himself—but he says never a word about how they impose upon the restaurant keepers. Oh, this is shameful!

---

[1]San Francisco *Alta California*, 28 November 1865, p. 1. For another item on the same theme, see "Closed Out" (no. 133).

B21. *Bribery! Corruption!*

30 November 1865

Clemens refers here to Evans' "Misapprehension Corrected," an item about two San Francisco street characters: "the old apple peddler on the southeast corner of Sacramento and Montgomery streets," and "the Rev. Mr. Crisis," salesman for *The World's Crisis,* an apocalyptic newspaper that predicts "the final and immediate burst up of the Universe."[1]

How MUCH fruit, peanuts and salvation did Fitz Smythe get for that first rate notice of the apple-peddler and the old street-preaching *Crisis* man? You are becoming considerably too brash, Fitz Smythe. You will have to be crowded down a little. You must stop using the columns of a great commercial paper to puff all the old bummers in town.

---

[1]San Francisco *Alta California,* 28 November 1865, p. 1.

B22. Drunk?

30 November 1865

Clemens here pokes fun at "A Fine Old Picture," a naive piece of art criticism that luxuriates in irrelevancies.[1] Part of the joke is Clemens' pretended ignorance that Evans' phrase "a genuine Horreman" refers to the Dutch painter John Horreman.

OR WHAT *was* the matter with the genial Fitz Smythe when he branched out on that high art criticism in Tuesday's *Alta?* He says one of the best *paintings* he has seen in San Francisco "is a genuine horreman," etc., (meaning *horseman,* of course.) Now how can a mere painting, on lifeless canvass be a "genuine horseman?" And then immediately he drops the horseman and goes to talking incoherently about something connected with an artist's studio. What natural connection can there be between a genuine horseman or bogus horseman, or yet a horseman of any kind, and an artist's studio? You have been getting drunk again, Fitz Smythe. You had better stop that, you know.

---

[1]San Francisco *Alta California,* 28 November 1865, p. 1.

B23. How Is That?

1 December 1865

Clemens' outraged bewilderment in this item is fully explained by Evans' article in the *Alta California* the day before:

HUMAN REMAINS FOUND.—A party reported to the Chief of Police, yesterday, that he had found the skeleton of a man with a black handkerchief around his neck, buried in the sand near the end of the Oakland Railroad wharf. The body must have been buried for some time, and the fact of the handkerchief being around the neck, while there was no other clothing, would lead to a suspicion of murder.[1]

WE DON'T so much mind Fitz Smythe's novel and irreverent familiarity—not to say novel and atrocious grammar—in speaking of "a skeleton with a black silk handkerchief around *his* neck"—we don't mind these queer little infelicities of composition which must of necessity frequently occur in the hurry of writing up a daily newspaper, but we *do* protest against "the fact of the handkerchief being around the neck, while there was no other clothing," being received as conclusive and damning evidence that deceased was "murdered!" Oh, this won't do, you know. This is the wildest blast of inspiration that has yet swept through the teeming brain of the great theorizer who traces all mysterious crimes back, step by step, to the bloody unknown goblin who gobbled up the unoffending Doe family in an obscure house up a dark alley at dead of night three years ago. Why is a black silk handkerchief around the throat of a comfortably clad skeleton a matter of no significance—and yet why, after all the other clothing has rotted away, does that same black silk handkerchief minutely proclaim that a terrible murder has been done? What is there so suspicious about a black silk handkerchief when it was unaccompanied by other clothing? How would it have been if the skeleton had worn one of Ward's shirts and no necktie at all? Fitz Smythe, you are wool-gathering. You are always haunted by some dark and dreadful theory or other. Fitz Smythe, you murdered that man and buried him in the sand, you know you did, and now you are just fixing yourself up to lay it all on your goblin with one of your fine theories.

---

[1]San Francisco *Alta California,* 30 November 1865, p. 1.

B24. *Delightful Romance*

5 December 1865

Clemens accurately summarizes Evans' article "Lively Candy," which appeared in the *Alta California* the day before.[1]

THE EXUBERANT Fitz Smythe has favored the world with another of his charming condensed romances. The scene is laid in a match factory, corner of Mission and Ninth streets. The principal characters are "a small China boy" and a squad of naughty "Melican" juveniles. The naughty boys steal a jar containing "sticks of phosphorus," which they mistake for "sticks of candy." The "Melican boys" burn their fingers and flee in disgust. Young China hastens to appropriate the abandoned spoil, and, getting burnt too, darts frantically away, yelling "H-i-e Y-a-a-h! Me smelly h—l!" This surpasses all Fitz Smythe's previous efforts—for it has a moral. We recommend its publication as a tract for distribution in Sunday Schools. What can more forcibly impress upon the youthful mind the wickedness of stealing—unless you're quite sure you are after the right article?

---

[1]San Francisco *Alta California*, 4 December 1865, p. 1.

B25. Our Active Police

12 December 1865

Clemens here alludes to "Shameful Attack on a Chinaman," which appeared in the *Morning Call* two days before.[1] Clemens was familiar with the *Call's* policy toward the Chinese in San Francisco, which had contributed to his dissatisfaction with the job of local reporter in 1864, when the *Call* censored one of his items on the subject. In January 1866 Clemens said in one of his letters to the Virginia City *Territorial Enterprise* that the virtue of the city's police was certified by "the fact that although many offenders of importance go unpunished, they infallibly snaffle every Chinese chicken-thief that attempts to drive his trade, and are duly glorified by name in the papers for it."[2]

THE CALL gives an account of an unoffending Chinese rag-picker being set upon by a gang of boys and nearly stoned to death. It concludes the paragraph thus: "He was carried to the City and County Hospital in an insensible condition, his head having been split open and his body badly bruised. The young ruffians scattered, and it is doubtful if any of them will be recognized and punished." If that unoffending man dies, and a murder has consequently been committed, it is doubtful whether his murderers will be recognized and punished, is it? And yet if a Chinaman steals a chicken he is sure to be recognized and punished, through the efforts of one of our active police force. If our active police force are not too busily engaged in putting a stop to petty thieving by Chinamen, and fraternizing with newspaper reporters, who hold up their wonderful deeds to the admiration of the community, let it be looked to that the boys who were guilty of this murderous assault on an industrious and unoffending man *are* recognized and punished. The *Call* says "some philanthropic gentlemen dispersed the miscreants;" these philanthropic gentlemen, if the police do their duty and arrest the culprits, can probably recognize them.

---

[1]San Francisco *Morning Call,* 10 December 1865, p. 3.
[2]"What Have the Police Been Doing?"—reprinted in the San Francisco *Golden Era* 14 (21 January 1866): 5. The sketch is scheduled to appear in the collection of social and political writings in The Works of Mark Twain.

B26. How Dare You?

19 December 1865

The rowdy "boys in blue," known locally as "Fourteeners" because they belonged to the Fourteenth Regiment of U.S. Infantry stationed at the Presidio, had been discussed by Clemens in "Facetious" (no. 131) and "Spirit of the Local Press" (no. 151). The article to which he refers in the present squib, "Outrages by Soldiers," appeared in the *Morning Call* on 16 December 1865.[1] It traced the lax law enforcement against marauding soldiers to their lawyers' argument that "having fought the battles of the Nation, they ought to be allowed more liberty than others." As Clemens ironically argues for this position, he alludes to a number of *Call* items that appeared about the Fourteeners in December 1865.[2]

THE LITTLE *Call* is down on "the boys in blue"—very down. It is most egregiously prejudiced against them. It doesn't understand the rights of "the boys in blue," and therefore it abuses them. It is systematically pursuing them with outrageous accusations. It accuses them of prodding inoffensive citizens with bayonets and things, of going a great way out of the way to steal divers property, of waylaying school children and confiscating their grub, and of getting caterwampously drunk. Now who ever knew of soldiers doing thus as aforesaid? Moreover, even if they do do thus, what then? Didn't they fight for their country, and haven't they *saved the country?* Well then. Very well then. After having saved the country, ain't they entitled to help themselves to just as much of it as they want? Don't the "spoils belong to the victors?" They should think so! The secret of this persecution of "the boys in blue" lies just here—they don't advertise in the little *Call*, and the little *Call* don't allow people to do as they "darn please," *unless they advertise in it.* Then it is all right. Don't you think now, little *Call*, that you had better sling away that subject and tackle a fresh one—"The Blue Laws of Connecticut," for instance, if you must "chaw up" something blue?

---

[1]San Francisco *Morning Call*, 16 December 1865, p. 1.

[2]San Francisco *Morning Call:* "Where Will It End?" and "Partially Heard," 16 December 1865, p. 1; "Stealing a Show-Case," "A Soldier Helps Himself," and "Grand Larceny," 16 December 1865, p. 3; "The Meanest Thing Yet," 17 December 1865, p. 1; "Another Outrage by Soldiers," 17 December 1865, p. 2.

APPENDIX C

MISCELLANEOUS FRAGMENTS
1864–1865

PUBLISHED HERE for the first time are two fragmentary holographs preserved in the Jean Webster McKinney Family Papers, now at Vassar. Both fragments were written for publication, the first being part of a longer manuscript, apparently abandoned, and the second being a false start, a gambit that did not inspire completion. They were preserved by the author, who gave them to his sister, Pamela, for safekeeping.

C1. [Excursion to Sacramento]

1864–1865

This fragment is written on stationery that Clemens used in 1864 and 1865, and it is evidently part of a narrative spoken to the author by someone else. Clemens himself went to Sacramento aboard the steamer *Antelope* with Captain Poole early in 1866, but it is not known what trip the present fragment refers to, or even whether it was written in 1864 or in 1865.

ting out the spars stirred my stagnant faculties and I soon began to feel cheerful and contented. All I needed, then, to make me entirely happy, was somebody to talk to. The Captain appeared to be the liveliest man at hand—I could hear him waltzing around on deck, giving quick, decided orders, in a loud voice, as fast as he could talk. I went up, and said I:

"Captain, when do you think we'll get to Sacramento?"

He glanced at me fiercely, and sung out:

"Look lively, now, look lively! and you men at the capstan, stand by for a surge!"

I was a good deal puzzled by his remarkable reply, and I thought he surely couldn't have understood me. I hesitated a moment and then said:

"I guess you didn't understand me, Captain. I asked you when you thought we'd be likely to——"

"Haul on that derrick-fall!"

That was all he said; and he yelled it in such a thundering voice, and glared on me so savagely that I involuntarily dropped back a step.

"No Sir," said I, "not that. I didn't say anything about hauling derrick-falls—what I meant to ask, was, if you didn't think we ought to——"

"Come ahead strong on both!—and tell 'em to open her out!"

And he looked at me that way again. Do you know I began to think he was getting as crazy as a loon? I did, and I thought I would test him again, with a plain, simple question. Said I:

"Captain, don't you think it's nice to be out in the moonlight, all by yourself, when it is just about warm enough not to be too warm, and just about cool enough not to make it uncomfortable to——"

"Go to the devil, you d—d impertinent meddlesome fool! don't you know any better than to come bothering me at such a moment as this?—carry the heel of that spar further for'ard!"

I will take my oath, Mark, he came near scaring me out of my clothes when he said that. I never was so surprised in my life. I could see by the first part of his remark that he was in his right mind for a moment, but I knew by the absurd jargon he wound up

C2. [*Letter to the* Californian]

June–December 1865

This fragment is written on the same stationery that Clemens used for "The Only Reliable Account" and "Angel's Camp Constable" (nos. 117 and 118). It appears to have been written sometime after Clemens had established a daily correspondence with the Virginia City *Territorial Enterprise* in late June 1865.

EDITORS CALIFORNIAN: In telegraphing the eastern news back over the mountains to the Virginia *Enterprise*, I am sometimes impelled to violate my instructions to send *all* telegraphic intelligence, so far as to gouge out and embezzle a dispatch for you occasionally. Because you don't get any eastern dispatches, you know, and they are all THE CALIFORNIAN lacks to make it an entirely readable and entertaining repository of poetry, ingenious dissertations and romance. I have kept back some dispatches for you this week, partly because I thought you would like them, and partly because I thought they were too important to be sent over the mountains at only two cents a word now when the weather is so rough on the "Kingsbury grade." As follows:

Washington. President Johnson drove out yesterday in his four-wheeled barouche, and took Tompkins of Michigan with

EXPLANATORY
NOTES

76. PARTING PRESENTATION

7.2   noble sons of the forest] The facetious use of Indian ter-
minology and the application of tribal names to white men
as epithets of distinction were common forms of humor. For
example, settlers who came to Nevada prior to 1860 were
known as "Pi-Utes." At the end of Mark Twain's printed
speech, the *Alta* reporter added: "Tim. McCarthy appeared
as the representative of the Pi-Utes, and D. Scannell for the
Shoshones."

7.15   graybacks] Probably a double pun. The term was used to
mean Confederate soldiers, as well as lice and such animals
as rabbits and squirrels.

8.1   High-you-muck-a-muck] An important person, especially
one who was arrogant or conceited. The expression may
have derived from Chinook jargon, "hiu mucka-muck,"
meaning "plenty to eat."

8.3   campoodies] A Piute word derived from the Spanish
"campo," meaning an "Indian hut or village." In chapter 51
of *The Innocents Abroad* Mark Twain compared the "dirt,
degradation and savagery" of Endor with an Indian
campoodie.

8.17   Captain Merritt] Israel John Merritt of New York City
(called J. J. Merritt by San Francisco newspapers) had been
in the salvage business since 1844. In 1865 he invented a
pontoon for raising sunken vessels, and eventually he developed Merritt's Wrecking Organization, the country's
largest salvage company (*National Cyclopædia of American Biography*, 5:131; New York *Times*, 15 December 1911,
p. 13).

8.20   greenbacks] These legal tender notes, issued to defray war
costs, were currently quoted at about fifty-two cents on the
dollar—roughly half face value. Californians were particularly reluctant to accept them in lieu of gold ("Pacific Board
of Brokers," San Francisco *Evening Bulletin*, 13 June 1864,
p. 3).

8.24   Winnemucca] Winnemucca and Washakie were well-
known Indian chiefs. Clemens may have invented the
others, although common names such as "Joe," "Jim," and
"John" were often part of the titles white men gave to Indian chiefs.

77. *"MARK TWAIN" IN THE METROPOLIS*

10.6   broken spirit of the contrite heart] Compare Ps. 51:17.

10.24   Dan] Clemens' friend and fellow *Enterprise* reporter Dan De
             Quille (William Wright). See the headnote to "The Illustri-
             ous Departed" (no. 32).

11.1   extraordinary decline of that stock] The cost of a share of
             Gould and Curry stock rose from $500 to $5,600 between
             March 1862 and July 1863. But by late March 1864 a share
             brought only $4,500, and in early June, $2,900. The most
             precipitous decline came between 21 June and 30 July 1864,
             when the price per share fell from $3,250 to $900 (San Fran-
             cisco *Alta California*, 3 August 1863, p. 1; ibid., 22 June
             1864, p. 6; San Francisco *Morning Call*, 3 June 1864, p. 3;
             ibid., 31 March 1864, p. 3; *Golden Era* 12 [7 August 1864]: 8).

11.8–9   Opera House . . . New Idea] Thomas Maguire's Opera
             House on Washington Street and the Metropolitan Theatre
             around the corner on Montgomery Street had long been
             dominating rivals in San Francisco's theatrical district.
             Maguire's Academy of Music, located to the south on Pine
             Street, opened in May 1864. The American Theatre, a prom-
             inant playhouse in the early 1850s, was used only occasion-
             ally during the 1860s. E. G. Bert's New Idea Melodeon on
             Commercial Street near Kearny, formerly the Union
             Theatre, was a variety and minstrel hall dating from May
             1853 (Estavan, *Theatre Research*, 15:58–70, 75, 98–99, 164;
             Langley, *Directory for 1864*, pp. 9, 431).

11.10   Museum] F. Gilbert's museum on Market Street opposite
             Second, then featuring such exhibits as "Prof. Hutchinson,
             The Lightning Calculator," and "The Little North Carolina
             Slave, The Smallest Woman in the World" (San Francisco
             Alta California, 20 June 1864, p. 6).

11.11   Circus company] John Wilson's circus, the Hippotheatron,
             which performed in a Jackson Street pavilion when in San
             Francisco. On June 10 the company left the city for a "tour
             through the interior of the state" (San Francisco *Alta
             California*, 9 June 1864, p. 6; "Hippotheatron," ibid., 10 June
             1864, p. 1).

11.13   Ella Zoyara] The name adopted by Omar Kingsley, a circus
             rider who was trained in Europe as a female impersonator
             and eventually became a major attraction at Wilson's cir-
             cus. His sex was frequently a matter for debate in the press
             (Gagey, *San Francisco Stage*, p. 108; "Of What Sex, Zoyara?"
             Californian 1 [28 May 1864]: 9).

11.14   Miss Caroline Richings] An accomplished pianist and the
             soprano prima donna of the Peter Richings English Opera
             Troupe, which opened at Maguire's Opera House on
             May 30. Born Caroline Reynoldson, she was Richings'
             adopted daughter. She lived at the Occidental Hotel, as did
             Clemens, who always spoke well of her performances
             ("Dramatic and Musical," *Californian* 1 [25 June 1864]: 4;
             San Francisco *Morning Call*, 29 May 1864, p. 1; "Personal,"
             Buffalo *Express*, 26 June 1871, p. 2; Langley, *Directory for
             1864*, p. 337).

11.21   Miss Annette Ince] A pupil of Peter Richings and a favorite
             tragedienne of western audiences since 1857. On June 10 she
             and Julia Dean Hayne became joint managers of the Met-
             ropolitan Theatre and began a successful season with the
             cast described in this sketch (Brown, *American Stage*, p.
             191; San Francisco *Morning Call*, 10 June 1864, p. 1).

11.21   Julia Dean Hayne] A leading western actress from 1856 to
             1865 who was well known to Clemens (see " 'Mark Twain's'
             Letter," no. 54, and " 'Mark Twain's' Letter," San Francisco
             Morning Call, 15 July 1863, p. 1).

11.23   Emily Jordan] A successful actress in the East and in En-
             gland who came to San Francisco in 1863. In August 1864
             Clemens reviewed her performance of the title role in
             Mazeppa (Brown, *American Stage*, pp. 198–199; *CofC*, pp.
             94–95).

11.23   Mrs. Judah] In 1852 at age forty Mariette Starfield Judah first
             played in San Francisco at the Jenny Lind Theatre. Over the
             next three decades she acquired a reputation as the "grand
             old woman" of the San Francisco stage (Estavan, *Theatre
             Research*, 5:100–103).

11.24   James H. Taylor] A veteran of the eastern stage since 1851,
             and a successful supporting actor in California during the
             mid-1860s (Brown, *American Stage*, p. 357).

11.24   Frank Lawlor] Lawlor began acting in California in 1857.
             Following years of successful appearances in the East and in
             England, he eventually returned to San Francisco as a direc-
             tor of the California Theatre (Brown, *American Stage*, p.
             214; Gagey, *San Francisco Stage*, p. 151).

11.24   Harry Courtaine] Courtaine came to San Francisco around
             1860 from London's Drury Lane Theatre. He was a talented
             actor, especially in comic roles, but was notorious for his
             alcoholism (Gagey, *San Francisco Stage*, p. 82).

11.24–25   Fred. Franks] During July and August of 1863 Franks acted in Virginia City, where Clemens must have observed him frequently (theater advertisements, Virginia City *Evening Bulletin,* July and August 1863).

12.10 Bank Exchange] The fashionable Bank Exchange Billiard Saloon on Montgomery Street reopened in early June after a complete renovation. It was well known to Clemens (Langley, *Directory for 1864,* p. 599; "Our S. F. Letter—IV," Unionville [Nev.] *Humboldt Register,* 11 June 1864, p. 2; AD, 26 May 1907, *MTE,* p. 364).

12.11 picture of Sampson and Delilah] Perhaps the painting of Samson and Delilah that the art critic Magilp reviewed for the *Morning Call* in March 1865. Magilp attributed the painting to "Jacobs," in the style of Rubens. Paul Emil Jacobs (1803–1866) specialized in painting biblical and classical scenes, and one of his works was called *The Capture of Samson* ("The California Art-Union," San Francisco *Morning Call,* 26 March 1865, p. 1; George C. Williamson, comp., *Bryan's Dictionary of Painters and Engravers,* 5 vols. [London: George Bell and Sons, 1904], s.v. "Jacobs, Paul Emil").

78. *THE EVIDENCE IN THE CASE OF SMITH* VS. *JONES*

14.9 Judge Shepheard] Philip W. Shepheard, a sea captain turned lawyer, became judge of the San Francisco police court in 1863 and served there until shortly before his death in December 1865. Clemens admired his wisdom and fairness (San Francisco *Evening Bulletin,* 18 December 1865, p. 5; see *CofC,* p. 155 and *passim*).

14.9 Police Court] The courtroom was in the City Hall on Portsmouth Square, the city's "center," bordered by Washington, Kearny, and Clay streets and Brenham Place.

15.34 Mr. Alfred Sowerby] Reminiscent of "Mr. Sowerberry," the name of the undertaker to whom Dickens' Oliver Twist was apprenticed.

19.25 slung-shot] a blackjack.

20.17–20 Two friends . . . John Ward] Clemens' good friend Lewis P. Ward and another, unidentified friend, were both arrested about June 23 (*CofC,* pp. 222–225).

20.33 assessments] As a disappointed speculator in Nevada mining stocks, Clemens shared the widespread bitterness of stockholders over the heavy assessments levied on them by mining companies that rarely paid dividends (*CofC,* pp. 236–242).

20.34   noblest works of God] Compare Pope's "An honest man's
             the noblest work of God" ("An Essay on Man," Epistle 4,
             line 248), and Burns's identical line in "The Cotter's Satur-
             day Night" (stanza 19).

79. EARLY RISING, AS REGARDS
EXCURSIONS TO THE CLIFF HOUSE

26.10   Harry, the stock-broker] Possibly John William Skae, whom
             Clemens had known in Nevada. Skae was in San Francisco,
             having recently made a record-breaking stagecoach trip
             from Virginia City to California (Ratay, *Pioneers*, p. 174).
             Skae accompanied Clemens on a later drive to the Cliff
             House (see "Concerning the Answer to That Conundrum,"
             no. 92).

27.26   Lone Mountain] A San Francisco hill, about halfway be-
             tween the ocean and the western margin of the bay, which
             in 1864 was the site of several large cemeteries (Lloyd,
             Lights and Shades, p. 364).

28.20   bar-keeper] Probably the proprietor, Captain Foster (Lloyd,
             Lights and Shades, pp. 69–70).

29.9   surcease of sorrow] Compare Poe's "The Raven," lines
             9–10.

29.30   Jewish cemeteries] The Gibboth Olom and Nevai Shalome
             cemeteries near Mission Dolores (Langley, *Directory for
             1864*, p. 580).

80. ORIGINAL NOVELETTE

32.17   Golden Age] The steamer *Golden Age* plied regularly be-
             tween San Francisco and the Isthmus of Panama.

81. WHAT A SKY-ROCKET DID

37.5–7   Mechanics' Fair . . . Christian Commission Fair] Clemens
             alludes first to an exhibition of machinery and manufac-
             tured items that was scheduled to be held in the Mechanics'
             Institute pavilion between September 3 and October 3, and
             then to a fund-raising fair scheduled to be held in Union
             Hall from August 24 to September 8 by the ladies of the
             United States Christian Commission to raise money for
             sick and wounded soldiers. Clemens eventually reported

both events for the *Call* (see *CofC*, pp. 98–115). "A Notable Conundrum" (no. 91) also grew out of his reporting the Mechanics' Institute Fair.

37.10   What shadows we are, and what shadows we pursue.] The phrase is taken verbatim from Edmund Burke's "Speech at Bristol, on Declining the Poll, 1780."

§82–85. [*MARK TWAIN ON THE NEW JOSH HOUSE*]

No notes.

86. [*SARROZAY LETTER FROM "THE UNRELIABLE"*]

52.21–22   Mike Nolan] The conductor was Michael N. Nolan (Langley, *Directory for 1864*, p. 304).

53.15–18   "The b—bawry . . . shed—"] A drunken version of the first stanza of Felicia Dorothea Hemans' "Casabianca," which reads:

> The boy stood on the burning deck,
>   Whence all but he had fled;
> The flame that lit the battle's wreck
>   Shone round him o'er the dead.

For Clemens' interest in this familiar poem, see the explanatory note on it for "Letter from Mark Twain" (no. 69.)

87. *INEXPLICABLE NEWS FROM SAN JOSÉ*

55.12–13   The Moral Phenomenon] Clemens probably acquired this nickname in Nevada. He used it again as part of the signature to his burlesque letter of application addressed to the *Californian* in August 1866 (see "The Moral Phenomenon," no. 191).

88. *HOW TO CURE HIM OF IT*

89. *DUE WARNING*

No notes.

90. *THE MYSTERIOUS CHINAMAN*

65.5   "No shabby *'door.'"*] Mark Twain's italics and his quotation marks around "door" are meant to clarify the joke. The word "shabby" is Chinese pidgin English for "savvy." Thus Chung says, "I don't understand the word 'door.'"

91. *A NOTABLE CONUNDRUM*

68.14   sanitary scarecrow] A life-size figure of a man into whose mouth fair-goers could deposit coins for the fund of the United States Sanitary Commission.

69.8   Art Gallery] A gallery immediately to the rear of the pavilion where California artists exhibited their paintings, engravings, sculptures, and photographs.

69.15   milk ranch] Probably a local euphemism for a saloon or liquor store that stayed open all night. An item in the *Call* stated, "The property on the southeast corner of Howard and Third streets, popularly known (between midnight and six A.M.) as the 'Milk Ranch,' has been sold." This "property" was indeed a liquor store—although not the one mentioned in the sketch, which was near Jackson Street ("The 'Milk Ranch,'" San Francisco *Morning Call*, 11 January 1865, p. 2; Langley, *Directory for 1864*, p. 237). On 21 November 1866, when Mark Twain visited San José, the editor of the San José *Evening Patriot* noted: "Mark Twain arrived by the cars yesterday evening. We had the pleasure of being with him for a half hour last night, drifting around until by some unknown force he was drawn into the Ranch. . . . We left in season for sweet repose, promising to be in at the trouble to-night" (p. 3).

69.16–17   Pioneer Soap Boiler and Candle Factor] The name is fictional: no such firm is listed in the San Francisco directories.

70.5   Weller's bust] Exhibit 800 of the fair was a bust of John B. Weller sculpted by Patrick J. Devine. Weller was a prominent Ohio lawyer and Democratic politician who had lost the race for governor of his state in 1848 by a narrow margin. Coming to California, he was elected United States senator in 1852, lost his bid for reelection in 1857, and became California's governor in 1858 (Oscar T. Shuck, ed., *Representative and Leading Men of the Pacific* [San Francisco: Bacon and Co., 1870], pp. 515–521). Early in September the managers of the fair tried to have Weller's bust removed from the gallery, presumably because of his southern leanings ("Abolition Malignity," San Francisco *Democratic Press,* 10 September 1864, p. 5). On the night of September 20 Frank Abell, described in the *Alta California* as a man "boiling over with patriotism," smashed the plaster bust. The *Call* reporter (presumably Clemens) wrote a punning account of the incident which began, "A man named Abell knocked Weller's bust to the floor, at the Fair, night before last, and improved it; at least he made a completer bust of it than it was before" ("Court Proceedings," San Francisco *Alta California,* 24 September 1864, p. 1; "Weller's Bust," San Francisco *Morning Call,* 22 September 1864, p. 1). The next day the *Call* published the pun-laden doggerel "Weller's Bust" on the front page. Abell paid Devine twenty-five dollars and was fined an additional twenty dollars in the police court ("The Weller-Buster," San Francisco *Morning Call,* 24 September 1864, p. 2).

71.4   Sanitary cheese] Like the sanitary scarecrow, the cheese was a means of collecting money for the Sanitary Fund and was often publicized in *Call* items. Made by Steele Brothers of Pescadero, in Santa Cruz County, the cheese weighed almost 4,000 pounds and measured 5'8" across and 1'10½" deep. It was situated in a central pagoda in the pavilion and could be viewed for a quarter ("A Philanthropic Nation" and "Two Great Cheeses," San Francisco *Morning Call,* 10 September 1864, p. 1).

92. *CONCERNING THE ANSWER TO THAT CONUNDRUM*

76.25   great law of compensation] Almost certainly an allusion to the doctrine popularized by Emerson in "Compensation" (1841). This is among the earliest—perhaps the earliest—of Clemens' allusions to Emerson's work (see also "Answers to Correspondents," no. 107).

77.8   Spring Valley Water Company] Mark Twain named this company in October 1863 while attacking the hypocrisy of San Francisco newspapers (see "A Bloody Massacre near Carson," no. 66).

77.13–14   memorandum . . . in my note-book] Clemens' notebook for this period does not survive (see *N&J1,* p. 63).

77.15   CALIFORNIAN office] Two weeks earlier Bret Harte announced that the *Californian* had moved to its new office at

326 Montgomery Street, between Pine and California
(*Californian* 1 [24 September 1864]: 8).

93. *STILL FURTHER CONCERNING THAT CONUNDRUM*

81.3   *Crown Diamonds*] *Les Diamants de la Couronne* was writ-
            ten in 1841 by Daniel François Auber. Clemens attended the
            opening performance of the opera by the Peter Richings En-
            glish Opera Troupe on 10 October 1864 at Maguire's Acad-
            emy of Music.

84.32   Miss Jenny Kempton . . . Mr. Peakes] Mrs. Jenny Kempton
            was a talented American contralto. Following her 1864 tour
            with the Richings troupe, she returned to the New York
            concert stage where, as a featured singer, she was active
            until 1871. Like Mrs. Kempton, W. J. Hill became well
            known as a concert singer in the East, where he continued
            to appear until 1883. Edward Seguin was born in the United
            States and trained in London and Paris; he returned home in
            1860, joined the Richings troupe in 1861, and remained with
            that group until about 1869. Henry C. Peakes also remained
            with the Richings troupe until about 1869. Thereafter, like
            Seguin, he sang with other English opera companies for
            many years (Brown, *American Stage,* p. 333; Odell, *New
            York Stage,* vols. 7–15 *passim*).

94. *WHEREAS*

88.1   Love's Bakery] In 1864 William Love operated a bakery on
            the southwest corner of Third and Minna streets (Langley,
            Directory for 1864, p. 254).

89.33   duffy] Of bread: doughy, half-baked, under-cooked.

90.28   Heuston & Hastings' omnipresent sign] H. M. Heuston and
            C. C. Hastings ran a men's clothing store at Montgomery
            and Sutter streets (Langley, *Directory for 1864,* p. 202). "Ol-
            lapod," an *Era* columnist, mentioned seeing many of their
            highway signs when out riding with "Martha Matilda" on
            the San Bruno road ("Ollapodrida," *Golden Era* 12 [9 Oc-
            tober 1864]: 5).

92.24–25   scalped by the Owens River Indians] From the 1850s until as
            late as 1865, Indian raids were directed against settlers in or
            near the Owens River valley of Mono and Inyo counties,
            California. Newspaper reports of such raids were frequent

(for example, "Murdered by Indians on Owens River," San Francisco *Evening Bulletin*, 30 November 1864, p. 3; "Indian Massacre in the Owens River Region," ibid., 16 January 1865, p. 3). In April 1862, when Clemens was in Aurora, he witnessed some of the military activity directed against the Indians (Clemens to Orion Clemens, 13 April 1862, *CL1*, letter 46).

95. *A TOUCHING STORY OF GEORGE WASHINGTON'S BOYHOOD*

95.14–15   "Old Dan Tucker,"] A song written by Daniel Emmett, published in 1843. Like "Home Sweet Home" and "Auld Lang Syne," which are mentioned later in the sketch, it might seem banal and tiresome on any instrument. When Mark Twain revised his text in 1873 for Chatto and Windus, he substituted "Days of Absence" for "Auld Lang Syne" (see the textual commentary).

96. *DANIEL IN THE LION'S DEN—AND OUT AGAIN ALL RIGHT*

102.38   Ackerman] This and all the names of the board members used in the sketch are fictitious. Eight are names of Dickens' characters, and at least five were standard comic favorites of Clemens': "Badger," "Billson," "Blivens," "Higgins," and "Snodgrass."

103.5–6   a sowing of unrighteousness and a harvest of sin] Perhaps a distant echo of the apocryphal Ecclesiasticus 7:3.

103.14   Ophir] This and all the other stocks named in the sketch were in real mines along the Comstock Lode.

103.15   Gould and Curry] Once worth $6,000 a share, Gould and Curry stock was undergoing a rapid depreciation at this time. Between the trading sessions of October 26 and November 3, it fell from $1,650 to $1,420 a share (San Francisco *Evening Bulletin*, 26 October 1864, p. 3; ibid., 3 November 1864, p. 3).

103.25   Kanaka language] Inasmuch as the percentage of Kanakas (Sandwich Islanders) in San Francisco's population was very small, Clemens' allusion here and in other sketches of the period may be partly explained by the lively interest taken in the Sandwich Islands by the city press: between mid-July and mid-October the *Evening Bulletin* alone published eleven letters from various correspondents on the islands.

104.26   Hale and Norcross] Sam and Orion Clemens owned stock in
            this company (*AMT,* p. 218).

104.30   Burning Moscow] At this time Burning Moscow was by far
            the most active stock on the market. On November 2 a
            share sold for under forty dollars, less than half the sale
            price of a week before ("Stock Review," San Francisco *Eve-
            ning Bulletin,* 2 November 1864, p. 3).

106.18–19   It is not worth while to mention names] Despite Clemens'
            assumption that this case was well known, it has not been
            identified.

106.32–33   as has been said of Woman, "The Broker that hesitates is
            lost!"] Compare "The woman that deliberates is lost"
            (Joseph Addison, *Cato,* act 4, scene 1, line 31).

97. *THE KILLING OF JULIUS CÆSAR "LOCALIZED"*

112.36   it is hinted by William Shakspeare] Clemens hints more
            darkly than Shakespeare did. In act 2, scene 3, Artemi-
            dorous soliloquizes from a paper clearly naming the as-
            sassins and predicting their intention of carrying out the
            conspiracy.

98. *A FULL AND RELIABLE ACCOUNT OF THE EXTRAORDINARY METEORIC SHOWER OF LAST SATURDAY NIGHT*

118.23   Veuve Clicquot] Veuve Clicquot Ponsardin, a famous dry
            champagne of Rheims.

119.19   Russ House] A leading San Francisco hotel on Montgomery
            Street between Pine and Bush (Langley, *Directory for 1864,*
            p. 460).

120.7   Great Menken] The flesh-colored tights worn by the star
            Adah Isaacs Menken in *Mazeppa* permitted Clemens to
            make this pun on "Great Bear" (*MTEnt,* p. 78).

120.18–25   Mercury . . . recognized by God] On 31 October 1864 Presi-
            dent Lincoln proclaimed Nevada the thirty-sixth state. Be-
            cause Mercury represented progress, wealth, and luck, it
            was appropriate for him to provide the flag in Portsmouth
            Square with its new star.

121.3   Charles Kean] This well-known Irish Shakespearian actor
            and his wife, Ellen Tree Kean, opened in San Francisco on
            8 October 1864 in *Henry VIII,* and thereafter played nightly
            to capacity audiences (Brown, *American Stage,* p. 201).

122.1–2   learned German] Clemens apparently invented this scholar.

122.6   that other benefactor] Clemens' exaggerated statement may
               allude to Kaspar von Barth (1587–1658), a prolific classical
               philologist and humanist, author of *Deutscher Phoenix*
               (1626) and many other volumes.

122.24   Olympic Club] Clemens was one of about four hundred
               members of the San Francisco Olympic Club, organized in
               1860. The club maintained a gymnasium on Sutter Street
               near Montgomery, where regular classes in gymnastics,
               boxing, and fencing were held (Langley, *Directory for 1864*,
               p. 566).

122.35   new Governor] Henry Good Blasdel, a wealthy mill and
               mine operator of Virginia City, was elected for the first of
               two terms as governor of Nevada in November 1864 (Phelps,
               Contemporary Biography, 2:124).

122.36–37   Governor of the Third House] In December 1863 Clemens
               had been elected governor of the Third House, a mock
               Nevada legislature that met after the regular legislative ses-
               sions and provided opportunity for jollification and for bur-
               lesque of legislative proceedings and political life in general
               (*MTEnt*, pp. 100–110).

123.6–7   Mr. Dick's astronomy] The Scottish writer Thomas Dick
               (1774–1857) wrote books on science, religion, and philoso-
               phy which were widely read in the United States. A child-
               hood interest in meteors supposedly motivated his career.
               His major works on astronomy were *Celestial Scenery*
               (1837), *The Sidereal Heavens* (1840), and *The Practical As-
               tronomer* (1845).

123.23   meteor by moonlight alone] A pun on the popular song
               "Meet Me by Moonlight Alone," words and music by Joseph
               Augustine Wade.

123.33–35   that time . . . Kingfisher] A reference to Skae's pun in
               "Concerning the Answer to That Conundrum" (no. 92).

                         99. LUCRETIA SMITH'S SOLDIER

128.7–8   Hon. T. G. Phelps] Timothy Guy Phelps, a San Francisco
               businessman and past member of the California Legislature,
               was a representative from California in the Thirty-seventh
               Congress (1861–1863).

128.10–11   Roman & Co. and Bancroft & Co.] H. H. Bancroft (later
               A. L. Bancroft) and Company and A. Roman and Company
               were the two leading West Coast publishers. Each firm

maintained a large city bookstore ("Literature and the Book Trade of San Francisco," San Francisco *Steamer Bulletin*, 17 June 1865, p. 3; Madeleine B. Stern, "Anton Roman, Argonaut of Books," *California Historical Society Quarterly* 28 [March 1949]: 1–18).

128.11   *Jomini's Art of War*] Baron Antoine Henri Jomini's most famous work, *Précis de l'art de la guerre* (1836), reflected his experience gained as a general of the French army in the Napoleonic wars and later as a general in chief in the service of Czar Nicholas I of Russia.

128.11–12   *Message of the President and Accompanying Documents*] A commonly used title for documents put out by departments of the federal government. President Lincoln's anticipated Fourth Annual Message would be delivered to Congress three days after Clemens' piece was published ("The President's Message," San Francisco *Evening Bulletin*, 8 December 1864, p. 2).

128.14–15   Overland Telegraph Company] This company was organized in 1861 to build the section of the transcontinental line between Carson City and Salt Lake City, a work completed that same year (Robert Luther Thompson, *Wiring a Continent* [Princeton: Princeton University Press, 1947], pp. 360, 367).

133.7   trail of the serpent] The ultimate allusion is to Thomas Moore's *Lalla Rookh*, lines 206–207 of the "Paradise and the Peri" section. But the more proximate allusion is probably to Mary Elizabeth Braddon's first novel, *The Trail of the Serpent*, originally published in 1861, but serialized in the *Era* from December 1863 to February 1864. In that novel, Valerie De Lancy, linked symbolically with Lucrezia Borgia, poisons her husband, Gaston De Lancy; he collapses in the final act of Donizetti's opera while singing to the prima donna playing Lucrezia Borgia. Charles Crocker, a San Francisco journalist whom Clemens knew, dramatized the novel, and his play was produced at the Opera House in San Francisco in September 1864 and was reviewed in the *Morning Call* ("Theatrical Record," San Francisco *Morning Call*, 25 September 1864, p. 1).

100. *AN UNBIASED CRITICISM*

137.4   EDITOR of THE CALIFORNIAN] Charles Henry Webb, editor and publisher of Clemens' 1867 collection of sketches, *The Celebrated Jumping Frog of Calaveras County, And other Sketches*.

137.16–17   three months' stay . . . Calaveras county] Clemens arrived
              at Jim Gillis' cabin on Jackass Hill, Tuolumne County, on
              4 December 1864 and was back in San Francisco by 26 Feb-
              ruary 1865. He interrupted his stay at Jackass Hill just after
              Christmas for a brief trip to Vallecito. He returned to Jack-
              ass Hill on January 3, stayed there until January 22, and
              then visited Angel's Camp, Calaveras County, until he
              started for home on February 20 (N&J1, pp. 68, 70, 71, 81,
              82). Angel's Camp is nine miles northwest, and Vallecito six
              miles north, of Jackass Hill. The famed Big Tree area, con-
              sisting of two stands of giant sequoia six miles apart, lies
              near the Stanislaus River more than twenty miles northeast
              of Angel's Camp.

138.1   Coon] In January 1865, while at Angel's Camp, Clemens
              wrote in his notebook: "Met Ben Coon, Ill river pilot here"
              (N&J1, p. 75). Albert Bigelow Paine identified Coon as the
              narrator of the jumping frog yarn that Clemens heard at
              Angel's Camp, although Clemens did not explicitly connect
              his notebook synopsis of the yarn with Coon (MTB, 1:271;
              N&J1, p. 80).

138.8   Murphy's] A mining camp, well established by 1849, about
              nine miles northeast of Angel's Camp.

138.9   San Andreas] A mining camp, settled in 1848, which be-
              came the Calaveras county seat; it is about twelve miles
              northwest of Angel's Camp.

138.13   Coddington] William Coddington, an early settler of
              Angel's Camp (Edna Bryan Buckbee, *Pioneer Days of
              Angel's Camp* [Angel's Camp: Calaveras Californian, 1932],
              p. 19). In the minutes of a meeting of Bear Mountain
              Masonic Lodge No. 76 at Angel's Camp on 8 February 1865,
              Coddington's name is listed as treasurer and Clemens'
              name as junior deacon (PH in MTP).

138.16   Dyer] Probably F. G. Dyer, the agent for Wells, Fargo and
              Company at Angel's Camp in the early 1860s (William H.
              Knight, ed., *Hand-Book Almanac for the Pacific States* [San
              Francisco: H. H. Bancroft and Co., 1863], p. 142).

138.22   Dick Stoker] Jim Gillis' partner and the original of Dick
              Baker in chapter 61 of *Roughing It*. Clemens pocket mined
              with Stoker and later remembered him with affection and
              admiration for his enactment of a part in a bawdy skit, "The
              Tragedy of the Burning Shame." Stoker lived comfortably at
              Jackass Hill until his death at age seventy-eight (AD,
              26 May 1907, MTE, pp. 360–361; Clemens to James N. Gil-
              lis, 26 January 1870, CL2, letter 154). Writing in his

notebook at Angel's Camp sometime after 30 January 1865, Clemens noted Stoker's arrival from Tuttletown, a small settlement about a mile from Jackass Hill. Clemens, Gillis, and Stoker left Angel's Camp together on February 20 (*N&J1*, pp. 77, 81).

138.25   'Lige Pickerell] Pickerell has not been identified. Clemens used the first name again in a sketch published some months later, "Uncle Lige" (no. 140).

138.38–   Parlor Theatricals . . . sewing-machine companies] The bur-
139.2   lesque of local election campaigns beginning at this point in the sketch makes use of three controversies agitating San Francisco newspapers early in 1865.

The parlor theatrical vs. *the Christian Commission controversy.* On 6 February 1865 the *Bulletin* published a letter from "Verbum Sat" asserting that a donation of ninety dollars raised at an amateur parlor theatrical had been rudely refused, solely because of its origin, by the treasurer of the Christian Commission, a national organization for aiding sick and wounded Union soldiers through voluntary public contributions. "Verbum Sat" asked a series of scathing questions along this line: "Is the 'Christian Commission' a body organized for charitable ends, or for the purpose of obtruding on the community the pharisaical doctrines which its officers may happen to entertain on questions of religion or morality?" This attack was especially sensational because its target was the well-known San Francisco banker Peder Sather. The following day "Verba Sap" acidly responded in defense of Sather. Before the controversy concluded in a kind of uneasy understanding, the *Bulletin* had published eight additional letters, including those from officials of the Christian Commission, the amateur actors, and assorted ironic and sarcastic readers (San Francisco *Evening Bulletin:* "The Financial Agent of the Christian Commission Sitting in Judgment on 'Parlor Theatricals,'" 6 February 1865, p. 3; "The Parlor Theatricals and Christian Commission Question," 7 February 1865, p. 3; "The Christian Commission and Parlor Theatricals," 8 February 1865, p. 2, accompanied by two additional letters; "The Christian Commission and Parlor Theatricals Again," 9 February 1865, p. 2, accompanied by four additional letters). The controversy spread to the *Call* as well ("The Christian Commission and the Drama," San Francisco *Morning Call*, 10 February 1865, p. 2; "The Christian Commission," ibid., 11 February 1865, p. 1).

The fireproof safe controversy. At 6:00 A.M. on 4 February 1865 three adjoining hay stores at the water's edge near Sacramento and Market streets burned to the ground. Five days later the *Bulletin* ran an advertisement from Joseph W. Stow, agent for Lillie's "Celebrated Chilled Iron Safes": "Lillie's Safe versus Tilton & McFarland. A Trial by Fire! Home Testimony!" Supported by affidavits from two of the burned-out companies, the advertisement asserted that the Lillie safe, red hot from the fire, had perfectly preserved its contents of papers and books, but that the contents of a Tilton and McFarland safe were saved from burning only by its falling into the bay when the floor gave way. On February 14 F. Tillman, agent for Tilton and McFarland safes, responded with a counter set of affidavits and blazing headlines. The controversy ended inconclusively with Stow's advertisement requesting the public to view the Tilton and McFarland safe at his store and judge for themselves (San Francisco *Evening Bulletin:* "Large Fire This Morning," 4 February 1865, p. 3; "Lillie's Safe versus Tilton & McFarland," 9 February 1865, p. 2; "Tilton & McFarland's Safe the Only Protection against Fire," 14 February 1865, p. 2; "The Tilton & McFarland Safe! Recently Burned on Market Street Tells Its Own Story," 17 February 1865, p. 2).

The sewing-machine controversy. For many years sewing-machine companies had advertised their products prominently in San Francisco newspapers. Grover and Baker, Florence, Folsom, Singer, Howe, Wheeler and Wilson, Taggart and Farr, Williams and Orvis, Ladd and Webster, and New England Family made strong claims and often supported them by testimonials and affidavits. Almost every year brought a skirmish, but early in 1865 the Grover and Baker and the Florence companies waged an all-out war over the credentials and honesty of the awards committee appointed at the Oregon State Fair and consequently over which machine deserved the blue ribbon. Charges of bribery, suppressed evidence, bogus reports, and illegal committee members flew back and forth. Of the three controversies, this one engendered the most joy of battle. The headline of one Grover and Baker advertisement for its "Celebrated Elastic Stitch Sewing Machine" adequately conveys the general tone: "The Lie Nailed! Ventilation of the Gross Mis-statements of the Florence Sewing Machine Agent. Trickery! Knavery! Deception, Lies, Are of No Avail! The Grover & Baker Sewing Machine Unscathed and the Miserably Imbecile and Grossly False Statements of the Agent of the Florence Sewing Machine Exposed! Gross Fraud upon the Public!" (For examples of advertisements see the *Golden Era* 13 for these dates: 22 January 1865, pp. 6, 7; 29 January 1865, p. 8; 12 February 1865, p. 8; 19 February 1865, p. 8. The *Californian* 2 [21 January 1865]: 14 is taken up entirely by the companies' conflicting statements and affidavits.)

139.15   Union Hotel] On 30 January 1865 Clemens wrote in his notebook, "Moved to the new hotel, just opened" (*N&J1*, p. 76).

139.26   Palladium of Freedom] In *Roughing It* Clemens commented, "Trial by jury is the palladium of our liberties. I do not know what a palladium is, having never seen a palladium, but it is a good thing no doubt at any rate" (*RI*, p. 316).

139.29   Rawhide Ranch] A rich mining town in Tuolumne County, about twelve miles southeast of Angel's Camp.

139.32   Cuyoté Flat] A site of rich placer mining in the early 1850s, a few miles below Vallecito in Calaveras County.

140.9–10   Esau . . . mess of pottage] Compare Gen. 25:32–34.

141.13   Columbia] An important mining camp that developed rapidly following a gold strike in 1850, about fourteen miles by road from Angel's Camp.

141.24   our reserve] The marching file of the drunken reserve forces carrying transparencies resembles the parades of McClellan's "Broom Rangers" and their Union counterparts during the 1864 presidential election campaign.

141.27   Tom Deer's] Clemens' mention of Tom Deer in his notebook suggests that he was an owner of the Morgan mine (*N&J1*, p. 74).

142.11   Morgan gold mine] The Morgan mine at Carson Hill, about four miles south of Angel's Camp, was an exceedingly rich claim discovered in 1850. Clemens referred to its yield in his notebook entries made at Angel's Camp (*N&J1*, p. 72).

142.26–27   picture store . . . Eureka Theatre] The shop of Jones, Wooll, and Sutherland, which specialized in artists' materials and picture framing, was a door or two away from the Eureka Theatre, a minstrel hall at 320 Montgomery Street (Langley, *Directory for 1865*, pp. 169, 247).

143.2   Esmeralda] Clemens prospected in Esmeralda County, Nevada, in the spring and summer of 1862 before joining the staff of the Virginia City *Territorial Enterprise* (see *MTB*, 1:193–204).

101. *IMPORTANT CORRESPONDENCE*

149.2   REV. BISHOP HAWKS] Francis Lister Hawks (1798–1866) was
          a noted Episcopal clergyman, educator, and author of books
          on American church and secular history. He held pastorates
          in both the North and South, including some in New York
          City in 1831–1843 and 1849–1862. He was a professor of
          divinity at Trinity College, Connecticut, and the first presi-
          dent of the University of Louisiana. He declined the office
          of bishop three times.

149.3–4   REV. PHILLIPS BROOKS ... AND REV. DR. CUMMINS] See
          the headnote to "Further of Mr. Mark Twain's Important
          Correspondence" (no. 102).

150.23   Rev. Dr. Wadsworth] Charles Wadsworth of Connecticut,
          Emily Dickinson's friend, was pastor of the Calvary Pres-
          byterian Church in San Francisco from 1862 to 1869, when
          he returned to a pastorate in Philadelphia. Clemens "called
          on Rev. Dr Wadsworth" on 3 December 1866, but failed to
          meet him. "I was sorry, because I wanted to make his ac-
          quaintance" (Clemens to Jane Clemens et al., 4 December
          1866, *CL1*, letter 115). He had earlier attended Wadsworth's
          church, probably on 4 March 1866, and described part of the
          sermon in a letter to the Virginia City *Territorial Enterprise*
          written shortly before his departure for the Sandwich Is-
          lands: "Dr. Wadsworth never fails to preach an able ser-
          mon," he said in part, "but every now and then, with an
          admirable assumption of not being aware of it, he will get
          off a firstrate joke and then frown severely at any one who is
          surprised into smiling at it. . . . Several people there on Sun-
          day suddenly laughed and as suddenly stopped again, when
          he gravely gave the Sunday school books a blast and spoke of
          'the good little boys in them who always went to Heaven,
          and the bad little boys who infallibly got drowned on Sun-
          day,' and then swept a savage frown around the house and
          blighted every smile in the congregation" ("Reflections on
          the Sabbath," *Golden Era* 14 [18 March 1866]: 3, reprinted in
          WIM, pp. 39–41). When Clemens returned from his trying
          experiences with the extravagantly religious *Quaker City*
          passengers, he gave his own ideal passenger list for a plea-
          sure excursion around the world on 20 November 1867, and
          included Wadsworth ("Letter from 'Mark Twain,'" written
          20 November 1867, published in the San Francisco *Alta
          California*, 8 January 1868, p. 1, reprinted in *TIA*, pp. 309–
          313). And when he returned to San Francisco in April 1868,
          Clemens attended a meeting of Wadsworth's newly formed

"Literary Society." " 'Mark Twain' was in the audience," the San Francisco *Alta California* reported on April 7, "and in response to an invitation by the management, took the platform in place of an absent singer, and made a speech, which was received with the liveliest applause" (p. 1). All of this evidence suggests that he found Wadsworth more personally congenial than the "hide-bound" members of the clergy.

150.24　　Rev. Mr. Stebbins] Horatio Stebbins of Massachusetts and Portland, Maine, served as pastor of the Geary Street First Unitarian Church from 1864 to 1899, succeeding Henry W. Bellows, who had filled the pulpit for six months after the death of Thomas Starr King. As president of the board of trustees of the College of California, Stebbins helped make the college into the state university, of which he was a regent for twenty-six years. Clemens poked good-natured fun at Stebbins a few months later in "The Cruel Earthquake" (no. 120), and on 4 December 1866 he said he was "thick as thieves with the Rev. Stebbings. . . . Stebbings is a regular brick" (Clemens to Jane Clemens et al., 4 December 1866, *CL1*, letter 115). He later used Stebbins—with disappointing results—as a character reference to Jervis Langdon (see *Mark Twain's Autobiography*, ed. Albert Bigelow Paine [New York: Harper and Brothers, 1924], 2:110).

150.37　　Rev. Mr. Thomas] The Reverend Eleazer Thomas, editor of the *California Christian Advocate*, was an officer, not the pastor, of the Powell Street Methodist Episcopal Church (Langley, *Directory for 1865*, pp. 427, 598).

151.16–17　he has gone to Europe] On 23 September 1864 Kip had sailed on the *Golden City* for Panama and Europe. Clemens heralded his return on 24 November 1865 in a notation headed "Kip, Kip, Hurrah!" ("Religious Intelligence," *Californian* 1 [24 September 1864]: 9; Langley, *Directory for 1865*, p. 19; "Mark Twain's Letters. Number 1," Napa County *Reporter*, 25 November 1865, p. 2).

152.24　　laborers in the vineyard] Compare Matt. 20:1.

152.26　　in the flesh] Compare Rom. 7:5 and 8:8–9.

152.38–39　Providence would take care of the young ravens] Compare Ps. 147:9.

153.21–22　little sparrows . . . ground unnoted] Compare Matt. 10:29.

154.16–17　editor of *Harper's Magazine* made three years ago] The statement Clemens remembered appeared in the "Editor's Easy Chair": "The editorial fraternity is not without some feeling of honor toward all private contributors and toward the public. They are not altogether ogres and giants. . . . Well, as we are not ogres, neither are we utterly vacuous judges, but just the most ordinary men and women. 'Fame!' said a famous man to the Easy Chair—'What is it? Who ought not to think the very smallest beer of himself when he sees that Martin Farquhar Tupper is famous?' " The article then went on to quote and criticize contributed poems (*Harper's New Monthly Magazine* 24 [December 1861]: 121–126).

154.21   Martin Farquhar Tupper] An English poet and moralist (1810–1889) whose uninspired and often fatuously sentimental compositions reached extremes of banality in his poems to and about children. See the explanatory note on Tupper for "City Marshal Perry" (no. 49).

154.30–31   faith without works] Compare James 2:20.

155.26   brevet member] In his sketch "Reflections on the Sabbath," Clemens termed himself a brevet member of Wadsworth's church and explained: "I was sprinkled in infancy, and look upon that as conferring the rank of Brevet Presbyterian. It affords none of the emoluments of the Regular Church— simply confers honorable rank upon the recipient and the right to be punished as a Presbyterian hereafter" (*WIM*, p. 40).

102. *FURTHER OF MR. MARK TWAIN'S IMPORTANT CORRESPONDENCE*

162.10–15   steamboat on the Mississippi . . . blow her up] A variation of the old superstition among sailors that a minister on board ship brings bad luck. In chapter 25 of *Life on the Mississippi* Uncle Mumford and Clemens agree that the combination of a gray mare and a preacher aboard a steamboat invariably breeds calamity.

103. *HOW I WENT TO THE GREAT RACE BETWEEN LODI AND NORFOLK*

166.14   "gallus" and unprepossessing aspect] On 12 September 1867 Clemens used the same slang term to describe camels in the Holy Land: "Camels are not beautiful, and their long under lip gives them an exceedingly 'gallus' expression" (Clemens to San Francisco *Alta California*, published 4 December

1867, reprinted in *TIA*, p. 184). In "Curious Dream" (no. 225), published on 30 April 1870, one of his characters referred to Anna Matilda Hotchkiss, a corpse with various portions missing, as having "a kind of swagger in her gait and a 'gallus' way of going with her arms akimbo and her nostrils in the air." The meaning is "impish, mischievous, impudent," deriving from "gallows," meaning "fit for the gallows, villainous, wicked" (Harold Wentworth, *American Dialect Dictionary* [New York: Thomas Y. Crowell Co., 1944], p. 241; *Lex*, p. 91).

104. *A VOICE FOR SETCHELL*

172.16   blue mass pills] A medicine prepared by combining finely divided mercury with glycerin, honey, confection of rose, and other substances. Blue pills made from the resulting mass were used as an alterative (George B. Wood and Franklin Bache, *The Dispensatory of the United States of America*, 15th rev. ed. [Philadelphia: J. B. Lippincott and Co., 1883], pp. 929–931).

173.2   Burton] The English actor William Evans Burton, who came to America in 1834. He managed theaters in Philadelphia and Baltimore before opening his Chambers Street Theatre (1848) and Burton's New Theatre (1856) in New York City. He was famous for the breadth and depth of his humorous portrayals, and he wrote plays, sketches, and reviews. Burton died in 1860.

["ANSWERS TO CORRESPONDENTS"
IN THE *CALIFORNIAN*]

§105. *ANSWERS TO CORRESPONDENTS*

179.1–3   Russ House Block . . . "I Love Land."] The Russ House was on Montgomery Street between Bush and Pine, an area with many real-estate offices. Presumably the inscription "I Love Land" was part of a realtor's advertisement.

179.5   Yes, my native land I love thee] The first line of the song "Missionary's Farewell," words by the Reverend Samuel F. Smith.

179.22   Quarter-less twain] The leadsman's call meaning one and three-quarters fathoms.

179.27   Mr. Gottschalk] Louis Moreau Gottschalk (1829–1869) was
              America's first internationally known concert pianist and
              composer. Born in New Orleans and trained in Paris, he
              made highly successful European appearances from 1845 to
              1852. Following his 1853 New York debut, he toured for
              many years in North and South America. He was influential
              as a popularizer of others' music and as an innovator in his
              use of Creole and Negro melodies in his own compositions.
              Gottschalk's first San Francisco concert on 10 May 1865
              initiated a series of successful western appearances, but in
              September a scandal involving two schoolgirls prompted his
              hurried departure from San Francisco and darkened his sub-
              sequent career. His articles in the *Atlantic Monthly* and
              the posthumous *Notes of a Pianist* (his journal for 1857–
              1868) reveal considerable literary ability (Louis Moreau
              Gottschalk, *Notes of a Pianist*, ed. Jeanne Behrend [New
              York: Alfred A. Knopf, 1964], pp. [ix]–xxxviii, 319–320;
              "Gottschalk's Concert," San Francisco *Alta California*,
              10 May 1865, p. 1).

179.33–34   Miss Adelaide Phillips] Adelaide Phillips, born in England
              in 1833, was initially a child actress and dancer and later
              became famous on the opera stage. As the contralto prima
              donna of Maguire's Italian Opera Troupe, she played at
              the Academy of Music from 2 May to 17 August 1865
              ("Amusements," *Golden Era* 13 [7 May 1865]: 5; 13 [13
              August 1865]: 4).

180.17   Signorina Sconcia] Olivia Sconcia of New York City was the
              soprano prima donna of Maguire's troupe. As Lady Harriet
              in Friedrich von Flotow's *Martha*, which opened at the
              Academy of Music on June 1, she sang "The Last Rose of
              Summer" in act 2 ("Amusements," San Francisco *Dramatic
              Chronicle*, 1 June 1865, p. 2).

§106. *ANSWERS TO CORRESPONDENTS*

183.5   "Lilly Dale"] A sentimental ballad by H. S. Thompson.

184.21–22   *Dramatic Chronicle*] This small, saucy San Francisco news
              sheet on the city's amusements had been started the preced-
              ing January by Charles and Michael H. de Young and was
              distributed free in theaters, restaurants, and other public
              places. It rapidly evolved into a full-fledged daily news-
              paper, and from 1 September 1868 was known as merely
              the *Chronicle*. Clemens joined its staff in October 1865
              (Clemens to Orion and Mollie Clemens, 19–20 October
              1865, *CL1*, letter 95).

184.22   poem] "For the Ladies," a poem "written for the Dramatic
            Chronicle," had appeared on 3 June 1865 (p. 2). Clemens
            quoted, in order, lines 1–2, 5–6, and the last four lines but
            two, which he omitted in order to sharpen his comic point.
            He italicized "Wear a smile."

185.39–40   *quarterless, Twain]* "Nom de Plume's" pun on Clemens'
            use of the leadsman's cry in the June 3 column (no. 105) is
            carried out in the river term "sounded."

185.41   5-scent shop] A five-cent shop was a saloon selling cheap
            low-quality liquor.

186.1   MELTON MOWBRAY] A town northeast of Leicester, England.

186.1   *Dutch Flat]* A town in Placer County, California, settled by
            two Germans in 1851. It is situated near the Bear River,
            about thirty miles northeast of Auburn.

186.11–12   "Johnny comes marching home."] Patrick Sarsfield Gil-
            more's song "When Johnny Comes Marching Home" was
            very popular in 1865, especially among Union soldiers mus-
            tered out of service.

                    §107. *ANSWERS TO CORRESPONDENTS*

191.4–5   "kings-*and*," . . . didn't fill] Presumably Clemens was refer-
            ring here to an unsuccessful draw intended to convert two
            pairs, king high, into a full house.

192.3–4   poet crop . . . this year] Perhaps an allusion to Bret Harte's
            Outcroppings, then in preparation (see the headnote).

192.11   Killickinick] Killikinick, or kinnikinnick, was a mixture of
            tobacco with the dried leaves and bark of such plants as the
            willow and sumac. California-grown tobacco, rated inferior
            for plugs, was often used to make killikinick ("Annual Re-
            view," San Francisco *Evening Bulletin,* 12 January 1865,
            p. 6).

192.12   old soldiers] Cigar or cigarette butts.

192.35–36   nice literary society] Probably the Howard Literary Club.
            On 7 April 1865 it had held its first "public entertainment,"
            which included the reading of an essay, a recitation, and a
            debate ("Literary Entertainment," San Francisco *Morning
            Call,* 8 April 1865, p. 3).

193.7–8   Love's Bakery] Clemens' sketch "Whereas" (no. 94), the tale
            of Aurelia's unfortunate young man, published in the
            Californian on 22 October 1864.

193.31–32   Stockton] The State Insane Asylum at Stockton.

193.33   Gold Hill *News*] This paper, known to Clemens from his
              days on the Virginia City *Territorial Enterprise*, had been
              badly fooled by his October 1863 hoax, "A Bloody Massacre
              near Carson" (no. 66), to which the *News* item alludes in
              the phrase "Dutch Nix joke." "Byron Busted" was pub-
              lished in the *News* on 13 June 1865 (p. 2).

194.27–28   *Flag* . . . wake of the *News*] The San Francisco *American
              Flag*, like the *News*, took seriously Clemens' feigned ignor-
              ance of Byron's verse. On July 1 the *Flag* printed an item
              ridiculing Clemens for having been taken in by "some
              wicked fellow at Dutch Flat." The item continued: "The
              Gold Hill News laughed out loud, and the victim of the
              ludicrous joke has been grumbling about it ever since.
              He . . . is as mad as a wet hen" ("Sticks in His Crop," San
              Francisco *American Flag*, 1 July 1865, p. 5). The *Flag* was a
              radical Union paper initially published in Sonora,
              Tuolumne County, by Daniel O. McCarthy, known for his
              fierce hatred of Copperheads. The paper began publication
              in San Francisco on 18 April 1864.

194.33–34   Let dogs . . . made them so!] From "Against Quarrelling and
              Fighting" by Isaac Watts. See the explanatory note on this
              poem for "City Marshal Perry" (no. 49).

195.23   just before the battle, mother] The title of a popular Civil
              War ballad by George F. Root.

195.27   Wolfe] The Irish poet Charles Wolfe. In 1853 Clemens had
              parodied his poem "The Burial of Sir John Moore" in "The
              Burial of Sir Abner Gilstrap" (no. 19).

196.6   *Monitor Silver Mines*] The mining property of the Monitor
              Gold and Silver Mining Company, with offices in San Fran-
              cisco, was at El Dorado Canyon, California. Clemens' refer-
              ence, however, may have been to the mines in the Monitor
              mining district near Silver Mountain, Nevada, an area he
              had visited in April 1864 (*MTEnt*, p. 182; William Wright,
              "Salad Days of Mark Twain," San Francisco *Examiner*,
              19 March 1893, pp. 13–14).

                    §108. *ANSWERS TO CORRESPONDENTS*

200.7–16   "Battle . . . Mechanic."] This letter had appeared in the
              San Francisco *Morning Call* on 18 June 1865 (p. 1). Beneath it
              the *Call* editor had added his mollifying reminder that only
              New Englanders customarily observed Bunker Hill day. The
              Evening Bulletin had also objected to the city's failure to

observe the occasion, asserting that "the patriotism of San Francisco seems to be napping to-day. . . . Not a flag waves from any of our hotels or public buildings" ("Anniversary of the Battle of Bunker Hill," San Francisco *Evening Bulletin,* 17 June 1865, p. 3).

201.20   *Flaming Loyalist*] The name best fits the San Francisco *American Flag,* the patriotic Union newspaper that stubbornly refused to concede that Clemens had recognized "The Destruction of Sennacherib" as Byron's.

203.5   Academy] The Academy of Music, where Maguire's Italian Opera Troupe was giving nightly performances.

206.21–22   writer in the *Golden Era*] The misquotation from Robert Burns's "To a Louse" came from a reader's unsigned contribution in the San Francisco *Golden Era* ("To Correspondents," *Golden Era* 13 [18 June 1865]: 4). Clemens' corrected version is accurate; the complete couplet reads, "O wad some power the giftie gie us / To see oursels as ithers see us!"

206.32–33   large oil painting . . . by J. Harrington] According to the *Call,* the picture represented St. Patrick illustrating the meaning of the Trinity, by means of a shamrock, as he preached before an assembly of Irish religious and secular leaders. On 4 July 1865 the picture was presented to the Second Irish Regiment by the Reverend John F. Harrington of St. Mary's Cathedral, a relative of the artist, who was on his way to Rome ("Presentation of an Historical Painting," San Francisco *Morning Call,* 6 July 1865, p. 3).

206.34   picture store] The store of Jones, Wooll, and Sutherland at 312 Montgomery Street (Langley, *Directory for 1865,* p. 247).

207.3–8   DISCOURAGING . . . *Chronicle.*] This item had appeared in the San Francisco *Dramatic Chronicle* on 20 June 1865 (p. 2).

§109. *ANSWERS TO CORRESPONDENTS*

211.12   Blucher] In *The Innocents Abroad* young Blucher, from the far West, is Mark Twain's outspoken traveling companion on the *Quaker City.*

211.13   Bilgewater's] Clemens' fondness for this name is shown by his use of it in "Angel's Camp Constable" (no. 118), in his letter to the San Francisco *Alta California* written on 20 December 1866 (*MTTB,* pp. 11–19), in chapter 77 of *Roughing It,* and in chapter 19 of *Adventures of Huckleberry*

Finn, where the "Dauphin" bestows it upon the "Duke of Bridgewater."

211.13–14   *Blood, Hair and the Ground Tore Up*] Clemens returned to this expressive phrase in "Ministerial Change" (no. 174) and in the *Alta* letter mentioned in the note above.

214.36–38   New York *Herald* . . . Mr. Forrest played "Othello"] The *Herald* column has not been identified. The famous actor Edwin Forrest played "Othello" in New York as early as 1826.

215.2–3   imaginary description . . . late Jacob Little] Jacob Little of Massachusetts was a multimillionaire New York financier and stockbroker noted for his bold operations. He was called the "Railway King" and the "great bear of Wall Street" ("Obituary," New York *Herald,* 29 March 1865, p. 4). Following his death on 28 March 1865, the *Herald* published a generalized description of his funeral service, supposedly held the day before, despite its postponement for twenty-four hours. The next day the *Herald* published its second notice of the service, this time a detailed and genuine account ("City Intelligence. Obsequies of Mr. Jacob Little," New York *Herald,* 31 March 1865, p. 5; "City Intelligence. Funeral of Mr. Jacob Little," ibid., 1 April 1865, p. 4).

216.25–28   The horse . . . I die!] Clemens composed these lines in imitation of the iambic tetrameter of Byron's poem "Mazeppa."

216.31–37   Sir Hilary . . . prayer:] This is the first stanza of Praed's "Good-Night," no. 3 in his "Charades and Enigmas" (*The Poems of Winthrop Mackworth Praed,* rev. and enl. ed. in 2 vols. [New York: W. J. Widdleton, 1865], 2:381). In the last line Clemens changed the word "two" to "four."

217.9   late *Democratic Press*] First published on 20 October 1863, this proslavery San Francisco newspaper vigorously supported Democratic party principles. Its equipment and offices were destroyed by a mob following news of Lincoln's assassination in April 1865.

217.11   BERIAH BROWN] Beriah Brown had been an editor and owner of the *Democratic Press* until it ceased publication. Reputedly the California governor-general of the secret rebel order known as the Knights of the Columbian Star, he was a radical leader of the California Democratic party and a fiery critic of Lincoln. In December 1865 Brown became editor of the Santa Rosa *Democrat* (United States War Department, *The War of the Rebellion: A Compilation of the Official*

Records of the Union and Confederate Armies, series 1, vol. 50, pt. 2, pp. 938–941, 1037; *CofC*, pp. 266–267, 270–272; "Are You There, Old Truepenny?" San Francisco *Dramatic Chronicle*, 21 December 1865, p. 3).

217.20–22   ANXIETY . . . *Era.*] From "To Correspondents," *Golden Era* 13 (25 June 1865): 4. A second item from the same column is quoted at 218.14–17.

217.20   General Halleck] Major General Henry Wager Halleck had recently been named commander of the Military Division of the Pacific. For many years he had been a prominent San Franciscan—as a leader in the California Constitutional Convention, as a member of the law firm of Halleck, Peachy, and Billings, and as a major general of the California militia. In 1861 he was commissioned a major general in the Union army and named to command the Department of the Missouri. The following year he was made military advisor to President Lincoln. Among his writings are *Elements of Military Art and Science* (1846) and *International Law; or, Rules Regulating the Intercourse of States in Peace and War* (1861).

217.24   Webster] Clemens' definitions of "approaching" and "maternity" are those found in the 1828 edition of Webster's dictionary.

218.14–17   MARK TWAIN . . . *Era.*] From "To Correspondents," *Golden Era* 13 (25 June 1865): 4. See Clemens' column of June 24 ("Answers to Correspondents," no. 108). Burns's line, as originally printed in the *Era* column that Clemens referred to, had the word "wad" (meaning "would") italicized. The *Era*'s response to Mark Twain's pointing out their substantive misquotation ("the" instead of "some," and "giftie tae gie" instead of "giftie gie") was to pretend that *"wad"* (italicized) was the only error. Clemens' response seems appropriate: "Are you wool-gathering, or is it I?" (218.18).

218.25–26   GOLD HILL NEWS . . . Dutch Nick's.] Clemens is referring to an item entitled "Mark Twain" in the Gold Hill *News* of 28 June 1865 (p. 2): "This old humbug, from Dutch Nick's, has a new subject for his peculiar style of red-herring criticism. He says his name is 'SOCRATES MURPHY.' Murther and turf, Murphy! Look out—Mark will sculp you as he did 'Misthress Hopkins'—with the red hair, at Dutch Nick's; or as he did Byron, at Dutch Flat." "Socrates Murphy" was the man who hummed an aria during an opera performance in Clemens' column of June 24 (no. 108).

§110. *ANSWERS TO CORRESPONDENTS*

223.26   coat-of-arms of California] The Great Seal of California,
          sometimes called the coat of arms, was adopted at the 1849
          Constitutional Convention. It depicts the goddess Minerva,
          typifying California full-born as a state. At her feet and
          slightly to the forefront a crouching grizzly bear feeds on
          clusters of grapes.

224.28   committee . . . late in the day] Following action by the
          board of supervisors on 29 May 1865, a citizens' committee
          of about seventy-five persons was selected, and it began to
          function on June 8 ("Board of Supervisors," San Francisco
          Evening Bulletin, 30 May 1865, p. 3; "Preparation for the
          Celebration of the Birthday of the American Republic," San
          Francisco *Alta California*, 9 June 1865, p. 1).

225.24   reporter of the *Alta*] Albert S. Evans, the local editor of the
          Alta and a long-time journalistic antagonist of Clemens'
          (see the headnotes to "Mark Twain on the New Josh
          House," nos. 82–85, and "Mark Twain Improves 'Fitz
          Smythe,'" nos. 129–135).

225.29–   "The most . . . summer breeze."] From "Celebration of the
226.24   Ninetieth Anniversary of Our National Independence" (San
          Francisco *Alta California*, 6 July 1865, p. 1). Clemens
          slightly shortened the passage he quoted: for details, see the
          textual apparatus.

226.27–31 reporter . . . on the *Call*] William K. McGrew, who had
          served as Clemens' assistant on the *Call* in September 1864,
          was now its local editor. (In 1906, Clemens recalled that his
          assistant was called "Smiggy McGlural." This may have
          been McGrew's nickname, or merely Clemens' faulty recol-
          lection. See AD, 13 June 1906, *MTE*, pp. 259–260.) McGrew
          moved to New York and went to work on the *Times*, but in
          October 1865, shortly before leaving San Francisco, he pub-
          lished an item satirizing Clemens, signing his article
          "McGrooge" ("A Sheik on the Move," San Francisco *Morn-
          ing Call*, 29 October 1865, p. 3; see *CofC*, p. 18).

226.32–40 STRAIGHTENING UP . . . laugh.] From the *Call* of 4 July 1865
          (p. 1). For details, see the textual commentary.

227.3   chief editor] Probably George E. Barnes or James J. Ayers
          (*CofC*, pp. 11–15).

227.5–17 A FINE DISPLAY . . . State.] From the *Call* of 4 July 1865 (p.
          1). For details, see the textual commentary.

227.20–30   THAT ARCH . . . '76."] From the *Call* of 4 July 1865 (p. 1). For details, see the textual commentary.

227.36–   "The triumphal . . . Stripes."] From "The Glorious Fourth,"
228.4   San Francisco *Evening Bulletin* of 3 July 1865 (p. 3). For details, see the textual commentary.

228.8–35   TRIUMPHAL ARCH . . . paintings.] From the San Francisco *American Flag* of 8 July 1865 (p. 4). For details, see the textual commentary.

228.39–40   I learned . . . Washoe judges] The reference is probably to the allegations of bribery brought in 1864 against judges George Turner, P. B. Locke, and John W. North in Nevada Territory because of their decisions in important mining lawsuits (Mack, *History*, p. 260).

230.20   Mercantile Library] Organized in 1853 and conveniently located at Montgomery and Bush streets, this library offered a collection of nineteen thousand volumes, then the largest in the city.

230.22–   From Webster's . . . *Independence.*] For bibliographical de-
231.35   tails of the dictionaries cited here, see the textual commentary, which also discusses the accuracy of the quotations as they appeared in the *Californian* printing of this column.

111. *ENTHUSIASTIC ELOQUENCE*

235.3   Olympic] The Olympic Theatre, formerly Gilbert's Melodeon, was at the corner of Clay and Kearny streets. Since 1859 it had been a leading variety house, along with the Bella Union and the Eureka Minstrel Hall.

235.13   Sam Pride] J. Wells Kelly, *Second Directory of Nevada Territory* (San Francisco: Valentine and Co., 1863), lists "Pride Samuel (colored) musician, bds with Mrs. Taylor" (p. 272). He had been performing in the West at least since 1862, when the San Francisco *Pacific Appeal* described him as "truly the Champion Banjoist of the world. . . . His performances are inimitable" ("Sam Pride's Original Colored Minstrels," San Francisco *Pacific Appeal*, 19 April 1862, p. 3).

235.13   Dashway cocktail] The Dashaway Association, which Clemens had covered as a reporter on the *Call*, was a temperance organization claiming three hundred members in its San Francisco chapter. Hot whisky punches fared badly in the chorus of the association's official song:

> Dash! dash the cup away!
> Dash! dash the cup away!
> In brotherhood, 'tis understood,
> We'll dash, dash the cup away!

[See *CofC*, pp. 54–55; "Dashaway Statistics for 1864," San Francisco *Morning Call*, 10 January 1865, p. 3; "The Dashaway Association," San Francisco *Evening Bulletin*, 5 January 1865, p. 3; *The Sacramento Bee's Centennial Album*, Part the Sixth, pp. CC–17.]

235.16–17   Brandreth's pills] "Brandreth's Vegetable Pills" were a patent medicine widely advertised for fever and ague and allegedly designed to "expel from the body all those evil geniuses that have had an agency in producing the disease" (advertisement, *Golden Era* 13 [9 July 1865]: 8).

112. *JUST "ONE MORE UNFORTUNATE"*

238.2   city prison] The jail underneath the police court in City Hall, at Kearny and Washington streets (Lloyd, *Lights and Shades*, pp. 136–137).

238.19   Industrial School] A city reformatory founded in 1859 to house and educate the "little waifs of society that have been picked up out of the highways and by ways of our city and rescued from a life of degradation and crime" (San Francisco *Evening Bulletin*, 22 May 1865, p. 5). It was situated six miles south of City Hall on Ocean House Road.

238.23   O, woman . . . humbug!] Compare *Hamlet*, act 1, scene 2, line 146: "Frailty, thy name is woman!"

239.1   blisters] Troublesome or annoying people (*Lex*, p. 22).

113. *ADVICE FOR GOOD LITTLE BOYS*

114. *ADVICE FOR GOOD LITTLE GIRLS*

No notes.

115. *MARK TWAIN ON THE COLORED MAN*

249.11   banner] The Negro contingent "bore the elegant banner of the 'Young Men's Benevolent Society'" ("Celebration of the Ninetieth Anniversary of Our National Independence," San Francisco *Alta California*, 6 July 1865, p. 1).

116. *THE FACTS*

258.25 Murray's] Lindley Murray's *English Grammar, Adapted to the Different Classes of Learners* (1795, revised 1818), for many years a grammatical authority in both England and the United States.

258.29 Calistoga] A hot springs resort in Napa County purchased in 1859 by Samuel Brannan, who intended to develop it as the "Saratoga of California." Its name resulted from a fortunate spoonerism, "Calistoga of Sarafornia" (Erwin G. Gudde, *California Place Names*, 2d ed. [Berkeley: University of California Press, 1960], p. 47).

259.12 gallinipper] A large mosquito.

261.15 Schuyler Colfax] In 1865 Schuyler Colfax (1823–1885), a Republican congressman from Indiana and Speaker of the House, led a widely publicized tour of the West to learn "by actual observation, more of this Pacific portion of the Republic, its resources and wants." After extensive travel he and his party were treated to a farewell banquet and ball at the Occidental Hotel the week following publication of this sketch ("The Colfax Party at the Farewell Banquet," San Francisco *Alta California*, 2 September 1865, p. 1). Four years later Colfax was inaugurated vice-president under Ulysses S. Grant, but he retired from political life in 1872 after being implicated in the Crédit Mobilier scandal.

[THREE VERSIONS OF THE "JUMPING FROG"]

§117. *THE ONLY RELIABLE ACCOUNT OF THE CELEBRATED JUMPING FROG OF CALAVERAS COUNTY*

273.2 CITY OF BOOMERANG] Clemens' fictional name for Angel's Camp is used both in this sketch and in "Jim Smiley and His Jumping Frog" (no. 119).

273.15 Lake Tulare] Formerly a lake thirty-five by fifty miles in the San Joaquin Valley south of Hanford, now converted to farm land.

275.35–36 beans and bacon . . . muddy coffee] Compare the entry made about January 24 in Clemens' notebook: "Beans & coffee *only* for breakfast & dinner every day at the French Restaurant at Angel's—bad, weak coffee—J told waiter must made mistake—he asked for café—this was day-before-yesterday's dishwater" (*N&J1*, p. 72).

277.2   Phelan and Kavanaugh] Michael Phelan won the first pro-
             fessional billiards championship in the United States in
             1859 and held the title through 1862. He had engaged in
             exhibition matches since 1851 and had lived for a time in
             San Francisco, but returned to New York City where he
             manufactured billiard tables. His book *Rules for the Gov-
             ernment of the Game of Billiards,* first published in 1850,
             went through many editions. Dudley Kavanaugh was a
             noted eastern billiards player and an associate of Phelan's.
             In 1858 he won a marathon eight-day tournament in New
             York City and was United States champion in 1863 and
             1864.

§118. *ANGEL'S CAMP CONSTABLE*

No notes.

§119. *JIM SMILEY AND HIS JUMPING FROG*

285.37   Dan'l Webster was the name of the frog] In 1907 William
             Lyon Phelps noted the appropriateness of naming the frog
             "Daniel Webster" and suggested that "the intense gravity of
             a frog's face, with the droop at the corners of the mouth,
             might well be envied by many an American Senator"
             ("Mark Twain," *North American Review* 185 [July 1907]:
             540–548, reprinted in *MTCH,* p. 266).

The portrait of Webster is taken from an engraving of a daguerreotype by John A. Whipple, published in *The Life, Eulogy, and Great Orations of Daniel Webster* (Rochester: Wilbur M. Hayward and Company, 1854). The illustration of the frog was drawn by True W. Williams for *Sketches, New and Old* (Hartford: American Publishing Company, 1875). Compare the device of naming the "little small bullpup" after Andrew Jackson.

[MARK TWAIN ON THE 1865 EARTHQUAKE]

§120. *THE CRUEL EARTHQUAKE*

291.21 And the earth shook and trembled!] Compare 2 Sam. 22:8 and Ps. 18:17.

292.15–19 O, Woman . . . angel thou] Compare Walter Scott, *Marmion,* canto 6, stanza 30:

> O Woman! in our hours of ease,
> Uncertain, coy, and hard to please,
> And variable as the shade
> By the light quivering aspen made;
> When pain and anguish wring the brow,
> A ministering angel thou!—

292.30 CHARLEY BRYAN] Charles H. Bryan of Ohio migrated to California late in the 1840s and began to practice law in Marysville. By 1852 he was Yuba County's district attorney, then state senator, and in 1854, at the age of 32, he was appointed the eighth justice of the California Supreme Court. Failing to retain his seat by election the following year, he returned to private practice in Marysville, and in 1859 moved to Nevada, where he had offices successively in Genoa, Carson City, and Virginia City. Clemens knew him as a successful lawyer deeply involved in mining litigation, and as an influential member of the first Nevada State Constitutional Convention. Bryan was also owner of the thoroughbred racehorse Lodi (Angel, *History,* pp. 78, 81, 555; J. Edward Johnson, *History of the Supreme Court Justices of California* [San Francisco: Bender-Moss Co., 1963], pp. 6, 50–51; "Washoe," Sacramento *Bee,* 7 September 1863, p. 2; clipping in Scrapbook 2, p. 63, MTP).

292.32 Joe Noques] The copy-text prints "Nongues," but no such name is listed in the Virginia City directories; it is probably a misprint for the last name of Joseph M. Noques, one of the town's attorneys. In August 1864 Noques, William M. Stewart, and Caleb Burbank were appointed by the Storey

County bar to recommend to President Lincoln a replacement for Judge John W. North, who had resigned under charges of corruption (Mack, *History,* pp. 260–261).

292.33   Cosmopolitan Hotel] The four-story Cosmopolitan Hotel, which opened on 1 September 1864 at Bush and Sansome streets, was noted for its elegant furnishings (Langley, *Directory for 1864,* pp. 6–7).

292.35   Sam Witgenstein] Witgenstein was in the mining business in Carson City and Virginia City (Kelly, *Second Directory,* p. 112).

293.1   Pete Hopkins] The former owner of the Magnolia Saloon in Carson City and an active turfman there. In September 1865 he had taken a position at San Francisco's Bay View Park and Race Track ("Personal," Gold Hill *News,* 19 September 1865, p. 2). Clemens apparently meant to tease him by using the name "Philip Hopkins" in his hoax "A Bloody Massacre near Carson" (no. 66).

§121. *POPPER DEFIETH YE EARTHQUAKE*

No notes.

§122. *EARTHQUAKE ALMANAC*

298.21   whence they cometh] Compare John 3:8.

299.23–24   Those of John Quincy Adams] Most of Adams' biographers give his last words as "This is the last of earth. I am content." William H. Seward gives the first phrase as "This is the end of earth" (*Life and Public Services of John Quincy Adams* [New York: C. M. Saxton, 1859], p. 400). Clemens would again allude to Adams' dying remarks in "The Last Words of Great Men" (no. 257), published in the Buffalo *Express* on 11 September 1869.

299.26   this mortal coil] *Hamlet,* act 3, scene 1, line 67.

§123. *THE GREAT EARTHQUAKE IN SAN FRANCISCO*

304.33   large four-story brick building] L. Popper's new building. See the headnote to "Popper Defieth Ye Earthquake" (no. 121).

307.34–35   attired like the Greek slave] That is, nude. The allusion is to Hiram Powers' statue "The Greek Slave," a female nude that caused a sensation when exhibited in 1851 at the London Crystal Palace exposition.

308.6   fire-telegraph] During the first three months of 1865, San Francisco installed a "fire alarm telegraph." This warning system was a complex network of signal boxes, bells, and gongs, all wired to a central station manned twenty-four hours a day by telegraph operators. A signal box, when activated, automatically indicated to the operator on duty the approximate location of the fire. The operator then set off gongs and bells in the appropriate fire stations and neighborhood and relayed information to the firemen. The system officially went into effect on 24 April 1865 (San Francisco *Evening Bulletin:* "Fire Alarm Telegraph—How It Progresses and How It Works," 9 January 1865, p. 3; "Fire Alarm Telegraph Matters," 16 March 1865, p. 3; "The Firemen Heard It That Time," 3 April 1865, p. 3). In May Clemens had called it "San Francisco's new toy— . . . the most lamentable humbug she has yet invested in" ("Fire Telegraph," San Francisco *Morning Call,* 16 May 1865, p. 1, reprinted from the Virginia City *Territorial Enterprise*).

308.23   shot tower] Thomas H. Selby and Company's tower for the manufacture of shot, bullets, sheet lead, and bar lead was an octagonal minaretlike structure one hundred and eighty feet high, at the corner of First and Howard streets.

308.31–32   Rev. Mr. Harmon] Reverend and Mrs. S. S. Harmon operated the Female College of the Pacific in Oakland.

309.8   Oakland talks and laughs again] The allusion is to a recent scandal in which the pianist Louis Gottschalk and his business agent, Charles Le Gay, were accused of seducing two girls from the Female College after the students were discovered climbing into a dormitory window at daybreak. Both men were forced to flee town in disgrace, and many parents removed their daughters from the school (Carson City *Appeal,* 17 September 1865, p. 3; see the explanatory note on Gottschalk for "Answers to Correspondents," no. 105).

124. *BOB ROACH'S PLAN FOR CIRCUMVENTING A DEMOCRAT*

313.4   S. H. Dwinelle] Clemens' account of the October 18 election results is accurate. Samuel H. Dwinelle was the incumbent judge of the Fifteenth District Court. He continued to hold this office until 1880, six years before his death.

313.6–7   Oh, 'Enery Villiam . . . thy shame!] Compare *Hamlet,* act 3,
             scene 4, line 82: "O shame! where is thy blush?"

314.1   Aleck Scott] Built in 1848 in St. Louis, the *Aleck Scott* was a
             boat of seven hundred tons still in the St. Louis–New Or-
             leans trade in 1859. It was converted into a ram for the
             United States Navy in 1862 (William M. Lytle, *Merchant
             Steam Vessels of the United States: 1807–1868* [Mystic,
             Conn.: The Steamship Historical Society of America, 1952],
             p. 5). Isaiah Sellers, the pilot whom Clemens ridiculed in
             "River Intelligence" (no. 24), was pilot of the *Aleck Scott* for
             many years.

314.6   plant] Meaning "bury," a favorite word of Clemens'. He
             used it, for example, in "Origin of Illustrious Men" (no.
             193), in chapter 47 of *Roughing It,* and in chapter 10 of
             Huckleberry Finn.

314.11   feet sticking out] As the ship's carpenter, Roach would have
             had the responsibility of building coffins for the dead, and
             perhaps even for supervising their burial en route. Yet it
             would appear that the corpse in this sketch was buried
             without the benefit of a coffin—not the usual practice. Ab-
             salom Grimes reported the river-bank burial of Clemens'
             friend Sam Bowen, who died while working as a pilot in
             1878. According to Grimes, when the erosion of the bank
             exposed Bowen's coffin, Clemens paid for having it removed
             and reinterred (*Absalom Grimes: Confederate Mail Runner,*
             ed. M. M. Quaife [New Haven: Yale University Press, 1925],
             pp. 18–19).

125. *SAN FRANCISCO LETTER*

No notes.

126. *STEAMER DEPARTURES*

322.9   General Rosecrans] William S. Rosecrans, one of the ablest
             and most popular northern generals during the early years of
             the Civil War. He was relieved of his command of the Army
             of the Cumberland after his defeat at Chickamauga by Gen-
             eral Bragg. Thereafter he was given relatively inactive as-
             signments. On 25 July 1865 he arrived in San Francisco on
             mining business. He was hailed as the "hero of Stony
             Creek" and a man who "belongs to the fighting order of
             generals" in contrast to a "dress parade hero" like General

McClellan. Large public welcomes were organized, attracting thousands of people (San Francisco *Evening Bulletin:* "Arrival of Gen. Rosecrans," 25 July 1865, p. 3; "Welcome to Rosecrans," 29 July 1865, p. 5; "Welcome to Gen. Rosecrans," 31 July 1865, p. 3; "Back Again," San Francisco *Morning Call,* 29 October 1865, p. 1).

322.11–12   scandalous meddling with the Oakland Seminaries] An allusion to the Gottschalk scandal. See the explanatory note to "Oakland talks and laughs again" for "The Great Earthquake in San Francisco" (no. 123).

322.14   Conness] Irish-born John Conness came to California soon after the discovery of gold. A miner and later a merchant, he served in the California Assembly before his election to the United States Senate (1863–1869) as a Union Republican. Clemens and Senator Conness met in Washington in 1867 ("Mark Twain in Washington," San Francisco *Alta California,* written 10 December 1867, published 15 January 1868, p. 1). Two months later Clemens said that the senator had offered to help make him postmaster of San Francisco and, indeed, had offered him any of five choice jobs in California. About one year later he said that Conness had urged him to accept appointment as minister to China, succeeding Anson Burlingame (Clemens to Jane Clemens and Pamela Moffett, 6 February 1868, *CL1,* letter 189; Clemens to Elisha Bliss, 4–6 February 1868, *CL1,* letter 188; Clemens to Olivia Langdon, 24 January 1869, *CL1,* letter 281).

127. *EXIT "BUMMER"*

325.25–26   Bummer's skin . . . that of Lazarus] The San Francisco *Morning Call* reported that Bummer's stuffed skin would "be placed for exhibition at a well-known saloon" ("When 'Bummer' Died," San Francisco *Morning Call,* 4 November 1865, p. 2). Lazarus' skin, stuffed in October 1863, appears to have been exhibited at various places in San Francisco, including the 1864 Fair of the Ladies' Christian Commission ("Lazarus Redivivus," San Francisco *Evening Bulletin,* 26 October 1863, p. 5).

128. *PLEASURE EXCURSION*

327.4   huge fortress at Black Point] Although there were a few cannons at Black Point (now Fort Mason), Mark Twain probably refers here to Fort Winfield Scott, a massive brick fortification constructed between 1853 and 1861 at Fort Point, the northernmost promontory of the San Francisco Peninsula, about three miles west of Black Point.

327.7–8   "When we were Marching Through Georgia,"] The song "Marching through Georgia" was written by Henry Clay Work. According to the *Alta* report of the trip, "Yankee Doodle," "Hail Columbia," and "A Little More Cider, Too" were other calliope numbers ("Trial Trip of the 'Rescue,' " San Francisco *Alta California*, 8 November 1865, p. 1).

[MARK TWAIN IMPROVES "FITZ SMYTHE"]

§129. [EDITORIAL "PUFFING"]

331.7–8   distinguished . . . Major-General] General Rosecrans; the departure of the *Colorado* is discussed in the headnote to "Steamer Departures" (no. 126).

§130. *THE OLD THING*

334.2   young Meyers] On 17 August 1864 Henry Meyers was knocked unconscious by a robber in his father's pawnshop on Commercial Street, a few doors from the *Call* office. Clemens reported the robbery in "Daring Attempt to Assassinate a Pawnbroker in Broad Daylight" (San Francisco *Morning Call*, 18 August 1864, p. 1, reprinted in *CofC*, pp. 199–202).

334.5–7   horrible wretch . . . below Santa Clara] On 2 September 1864 Charles L. Wiggins, clerk to Mayor Coon, was chloroformed and robbed in his rooming house by James Mortimer, a well-known desperado ("Daring and Successful Chloroform Robbery," San Francisco *Alta California*, 7 September 1864, p. 1). Detective George W. Rose arrested Mortimer near Belmont, but he escaped on September 9 after severely wounding Rose—an episode Clemens reported in "Attempted Assassination of a Detective Officer" (San Francisco *Morning Call*, 11 September 1864, p. 3, reprinted in *CofC*, pp. 202–204).

334.8–12   killed the lone woman . . . another dark alley] Clemens alludes here to the murders of prostitutes in Pike Street, Waverly Place, and Stout's Alley—crimes which Evans attempted to link with the assault on Meyers (see the next note).

334.14–16   whole batch . . . one imaginary scoundrel] On 18 August
1864, referring to the assault on Meyers, Evans wrote,
"Many people, remembering the mysterious murders of the
prostitutes in Waverly Place and Stout's Alley, believe the
perpetrator of all these crimes is one and the same person,
and the matter becomes the more horrible from the terrible
veil of mystery which enshrouds it." The next day Evans
listed various possibilities for the identity of the robber or
robbers: "a party of Mongolian Thugs," an enemy of the
proprietor, a customer acting on impulse, or the murderer of
a French prostitute in Pike Street the year before ("A Strange
Affair," San Francisco *Alta California*, 18 August 1864, p. 1;
"The Commercial Street Mystery," ibid., 19 August 1864, p.
1). It was this line of reasoning that Evans capped in November 1865 with his remarks in "Daring Hotel Robbery"
(see the headnote). Contrary to Clemens' assertion in the
sketch, however, Evans did not suggest that Mortimer,
"who half-murdered detective officer Rose," was linked
with any unsolved crimes.

§131. *SAN FRANCISCO LETTER*

337.3   fine Christmas poem appears in the *Alta*] Clemens quoted
and paraphrased "Christmas Comes But Once a Year" (San
Francisco *Alta California*, 22 December 1865, p. 1). Here is
the original text in full:

> The holidays are approaching. We hear of them and see
> their signs every day. The children tell you every morning
> how long it is till New Year. The pavements are covered
> with boxes, which have arrived by steamer, and are being
> unpacked in anticipation of an unusual demand. The win-
> dows of the shops along Montgomery street are brilliant
> with articles of ornament and luxury; the more substantial
> goods, which during the last eleven months occupied the
> place, having been put aside for a few weeks. Silks, satins,
> laces, articles of silver and gold, jewels, porcelain from
> Sevres and Dresden, Bohemian and Venitian glass, pictures,
> engravings, bronzes of the finest workmanship and the
> most extravagant price, attract the eyes at every step along
> the promenades of fashion. The hotels are crowded with
> visitors who have come from the interior to enjoy the
> amusements of the metropolis, or to find a more extensive
> market and lower prices for their holiday purchases than
> their country towns afford. The abundant and early rains
> have promised a year of prosperity, and the dry and sunny
> weather which has prevailed for two weeks past offers

facilities for reaching the city, and for enjoyment after getting here. The ocean beach during the day, and the theatres
during the evening, show a throng of strangers as well as of
residents. All the appearances indicate that this holiday
season in San Francisco will be one of unusual liveliness
and brilliancy.

As Henry Nash Smith pointed out in 1957, Clemens' rendering of this passage into blank verse testified to "his intense
interest in the theater; for his 'blank verse' is imitated from
nineteenth-century theatrical pseudo-Shakespearian verse
of the sort used by Bulwer-Lytton in *The Lady of Lyons*"
(*MTCor*, p. 81).

338.34   a scintillation of Fitz Smythe's in the same column] Just
below the editorial quoted above, Evans published "Beauty
and Booty," in which he referred to "one of the nip-
tomaniacs of the gallant Fourteenth," who stole some
boots.

338.35   thieving scalliwags of the Fourteenth Infantry] The Fourteenth Regiment of U.S. Infantry, which had served under
General Sherman, arrived at the Presidio barracks in November. According to the *Call*, recent recruits to the Fourteenth were "rapscallions . . . from the slums and purlieus
of New York," who replaced the regiment's "dead heroes."
The *Call* also claimed that, since the arrival of the regiment, the police department and police court were spending
half their time arresting and trying "Fourteeners" for crimes
of all sorts in San Francisco, from drunk and disorderly conduct to attempted murder ("The Fourteeners," San Francisco *Morning Call*, 6 January 1866, p. 1; "A Hard Set," ibid.,
7 December 1865, p. 3). This contention is supported by a
large number of local items in the city press, during November and December, recording thefts and other crimes by
soldiers. By early January the problem had eased, following
the dispatch of many of the troops to Arizona.

339.22   Mayo and Aldrich] Frank Mayo was a popular actor who had
begun his stage career in San Francisco in 1856; in 1865 he
returned East for a series of theater engagements. (See the
explanatory note on him for " 'Mark Twain's' Letter," no.
54.) Louis Aldrich made his acting debut in Ohio in 1850
while still a boy. He and Mayo met as members of Maguire's
San Francisco Opera House company in 1863.

339.28   Keans] Charles John Kean (son of Edmund Kean) and his
wife, Ellen Tree Kean, famous Irish actors who were currently giving farewell performances in preparation for returning home from their world tour, begun in 1863.

340.7   I make an extract] Clemens doubtless approved of this rather critical view of business and stock speculation in San Francisco. In an *Enterprise* letter probably written the week before, he said in part: "Out, out upon these vain theatricals, these tinsel trappings of folly! Bring us shrouds, and coffins, and the tolling of bells, and the waving of sable plumes, and the solemn pomp of the passing funeral! What are the poor vanities of this world unto this people, who 'called' their persecuted Washoe with 'two pairs and a jack,' and she answered with a 'king full?' They digged the props from under Washoe, and she fell on them" ("Feels Somber," San Francisco *Morning Call,* 22 December 1865, p. 1).

341.20   Listen to the *Alta:*] Clemens quoted most of the last two paragraphs of a full-column editorial, "The Condition of Mother Earth" (San Francisco *Alta California,* 22 December 1865, p. 2). He omitted the last part of the final paragraph, which read: "But knowing the ease with which cause may be mistaken for effect, and things can be connected which have no possible relation to each other, we leave all such speculations, till science has made some further progress, to the adventurous school of philosophy, for which no gordion knot is too intricate to be untied. The only conclusion that we propose to draw, is the very obvious one that there must be something wrong somewhere. We could not very well haul up anywhere else, when we look abroad and see the troubles, not only in the earth itself, but among those who dwell thereon."

§132. *FITZ SMYTHE'S HORSE*

346.24   old General Macdowl] Major General Irvin McDowell, commander of the Department of California since 1 July 1864. Clemens came to know him while reporting for the *Morning Call* (see *CofC,* pp. 247–250).

§133. *CLOSED OUT*

No notes.

§134. *TAKE THE STAND, FITZ SMYTHE*

350.1   "Amigo," of the Gold Hill *News*] Evans' weekly column in the Gold Hill *News* began on 2 July 1864 and was signed "Amigo."

350.12   Barney Olwell] On 13 January 1865 Barney Olwell killed James Irwin. He was later convicted of murder in the first degree and hanged on 22 January 1866. Evans' report of the execution called Olwell "a brute of the lowest type, hardly entitled to be considered a man; he committed a brutal murder in cold blood and with malice aforethought" ("Our San Francisco Correspondence," Gold Hill *News*, 29 January 1866, p. 2). Evans' items on Olwell were, despite Clemens' gibe to the contrary, consistently critical of him.

351.2   Ansbro] Thomas Ansbro of the San Francisco police force (Langley, *Directory for 1865*, p. 61).

351.7   Chappell] Jacob G. Chappell, also of the police force (Langley, *Directory for 1865*, p. 116).

352.9   WHERE ARE THE POLICE?] Signed "W. W.," this letter appeared in the San Francisco *Morning Call* on 3 February 1866 (p. 1). Clemens made no changes.

§135. *REMARKABLE DREAM*

355.9   Ananias] See Acts 5:1–10. Ananias, a disciple in the church at Jerusalem, conspired with his wife, Sapphira, to hold back money derived from the sale of land and intended for the church. Peter denounced the falsehood, and because the couple "lied . . . unto God" they were killed by divine wrath.

357.17   Baron de Munchausen] Baron Karl Friedrich Hieronymous von Münchhausen (1720–1797) was a German hunter and soldier who had served with distinction in Russian campaigns against the Turks. His name is proverbially associated with absurdly exaggerated exploits, from the attribution to him of a collection of fantastic tales entitled *Baron Munchausen's Narrative of his Marvellous Travels and Campaigns in Russia* (London: Smith, 1785). The actual author was probably Rudolf Erich Raspe (1737–1794), a scholar whose reputation for genius was surpassed only by his notoriety as a swindler (Thomas Seccombe, introduction to *The Surprising Adventures of Baron Munchausen* [London: Lawrence and Bullen, 1895], pp. v–xxviii).

357.25   world."] At this point in the Yale Scrapbook (p. 40) Mark Twain added a footnote: "The Baron's shameful satire was aimed at the police—they wear gray in San Francisco."

357.29   Thomas Pepper] Tom Pepper was a legendary nautical liar who was expelled from hell because of his unbelievable yarns (William Henry Smyth, *The Sailor's Word Book* [London: Blackie and Son, 1867], p. 685).

136. "MARK TWAIN" ON THE LAUNCH
OF THE STEAMER "CAPITAL"

361.1   MR. MUFF NICKERSON] Mulford Nickerson was known as a
         prominent turfman and good fellow. In April 1865, for in-
         stance, he was listed as a performer in a burlesque circus
         program. Clemens' acquaintance with him has not been
         otherwise documented ("Medley Circus of California,"
         Golden Era 13 [30 April 1865]: 4; "The New Play," San
         Francisco *Examiner,* 22 September 1865, p. 3).

363.25–26 scriptural panorama] The panorama show presented a
         continuous picture—in this case, made up from scenes of
         biblical events—painted on a long canvas that was un-
         rolled slowly to the accompaniment of the panoramist's
         commentary.

365.12–13 "Oh, a life . . . rolling deep!"] From "A Life on the Ocean
         Wave" (1838), music by Henry Russell and words by Epes
         Sargent.

365.35–36 "Come rise up . . . with me!"] From "Willie Reilly," an Irish
         folk song.

137. THE PIONEERS' BALL

369.6   Colfax party] An allusion to the testimonial send-off for
         Schuyler Colfax held the preceding August. See the
         explanatory note on Colfax for "The Facts" (no. 116).

369.16   Mrs. C. N. . . . white kid gloves] Mrs. C. N.'s scanty cos-
         tume is comparable to that of several belles at the ball of the
         San Francisco Olympic Club a month earlier: "Miss B. wore
         a pair of slippers. . . . Miss D. had on a watch, and one Os-
         trich feather" (*Golden Era* 13 [15 October 1865]: 5).

138. THE GUARD ON A BENDER

372.2   Provost Guard] The provost marshal of the Department of
         California was Major Alfred Morton, with offices at 416
         Washington Street (Langley, *Directory for 1865,* p. 622).

372.3   mint] The San Francisco mint was on Commercial Street
         near Montgomery, next door to the *Call* building (Langley,
         Directory for 1865, pp. 325, 593).

372.5   "Blue Wing" saloon] At 140 Montgomery Street (*CofC,*
         p. 11).

372.22   Wells, Fargo & Co's building] At Montgomery and Califor-
         nia streets (Langley, *Directory for 1865,* p. 449).

373.10   Lick House] On Montgomery Street between Sutter and
            Post (Langley, *Directory for 1865*, p. 277).

373.10   Occidental Market] From Market to Sutter streets, between
            Sansome and Montgomery (Langley, *Directory for 1865*,
            p. 345).

373.10–11   St. Mary's Cathedral] Archbishop Joseph S. Alemany's
            Gothic cathedral at California and Dupont streets (Langley,
            Directory for 1865, pp. 600–601).

139. *BENKERT COMETH!*

No notes.

140. *UNCLE LIGE*

378.6   bit house] In a bit house beer sold for twelve and one-half
            cents, or one bit, twice the cost of beer in ordinary saloons
            and bars (Ratay, *Pioneers*, p. 259 n. 1).

378.7   faro bank] Both the establishment where faro is played and
            the capital ventured in the game by the dealer at the faro
            table.

378.18   Diggers] A small group of Indians of southwestern Utah and
            California, so called because they lived on roots dug up from
            the ground. Clemens typically associated them with de-
            graded humanity.

379.15   Reeseriv'] Reese River, a mining district in Lander County,
            Nevada, was the site of a major mining rush in the early
            1860s.

379.37   cholera] The disease was epidemic in North America during
            1866 and 1867.

141. *WEBB'S BENEFIT*

383.21   Mr. Barry] William Barry, a comedian, was part of the acting
            company attached to Maguire's Opera House in San Fran-
            cisco (Langley, *Directory for 1865*, p. 71).

142. *A RICH EPIGRAM*

No notes.

143. *A GRACEFUL COMPLIMENT*

390.13   William B. Astor] Following the death of his father, John Jacob Astor, in 1848, William Backhouse Astor was reputed to be the country's wealthiest man.

391.16   Frank Soulé] Soulé and Clemens were colleagues on the *Morning Call* in 1864. Sixteen years later Clemens remembered him as "one of the sweetest and whitest & loveliest spirits that ever wandered into this world by mistake" (*MTHL*, 1:325). Soulé took an advanced degree in journalism at Wesleyan College a few years before coming to California in 1849. For more than thirty years he worked on numerous San Francisco newspapers and in the mid-sixties served in the U.S. Customs House. He was one of the authors of *The Annals of San Francisco*. In addition, he composed a large amount of mediocre poetry, for some of which Clemens tried to help him find a publisher in 1880. Soulé was also collector of Internal Revenue in San Francisco for four years (John M. Hoffman, "Vignette of a Mystic in California," *Beta Theta Pi Magazine* 94 [May 1967]: 323–324).

391.34–35   enormous national debt] The public debt had risen from a prewar level of $65,000,000 to the sum of $2,808,549,437 by late 1865 (*Report of the Secretary of the Treasury on the State of the Finances for the Year 1865* [Washington: The Government Printing Office, 1865], pp. 17, 253).

144. *"CHRISTIAN SPECTATOR"*

394.24   Bishop Pierce] George Foster Pierce helped to organize the Methodist Episcopal Church, South, and in 1854 was elected bishop. Earlier he had been president of Georgia Female College (now Wesleyan College) at Macon, and then president of Emory College, Oxford, Georgia. After the war he worked assiduously to establish the western conferences of the church. *Bishop Pierce's Sermons and Addresses* was published in 1866.

395.3   Ward's shirts] The firm of S. W. H. Ward and Son of 323 Montgomery Street manufactured—and widely advertised—shirts for men (Langley, *Directory for 1865*, p. 445).

395.21   Chief Burke, or Blitz, or Lees] Clemens was well acquainted with Chief of Police Martin J. Burke, the tireless and clever detective Bernard S. Blitz, and Captain Isaiah W. Lees, later chief of police. In 1866 Clemens' charges of mismanagement and corruption in the police force focused on Burke's handling of his job.

145. *MORE ROMANCE*

397.3–4   in the days ... long time ago] Edwin Ransford's "In the Days When We Went Gypsying" includes the lines "In the days when we went gypsying / A long time ago."

146. *GRAND FETE-DAY AT THE CLIFF HOUSE*

400.10   JIM EOFF] An excellent trainer and driver of horses. In a sensational 1863 trial he had been acquitted of murder charges for having shot and killed William D. Chapman during a dispute at the Willows Race Track (San Francisco *Morning Call*, 2 May 1863, p. 1).

400.12   HARRIS COVEY] Co-owner of the Fashion Livery and Sale Stable on Sutter Street (Langley, *Directory for 1865*, p. 361).

400.12–13 BILLY WILLIAMSON] William F. Williamson was the popular proprietor of the Bay View Park and Race Track on San Bruno Road (Langley, *Directory for 1865*, p. 458).

400.15   JEROME LELAND] With his brother Lewis, Leland was co-proprietor of the Occidental Hotel, known for its superior catering. The "famous cow" may have been a prize animal purchased to feed the patrons of the Occidental.

400.18   COMMODORE PERRY CHILDS] Possibly George E. Childs, bookkeeper for the Occidental (Langley, *Directory for 1865*, p. 117).

401.1   MICHAEL REESE] Reese was a native of Bavaria who had come to the United States as a youth and then to California in 1850. In spite of various financial set-backs he eventually became one of San Francisco's wealthiest men ("Pioneer Obituaries. Michael Reese," San José *Pioneer*, 10 August 1878, p. 2). After Reese was sued for breach of contract of marriage in February 1866, Clemens was consistently critical of his integrity (see "Michael," no. 177; "A San Francisco Millionaire," no. 180; "Reflections on the Sabbath," *Golden Era* 14 [18 March 1866]: 3, reprinted in WIM, pp. 39–41).

401.6   Emperor Norton] Joshua A. Norton, who lost his fortune in 1853 and as a result became a likable lunatic. See the explanatory note on him for "The Lick House Ball" (no. 65).

147. *MACDOUGALL VS. MAGUIRE*

148. *THE CHRISTMAS FIRESIDE*

149. *ENIGMA*

No notes.

150. *ANOTHER ENTERPRISE*

414.3   John L. Stephens] This steamer was commanded by Edgar Wakeman for the Mexican Steamship Line and left San Francisco monthly for Mexican ports. It returned with its cargo of oysters on December 22 ("Arrived," San Francisco *Evening Bulletin*, 23 December 1865, p. 5).

415.30   Alexander Von Humboldt] Baron Friederich Heinrich Alexander von Humboldt (1769–1859), the world-famous naturalist, explorer, and diplomat.

151. *SPIRIT OF THE LOCAL PRESS*

418.17   'Fourteener' items] The "Fourteeners" were the soldiers of the Fourteenth Regiment of U.S. Infantry, and had been the subject of numerous recent items in the press about crimes committed in San Francisco. See the explanatory note on the Fourteenth Infantry for "San Francisco Letter" (no. 131).

152. *CONVICTS*

No notes.

TEXTUAL
APPARATUS

But that which is most difficult is not always most important, and to an editor nothing is a trifle by which his authour
is obscured.

—Samuel Johnson, "Preface to Shakespeare"

An individual textual apparatus for each sketch provides everything needed to reconstruct the copy-text and Mark Twain's revisions (whenever any survives). Each apparatus usually, but not
invariably, includes the elements described below. A description of
texts follows the guide to the apparatus in this volume; it identifies textually significant editions of Mark Twain's sketches and
specifies the copies collated and examined in the preparation of
this collection. A list of word divisions in this volume, which
records ambiguous compounds hyphenated in the present edition
at the end of a line, is given at the end of the entire apparatus to
facilitate accurate quotation of Mark Twain's texts.

Textual Commentary.   This section gives the copy-text and
specifies the copy or copies used; it discusses problems or unusual
features of the text; and under a subheading, "Reprintings and
Revisions," gives the history of the sketch and characterizes Mark
Twain's revisions of it.

Textual Notes.   This section discusses emendations or decisions not to emend: it calls attention to possible errors left un-
emended in the text, to problems in establishing particular readings,
and to variants in the reprinting history which are especially
problematic.

Emendations of the Copy-Text.   This section records every departure in this edition from the copy-text, with the exception of
the typographical features discussed above. It also records the
resolution of doubtful or ambiguous readings. In each entry, the
reading of this edition is given first, with its source identified by a
symbol in parentheses; it is separated by a centered dot from the
rejected copy-text reading on the right, thus:

daguerreotype (JF1) • daguerreotpe

A wavy dash (~) to the right of the dot stands for the word on the left and signals that a mark of punctuation is being emended; a caret (ʌ) indicates the absence of a punctuation mark; and the symbol I-C follows any emendation whose source is not an authoritative text, even if the same correction was made in a derivative edition, thus:

> cold. (I-C) • ~?
> moment. (I-C) • ~ʌ

Emendations marked with an asterisk in the left margin are discussed in the textual notes. A vertical rule indicates the end of a line in the copy-text, thus:

> footsteps (I-C) • foot-|steps
> secret? These (I-C) • ~?—|~

Italicized words in square brackets, such as [*not in*], [*no* ¶], and [*torn*], are editorial. Doubtful readings are recorded with the following notation:

Cairo (I-C) • Ca[ ]o [*torn*]	*ir* not present, tear in copy-text
long (I-C) • lon[g] [*torn*]	*g* unclear, tear in copy-text
every (I-C) • eve[r]y	*r* unclear in copy-text
meant, (I-C) • ~[,]	comma unclear in copy-text
eat; (I-C) • ~[:]	semicolon unclear, possibly colon
notion. (I-C) • ~[ʌ]	space for period in copy-text
saw (I-C) • saw/has seen	alternate reading left standing in copy-text

Emendations and Adopted Readings. This section replaces *Emendations of the Copy-Text* when the text is established from radiating or composite texts. It records all variants, substantive and accidental, among the relevant texts, which are identified by abbreviations with superscript numbers; the numbers are assigned according to the chronology of publication and do not indicate relative authority of the texts. Thus the following entry shows that three texts agree with each other against a fourth, and the majority reading has been adopted in this collection:

savan (P^{1-2}, P^4) • *savan* (P^3)

And the following entry shows that a compound hyphenated at the end of a line in one text and rendered solid in another is resolved in accord with the two that render it hyphenated:

fore-finger (P^{1-2}) • fore-|finger (P^3); forefinger (P^4)

An entry that rejects all of the radiating texts in favor of an editorial emendation appears as follows:

mixture. (I-C) • ~, (P^{1-4})

Diagram of Transmission and Historical Collation. These elements appear in the textual apparatus only for sketches reprinted or revised by Mark Twain. We give a diagram every time there is a chain of transmission, and it is essential for reading the entries in the historical collation. A list of the texts collated for each sketch immediately precedes the collation, which records all substantive variants in them. In addition, because Mark Twain is known to have concerned himself with revising emphasis (italics and exclamation points) as well as paragraphing, such variants in accidentals are likewise recorded. When Mark Twain demonstrably corrected or revised other accidentals—spelling, punctuation, and so on—in any of the surviving marked copies (YS**MT**, JF1**MT**, HWa**MT**, HWb**MT**, and MTSk**MT**), the full history of the particular accidental variant is also recorded.

In each collation entry the reading of this edition is given first, followed by symbols for the texts that agree with it; it is separated by a centered dot from its variants, which are identified by the

appropriate symbols (given in the list of texts collated). A sample
chain of transmission is given in figure 1 to facilitate understanding the examples that follow. Each transmission diagram in the
individual apparatuses is essential to reading the collation for that
sketch, because although the pattern of transmission is similar
for many sketches, it varies in significant ways from sketch to
sketch.

Symbols joined by a dash (–) indicate that the reading appeared
in the first text noted and was transmitted as far as the second.
Thus the entry

    git (GE–JF4) • get (JF3–SkNO)

indicates that the original dialect word was accurately transmitted from the *Golden Era* (GE) through JF1 and JF2 to JF4; but that
Hotten altered it to "get" in his JF3, from where it was transmitted to HWa, then to HWb, and ultimately to SkNO, without being
corrected by Mark Twain. A plus sign (+) indicates that the reading appears in the given text and in all printings derived from it.
Thus the entry

    [¶] If (GE) • [*no* ¶] If (JF1+)

indicates that a paragraph break appears at this point in GE, but
not in JF1 or in any subsequent reprinting deriving from it. A more
complicated entry, involving Mark Twain's revision, appears
thus:

    believe I threw (GE–MTSk, GE–HWa) • believed I had
    thrown (HWa**MT**–SkNO)

Here several complexities are recorded. The reading of the present
edition and of the copy-text was, in this case, successfully transmitted from GE through JF1, JF2, and JF4 to MTSk; it was also
transmitted from GE through JF1, JF2, and JF3 to HWa. Mark
Twain encountered it there and revised it to the variant reading in
HWa**MT**, which was incorporated in HWb and subsequently reprinted in SkNO. A still more complicated entry appears thus:

    and ate . . . healthy. [¶] After (GE–JF2; GE–HWa) • and

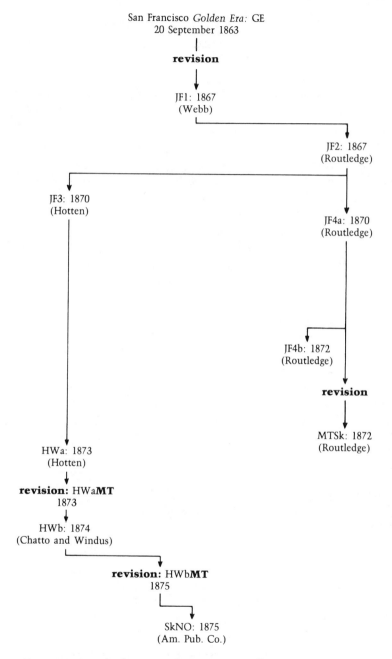

FIGURE 1. Sample diagram of transmission (from "How to Cure a Cold," no. 63).

eat . . . healthy. [¶] After (JF4); and—— [¶] After (MTSk);
and—here is food for the imagination. [¶] After
(HWaMT–SkNO)

The original reading was transmitted successfully from GE
through JF1 to JF2; it was also successfully transmitted from GE
through JF1, JF2, and JF3 to HWa. JF4 altered "ate" to "eat" without authority. Mark Twain revised the JF4 text by striking out the
passage following "and" and substituting an expressive long dash
in MTSk. But when he revised HWaMT, he revised differently: he
again deleted the matter after "and," but substituted another dash
and the phrase "here is food for the imagination." This revision
was incorporated in HWb and subsequently reprinted in SkNO.

The historical collation preserves all substantive variants in the
texts collated, whether or not they originated with Mark Twain.
But the history of reprinting and revision given in the textual
introduction permits us to make certain discriminations between
variants which Mark Twain certainly made, and those which he
could not possibly have made.

(1) Variants that first appear in JF2, JF3, JF4, Scrs, EOps, PJks,
and HWa *cannot be authorial.*

(2) Variants that first appear in JF1, CD, MTSk, HWb, Sk#1,
and SkNO *may be authorial,* but may also have been introduced
by editors or compositors.

(3) Variants for which we have documentary evidence in the
form of Mark Twain's autograph changes—YSMT, JF1MT,
HWaMT, HWbMT, and MTSkMT (and a few stray examples of
printer's copy in other forms)—*are certainly authorial,* and are so
indicated in the collation by the symbol MT. Any variant that
arises in JF1, HWb, or SkNO can be certainly attributed to Mark
Twain when the revision appears first in the marked printer's
copy.

The textual apparatus may contain other elements that are more
or less self-explanatory. In the items where copy-text is a holograph, we include a section called *Alterations in the Manuscript,*
which reports the author's cancellations, substitutions, and revisions. Essential corrections that Mark Twain made as he wrote or

reread his work are not recorded: letters or words that have been mended or traced over, or canceled and rewritten merely for clarity; false starts and slips of the pen; corrected eye skips; and words or phrases that have been inadvertently repeated, then canceled.

Special collations are provided when a potentially authoritative text—for instance, a contemporary reprinting of uncertain origin—has *not* been used to establish the present text because it is probably derivative. The variants are recorded as a check on this decision.

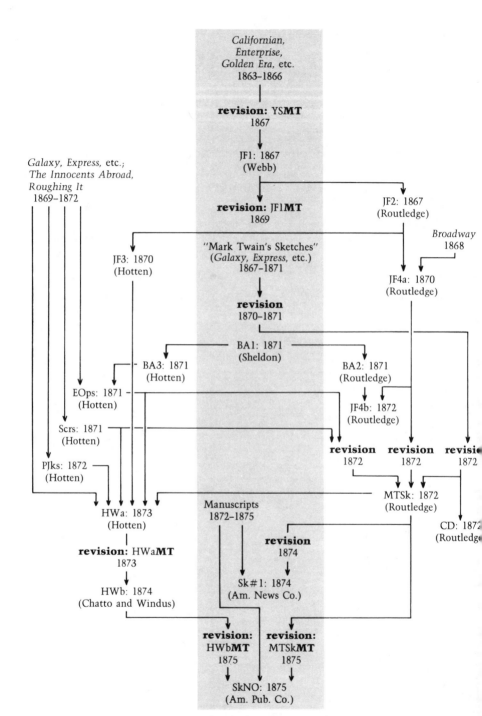

FIGURE 2. History of reprinting and revision.

Description of Texts

The following list identifies and briefly characterizes textually significant editions, impressions, and issues of Mark Twain's early tales and
sketches used in the preparation of the present collection. These include
editions for which Mark Twain prepared the printer's copy, as well as
editions that he did not so prepare but that form part of the chain of
transmission. Individual journal printings and manuscripts, and several
minor editions that affect only a few sketches, are not included in this
list but are of course defined in the textual commentaries. Also excluded,
but listed at the end, are a group of editions found to be derivative and
without textual significance.

Bibliographical terms used here follow the definitions of Fredson Bow-
ers in *Principles of Bibliographical Description* (New York: Russell and
Russell, 1962) and of G. Thomas Tanselle in "The Bibliographical Con-
cepts of *Issue* and *State*" (*PBSA* 69 [1975]: 17–66). Sight collation means
the collation of two or more copies printed from different settings of
type. Machine collation means the collation on the Hinman collator of
two copies printed from the same typesetting or from plates cast from the
same typesetting. (The Hinman machine superimposes the images of the
two copies on each other and thereby enables the operator to detect even
minute typographic differences.)

Following the description of texts is a list of the specific copies of each
edition or issue used in the preparation of this collection.

YSMT   The Yale Scrapbook, which contains clippings from the Virginia City *Territorial Enterprise, Californian,* San Francisco
Golden Era, San Francisco *Dramatic Chronicle,* Sacramento
Union, and other unidentified newspapers (Yale). The clippings were published between mid-December 1863 and late
October 1866. Many of them were revised by Mark Twain,
and the scrapbook supplied most of the printer's copy for JF1.

JF1   *The Celebrated Jumping Frog of Calaveras County, And
other Sketches.* By Mark Twain. Edited by John Paul. New
York: C. H. Webb, 1867. *BAL* 3310. An authorized American
edition. All of the sketches in JF1 were set from newspaper
and journal printings—many of them unauthoritative reprints, and most of them taken as clippings from **YSMT**.
Machine collation shows no authoritative changes in the
plates through 1870, when Mark Twain had them destroyed.

JF1MT   The copy of an 1869 impression of JF1 revised by Mark Twain
(Doheny).

JF2   *The Celebrated Jumping Frog of Calaveras County, And
other Sketches.* By Mark Twain. Edited by John Paul. London: George Routledge and Sons, 1867. *BAL* 3586. An unau-

577

thorized English edition, set from JF1. JF2 was used as printer's copy in setting both Hotten's unauthorized JF3 and the Routledges' authorized JF4a.

JF3   *The Jumping Frog and Other Humourous Sketches.* By Mark Twain. [Samuel L. Clemens.] From the Original Edition. London: John Camden Hotten, [1870]. *BAL* 3587. An unauthorized English edition, set from JF2. The plates (or duplicate plates) of JF3 were used to supply the text of JF3 in Hotten's *A 3rd Supply of Yankee Drolleries* [1870], listed in *BAL*, p. 246. JF3 served as printer's copy for portions of Hotten's unauthorized HWa.

JF4

JF4a   *The Celebrated Jumping Frog of Calaveras County, And other Sketches.* By Mark Twain. London: George Routledge and Sons, 1870. *BAL* 3319. The earliest issue of an authorized English edition, set from JF2. JF4a contained what advertisements (and perhaps the cover, which we have not seen) called "a New Copyright Chapter," "Cannibalism in the Cars" (no. 232). Mark Twain did not revise the printer's copy for JF4a, but he did use a copy of it to prepare part of the printer's copy for the Routledges' authorized MTSk.

JF4b   *Mark Twain's Celebrated Jumping Frog of Calaveras County And other Sketches. With the Burlesque Autobiography and First Romance.* London: George Routledge and Sons, [1872]. *BAL* 3338. An authorized reissue of JF4a. To produce this reissue, or "author's edition, with a copyright chapter and Mark Twain's Autobiography" (as the cover announced), the Routledges added two sketches to the plates of JF4a ("An Awful—Terrible Medieval Romance" and "A Burlesque Autobiography," nos. 276 and 355). Mark Twain did not revise the printer's copy for JF4b, which is textually identical with JF4a except for the new sketches. Machine collation shows no authoritative changes in the plates through 1900.

BA1   *Mark Twain's (Burlesque) Autobiography and First Romance.* New York: Sheldon and Company, [1871]. *BAL* 3326. An authorized American edition. BA1 served as printer's copy for the Routledges' unauthorized BA2, and possibly for Hotten's unauthorized BA3 as well. Machine collation of BA1 shows no authorial changes in the plates through 1882, when Mark Twain had them destroyed.

BA2   *Mark Twain's (Burlesque) Autobiography and First Romance.* London: George Routledge and Sons, [1871]. *BAL* 3595. An unauthorized English edition, set from BA1.

BA3 *Mark Twain's (Burlesque) 1. Autobiography. 2. Mediæval Romance. 3. On Children.* London: John Camden Hotten, [1871]. *BAL* 3329. An unauthorized English edition, set from BA1 or BA2 with the addition of two pieces not by Mark Twain.

EOps *Eye Openers: Good Things, Immensely Funny Sayings & Stories That Will Bring a Smile upon the Gruffest Countenance.* By Mark Twain. London: John Camden Hotten, [1871]. *BAL* 3331. An unauthorized English edition. Hotten reprinted many sketches from the *Galaxy* and a few from newspapers. Mark Twain revised a copy of EOps, which served as printer's copy for portions of the authorized Routledge MTSk. EOps also served as printer's copy for portions of Hotten's unauthorized HWa.

Scrs *Screamers: A Gathering of Scraps of Humour, Delicious Bits, & Short Stories.* By Mark Twain. London: John Camden Hotten, [1871]. *BAL* 3333. An unauthorized English edition. Scrs reprinted many sketches from the *Galaxy*, two from JF3, and one from the Buffalo *Express*. It also reprinted six sketches that were not by Mark Twain; later impressions of Scrs omit the final sketch ("Vengeance"), which was not Mark Twain's. Mark Twain revised a copy of Scrs, which served as printer's copy for portions of the authorized Routledge MTSk. Scrs also served as printer's copy for portions of Hotten's unauthorized HWa.

PJks *Practical Jokes with Artemus Ward, Including the Story of the Man Who Fought Cats.* By Mark Twain and Other Humourists. London: John Camden Hotten, [1872]. *BAL* 3342. An unauthorized English edition. PJks reprinted sketches from the *Galaxy*, the Buffalo *Express*, and *Roughing It*; it included many sketches not by Mark Twain. It served as printer's copy for portions of Hotten's unauthorized HWa.

CD *A Curious Dream; and Other Sketches.* By Mark Twain. Selected and Revised by the Author. Copyright. London: George Routledge and Sons, [1872]. *BAL* 3340. An authorized English edition. Mark Twain prepared the printer's copy for CD by revising clippings from the *Galaxy*, Buffalo *Express*, New York *Tribune*, *Packard's Monthly*, Newark (N.J.) *Press*, and *American Publisher*. These revised clippings also served as printer's copy for portions of the authorized Routledge MTSk. Machine collation of CD reveals only six minor textual variants, none of them authorial, which occurred sometime between the 1872 and 1892 impressions.

MTSk   *Mark Twain's Sketches.* Selected and Revised by the Author.
        Copyright Edition. London: George Routledge and Sons,
        1872. *BAL* 3341. An authorized English edition. Mark Twain
        prepared printer's copy for MTSk by revising copies of JF4a,
        EOps, and Scrs. He or his publisher also included the fifteen
        sketches prepared as clippings for CD. The plates of MTSk
        were sold to Chatto and Windus in 1892, who reissued MTSk
        in 1897. Machine collation reveals only minor changes and
        corrections, none of them authorial. Mark Twain used
        MTSk as printer's copy for portions of the American News
        Company's authorized Sk#1 and the American Publishing
        Company's authorized SkNO.

MTSk**MT** The copy of an 1872 impression of MTSk revised by Mark
        Twain to serve as printer's copy for SkNO (MTP).

HW

HWa   *The Choice Humorous Works of Mark Twain.* Now First
        Collected. With Extra Passages to the "Innocents Abroad,"
        Now First Reprinted, and a Life of the Author. Illustrations
        by Mark Twain and other Artists; also Portrait of the Author.
        London: John Camden Hotten, [1873]. *BAL* 3351. An unau-
        thorized English edition. HWa reprinted sketches from Hot-
        ten's own JF3, EOps, Scrs, and PJks, as well as all of *The
        Innocents Abroad.* It also reprinted seven sketches from
        MTSk or CD and extracts from *Roughing It,* as well as a few
        sketches not by Mark Twain. In 1873 Mark Twain revised a
        set of HWa sheets, and the plates were altered to follow his
        corrections and produce the authorized reissue HWb, pub-
        lished by Chatto and Windus, Hotten's successors.

HWa**MT**   The set of sheets of HWa revised by Mark Twain and used to
        produce HWb (Rare Book Room, New York Public Library,
        *KL).

HWb   *The Choice Humorous Works of Mark Twain.* Revised and
        Corrected by the Author. With Life and Portrait of the Au-
        thor, and Numerous Illustrations. London: Chatto and Win-
        dus, 1874. *BAL* 3605. An authorized reissue of HWa. The
        plates of HWa were altered for HWb to follow Mark Twain's
        corrections on HWa**MT**. Machine collation of HWb reveals
        no further authorial changes in the plates.

HWb**MT**   The copy of an 1874 impression of HWb revised by Mark
        Twain and used as printer's copy for SkNO (Doheny).

Sk#1   *Mark Twain's Sketches. Number One.* Authorised Edition.
        With Illustrations by R. T. Sperry. New York: American
        News Company, [1874]. *BAL* 3360. An authorized American

edition. Sk#1 reprinted ten sketches from MTSk, several of them further revised by Mark Twain, and three sketches not previously published. Machine collation was not performed because no later impression could be obtained.

SkNO *Mark Twain's Sketches, New and Old.* Now First Published in Complete Form. Hartford and Chicago: American Publishing Company, 1875. *BAL* 3364. An authorized American edition. SkNO drew the bulk of its sketches from copies of MTSk and HWb which Mark Twain revised—MTSk**MT** and HWb**MT**—and the rest of its sketches from manuscripts and revised clippings. Machine collation reveals that in the first impression a new preface replaced that of the publisher's prospectus, which was otherwise printed from the plates of SkNO. Later impressions of SkNO made minor corrections and dropped one sketch ("From 'Hospital Days' ") which was not written by Mark Twain.

DERIVATIVE EDITIONS

The following editions were found to be derivative and without textual significance—that is, Mark Twain played no part in their production, and he did not subsequently revise their texts or anything deriving from their texts. We follow the order of *BAL*.

Beadle's Dime Book of Fun No. 3. New York: Beadle and Company, [1866]. *BAL* 3309.

The Piccadilly Annual of Entertaining Literature. London: John Camden Hotten, [1870]. *BAL* 3323.

Mark Twain's Memoranda. From the Galaxy. Toronto: Canadian News and Publishing Company, 1871. *BAL* 3327.

Autobiography, (Burlesque.) First Romance, and Memoranda. By Mark Twain. Toronto: James Campbell and Son, [1871]. *BAL* 3334.

A Book for an Hour, Containing Choice Reading and Character Sketches. A Curious Dream, and Other Sketches, Revised and Selected for This Work by the Author Mark Twain. New York: B. J. Such, 1873. *BAL* 3352.

Sketches by Mark Twain. Toronto: Belfords, Clarke and Co., 1879. *BAL* 3384.

Mark Twain's Library of Humor. New York: Charles L. Webster and Company, 1888. *BAL* 3425.

Sketches New and Old, vol. 19 of *The Writings of Mark Twain.* Autograph Edition. Hartford: American Publishing Company, 1899. *BAL* 3456.

The $30,000 Bequest and Other Stories by Mark Twain. New York and London: Harper and Brothers, 1906. *BAL* 3492.

The Celebrated Jumping Frog of Calaveras County, and Other Sketches. Melbourne: George Robertson, 1868. *BAL* 3588.

Information Wanted and Other Sketches. London: George Routledge and Sons, [1876]. *BAL* 3608.

Sketches by Mark Twain. Now First Published in Complete Form. Toronto: Belfords, Clarke and Co., 1880. *BAL* 3624.

Sketches by Mark Twain. Leipzig: Bernhard Tauchnitz, 1883. *BAL* 3632.

Sketches New and Old. Hartford: American Publishing Company, 1893. *BAL* 3651.

Mark Twain's Sketches. Selected and Revised by the Author. A New Edition. London: Chatto and Windus, 1897. *BAL* 3657.

Editorial Wild Oats. New York and London: Harper and Brothers, 1905. *BAL* 3665.

A 3rd Supply of Yankee Drolleries: The Most Recent Works of the Best American Humourists. London: John Camden Hotten, [1870]. *BAL,* p. 246.

Fun for the Million. A Gathering of Choice Wit and Humour, Good Things, and Sublime Nonsense by Jerrold, Dickens, Sam Slick, Mark Twain . . . and a Host of other Humourists. London: John Camden Hotten, [1873]. *BAL,* p. 247.

The Celebrated Jumping Frog of Calaveras County, and Other Sketches. By Mark Twain. Toronto: A. S. Irving, 1870. Not in *BAL.*

TEXTS COLLATED

The following copies were used in machine and sight collations or examined in the course of preparing this edition. In addition, variant readings discovered in collations were exhaustively checked in every relevant copy available to the editors.

JF1   Copies machine collated: 1867 impression (MTP Armes), 1867 impression, variant state with unprinted page 198 (PH of copy at CWB), 1868 impression (Iowa xPS 1322.C4.1868), 1870 impression (University of North Carolina 817.C625.ce).

   Copies sight collated or examined: 1867 impression (MTP Webster), 1868 impression (Bancroft F855.1.C625c), 1869 impression (Bancroft F855.1.C625c), 1870 impression (Iowa xPS 1322.C4.1870).

JF2   Copies sight collated: 1867 impression (PH of copy at Texas), 1867 impression (MTP).

JF3   Copies machine collated: [1870] impression (PH of copy at Texas), [1870] impression, included in *A 3rd Supply of Yankee Drolleries* (PH of copy at British Museum, 12316.cc.27), [1882] impression, George Routledge and Sons (PH of copy at British Museum, 12316.d.34).

   Copy examined: [1877] impression, Ward, Lock, and Co. (MTP Appert).

JF4   Copies machine collated: JF4a 1870 impression (PH of copy at Texas, Clemens 7aa), JF4b [1872] impression, *BAL* "first" (Houghton Library, Harvard University, AL1059.38), JF4b [1872?] impression, *BAL* "third" (MTP), JF4b [1900] impression (Robert H. Hirst collection).

   Copies sight collated or examined: JF4b [1872?] impression, *BAL* "second" (PH of copy at University of Michigan,

PS1322.J8.1873), JF4b [1872?] impression, *BAL* "third" (Charles Cornman collection).

BA1   Copies machine collated: [1871] impression (MTP green cover), [1871] impression (MTP brown cover), [1871] impression (MTP purple cover).

        Copies sight collated or examined: [1871] impression (MTP Judd, paper cover), [1871] impression (MTP paper cover), [1871] impression (Berkeley 957.C625.ma).

BA2   Copy sight collated: [1871] impression (PH of copy at University of Virginia).

BA3   Copies sight collated or examined: [1871] impression (PH of copy at Texas), [1871] impression (PH of copy at Yale).

EOps   Copies machine collated: [1871] impression (PH of copy at Texas), [1871 or later] impression (Yale Ix.H251.867ce).

        Copy examined: [1875] impression, Ward, Lock and Co. (University of British Columbia PS1303.W3).

Scrs   Copies machine collated: [1871] impression (Yale Ix.H251.867ce), [1871 or later] impression, without final sketch (University of Indiana PS1303.H834.1872).

        Copies sight collated or examined: [1871 or later] impression, without final sketch (MTP paper cover), [1871 or later] impression, without final sketch (MTP rebound copy).

PJks   Copy sight collated: [1872] impression (PH of copy at University of Illinois, 817.C859p).

CD   Copies machine collated: [1872] impression (PH of copy at Texas, Clemens 86), [1892] impression (University of Chicago PS1322.C74.1892), [1900] impression (Robert H. Hirst collection).

        Copy examined: [1872 or later] impression (Robert H. Hirst collection).

MTSk   Copies machine collated: [1872] impression (MTP), [1897] impression, Chatto and Windus (Bowdoin College PS1319.A1.1897). Copy partially machine collated: [1872] impression, revised by Mark Twain (MTSk**MT**, MTP).

HW   Copies machine collated: HWa [1873] impression (Texas Clemens B33), HWb 1874 impression (PH of copy at CWB), HWb 1877 impression (Texas Clemens B34), HWb 1878 impression (MTP), HWb 1902 impression (McMaster University PS1302.C5.1902), HWb 1922 impression (University of Cincinnati PS1302.C5.1922).

Sk#1   Copies sight collated or examined: [1874] impression (Iowa xPS1322.S47.1874), [1874] impression (Berkeley FILM 4274.-PR.v.2.reel C16).

SkNO   Copies machine collated: publisher's prospectus (MTP Tufts), publisher's prospectus (MTP), 1875 impression (MTP copy 3), 1875 impression (MTP copy 4), 1875 impression (Texas Clemens 118), 1887 impression (University of Virginia PS1319.A1.1887), 1893 impression (Texas Clemens 129b).

Copies sight collated or examined: publisher's prospectus (PH of copy at Yale), 1875 impression (MTP copy 2), 1875 impression (MTP copy 5), 1875 impression (MTP Hearst), 1892 impression (Princeton University 3679.7.382.11).

76. *PARTING PRESENTATION*

Textual Commentary

The first printing in the San Francisco *Alta California* for 13 June 1864 (p. 1) is copy-text. Copy: PH from Bancroft. The text was preceded by a paragraph, possibly by Mark Twain as well, that said the *Alta* had "secured a copy of this eloquent production" which it gave to its readers "verbatim" (see the headnote). This "copy" was almost certainly Mark Twain's manuscript, now lost, rather than a transcription made by someone else. There are no textual notes.

Emendations of the Copy-Text

7.13	very (I-C) • vary
7.17	these (I-C) • th[e]se
7.23	McClellan, (I-C) • ~.
8.5	land: (I-C) • ~ [:]
8.8	savage (I-C) • [s]avage
8.22	to-morrow (I-C) • to-|morrow
8.25	Buckskin (I-C) • Buck-|skin
8.25–26	Rivers; (I-C) • ~ [:]
8.26	Washakee (I-C) • Wash[a]kee
8.32	-a-muck (I-C) • -~∧~

77. *"MARK TWAIN" IN THE METROPOLIS*

Textual Commentary

The first printing in the Virginia City *Territorial Enterprise,* probably sometime between 17 and 23 June 1864, is not extant. The sketch survives in the only known contemporary reprinting of the *Enterprise,* the San Francisco *Golden Era* 12 (26 June 1864): 3, which is copy-text. Copies: PH from Bancroft and from Yale.

Textual Notes

12.21   MARK TWAIN.] As in the copy-text, which did not, however, reprint the author's normal letter greeting to "EDS. ENTERPRISE." Since the item is nevertheless a letter, we have retained the author's signature.

Emendations of the Copy-Text

10.1	To (I-C) • "To
10.7	Limburger (I-C) • Limberger
10.13	12 (I-C) • I2
10.17	siege (I-C) • seige
11.10	Museum (I-C) • Musenm
11.19	visitor (I-C) • vistor
11.20	lessees (I-C) • leesees
11.27	because, (I-C) • ~[,]
11.30	funny?) (I-C) • ~.∧
11.36	one (I-C) • ono

78. *THE EVIDENCE IN THE CASE OF SMITH* VS. *JONES*

Textual Commentary

The first printing in the San Francisco *Golden Era* 12 (26 June 1864) : 4 is copy-text. Copies: PH from Bancroft and from Yale.

Textual Notes

14.1	REPORTED BY MARK TWAIN.] Although by-lines have in general been silently omitted, these words have been judged a necessary subtitle and retained.
14.9	Shepheard] The copy-text twice misspelled the name of Judge Philip W. Shepheard by omitting the *a*.

Emendations of the Copy-Text

*14.9	Shepheard (I-C) • Shepherd
17.1	red-headed (I-C) • red-|headed
17.2	Limburger (I-C) • Limberger
18.1	*Witness.* (I-C) • ~∧
18.36	in—" (I-C) • ~—∧
19.12	"There (I-C) • ∧~
19.19	can't (I-C) • cant
19.31	slung-shot (I-C) • slung-|shot
19.37	talking (I-C) • talknig
20.4	others swore (I-C) • other swore
20.6	straightforward (I-C) • straight-|forward
*20.11	Shepheard (I-C) • Shepherd
21.8	pronounced. (I-C) • pronounced. MARK TWAIN.

79. *EARLY RISING, AS REGARDS*
EXCURSIONS TO THE CLIFF HOUSE

Textual Commentary

The first printing in the San Francisco *Golden Era* 12 (3 July 1864): 4 is copy-text. Copies: clipping in Scrapbook 3, pp. 159–160, MTP; PH from Bancroft and from Yale. There are no textual notes.

Emendations of the Copy-Text

24.4	it. (I-C) • ~[ʌ]
25.37	before! (I-C) • ~?
26.1	unhandsome (I-C) • undhandsome
26.25	thoroughly (I-C) • thorougly
27.3	programme, (I-C) • ~,"
27.8	ice-bergs (I-C) • ice-|bergs
28.20	bar-keeper (I-C) • bar-|keeper
30.24	sentiment. (I-C) • sentiment. | MARK TWAIN.

80. *ORIGINAL NOVELETTE*

Textual Commentary

The first printing in the San Francisco *Morning Call* for 4 July 1864 (p. 2) is copy-text. Copy: PH from Bancroft. There are no textual notes.

Emendations of the Copy-Text

32.1	drawback (I-C) • draw-|back
32.6	I.—About (I-C) • ~.—|~
32.8	Chapter (I-C) • Chap[ ]er
32.11	III.—These (I-C) • ~.—|~
32.13	arrive. (I-C) • ~ʌ
32.18	V. (I-C) • ~ʌ
32.24	rudder (I-C) • ru[d]der

81. *WHAT A SKY-ROCKET DID*

Textual Commentary

The first printing in the San Francisco *Morning Call* for 12 August 1864 (p. 1) is copy-text. Copy: PH from Bancroft. There are no textual notes.

Emendations of the Copy-Text

36.11   said (I-C) • s[a]id
36.14   substantiated (I-C) • substan[t]iated
36.19   running (I-C) • runring
37.8   smart (I-C) • sm[a]rt

[MARK TWAIN ON THE NEW JOSH HOUSE]

§82. *THE NEW CHINESE TEMPLE*

Textual Commentary

The first printing in the San Francisco *Morning Call* for 19 August 1864
(p. 3) is copy-text. Copies: clipping in Scrapbook 5, p. 41, MTP; PH from
Bancroft. There are no textual notes.

Emendations of the Copy-Text

41.25   candle-supports (I-C) • candle[-]supports

§83. *THE CHINESE TEMPLE*

Textual Commentary

The first printing in the San Francisco *Morning Call* for 21 August 1864
(p. 1) is copy-text. Copies: clipping in Scrapbook 4, p. 7, MTP; PH from
Bancroft. There are no textual notes or emendations.

§84. *THE NEW CHINESE TEMPLE*

Textual Commentary

The first printing in the San Francisco *Morning Call* for 23 August 1864
(p. 3) is copy-text. Copies: clipping in Scrapbook 5, p. 41, MTP; PH from
Bancroft. There are no textual notes.

Emendations of the Copy-Text

45.6   unchristian (I-C) • un-|christian
45.17   halls (I-C) • hal[l]s
45.20   there, (I-C) • ~.
46.4   were (I-C) • we[ ]e

46.12   in the (I-C) • i[n] the
46.19   sing-song (I-C) • sing-|song

§85. *SUPERNATURAL IMPUDENCE*

Textual Commentary

The first printing in the San Francisco *Morning Call* for 24 August 1864 (p. 2) is copy-text. Copy: clipping in Scrapbook 4, p. 7, MTP. Mark Twain quoted Albert S. Evans' article "Opening of a New Temple," San Francisco *Alta California,* 23 August 1864, p. 1 (Alta), near the beginning of his sketch. Either he or the compositor corrected one ambiguity (by supplying a comma after "easy" at 47.7) and made three other changes. We have retained the correction, but emended the other changes by restoring the readings in the first printing of Evans' sketch. There are no textual notes.

Emendations of the Copy-Text

47.8   who (Alta) • ~,
47.9   very young (Alta) • young
47.12   around (Alta) • ~,

86. [*SARROZAY LETTER FROM "THE UNRELIABLE"*]

Textual Commentary

The manuscript of this sketch, probably written sometime between 15 and 22 August 1864, survives in the Jean Webster McKinney Family Papers, Vassar. It is copy-text. The piece is written in brown or black ink on six leaves, each of which measures 11⅝ by 7¼ inches. The first two leaves are unnumbered; the last four are numbered 2–5. The stationery is cream-colored laid paper with thirty-two blue horizontal rules, embossed in the upper left corner with a crown. The paper is identical with that used for two other sketches (also at Vassar), "The Only Reliable Account of the Celebrated Jumping Frog of Calaveras County" (no. 117) and "Angel's Camp Constable" (no. 118), both presumably written in late 1865. Someone, not the author, has written "Oldest Mark Twain signature in existence" on the first manuscript leaf.

 The details of composition and revision evident in the manuscript are recorded below. It should be noted here, however, that the author first signed his *nom de plume* to the drunken letter (53.27), later canceled the signature and substituted "THE UNRELIABLE," and finally added the prefatory letter (51.1–12), which he signed "MARK TWAIN." The first leaf, which is unnumbered, was clearly added after the author had completed the original sketch in five leaves. There are no textual notes.

Emendations of the Copy-Text

51.18	Saffercisco's (I-C) • Saffer-|cisco's
52.17	s—sociating (I-C) • s—cociating
52.3	unstand (I-C) • un-|stand
53.1	sometimes. Everything (I-C) • ~—.|~
53.13	newsper (I-C) • news-|per

Alterations in the Manuscript

51.18	editor] *interlined with a caret.*
51.20	two] *follows 'two' written and canceled twice.*
51.20	Morring] *interlined with a caret above canceled* 'Morning'.
51.21	nev'] *follows canceled* 'never': 'er' *wiped out and* 'nev' *canceled.*
51.22	newsper men] *interlined with a caret above canceled* 're-porters'.
52.1	Georshe,] *interlined with a caret above canceled* 'Jorshe,'.
52.1	(Hic!)] *written over wiped-out* 'Shamed'.
52.4	Warrum] 'W' *written over wiped-out* 'w'.
52.8	scarrered] 'ered' *written over wiped-out* 'ed'.
52.15	don'] *originally* 'don't'; 't' *wiped out.*
52.16	ch(ic!)urch!] *follows canceled* 'church!'.
52.17	drunken] *follows canceled* 'dr—'.
52.17	beasts. Beauriful girls here,] *originally* 'beasts; beauriful girls, here'; *the semicolon altered to a period,* 'beauriful girls, here' *canceled, and* 'Beauriful girls here,' *added.*
52.19	buggies—] *dash mended from a period.*
52.23	lemme] *interlined with a caret above canceled* 'let me'.
52.25	strong.] *interlined with a caret above canceled* 'proper.'
52.26	person] *written over wiped-out* 'steady'.
52.30	Said] *follows canceled* 'Says he, "You suit me! You're—(hic!)—you're a nice boy—nice, clean boy. If you hadn't held her down'.
52.33	on that train.] *follows canceled* 'that day.'
52.38	shot] 'o' *written over* 'i'.
53.2	you] *interlined with a caret.*

53.10	I] *follows canceled* 'it hadn't been for me'.
53.12	s-streets] *interlined with a caret above canceled* 'streets'.
53.12	in] *follows canceled* 'in'.
53.13	I'm sleepy] 'm' *squeezed in.*
53.14	c-cow-catcher] 'c-' *squeezed in.*
53.21	thing] *originally* 'thi-'; 'ng' *written over the wiped-out hyphen.*
53.24	b-bawry] *follows canceled* 'b-ba'.
53.24	d-drake"] *squeezed in following canceled* 'd-dock, d-dog—'.
53.25	beauriful] 'bea' *written over wiped-out* 'bu'.
53.27	THE UNRELIABLE.] *follows canceled* 'Mark Twain'.

87. *INEXPLICABLE NEWS FROM SAN JOSÉ*

Textual Commentary

The first printing in the San Francisco *Morning Call* for 23 August 1864 (p. 1) is copy-text. Copies: clipping in Scrapbook 5, pp. 41–42, MTP; PH from Bancroft. The author's holograph of an earlier version survives (MS); it is published for the first time in this collection as "Sarrozay Letter from 'the Unreliable' " (no. 86). Since Mark Twain copied portions of the earlier version into the present sketch, quoting them as parts of a "letter from an intelligent correspondent, dated 'Sarrozay, (San José?) Last Sunday,' " it is tempting to regard the accidentals of the earlier manuscript as more authoritative than those of the *Call* printing where these coincide. But comparison of the manuscript with the *Call* version shows that Mark Twain extensively rewrote the quoted portions of his original letter, and study of the manuscript shows that even in the earlier version he was tinkering with the accidentals as well as the substantives of his text. Where the accidentals of the *Call* (written within days of the manuscript) vary from the accidentals of the holograph, the difference is therefore as likely to be the result of the author's deliberate choice as of the compositor's changes. The word "sp-sp-sp(ic!)irits" in the *Call*, for example, is just as likely to render Mark Twain's intention as the manuscript reading "sp—sp—sp(ic!)—irits." We have therefore not emended from MS except to resolve doubtful readings in the *Call*. There are no textual notes.

Emendations of the Copy-Text

55.17	turpentine (MS) • turpent[i]ne
55.22	Flag (MS) • F[l]ag

88. *HOW TO CURE HIM OF IT*

Textual Commentary

The first printing in the San Francisco *Morning Call* for 27 August 1864 (p. 3) is copy-text. Copies: clipping in Scrapbook 4, p. 7, MTP; PH from Bancroft. There are no textual notes.

Emendations of the Copy-Text

58.4   subject (I-C) • su[b]ject
58.7   himself (I-C) • h[i]mself

89. *DUE WARNING*

Textual Commentary

The first printing in the San Francisco *Morning Call* for 18 September 1864 (p. 3) is copy-text. Copies: PH from Bancroft and from Yale. There are no textual notes.

Emendations of the Copy-Text

60.6   opportunity (I-C) • oppor[t]unity
60.17   coincidence. (I-C) • ~[∧]
60.18   coincidence (I-C) • coin[   ]idence
60.23   against (I-C) • aga[i]nst

90. *THE MYSTERIOUS CHINAMAN*

Textual Commentary

A photofacsimile of the manuscript of this poem, tipped into a copy of *Memories of Mark Twain and Steve Gillis* (Sonora, Calif.: The Banner, 1924), following p. 82, and now in the Doheny collection (acquisition number 6974), is copy-text. The manuscript itself has not been found. Folds and one ink-blot in the manuscript obscure a few letters, occasioning some emendation. At the top of the manuscript Mark Twain wrote, "(Written for M. E. G.'s Album.)."

Emendations of the Copy-Text

64.8   more." (I-C) • ~.∧
64.14   you" (I-C) • y[   ]u∧ [*fold*]
64.16   Chung (I-C) • Ch[   ]ng [*fold*]
64.16   there (I-C) • th[   ]re [*fold*]
64.17   beguiling (I-C) • begu[   ]ling [*fold*]

64.18	bore (I-C) • bor[ ] [blot]
64 note	imperatively (I-C) • imper[ ]tively [fold]
65.3	ere (I-C) • er[ ] [fold]
65.11	"No (I-C) • ["]No [fold]

Alterations in the Manuscript

64.20	Raven] *originally* 'craven'; 'R' *written over* 'cr'.

91. *A NOTABLE CONUNDRUM*

Textual Commentary

The first printing in the *Californian* 1 (1 October 1864): 9 is copy-text. Copies: Bancroft; PH of the Yale Scrapbook, pp. 29–29A. Since Mark Twain preserved a clipping of the sketch in the Yale Scrapbook, he may have considered reprinting it in JF1. Probably sometime in January or early February 1867, however, he struck through the clipping, and the sketch was not reprinted during his lifetime. There are no textual notes.

Emendations of the Copy-Text

69.13	sur-charged (I-C) • sur-|charged
71.8	was. (I-C) • was. | MARK TWAIN.

92. *CONCERNING THE ANSWER TO THAT CONUNDRUM*

Textual Commentary

The first printing in the *Californian* 1 (8 October 1864): 1 is copy-text. Copies: Bancroft; clipping in Scrapbook 4, pp. 16–17, MTP; PH of the Yale Scrapbook, pp. 31–32. Since Mark Twain preserved a clipping of the *Californian* in the Yale Scrapbook, where he slightly revised it, he must have considered reprinting the sketch in JF1. The revised clipping remains intact in the scrapbook; the sketch was not reprinted in JF1, or during Clemens' lifetime.

Textual Notes

74 title	*the Answer to That*] Mark Twain canceled these words on the Yale Scrapbook clipping (whose title was printed in all capital letters) and substituted "A REMARKABLE," presumably because the original title alluded to the previous *Californian* sketch "A Notable Conundrum" (no. 91), and he had already decided not to reprint that one (see the preceding textual commentary).

74.13   waves] Mark Twain canceled this word and substituted
               "billows" in the Yale Scrapbook. Then, probably noticing
               that his text used the word "billows" a few lines below, he
               canceled his revision and restored the original word by writ-
               ing "stet."

75.5–6   and the old, old story of man's falter and woman's fall,]
               Mark Twain canceled this phrase in the Yale Scrapbook,
               presumably to eliminate the hint of sexual misconduct for
               his new eastern audience.

Emendations of the Copy-Text

78.7   sir.)" (I-C) • ~."）
78.26–27   culture, (I-C) • ~[.]
78.37   Napoleon. (I-C) • Napoleon. MARK TWAIN.

Alterations in the Yale Scrapbook

74 *title*   *the Answer to That*] *canceled;* 'A REMARKABLE' *written*
               in the margin with a line to indicate placement.

74.13   waves] *canceled;* 'billows' *written in the margin and then*
               canceled; 'waves' *restored by* 'stet.' *with a line to indicate*
               placement.

75.5–6   and the . . . fall,] *canceled.*

93. *STILL FURTHER CONCERNING THAT CONUNDRUM*

Textual Commentary

The first printing in the *Californian* 1 (15 October 1864): 1 is copy-text.
Copies: Bancroft; clipping in Scrapbook 4, pp. 17–18, MTP; PH of the Yale
Scrapbook, pp. 30–31. Since Mark Twain preserved a clipping of the
Californian in the Yale Scrapbook (**YSMT**), where he revised it, he must
have considered reprinting the sketch in JF1. The revised clipping remains intact in the scrapbook; the sketch was not reprinted in JF1, or
during Clemens' lifetime.

Textual Notes

83.20   stolidity] Copy-text "solidity" is probably an error. In the
               Yale Scrapbook clipping Mark Twain changed "solidity" to
               "stolidity," and we have adopted his change as a correction
               of the copy-text.

84.37–85.9   I believe . . . lively.] Mark Twain canceled these concluding
               two paragraphs in the Yale Scrapbook clipping, perhaps be-
               cause the first alluded facetiously to his being hired "for
               some years" to write opera criticism, and because the final

paragraph referred to his unanswered conundrum. Since he had evidently decided not to reprint the initial sketch ("A Notable Conundrum," no. 91), he eliminated the reference to it, even though he did not change his title.

85.3   MARK TWAIN.] Although this sketch is not self-evidently a letter to the editor of the *Californian*, the postscript that immediately follows the signature implies that this is the form in Mark Twain's mind, and we have therefore retained his signature as in the copy-text.

Emendations of the Copy-Text

82.34   chieftain's (I-C) • chieftan's
*83.20   stolidity (**YSMT**) • solidity
84.3   evening (I-C) • evenng

Alterations in the Yale Scrapbook

82.13   very] *canceled.*
83.20   stolidity] *corrected from* 'solidity'.
84.37–85.9 I believe . . . lively.] *canceled.*

94. WHEREAS

Textual Commentary

The first printing in the *Californian* 1 (22 October 1864): 1 is copy-text. Copies: Bancroft; clipping in Scrapbook 4, pp. 18–19, MTP; PH of the Yale Scrapbook, pp. 10–12.

Reprintings and Revisions. Mark Twain revised a clipping from the *Californian* in the Yale Scrapbook, where it remains intact. He retitled the sketch "LOVE'S BAKERY. *To which is added the Singular History of Aurelia Maria*" (see figure 94A). He substituted "Plantation Bitters" for "Heuston & Hastings," the name of a San Francisco firm, presumably because the former was more widely known. He corrected an error by inserting "heaven" in the phrase "of heaven itself." He also broke the long summary paragraph (beginning at 91.15) into seven shorter paragraphs; and he inserted "Aurelia" at 93.8. The author's intention in January or February 1867 was evidently to reprint the entire sketch as he had revised it.

JF1, however, reprinted only the second half, omitting the long introductory section about Love's Bakery. The sketch was retitled "Aurelia's Unfortunate Young Man" and incorporated several smaller changes not entered in the scrapbook, as well as Mark Twain's scrapbook alterations: his changes in paragraphing and his insertion of "Aurelia" all appeared in the JF1 printing—strong presumptive evidence that the scrapbook clipping served as printer's copy.

But as we have argued in the textual introduction (volume 1, pp. 526–527), it is still not clear why, if the clipping was indeed printer's copy, it was not removed from the scrapbook. Perhaps the procedure of removing clippings for the printer's convenience was adopted only after "Whereas" and the "Jumping Frog" sketch—the first two items in JF1—were typeset. Or perhaps a duplicate clipping, now lost, was used as printer's copy instead, after the author's revisions had been transferred to it. In any case, "Whereas" was demonstrably edited further after Mark Twain had revised it in the scrapbook—either in proof, or on a duplicate clipping (see the textual note at 91.3–4). On balance, it seems likely that these slight later alterations were made by the editor of JF1, Charles Henry Webb, and that it was also he who decided to shorten the sketch. Nevertheless, the possibility of authorial tinkering cannot be completely ruled out.

The reprinting of the JF1 text is described in the textual introduction. Routledge reprinted JF1 in 1867 (JF2), and Hotten in turn reprinted JF2 in 1870 (JF3); Routledge also reprinted JF2 in 1870 (JF4a) and, using the JF4 plates, reissued the book in 1872 (JF4b). None of these texts was revised by the author, although the compositors of JF2 and JF3 introduced several minor errors and sophistications: "came" for "come" (91.3); "with" for "like" (91.24); and "truly" for "true" (92.31). When Mark Twain prepared the printer's copy for MTSk in March or April 1872, he revised a copy of JF4a, making two changes: "infernal" became "singular" (93.8), and "all right, you know" became "safe" (93.10–11). The compositor introduced one obvious error, making 93.7–8 read "It does not seem to me that there is not much risk"; the error may reflect the author's effort, unclear or misinterpreted, to move "not" from its original position to one just before "much."

One year later (1873) Hotten reprinted the JF3 text in HWa. When Mark Twain revised this book for Chatto and Windus in the fall of 1873 (HWaMT), he made a number of small changes. He corrected an error deriving from JF3, restoring "like" for "with." He deleted "tearful" (92.3) and changed "be" to "have been" (92.11). And instead of changing "infernal" to "singular," as he had done for MTSk, he deleted it. All of the HWaMT changes were incorporated in HWb, published in 1874. HWb also reprinted an error ("This" instead of "That" at 92.25) first introduced by the compositor of HWa.

In 1874 Mark Twain reprinted the sketch in Sk#1, using a copy (now lost) of MTSk as printer's copy. He made no revisions, but he or his compositor did correct the error introduced by the MTSk compositor, reverting to his original reading: "It does not seem to me that there is much risk." In 1875, when Mark Twain came to reprint the sketch in SkNO, he entered the title "Aurelia's Unfortunate Young Man" as item 63 in the Doheny table of contents (see figure 23G in the textual introduction, volume 1, p. 630). The sketch was included in a group, items

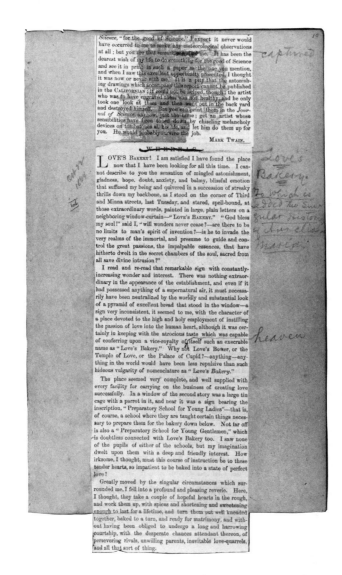

FIGURE 94A. Page 10 of the Yale Scrapbook, which, along with page 12, contains most of the revisions inscribed by Mark Twain. The revisions seen here were not incorporated in JF1. At the top are the final lines of "A Full and Reliable Account" (no. 98): Mark Twain changed "corralled" to "captured."

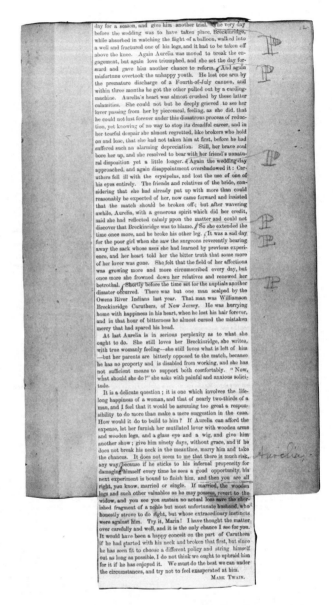

day for a season, and give him another trial. The very day before the wedding was to have taken place, Breckinridge, while absorbed in watching the flight of a balloon, walked into a well and fractured one of his legs, and it had to be taken off above the knee. Again Aurelia was moved to break the engagement, but again love triumphed, and she set the day forward and gave him another chance to reform. And again misfortune overtook the unhappy youth. He lost one arm by the premature discharge of a Fourth-of-July cannon, and within three months he got the other pulled out by a carding-machine. Aurelia's heart was almost crushed by these latter calamities. She could not but be deeply grieved to see her lover passing from her by piecemeal, feeling, as she did, that he could not last forever under this disastrous process of reduction, yet knowing of no way to stop its dreadful career, and in her tearful despair she almost regretted, like brokers who hold on and lose, that she had not taken him at first, before he had suffered such an alarming depreciation. Still, her brave soul bore her up, and she resolved to bear with her friend's unnatural disposition yet a little longer. Again the wedding-day approached, and again disappointment overshadowed it : Caruthers fell ill with the erysipelas, and lost the use of one of his eyes entirely. The friends and relatives of the bride, considering that she had already put up with more than could reasonably be expected of her, now came forward and insisted that the match should be broken off; but after wavering awhile, Aurelia, with a generous spirit which did her credit, said she had reflected calmly upon the matter and could not discover that Breckinridge was to blame. So she extended the time once more, and he broke his other leg. It was a sad day for the poor girl when she saw the surgeons reverently bearing away the sack whose uses she had learned by previous experience, and her heart told her the bitter truth that some more of her lover was gone. She felt that the field of her affections was growing more and more circumscribed every day, but once more she frowned down her relatives and renewed her betrothal. Shortly before the time set for the nuptials another disaster occurred. There was but one man scalped by the Owens River Indians last year. That man was Williamson Breckinridge Caruthers, of New Jersey. He was hurrying home with happiness in his heart, when he lost his hair forever, and in that hour of bitterness he almost cursed the mistaken mercy that had spared his head.

At last Aurelia is in serious perplexity as to what she ought to do. She still loves her Breckinridge, she writes, with true womanly feeling—she still loves what is left of him —but her parents are bitterly opposed to the match, because he has no property and is disabled from working, and she has not sufficient means to support both comfortably. " Now, what should she do ?" she asks with painful and anxious solicitude.

It is a delicate question ; it is one which involves the lifelong happiness of a woman, and that of nearly two-thirds of a man, and I feel that it would be assuming too great a responsibility to do more than make a mere suggestion in the case. How would it do to build to him ? If Aurelia can afford the expense, let her furnish her mutilated lover with wooden arms and wooden legs, and a glass eye and a wig, and give him another show ; give him ninety days, without grace, and if he does not break his neck in the meantime, marry him and take the chances. It does not seem to me that there is much risk, any way, because if he sticks to his infernal propensity for damaging himself every time he sees a good opportunity, his next experiment is bound to finish him, and then you are all right, you know, married or single. If married, the wooden legs and such other valuables as he may possess, revert to the widow, and you see you sustain no actual loss save the cherished fragment of a noble but most unfortunate husband, who honestly strove to do right, but whose extraordinary instincts were against him. Try it, Maria ! I have thought the matter over carefully and well, and it is the only chance I see for you. It would have been a happy conceit on the part of Caruthers if he had started with his neck and broken that first, but since he has seen fit to choose a different policy and string himself out as long as possible, I do not think we ought to upbraid him for it if he has enjoyed it. We must do the best we can under the circumstances, and try not to feel exasperated at him.

MARK TWAIN.

56–63, that we have conjectured the author intended to have typeset from a revised copy of Sk#1, now lost (see volume 1, pp. 634–635). He canceled the sketch in HWb**MT**, and made no revisions of it in MTSk**MT**, the two other sources available to the compositors of SkNO. Unable to find the copy of Sk#1, and discovering that the sketch was canceled in HWb**MT**, they set it from MTSk**MT**. Mark Twain may have read proof on this sketch for SkNO, and either he or the compositors again corrected the MTSk error. But collation shows that SkNO contained a faithful reprint of the MTSk text: there were no further authorial revisions.

Mark Twain had revised the JF1 printing of this sketch well before making most of the revisions discussed above. Sometime in 1869 he made two small revisions in the Doheny copy of the *Jumping Frog*, JF1**MT**, canceling "tearful" and "infernal" (92.3 and 93.8). Although collation shows that JF1**MT** was not used as printer's copy for any known reprinting, the revisions it contains are often strikingly similar, even identical, to those the author made on HWa**MT** and elsewhere.

The diagram of transmission is given below.

Textual Notes

88.24–89.1   vice-royalty of heaven itself] Copy-text "vice-royalty of itself" is an error that makes nonsense of the sentence. We have adopted Mark Twain's correction as inscribed in **YSMT**.

91.3–4   case . . . personally] JF1 altered these words to "following case" and "perfectly." Neither change was inscribed in the scrapbook. The first appears to be an adjustment for the omission of the preceding introductory passage and is here conjecturally attributed to Webb. The second revision may have been Mark Twain's, but only if a duplicate clipping was used as printer's copy. It therefore seems somewhat more likely that the change was made by Webb, in proof.

91.27   trial. The] Here, and at five subsequent points, Mark Twain inserted new paragraph breaks in **YSMT**; these were followed in the JF1 printing. There is a strong possibility that the author was restoring the form of his original manuscript. But in the absence of indubitable evidence that the copy-text is erroneous, we have regarded these changes as revisions made for JF1 and not adopted them here.

Emendations of the Copy-Text

*89.1   heaven (**YSMT**) • [*not in*]
90.4   lady-fingers (I-C) • lady-|fingers
92.37   life-long (I-C) • life-|long
93.23   him. (JF1) • him. | MARK TWAIN.

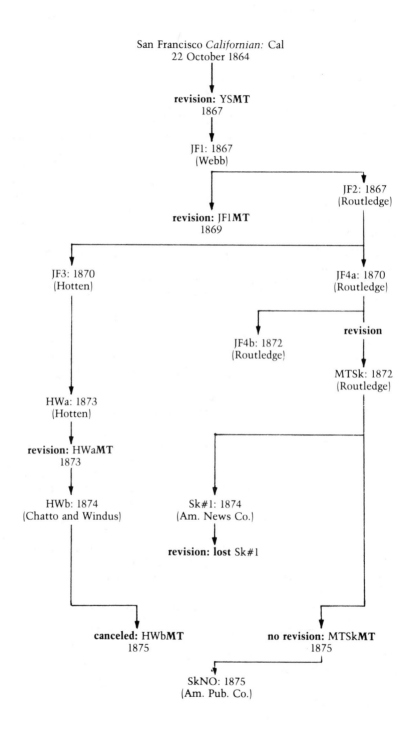

Historical Collation

Texts collated:

Cal "Whereas," *Californian* 1 (22 October 1864): 1.

YSMT Clipping of Cal revised by Mark Twain in the Yale Scrapbook.

    [*"Aurelia's Unfortunate Young Man" in the following*]

JF1 *Jumping Frog* (New York: Webb, 1867), pp. 20–25. Reprints part of Cal with authorial revisions and corrections identical with those in **YSMT**.

JF1**MT** The copy of an 1869 impression of JF1 revised by Mark Twain. The revisions were not reprinted.

JF2 *Jumping Frog* (London: Routledge, 1867), pp. 21–25. Reprints JF1 with few errors.

JF3 *Jumping Frog* (London: Hotten, 1870), pp. 28–31. Reprints JF2 with few errors.

JF4 *Jumping Frog* (London: Routledge, 1870 and 1872), pp. 16–20. Reprints JF2 without substantive error.

MTSk *Mark Twain's Sketches* (London: Routledge, 1872), pp. 239–242. Reprints JF4 with authorial revisions and few errors.

MTSk**MT** Copy of MTSk revised by Mark Twain, who made no changes in this sketch.

HWa *Choice Humorous Works* (London: Hotten, 1873), pp. 388–390. Reprints JF3 with few errors.

HWa**MT** Sheets of HWa revised by Mark Twain, who made four changes in this sketch.

HWb *Choice Humorous Works* (London: Chatto and Windus, 1874), pp. 383–385. Reprints HWa with authorial revisions from HWa**MT**.

HWb**MT** Copy of HWb revised by Mark Twain, who canceled this sketch.

Sk#1 *Mark Twain's Sketches. Number One* (New York: American News Company, 1874), pp. 23–25. Reprints MTSk without authorial revisions.

SkNO *Sketches, New and Old* (Hartford: American Publishing Company, 1875), pp. 253–256. Reprints MTSk**MT** without authorial revisions.

Collation:

88 *title* *Whereas* (Cal) • LOVE'S BAKERY. | *To which is added the Singular History of Aurelia Maria.* (**YSMT**); Aurelia's Unfortunate Young Man (JF1+)

88.1–91.2   Love's ... powerless. (Cal) • [not in] (JF1+)
89.1   heaven (YSMT) • [not in] (Cal)
90.28   Heuston & Hastings' (Cal) • "'Plantation Bitters' " (YSMT)
91.3   case (Cal) • following case (JF1+)
91.3   come (Cal-JF1) • came (JF2+)
91.4   personally (Cal) • perfectly (JF1+)
91.24   like (Cal-Sk#1, Cal-SkNO, HWaMT-HWb) • with (JF3–HWa)
91.27   [no ¶] The (Cal) • [¶] The (YSMT+)
91.33   [no ¶] And (Cal) • [¶] And (YSMT+)
92.3   tearful despair (Cal-Sk#1, Cal-SkNO, Cal-HWa) • despair (JF1MT, HWaMT-HWb)
92.7   [no ¶] Again (Cal) • [¶] Again (YSMT+)
92.11   be (Cal-Sk#1, Cal-SkNO, Cal-HWa) • have been (HWaMT-HWb)
92.16   [no ¶] So (Cal) • [¶] So (YSMT+)
92.17   [no ¶] It (Cal) • [¶] It (YSMT+)
92.23   [no ¶] Shortly (Cal) • [¶] Shortly (YSMT+)
92.25   That (Cal-Sk#1, Cal-SkNO, Cal-JF3) • This (HWa-HWb)
92.31   true (Cal-JF1) • truly (JF2+)
93.8   much (Cal-JF4, Cal-HWb, Sk#1, SkNO) • not much (MTSk)
93.8   way, (Cal) • way, Aurelia, (YSMT+)
93.8–9   infernal propensity (Cal-JF4, Cal-HWa) • singular propensity (MTSk-Sk#1, MTSk-SkNO); propensity (JF1MT, HWaMT-HWb)
93.10–11   all right, you know (Cal-JF4, Cal-HWb) • safe (MTSk-Sk#1, MTSk-SkNO)
93.13–14   fragment (Cal-Sk#1, Cal-SkNO, Cal-HWa) • fragments (HWb)
93.16   Maria! (Cal-JF4, Cal-HWb) • ~. (MTSk-Sk#1, MTSk-SkNO)
93.23   him. (JF1+) • him. | MARK TWAIN. (Cal)

95. *A TOUCHING STORY OF GEORGE WASHINGTON'S BOYHOOD*

Textual Commentary

The first printing in the *Californian* 1 (29 October 1864): 1 is copy-text. Copies: Bancroft; clipping in Scrapbook 4, pp. 20–21, MTP.

Reprintings and Revisions. The sketch was reprinted in JF1, very slightly revised, almost certainly from a clipping of the *Californian.* No trace of such a clipping survives in the Yale Scrapbook, presumably because the sketch was among those removed from the front part of the scrapbook when whole leaves were cut out. Two verbal changes appear in the JF1 printing: the insertion of "in fact," before "I am anxious" at 98.15 and the substitution of "bassoon-sophomore" for "bassoon-sharp" at 96.3. Both changes are consistent with holograph revisions Mark Twain made elsewhere in the Yale Scrapbook, but both could easily have been made by Charles Henry Webb as well.

The reprinting of the JF1 text is described in the textual introduction. Routledge reprinted JF1 in 1867 (JF2), and Hotten in turn reprinted JF2 in 1870 (JF3). Routledge also reprinted JF2 in 1870 (JF4a) and, using the unaltered plates of JF4a, reissued the book in 1872 (JF4b). None of these texts was revised by the author, but the compositors of JF2, JF3, and JF4a made several minor errors and sophistications: "sailed" instead of "sallied" (96.1); "burnt" instead of "burned" (96.2); "he" instead of "the" (96.34); "borders" instead of "boarders" (97.16); "smash" instead of "mash" (97.27); and "me" at 98.29 omitted. When Mark Twain prepared the printer's copy for MTSk in March or April 1872, he revised a copy of JF4a and evidently decided to omit this sketch: it was not reprinted in MTSk.

One year later (1873) Hotten reprinted the JF3 text in HWa, perpetuating two of its errors: "sailed" and "smash" (96.1 and 97.27). When Mark Twain revised this book for Chatto and Windus in the fall of 1873 (HWa**MT**), he made eight changes. He corrected the error deriving from JF2, restoring "sallied" where HWa had "sailed." He substituted "Days of Absence" for "Auld Lang Syne" three times (96.37–38, 97.8, and 97.30–31). He canceled the sentence at 97.37–98.1: "I reflected, though, that if I could only have been allowed to give this latter just one more touch of the variations, he would have finished the old woman." And he made his expression somewhat less strenuous in three cases, canceling "a disgusting and" (96.36), "vilest and" (97.3), and "feeling" (98.7). All of the HWa**MT** changes were incorporated in HWb, published in 1874.

When in 1875 Mark Twain prepared the printer's copy for SkNO, he revised the sketch in HWb**MT**, canceling "under the exquisite torture" (96.1), "dreadful" (96.31), and "devoutly" (98.6) before deciding to cancel the whole sketch. It was not listed in the Doheny table of contents and was not subsequently reprinted.

Mark Twain had revised the JF1 printing of this sketch well before any of the revisions discussed above. Sometime in 1869 he made several alterations in the Doheny copy of the *Jumping Frog,* JF1**MT**; these are typically concerned with removing improprieties: three times he canceled or modified exclamatory references to God (96.32, 98.8, and 98.8), and he made other comparable efforts to give the sketch a less rambunctious tone. Although collation shows that JF1**MT** was never used as printer's copy for any known reprinting, the revisions it contains are often strikingly similar to, even identical with, those Mark Twain made on HWa**MT** and HWb**MT**.

There are no textual notes. The diagram of transmission is given below.

Emendations of the Copy-Text

98.20	door. (JF1) • ~ [ʌ]
99.9	touching. (JF1) • touching. | MARK TWAIN.

Historical Collation

Texts collated:

Cal	"A Touching Story of George Washington's Boyhood," *Californian* 1 (29 October 1864): 1.
JF1	*Jumping Frog* (New York: Webb, 1867), pp. 132–140. Reprints Cal with two possibly authorial revisions.
JF1**MT**	The copy of an 1869 impression of JF1 revised by Mark Twain. The revisions were not reprinted.
JF2	*Jumping Frog* (London: Routledge, 1867), pp. 124–131. Reprints JF1 with few errors.
JF3	*Jumping Frog* (London: Hotten, 1870), pp. 93–97. Reprints JF2 with few errors.
JF4	*Jumping Frog* (London: Routledge, 1870 and 1872), pp. 114–120. Reprints JF2 with few errors.
HWa	*Choice Humorous Works* (London: Hotten, 1873), pp. 544–547. Reprints JF3 with no further errors.
HWa**MT**	Sheets of HWa revised by Mark Twain, who made eight changes in this sketch.
HWb	*Choice Humorous Works* (London: Chatto and Windus, 1874), pp. 518–521. Reprints HWa with authorial revisions from HWa**MT**.
HWb**MT**	Copy of HWb revised by Mark Twain, who revised, then canceled this sketch.

Collation:

96.1	under the exquisite torture (Cal–JF4, Cal–HWb) • [*canceled*] (HWb**MT**)
96.1	sallied (Cal–JF1, HWa**MT**–HWb) • sailed (JF2–JF4, JF2–HWa)
96.2	burned (Cal–HWb) • burnt (JF4)
96.3	bassoon-sharp (Cal) • bassoon-sophomore (JF1+)

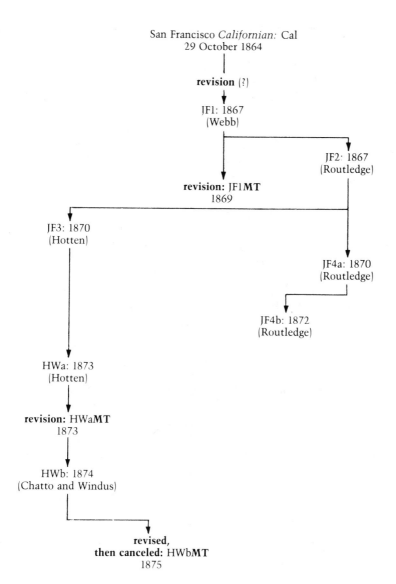

San Francisco *Californian:* Cal
29 October 1864

revision (?)

JF1: 1867
(Webb)

JF2: 1867
(Routledge)

revision: JF1**MT**
1869

JF3: 1870
(Hotten)

JF4a: 1870
(Routledge)

JF4b: 1872
(Routledge)

HWa: 1873
(Hotten)

revision: HWa**MT**
1873

HWb: 1874
(Chatto and Windus)

**revised,
then canceled:** HWb**MT**
1875

96.4   [*no* ¶] I (Cal) • [¶] I (JF1+)

96.19   my (Cal–JF4, Cal–HWb) • the/my (JF1**MT**)

96.25   be (Cal–HWb) • he (JF4)

96.31   dreadful (Cal–JF4, Cal–HWb) • [*canceled*] (JF1**MT**, HWb**MT**)

96.32   God (Cal–JF4, Cal–HWb) • Heaven (JF1**MT**)

96.34   the (Cal–HWb) • he (JF4)

96.36   a disgusting and (Cal–JF4, Cal–HWa) • an (JF1**MT**, HWa**MT**-HWb)

96.37–38   Auld Lang Syne (Cal–JF4, Cal–HWa) • Days of Absence (HWa**MT**-HWb)

97.3   vilest and (Cal–JF4, Cal–HWa) • [*canceled*] (JF1**MT**, HWa**MT**); [*not in*] (HWb)

97.8   Lang Syne (Cal–JF4, Cal–HWa) • Days of Absence (HWa**MT**-HWb)

97.13   desperate (Cal–JF4, Cal–HWb) • [*canceled*] (JF1**MT**)

97.16   boarders (Cal–HWb) • borders (JF4)

97.27   mash (Cal–JF4) • smash (JF3–HWb)

97.30–31   Auld Lang Syne (Cal–JF4, Cal–HWa) • Days of Absence (HWa**MT**-HWb)

97.37–98.1   I . . . woman. (Cal–JF4, Cal–HWa) • [*canceled*] (JF1**MT**, HWa**MT**); [*not in*] (HWb)

98.6   devoutly (Cal–JF4, Cal–HWb) • [*canceled*] (HWb**MT**)

98.7   with feeling unction, and (Cal–JF4, Cal–HWa) • [*canceled*] (JF1**MT**); with unction, and (HWa**MT**-HWb)

98.8   God (Cal–JF4, Cal–HWb) • [*canceled*] (JF1**MT**)

98.8   God (Cal–JF4, Cal–HWb) • [*canceled*] (JF1**MT**)

98.15   die—(Cal) • die—in fact, (JF1+)

98.19   peculiarly (Cal–JF4, Cal–HWb) • [*canceled*] (JF1**MT**)

98.23   the accordeon (Cal–JF4, Cal–HWb) • [*canceled*] (JF1**MT**)

98.29   me (Cal–JF4) • [*not in*] (JF3–HWb)

99.9   touching. (JF1+) • touching. | Mark Twain. (Cal)

96. *DANIEL IN THE LION'S DEN—AND OUT AGAIN ALL RIGHT*

Textual Commentary

The first printing in the *Californian* 1 (5 November 1864): 9 is copy-text. Copies: Bancroft; clipping in Scrapbook 4, pp. 21–22, MTP; PH of the Yale Scrapbook, pp. 2–6. Since Mark Twain preserved a clipping of the

Californian in the Yale Scrapbook, where he slightly revised it, he must have considered reprinting the sketch in JF1. The revised clipping remains intact in the scrapbook; the sketch was not reprinted in JF1, or during Clemens' lifetime. There are no textual notes.

Emendations of the Copy-Text

101.23	it (I-C) • [*not in*]
102.5	think (I-C) • tnink
102.14	semi-circular (I-C) • semi-|circular
103.36–37	thirty, . . . payment,)' (I-C) • ~,' . . . ~,)∧
105.6	"Silence (I-C) • ∧~
106.38	cross-counter (I-C) • cross-|counter
107.23	there!" (I-C) • there!" MARK TWAIN.

Alterations in the Yale Scrapbook

105.13	Slushbuster] *altered to* 'Blucher'.
105.14	Hogwash] *altered to* 'Muggins'.
107.16	Paradise] *altered to* 'the New Jerusalem'.
107.21	Humph!] *canceled.*
107.22	heaven,] *altered to* 'Paradise, maybe,'.

97. THE KILLING OF JULIUS CAESAR "LOCALIZED"

Textual Commentary

The first printing in the *Californian* 1 (12 November 1864): 1 is copy-text. Copies: Bancroft; clipping in Scrapbook 4, pp. 23–24, MTP.

Reprintings and Revisions. The sketch was reprinted in JF1, very slightly altered, almost certainly from a clipping of the *Californian.* No trace of such a clipping survives in the Yale Scrapbook, presumably because the sketch was among those removed from the front part of the scrapbook when whole leaves were cut out. None of the changes—"and" omitted (110.2); "Oh!" instead of "O," (111.2); "did not" instead of "didn't" (111.11); "are" instead of "were" (112.27); the addition of "to" (112.34)—is convincingly authorial. The change from "and" to "&" (112.24) may be authorial, while the substitution of "an't" for "ain't" (111.2) is demonstrably not authorial (see the textual note). All of the changes in JF1 are, therefore, here attributed to Charles Henry Webb.

The reprinting of the JF1 text is described in the textual introduction. Routledge reprinted JF1 in 1867 (JF2), and Hotten in turn reprinted JF2 in 1870 (JF3). Routledge also reprinted JF2 in 1870 (JF4a) and, using the unaltered plates of JF4a, reissued the book in 1872 (JF4b). None of these texts was revised by the author, although the compositors of JF2, JF3, and

JF4a made several small errors: "aggravating" instead of "aggravated" (110.7); "in" omitted (111.16); *"Faces"* instead of *"Fasces"* (111.18); "Cimba" instead of "Cimber" (114.9); and "Police!" instead of "Po-LICE!" (114.21–22). When Mark Twain prepared the printer's copy for MTSk in March or April 1872, he revised a copy of JF4a and evidently made one large deletion at the end of the first paragraph (110.22–111.6), containing his supposed words to the dying Caesar. Collation suggests that he also corrected two errors (*"Faces"* and "Police!") introduced by the JF4a compositor, and it may have been he who altered "sprang" to "sprung" (114.5).

One year later (1873) Hotten reprinted the JF3 text in HWa. His compositors made two small errors: "button-holding" instead of "button-holing" (110.21) and "persual" instead of "perusal" (112.30). When Mark Twain revised this book for Chatto and Windus in the fall of 1873 (HWaMT), he made three changes. He deleted "sneaking" (113.31) and changed "d—d" to "hanged" (114.2). And he again deleted his supposed words to the dying Caesar, this time wholly removing the last two sentences of the first paragraph, as well as the subsequent paragraph about the technique of "localizing" (110.19–111.14). The error "button-holding" was removed with this deletion; the error "Cimba" introduced by JF3 persisted, as did the error "persual." All of the HWaMT changes were incorporated in HWb, published in 1874.

When in 1875 Mark Twain came to reprint the sketch in SkNO, he entered the title "The Killing of Julius Caesar Localized" as item 24 in the Doheny table of contents (see figure 23C in the textual introduction, volume 1, p. 626). He did not revise the sketch in either HWbMT or MTSkMT, the two sources available to the compositors of SkNO. Since he did not cancel it in HWbMT, the presumption must be that he intended the compositors to use this text, which they did. Collation shows that SkNO contained a faithful reprinting of the HWb text, correcting two errors ("Cimba" and "persual") introduced by JF3 and HWa, but containing no further revisions by Mark Twain.

The diagram of transmission is given below.

Textual Notes

111.2   ain't] The JF1 compositor (or editor) altered this word to "an't," an error that appeared also in the JF1 reprinting of "Jim Smiley and His Jumping Frog" (no. 119). Since Clemens demonstrably restored his original spelling of "ain't" in the later sketch, it is unlikely that he authorized this JF1 change, even though it persisted in all subsequent reprintings.

112.24   Demosthenes and Thucydides'] JF1 corrected the transposed letters in the copy-text error "Thucidýdes' " but it also

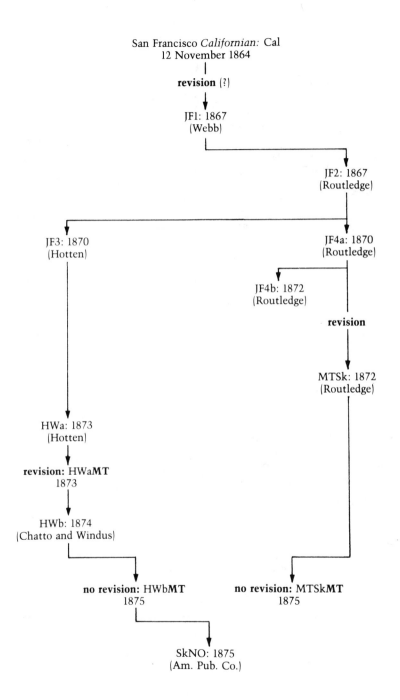

San Francisco *Californian:* Cal
12 November 1864

revision (?)

JF1: 1867
(Webb)

JF2: 1867
(Routledge)

JF3: 1870
(Hotten)

JF4a: 1870
(Routledge)

JF4b: 1872
(Routledge)

revision

MTSk: 1872
(Routledge)

HWa: 1873
(Hotten)

revision: HWaMT
1873

HWb: 1874
(Chatto and Windus)

no revision: HWbMT
1875

no revision: MTSkMT
1875

SkNO: 1875
(Am. Pub. Co.)

added an *s* after the apostrophe and changed "and" to "&," presumably because the ampersand was appropriate for the name of a business. Although it is tempting to regard these refinements as Mark Twain's corrections of the copy-text, we lack the holograph evidence that would make this certain. We have, therefore, adopted only the spelling correction. The added *s* and the ampersand may be the author's correction or revision, or they may wholly lack his authority.

114.21–22   PO-LICE! PO-LICE!] The JF4a compositor omitted the hyphens, thereby losing some of the oral validity of the words as printed in the copy-text. The MTSk text was set from a revised copy of JF4a, and it restored the hyphens. Since it is unlikely that the MTSk compositor volunteered such a revision, it seems reasonable to suppose that Mark Twain corrected the printer's copy.

Emendations of the Copy-Text

110.4   OCCURRENCE.] (I-C) • ~.∧
111.30   Mr. (JF1) • M.r
*112.24   Thucydides' (I-C) • Thucydydes'
112.34   to (JF1) • [*not in*]
113.6   Popilius (I-C) • Papilius
113.27   Decius, (I-C) • ~∧
114.2   stay (JF1) • st[a]y
114.28   Ligarius (I-C) • Legarius
114.31   overpowered (JF1) • over-|powered
115.14   accordingly. (JF1) • accordingly. MARK TWAIN.

Historical Collation

Texts collated:

Cal   "The Killing of Julius Cæsar 'Localized,' " *Californian* 1 (12 November 1864): 1.

JF1   *Jumping Frog* (New York: Webb, 1867), pp. 94–109. Reprints Cal without demonstrably authorial revision.

JF2   *Jumping Frog* (London: Routledge, 1867), pp. 92–101. Reprints JF1 with few errors.

JF3   *Jumping Frog* (London: Hotten, 1870), pp. 75–81. Reprints JF2 without further error.

JF4   *Jumping Frog* (London: Routledge, 1870 and 1872), pp. 85–93. Reprints JF2 with few errors.

MTSk   *Mark Twain's Sketches* (London: Routledge, 1872), pp. 264-271. Reprints JF4 with authorial revisions.

MTSk**MT**   Copy of MTSk revised by Mark Twain, who made no changes in this sketch.

HWa   *Choice Humorous Works* (London: Hotten, 1873), pp. 509-513. Reprints JF3 with few errors.

HWa**MT**   Sheets of HWa revised by Mark Twain, who made three changes in this sketch.

HWb   *Choice Humorous Works* (London: Chatto and Windus, 1874), pp. 488-491. Reprints HWa with authorial revisions from HWa**MT**.

HWb**MT**   Copy of HWb revised by Mark Twain, who made no changes in this sketch.

SkNO   *Sketches, New and Old* (Hartford: American Publishing Company, 1875), pp. 162-166. Reprints HWb**MT** without authorial revisions.

Collation:

110.2   AND TAKEN (Cal) • taken (JF1+)

110.7   aggravated (Cal) • aggravating (JF2+)

110.19-22   In . . . note-book; (Cal-MTSk, Cal-HWa) • [*canceled*] (HWa**MT**); [*not in*] (HWb-SkNO)

110.21   button-holing (Cal–MTSk, Cal–JF3) • button-holding (HWa)

110.22-   and . . . hounds! (Cal-JF4, Cal-HWa) • [*not in*] (MTSk);
111.6   [*canceled*] (HWa**MT**); [*not in*] (HWb-SkNO)

111.2   O, (Cal) • Oh! (JF1-JF4, JF1-HWa)

111.2   ain't (Cal) • an't (JF1-JF4, JF1-HWa)

111.7-14   Ah! . . . thing. (Cal–MTSk, Cal–HWa) • [*canceled*] (HWa**MT**); [*not in*] (HWb-SkNO)

111.11   didn't (Cal) • did not (JF1-MTSk, JF1-HWa)

111.16   in (Cal-SkNO) • [*not in*] (JF4-MTSk)

111.18   *Fasces* (Cal-SkNO, MTSk) • *Faces* (JF4)

112.24   and (Cal, JF2+) • & (JF1)

112.27   were (Cal) • are (JF1+)

112.30   perusal (Cal–MTSk, Cal–JF3, SkNO) • persual (HWa-HWb)

112.34   to (JF1+) • [*not in*] (Cal)

113.31   fawning, sneaking (Cal–MTSk, Cal–HWa) • fawning (HWa**MT**-SkNO)

114.2   d—d (Cal–MTSk, Cal–HWa) • hanged (HWa**MT**–SkNO)
114.5   sprang (Cal–JF4, Cal–SkNO) • sprung (MTSk)
114.9   Cimber (Cal–MTSk, SkNO) • Cimba (JF3–HWb)
114.21-22   Po·lice! Po·lice! (Cal–SkNO, MTSk) • Police! Police! (JF4)
115.14   accordingly. (JF1+) • accordingly. Mark Twain. (Cal)

98. *A FULL AND RELIABLE ACCOUNT OF THE EXTRAORDINARY METEORIC SHOWER OF LAST SATURDAY NIGHT*

Textual Commentary

The first printing in the *Californian* 1 (19 November 1864): 9 (Cal) is copy-text for everything but the telegram from Benjamin Silliman quoted in the first paragraph. Collation shows that the Cal printer's copy for this telegram was probably a clipping of a newspaper article, "The Periodic Shower of Meteors," San Francisco *Morning Call*, 11 November 1864, p. 1 (MC), which is copy-text from 118.3 through 118.13. One change that Mark Twain probably made in the telegram text ("from" added at 118.6) is introduced into the present text as a needed emendation from Cal. Copies: PH from Bancroft (MC); clipping in Scrapbook 4, pp. 24–25, MTP (Cal); PH of the Yale Scrapbook, pp. 6–10 (Cal).

Silliman's telegram also appeared in "Meteoric Showers," San Francisco *Alta California*, 11 November 1864 (p. 1), and in "Star-Gazers, Be Watchful!" San Francisco *Evening Bulletin*, 11 November 1864 (p. 3). Since all three printings (*Alta, Bulletin,* and *Call*) radiate independently from the original telegram, it is possible to reconstruct a slightly more accurate text of it than appeared in any of the newspapers. But since this hypothetical reconstruction varies from MC in only trivial ways, we have not used such a reconstruction here. We bear in mind Mark Twain's example of the "learned German who has devoted half his valuable life to determining what materials a butterfly's wing is made of, and to writing unstinted books upon the subject" (122.1–4). The historical collation records the substantive variants between Cal and MC.

Since Mark Twain preserved a clipping of the *Californian* in the Yale Scrapbook, where he slightly revised it, he must have considered reprinting the sketch in JF1. Probably sometime in mid-February 1867 he listed it as "Dream of Stars" in the back of the scrapbook, along with six other sketches that did not "run average" (see the textual introduction, volume 1, pp. 538–539). The revised clipping remains intact in the scrapbook, perhaps because of its length, perhaps because the editor saw no easy way to adapt the humor of intoxication to an eastern audience. The sketch was not reprinted in JF1, or during Clemens' lifetime.

Textual Notes

118.11   American Journal of Science] Cal prints this title, here and
          at 118.18, 120.13, 122.30–31, 124.1, and 124.13, in italic type.
          It is possible that Clemens italicized the title in the clipping
          which here served as his printer's copy, but it seems more
          likely that the consistent styling was imposed, at least in
          this case, by the compositor.

118.12   for the good of science] Although Mark Twain later quotes
          this phrase as "for the good of Science" (124.2), using a
          mock-honorific capital letter, we have not emended in
          either case, since the slight distortion of Silliman's telegram
          may be intentional.

Emendations of the Copy-Text

[Copy-text from 118.3 through 118.13 is MC]

118.6   from (Cal) • [*not in*]

          [Copy-text from 118.14 through 124.17 is Cal]

118.23   Clicquot (I-C) • Cliquot
119.3   telescopic (I-C) • telescop[i]c
121.33   conceive (I-C) • conceiv[e]

Historical Collation

Texts collated: Cal and MC (see the commentary above).

Collation:

118.6   from (Cal) • [*not in*] (MC)
118.8   in (MC) • [*not in*] (Cal)

Alterations in the Yale Scrapbook

120.25   says] *altered to* 'said'.
120.25–26 her . . . her] *altered to* 'it . . . it'.
122.34   tackle] *altered to* 'take to'.
122.35–38 You . . . it.] *canceled.*
124.4   corralled] *altered to* 'captured'.

99. LUCRETIA SMITH'S SOLDIER

Textual Commentary

The first printing in the *Californian* 2 (3 December 1864): 9 is copy-text.
Copies: Bancroft; PH from Yale.

Reprintings and Revisions. The sketch was reprinted in JF1, probably from an edited clipping of the *Californian*. Such a clipping might have been removed from the front part of the Yale Scrapbook when whole leaves were cut out, in which case variants in JF1 would almost certainly reflect revisions made by Mark Twain in the scrapbook. But no trace of such a clipping or of Mark Twain's revisions (assuming he made some) now survives in the scrapbook, and any argument for authorial revision in JF1 must rest heavily on the evidence of collation. Among half a dozen minor variants introduced by JF1, only one may be plausibly attributed to the author: the moderating change to "weeks" instead of "weeks and weeks" (131.24) is characteristic, even though it could easily be the result of compositorial oversight instead. Most of these minor variants are clearly not characteristic, however, and must be attributed to the compositor or the editor of JF1: "own" for "old" (129.16); "next" for "the next" (130.27); "fife" for "a fife" (130.27-28); "surgeon" for "surgeons" (132.10); and "fluttering" for "a fluttering" (132.24), as well as several changes in emphasis (italics and exclamation points). On the other hand, JF1 did introduce some slightly more substantial changes that are plausibly authorial. All of these cluster in the opening paragraph, which JF1 changed from a "NOTE FROM THE AUTHOR" addressed to *"Mr. Editor"* into a briefer and less topical introduction. Mark Twain's reference to "stories in *Harper's Weekly*" became the more general "stories which have lately been so popular" (128.2); his telltale reference to a story "which I now forward to you for publication" became the noncommital "which is now completed" (128.4); his allusion to "the Hon. T. G. Phelps, who has so long and ably represented this State in Congress" (128.7-9) was omitted; the statement that "I should make honorable mention of the obliging publishing firms Roman & Co. and Bancroft & Co., of this city, who loaned" him several books was shortened to say simply "I should confess that I have drawn largely on" those books (128.9-11). Finally, Mark Twain's allusion to the "inspiration" he had drawn from the "excellent beer" supplied by a local brewery (128.16-20) was also omitted, perhaps in the interest of decorum. These changes conform to a pattern of revision repeated throughout the sketches included in JF1, and all or part of them may well have been instituted by Mark Twain on the clipping presumably drawn from the Yale Scrapbook. But Charles Henry Webb, following the example of Mark Twain's revisions elsewhere in the scrapbook, could easily have supplied these changes for the author—and if he did so, it would help to account for their somewhat neutral and colorless character. In the absence of concrete holographic evidence, and especially in the absence of distinctively authorial revisions, it is necessary to treat all of the JF1 variants as editorial in origin.

Whether or not Mark Twain revised the text for JF1, all but one of its variants were perpetuated in subsequent reprintings. The reprinting of the JF1 text is described in the textual introduction. Routledge reprinted JF1 in 1867 (JF2), and Hotten in turn reprinted JF2 in 1870 (JF3). Routledge also reprinted JF2 in 1870 (JF4a) and, using the unaltered plates of JF4a, reissued the book in 1872 (JF4b). None of these texts was revised by Mark Twain, although the compositor of JF2 made a number of errors and sophistications that were incorporated in JF3 and JF4a: "of" instead of "at" (128.6); "and" instead of "&" (129.5); "his name to" omitted (130.19). When Mark Twain prepared the printer's copy for MTSk in March or April 1872, he presumably revised a copy of JF4a, making two deletions: he omitted Lucretia's internal monologue (" 'Drat it!' The words were in her bosom, but she locked them there, and closed her lips against their utterance" at 131.22–23); and he removed "and slobbering" from a later speech (133.1). Either he or the compositor corrected one variant introduced by JF1, restoring the indefinite article before "fife" (130.27–28), and altered "upon" to "up on" (130.28). And Mark Twain probably corrected an error deriving from the original *Californian* printing, restoring "trail" where all previous texts had "tail" in the phrase quoted from *Lalla Rookh*, "the trail of the serpent is over us all" (133.7)—a correction adopted in the present text.

One year later (1873) Hotten reprinted the JF3 text in HWa. His compositors made many minor changes in punctuation, but only one substantive change (also minor): "an" instead of "a" at 132.4. When Mark Twain revised this book for Chatto and Windus in the fall of 1873 (HWaMT), he duplicated some of the changes he presumably made one year earlier for MTSk: he again deleted Lucretia's slang monologue and the reference to "slobbering" (131.22–23 and 133.1), but he did not repeat his earlier correction of "tail" to "trail," nor the minor corrections made by him or the MTSk compositor at 130.27–28 and 130.28. All of the HWaMT changes were made in the HWa plates and incorporated in HWb, published in 1874.

When in 1875 Mark Twain came to reprint the sketch in SkNO, he entered the title "Lucretia Smith's Soldier" as item 49 in the Doheny table of contents (see figure 23F in the textual introduction, volume 1, p. 629). He marked this entry, as he marked four others (items 12, 20, 52, and 67), with a circled cross, perhaps to indicate only tentative approval. He did not revise the sketch in either HWbMT or MTSkMT, the two sources available to the compositors of SkNO. Since he did not cancel it in HWbMT, the presumption must be that he intended the compositors to use that text. They, however, entered the page number (196S) to indicate that they had found it listed on page 196 in the table of contents for MTSkMT. At some point, however, Mark Twain or Elisha Bliss decided not to include the sketch in SkNO: Bliss has written on the Doheny table of contents, "(Not set)."

The diagram of transmission is as follows:

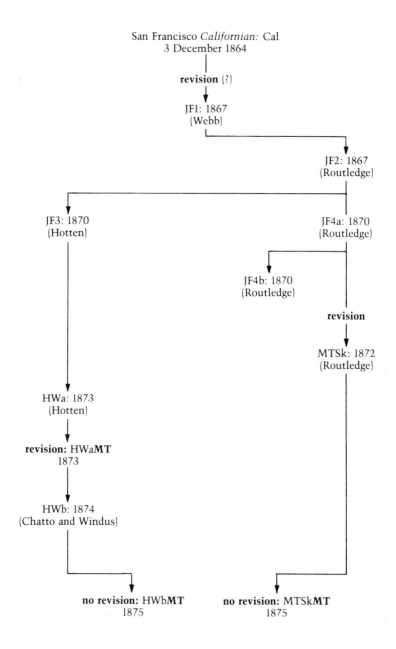

San Francisco *Californian:* Cal
3 December 1864

revision (?)

JF1: 1867
(Webb)

JF2: 1867
(Routledge)

JF3: 1870
(Hotten)

JF4a: 1870
(Routledge)

JF4b: 1870
(Routledge)

revision

MTSk: 1872
(Routledge)

HWa: 1873
(Hotten)

revision: HWa**MT**
1873

HWb: 1874
(Chatto and Windus)

no revision: HWb**MT**
1875

no revision: MTSk**MT**
1875

Textual Notes

133.7   trail of the serpent] The copy-text and all subsequent re-
            printings except MTSk give "tail of the serpent." But since
            Mark Twain's allusion is clear (see the headnote to this
            sketch), and since he may well have corrected the error in
            preparing the printer's copy for MTSk, we have adopted the
            MTSk reading as a necessary correction of the copy-text.

Emendations of the Copy-Text

128.10   Bancroft (I-C) • of Bancroft
128.15   returning (JF1) • returnlng
128.19   manufactured (I-C) • mauufactured
128.20   Kearny (I-C) • Kearney
128.26   M. (I-C) • ~,
129.6   Post-office (I-C) • Post-|office
129.33   his (JF1) • hls
130.31   "Oh (JF1) • '~
132.34   crash (JF1) • orash
132.34   again (JF1) • agaln
*133.7   trail (MTSk) • tail
133.10   yet. (JF1) • yet. | MARK TWAIN.

Historical Collation

Texts collated:

Cal   "Lucretia Smith's Soldier," *Californian* 2 (3 December
            1864): 9.
JF1   *Jumping Frog* (New York: Webb, 1867), pp. 89–98. Prints an
            edited Cal without demonstrable revision by Mark Twain.
JF2   *Jumping Frog* (London: Routledge, 1867), pp. 82–91. Re-
            prints JF1 with few errors.
JF3   *Jumping Frog* (London: Hotten, 1870), pp. 84–89. Reprints
            JF2 without further error.
JF4   *Jumping Frog* (London: Routledge, 1870 and 1872), pp.
            76–84. Reprints JF2 without further error.
MTSk   *Mark Twain's Sketches* (London: Routledge, 1872), pp.
            196–203. Reprints JF4 with Mark Twain's revisions.
MTSk**MT** Copy of MTSk revised by Mark Twain, who made no
            changes in this sketch.
HWa   *Choice Humorous Works* (London: Hotten, 1873), pp. 532–
            535. Reprints JF3 with few errors.

HWaMT   Sheets of HWa revised by Mark Twain, who made two
               changes in this sketch.

HWb   *Choice Humorous Works* (London: Chatto and Windus,
               1874), pp. 506–509. Reprints HWa with authorial revisions
               from HWaMT.

HWbMT   Copy of HWb revised by Mark Twain, who made no changes
               in this sketch.

Collation:

128.1   [NOTE . . . *Editor:* (Cal) • *[not in]* (JF1+)

128.2   in . . . *Weekly* (Cal) • which have lately been so popular
               (JF1+)

128.4   I . . . publication (Cal) • is now completed (JF1+)

128.6   at (Cal–JF1) • of (JF2+)

128.7–9   The . . . Congress. (Cal) • *[not in]* (JF1+)

128.9–11   make . . . me (Cal) • confess that I have drawn largely on
               (JF1+)

128.16–20   The . . . Kearny. (I-C) • *[not in]* (JF1+); The . . . Kearney.
               (Cal)

128.26   M. T. (I-C) • *[not in]* (JF1+); M, T. (Cal)

129.5   & (Cal–JF1) • and (JF2+)

129.16   old (Cal) • own (JF1+)

130.7   Lucretia, (Cal) • ~! (JF1+)

130.14   arms! (Cal) • ~. (JF1+)

130.19   his name to (Cal–JF1) • *[not in]* (JF2+)

130.27   the next (Cal) • next (JF1+)

130.27–28   a fife (Cal, MTSk) • fife (JF1–JF4, JF1–HWb)

130.28   upon (Cal–JF4, Cal–HWb) • up on (MTSk)

130.31   Oh, (Cal) • ~! (JF1+)

131.22–23   life. "Drat . . . utterance. (Cal–JF4, Cal–HWa) • life. (MTSk,
               HWaMT–HWb)

131.24   and weeks (Cal) • *[not in]* (JF1+)

132.1–2   R. D. . . . wounded! (Cal) • *R. D. Whittaker, private soldier,*
               desperately wounded! (JF1+)

132.4   a hospital (Cal–MTSk, Cal–JF3) • an hospital (HWa–HWb)

132.10   surgeons (Cal) • surgeon (JF1+)

132.24   a fluttering (Cal) • fluttering (JF1+)

132.29   here! . . . matter! Alas! (Cal–MTSk) • ~? . . . ~? ~. (JF3);
               ~? . . . ~? ~! (HWa–HWb)

132.36   O (Cal) • Oh! (JF1+)

133.1	snuffling and slobbering (Cal–JF4, Cal–HWa) • snuffling (MTSk, HWa**MT**–HWb)
133.6	Smith. (Cal–MTSk, Cal–JF3) • ~! (HWa–HWb)
133.7	trail (MTSk) • tail (Cal–JF4, Cal–HWb)
133.10	yet. (JF1+) • yet. | Mark Twain.

100. *AN UNBIASED CRITICISM*

Textual Commentary

The first printing in the *Californian* 2 (18 March 1865): 8–9 is copy-text. Copies: Bancroft; PH from Yale; PH of the Yale Scrapbook, pp. 17–18.

Reprintings and Revisions. Only a part of this sketch, retitled "Literature in the Dry Diggings," was reprinted in JF1: the section about Coon and his "mighty responsible old Webster-Unabridged." The printer's copy for the JF1 printing was drawn from the Yale Scrapbook, where Mark Twain revised a clipping of the *Californian* printing. Only the portion not reprinted in JF1 (from "but" at 138.36 to the end) survives in the scrapbook; it is preceded by three page stubs, indicating that the scrapbook pages that once held the preceding portion of the clipping were scissored out to serve as the printer's copy. Mark Twain demonstrably revised that portion of the scrapbook clipping which remains intact, substituting "fearful" for "rough" (141.22), deleting "which is the richest in the world at the present time, perhaps" (142.11–12), and correcting one typographical error, at 143.7. This evidence suggests that at least some of the variants in the JF1 printing reflect changes Mark Twain made on the now lost printer's copy: only he would be likely to change "Jackass" to "Jackass Gulch" (138.9), and it was probably he who deleted the exclamation "by G—d" (138.9) and substituted "cuss" for "d—n" (138.19). Nevertheless, some changes can more plausibly be attributed to the compositor: the transposition of "ever I" from "I ever" (138.7) and the omission of "me" from "understand me" (138.18). The revised scrapbook clipping suggests that the author's intention in January or February 1867 was to reprint the entire sketch. The decision to include only a small portion of it in JF1 was therefore probably made by Charles Henry Webb, who was then obliged to make some further adjustments in order to isolate the section about Coon and his dictionary. Webb presumably deleted the introductory portion (137.1–12), gave the sketch its new title, and supplied a revised version of the first sentence in the third paragraph: "Although a resident of San Francisco, I never heard much about the 'Art Union Association' of that city until I got hold of some old newspapers during my three months' stay in the Big Tree region of Calaveras county." Although it is conceivable that the author made these revisions, or helped Webb make them, one circumstance strongly implies that Webb acted more or less independently. When Mark Twain revised the text of

"Literature in the Dry Diggings" in HWa**MT** (1873), he deleted this revised sentence—perhaps because he recognized it as not wholly authentic. In any case, the JF1 text contains variants that are almost certainly
Mark Twain's work, as well as some that must be attributed to his editor
and to his compositor.

The reprinting of the JF1 text is described in the textual introduction.
Routledge reprinted JF1 in 1867 (JF2), and Hotten in turn reprinted JF2 in
1870 (JF3). Routledge also reprinted JF2 in 1870 (JF4a) and, using the
unaltered plates of JF4a, reissued the book in 1872 (JF4b). Although none
of these texts was revised by the author, a number of minor errors were
introduced by the compositors of JF3 and JF4a: for example, "We'll"
instead of "Well" (138.4), "Sam" instead of "San" (138.9), and an added
comma after "all-firedest" (138.26). When Mark Twain prepared the
printer's copy for MTSk in March or April 1872, he presumably marked a
copy of JF4a. Collation suggests that he made no revisions in this sketch,
but may have corrected some of the obvious errors introduced by the JF4a
compositor. Even so, the MTSk compositor made four additional errors,
such as "well well" for "well" (138.19), "loose" for "lose" (138.21), and, as
in JF3, an added comma after "all-firedest."

One year later (1873) Hotten reprinted the JF3 text in HWa. When Mark
Twain revised this book for Chatto and Windus in the fall of 1873
(HWa**MT**), he canceled the sentence first introduced in JF1 (discussed
above) and deleted the comma that had been supplied after "all-firedest."
The HWa**MT** changes were made in the plates of HWa and were incorporated in HWb, which was published in 1874 and made no further errors or
sophistications.

When in 1875 Mark Twain prepared the printer's copy for SkNO, he
canceled this sketch in HWb**MT** and indicated, by canceling the entry
"Literature in the Dry Diggings" in the table of contents for MTSk**MT**,
that he did not intend to reprint it (see figure 24 in the textual introduction, volume 1, p. 638). He did not list the sketch in the Doheny table of
contents, and he did not subsequently reprint it.

The diagram of transmission is given below.

Textual Notes

138.2   Angel's] The copy-text reading "Angels'" here and at
             139.15, 142.15, and 142.19 has been emended to the correct
             spelling, "Angel's." In his notebooks and manuscripts for
             this period, Mark Twain spelled the name correctly about
             one third of the time, dividing the remaining two-thirds
             between "Angels" and "Angels'" (*N&J1*, pp. 70–72, 76, 77,
             81, 82; "Angel's Camp Constable," no. 118).

138.26   all-firedest dryest] The MTSk and the JF3 compositor independently supplied a comma after "firedest." Although
             Mark Twain rarely corrected punctuation when he revised,

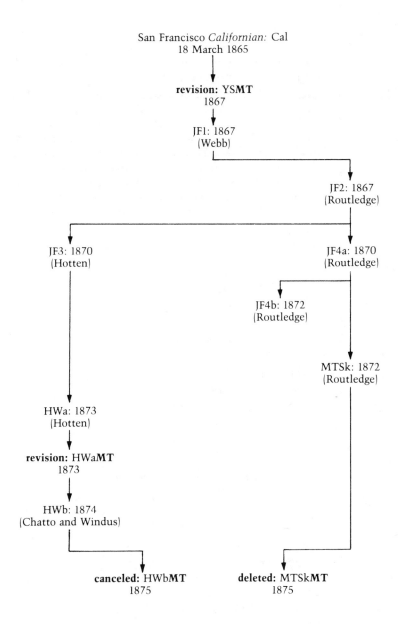

San Francisco *Californian:* Cal
18 March 1865

revision: YSMT
1867

JF1: 1867
(Webb)

JF2: 1867
(Routledge)

JF3: 1870
(Hotten)

JF4a: 1870
(Routledge)

JF4b: 1872
(Routledge)

MTSk: 1872
(Routledge)

HWa: 1873
(Hotten)

revision: HWaMT
1873

HWb: 1874
(Chatto and Windus)

canceled: HWbMT
1875

deleted: MTSkMT
1875

he did delete this comma in HWa**MT** (which derived from
JF3), for in addition to altering the rhythm of Coon's speech,
the comma changed his meaning by removing "all-firedest"
from its modifying control of "dryest."

138.36   but] The clipping that survives in the Yale Scrapbook begins
with this word and continues to the end of the sketch. Part
of the final three paragraphs was rendered illegible when a
clipping of "Answers to Correspondents" (no. 107), which
had been pasted to the other side of the page, was peeled and
partly cut away from the scrapbook page. Although the sequence of events remains uncertain, it is conceivable that
the damaged clipping contributed to Webb's decision to reprint only the first part of "A Unbiased Criticism."

Emendations of the Copy-Text

*138.2   Angel's (I-C) • Angels'
138.2   Camp. (I-C) • ~,
*139.15   Angel's (I-C) • Angels'
139.22   *Burglar* (I-C) • *Burlar*
140.2   *Party'* (I-C) • ~∧
140.33   handbills (I-C) • hand-|bills
*142.15   Angel's (I-C) • Angels'
*142.19   Angel's, (I-C) • Angels,'
143.7   mother (**YSMT**) • tmoher
143.33   drink." (I-C) • drink." | Mark Twain.

Historical Collation

Texts collated:

Cal   "An Unbiased Criticism," *Californian* 2 (18 March 1865):
8–9.

YSMT   Clipping of Cal, from "but" (138.36) to the end, revised by
Mark Twain in the Yale Scrapbook.

              [*"Literature in the Dry Diggings" in the following*]

JF1   *Jumping Frog* (New York: Webb, 1867), pp. 82–84. Reprints
the part of Cal not now in the Yale Scrapbook with authorial and editorial revisions.

JF2   *Jumping Frog* (London: Routledge, 1867), pp. 76–78. Reprints JF1 without substantive error.

JF3   *Jumping Frog* (London: Hotten, 1870), pp. 58–59. Reprints
JF2 with several errors.

JF4   *Jumping Frog* (London: Routledge, 1870 and 1872), pp.
70–72. Reprints JF2 with several errors.

MTSk   *Mark Twain's Sketches* (London: Routledge, 1872), pp. 352–353. Reprints JF4 with possibly authorial corrections but no revisions, as well as several errors.

MTSk**MT**   Copy of MTSk revised by Mark Twain, who made no changes in this sketch but deleted it in the table of contents.

HWa   *Choice Humorous Works* (London: Hotten, 1873), pp. 438–439. Reprints JF3 without substantive error.

HWa**MT**   Sheets of HWa revised by Mark Twain, who made two changes in this sketch.

HWb   *Choice Humorous Works* (London: Chatto and Windus, 1874), p. 426. Reprints HWa with authorial revisions from HWa**MT**.

HWb**MT**   Copy of HWb revised by Mark Twain, who canceled this sketch.

Collation:

137 *title*   *An Unbiased Criticism* (Cal) • Literature in the Dry Diggings (JF1+)

137.1–12   THE . . . matters. (Cal) • [*not in*] (JF1+)

137.13–17   After . . . county; [up (Cal) • Although a resident of San Francisco, I never heard much about the "Art Union Association" of that city until I got hold of some old newspapers during my three months' stay in the Big Tree region of Calaveras county. Up (JF1-MTSk, JF1-HWa); Up (HWa**MT**-HWb)

138.4   Well (Cal-JF2, MTSk, Cal-HWb) • We'll (JF4)

138.7   I ever (Cal) • ever I (JF1+)

138.9   Jackass (Cal) • Jackass Gulch (JF1+)

138.9   by G—d (Cal) • [*not in*] (JF1+)

138.9   San (Cal-JF2, MTSk, Cal-HWb) • Sam (JF4)

138.13   'em's (Cal-JF2) • em's (JF4-MTSk, JF3-HWb)

138.15–16   middle (Cal-JF2, MTSk, Cal-HWb) • midddle (JF4)

138.18   me (Cal) • [*not in*] (JF1+)

138.19   d—n (Cal) • cuss (JF1+)

138.19   well (Cal-JF4, Cal-HWb) • well well (MTSk)

138.21   lose (Cal-JF4, Cal-HWb) • loose (MTSk)

138.25   'Lige (Cal-JF4, Cal-HWb) • 'Liege (MTSk)

138.26   all-firedest (Cal-JF4, HWa**MT**-HWb) • all-firedest, (MTSk, JF3-HWa)

138.36–143.33   but . . . drink." (Cal-YS**MT**) • [*not in*] (JF1+)

141.22   rough (Cal) • fearful (YS**MT**)

142.11-12   which . . . perhaps, (Cal) • [canceled] (YSMT)
143.7   mother (YSMT) • tmoher (Cal)
143.33   drink." (I-C) • drink." | MARK TWAIN. (Cal–YSMT)

101. *IMPORTANT CORRESPONDENCE*

Textual Commentary

The first printing in the *Californian* 2 (6 May 1865): 9 is copy-text. Copies: Bancroft; PH from Yale; PH of the Yale Scrapbook, pp. 32A–33A. Since Mark Twain slightly revised a clipping of the *Californian* in the Yale Scrapbook, he may have considered reprinting the sketch in JF1. The revised clipping is intact. Mark Twain did not reprint the sketch in JF1 or elsewhere.

Textual Notes

149.4   CUMMINS] The copy-text reading "CUMMINGS" here and at
             156.28 probably reflects Mark Twain's error in his manu-
             script, since his source in the San Francisco *Evening Bulle-
             tin* (see the headnote) made the same error. We have
             emended here and in the companion sketch (no. 102) to
             correct the misspelling.

154.35   lightening] Possibly a misspelling. Webster's 1828 diction-
             ary gives the spelling as "lightning" but adds, "that is,
             lightening, the participle present of *lighten*." Since the
             spelling of the copy-text is not unambiguously mistaken,
             we have not emended.

Emendations of the Copy-Text

*149.4   CUMMINS (I-C) • CUMMINGS
152.30 $7,000 (I-C) • $7.000
156.28   Cummins (I-C) • Cummings
156.31   same. (I-C) • same. | MARK TWAIN.

Alterations in the Yale Scrapbook

154.25-31   But . . . doctrine.] *canceled.*

102. *FURTHER OF MR. MARK TWAIN'S IMPORTANT CORRESPONDENCE*

Textual Commentary

The first printing in the *Californian* 2 (13 May 1865): 9 is copy-text. Copies: Bancroft; PH from Yale; PH of the Yale Scrapbook, pp. 34–34A.

Mark Twain revised a clipping of the *Californian* in the Yale Scrapbook and probably considered reprinting the sketch in JF1 together with its companion piece, "Important Correspondence" (no. 101). Some time after the main selections for JF1 had been made, he listed it as "Portion after Hawks" in the back of the scrapbook, along with six other sketches that did not "run average" (see the textual introduction, volume 1, pp. 538–539). The revised clipping remains intact in the scrapbook. Mark Twain did not reprint the sketch in JF1 or elsewhere. There are no textual notes.

Emendations of the Copy-Text

159.4	Cummins (I-C) • Cummings
160.3	CUMMINS (I-C) • CUMMINGS
160.8	DR. CUMMINS (I-C) • DR∧ CUMMINGS
161.9	flock; (I-C) • ~[:]
162.16	night. (I-C) • night. | MARK TWAIN.

Alterations in the Yale Scrapbook

159 *title*– 160.29	Further . . . excited:] *canceled.*
160 *note*	*Excuse . . . M. T.] *canceled.*
161.36	brashly] *altered to* 'hastily'.

103. *HOW I WENT TO THE GREAT RACE BETWEEN LODI AND NORFOLK*

Textual Commentary

The first printing in the *Californian* 3 (27 May 1865): 9 is copy-text. Copies: Bancroft; PH from Yale; PH of the Yale Scrapbook, pp. 15–16. Since Mark Twain preserved a clipping of the *Californian* in the Yale Scrapbook, where he slightly revised it, he must have considered reprinting the sketch in JF1. The revised clipping remains intact in the scrapbook. Mark Twain did not reprint the sketch in JF1 or elsewhere. There are no textual notes.

Emendations of the Copy-Text

165.24	present (I-C) • pretent
168.11	*will* (I-C) • *wi[ ]l*
168.27	forever. (I-C) • forever. MARK TWAIN.

Alterations in the Yale Scrapbook

165.5	Incidental] *altered to* 'Great Sahara'.
165.6	names,] *a closing bracket written over the comma.*

165.6–8	to prevent . . . is.]] *canceled.*
165.10	Incidental Hotel] *altered to* 'Great Sahara'.
166.25	off] *altered to* 'off & ticketing'.
166.28	"neck-or-nothing"] *the quotation marks deleted.*
166.33	Incidental] *altered to* 'Great Sahara'.
167.21	Incidental] *altered to* 'Great Sahara'.

104. *A VOICE FOR SETCHELL*

Textual Commentary

The first printing in the *Californian* 3 (27 May 1865): 9 is copy-text. Copies: Bancroft; PH from Yale; PH of the Yale Scrapbook, p. 51. Since Mark Twain preserved a clipping of the *Californian* in the Yale Scrapbook, he may have considered reprinting it in JF1. Probably sometime in January or February 1867, however, he struck through the clipping, and did not reprint it in JF1 or elsewhere. There are no textual notes.

Emendations of the Copy-Text

172.14	naturally and (I-C) • naturally an[d]
173.15	extravagantly. (I-C) • ~[,]
173.16	honest. (I-C) • honest. X.

["ANSWERS TO CORRESPONDENTS" IN THE *CALIFORNIAN*]

§105. *ANSWERS TO CORRESPONDENTS*

Textual Commentary

The first printing in the *Californian* 3 (3 June 1865): 4 is copy-text. Copies: Bancroft; PH from Yale; PH of the Yale Scrapbook, pp. 18A–19.

Reprintings and Revisions. Mark Twain revised clippings of this sketch and four similar sketches from the *Californian* (nos. 105–109) in the Yale Scrapbook, rejecting portions of each and revising others to assemble a composite sketch for JF1. Only one section of the present sketch, from 178.30 to 179.35, survives in the scrapbook (p. 19), where Mark Twain struck through it in ink, but it is apparent that a complete clipping of the *Californian* was once present, that the author revised it, and that portions were then peeled away to serve as printer's copy for JF1. The missing portions appear to have been only slightly altered: Mark Twain supplied a new title, in pencil, for his intended composite version, and some undeciphered pencil marks on the section beginning at 179.36

show that he also made some unidentified revision there (see figures 105A-B below). For details of the JF1 composite text and its subsequent reprinting and revision, see the textual commentary for "Burlesque 'Answers to Correspondents' " (no. 201). Only the alterations made by Mark Twain in the Yale Scrapbook are recorded here, where they can be keyed to the complete text of the original *Californian* sketch. There are no textual notes.

Emendations of the Copy-Text

177.1	LOVER. (I-C) • ~$_\wedge$
178.35	and I (I-C) • and 1
179.37	landlord (I-C) • land[$_\wedge$]|lord
179.38	harassing (JF1) • harrassing

Alterations in the Yale Scrapbook

177 *title*	*Answers to Correspondents*] *altered to* 'BURLESQUE "ANSWERS TO CORRESPONDENTS." '
177.1– 178.29	DISCARDED . . . comfort.] *peeled away.*
178.30– 179.35	MR. . . . "Scasely."] *canceled.*
179.36– 180.25	PERSECUTED . . . it.] *peeled away.*

§106. ANSWERS TO CORRESPONDENTS

Textual Commentary

The first printing in the *Californian* 3 (10 June 1865): 9 is copy-text. Copies: Bancroft; PH from Yale; PH of the Yale Scrapbook, pp. 19A–20A.

Reprintings and Revisions. Mark Twain revised clippings of this sketch and four similar sketches from the *Californian* (nos. 105–109) in the Yale Scrapbook, rejecting portions of each and revising others to assemble a composite sketch for JF1. Only one section of the present sketch, from 184.18 to 185.41, survives in the scrapbook (pp. 20–20A), where Mark Twain struck through most of it; but it is apparent that a complete clipping of the *Californian* was once present, that the author revised it, and that portions were then peeled away to serve as printer's copy for JF1. A reconstruction of the missing portions as Mark Twain revised them helps to determine what changes he made (see figures 3–4 in the textual introduction, volume 1, pp. 514–515, and figures 106A–B below). For details of the JF1 composite text and its subsequent reprinting and revision, see the textual commentary for "Burlesque 'Answers to Correspondents' " (no. 201). Only the alterations made by Mark Twain in

FIGURE 105A. Page 18A of the Yale Scrapbook. The compilers of JF1 were evidently forced to use scissors when the middle portion of the clipping would not peel away from the scrapbook page without tearing.

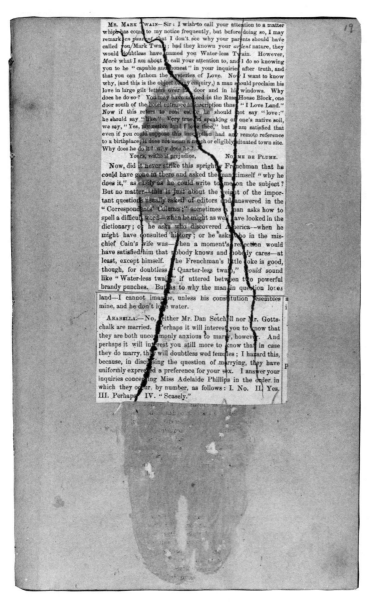

MR. MARK TWAIN—Sir: I wish to call your attention to a matter which has come to my notice frequently, but before doing so, I may remark *en passant* that I don't see why your parents should have called you Mark Twain; had they known your *ardent* nature, they would doubtless have named you Water-less Twain. However, *Mark* what I am about to call your attention to, and I do so knowing you to be " capable and honest " in your inquiries after truth, and that you can fathom the mysteries of Love. Now I want to know why, (and this is the object of my enquiry,) a man should proclaim his love in large gilt letters over his door and in his windows. Why does he do so ? You may have noticed in the Russ House Block, one door south of the hotel entrance an inscription thus: " I Love Land." Now if this refers to real estate, he should not say "love:" he should say "like." Very true in speaking of one's native soil, we say, " Yes, my native land I love thee," but I am satisfied that even if you could suppose this inscription had any remote reference to a birthplace, it does not mean a ranch or eligibly situated town site. Why does he do it ? why does he ?

Yours, without prejudice,   NOMME DE PLUME.

Now, did it never strike this sprightly Frenchman that he could have gone in there and asked the man himself " why he does it," as easily as he could write to me on the subject ? But no matter—this is just about the weight of the important questions usually asked of editors and answered in the " Correspondents' Column ;" sometimes a man asks how to spell a difficult word—when he might as well have looked in the dictionary ; or he asks who discovered America—when he might have consulted history ; or he asks who in the mischief Cain's wife was—when a moment's reflection would have satisfied him that nobody knows and nobody cares—at least, except himself. The Frenchman's little joke is good, though, for doubtless " Quarter-less twain," would sound like " Water-less twain," if uttered between two powerful brandy punches. But as to why the man in question loves land—I cannot imagine, unless his constitution resembles mine, and he don't love water.

ARABELLA.—No, neither Mr. Dan Setchell nor Mr. Gottschalk are married. Perhaps it will interest you to know that they are both uncommonly anxious to marry, however. And perhaps it will interest you still more to know that in case they do marry, they will doubtless wed females ; I hazard this, because, in discussing the question of marrying, they have uniformly expressed a preference for your sex. I answer your inquiries concerning Miss Adelaide Phillips in the order in which they occur, by number, as follows : I. No. II. Yes. III. Perhaps. IV. " Scasely."

FIGURE 105B. Page 19 of the Yale Scrapbook.

FIGURE 106A. Page 19A of the Yale Scrapbook, showing the evidence for Mark Twain's conjectured alteration of "yowling" to "howling."

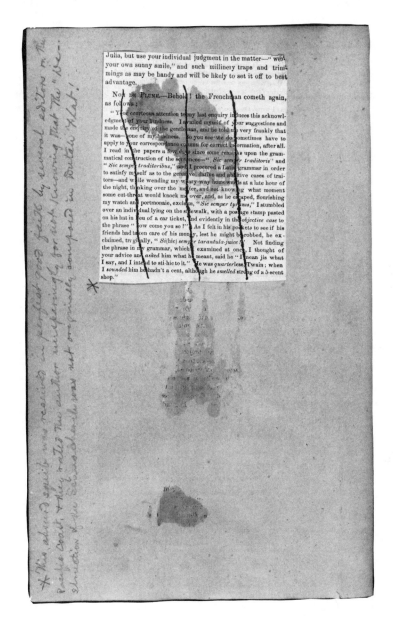

FIGURE 106B. Page 20A of the Yale Scrapbook, showing Mark Twain's added footnote.

the Yale Scrapbook are recorded here, where they can be keyed to the complete text of the original *Californian* sketch.

Textual Notes

183.25–28 Tenthly . . . Eleventhly] Mark Twain omitted "Ninthly." Although "Ninthly . . . Tenthly" would be arithmetically correct, it would be comically deficient. The author clearly intends to raise a smile with his long enumeration and particularly with his silly word "Eleventhly." Since emendation would sacrifice humor for mere arithmetic precision, we have not corrected the inaccuracy.

185.27 genative] The first of two spelling errors in the Frenchman's letter (see also *"tyranis"* at 185.31). Although the errors may be Mark Twain's oversight, the possibility that they are intended signs of the Frenchman's ignorance cannot be excluded, and we have therefore not emended in either case.

Emendations of the Copy-Text

182.19 beleaguered (JF1) • beleagured
183.5 Lilly (I-C) • Lily
185.4 smile.' " (I-C) • ~.ᴧ"
185.25 'Sic . . . traditoris' (I-C) • "~ . . . ~"
185.25 'Sic . . . traditoribus,' (I-C) • "~ . . . ~,"
185.31 'Sic . . . tyranis,' (I-C) • "~ . . . ~,"
185.34 'how . . . so?' (I-C) • "~ . . . ~?"
185.36 'Si(hic) . . . juice!' (I-C) • "Si(hic) . . . ~!"
185.38–39 'I . . . it.' (I-C) • "~ . . . ~."
186.7 Galilee." (JF1) • ~.'
186.26 mistaken (I-C) • mistakan

Alterations in the Yale Scrapbook

182.1–
184.17 Amateur . . . Selkirk.] *peeled away.*

183.20 yowling] *altered to* 'howling'.
183.27 be] *altered to* 'would be'.
184.6 you] *deleted.*
184.18–
185.12 Julia . . . fashions,] *canceled in pencil.*

185.6–7 grand-discounts] *altered to* 'discounts'.
185.12–15 Julia . . . advantage.] *left uncanceled.*
185.16–
185.41 Nom . . . shop."] *canceled in ink.*

186.1–   MELTON . . . mistaken.] *peeled away.*
186.26

186.1   MELTON] *an asterisk and the following footnote added:*
            '*This absurd squib was received in perfect good faith by
            several editors on the Pacific Coast, & they rated the author
            unsparingly for not knowing that the "Destruction of the
            Sennacherib was not originally composed in Dutch Flat!'

§107. *ANSWERS TO CORRESPONDENTS*

Textual Commentary

The first printing in the *Californian* 3 (17 June 1865): 4 (Cal) is copy-text
for all but the item Mark Twain quotes from the Gold Hill *News*, 13 June
1865, p. 2 (GHN), which is copy-text from 193.34 through 194.19. Collation suggests that a clipping of GHN was part of Mark Twain's manuscript: a dozen or so minor changes and corrections, most of them in
the system of quotation marks, were presumably introduced by Mark Twain
or his compositor and are here adopted as needed emendations of GHN
from Cal. Since in this case all variants between Cal and GHN are listed
in the record of emendations, no historical collation for these texts
has been supplied. Copies: Bancroft; PH from Yale (Cal); PH from
Bancroft (GHN).

Reprintings and Revisions. Mark Twain revised clippings of this
sketch and four similar sketches from the *Californian* (nos. 105–109) in
the Yale Scrapbook, rejecting portions of each and revising others to
assemble a composite sketch for JF1. None of the *Californian* clipping for
the present sketch survives in the scrapbook, but it is apparent that a
clipping for all but the portion following "Tobacco" (192.34) once occupied pages 22A and 23; the remainder of the sketch was evidently
never in the scrapbook. Mark Twain revised the clipping on these pages
before it was peeled away to serve as printer's copy for JF1. A reconstruction of the missing portions as Mark Twain revised them helps determine what changes he made (see figures 9–11 in the textual introduction,
volume 1, pp. 522–524, and figure 107 below). For details of the JF1 composite text and its subsequent reprinting and revision, see the textual
commentary for "Burlesque 'Answers to Correspondents' " (no. 201).
Only the alterations made by Mark Twain in the Yale Scrapbook are
recorded here, where they can be keyed to the complete text of the
original *Californian* sketch.

Textual Notes

190.18–20   "ornery" and unloveable . . . ceaseless and villainous] As
            figure 10 in the textual introduction shows, these two pairs
            of adjectives occur in two adjacent lines in Cal. But Mark

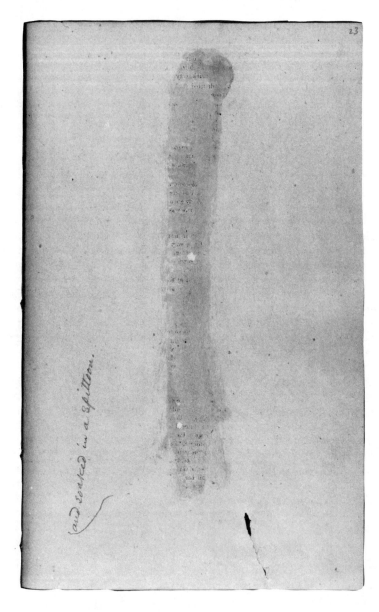

FIGURE 107. Page 23 of the Yale Scrapbook, showing Mark Twain's added phrase at 192.17.

Twain's autograph change in the Yale Scrapbook ("wretched") cannot now be reconstructed precisely enough for us to be certain whether he intended to substitute "wretched" for one pair of adjectives or for only one word in either pair, in part because the JF1 composite text of "Burlesque 'Answers to Correspondents' " did not incorporate his scrapbook revision. But when Mark Twain revised a copy of JF4a as printer's copy for MTSk, he presumably substituted "disagreeable" for the first pair and "tiresome" for the second. And when he revised HWb**MT** (which derived independently from JF1) in 1875, he allowed the first pair to stand unchanged, but deleted "ceaseless and" from the second. It therefore seems less likely that he ever intended to substitute "wretched" for only one word in the two pairs than that he sought in different ways to avoid two sets of paired adjectives. We have accordingly conjectured that he substituted "wretched" for "ceaseless and villainous" in the scrapbook, just as he appears to have substituted "tiresome" for the same words in MTSk.

190.21   a particle of] As figure 9 in the textual introduction shows, Mark Twain's marginal inscription of "any" in the Yale Scrapbook cannot now be demonstrably linked with the word or words it was meant to replace, in part because the JF1 composite text did not adopt the change. Since the MTSk printing of "Burlesque 'Answers to Correspondents' " substituted "any" for "a particle of," we have conjectured that Mark Twain made the same substitution in his original revision in the scrapbook.

192.17   chopping-machine.] In the Yale Scrapbook Mark Twain added the phrase "and soaked in a spittoon" after "chopping-machine," a change that is reflected in the JF1 composite text of "Burlesque 'Answers to Correspondents' " (see figure 107 below).

Emendations of the Copy-Text

[Copy-text from 189.1 through 193.33 is Cal]

189.4	injured, (JF1) • ~[,]
189.16	time. (JF1) • ~-
191.7	say, (JF1) • ~'
191.27	prayer 'n (JF1) • pray'er'n
192.20	sold (JF1) • so[l]d
193.19	good thing (I-C) • goodthing
193.29	auger (I-C) • augur

[*Copy-text from 193.34 through 194.19 is GHN*]

193.34	"BYRON (Cal) • ∧~
193.37	CALIFORNIAN (Cal) • *Californian*
194.1	'Answers to Correspondents.' (Cal) • "~~~."
194.3	CALIFORNIAN (Cal) • *Californian*
194.4	'lot of doggerel.' (Cal) • "~~~."
194.5	'fix' (Cal) • "~"
194.7	" 'Melton (Cal) • "∧~
194.8	us (Cal) • [*not in*]
194.8	of (Cal) • [*not in*]
194.9	verse: (Cal) • ~;
194.10–13	'The . . . Galilee.' (Cal) • "~ . . . Galile[ ]."
194.12	the sea, (Cal) • sea[.]
194.14	" 'There (Cal) • ∧∧~
194.19	blubber.' " (Cal) • ~.∧∧

[*Copy-text from 194.20 through 196.15 is Cal*]

194.33–34	'Let . . . so!' " (I-C) • "~ . . . ~!∧"
195.17	warm-hearted (I-C) • warm-|hearted
195.18	broken-hearted (I-C) • broken-|hearted
196.14	bunch-grass (I-C) • bunch-|grass

Alterations in the Yale Scrapbook

189.1– 192.34	MORAL . . . Tobacco."] *peeled away.*
190.12	greenbacks] *the following footnote added:* '*It is hardly worth while to explain that <the circulating med> gold & silver coin form the circulating medium on the Pacific coast.'
190.19–20	ceaseless and villainous] *altered to* 'wretched'.
190.21	a particle of] *altered to* 'any'.
192.17	chopping-machine.] *altered to* 'chopping-machine and soaked in a spittoon.'

§108. ANSWERS TO CORRESPONDENTS

Textual Commentary

The first printing in the *Californian* 3 (24 June 1865): 4 (Cal) is copy-text for all but the item Mark Twain quotes from the San Francisco *Morning Call,* 18 June 1865, p. 1 (MC), which is copy-text from 200.7 through

200.16, and the article he quotes from the San Francisco *Dramatic Chronicle*, 20 June 1865, p. 2 (DC), which is copy-text from 207.3 through 207.8. Collation suggests that a transcription of MC and a clipping of DC were probably part of Mark Twain's manuscript. Some of the minor corrections and revisions of the quoted material were presumably introduced by him and are adopted here as needed emendations of MC and DC from Cal. Since not all variants between Cal and the material quoted are adopted, however, a historical collation of these texts is provided. Copies: Bancroft (Cal); PH from Yale (Cal); PH of the Yale Scrapbook, pp. 21–22 (Cal); PH from Bancroft (MC and DC).

Reprintings and Revisions. Mark Twain revised clippings of this sketch and four similar sketches from the *Californian* (nos. 105–109) in the Yale Scrapbook (YS**MT**), rejecting portions of each and revising others to assemble a composite sketch for JF1. Only one portion of the present sketch, from the title through 202.31 ("industry?"), survives in the scrapbook (pp. 21–21A), but it is apparent that a complete clipping of the *Californian* was once present, that the author revised it, and that the missing portions were then peeled away to serve as printer's copy for JF1. Reconstruction of the missing portions as Mark Twain revised them helps to determine what changes he made (see figures 6–7 in the textual introduction, volume 1, pp. 518–519, and figures 108A–B below). For details of the JF1 composite text and its subsequent reprinting and revision, see the textual commentary for "Burlesque 'Answers to Correspondents' " (no. 201). Only the alterations made by Mark Twain in the Yale Scrapbook are recorded here, where they can be keyed to the complete text of the original *Californian* sketch; two of these changes are adopted as needed corrections of the copy-text.

Textual Notes

200.10–12   Glorious Anniversary . . . *Custom House?*] The capital letters in "Glorious" and in *"Great"* as well as the italics in *"our Great Ensign of Freedom does not appear on the Custom House?"* are emendations of MC adopted from Cal. Mark Twain's allusion to the effect of "stunning capitals" (201.7) and his general satiric purpose both imply that it was he who imposed these changes in the material being quoted.

202.10   tried] It is tempting to regard "tried" as a typographical error for "tired," especially since a few lines later the servant is described as "exhausted" (202.15). But in the absence of a manuscript, or of holograph correction in the Yale Scrapbook, the reading of the copy-text, "tried" (meaning "found good, faithful, worthy"), must be permitted to stand.

204.4   Here] Cal omits a paragraph break at this point, thereby creating a minor inconsistency, which Mark Twain noticed

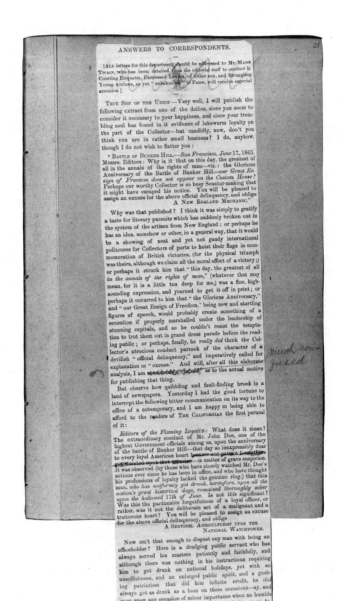

[ALL letters for this department should be addressed to Mr. MARK TWAIN, who has been detailed from the editorial staff to conduct it. Courting Etiquette, Distressed Lovers, of either sex, and Struggling Young Authors, as yet "unbeknown" to Fame, will receive especial attention.]

TRUE SON OF THE UNION.—Very well, I will publish the following extract from one of the dailies, since you seem to consider it necessary to your happiness, and since your trembling soul has found in it evidence of lukewarm loyalty on the part of the Collector—but candidly, now, don't you think you are in rather small business? I do, anyhow, though I do not wish to flatter you:

"BATTLE OF BUNKER HILL.—*San Francisco, June* 17, 1865. Messrs. Editors: Why is it that on this day, the greatest of all in the annals of the rights of man—viz.: the Glorious Anniversary of the Battle of Bunker Hill—*our Great En sign of Freedom does not appear on the Custom House?* Perhaps our worthy Collector is so busy Senator-making that it might have escaped his notice. You will be pleased to assign an excuse for the above official delinquency, and oblige
A NEW ENGLAND MECHANIC."

Why was that published? I think it was simply to gratify a taste for literary pursuits which has suddenly broken out in the system of the artisan from New England ; or perhaps he has an idea, somehow or other, in a general way, that it would be a showing of neat and yet not gaudy international politeness for Collectors of ports to hoist their flags in commemoration of British victories, (for the physical triumph was theirs, although we claim all the moral effect of a victory ;) or perhaps it struck him that " this day, the greatest of all *in the annals of the rights of man,*" (whatever that may mean, for it is a little too deep for me), was a fine, highsounding expression, and yearned to get it off in print ; or perhaps it occurred to him that " the Glorious Anniversary," and " our Great Ensign of Freedom," being new and startling figures of speech, would probably create something of a sensation if properly marshalled under the leadership of stunning capitals, and so he couldn't resist the temptation to trot them out in grand dress parade before the reading public ; or perhaps, finally, he really *did* think the Collector's atrocious conduct partook of the character of a devilish " official delinquency," and imperatively called for explanation or " excuse." And still, after all this elaborate analysis, I am ~~specifically mixed~~ as to the actual motive for publishing that thing.

But observe how quibbling and fault-finding breed in a land of newspapers. Yesterday I had the good fortune to intercept the following bitter communication on its way to the office of a cotemporary, and I am happy in being able to afford to the readers of THE CALIFORNIAN the first perusal of it:

Editors of the Flaming Loyalist: What does it mean? The extraordinary conduct of Mr. John Doe, one of the highest Government officials among us, upon the anniversary of the battle of Bunker Hill—that day so inexpressibly dear to every loyal American heart ~~because our patriot forefathers got scalded upon that occasion~~—is matter of grave suspicion. It was observed (by those who have closely watched Mr. Doe's actions ever since he has been in office, and who have thought his professions of loyalty lacked the genuine ring,) that this man, *who has uniformly got drunk, heretofore, upon all the nation's great historical days, remained thoroughly sober upon the hallowed 17th of June.* Is not this significant? Was this the pardonable forgetfulness of a loyal officer, or rather, was it not the deliberate act of a malignant and a traitorous heart? You will be pleased to assign an excuse for the above official delinquency, and oblige
A SENTINEL AGRICULTURIST UPON THE NATIONAL WATCHTOWER.

Now isn't that enough to disgust any man with being an officeholder? Here is a drudging public servant who has always served his masters patiently and faithfully, and although there was nothing in his instructions requiring him to get drunk on national holidays, yet with an unselfishness, and an enlarged public spirit, and a gushing patriotism that did him infinite credit, he *did* always get as drunk as a loon on these occasions—ay, and even upon any occasion of minor importance when an humble effort on his part could shed additional lustre upon hi

FIGURE 108A. Page 21 of the Yale Scrapbook. Mark Twain revised this early part of the clipping, but it was not removed and therefore was not part of the JF1 composite text (no. 201).

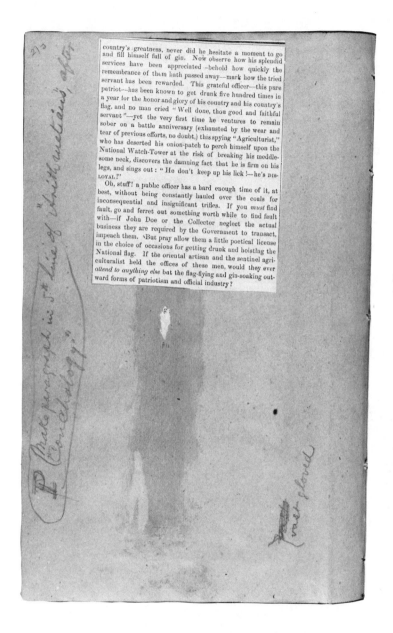

country's greatness, never did he hesitate a moment to go and fill himself full of gin. Now observe how his splendid services have been appreciated –behold how quickly the remembrance of them hath passed away—mark how the tried servant has been rewarded. This grateful officer—this pure patriot—has been known to get drunk five hundred times in a year for the honor and glory of his country and his country's flag, and no man cried "Well done, thou good and faithful servant"—yet the very first time he ventures to remain sober on a battle anniversary (exhausted by the wear and tear of previous efforts, no doubt,) this spying "Agriculturist," who has deserted his onion-patch to perch himself upon the National Watch-Tower at the risk of breaking his meddlesome neck, discovers the damning fact that he is firm on his legs, and sings out : "He don't keep up his lick !—he's DIS-LOYAL !"

Oh, stuff! a public officer has a hard enough time of it, at best, without being constantly hauled over the coals for inconsequential and insignificant trifles. If you *must* find fault, go and ferret out something worth while to find fault with—if John Doe or the Collector neglect the actual business they are required by the Government to transact, impeach them. But pray allow them a little poetical license in the choice of occasions for getting drunk and hoisting the National flag. If the oriental artisan and the sentinel agriculturalist held the offices of these men, would they ever *attend to anything else* but the flag-flying and gin-soaking outward forms of patriotism and official industry?

FIGURE 108B. Page 21A of the Yale Scrapbook, showing Mark Twain's instruction for making a new paragraph at 204.4, and evidence for his conjectured revision of "ample" to "vast gloved."

as he revised the clipping in the Yale Scrapbook. "Make paragraph in 5ᵗʰ line of 'Arithmeticus,' after 'Conchology' " he wrote. The change is adopted here as a correction, rather than a revision, of the copy-text. See figure 108B.

204.23 blow your brains out] Cal omits "your," an error corrected by Mark Twain in the Yale Scrapbook; we have adopted his correction here (see figures 6–7 in the textual introduction).

205.10 It] Mark Twain inserted a new paragraph break before this word in the Yale Scrapbook clipping (see figures 6–7 in the textual introduction). It is tempting to regard this change as a restoration of Mark Twain's original manuscript form, but in the absence of that manuscript it must be regarded as a revision for the JF1 composite version, and we have therefore not adopted the change in the present text.

Emendations of the Copy-Text

[Copy-text from 200.1 through 200.6 is Cal]

200.1 Union. (I-C) • ~[.]

[Copy-text from 200.7 through 200.16 is MC]

200.7 "Battle of Bunker Hill (I-C) • **Battle of Bunker Hill** [*Cal has ¶*]

200.9 [*no* ¶] Messrs. Editors: (Cal) • [¶] Editors Morning Call:—

*200.10 Glorious (Cal) • glorious

*200.11–12 *our Great . . . House?* (Cal) • our great Ensign of Freedom does not appear on the Custom House?

200.13 busy (Cal) • busily engaged in

200.16 Mechanic." (Cal) • ~.ₐ

[Copy-text from 200.17 through 207.2 is Cal]

203.17 footmen (JF1) • foot-|men

*204.4 [¶] Here (**YSMT**) • [*no* ¶] Here

*204.23 your (**YSMT**) • [*not in*]

205.25 butter, (JF1) • ~[,]

206.3 plain-spoken (JF1) • plain-|spoken

206.33 432,' (I-C) • ~,ₐ

[Copy-text from 207.3 through 207.8 is DC]

207.3 Discouraging (Cal) • **Discouraging**

207.5 Sennacherib (Cal) • Sennecharib

207.8 —*Dramatic Chronicle.* (Cal) • [*not in*]

Historical Collation

Texts collated: Cal, MC, and DC (see the commentary above).

Collation:

200.7	"BATTLE (I-C) • **Battle** (MC); [¶] "BATTLE (Cal)
200.9	[no ¶] Messrs. Editors: (Cal) • [¶] EDITORS MORNING CALL:— (MC)
200.11-12	our Great . . . House! (Cal) • our great Ensign of Freedom does not appear on the Custom House? (MC)
200.13	busy (Cal) • busily engaged in (MC)
207.6	that (DC) • [not in] (Cal)
207.8	"a key" (DC) • a "key" (Cal)
207.8	—Dramatic Chronicle. (Cal) • [not in] (DC)

Alterations in the Yale Scrapbook

201.13	considerably "mixed"] altered to 'much confused'.
201.24-25	because . . . occasion] canceled.
202.32–207.10	SOCRATES . . . think?] peeled away.
203.22	ample] altered to 'vast gloved'.
204.4	[¶] Here] paragraph break added.
204.21	quote poetry] altered to 'swear'.
204.23	your] added.
204.35	forever."] an asterisk and the following footnote added: '*The ensuing statement of the baby's performances is almost literally true.'
205.10	It] paragraph break added.

§109. ANSWERS TO CORRESPONDENTS

Textual Commentary

The first printing in the *Californian* 3 (1 July 1865): 4–5 (Cal) is copy-text for all but the two items that Mark Twain quotes from the San Francisco *Golden Era* 13 (25 June 1865): 4 (GE), which is copy-text at 217.20–22 and 218.14–17. Collation suggests that clippings of GE were part of Mark Twain's manuscript: Cal reproduced GE without substantive error, except for one inadvertent omission ("verily" at 218.16). Since this is the only variant between Cal and GE, no historical collation for these texts has been provided. The quotation from Winthrop Macworth Praed (216.31–38) does not vary substantively from the 1865 edition of his works cited in the explanatory notes, except in two obviously deliberate changes: "four" instead of "two," and the addition of "GEE-WHILLIKINS."

Since the precise source of Mark Twain's quotation is not known, however, the copy-text remains the first printing of this sketch, Cal. Likewise, since the exact edition of Webster's dictionary, which served as the source of the quotation at 217.25-26, is not known, Cal remains copy-text for this passage also. Copies: Bancroft (Cal); PH from Yale (Cal); PH of the Yale Scrapbook, pp. 27A-28A (Cal); PH from Bancroft (GE).

Reprintings and Revisions. Mark Twain revised clippings of this sketch and four similar sketches from the *Californian* (nos. 105-109) in the Yale Scrapbook (YSMT), rejecting portions of each and revising others to assemble a composite sketch for JF1. Only one portion of the present sketch, from "correct" (211.21) to "two l's" (216.22), now survives in the scrapbook (pp. 27A-28A), but it is evident that a clipping for the portion from the title through "at once" (211.21) once occupied the top of page 27A; the remainder of the sketch was evidently never in the scrapbook. Mark Twain canceled the parts of the sketch that remain in the scrapbook, except for the section called "MARY, *Rincon School,*" which survives uncanceled. He slightly revised this section, and sometime after the main selections for JF1 had been made, he listed it as "Geewhillikens" in the back of the scrapbook, along with six other sketches that did not "run average" (see the textual introduction, volume 1, pp. 538-539). Mark Twain may have considered using this section as a separate piece, and he almost certainly intended using other parts of the sketch for his composite version "Burlesque 'Answers to Correspondents' " (no. 201). Yet even though a section of the Cal clipping was scissored out of the scrapbook, no part of the sketch was included in the composite sketch, and Mark Twain did not subsequently reprint any of it.

Textual Notes

215.32-33   neither... nor] Mark Twain corrected the Cal reading
              "either... or" on YSMT. Although this change might be
              construed as a revision, it seems somewhat more likely that
              through either his own or the compositor's error, Mark
              Twain's text in Cal did not say what he meant; we have
              therefore adopted the change as a needed correction of the
              copy-text. It should be noted that Mark Twain's correction
              was inconsistent with his (or the compositor's) practice
              elsewhere in this sketch: for example, the form "neither...
              or" at 212.17. Webster's 1828 dictionary suggested that al-
              though "*neither,* in the first part of a negative sentence, is
              followed by *nor,* in the subsequent part... *or* would be
              most proper, for the negative in *neither,* applies to both
              parts of the sentence." Mark Twain is known to have used
              Webster's dictionary, and he may therefore be responsible
              for the use elsewhere of the form "neither... or." Although

the correction he supplied on **YSMT** is at variance with this single-negative style, we have adopted it as more demonstrably authorial than the reading in Cal.

Emendations of the Copy-Text

[*Copy-text from the title through 217.19 is Cal*]

211.12	"Lord Blucher," (I-C) • '~~,'
212.1	"Lord Blucher" (I-C) • '~~'
212.1–2	"Viscount Cranberry," (I-C) • '~~,'
212.4	"Lord Blucher's" (I-C) • 'Lord Blucher's'
212.6–7	"Speak . . . ter-r-raitor!" (I-C) • 'Speak . . . ter-r-raitor!'
213.19	death-bed (I-C) • death-|bed
214.4	"Lord Blucher" (I-C) • '~~'
214.8	"Viscount," (I-C) • '~,'
214.10	"fever-heat" (I-C) • 'fever-heat'
214.10	"zero" (I-C) • '~'
214.18	"Lord Blucher" (I-C) • '~~'
214.37	Forrest's (I-C) • Forest's
*215.32–33	neither . . . nor (**YSMT**) • either . . . or
216.4	remark, (I-C) • ~.

[*Copy-text from 217.20 through 217.22 is GE*]

217.22	—*Golden Era.* (Cal) • [*not in*]

[*Copy-text from 218.14 through 218.17 is GE*]

218.17	—*Golden Era.* (Cal) • [*not in*]

Alterations in the Yale Scrapbook

211 *title*–21	*Answers . . . once*] *scissored out.*
211.21– 215.18	*correct . . . contained.*] *canceled.*
215.32–33	neither . . . nor] *altered from* 'either . . . or'.
216.20–22	We . . . two l's,] *canceled.*
216.22– 218.31	which . . . elegance.] *never present.*

§110. *ANSWERS TO CORRESPONDENTS*

Textual Commentary

The first printing in the *Californian* 3 (8 July 1865): 4–5 (Cal) is copy-text, except where Mark Twain quotes from newspaper articles and dictionaries. Collation suggests that he pasted clippings of these articles into his manuscript, since there are so few variants between Cal and the newspapers it reprints. The original newspaper printings are copy-text for the material quoted:

AC   "Celebration of the Ninetieth Anniversary of Our National Independence," San Francisco *Alta California*, 6 July 1865, p. 1, is copy-text from 225.29 through 226.24;

MC   "Straightening Up," "A Fine Display," and "That Arch," San Francisco *Morning Call*, 4 July 1865, p. 1, are copy-text from 226.32 through 226.40, 227.5 through 227.17, and 227.20 through 227.30;

EB   "The Glorious Fourth," San Francisco *Evening Bulletin*, 3 July 1865, p. 3, is copy-text from 227.36 through 228.4;

AF   "Triumphal Arch," San Francisco *American Flag*, 8 July 1865, p. 4, is copy-text from 228.8 through 228.35.

Copies: Bancroft (Cal); PH from Bancroft (AC, MC, EB); California State Library, Sacramento (AF).

Mark Twain's quotations from dictionaries present a somewhat more puzzling situation. He surely would not have scissored out passages from any of the dictionaries he consulted "in the Mercantile Library" (230.20) in order to provide copy for the Cal compositor; and it seems unlikely that he would have borrowed the books and carried them to the *Californian* offices for typesetting. The most likely explanation is that he transcribed the dictionary entries and inserted these transcriptions into his manuscript, modifying the wording here and there (condensing certain definitions and eliminating pronunciation indications, for example) and perhaps styling the type format for a uniform appearance. Although most of the books in the Mercantile Library were destroyed in the 1906 earthquake, its catalogs for 1854, 1861, and 1874 are now preserved in the library of the Mechanics' Institute in San Francisco. These catalogs have made it possible to identify which edition of each dictionary Mark Twain consulted. Therefore, we have designated these editions as copy-text, using the same impression as the author whenever possible. The quoted material is emended in two ways: to follow the substantive changes that Mark Twain clearly intended to make in the original, and to make uniform the rendering of "Bɪʟк" with a capital and small capital letters. Thus pronunciation indications omitted in Cal have been emended out of the copy-text, while the minimal styling mentioned has been emended in. The result is a text that renders the quoted material more accurately than did Cal, whenever it seems likely that variants between the copy-texts and Cal were caused by inadvertent errors on the part of the author or compositor. All substantive variants are recorded in the historical collation. Mark Twain did not preserve a clipping of this piece in the Yale Scrapbook, and it was not reprinted.

Webster	Noah Webster, *An American Dictionary of the English Language*, 2 vols. [New York: S. Converse, 1828], is copy-text from 230.23 through 230.27.
Walker	B. H. Smart, *Walker's Pronouncing Dictionary of the English Language*, 6th ed. [London: Longman and Co., 1860], is copy-text for 230.29.
Wright	Thomas Wright, *The Universal Pronouncing Dictionary and General Expositor of the English Language*, 5 vols. [London and New York: London Printing and Publishing Company, 1852–1856], is copy-text for 230.31.
Worcester	Joseph E. Worcester, *A Dictionary of the English Language* [Boston: Hickling, Swan, and Brewer, 1860], is copy-text from 230.33 through 230.35.
Spiers	A. Spiers, *Spiers and Surenne's French and English Pronouncing Dictionary* [New York: D. Appleton and Company, 1856], is copy-text for 230.37. Mark Twain apparently used the 1862 impression of this edition, which we were unable to obtain. The 1856 and 1867 impressions are identical, however, from which we infer that the 1862 edition was also unaltered.
Adler	George J. Adler, *A Dictionary of the German and English Languages*, 2nd rev. ed. [New York: D. Appleton and Co., 1849], is copy-text from 231.2 through 231.4. Mark Twain used the 1854 impression; we could obtain only the 1849 and 1868 impressions, which are identical.
Seoane	Mariano Velázquez de la Cadena, *A Pronouncing Dictionary of the Spanish and English Languages* [New York: D. Appleton and Co., 1852], is copy-text from 231.6 through 231.7. Mark Twain used the 1857 impression; we could obtain only the 1852 and 1875 impressions, which are identical.
Johnson	Samuel Johnson, *A Dictionary of the English Language* [London: Henry G. Bohn, 1854], is copy-text from 231.9 through 231.14.
Richardson	Charles Richardson, *A New Dictionary of the English Language*, 2 vols. [Philadelphia: E. H. Butler and Co., 1851], is copy-text from 231.16 through 231.35.

Textual Notes

226.2–3	arch was . . . evening.] The two emendations of the AC text here accord with the substantive readings of Cal and represent deletions that Mark Twain presumably made on the clipping of AC. The possibility that the Cal compositor inadvertently skipped over the material has been rejected.

227.39–40   [Here ... detail.]   ] The bracketed sentence appears only in
            Cal, where Mark Twain presumably interpolated it by
            marking a clipping of EB, which serves as copy-text here.
            We have adopted the sentence to accord with the reading
            of Cal and recorded the deleted EB passage in the list of
            emendations.

230.31   To deceive; to defraud] Cal shortened the definition as it
            appeared in Wright's dictionary, which is copy-text here,
            presumably because Mark Twain did not want to repeat the
            definition already quoted from Webster's (230.25–26). We
            have emended Wright to conform to the reading of Cal.

230.33–34   To cheat ... to elude.] Cal omits this passage, and it may be
            that Mark Twain so directed the Cal compositor. It seems
            somewhat more likely, however, that the compositor or
            Mark Twain simply miscopied the entry. We have not,
            therefore, emended the copy-text, which is Worcester's dic-
            tionary for these two lines.

Emendations of the Copy-Text

[*Copy-text from 221* title *through 225.28 is Cal*]

221.8   arch-traitors (I-C) • arch-|traitors
222.28   barber-shop (I-C) • barber-|shop

[*Copy-text from 225.29 through 226.24 is AC*]

225.29   [¶] "The (Cal) • [*no* ¶] ‸~
225.32   at (Cal) • At
*226.2   arch (Cal) • arch, or rather quadruple arch, for such it really
            was, as there were four pillars at the four corners of the
            street, from which arose four arches, one for each street-
            front on both California and Montgomery streets,
*226.3   evening. (Cal) • evening. The height of each arch was fifty-
            four feet, and the width from pillar to pillar was thirty-four
            feet.
226.11   'Mine ... Lord,' (Cal) • "~ ... ~,"
226.13   'Honor ... Republic.' (Cal) • "~ ... ~."
226.24   breeze." (Cal) • ~.‸

[*Copy-text from 227.5 through 227.17 is MC*]

227.6   this (Cal) • ~,
227.9   M. F. (Cal) • F. M.

[*Copy-text from 227.36 through 228.4 is EB*]

227.36   "The (Cal) • ‸~

*227.39–40   [Here . . . detail.] The arches (Cal) • The arch, or rather the arches, for there are four, rise from four massive pillars 30 feet in height, the tops of the arches reaching nearly 50 feet from the ground and spanning the whole width of the street. They

228.4   Stripes." (Cal) • ~.∧

             [Copy-text from 228.8 through 228.35 is AF]

228.8   [¶] Triumphal Arch.—A (Cal) • *[centered]* **Triumphal Arch.** [¶] A

228.34   creditably (Cal) • creditable

             [Copy-text from 230.23 through 230.27 is Webster]

230.23   Bilk (Cal) • BILK
230.27   Bilked (Cal) • BILK'ED

             [Copy-text for 230.29 is Walker]

230.29   Bilk, (Cal) • BILK=bĭlk,

             [Copy-text for 230.31 is Wright]

*230.31   Bilk. To deceive; to defraud. (Cal) • Bilk, *bilk,* v. a. *(A. S.)* To frustrate or disappoint; to deceive or defraud, by non-fulfilment of engagement; to cheat.

             [Copy-text from 230.33 through 230.35 is Worcester]

230.33   Bilk (Cal) • BĬLK
230.33   deride.] (I-C) • deride.] [*i.* bilked; *pp.* bilking, bilked.]

             [Copy-text for 230.37 is Spiers]

230.37   Bilk, (Cal) • BILK [bĭlk]
230.37   (argot) (Cal) • † (argot)

             [Copy-text from 231.2 through 231.4 is Adler]

231.2   Bilk (Cal) • BILK

             [Copy-text from 231.6 through 231.7 is Seoane]

231.6   Bilk. (Cal) • BILK [bilc]

             [Copy-text from 231.16 through 231.35 is Richardson]

231.16   Bilk (Cal) • BILK

Historical Collation

Texts collated: Cal, AC, MC, EB, AF, Webster, Wright, Walker, Worcester, Spiers, Adler, Seoane, Johnson, and Richardson (see the commentary above).

Collation:

225.29   [¶] "The (Cal) • [no ¶] ∧~ (AC)

226.2   arch (Cal) • arch, or rather quadruple arch, for such it really
            was, as there were four pillars at the four corners of the
            street, from which arose four arches, one for each street-
            front on both California and Montgomery streets, (AC)

226.3   evening. (Cal) • evening. The height of each arch was fifty-
            four feet, and the width from pillar to pillar was thirty-four
            feet. (AC)

226.11   [¶] 'Mine (I-C) • [¶] "Mine (AC); [no ¶] 'Mine (Cal)

226.13   [¶] 'Honor (I-C) • [¶] "Honor (AC); [no ¶] 'Honor (Cal)

226.13   our (AC) • the (Cal)

226.14   [¶] The (AC) • [no ¶] The (Cal)

226.18–19   evergreen wreaths (AC) • evergreens, wreaths (Cal)

227.9   M. F. (Cal) • F. M. (MC)

227.22   dignified (MC) • designated (Cal)

227.23   [¶] "The (MC) • [no ¶] "The (Cal)

227.37–38   Montgomery and California (EB) • California and Mont-
            gomery (Cal)

227.39–40   [Here . . . detail.] The arches (Cal) • The arch, or rather the
            arches, for there are four, rise from four massive pillars 30
            feet in height, the tops of the arches reaching nearly 50 feet
            from the ground and spanning the whole width of the street.
            They (EB)

228.1   evergreen (EB) • evergreens (Cal)

228.8   [¶] TRIUMPHAL ARCH.—A (Cal) • [centered] **Triumphal
            Arch.** [¶] A (AF)

228.16   each of (AF) • [not in] (Cal)

228.34   creditably (Cal) • creditable (AF)

230.24   exult (Webster) • vault (Cal)

230.29   BILK, (Cal) • BILK=bĭlk, (Walker)

230.31   BILK. To deceive; to defraud. (Cal) • BILK, *bilk*, v. a. *(A. S.)*
            To frustrate or disappoint; to deceive or defraud, by nonful-
            filment of engagement; to cheat. (Wright)

230.33–34   deride.] To . . . elude. (I-C) • deride.] [*i.* BILKED; *pp.* BILKING,
            BILKED.] To . . . elude. (Worcester); deride; to defraud. (Cal)

230.37   BILK, (Cal) • BILK [bĭlk] (Spiers)

230.37   (argot) (Cal) • † (argot) (Spiers)

231.2   betrügen (Adler) • betragen (Cal)

231.6   BILK. (Cal) • BILK [bilc] (Seoane)

231.9   *Lye* (Johnson) • Lye (Cal)
231.11   *Dryd.* (Johnson) • *Dryden.* (Cal)
231.18   *explained* (Richardson) • explained (Cal)
231.21   [¶] To (Richardson) • [*no* ¶] To (Cal)

111. *ENTHUSIASTIC ELOQUENCE*

Textual Commentary

The first printing in the San Francisco *Dramatic Chronicle* for 23 June 1865 (p. 2) is copy-text. Copy: PH from Bancroft. There are no textual notes.

Emendations of the Copy-Text

235.1   I HAVE (I-C) • "~~
235.5   "tum, tum." (I-C) • '~, ~.'
235.6   "tum, tum," (I-C) • '~, ~,'
235.6   instrument (I-C) • instrumens
235.8   "tum, tum." (I-C) • '~, ~.'
235.20   banjo! (I-C) • ~!"

112. *JUST "ONE MORE UNFORTUNATE"*

Textual Commentary

The first printing in the Virginia City *Territorial Enterprise*, probably sometime between 27 and 30 June 1865, is not extant. The sketch survives in the only known contemporary reprinting of the *Enterprise*, the Downieville (Calif.) *Mountain Messenger* for 1 July 1865 (p. 1), which is copy-text. Copy: PH from Bancroft. There are no textual notes.

Emendations of the Copy-Text

238.1   IMMORALITY (I-C) • "~
238.3   myself— (I-C) • ~[∧]
238.7   school-girl, (I-C) • school-girl.
238.10   straightforward (I-C) • straight-|forward
238.12   Holborn (I-C) • Halborn
238.12   living, (I-C) • ~.
238.17   heifer (I-C) • [h]eifer
238.17   child, (I-C) • ~.
239.2   and (I-C) • a
239.3   that (I-C) • [t]hat

239.6   some of (I-C) • some
239.10   Bill," (I-C) • ~",
239.10   Mike, (I-C) • ~.

113. ADVICE FOR GOOD LITTLE BOYS

Textual Commentary

The first printing in the San Francisco *Youths' Companion*, probably on
1 July 1865, is not extant. The sketch survives in the only known contemporary reprinting of the *Companion*, the Yreka City (Calif.) *Weekly
Union* for 8 July 1865 (p. 1), which is copy-text. Copy: PH from Bancroft.

Textual Notes

242.19   cat by the tail] Copy-text "cat by a tail" implies a cat with
             more than one tail. Since the "advice" given in the sketch is
             not itself written in vernacular, and since the copy-text
             (twice removed from Mark Twain's manuscript) has five
             additional manifest errors, we have emended.

Emendations of the Copy-Text

242.3   another boy's (I-C) • an-| another's boys
242.4   unless (I-C) • uless
242.4   can't (I-C) • can
242.8   not at (I-C) • not
242.10   to a (I-C) • to
242.15   grandpapa (I-C) • grand-|papa
*242.19   the tail (I-C) • a tail

114. ADVICE FOR GOOD LITTLE GIRLS

Textual Commentary

The first printing, probably in the San Francisco *Youths' Companion* for
1 or 8 July 1865, is not extant. The sketch survives in the earliest known
reprinting in JF1, pp. 164–166, which is copy-text. Copies: 1867 impression (MTP Armes) and 1870 impression (University of North Carolina
817.C625.ce).

Reprintings and Revisions. This is the only sketch in JF1 for which
no periodical printing has been found. It is possible, but unlikely, that
Clemens wrote it for JF1, which would then constitute its first printing.
It seems somewhat more likely that it was reprinted in JF1, either from
the San Francisco *Youths' Companion* or from some unidentified reprint-

ing. Because no earlier printing has been found, it is impossible to detect any revisions that Clemens may have made in his sketch in January or February 1867, while preparing the JF1 printer's copy.

The JF1 text was reprinted in a way that deviates slightly from the usual pattern as described in the textual introduction. As usual, Routledge reprinted JF1 in 1867 (JF2), and Hotten in turn reprinted JF2 in 1870 (JF3). Routledge also reprinted JF2 in 1870 (JF4a) and, using the unaltered plates of JF4a, reissued the book in 1872 (JF4b). None of these texts was revised by the author, and the compositors made only one substantive error: JF3 printed "aggravated" instead of "aggravating" (244.3). When Mark Twain prepared the printer's copy for MTSk in March or April 1872, he revised a copy of JF4a and evidently made one revision in this sketch: he changed "rope him in" to "beguile" (244.11).

One year later (1873), however, Hotten reprinted the sketch in HWa, taking his text not from JF3 (as he did for all but two sketches), but from MTSk. His compositors made no substantive errors, and they of course incorporated the one change that the author had made for MTSk. When Mark Twain revised HWa for Chatto and Windus in the fall of 1873 (HWa**MT**), he made four changes. He deleted "artless" (244.13), "eminently" (244.15), and "and disaster" (244.16). He also changed the dash after "people" (245.11) to a comma. All of the HWa**MT** changes were incorporated in HWb, published in 1874.

When in 1875 Mark Twain came to reprint the sketch in SkNO, he entered the title "Advice to Good Little Girls" as item 46 in the Doheny table of contents (see figure 23E in the textual introduction, volume 1, p. 628). He revised the sketch slightly in HWb**MT**, adding "him" after his earlier revision "beguile." He did not revise it in MTSk**MT**, nor did he clearly indicate in the table of contents for that volume that it was elsewhere revised. Although Clemens obviously intended to have the sketch reprinted from HWb**MT**, the printers entered "321S" beside the item in the Doheny table of contents, indicating that they had found it on page 321 of MTSk**MT**. The sketch was not finally reprinted in SkNO: someone, possibly the author, has drawn a cross through it and the next two items in the Doheny table of contents. They were also omitted.

There are no emendations of the copy-text or textual notes. The diagram of transmission is given below.

Historical Collation

Texts collated:

JF1   *Jumping Frog* (New York: Webb, 1867), pp. 164–166. Probably reprints the San Francisco *Youths' Companion,* which is not extant.

JF2   *Jumping Frog* (London: Routledge, 1867), pp. 155–157. Reprints JF1 without substantive error.

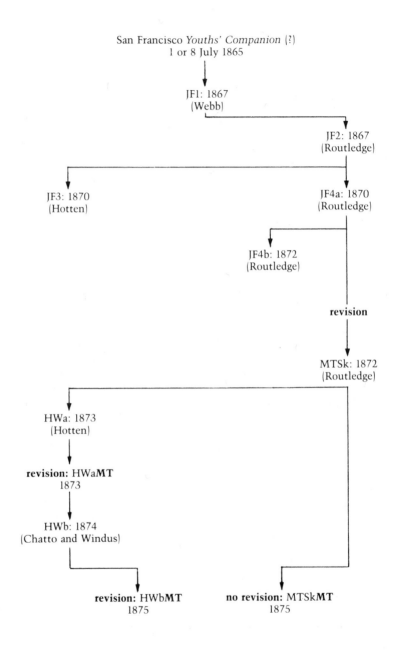

San Francisco *Youths' Companion* (?)
1 or 8 July 1865

JF1: 1867
(Webb)

JF2: 1867
(Routledge)

JF3: 1870
(Hotten)

JF4a: 1870
(Routledge)

JF4b: 1872
(Routledge)

revision

MTSk: 1872
(Routledge)

HWa: 1873
(Hotten)

revision: HWaMT
1873

HWb: 1874
(Chatto and Windus)

revision: HWbMT
1875

no revision: MTSkMT
1875

JF3   *Jumping Frog* (London: Hotten, 1870), pp. 131–132. Reprints JF2 with one error.

JF4   *Jumping Frog* (London: Routledge, 1870 and 1872), pp. 142–143. Reprints JF2 without error.

MTSk   *Mark Twain's Sketches* (London: Routledge, 1872), pp. 321–322. Reprints JF4 with one revision by Mark Twain.

MTSk**MT**   Copy of MTSk revised by Mark Twain, who made no changes in this sketch.

HWa   *Choice Humorous Works* (London: Hotten, 1873), p. 382. Reprints MTSk without substantive error.

HWa**MT**   Sheets of HWa revised by Mark Twain, who made four changes in this sketch.

HWb   *Choice Humorous Works* (London: Chatto and Windus, 1874), pp. 377–378. Reprints HWa with authorial revisions from HWa**MT**.

HWb**MT**   Copy of HWb revised by Mark Twain, who made one change in this sketch.

Collation:

244.3   aggravating (JF1–HWb) • aggravated (JF3)

244.11   rope him in (JF1–JF4, JF1–JF3) • beguile (MTSk–HWb); beguile him (HWb**MT**)

244.13   artless simplicity (JF1–HWa, JF1–JF3) • simplicity (HWa**MT**–HWb)

244.15   eminently plausible (JF1–HWa, JF1–JF3) • plausible (HWa**MT**–HWb)

244.16   ruin and disaster. (JF1–HWa, JF1–JF3) • ruin. (HWa**MT**–HWb)

245.11   people— (JF1–HWa, JF1–JF3) • ~, (HWa**MT**–HWb)

115. *MARK TWAIN ON THE COLORED MAN*

Textual Commentary

The first printing in the Virginia City *Territorial Enterprise*, probably sometime between 7 and 19 July 1865, is not extant. The sketch survives in the only known contemporary reprinting of the *Enterprise*, the San Francisco *Golden Era* 13 (23 July 1865): 2, which is copy-text. Copy: PH from Bancroft. There are no textual notes.

Emendations of the Copy-Text

248.1   AND (I-C) • "~

248.1   procession (I-C) • procession of the procession

248.15   fellow-citizens (I-C) • fellow[-]citizens
248.15   short-sighted (I-C) • short-|sighted
249.9   ranks, (I-C) • ~[.]
249.17   out. (I-C) • ~."

116. *THE FACTS*

Textual Commentary

The first printing in the *Californian* 3 (26 August 1865): 5 is copy-text. Copies: Bancroft; PH from Yale; PH of the Yale Scrapbook, pp. 13–14.

Reprintings and Revisions. Only a part of this sketch, retitled "An Item Which the Editor Himself Could Not Understand," was reprinted in JF1: the section devoted to Johnny Skae's *"Distressing Accident"* and the initial reaction to it. The printer's copy for the JF1 printing was drawn from the Yale Scrapbook, where Mark Twain revised a clipping of the *Californian*. Only the portion not reprinted in JF1 (from "But" at 257.29 to the end) survives in the scrapbook; it is preceded by three page stubs, indicating that the scrapbook pages which once held the preceding portion of the clipping were scissored out to serve as the printer's copy. Mark Twain demonstrably revised that portion of the scrapbook clipping which remains intact, substituting "streams" for "stream" (259.11), "legs" for "body" (259.11), and "leer" for "slobber" (259.19). This evidence suggests that some of the variants in the JF1 printing may reflect changes Mark Twain made on the now lost printer's copy: for example, the substitution "the office where we are sub-editor" for "our office" (254.7). Nevertheless, most of the changes can more plausibly be attributed to the compositor or the editor. Indeed, the revised scrapbook clipping suggests that the author's intention in January or February 1867 was to reprint the entire sketch. The decision to include only a small portion of it in JF1 was therefore probably made by Charles Henry Webb, who was obliged to make only a few minor adjustments, such as removing the reference to the *Californian* at 255.27 perhaps, or changing Mark Twain's habitual "who" to "whom" at 257.25. Although it is conceivable that Mark Twain contributed minor changes to the text as reprinted in JF1, none of its variants is distinctively authorial, and they are all here attributed to Webb.

The reprinting of the JF1 text is described in the textual introduction. Routledge reprinted JF1 in 1867 (JF2), and Hotten in turn reprinted JF2 in 1870 (JF3). Routledge also reprinted JF2 in 1870 (JF4a) and, using the unaltered plates of JF4a, reissued the book in 1872 (JF4b). Although none of these texts was revised by the author, the compositors introduced a number of minor errors. For example, "snuffling" became "snuffing" (256.2) in JF2, "its" became "his" (255.7) in JF4, and "information"

(256.26) was omitted from JF3. When Mark Twain prepared the printer's copy for MTSk in March or April 1872, he revised a copy of JF4a and presumably made a dozen revisions and corrections in this sketch. Collation shows that he corrected the error "snuffing" back to "snuffling," but did not restore "its." He modified the rambunctious tone of his language by removing words such as "blasted" (255.21), "very" (255.28), "got" (255.34), "unfortunate" (256.31–32), "driveling" (257.5), and "infernal" (257.16). He also changed "boss-editor" to "chief editor" (255.28), "blazes" to "grass" (256.2), and tightened the syntax in several places by adding "that."

One year later (1873), Hotten reprinted the JF3 text in HWa. When Mark Twain revised this book for Chatto and Windus in the fall of 1873 (HWa**MT**), he made only four changes. He again corrected the error "snuffing" that he had earlier corrected in MTSk, and instead of deleting "blasted" and "infernal" (255.21 and 257.16) he changed them to "single" and "exasperating," while also deleting "distressing" at 257.16. The HWa**MT** changes were made in the plates of HWa and incorporated in HWb, which was published in 1874 and introduced no new errors.

When in 1875 Mark Twain prepared the printer's copy for SkNO, he revised this sketch extensively in HWb**MT**, leaving it unrevised in MTSk**MT**. He entered the title "An Item which the Editor himself could not understand" as item 31 of the Doheny table of contents (see figure 23D in the textual introduction, volume 1, p. 627). Mark Twain made some seventeen corrections and revisions. He again deleted "very," "got," and "unfortunate." He changed "boss-editor" to "head editor" (255.28), "earthly" to "sort of" (255.35), and again supplied a second "that" at 255.32. He also canceled two longer phrases: the injunction "to go to blazes with it" (256.2), and the sentence "He says every man he meets has insinuated that somebody about THE CALIFORNIAN office has gone crazy" (255.36–37). He changed Johnny Skae's name to "Bloke" throughout the text, but not in the title: SkNO used the Doheny table of contents title in its table of contents, but the sketch itself was retitled "Mr. Bloke's Item," perhaps because Mark Twain or Bliss made the change in proof. SkNO incorporated all of the changes imposed by Mark Twain on the printer's copy.

Mark Twain had revised the JF1 printing of this sketch twice before making most of the revisions discussed above. Sometime in 1869 he made ten revisions in the Doheny copy of the *Jumping Frog*, JF1**MT**, some of which duplicate later changes (the cancellation of "blasted" and the substitution "chief editor" for "boss editor"). Other revisions conform to the generally cautious intention of the JF1**MT** changes: for example, the substitution "full of hope" for the more reckless original phrase, "in the full hope of a glorious resurrection" (255.17–18). All of the JF1**MT** revisions are recorded in the historical collation. Mark Twain also revised one portion of the text, Johnny Skae's *"Distressing Accident"* item, before reprinting it in "Favors from Correspondents," *Galaxy* 10 (October 1870): 576, from a copy of JF1. He made one substantive revision, substituting "solitary" for "blasted" (255.21). This variant is not recorded in the historical collation.

The diagram of transmission is given below.

Emendations of the Copy-Text

254.2	MARK (I-C) • MAKK
255.1	*Accident.* — (I-C) • ~∧—
255.21	world. (I-C) • ~[∧]
256.8	blasphemy. (I-C) • ~[∧]
257.19	it. (I-C) • ~[∧]
259.24	wishy-washy (I-C) • wishy-|washy
260.6	rhythm (I-C) • rythm
260.16	CALIFORNIAN.) (I-C) • ~[∧])
261.9	wool-gathering (I-C) • wool-|gathering
261.19	Skae. (I-C) • Skae. | MARK TWAIN.

Historical Collation

Texts collated:

Cal	"The Facts," *Californian* 3 (26 August 1865): 5.
YSMT	Clipping of Cal from 257.29 to the end, revised by Mark Twain in the Yale Scrapbook.

["*An Item Which the Editor Himself Could Not Understand*" *in the following*]

JF1	*Jumping Frog* (New York: Webb, 1867), pp. 110–115. Reprints part of Cal with editorial changes but no identifiable authorial revisions.
JF1MT	The copy of an 1869 impression of JF1 revised by Mark Twain. It was not used as printer's copy for any known reprinting.
JF2	*Jumping Frog* (London: Routledge, 1867), pp. 102–107. Reprints JF1 with one error.
JF3	*Jumping Frog* (London: Hotten, 1870), pp. 71–73. Reprints JF2 with two errors.
JF4	*Jumping Frog* (London: Routledge, 1870 and 1872), pp. 94–99. Reprints JF2 with one error.
MTSk	*Mark Twain's Sketches* (London: Routledge, 1872), pp. 272–276. Reprints JF4 with a dozen revisions by Mark Twain.
MTSkMT	Copy of MTSk revised by Mark Twain, who made no changes in this sketch.

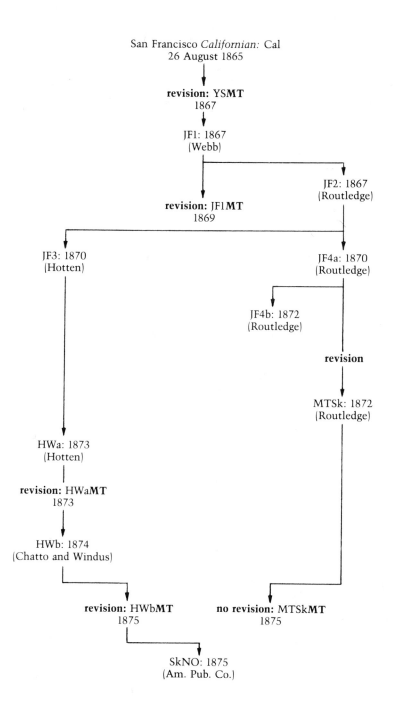

San Francisco *Californian:* Cal
26 August 1865

revision: YSMT
1867

JF1: 1867
(Webb)

JF2: 1867
(Routledge)

revision: JF1MT
1869

JF3: 1870
(Hotten)

JF4a: 1870
(Routledge)

JF4b: 1872
(Routledge)

revision

MTSk: 1872
(Routledge)

HWa: 1873
(Hotten)

revision: HWaMT
1873

HWb: 1874
(Chatto and Windus)

revision: HWbMT
1875

no revision: MTSkMT
1875

SkNO: 1875
(Am. Pub. Co.)

HWa   *Choice Humorous Works* (London: Hotten, 1873), pp. 483–485. Reprints JF3 without additional error.

HWa**MT**   Sheets of HWa revised by Mark Twain, who made four changes in this sketch.

HWb   *Choice Humorous Works* (London: Chatto and Windus, 1874), pp. 469–471. Reprints HWa with authorial revisions from HWa**MT**.

HWb**MT**   Copy of HWb revised by Mark Twain, who made seventeen changes in this sketch.

[*"Mr. Bloke's Item" in the following*]

SkNO   *Sketches, New and Old* (Hartford: American Publishing Company, 1875), pp. 167–170. Reprints HWb with authorial revisions from HWb**MT**.

Collation:

254 *title*   *The Facts* (Cal) • An Item Which the Editor Himself Could Not Understand (JF1–MTSk, JF1–HWb); Mr. Bloke's Item (SkNO)

254.1–6   CONCERNING . . . *Mysterious.* — (Cal) • [*not in*] (JF1+)

254.6   Skae (Cal–MTSk, Cal–HWb) • Bloke (HWb**MT**–SkNO)

254.7   our office (Cal) • the office where we are sub-editor (JF1+)

254.8   profound and (Cal–MTSk, Cal–SkNO) • [*canceled*] (JF1**MT**)

254.14   Oh (Cal) • oh! (JF1+)

254.16   Our (Cal) • The (JF1+)

255.3   usual (Cal–MTSk, Cal–SkNO) • [*canceled*] (JF1**MT**)

255.4   only (Cal–MTSk, Cal–SkNO) • [*canceled*] (JF1**MT**)

255.7   its (Cal–JF2, Cal–SkNO) • his (JF4–MTSk)

255.16   lookout (Cal–MTSk, Cal–SkNO) • alert (JF1**MT**)

255.17–18   in . . . resurrection (Cal–MTSk, Cal–SkNO) • full of hope (JF1**MT**)

255.19   guile, as it were (Cal–MTSk, Cal–SkNO) • guile (JF1**MT**)

255.21   every blasted (Cal–JF4, Cal–HWa) • every (JF1**MT**, MTSk); single (HWa**MT**–SkNO)

255.23   die we can do it (Cal–MTSk, Cal–SkNO) • die, we can (JF1**MT**)

255.24   hearts (Cal–MTSk, Cal–HWb) • heart (SkNO)

255.24–25   and sincerity (Cal–MTSk, Cal–SkNO) • [*canceled*] (JF1**MT**)

255.27   (SECOND . . . CALIFORNIAN.) (Cal) • [*not in*] (JF1+)

255.28   boss-editor (Cal–JF4, Cal–HWb) • chief editor (JF1**MT**, MTSk); head editor (HWb**MT**–SkNO)

255.28	very mischief (Cal–JF4, Cal–HWb) • mischief (MTSk, HWb**MT**-SkNO)
255.32	says that (Cal–JF4, Cal–HWb) • says that that (MTSk, HWb**MT**-SkNO)
255.33	Johnny Skae's (Cal–MTSk, Cal–HWb) • Mr. Bloke's (HWb**MT**-SkNO)
255.34	has got (Cal–JF4, Cal–HWb) • has (MTSk, HWb**MT**-SkNO)
255.34	in it (Cal–JF4, Cal–SkNO) • [not in] (MTSk)
255.35	earthly (Cal–MTSk, Cal–HWb) • sort of (HWb**MT**-SkNO)
255.36–37	it. He says . . . crazy. (Cal–JF4, Cal–HWb) • it. He says that . . . crazy. (MTSk); it. (HWb**MT**-SkNO)
256.1	Johnny Skae (Cal–MTSk, Cal–HWb) • Mr. Bloke (HWb**MT**-SkNO)
256.2	hour, and . . . it'— (Cal–MTSk, Cal–HWb) • hour; (HWb**MT**-SkNO)
256.2	blazes (Cal–JF4, Cal–HWb) • grass (MTSk)
256.2	snuffling (Cal–JF1, MTSk, HWa**MT**-SkNO) • snuffing (JF2–JF4, JF2–HWa)
256.9	just read (Cal–MTSk, Cal–HWb) • read (HWb**MT**-SkNO)
256.26	information (Cal--MTSk, HWb**MT**-SkNO) • [not in] (JF3–HWb)
256.29	Skae (Cal–MTSk, Cal–HWb) • Bloke (HWb**MT**-SkNO)
256.31–32	the unfortunate (Cal–JF4, Cal–HWb) • the (MTSk, HWb**MT**-SkNO)
257.5	driveling (Cal–JF4, Cal–SkNO) • [not in] (MTSk)
257.6	gesticulating (Cal–JF4, Cal–SkNO) • gesticulation (MTSk)
257.14	Skae (Cal–MTSk, Cal–HWb) • Bloke (HWb**MT**-SkNO)
257.16	infernal imaginary distressing (Cal–JF4, Cal–HWa) • imaginary distressing (MTSk); exasperating imaginary (HWa**MT**-SkNO)
257.17	his (Cal–MTSk) • this (JF3–SkNO)
257.23	Skae's (Cal–MTSk, Cal–HWb) • Bloke's (HWb**MT**-SkNO)
257.25	who (Cal) • whom (JF1+)
257.27	cipher (Cal–MTSk, HWb**MT**-SkNO) • cypher (JF3–HWb)
257.29–261.19	But . . . Skae. (Cal, YS**MT**) • [not in] (JF1+)
259.11	stream (Cal) • streams (YS**MT**)
259.11	body (Cal) • legs (YS**MT**)
259.19	slobber (Cal) • leer (YS**MT**)
261.19	Skae. (I-C) • Skae. | Mark Twain. (Cal, YS**MT**)

[THREE VERSIONS OF THE JUMPING FROG]

§117. *THE ONLY RELIABLE ACCOUNT OF THE CELEBRATED JUMPING FROG OF CALAVERAS COUNTY*

Textual Commentary

The manuscript of this sketch, probably written in September or early October 1865 but never published, survives in the Jean Webster McKinney Family Papers, Vassar. It is copy-text. The piece is written in brown or black ink on eleven leaves numbered consecutively by Mark Twain. The first six leaves are unlined cream-colored wove stationery measuring 12½ by 7⅞ inches, with an embossment of the Capitol in the lower right corner. The last five leaves are cream-colored wove paper with thirty-two horizontal rules, measuring 11⅝ by 7⅜ inches, with an embossment of a crown in the upper left corner. The second of these stationeries is also used in "Angel's Camp Constable" (no. 118), in "Sarrozay Letter from 'the Unreliable' " (no. 86), as well as in the fragment reproduced in Appendix C2, volume 2: the partial letter to "Editors Californian" written sometime in the latter part of 1865.

On the back of the first leaf of the manuscript Mark Twain wrote "The Frog." He then canceled this and wrote "Boomerang." Finally, in pencil, he added "Letter to Tribune."

Textual Notes

274.12   BOOMERANG—PAST.] Mark Twain revised this heading in the manuscript by adding "—PAST." In doing so, he inadvertently left standing a period after "BOOMERANG," and we have therefore emended to correct the oversight.

Emendations of the Copy-Text

274.2   farm-house (I-C) • farm-|house
274.9   broken-hearted (I-C) • broken-|hearted
*274.12 BOOMERANG (I-C) • ~.
276.11   fly-blown (I-C) • fly-|blown
276.12   threadbare (I-C) • thread-|bare
276.36   chipped (I-C) • ~.
277.2   made (I-C) • accom/made
278.2   birthright (I-C) • birth-|right

Alterations in the Manuscript

273.1   the] *written over wiped-out* 'Mr.'
273.3   WHEELER,] *originally followed by* 'formerly', *which was wiped out;* 'in former times' *written over, then canceled.*

273.12	Simon] 'Si' *written over wiped-out* 'the'.
273.13	times, [though] *originally* 'times,—though'; *the open parenthesis written over the dash, canceling it.*
273.14–15	the picturesque borders of Lake Tulare,] *interlined with a caret above canceled* 'Oro Fino Flat'.
274.3	its] *interlined with a caret following canceled* 'the'.
274.3	outlines] *follows canceled* 'picture'.
274.4	the] *written over a wiped-out dash.*
274.5	proceeded] *written over wiped-out* 'journeyed'.
274.6	my] *written over wiped-out* 'our'.
274.12	—PAST.] *added.*
274.22	their] *followed by canceled* 'muddy,'.
274.28	grand] *followed by canceled* 'military'.
274.30–31	fulminated] *follows canceled* 'fired'.
274.31–32	a newspaper] 'a' *interlined with a caret;* 's' *on* 'newspapers' *canceled.*
274.35	also] *interlined with a caret.*
275.3	BOOMERANG] *written over wiped-out* 'Behold the'.
275.3	—PRESENT.] *added.*
275.7	Where] *written over wiped-out* 'Once'.
275.10	banquets] *written over wiped-out* 'suppers,'.
275.10	ten-pins] *written over wiped-out* 'billiards'.
275.11	stragglers] 'gg' *mended from* 'ng'; 'lers' *added.*
275.20	the] 'e' *mended from* 'y'.
275.26	a piano] *followed by canceled* '&'.
275.26	in it, and also a young] *written over wiped-out* 'a young lady in'.
275.27	now] *interlined with a caret above canceled* 'to-day'.
275.27	a wide-spread] *follows canceled* 'a wide-spread' *and interlined without a caret above canceled* 'an'.
275.27	of] *interlined with a caret after canceled* 'of leaning, bulging,'.
275.28	surrounded] *written over* 'in' *following canceled* 'with broken windows, & shutters hanging by one hinge in'.
275.34	costly] *written over wiped-out* 'costly'.
275.35	rich] *interlined with a caret above canceled* 'expensive'.
275.35	must put] *written over wiped-out* 'will be'.
276.10	single] 's' *written over wiped-out* 'b'.
276.13	and is] 'is' *interlined with a caret.*

276.13   places] 's' *mended from* 'd'.

276.13   one of the] *written over wiped-out* 'the pockets'.

276.13   piano is] 'is' *interlined without a caret above canceled* 'was'.

276.14   are] *interlined with a caret above canceled* 'were'.

276.14   willow] *interlined with a caret.*

276.15   are] *interlined without a caret above canceled* 'were'.

276.15   get] *interlined without a caret above canceled* 'got'.

276.16   stand] *interlined without a caret above canceled* 'stood'.

276.17   want] *mended from* 'wanted'.

276.17   don't] *interlined without a caret above canceled* 'didn't'.

276.17   can] *interlined without a caret above canceled* 'could'.

276.19   have] *interlined without a caret above canceled* 'had'.

276.19   from] *written over wiped-out* 'ca' *or* 'co'.

276.20   can] *interlined without a caret above canceled* 'could'.

276.20   at all] *follows canceled* 'at all'.

276.21   balls] *follows canceled* 'colors of the'.

276.22   is] *interlined without a caret above canceled* 'was'.

276.23   is] *interlined without a caret above canceled* 'was'.

276.24   look] *mended from* 'looked'.

276.24   will] *interlined without a caret above canceled* 'would'.

276.25   is] *interlined without a caret above canceled* 'was'.

276.26   play] *mended from* 'played'.

276.26   will] *interlined without a caret above canceled* 'would'.

276.27   requires] 's' *written over* 'd'.

276.28   is] *interlined without a caret above canceled* 'was'.

276.29   is] *interlined without a caret above canceled* 'was'.

276.29   isn't] *interlined without a caret above canceled* 'wasn't'.

276.32   hint] *mended from* 'hinted'.

276.33   is] *interlined without a caret above canceled* 'was'.

276.34   withers] 's' *written over* 'ed'.

276.34   lofty] *interlined without a caret above canceled* 'grand'.

276.36   are] *interlined without a caret above canceled* 'were'.

276.36   chipped] *followed by period left standing.*

276.37   are] *interlined without a caret above canceled* 'were'.

276.38   bounce] *mended from* 'bounced'.

276.38   scamper] *mended from* 'scampered'.

276.38   clatter] *mended from* 'clattered'.

276.38   as if] *interlined without a caret above canceled* 'like'.

277.2   did see] *interlined without a caret above canceled* 'saw'.

277.2   shots] *interlined without a caret above canceled* 'others'.

277.2   made] *written over* 'accomp' *and interlined without a caret above canceled* 'made'; 'accom' *interlined without a caret between* 'made' *and canceled* 'made' *and left standing.*

277.5   we will say] *interlined with a caret.*

277.6   back] *interlined with a caret.*

277.8   rules of] 'of' *written over wiped-out* 'to'.

277.10   once more,] *interlined without a caret above canceled* 'again,'.

277.11   red;"] *the semicolon mended from a period.*

277.11   very] *added in left margin.*

277.21   describe] *written over wiped-out* 'picture it'.

277.24   presumption] 'ion' *mended from* 'uous'.

277.25   hope] *written over wiped-out* 'expect'.

277.32   The ancient] *written over wiped-out* 'But will'.

277.35   barkeeper] 'k' *written over a hyphen.*

277.35   5] *interlined with a caret.*

278.1–2   new empire] *written over wiped-out* 'proud'.

278.3   New] 'N' *written over* 'n'.

§118. *ANGEL'S CAMP CONSTABLE*

Textual Commentary

The manuscript of this sketch, probably written in September or early October 1865 but never published, survives in the Jean Webster McKinney Family Papers, Vassar. It is copy-text. The piece is written in brown or black ink on five leaves numbered consecutively by Mark Twain. All five leaves are cream-colored wove paper with thirty-two horizontal rules, measuring 11⅝ by 7⅜ inches, with an embossment of a crown in the upper left corner. The same paper is used in "The Only Reliable Account" (no. 117) and in the fragment reproduced in Appendix C2, volume 2, as well as in "Sarrozay Letter from 'the Unreliable' " (no. 86), written in 1864. Mark Twain wrote the title on the back of the first leaf. There are no textual notes.

Emendations of the Copy-Text

279.14   enthusiasm (I-C) • unthusiasm

280.4   there's (I-C) • there

280.8   fighting— (I-C) • ~.—

280.15   "I (I-C) • ∧~
280.18-19   'Hell . . . riot,' . . . 'In . . . peace' (I-C) • "~ . . . ~,'' . . .
              "~ . . . ~"
280.23-26   "Then . . . ' 'Nother . . . it.' (I-C) • ∧~ . . . " 'Nother . . . ~."
280.30-   "Well . . . 'O . . . all.' . . . slouch." (I-C) • ∧~ . . . "O . . .
281.13   ~." . . . ~.∧

              Alterations in the Manuscript

279.3   not] *interlined with a caret.*
279.3   laugh] *followed by a canceled comma and canceled* 'while
              he was'.
279.5   fortified] *interlined without a caret above canceled*
              'provided'.
279.8   formerly] 'f' *written over* 'a'.
279.14-15   the smooth] *follows canceled* 'his monotonous'.
279.15   voice.] *follows canceled* 'manner of speaking' *and a period
              left standing.*
280.16   noticing] 'c' *written over* 'n'.
280.17-18   sung . . . riot,'] *interlined with a caret above canceled*
              'says'.
280.26   fellers] 'er' *written over wiped-out* 'ow'.
280.27   engaged] 'en' *written over wiped-out* 'ou'.
280.31   in] *written over wiped-out* 'to'.
280.32   one] *written over wiped-out* 'the'.
280.35   say] 'y' *possibly written over* 'i'.
280.38   do you s'pose I've] *interlined with a caret above canceled*
              'have I'.
281.2   reckon] *interlined without a caret above canceled*
              'suppose'.
281.5   Well] *follows a canceled dash.*
281.9   knowed] *interlined without a caret above canceled* 'knew'.
281.9   busting] *follows canceled* 'putting'.

              §119. *JIM SMILEY AND HIS JUMPING FROG*

              Textual Commentary

The first printing in the New York *Saturday Press* 4 (18 November 1865):
248-249 (SP) is copy-text. Copies: New York Public Library; PH from
Yale; PH of the Yale Scrapbook, pp. 23A-26A; PH in MTP. The present
text reprints SP, corrected but unrevised. A second version of the tale,

incorporating revisions made by Mark Twain as late as 1874, will appear in its chronological position in this collection as "The Notorious Jumping Frog of Calaveras County" (no. 363).

Reprintings and Revisions. Two factors encouraged Mark Twain to expend more than his usual energy in revising and correcting this sketch: its great fame, and its extensive use of Pike County dialect (David Carkeet, "The Dialects in *Huckleberry Finn*," *American Literature* 51 [November 1979]: 326). Its fame assured that it would be frequently reprinted (ten times in ten years). Its dialect assured that Mark Twain would continue to tinker with the consistency and the form of dialect spellings, and that he would need to correct the frequent errors of his compositors and editors, who tended both to normalize unusual spellings ("risk" instead of "resk") and to supply nonstandard spellings which he did not want ("cal'klated" instead of his original "cal'lated"). Fortunately, Mark Twain's efforts at revision and correction need not be inferred wholly from the evidence of collation. Two sets of holograph changes—one on the Yale Scrapbook clipping (YS**MT**) and one on the 1869 Doheny *Jumping Frog* (JF1**MT**)—demonstrate how he attended to what might otherwise be treated as compositorial changes in spelling and punctuation. Thus, even when we have only the evidence of collation, a demonstrable pattern does emerge: Mark Twain revised and corrected his text in order to increase the number and the consistency of the nonstandard spellings. For a full discussion of problematic variants, however, see the textual commentary to "The Notorious Jumping Frog of Calaveras County."

Since Mark Twain was in San Francisco when the sketch first appeared in New York (SP), he could not control the accuracy of that printing, which was presumably based on his manuscript, now lost. Less than a month after SP, however, Bret Harte reprinted the sketch in the San Francisco *Californian* 4 (16 December 1865): 12 (Cal). Since Harte and Mark Twain were colleagues on the *Californian*, the author certainly had the opportunity to revise a clipping of SP before it was reprinted in Cal. Collation shows that while Mark Twain revised the printer's copy, introducing a handful of changes only he could have made, he did not read or correct the Cal reprinting in proof, for it contained a number of demonstrable errors as well. Mark Twain may have supplied two needed closing quotation marks toward the end of the sketch (287.11 and 287.28), both corrections adopted in the present text. He probably gave the sketch its new title, "The Celebrated Jumping Frog of Calaveras County," for he had used these words one month earlier in the unfinished draft: "The Only Reliable Account of the Celebrated Jumping Frog of Calaveras County" (no. 117). He may also have substituted the real place name "Angel's Camp" for the fictional name "Boomerang" used in SP and in the draft. Five revisions of the dialect are also probably the author's changes: "came" became the nonstandard "come" (285.6); "gave" became "give" (285.10); "his'on" became "his'n" (285.20); "throwed" became "throw'd" (287.27); and "sit" became "set" (287.37). Finally, the name "Smiley" was supplanted throughout by "Greeley," almost certainly because Mark Twain made the change. In an interview published in the Adelaide (South Australian) *Register* on 14 October 1895—thirty years after SP was published—he said that his protagonist "was a real character, and his name was Greeley. The way he got the name of Smiley was this—I wrote the story for the New York *Saturday Gazette,* a perishing weekly so-called literary newspaper. . . . They had not enough 'G's,' and so they changed Greeley's name to 'Smiley.' That's a fact" (Louis J. Budd, ed., *A Listing of and Selection from Newspaper and Magazine Interviews with Samuel L. Clemens: 1874–1910* [Arlington, Texas: American Literary Realism, 1977], p. 63). Although this explanation smacks of printer's lore, it does imply that Mark Twain's original intention was to name the character "Greeley" and that he therefore took the opportunity afforded by the *Californian* to restore his first choice. On the other hand, the Cal reprinting was far from perfect, for Mark Twain demonstrably corrected some eight errors when he revised YS**MT** and JF1**MT**, and he probably corrected a ninth in preparing Sk#1, changing "sat me down" back to "sat down" (283.2); "sitting" back to "setting" (283.33); restoring "him" (284.9); "catching" back to "ketching" (285.32); "send" back to "set" (285.36); restoring "lively" (287.13); "wa'nt" to "warn't" (formerly "wasn't") (287.15); "an" back to "a" (287.16); and "shoulders" back to "shoulder" (287.22). An additional five changes made in Cal—most of them omissions and regularizations of the dialect ("been" instead of "ben"; "went" instead of "went out"; "to see" instead of "to go and see") are here attributed to the compositor even though Mark Twain never restored the original readings.

The author himself pasted a clipping of Cal in the Yale Scrapbook, and sometime in early 1867 he revised that clipping for reprinting in JF1: the four pages originally containing the clipping of Cal are reproduced in photofacsimile in the textual introduction (figures 13–18, volume 1, pp. 528–533). Mark Twain demonstrably corrected five of the errors introduced by Cal, and made six revisions of his text. He added a footnote to explain the circumstances of composition: "Originally written, by request, for Artemus Ward's last book, but arrived in New York after that work had gone to press." He changed "he was on the road" to "it took him to make the trip" (284.4); "Providence" to "Prov'dence" (284.11); "for'castle" to "fo'castle" (284.31); "he" to "*he*" (284.36); and "came" to "come" (285.2). He also reversed his decision of the previous December, reverting to the name "Smiley" throughout the text.

At some time after this initial revision—probably after Webb had agreed to edit JF1 for Mark Twain—the first three paragraphs were peeled away from the scrapbook page, presumably remounted, and then further revised to remove all allusions to Artemus Ward. It is by no means certain that Mark Twain made these changes, especially since one correction that he demonstrably made—the deletion of "me" at 283.2—was evidently not transferred to the new copy and was not incorporated in JF1. Only the first page of the clipping was removed from the scrapbook, however, presumably because it alone required more extensive editing than the scrapbook margin permitted. The other sections remained in place, except for the last one: at some point it too was peeled away from a page that had been scissored out. The clipping was remounted, out of order, in the scrapbook—and two corrections presumably inscribed on the original scrapbook page (the restored word "lively" and the deletion of *n* from "an" at 287.13 and 287.16) were both lost and did not appear in JF1.

Collation demonstrates that JF1 was set from a revised clipping of Cal, and that it followed six of the eleven revisions and corrections inscribed by Mark Twain on the scrapbook clipping. Of the five changes not followed, one was the footnote about Artemus Ward (now superfluous because of the revisions imposed on the early paragraphs); another was the phrase written almost vertically in the left scrapbook margin, "it took him to make the trip" (omitted in favor of the original reading, clearly legible beneath the canceling pencil marks); and three were the corrections ("me," "lively," and "a" for "an") that had been lost when clippings were removed and remounted. The loss of these last three corrections is strong evidence that the YSMT clipping was either the printer's copy, or the immediate source of the printer's copy for JF1. The close correspondence between YSMT and JF1 on six changes, and the understandable failure to follow four of the five remaining changes, makes this inference all but inescapable. It is possible that Mark Twain or Webb, instead of using the YSMT clipping, used a duplicate of Cal to which the scrapbook changes were transferred (albeit imperfectly). This supposed duplicate would account for the failure to follow the revised phrase "it took him to make the trip," and it would also help to explain some further variants in JF1 that are suspiciously like authorial revisions: "hang" instead of "curse" (288.8), "he'd been doin' " instead of "he'd done" (286.3), as well as spelling changes that make Wheeler's dialect even more extreme Pike County ("jest" instead of "just," "j'int" instead of "joint," and "p'ints" instead of "points"). Since these changes conform to Mark Twain's pattern of increasing the number of nonstandard usages in Simon Wheeler's narrative, it is tempting to attribute them to the author. If he made them, however, he must have done so on a duplicate clipping, for they do not appear in YSMT, and Mark Twain was emphatic in saying that he did not read proof for JF1: "It is full of damnable errors of grammar & deadly inconsistencies of spelling in the Frog sketch because I was away & did not read the proofs" (Clemens to Bret Harte, 1 May 1867, *CL1*, letter 130). Such a duplicate clipping cannot be ruled out, but if a duplicate was used, it now seems unlikely that Mark Twain added revisions to it or that he carefully scrutinized the transfer of his YS**MT** changes to the new clipping. The alternative is that Webb, not Mark Twain, made the additional changes, either in proof or on a duplicate clipping, and that it was precisely these further changes to which Mark Twain objected in his letter to Harte. For example, although JFl regularly printed "an't" instead of "ain't," Mark Twain's holograph corrections on JFl**MT** show that he tried to restore his original spelling throughout. Likewise, he restored the italics for "*him*" (283.25), changed "came" back to "come" (283.21), removed an unauthorized comma after "flush" (283.30), changed "risk" back to "resk" twice (284.12 and 286.22), changed "wan't" back to "warn't" (284.28), changed "by" back to "in" (285.4), and changed "cal'klated" and "edercate" back to "cal'lated" and "educate" (285.26). These corrections indicate that the editor or compositor of JFl had volunteered changes in the dialect spellings which Mark Twain did not want. The fact that the author did not also restore "points" where JFl had "p'ints," for example, cannot exempt such changes from the suspicion that they too were volunteered by the JFl editor or compositor. Although it is still conceivable that Mark Twain made changes on a duplicate clipping which do not appear in YS**MT**, these further changes cannot now be distinguished from those which were demonstrably imposed by the editor and later rejected by Mark Twain. Accordingly, JFl variants that do not have the warrant of holograph evidence are here attributed to Webb.

The reprinting of the JFl text is described in the textual introduction. Routledge reprinted JFl in 1867 (JF2), and Hotten in turn reprinted JF2 in 1870 (JF3). Routledge also reprinted JF2 in 1870 (JF4a) and, using the unaltered plates of JF4a, reissued the book in 1872 (JF4b). None of these texts was revised by the author, but the compositors made several minor errors: "solit'ry" instead of "solitry" (283.28); "sitting" instead of "setting" (283.33); "follow" instead of "foller" (284.2); "upon" instead of "up on" (284.30); "any" instead of "ary" (286.24); and "prised" instead of "prized" (287.4). When Mark Twain prepared the printer's copy for MTSk in March or April 1872, he revised a copy of JF4a and made extensive changes in wording and spelling. (Three years earlier he had extensively revised the Doheny copy of the *Jumping Frog* book, JFl**MT**, and although this copy was never used for printer's copy in any known reprinting, its holograph changes were frequently duplicated in MTSk.) Mark Twain continued his revision and correction of the dialect, changing "wasn't" to "warn't" (283.20), "came" to "come" (283.21), "any" to "ary" (283.29), "sitting" to "setting" (283.33), "risk" to "resk" (284.12), "saw" to "see" (285.6), "cal'klated" to "cal'lated" and "edercate" to "educate" (285.26), "kept" to "kep' " (286.13), and "jump" to "*git*" (287.12). He altered several phrases to improve the dialect rendering: "get" became "get to—to" (284.1), "asked" became "up and asked him" (284.9), "shine savage like the furnaces" became "shine wicked you hear *me*" (284.32); "an anvil" became "a church" (287.16); "lifted him up" became "hefted him" (287.29). He again corrected "sat me down" to "sat down" (283.2), and again restored "lively" at 287.13. And, as he had done on JF1**MT**, Mark Twain deleted two sentences at 283.12–15 to avoid explaining his own humor: "To me, the spectacle of a man drifting serenely along through such a queer yarn without ever smiling was exquisitely absurd. As I said before, I asked him to tell me what he knew of Rev. Leonidas W. Smiley, and he replied as follows." Similarly, Mark Twain revised the concluding sentence about as he had done on JF1**MT**. He replaced " 'Oh, hang Smiley and his afflicted cow!' I muttered, good-naturedly, and bidding the old gentleman good-day, I departed" with the following: "Lacking both time and inclination, I did not wait to hear about the afflicted cow, but took my leave." (Compare JF1**MT**: "For lack of time & inclination, I did not tarry to hear about the afflicted cow, but took my departure.")

One year later (1873) Hotten reprinted JF3 in HWa. Despite Mark Twain's earlier revision of MTSk, when he revised HWa for Chatto and Windus in the fall of 1873 (HWa**MT**), he made no corrections or revisions in this sketch, which was reprinted in HWb the following year from the unaltered plates of HWa. In 1874, however, Mark Twain again reprinted the sketch in Sk#1, using a copy of MTSk (now lost) as printer's copy. He changed the title from the "Celebrated" to the "Notorious Jumping Frog of Calaveras County" and he presumably made some twenty adjustments in the dialect spelling and wording. Typically, Mark Twain restored five SP readings that had been corrupted in Cal, JF1, and JF4: "what" became "that" (283.24), "him" became "*him*" (283.25), "wan't" became "warn't" (284.28), "by" became "in" (285.4), and "catching" became "ketching" (285.32). Mark Twain continued to revise his dialect as well: "kept" became "kep' " (285.33), a change in keeping with MTSk "kep' " at 286.13; "far" became "fur" (285.34); "he would" became "he'd" (284.6); "again" became "agin" (286.1); "across" became "acrost" (286.15), a change made earlier on JF1**MT**; "wan't" became "warn't" (287.15); and "this way" became "so" (287.22). He corrected an error introduced by the MTSk compositor: "he had been doin' " was restored to JF1 "he'd been doin' " (286.3). Mark Twain also added "he says" to two phrases (286.27–28 and 287.23), and supplied "However" at the beginning of the concluding sentence (288.9).

Mark Twain is known to have revised his text one more time. Early in 1875 he prepared the printer's copy for SkNO, and he listed this sketch as item 3, "The Jumping Frog," in the Doheny table of contents. But shortly before submitting his printer's copy to Elisha Bliss, Mark Twain decided not to print the sketch by itself, but to publish for the first time a piece written in 1873, "The 'Jumping Frog.' In English. Then in French" (no. 364). This piece did include the "Jumping Frog" sketch, however, and collation shows that this portion of the SkNO piece was set from a revised copy of Sk#1, now lost. Mark Twain made two notable changes: he rejected his revision in MTSk, "shine wicked, you hear *me*," in favor of a reading similar to the original one, "shine like the furnaces" (284.32); and he added some musing comments to the beginning of the sentence at 283.17 ("There was a feller"): "Rev. Leonidas W. H'm, Reverend Le— well, there" (a change virtually identical with one he had written on JF1**MT**: "Reverent Leonidas W. H'm. Reverent Le—— well, there." These and a few other variants that appear in the "Jumping Frog" text of the longer piece in SkNO are reported in the historical collation given below, even though they are pertinent to no. 364 as well. All known variants between 1865 and 1875 are, therefore, reported in the historical collation of the present sketch. Since Mark Twain's revisions of JF1**MT** were very complex and sometimes incomplete, we have adopted the form used for *Alterations in the Manuscript* to report many of them.

Mark Twain also revised a copy of HWb (1878 impression in MTP) to use for oral reading. The few variants he introduced in this sketch are reported only in the textual notes.

The diagram of transmission is given below.

Textual Notes

282.1–24   Mr. . . . him.] This entire opening passage is canceled in Mark Twain's copy of HWb marked for reading. (The piece actually begins with "In compliance" in HWb.)

283.2   sat] Mark Twain probably changed Cal "sat me" to "sat" on YS**MT**, although the correction was not followed in JF1: see the reconstruction of the revised clipping (figures 13–14, volume 1, pp. 528–529). Mark Twain made the same correction on JF1**MT** and probably on MTSk as well. For another interpretation of the YS**MT** deletion mark, see the next note.

283.5   turned] Mark Twain may have revised this word on YS**MT** to read "tuned," the reading of JF1 and all subsequent texts: the reconstruction of the revised clipping cannot exclude the possibility that the author deleted the *r* of "turned" instead of the word "me" (283.2), or with the same stroke that was intended to delete that word. But even if Mark Twain changed "turned" to "tuned" on YS**MT**, his change is here regarded as a revision, not a correction of the copy-text, and it has not been adopted in the present text.

283.30   or you find him busted] JF1 altered "you" to "you'd," bringing it into conformity with the previous phrase "you'd find him flush." The change does not appear on YS**MT**, and is

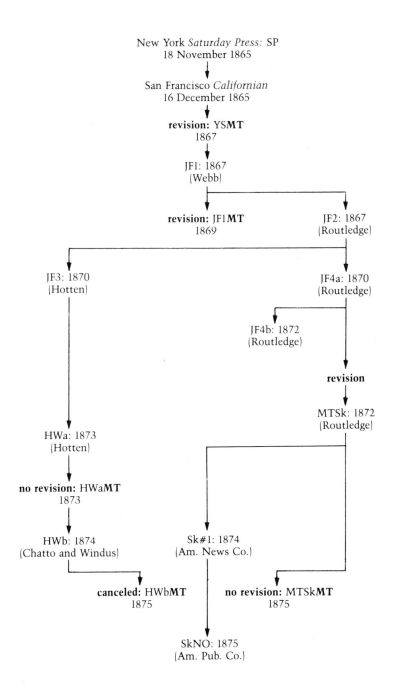

New York *Saturday Press:* SP
18 November 1865

San Francisco *Californian*
16 December 1865

revision: YS**MT**
1867

JF1: 1867
(Webb)

revision: JF1**MT**   JF2: 1867
1869   (Routledge)

JF3: 1870   JF4a: 1870
(Hotten)   (Routledge)

                    JF4b: 1872
                    (Routledge)

                    revision

                    MTSk: 1872
                    (Routledge)

HWa: 1873
(Hotten)

no revision: HWa**MT**
1873

HWb: 1874   Sk#1: 1874
(Chatto and Windus) (Am. News Co.)

        canceled: HWb**MT**   **no revision:** MTSk**MT**
        1875   1875

                    SkNO: 1875
                    (Am. Pub. Co.)

probably editorial or compositorial in origin. Compare the change from "you'd" to "you" at 285.29 that occurs in Sk#1, presumably a result of Mark Twain's revision.

284.25   blowing her nose] This phrase is canceled in the HWb reading copy.

286.3   do.] In the HWb reading copy, this word is followed by the added sentence *"That's* the kind of frog he was."

286.23   Smiley] The Cal clipping from here to the end of the sketch was peeled off its original page in **YSMT** and repasted onto another page (see the textual introduction, volume 1, p. 527, and figures 17–18, pp. 532–533). As a result, some of Mark Twain's marginal revisions were lost, although there are still marks on the clipping itself indicating cancellations and additions. In the following instances "Greeley" was canceled, but no marginal "Smiley" is extant: 286.23, 286.38, 287.17, 287.25, 288.1, and 288.3. In four other cases, there is an *S* visible, which has been reported as "S[miley]" in the collation: 286.27, 286.30, 287.2, and 288.8. The "Greeley" at 288.6 was inadvertently left uncanceled.

287.31   he belched out about a] The word "about" was omitted in JF1, possibly because the Cal clipping in **YSMT** was torn here (see figure 18, volume 1, p. 533). On his reading copy of HWb, Mark Twain altered the phrase to read "out comes a."

287.35–   [Here . . . departed.] This passage is canceled in Mark
288.9   Twain's reading copy of HWb.

287.13–16 lively . . . a anvil] On **YSMT**, there is a penciled caret after "off," indicating that a word was to be inserted, and the *a* of "an" is marked through (see figure 18, volume 1, p. 533). Collation of SP against Cal indicates that Mark Twain added the word "lively" and changed "an" to "a," revisions that have been reported as "[lively]" and "[a]" in the collation.

Emendations of the Copy-Text

282.15   Boomerang (I-C) • Noomerang
283.22   anything (Cal) • any-|thing
287.11   word." (Cal) • ~.$_\wedge$
287.28   somehow" (I-C) • ~$_\wedge$

Historical Collation

Texts collated:

SP   "Jim Smiley and His Jumping Frog," New York *Saturday Press* 4 (18 November 1865): 248–249.

[*"The Celebrated Jumping Frog of Calaveras County"* in
the following]

Cal　　　*Californian* 4 (16 December 1865): 12. Reprints SP with authorial revisions and as many errors.

YSMT　　Part of a clipping of Cal in the Yale Scrapbook, pp. 23A-
26A. Revised and corrected by Mark Twain; served as
printer's copy, or the proximate source of copy, for JF1.

JF1　　　*Jumping Frog* (New York: Webb, 1867), pp. 7-19. Reprints
YSMT with editorial revisions.

JF1**MT**　The copy of an 1869 impression of JF1 revised by Mark
Twain. There are extensive revisions and corrections in this
sketch, although it was not used as printer's copy for any
known reprinting.

JF2　　　*Jumping Frog* (London: Routledge, 1867), pp. 9-20. Reprints
JF1 with few errors.

JF4　　　*Jumping Frog* (London: Routledge, 1870 and 1872), pp. 5-15.
Reprints JF2 with few errors.

MTSk　　*Mark Twain's Sketches* (London: Routledge, 1872), pp.
13-21. Reprints JF4 with extensive authorial revisions and
corrections.

MTSk**MT**　Copy of MTSk revised by Mark Twain, who made no
changes in this sketch.

[*"The Jumping Frog of Calaveras County"* in the following]

JF3　　　*Jumping Frog* (London: Hotten, 1870), pp. 15-22. Reprints
JF2 with few errors.

HWa　　*Choice Humorous Works* (London: Hotten, 1873), pp. 361-
365. Reprints JF3 with few errors.

HWa**MT**　Sheets of HWa revised by Mark Twain, who made no
changes in this sketch.

HWb　　*Choice Humorous Works* (London: Chatto and Windus,
1874), pp. 361-365. Reprints HWa from unaltered plates.

HWb**MT**　Copy of HWb revised by Mark Twain, who made no changes
in this sketch.

[*"The Notorious Jumping Frog of Calaveras County"* in the
following]

Sk#1　　*Mark Twain's Sketches, No. 1* (New York: American News
Company, 1874), pp. 9-12. Reprints MTSk with authorial
revisions.

SkNO　　*Sketches, New and Old* (Hartford: American Publishing
Company, 1875), pp. 29-35. Reprints Sk#1 with authorial
revisions, as part of a longer sketch, no. 364.

Collation:

282 *title*   *Jim Smiley and His Jumping Frog* (SP) • The Celebrated
Jumping Frog of Calaveras County (Cal–JF4); The Cele-
brated Jumping Frog of Calaveras County* | [*footnote*]
*—Originally written, by request, for Artemus Ward's last
book, but arrived in New York after that work had gone to
press. (YSMT); The Jumping Frog of Calaveras County
(JF3–HWb); The Celebrated Jumping Frog of Calaveras*
County | [*footnote*] *Pronounced Cal-e-*va*-ras. (MTSk); The
Notorious Jumping Frog of Calaveras* County | [*footnote*]
*Pronounced Cal-e-*va*-ras. (Sk#1–SkNO)

282.1–2   Mr. . . . Well (SP–Cal) • In compliance with the request of
a friend of mine, who wrote me from the East (JF1+)

282.2   -natured, garrulous (SP+) • [*canceled, then restored*]
(JF1**MT**)

282.3   I (SP–Cal) • [*not in*] (JF1+)

282.3   your friend (SP–Cal) • my friend's friend (JF1+); one
(JF1**MT**)

282.3   Leonidas W. Smiley (SP, **YSMT**, Sk#1–SkNO) • Leonidas
W. Greeley (Cal); *Leonidas W.* Smiley (JF1–HWb, JF1–MTSk)

282.4   you requested me (SP–Cal) • requested (JF1+)

282.4–5   If . . . it. (SP–Cal) • [*not in*] (JF1+)

282.6   lurking (SP+) • [*canceled*] (JF1**MT**)

282.6   your Leonidas W. Smiley (SP, **YSMT**) • your Leonidas W.
Greeley (Cal); *Leonidas W.* Smiley (JF1+)

282.7   you never (SP–Cal) • my friend never (JF1+)

282.7   you only (SP–Cal) • he only (JF1+)

282.9   infamous (SP+) • execrable (JF1**MT**)

282.9   Smiley (SP, **YSMT**+) • Greeley (Cal)

282.10   nearly to (SP–HWb, SP–JF4) • to (JF1**MT**, MTSk–SkNO)

282.10   infernal (SP–HWb, SP–JF4) • [*altered to 'infamous', then
both adjectives canceled*] (JF1**MT**); exasperating (MTSk–
SkNO)

282.11   tedious (SP–HWb, SP–Sk#1) • as tedious (SkNO)

282.11–12   your design . . . that it (SP–Cal) • the design, it certainly
(JF1–HWb, JF1–JF4); the design, it (JF1**MT**, MTSk–SkNO)

282.14   little old (SP) • old (Cal–HWb, Cal–JF4); [*not in*] (MTSk–
SkNO)

282.14   ancient (SP–HWb, SP–JF4) • decayed (MTSk–SkNO)

282.15   of Boomerang (I-C) • of Noomerang (SP); of Angel's (Cal+);

	['of Angel's' *altered to* 'at Angel's'; 'at Angel's' *then altered to* 'at Jesus Maria'; *then* 'of Angel's' *restored*] (JF1**MT**)
282.20	named Leonidas W. Smiley (SP, YS**MT**) • named Leonidas W. Greeley (Cal); named *Leonidas W. Smiley* (JF1+); ['Smiley' *altered to* '——', *then restored*] (JF1**MT**)
282.20	Rev. Leonidas W. Smiley (SP, YS**MT**) • Rev. Leonidas W. Greeley (Cal); *Rev. Leonidas W. Smiley* (JF1+)
282.21	who . . . heard (SP+) • ~, . . . ~, (JF1**MT**)
282.22	this village of Boomerang (SP) • Angel's Camp (Cal+); ['Angel's' *altered to* 'J. Maria', *then restored*] (JF1**MT**)
282.23	Smiley (SP, JF1+) • Greeley (Cal)
283.2	sat (SP, YS**MT**, JF1**MT**, MTSk–SkNO) • sat me (Cal–HWb, Cal–JF4)
283.3	follows this paragraph (SP+) • [*altered to* 'I shall here produce', *then restored*] (JF1**MT**)
283.5	quiet, gently-flowing (SP) • gentle-flowing (Cal+)
283.5	turned the (SP–Cal) • tuned the (JF1–HWb, JF1–MTSk); tuned his (Sk#1–SkNO)
283.10	important matter (SP+) • [*underlined, then the underlining canceled*] (JF1**MT**)
283.11	finesse (SP) • *finesse* (Cal+)
283.12–15	To . . . follows. I (SP–HWb, SP–JF4) • I (JF1**MT**, MTSk–SkNO)
283.15	Smiley (SP, YS**MT**+) • Greeley (Cal)
283.17	There (SP–HWb, SP–Sk#1) • Reverent Leonidas W. H'm. Reverent Le—— well, there (JF1**MT**); Rev. Leonidas W. H'm, Reverend Le— well, there (SkNO)
283.17	Smiley (SP, JF1+) • Greeley (Cal)
283.20	wasn't (SP–HWb, SP–JF4) • warn't (JF1**MT**, MTSk–SkNO)
283.21	come (SP–Cal, JF1**MT**, MTSk–SkNO) • came (JF1–HWb, JF1–JF4)
283.24	sides— (SP+) • sides. Yes he would. (JF1**MT**)
283.24	that (SP–HWb, Sk#1–SkNO) • what (JF4–MTSk)
283.25	*him* (SP–Cal, JF1**MT**, Sk#1–SkNO) • him (JF1–HWb, JF1–MTSk)
283.28	solitry (SP–JF1) • solit'ry (JF2+)
283.28	what (SP) • [*not in*] (Cal+)
283.28	offer (SP+) • up and offer (JF1**MT**)
283.29	any (SP–HWb, SP–JF4) • ary (JF1**MT**, MTSk–SkNO)
283.30	flush (SP–Cal, JF1**MT**, JF4–SkNO) • ~, (JF1–HWb)

283.30   you (SP–Cal) • you'd (JF1+)
283.33   setting (SP, YS**MT**–JF3, MTSk–SkNO) • sitting (Cal, JF4, HWa–HWb)
283.35   reglar (SP–Cal) • reg'lar (JF1+)
283.37   see (SP–Cal, MTSk–SkNO) • seen (JF1–HWb, JF1–JF4)
284.1   get (SP–HWb, SP–JF4) • get to—to (JF1**MT**, MTSk–SkNO)
284.2   foller (SP–HWb) • follow (JF4–SkNO)
284.4   he . . . road (SP+) • it took him to make the trip (YS**MT**)
284.5   Smiley (SP, JF1+) • Greeley (Cal)
284.6   he would (SP–HWb, SP–MTSk) • he'd (Sk#1–SkNO)
284.6   *anything* (SP–Cal) • *any* thing (JF1+)
284.8   seemed (SP+) • 'peared (JF1**MT**)
284.8   save her (SP+) • fetch her round (JF1**MT**)
284.9   Smiley (SP, YS**MT**+) • Greeley (Cal)
284.9   asked him (SP, JF1**MT**) • asked (Cal–HWb, Cal–JF4); up and asked him (MTSk–SkNO)
284.10   considerable (SP–HWb, SP–Sk#1) • considable (SkNO)
284.11   Providence (SP–Cal) • Prov'dence (YS**MT**+)
284.12   Smiley (SP, YS**MT**+) • Greeley (Cal)
284.12   says (SP+) • up and says (JF1**MT**)
284.12   resk (SP–Cal, JF1**MT**, MTSk–SkNO) • risk (JF1–HWb, JF1–JF4)
284.13   that (SP–HWb, SP–MTSk) • [*not in*] (Sk#1–SkNO)
284.14   Smiley (SP, YS**MT**+) • Greeley (Cal)
284.15–16 because, of course, (SP–HWb, SP–MTSk) • ~∧~~∧ (JF1**MT**, Sk#1–SkNO)
284.18   distemper (SP+) • bronchitis (JF1**MT**)
284.21   spraddling (SP–Cal) • straddling (JF1+)
281.25   always (SP–HWb, SP–MTSk) • *always* (Sk#1–SkNO)
284.26   down. (SP+) • ['Indeed *would* she.' *added after* 'down.' *and then canceled;* 'You bet you.' *added in its place*] (JF1**MT**)
284.28   warn't (SP–Cal, JF1**MT**, Sk#1–SkNO) • wan't (JF1–HWb, JF1–MTSk)
284.28   but (SP+) • only (JF1**MT**)
284.28   ornery (SP, JF1+) • onery (Cal)
284.30   up on (SP–JF1, MTSk–SkNO) • upon (JF2–HWb, JF2–JF4)
284.31   like . . . steamboat (SP+) • [*canceled, then restored*] (JF1**MT**)
284.31   for'castle (SP–Cal) • fo'castle (YS**MT**+)

284.32	savage like the furnaces (SP-HWb, SP-JF4) • [altered to 'savage you bet you', then restored] (JF1**MT**); wicked, you hear me (MTSk-Sk#1); like the furnaces (SkNO)
284.32	And (SP+) • ['don't you know' added after 'And', then canceled] (JF1**MT**)
284.36	he (SP-Cal) • he (YS**MT**+)
284.39	just (SP-Cal) • jest (JF1+)
284.39	joint (SP-Cal) • j'int (JF1+)
284.39	legs (SP) • leg (Cal+)
285.1	just (SP-Cal, SkNO) • jest (JF1-HWb, JF1-Sk#1)
285.2	Smiley (SP, YS**MT**+) • Greeley (Cal)
285.2	came (SP-Cal) • come (YS**MT**+)
285.3	harnessed (SP+) • tackled (JF1**MT**)
285.4	sawed (SP-JF2, SP-SkNO) • saw'd (JF3-HWb)
285.4	in (SP-Cal, JF1**MT**, Sk#1-SkNO) • by (JF1-HWb, JF1-MTSk)
285.6	came (SP) • come (Cal+)
285.6	saw (SP-HWb, SP-JF4) • see (JF1**MT**, MTSk-SkNO)
285.7	imposed on, and how (SP+) • [canceled, then restored] (JF1**MT**)
285.10–19	He . . . talent. (SP+) • [passage revised (see below), then canceled] (JF1**MT**)
285.10	gave (SP, HWa-HWb) • give (Cal-JF3, Cal-SkNO)
285.10	Smiley (SP, JF1+) • Greeley (Cal)
285.14	and laid (SP+) • [altered to '& went & laid', then restored; entire passage then canceled] (JF1**MT**)
285.17–18	don't stand to reason (SP+) • [altered to 'don't stand to reason—Now does it?'; then 'Now does it?' canceled; entire passage then canceled] (JF1**MT**)
285.19–20	It . . . I (SP+) • [canceled, apparently in error, then restored] (JF1**MT**)
285.20	his'on (SP) • his'n (Cal+)
285.22	Smiley (SP, YS**MT**+) • Greeley (Cal)
285.22	rat-terriers (SP) • rat-tarriers (Cal+)
285.26	cal'lated (SP-Cal, JF1**MT**, MTSk-SkNO) • cal'klated (JF1-HWb, JF1-JF4)
285.26	educate (SP-Cal, JF1**MT**, MTSk-SkNO) • edercate (JF1-HWb, JF1-JF4)
285.28	hunch (SP) • punch (Cal+)
285.29	you'd (SP-HWb, SP-MTSk) • you (Sk#1-SkNO)

285.31   come (SP-JF3, SP-SkNO) • came (HWa-HWb)

285.32   ketching (SP, Sk#1-SkNO) • catching (Cal-HWb, Cal-MTSk)

285.33   kept (SP-HWb, SP-MTSk) • kep' (Sk#1-SkNO)

285.34   far (SP-HWb, SP-MTSk) • fur (Sk#1-SkNO)

285.34   Smiley (SP, **YSMT**+) • Greeley (Cal)

285.35   most (SP-HWb) • 'most (JF4-SkNO)

285.36   set (SP, **YSMT**+) • sent (Cal)

285.36   this (SP+) • this very (JF1**MT**)

285.37   Flies! (SP-Cal) • ~, (JF1+)

285.38   flies, (SP-Cal) • ~! (JF1+)

285.38   spring (SP+) • skip (JF1**MT**)

286.1   again (SP-HWb, SP-MTSk) • agin (Sk#1); ag'in (SkNO)

286.3   he'd done (SP-Cal) • he'd been doin' (JF1-HWb, JF1-JF4, Sk#1-SkNO); he had been doin' (MTSk)

286.3   do. (SP+) • ['still he'd—well' *added after* 'do.', *then canceled*] (JF1**MT**)

286.7   strong suit (SP+) • [*underlined, then the underlining canceled*] (JF1**MT**)

286.8   Smiley (SP, **YSMT**+) • Greeley (Cal)

286.9   Smiley (SP, **YSMT**+) • Greeley (Cal)

286.11   ben (SP) • been (Cal+)

286.13   Smiley (SP, JF1+) • Greeley (Cal)

286.13   kept (SP-HWb, SP-JF4) • kep' (JF1**MT**, MTSk-SkNO)

286.14   bet. (SP+) • bet. But the boys all knowed *him.* (JF1**MT**)

286.15   across (SP-HWb, SP-MTSk) • acrost (JF1**MT**, Sk#1-SkNO)

286.17   box?'' (SP+) • box?'' (Oh he was deep—he was awful deep, that feller was) (JF1**MT**)

286.18   Smiley (SP, **YSMT**+) • Greeley (Cal)

286.19   ain't (SP-Cal, JF4-SkNO) • an't (JF1-HWb)

286.20   feller (SP+) • [*altered to* 'feller you know he', *then to just* 'feller he'] (JF1**MT**)

286.23   Smiley (SP, JF1+) • Greeley (Cal); ['Greeley' *canceled*] (YS**MT**)

286.24   ary (SP-JF1) • any (JF2+)

286.26   particular (SP, JF1+) • particlar (Cal)

286.27   give (SP-SkNO) • gave (JF3-HWb)

286.27   Smiley (SP, JF1+) • Greeley (Cal); S[miley] (YS**MT**)

286.27-28   Well—I (SP-HWb, SP-MTSk) • Well,'' he says, ''I (Sk#1-SkNO)

286.28   points (SP–Cal) • p'ints (JF1+)

286.30   Smiley (SP, JF1+) • Greeley (Cal); S[miley] (YS**MT**)

286.32   ain't (SP–Cal, JF3–HWb, MTSk–SkNO) • an't (JF1–JF4)

286.33   resk (SP–Cal, JF1**MT**, MTSk–SkNO) • risk (JF1–HWb, JF1–JF4)

286.34   ary (SP–Cal) • any (JF1+)

286.35   feller (SP+) • feller he (JF1**MT**)

286.36   ain't (SP–Cal, JF1**MT**, MTSk–SkNO) • an't (JF1–HWb, JF1–JF4)

286.37   had (SP+) • *had* (JF1**MT**)

286.38   Smiley (SP, JF1+) • Greeley (Cal); ['Greeley' *canceled*] (YS**MT**)

287.2   Smiley's (SP, JF1+) • Greeley's (Cal); S[miley's] (YS**MT**)

287.3   hisself (SP+) • 'mself (JF1**MT**)

287.5   quail-shot (SP+) • quail-shot yes he did (JF1**MT**)

287.6   Smiley (SP, JF1+) • Greeley (Cal); ['Greeley' *canceled*] (YS**MT**)

287.6   out (SP) • [*not in*] (Cal+)

287.7   slopped (SP+) • ['slop-|ped' *altered to* 'slop-| & slop & slop|ped', *then restored*] (JF1**MT**)

287.8   give (SP–SkNO) • gave (JF3–HWb)

287.10   Now (SP+) • Now, Cap, (JF1**MT**)

287.11   Dan'l's (SP–Cal, JF1**MT**, MTSk–SkNO) • Dan'l (JF1–HWb, JF1–JF4)

287.12   jump (SP–HWb, SP–JF4) • git (JF1**MT**); *git* (MTSk–SkNO)

287.13   from (SP+) • [*canceled*] (JF1**MT**)

287.13   lively (SP, JF1**MT**, MTSk–SkNO) • [*not in*] (Cal–HWb, Cal–JF4); [lively] (YS**MT**)

287.14   Dan'l (SP+) • Dan'l he (JF1**MT**)

287.15   wasn't (SP) • wan't (Cal–HWb, Cal–MTSk); warn't (JF1**MT**, Sk#1–SkNO)

287.15   budge (SP+) • budge a peg (JF1**MT**)

287.16   a anvil (SP) • an anvil (Cal–HWb, Cal–JF4); [a] anvil (YS**MT**); a church (JF1**MT**, MTSk–SkNO)

287.17   Smiley (SP, JF1+) • Greeley (Cal); ['Greeley' *canceled*] (YS**MT**)

287.22   shoulder (SP, JF1**MT**, JF2+) • shoulders (Cal–JF1)

287.22   this way (SP–HWb, SP–MTSk) • so (Sk#1–SkNO)

287.23   Well—*I* (SP–HWb, SP–MTSk) • Well," he says, "*I* (Sk#1–SkNO)

287.23   points (SP–Cal) • p'ints (JF1+)

287.25   Smiley (SP, JF1+) • Greeley (Cal); ['Greeley' *canceled*] (YS**MT**)
287.27   throwed (SP, JF3–HWb) • throw'd (Cal–SkNO)
287.27   ain't (SP–Cal, JF1**MT**, MTSk–SkNO) • an't (JF1–HWb, JF1–JF4)
287.29   lifted him up (SP–HWb, SP–JF4) • hefted him (JF1**MT**, MTSk–SkNO)
287.31   about (SP–Cal) • [*not in*] (JF1+)
287.36   go and see (SP) • see (Cal+)
287.37   sit (SP) • set (Cal+)
287.38   ain't (SP–Cal, JF1**MT**, JF3–HWb, MTSk–SkNO) • an't (JF1–JF4)
287.39   by your leave, (SP+) • [*canceled*] (JF1**MT**)
288.1   enterprising (SP+) • [*canceled, then restored*] (JF1**MT**)
288.1   vagabond (SP+) • [*canceled*] (JF1**MT**)
288.1   Jim Smiley (SP) • Jim Greeley (Cal); Jim (YS**MT**); *Jim* Smiley (JF1+)
288.2–3   Rev. Leonidas W. Smiley (SP) • Rev. Leonidas W. Greeley (Cal); Rev. Leonidas W. (YS**MT**); *Rev. Leonidas W.* Smiley (JF1–HWb, JF1–MTSk); *Rev. Leonidas W.* Smiley (Sk#1–SkNO)
288.6   Smiley (SP, JF1+) • Greeley (Cal); Smiley he (JF1**MT**)
288.6   cow (SP+) • cow you know, ['cow' *underlined, then the underlining canceled*] (JF1**MT**)
288.7   tail (SP+) • tail at all ['tail' *underlined, then the underlining canceled*] (JF1**MT**)
288.7   just (SP–Cal, HWa–HWb) • jest (JF1–JF3, JF1–SkNO)
288.8–9   "O . . . departed. (SP–HWb, SP–JF4) • For lack of time & inclination, I did not tarry to hear about the afflicted cow, but took my departure. (JF1**MT**); Lacking both time and inclination, I did not wait to hear about the afflicted cow, but took my leave. (MTSk); However, lacking both time and inclination, I did not wait to hear about the afflicted cow, but took my leave. (Sk#1–SkNO)
288.8   O, curse (SP–Cal) • Oh! hang (JF1–HWb, JF1–JF4)
288.8   Smiley (SP, JF1–HWb, JF1–JF4) • Greeley (Cal); S[miley] (YS**MT**)
288.8–9   I . . . and (SP–HWb, SP–JF4) • [*altered to '—now I've got enough.', then the entire sentence 'Oh! . . . departed.' canceled and altered to read as described above at 288.8–9*] (JF1**MT**)
288.10–11 Yours, truly, | Mark Twain. (SP–Cal) • [*not in*] (JF1+)

[MARK TWAIN ON THE 1865 EARTHQUAKE]

§120. *THE CRUEL EARTHQUAKE*

Textual Commentary

The first printing in the Virginia City *Territorial Enterprise*, probably on 10 or 11 October 1865, is not extant. The sketch survives in the only known contemporary reprinting of the *Enterprise*, the Gold Hill *News* for 13 October 1865 (p. 2), which is copy-text. Copy: PH from Bancroft.

Textual Notes

292.32   Noques] Copy-text "Nongues" is here judged an error because that name does not appear in any Virginia City directory. We conjecture that the Gold Hill *News* or the *Enterprise* printed "Nongues" for "Noques" and have so emended. See the explanatory note.

Emendations of the Copy-Text

291.17   luck." (I-C) • ~.∧
292.1   earthquake (I-C) • earth-|quake
292.21   their shawls (I-C) • sheir shawls
292.24   earthquake (I-C) • earth-|quake
*292.32   Noques (I-C) • Nongues
293.5   earthquake (I-C) • earth-|quake

§121. *POPPER DEFIETH YE EARTHQUAKE*

Textual Commentary

The first printing in the Virginia City *Territorial Enterprise*, sometime between 15 and 31 October 1865, is not extant. The sketch survives in the only known contemporary reprinting, a damaged clipping from an unidentified newspaper in the Yale Scrapbook (pp. 38A–39) and in a photograph of the clipping on page 39, now pasted to page 42 of the scrapbook. The original clipping and the photograph of it are here designated copy-text.

The clipping was originally pasted near the bottom of page 39 in the scrapbook. The last four lines of it extended over the bottom edge of the page, and they were later torn off and repasted to the previous page, 38A. One of the previous owners of the scrapbook, probably J. H. Morse, photographed the clipping on page 39 when it was slightly less damaged than it now appears and pasted this photograph to page 42. By conflating these fragments we have recovered most, but not all, of the text. Portions

of the last three sentences are wholly lost. We have, nevertheless, conjectured what words are missing and emended them into the present text,
basing our guesses on the size of the gaps in each line as well as on the
context. Several equally plausible variations are possible, however, as the
reader may see for himself by trying to complete the missing words in
figure 121. Mark Twain canceled the clipping in early 1867 when he
revised the scrapbook, presumably because he did not intend to collect it
in JF1. He did not subsequently reprint it. There are no textual notes.

Emendations of the Copy-Text

296.14	think . . . were (I-C) • [think] (If I] [torn]
296.14–15	earthquake . . . such (I-C) • ear[thqu] [torn]
296.15	Popper. . . . that I (I-C) • Popper [torn]
296.16	down . . . took (I-C) • do[wn] [torn]
296.16	shake. (I-C) • shake.—Mark Twain, in the E [torn]

§122. *EARTHQUAKE ALMANAC*

Textual Commentary

The first printing in the San Francisco *Dramatic Chronicle* for 17
October 1865, p. 3 (DC), is copy-text. Copy: PH from Bancroft.
    Reprintings and Revisions. The San Francisco *Golden Era* 13 (22
October 1865): 1 reprinted the sketch from DC, but collation shows no
authorial changes, and that reprinting is here treated as derivative. The
sketch was reprinted in JF1, probably from a clipping of DC rather than of
the *Golden Era,* for JF1 preserves the exclamation point after "Shed!"
(299.27) while the *Era* does not. No evidence of the clipping now survives
in the Yale Scrapbook, which was nevertheless the likely source for JF1
printer's copy. JF1 contained several substantive changes. The title was
altered to "A Page from a Californian Almanac"; the greeting "Eds.
Chronicle" and the signature "Mark Twain" were both omitted; "for
this latitude" became "for the latitude of San Francisco" (298.7); and
"look out for" became "look for" (299.4). Although it is possible that
Mark Twain made some or all of these changes, they contain nothing
distinctively authorial, and in the absence of further evidence they are
here attributed to his editor, Charles Henry Webb.
    The reprinting of the JF1 text is described in the textual introduction.
Routledge reprinted JF1 in 1867 (JF2), and Hotten in turn reprinted JF2 in
1870 (JF3). Routledge also reprinted JF2 in 1870 (JF4a) and, using the
unaltered plates of JF4a, reissued the book in 1872 (JF4b). None of these
texts was revised by the author, although the compositor of JF3 made one
error ("Some" instead of "Same" at 298.16). When Mark Twain prepared
the printer's copy for MTSk in March or April 1872, he revised a copy of

POPPER DEFIETH YE EARTHQUAKE.—Where's Ajax now, with his boasted defiance of the lightning? Who is Ajax to Popper, and what is lightning to an earthquake? It is taking no chances to speak of to defy the lightning, for it might pelt away at you for a year and miss you every time—but I don't care what corner you hide in, if the earthquake comes it will shake you; and if you will build your house weak enough to give it a fair show, it will melt it down like butter. Therefore, I exalt Popper above Ajax, for Popper defieth the earthquake. The famous shake of the 8th of October snatched the front out of Popper's great four-story shell of a house on the corner of Third and Mission as easily as if it had been mere pastime; yet I notice that the reckless Popper is rebuilding it again just as thin as it was before, and using the same old bricks. Is this paying proper re-

an ear.... insolence from Popper would shake that shell down.... my last shake.—MARK TWAIN, in the

FIGURE 121. The two fragments on pages 38A and 39 of the Yale Scrapbook are here brought into conjunction to simulate the original clipping.

JF4a and presumably made four changes: he omitted the allusion to John 3:8—"more especially when they blow from whence they cometh and whither they listeth. N.B.—Such is the nature of winds" (298.20-22); he changed "Go slow" to "Stand by for a surge" (299.14) and "slathered" to "shied" (299.16); and he probably changed "some" to "somewhat" (299.29).

One year later (1873) Hotten reprinted the JF3 text in HWa. His compositors repeated the error introduced in JF3 ("Some" instead of "Same") but made no further errors. When Mark Twain revised this book for Chatto and Windus in the fall of 1873 (HWaMT), he made one revision ("increases" instead of "increased" at 298.14) but then canceled the whole sketch, writing "Leave out this puling imbecility"; it was not reprinted in HWb. He again canceled it in the table of contents for MTSkMT in 1875, and he did not subsequently reprint it.

There are no textual notes. The chain of transmission is given below.

Emendations of the Copy-Text

298.18	east'ard (JF1) • east-|'ard
299.19	exhilarating (JF1) • exhilerating
299.31	spinning (JF1) • epinning

Historical Collation

Texts collated:

DC   "Earthquake Almanac," San Francisco *Dramatic Chronicle*, 17 October 1865, p. 3.

            ["A Page from a Californian Almanac" in the following]

JF1   *Jumping Frog* (New York: Webb, 1867), pp. 141–143. Reprints DC without demonstrable revision by Mark Twain.

JF2   *Jumping Frog* (London: Routledge, 1867), pp. 132–134. Reprints JF1 without substantive error.

JF3   *Jumping Frog* (London: Hotten, 1870), pp. 104–105. Reprints JF2 with one error.

JF4   *Jumping Frog* (London: Routledge, 1870 and 1872), pp. 121–123. Reprints JF2 without further error.

MTSk   *Mark Twain's Sketches* (London: Routledge, 1872), pp. 153–155. Reprints JF4 with Mark Twain's revisions.

MTSkMT   Copy of MTSk revised by Mark Twain, who made no changes in this sketch and deleted it in the table of contents.

HWa   *Choice Humorous Works* (London: Hotten, 1873), pp. 559–560. Reprints JF3 without further error.

HWaMT   Sheets of HWa revised by Mark Twain, who first revised and then canceled this sketch.

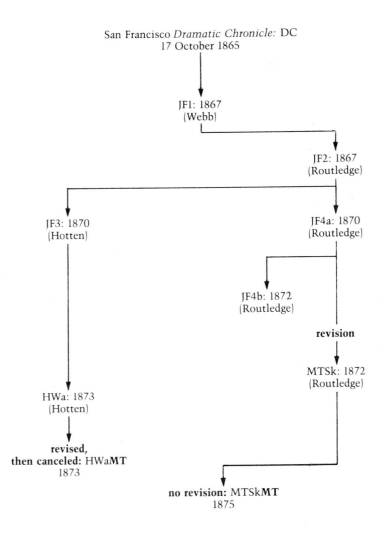

San Francisco *Dramatic Chronicle:* DC
17 October 1865

JF1: 1867
(Webb)

JF2: 1867
(Routledge)

JF3: 1870
(Hotten)

JF4a: 1870
(Routledge)

JF4b: 1872
(Routledge)

revision

MTSk: 1872
(Routledge)

HWa: 1873
(Hotten)

**revised,
then canceled:** HWa**MT**
1873

no revision: MTSk**MT**
1875

Collation:

298 *title*   *Earthquake Almanac* (DC) • A Page from a Californian Almanac (JF1+)

298.1   EDS. CHRONICLE:— (DC) • [*not in*] (JF1+)

298.7   for this latitude (DC) • for the latitude of San Francisco (JF1+)

298.14   increased (DC–MTSk, DC–HWa) • increases (HWa**MT**)

298.16   Same (DC–MTSk) • Some (JF3–HWa)

298.20–22   uncertain . . . winds. (DC–JF4, DC–HWa) • uncertain.
            (MTSk)
299.2   under. (DC) • ~! (JF1+)
299.4   out (DC) • [not in] (JF1+)
299.14   Go slow (DC–JF4, DC–HWa) • Stand by for a surge (MTSk)
299.16   slathered (DC–JF4, DC–HWa) • shied (MTSk)
299.29   some (DC–JF4, DC–HWa) • somewhat (MTSk)
299.32   MARK TWAIN. (DC) • [not in] (JF1+)

§123. *THE GREAT EARTHQUAKE IN SAN FRANCISCO*

Textual Commentary

The first printing in the New York *Weekly Review* for 25 November 1865
(p. 5) is copy-text. Copy: PH from the New York Public Library. There are
no textual notes.

Emendations of the Copy-Text

303.4–5   earthquake (I-C) • earth-|quake
303.13   earthquakes (I-C) • earth-|quakes
303.24   north-west (I-C) • north-|west
304.31   earthquake (I-C) • earth-|quake
305.17   charged (I-C) • changed
306.5   shipwrecked (I-C) • ship-|wrecked
307.15   billiard-cue (I-C) • billiard[-]cue
307.27   earthquake (I-C) • earth-|quake
308.2   earthquake (I-C) • earth-|quake
308.20   fire-walls (I-C) • fire-|walls
308.29   earthquake (I-C) • earth-|quake
309.4   quarter-horse (I-C) • quarter-|horse
309.27   earthquake (I-C) • earth-|quake

124. *BOB ROACH'S PLAN FOR CIRCUMVENTING A DEMOCRAT*

Textual Commentary

The first printing in the Virginia City *Territorial Enterprise*, probably
sometime between 21 and 24 October 1865, is not extant. The sketch
survives in the only known contemporary reprinting of the *Enterprise*,
the San Francisco *Examiner* for 30 November 1865 (p. 1), which is copy-
text. Copy: PH from Bancroft. There are no textual notes.

Emendations of the Copy-Text

313.19   ice-cream (I-C) • ice-|cream
314.1   Aleck (I-C) • Alec
314.4   used (I-C) • use

125. [*SAN FRANCISCO LETTER*]

Textual Commentary

The first printing appeared in the Virginia City *Territorial Enterprise*, probably sometime between 26 and 28 October 1865 (TEnt). The only known copy of this printing, part of a clipping in the Yale Scrapbook (p. 39), is copy-text from "mustered" (318.13) through "taste." (320.3). The first printing for the opening section of the letter (317.1–318.12) is not extant. This section survives in the only known contemporary reprinting of the *Enterprise*, the San Francisco *Evening Bulletin* for 30 October 1865, p. 3 (EB), which is copy-text. Copies: PH from Bancroft (EB) and from Yale (TEnt).

We have conjectured that the section preserved in TEnt and the section preserved in EB are in fact from the same letter to the *Enterprise*. We have adopted the title typically used by that paper for Mark Twain's daily letter to it during the last part of 1865, several examples of which are preserved in the Yale Scrapbook. The letter probably had a dateline reading "SAN FRANCISCO, Oct. 24," if it was like other letters written about this time. The TEnt clipping in the scrapbook preserves only the last four words of a section of the letter now wholly lost, and there may well have been sections both before and after "A Love of a Bonnet Described" that are not preserved. Ellipsis points indicate that material has been or may have been lost.

Mark Twain canceled the clipping of TEnt in the scrapbook. Since it follows a page stub that might well have held the earlier part of the letter, there is some possibility that this unidentified section was removed to serve as printer's copy for JF1. None of the letter, however, was reprinted in JF1, and Mark Twain did not subsequently reprint it. There are no textual notes.

Emendations of the Copy-Text

[*Copy-text from 317.1 through 318.12 is EB*]

317.17   beautiful (I-C) • beauti[f]ul

[*Copy-text from 318.13 through 320.3 is TEnt*]

318.28   sweethearts (I-C) • sweet-|hearts
320.1   most (I-C) • m[ ]t

126. STEAMER DEPARTURES

Textual Commentary

The first printing in the Virginia City *Territorial Enterprise*, probably between 31 October and 2 November 1865, is not extant. The sketch survives in the only known contemporary reprinting of the *Enterprise*, a clipping from an unidentified newspaper in the Yale Scrapbook (p. 34A), which is copy-text. Clemens struck through the clipping in pencil, probably in January or February 1867, indicating that he did not intend to reprint it in JF1. There are no textual notes or emendations.

127. EXIT "BUMMER"

Textual Commentary

The first printing in the Virginia City *Territorial Enterprise* for 8 November 1865 is not extant. The sketch is preserved in the only known contemporary reprinting of the *Enterprise*, the *Californian* 3 (11 November 1865): 12, which is copy-text. Copies: Bancroft; PH from Yale. There are no textual notes.

Emendations of the Copy-Text

325.1	The (I-C) • ''~
325.1	"Bummer" (I-C) • '~'
325.3	"Lazarus" (I-C) • '~'
325.9–10	"died . . . on" (I-C) • '~ . . . ~'
325.26	and (I-C) • ahd
325.26	Lazarus. (I-C) • ~."

128. PLEASURE EXCURSION

Textual Commentary

The first printing in the Virginia City *Territorial Enterprise*, sometime between 9 and 12 November 1865, is not extant. The sketch survives in two contemporary reprintings of the *Enterprise:*

P¹   " 'Mark Twain's' Trial Trip," San Francisco *Golden Era* 13 (19 November 1865): 5.

P²   "Pleasure Excursion," San Francisco *Examiner*, 2 December 1865, p. 1.

Copies: PH from Bancroft. The sketch is a radiating text: there is no copy-text. All variants are recorded in a list of emendations and adopted readings, which also records any readings unique to the present edition, identified as I-C.

The independence of P¹ and P² is guaranteed by obviously authorial passages unique to each printing. Neither P¹ nor P² reproduces Mark Twain's entire letter to the *Enterprise,* or even the whole of this section of the letter: P¹ omits most of the opening sentence, which is preserved only in P², but it includes the second sentence, which is omitted in P². The diagram of transmission is as follows:

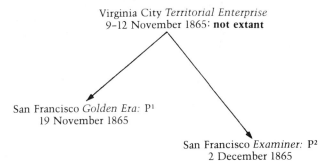

Virginia City *Territorial Enterprise*
9–12 November 1865: **not extant**

San Francisco *Golden Era:* P¹
19 November 1865

San Francisco *Examiner:* P²
2 December 1865

Emendations and Adopted Readings

327 *title*	*Pleasure Excursion* (P²) • "Mark Twain's" Trial Trip (P¹)
327.1–6	WE . . . Gate; (P²) • [*not in*] (P¹)
327.1	WE (I-C) • "~ (P²)
327.3	sand-hills (I-C) • sand-|hills (P²)
327.6	I (P²) • "~ (P¹)
327.7–9	All . . . line. (P¹) • * * * * * * * (P²)
327.7–8	"When . . . Georgia," (I-C) • '~ . . . ~,' (P¹)
327.11	the others (P¹) • others (P²)
327.13	know, (P²) • ~∧ (P¹)
327.14	I am (P¹) • 1 am (P²)
327.18	wind-mill (P²) • windmill (P¹)
327.18–19	handsprings (P¹) • hand-|springs (P²)
327.19	"mumble peg," (P²) • '~~,' (P¹)
328.2	circumstances (P²) • circustances (P¹)
328.3	hundred, (P¹) • ~∧ (P²)
328.4	excursion. (I-C) • ~." (P¹·²)

129. [*EDITORIAL "PUFFING"*]

Textual Commentary

The first printing in the Virginia City *Territorial Enterprise,* probably between 15 and 18 November 1865, is not extant. The sketch survives in the only known contemporary reprinting of the *Enterprise,* the San Francisco *Examiner* for 20 November 1865 (p. 3), which is copy-text. Copy: PH from Bancroft.

Textual Notes

331.13   raal] Mark Twain is affecting a mild Irish accent in this portion of the sketch (see also "Moike" and "ould"), so that even though "raal" may be a compositorial error and less than accurate in its dialect rendering, we have not emended the spelling of the copy-text.

Emendations of the Copy-Text

331.1   Let (I-C) • "∼
331.1–3   "John . . . citizens," (I-C) • '∼ . . . ∼'
331.3   "to . . . nativity," (I-C) • '∼ . . . ∼'
331.5–7   "but . . . again" (I-C) • '∼ . . . ∼'
331.14   it. (I-C) • ∼."

130. THE OLD THING

Textual Commentary

The first printing in the Virginia City *Territorial Enterprise* for 18 November 1865 is not extant. The sketch survives in the only known contemporary reprinting of the *Enterprise,* the *Californian* 3 (25 November 1865): 12, which is copy-text. Copies: Bancroft; PH from Yale. There are no textual notes.

Emendations of the Copy-Text

334.2   Meyers (I-C) • Myers
334.13   perpetrator (I-C) • perpretator
334.16–17   "Here . . . yours," (I-C) • '∼ . . . ∼'
334.22–23   "Here . . . work." (I-C) • '∼ . . . ∼'
335.3–4   "The Mysterious" (I-C) • '∼∼'
335.6   Smythe (I-C) • "∼
335.13   mien (I-C) • mein
335.13–14   "Here . . . know," (I-C) • '∼ . . . ∼'
335.14   House. (I-C) • ∼."

§131. SAN FRANCISCO LETTER

Textual Commentary

The first printing appeared in the Virginia City *Territorial Enterprise,* probably on 24 or 26 December 1865 (TEnt). The only known copy of this printing, in a clipping in the Yale Scrapbook (pp. 54–55), is copy-text for all but four items that Mark Twain quotes from San Francisco newspapers:

AF   "California and Nevada—Both under the False Financial Rule," San Francisco *Weekly American Flag,* 30 December 1865, p. 4, is copy-text from 340.8 through 340.27;

MC   "The 'Territorial Enterprise' " and "Changed," San Francisco *Morning Call,* 22 December 1865, p. 1, is copy-text from 340.31 through 340.35;

AC   "The Condition of Mother Earth," San Francisco *Alta California,* 22 December 1865, p. 2, is copy-text from 341.21 through 342.4.

The article that Mark Twain quotes and paraphrases from the San Francisco *Alta California* at 337.7 through 338.28 has been so completely altered by him that copy-text is necessarily TEnt. On the other hand, collation suggests that clippings of AF, MC, and AC were part of Mark Twain's manuscript. Two minor changes in the text of AC are here presumed to be revisions imposed by him, and are adopted as needed emendations of AC from TEnt, while one substantive variant between AF and TEnt is presumed to be compositorial and has been rejected. The reader may consult the original of the *Alta* paraphrase in the explanatory notes. Copies: PH of the Yale Scrapbook, pp. 54–55 (TEnt); PH from Bancroft (MC, AC); California State Library, Sacramento (AF).

The opening section of the letter—"How Long, O Lord, How Long?"—is omitted from the present text. It is scheduled to appear in the collection of social and political writings in The Works of Mark Twain. There are no textual notes.

Emendations of the Copy-Text

[*Copy-text from 337.1 through 340.7 is TEnt*]

338.7	The (I-C) • Th[e]
338.27	withal!" (I-C) • ~!∧
339.24	Stock (I-C) • [S]tock
340.5	greenbacks (I-C) • green-|backs

[*Copy-text from 340.8 through 340.27 is AF*]

340.26	public (TEnt) • pub[l]ic

[*Copy-text from 341.21 through 342.4 is AC*]

341.34	an (TEnt) • a very
342.4	cholera. (TEnt) • ~;

Historical Collation

Texts collated: TEnt, AF, MC, AC (see the commentary above).

Collation:

340.12   house (AF) • home (TEnt)
341.34   an (TEnt) • a very (AC)

§132. *FITZ SMYTHE'S HORSE*

Textual Commentary

The first printing in the Virginia City *Territorial Enterprise*, probably sometime between 16 and 18 January 1866, is not extant. The sketch survives in two contemporary reprintings of the *Enterprise:*

P[1]   "Fitz Smythe's Horse," San Francisco *Golden Era* 14 (21 January 1866): 5.

P[2]   "Mark Twain on Fitz Smythe's Horse," *Beadle's Dime Book of Fun No. 3* (New York: Beadle and Company, [1866]), pp. 75–77.

Copies: PH from Bancroft (P[1]); PH from Yale (P[2]). The sketch is a radiating text: there is no copy-text. All variants are recorded in a list of emendations and adopted readings, which also records any readings unique to the present edition, identified as I-C.

The independence of P[1] is guaranteed by its date of publication: P[2] was not advertised for sale until late in April 1866 (*BAL*, 3309). P[2] cannot derive from P[1] because it contains one superior reading that it seems unlikely a compositor would supply: "thinks he" instead of P[1] "think she" (346.24). P[2] does, however, make a number of errors, so that when variants are wholly indifferent we have preferred P[1]. It is possible that P[2] derives from an unidentified reprinting of the lost *Enterprise* instead of the *Enterprise* itself: this would account for its high incidence error. But even though P[2] may stand at somewhat greater remove from the first printing, we have conjectured that both P[1] and P[2] derive independently from it, and each may therefore preserve authorial readings among its variants.

There are no textual notes. The diagram of transmission is as follows:

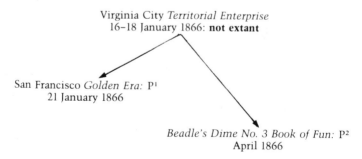

Virginia City *Territorial Enterprise*
16–18 January 1866: **not extant**

San Francisco *Golden Era:* P[1]
21 January 1866

Beadle's Dime No. 3 Book of Fun: P[2]
April 1866

Emendations and Adopted Readings

345 *title*	*Fitz Smythe's Horse* (P¹) • Mark Twain on Fitz Smythe's Horse (P²)
345.3	looks (P¹) • looked (P²)
345.3	dejected and (P¹) • [*not in*] (P²)
345.6	exchanges (P²) • exchanges (P¹)
345.9	him. (P¹) • ~! (P²)
345.11	et (P¹) • eat (P²)
345.15	gate (P²) • gait (P¹)
345.15	it; (P²) • ~: (P¹)
345.16	*Altas* and *Bulletins* (P¹) • Altas and Bulletins (P²)
345.17	a chawin' (P¹) • a-chawin' (P²)
345.18	a-n-y-thing (P¹) • a-n-y∧thing (P²)
345.18	boy, (P¹) • ~∧ (P²)
345.20	bible (P¹) • Bible (P²)
345.21	*he* (P¹) • he (P²)
345.22	anything (P¹) • any thing (P²)
346.3	why, (P¹) • ~∧ (P²)
346.4	a old tom cat (P¹) • an old tom-cat (P²)
346.4	that there (P²) • them there (P¹)
346.5	yonder, (P¹) • ~∧ (P²)
346.5	a sunning (P¹) • sunning (P²)
346.6	a hanging on and a grabbling (P¹) • a-hanging on, grabbing (P²)
346.7	around (P¹) • around, and (P²)
346.10	know, (P¹) • ~∧ (P²)
346.11	it ain't likely, (P¹) • [*not in*] (P²)
346.12	of not (P¹) • of (P²)
346.16	all (P¹) • all of (P²)
346.16	bet (P¹) • bet you (P²)
346.22	a jolting (P¹) • a-jolting (P²)
346.23	close pin (P¹) • clothes-pin (P²)
346.24	thinks he (P²) • think she (P¹)
346.24	Macdowl (I-C) • Mac-|dowl (P¹); Macdowel (P²)
346.25	a going (P¹) • a-going (P²)
346.25	hornisswoggle (P²) • horniss-|woggle (P¹)
346.25	goblin (P²) • gobbling (P¹)

346.26   *down* (P¹) • down (P²)
346.26-27   him. . . . coming!" (P²) • ∼." . . . ∼!∧ (P¹)
346.28   that I (P¹) • I (P²)
346.30   now (P¹) • not (P²)
346.33   frivolous (P¹) • ∼, (P²)
346.33   anyways (P¹) • any ways (P²)

§133. *CLOSED OUT*

Textual Commentary

The first printing appeared in the Virginia City *Territorial Enterprise*, probably on 30 or 31 January 1866. The only known copy of this printing, in a clipping in the Yale Scrapbook (pp. 36A–37), is copy-text. Mark Twain struck through the entire clipping while selecting material for JF1 in January or February 1867. There are no textual notes or emendations.

§134. *TAKE THE STAND, FITZ SMYTHE*

Textual Commentary

The first printing appeared in the Virginia City *Territorial Enterprise*, probably on 6 or 7 February 1866 (TEnt). The only known copy of this printing, in a clipping in the Yale Scrapbook, pp. 47–48, is copy-text for all but the passage that Mark Twain quotes from the San Francisco *Morning Call*, 3 February 1866, p. 1 (MC), which is copy-text from 352.9 through 352.25. Mark Twain presumably dropped the signature from the passage quoted, and this change is adopted as a needed emendation of MC from TEnt, while two further changes in spacing and paragraphing are rejected as compositorial. Copy: PH from Bancroft (MC). Mark Twain struck through the scrapbook clipping early in 1867, presumably because he did not intend to reprint it in JF1. There are no textual notes.

Emendations of the Copy-Text

[Copy-text from the title through 352.8 is TEnt]

351.1   flattery. (I-C) • ∼?
351.2   saw him (I-C) • saw kim
351.7   Chappell (I-C) • Chappelle
351.31   altogether." (I-C) • ∼.∧
352.1   get (I-C) • yet

[Copy-text from 352.9 through 352.25 is MC]

352.25   officer? (TEnt) • officer? | W. W.

Historical Collation

Texts collated: TEnt and MC (see the commentary above).

Collation:

352.9	WHERE (I-C) • **Where** (MC); [¶] WHERE (TEnt)
352.10	[¶] EDITORS (MC) • [*no* ¶] *Editors* (TEnt)
352.25	officer? (TEnt) • officer? | W. W. (MC)

§135. *REMARKABLE DREAM*

Textual Commentary

The first printing appeared in the Virginia City *Territorial Enterprise,* probably sometime between 8 and 10 February 1866. The only known copy of this printing, in a clipping in the Yale Scrapbook, pp. 40–40A (YSMT), is copy-text. Since Mark Twain extensively revised this sketch, he must have considered reprinting it in JF1. The revised clipping remains intact in the scrapbook, however, and Mark Twain did not reprint it in JF1 or elsewhere. We have adopted one change in YSMT as a correction.

Textual Notes

355.21	Smythe] Clemens replaced this name with "Raymond" here and again at 356.10 in **YSMT.** At 356.18 and 356.26 he merely canceled "Smythe," expecting his editor or compositor to supply the new name in its place. At 357.10 he made a fuller substitution, however, crossing out "Armand Leonidas Fitz Smythe Amigo Stiggers" and writing "Armand Adolphus Fitz Raymond" instead.
357.13	the] In **YSMT** Clemens replaced the definite article with a marginal *a* by drawing an insert line to canceled "the." He also corrected the misspelling in the *Enterprise,* "Munchusen" (357.17), by drawing another line from the same marginal *a* to that word. We have deemed the first change a revision, and have not adopted it. We have deemed the second a correction of the copy-text, and have emended.

Emendations of the Copy-Text

356.10	'Brother Smythe' (I-C) • "~~"
356.12	from (I-C) • form
356.13	Twain, (I-C) • ~.
357.17	Munchausen (**YSMT**) • Munchusen
358.9	sunburned (I-C) • sun-|burned

358.36   and brimstone (I-C) • brimstone

Alterations in the Yale Scrapbook

355.16–17   it. . . . didn't] *altered to* 'it, didn't'.
355.21   Smythe——] *altered to* 'Raymond—'.
356.10   Fitz Smythe] 'Smythe' *altered to* 'Raymond'.
356.11   *Alta*] *altered to* 'Alpha'.
356.18   seconds!] *altered to* 'seconds!—gracious'.
356.18   Smythe] *canceled.*
356.26   Smythe's] *canceled.*
356.37   hell] *altered to* 'Hades'.
357.5   now] *altered to* 'then'.
357.10   Armand Leonidas Fitz Smythe Amigo Stiggers] *altered to* 'Armand Adolphus Fitz Raymond'.
357.13   the] *altered to* 'a'.
357.17   Munchausen] *corrected from* 'Munchusen'.
357.25   world."] *an asterisk and the following footnote added:* '*The Baron's shameful satire was aimed at the police— they wear gray in San Francisco.'
357.31   hell] *altered to* 'the other place'.
358.15   hell] *altered to* 'Perdition'.
358.39   Smythe.] *an asterisk and the following footnote added:* '*Published in the course of a newspaper controversy with a newspaper and correspondent who signed himself "Armand Adolphus Fitz Raymond." '

136. "MARK TWAIN" ON THE LAUNCH OF THE STEAMER "CAPITAL"

Textual Commentary

The first printing in the *Californian* 3 (18 November 1865): 9 is copy-text. Copies: Bancroft; PH from Yale.

Reprintings and Revisions. This sketch was frequently reprinted in the United States without Mark Twain's authority. For example, in April 1866 *Beadle's Dime Book of Fun No. 3* (*BAL* 3309) reprinted the "Scriptural Panoramist" section together with an introduction and conclusion clearly not by Mark Twain. "If I were in the east, now," Clemens wrote his sister on 22 May 1866, "I could stop the publication of a piratical book which has stolen some of my sketches" (*CL1*, letter 104). A few months later, the *Californian* noted that the sketch was "going the rounds of the Eastern press wrongly credited to the *Alta California*. It was written more than a year ago, at the time the steamer *'Capital'* was launched, for THE CALIFORNIAN" ("The Story of a Scriptural Panoramist," *Californian* 5 [17 November 1866]: 5). On this occasion the *Californian* itself paraphrased the frame story and reprinted an edited text of the "Scriptural Panoramist" section. Although Mark Twain was lecturing in San Francisco at this time and therefore could have edited the sketch for the *Californian*, collation discloses no distinctively authorial changes. Both the reprinting in *Beadle's Dime Book* and in the *Californian* are here regarded as derivative and their variants are not recorded in the historical collation.

The sketch was reprinted in JF1 from an edited clipping of the *Californian*, probably taken from the Yale Scrapbook. No trace of such a clipping or of Mark Twain's holograph revisions (if he made any) survives, presumably because the sketch was among those removed from the front part of the scrapbook when whole leaves were scissored out. Only very minimal revisions were imposed on the JF1 text. It is conceivable that Mark Twain restored his characteristic spelling "staid" (instead of "stayed") at 363.19, or that he removed "Mark Twain" from the title, or changed "story" to "history" at 363.23. He may also have made several substantial deletions in the frame story, reducing the first three paragraphs to a few sentences in JF1. But in the absence of holograph evidence or of more distinctively authorial revisions, all of the changes made for JF1 must be attributed to Charles Henry Webb.

The reprinting of the JF1 text is described in the textual introduction. Routledge reprinted JF1 in 1867 (JF2), and Hotten in turn reprinted JF2 in 1870 (JF3). Routledge also reprinted JF2 in 1870 (JF4a) and, using the unaltered plates of JF4a, reissued the book in 1872 (JF4b). None of these texts was revised by the author, but the compositors made several minor errors, such as "ran" instead of "run" (364.14), "around" instead of "round" (365.10), "super" instead of "supes" (365.21), and "wrapt" instead of "rapt" (363.9). Meanwhile, Hotten had also reprinted the sketch in Scrs in 1871, drawing his text not from JF3 but from an unidentified reprinting of the *Californian*. Either because of Hotten's editing or because of his source for the text, Scrs contained almost two dozen substantive errors and sophistications, and it wholly omitted the frame story about Muff Nickerson.

When Mark Twain prepared the printer's copy for MTSk in March or April 1872, he had a choice between two reprinted texts of this sketch, one in Scrs and one in JF4a. Collation shows that he chose JF4a, revising it more extensively than any other sketch (save no. 119) reprinted in MTSk. Apparently both the quasi-religious subject matter and the highly vernacular narration of the sketch brought out Mark Twain's conservative feelings in 1872. While he revised away the frame story completely,

he also made numerous changes to eliminate both the narrator's skeptical remarks and much of his vulgar language. For instance, he altered a
phrase that compared the panorama show to "a camp-meeting revival"
(364.5), and he deleted a somewhat racy description of the audience, who,
he had said, were "mostly middle-aged and old people who belonged to
the church and took a strong interest in Bible matters," while "the balance were pretty much young bucks and heifers—*they* always come out
strong on panoramas, you know, because it gives them a chance to taste
one another's mugs in the dark" (364.7–12). He made some twenty revisions of the narrator's diction, transforming the wild inventiveness of
Muff Nickerson's western slang into something both tamer and more
comprehensible to an English audience. For example, "wooden-headed
old slab" became "simple old creature" (363.26); "rough" became "rasping" (363.32); "simple" became "poor" (364.1); "stunning" became
"smart" (364.2); "corral" became "capture" (364.6); "mud-dobber" became "pianist" or "musician" (364.14 and 364.29); "tackled" was omitted (364.14); "grind out" became "unwind" (364.16); "piano sharp"
became "pianist" (364.34); "grit" became "pluck" (365.2); "started in
fresh" became "began again" (365.2); "snickering" became "laughter"
(365.14); "mighty" became "very" (365.21); "ass" became "muggins"
(365.34); "huff" became "fury" (366.2); "It was rough on the audience,
you bet you" became simply "My!" (366.1); and the final explosion of the
proprietor—"That lets you out, you know, you chowder-headed old
clam! Go to the door-keeper and get your money, and cut your stick!—
vamose the ranch!" and so on (366.6–9)—was reduced to a simple dash,
followed by the comment, "But what he said was too vigorous for repetition, and is better left out."

One year later (1873) Hotten reprinted the Scrs text in HWa. Despite
Mark Twain's extensive and careful revision for MTSk, when he revised
HWa for Chatto and Windus in the fall of 1873 (HWa**MT**), he made only
two corrections and one minor revision. Both the Scrs text and the reprinting in HWa contained dozens of errors and sophistications. Hotten
(or his source), like Mark Twain before him, had reduced the sketch to
the core story about the panoramist, and he had retitled it "A Travelling
Show." Both Scrs and HWa changed "gritted" to "grated" (365.16);
"piano sharp" to "pianist sharp" (364.34); "belonged" to "belong"
(364.8); and "proprieties" to "proprietors" (363.32). Hotten had made
some rather bold changes in the diction: "illustrates" became "repre-
sents" (365.23); "rare ability" became "marvellous skill"(365.25). Apparently sensing that the HWa text was not wholly reliable, Mark Twain
made one marginal comment directed at Hotten's successors, Chatto and
Windus. When he came across the error "proprietors" he made the correction and added in the margin: "I hope the new firm has hired a *proof-
reader* instead of a shoemaker." Chagrined at his own harshness, perhaps,
he canceled that and wrote simply: "The proof-reading on this book must

have been very hurriedly done, or else done by a novice." He went on to correct only one additional error in this sketch, however, replacing the error "Ri-d-ley" with the correct reading "Ri-i-ley" (365.35), and he slightly modified what became the concluding sentence of the sketch (366.9). Either he could not detect or did not trouble to restore most of the substituted readings imposed by Hotten and his compositors.

When in 1875 Mark Twain prepared the printer's copy for SkNO, he revised the sketch in HWb**MT**, deleted it from the table of contents for MTSk**MT**, and entered "The Scriptural Panoramist" as item 75 in the Doheny table of contents (see figure 23H in the textual introduction, volume 1, p. 631). The printers entered the correct HWb page number (375) on this table of contents, and the text in SkNO was set from the revised and corrected HWb**MT**. Mark Twain supplied the new title, corrected "girt" to "grit" (365.2), changed "grated" to "gritted" (365.16), altered "mugs" to "complexions" (364.11), and made only one additional change, substituting "Whe-ew!" for "It was rough on the audience, you bet" (366.1)—a change parallel to but not duplicating the change he had made in MTSk two years earlier. The SkNO text therefore incorporated most of the unauthoritative readings that first appeared in Scrs, but did not incorporate the relatively conservative revisions Mark Twain had made for MTSk in 1872.

The diagram of transmission is given below.

Textual Notes

366.9   dismiss—"] When Mark Twain revised this sentence in
           HWa**MT**, he found that it ended not with a dash to indicate
           interruption, but with a simple period—a change that had
           originated in the Scrs printing. Instead of restoring his orig-
           inal text, Mark Twain added two words, "the house," to
           complete the sentence.

Emendations of the Copy-Text

361.2   Assist (I-C) • Asssist
361.15   everything (I-C) • every-|thing
361.18–19 awe-inspiring (I-C) • awe-|inspiring
361.22   could (I-C) • cou[ ]d
362.2   arrayed (I-C) • a[ ]rayed
363.2   kind-hearted (JF1) • kind-|hearted
363.30   first-rate (JF1) • first-|rate
364.6   showman (JF1) • show-|man
364.13   Well (JF1) • "~
365.9   deep!" (JF1) • ~!∧
366.6   lets (JF1) • let's

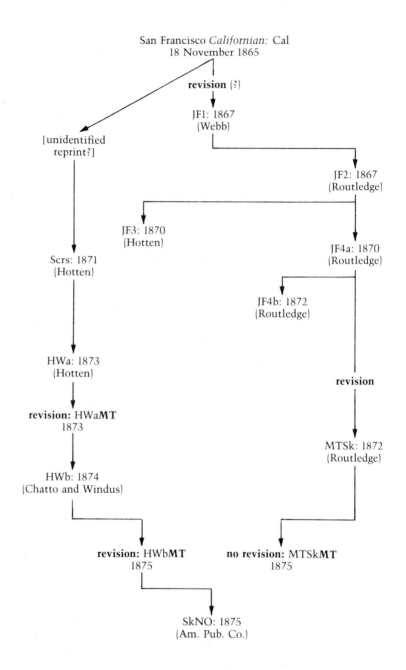

San Francisco *Californian:* Cal
18 November 1865

revision (?)

JF1: 1867
(Webb)

[unidentified
reprint?]

JF2: 1867
(Routledge)

JF3: 1870
(Hotten)

Scrs: 1871
(Hotten)

JF4a: 1870
(Routledge)

JF4b: 1872
(Routledge)

HWa: 1873
(Hotten)

revision

revision: HWaMT
1873

MTSk: 1872
(Routledge)

HWb: 1874
(Chatto and Windus)

revision: HWbMT
1875

no revision: MTSkMT
1875

SkNO: 1875
(Am. Pub. Co.)

Historical Collation

Texts collated:

Cal   " 'Mark Twain' on the Launch of the Steamer 'Capital,' " *Californian* 3 (18 November 1865): 9.

[*"The Launch of the Steamer Capital" in the following*]

JF1   *Jumping Frog* (New York: Webb, 1867), pp. 151–161. Reprints Cal with omissions and minor revisions not demonstrably by Mark Twain.

JF2   *Jumping Frog* (London: Routledge, 1867), pp. 144–152. Reprints JF1 with few errors.

JF3   *Jumping Frog* (London: Hotten, 1870), pp. 98–103. Reprints JF2 with few additional errors.

JF4   *Jumping Frog* (London: Routledge, 1870 and 1872), pp. 132–139. Reprints JF2 with few additional errors.

[*"The Entertaining History of the Scriptural Panoramist" in the following*]

MTSk   *Mark Twain's Sketches* (London: Routledge, 1872), pp. 204–207. Reprints JF4 heavily edited by Mark Twain.

MTSk**MT**   Copy of MTSk revised by Mark Twain, who made no changes in this sketch and deleted it in the table of contents.

[*"A Travelling Show" in the following*]

Scrs   *Screamers* (London: Hotten, 1871), pp. 146–150. Reprints an unidentified edited version of Cal.

HWa   *Choice Humorous Works* (London: Hotten, 1873), pp. 377–379. Reprints Scrs with few additional errors.

HWa**MT**   Sheets of HWa revised by Mark Twain, who made three changes in this sketch.

HWb   *Choice Humorous Works* (London: Chatto and Windus, 1874), pp. 375–377. Reprints HWa with authorial revisions from HWa**MT**.

[*"The Scriptural Panoramist" in the following*]

HWb**MT**   Copy of HWb revised by Mark Twain, who made five changes in this sketch.

SkNO   *Sketches, New and Old* (Hartford: American Publishing Company, 1875), pp. 296–299. Reprints HWb with authorial revisions from HWb**MT**.

Collation:

361 *title*   *"Mark Twain" on the Launch of the Steamer "Capital"* (Cal) • The Launch of the Steamer Capital (JF1–

JF4, JF1–JF3); The Entertaining History of the Scriptural
Panoramist (MTSk); A Travelling Show (Scrs–Hwb); The
Scriptural Panoramist (HWb**MT**–SkNO)

361.1– 363.20	I get . . . attentively to (Cal–JF4, Cal–JF3) • [not in] (MTSk, Scrs–SkNO)
361.10– 362.3	He . . . enchantment! (Cal) • [not in] (JF1–JF4, JF1–JF3)
362.4–14	I could . . . together. (Cal) • [not in] (JF1–JF4, JF1–JF3)
362.17–20	I tried . . . water!" (Cal) • [not in] (JF1–JF4, JF1–JF3)
363.9	rapt (Cal–JF3) • wrapt (JF4)
363.21–23	THE . . . language.] (Cal–MTSk, Cal–JF3) • [not in] (Scrs– SkNO)
363.23	story (Cal) • history (JF1–MTSk, JF1–JF3)
363.25	of a (Cal–MTSk, Cal–JF3) • of (Scrs–SkNO)
363.26	wooden-headed old slab (Cal–JF4, Cal–JF3, Scrs–SkNO) • simple old creature (MTSk)
363.30	didn't (Cal–MTSk, Cal–JF3) • don't (Scrs–SkNO)
363.32	rough (Cal–JF4, Cal–JF3, Scrs–SkNO) • rasping (MTSk)
363.32	proprieties (Cal–MTSk, Cal–JF3, HWa**MT**–SkNO) • propri- etors (Scrs–HWa)
364.1	simple (Cal–JF4, Cal–JF3, Scrs–SkNO) • poor (MTSk)
364.2	stunning (Cal–JF4, Cal–JF3, Scrs–SkNO) • smart (MTSk)
364.4	get (Cal–JF4, Cal–JF3) • to get (MTSk, Scrs–SkNO)
364.5	like a camp-meeting revival (Cal–JF4, Cal–JF3, Scrs–SkNO) • to an appreciation of it (MTSk)
364.6	corral (Cal–JF4, Cal–JF3, Scrs–SkNO) • capture (MTSk)
364.7–13	mostly . . . Well, (Cal–JF4, Cal–JF3, Scrs–SkNO) • [not in] (MTSk)
364.8	belonged (Cal–JF4, Cal–JF3) • belong (Scrs–SkNO)
364.10	*they* (Cal–JF4, Cal–JF3) • they (Scrs–SkNO)
364.11	mugs (Cal–JF4, Cal–JF3) • mug (Scrs–HWb); complexions (HWb**MT**–SkNO)
364.14	and the (Cal–JF4, Cal–JF3, Scrs–SkNO) • the (MTSk)
364.14	mud-dobber . . . run (Cal–JF1) • mud-dobber . . . ran (JF2– JF4, JF2–JF3, Scrs–SkNO); pianist ran (MTSk)
364.15	down (Cal–JF4, Cal–JF3, Scrs–SkNO) • down his instru- ment (MTSk)
364.15	she (Cal–JF4, Cal–JF3, Scrs–SkNO) • it (MTSk)
364.16	fellows (Cal–JF4, Cal–JF3, Scrs–SkNO) • supes (MTSk)
364.16	grind out (Cal–JF4, Cal–JF3, Scrs–SkNO) • unwind (MTSk)

364.18	on (Cal–MTSk, Cal–JF3) • over (Scrs–SkNO)
364.18	eye (Cal–MTSk, Cal–JF3) • eyes (Scrs–SkNO)
364.26	in a (Cal–MTSk, Cal–JF3) • into the (Scrs–SkNO)
364.29	mud-dobber (Cal–JF4, Cal–JF3, Scrs–SkNO) • musician (MTSk)
364.29–30	the second the speech was finished he (Cal–MTSk, Cal–JF3) • when the second speech was finished (Scrs–SkNO)
364.31	Oh, (Cal, Scrs–SkNO) • ~! (JF1–MTSk, JF1–JF3)
364.34	piano sharp (Cal–JF4, Cal–JF3) • pianist (MTSk); pianist sharp (Scrs–SkNO)
365.2	grit (Cal–JF4, Cal–JF3, Scrs–HWa, HWbMT–SkNO) • pluck (MTSk); girt (HWb)
365.2	started in fresh (Cal–JF4, Cal–JF3, Scrs–SkNO) • began again (MTSk)
365.7	invokes! (Cal–MTSk, Cal–JF3, Scrs) • ~? (HWa–SkNO)
365.8	writings! (Cal–MTSk, Cal–JF3) • ~? (Scrs–SkNO)
365.10	around (Cal–MTSk, Scrs–SkNO) • round (JF3)
365.10	Oh, (Cal, Scrs–SkNO) • ~! (JF1–MTSk, JF1–JF3)
365.10	lovely! (Cal–MTSk, Cal–JF3) • ~, (Scrs–SkNO)
365.12	Oh, (Cal) • ~! (JF1–MTSk, JF1–JF3); [not in] (Scrs–SkNO)
365.13	deep! (Cal–JF4, Cal–JF3, Scrs–SkNO) • ~? (MTSk)
365.14	snickering turned on (Cal–JF4, Cal–JF3, Scrs–SkNO) • laughter (MTSk)
365.15	old (Cal–JF4, Cal–JF3, Scrs–SkNO) • [not in] (MTSk)
365.16	gritted (Cal–MTSk, Cal–JF3, HWbMT–SkNO) • grated (Scrs–HWb)
365.20	any how (Cal–MTSk, Cal–JF3) • any way (Scrs–SkNO)
365.21	mighty (Cal–JF4, Cal–JF3, Scrs–SkNO) • very (MTSk)
365.21	supes (Cal–MTSk, Scrs–SkNO) • super (JF3)
365.21–22	to grinding (Cal–JF4, Cal–JF3) • [not in] (MTSk); grinding (Scrs–SkNO)
365.23	illustrates (Cal–MTSk, Cal–JF3) • represents (Scrs–SkNO)
365.25	rare ability (Cal–MTSk, Cal–JF3) • marvellous skill (Scrs–SkNO)
365.29	awakening (Cal–MTSk, Cal–JF3) • awakened (Scrs–SkNO)
365.34	ass (Cal–JF4, Cal–JF3, Scrs–SkNO) • muggins (MTSk)
365.35	Ri-i-ley (Cal–MTSk, Cal–JF3, HWaMT–SkNO) • Ri-d-ley (Scrs–HWa)
366.1	It . . . bet you. (Cal–JF4, Cal–JF3) • My! (MTSk); It . . . bet. (Scrs–HWb); Whe-ew! (HWbMT–SkNO)

366.2   huff (Cal–JF4, Cal–JF3, Scrs–SkNO) • fury (MTSk)

366.5-9   says: . . . dismiss—" (Cal–JF4, Cal–JF3) • says—— [¶] But
             what he said was too vigorous for repetition, and is better
             left out. (MTSk); says— . . . dismiss." (Scrs–HWa); says—
             . . . dismiss the house." (HWaMT-SkNO)

366.6   lets (JF1–JF4, JF1–JF3, Scrs–SkNO) • let's (Cal)

366.6   clam! (Cal–JF4, Cal–JF3, Scrs–HWa) • ~: (HWb–SkNO)

366.7   stick! (Cal–JF4, Cal–JF3) • ~∧ (Scrs–SkNO)

366.10-24   "By . . . man. (Cal–JF4, Cal–JF3) • [not in] (MTSk, Scrs–
             SkNO)

366.13   [no ¶] "What (Cal) • [¶] "What (JF1–JF4, JF1–JF3)

366.18   MARK TWAIN. (Cal) • [not in] (JF1–JF4, JF1–JF3)

366.21   glass (Cal–JF4) • a glass (JF3)

137. THE PIONEERS' BALL

Textual Commentary

The first printing in the Virginia City *Territorial Enterprise,* probably on
19 or 21 November 1865, is not extant. The sketch survives in two contemporary reprintings of the *Enterprise:*

P¹   "The Pioneer Ball," *Californian* 3 (25 November 1865): 12.

P²   " 'Mark Twain'—The Pioneers' Ball," San Francisco *Golden Era* 13
      (26 November 1865): 5.

Copies: Bancroft (P¹) and PH from Bancroft (P²). The sketch is a radiating
text: there is no copy-text. All variants are recorded in a list of emendations and adopted readings, which also records any readings unique to the
present edition, identified as I-C. The independence of P¹ is guaranteed by
its date of publication—one day before P². The independence of P² is
guaranteed by the first paragraph, which is clearly authorial and occurs
only in P². Since both printings derive independently from the lost *Enterprise,* each may preserve authorial readings among its variants. It is possible, but very unlikely, that the JF1 text was set from an *Enterprise*
clipping, now lost, taken from the Yale Scrapbook. But collation suggests
that JF1 might easily derive from a clipping of P¹, and we have therefore
not used it to help reconstruct the *Enterprise* text.

   Reprintings and Revisions. The printer's copy for JF1 cannot be certainly established, but it was probably a clipping of P¹ that Mark Twain or
Charles Henry Webb found in the Yale Scrapbook. If so, either the author
or his editor supplied a new title (" 'After' Jenkins"), derived from the
introductory remark in P¹ that the sketch was "a clever satire on Jenkins." A new introductory paragraph was also supplied, probably by
Webb. The only other substantive revision was the deletion of "late of

your State" (370.13). In the absence of distinctively authorial revisions, all of the variants in JF1 are here attributed to Webb.

The reprinting of the JF1 text is described in the textual introduction. Routledge reprinted JF1 in 1867 (JF2), introducing one error: "great" instead of "good" (370.14). Hotten in turn reprinted JF2 in 1870 (JF3). Routledge also reprinted JF2 in 1870 (JF4a) and, using the unaltered plates of JF4a, reissued the book in 1872 (JF4b). None of these texts was revised by the author, and JF2's small error was followed in all subsequent reprintings.

When Mark Twain prepared the printer's copy for MTSk in 1872, he revised a copy of JF4a and presumably deleted the last sentence of the sketch, as well as making two changes: "prancing" instead of "slopping" (370.23) and "deceive" instead of "fool" (370.27). One year later, Hotten reprinted the JF3 text in HWa. When Mark Twain revised this book for Chatto and Windus in the fall of 1873 (HWaMT), he deleted the last two paragraphs but made no verbal revisions. Contrary to the usual pattern, only part of his revisions was followed by HWb: the compositors retained the first of the two deleted paragraphs and omitted only the second, perhaps in an effort to save labor in repaging HWb.

When in 1875 Mark Twain came to reprint the sketch in SkNO, he entered the title " 'After' Jenkins" as item 25 in the Doheny table of contents (see figure 23C in the textual introduction, volume 1, p. 626). The compositors supplied the appropriate page number for the sketch in MTSk (99S), but collation shows that they ultimately set it from the text in HWbMT. (Mark Twain did not revise the sketch in either HWbMT or MTSkMT, although he had canceled it in the table of contents for the latter, indicating his preference for the former.) Notably, the SkNO text contained several revisions, all of them deletions. The sketch did not appear as the twenty-fifth but as the forty-eighth item in the collection, and it was apparently used by Elisha Bliss to help fill out a short page following the last five lines of "Aurelia's Unfortunate Young Man," an edited version of "Whereas" (no. 94). Four early paragraphs were consolidated into one; part of one and all of two paragraphs were omitted, including the last paragraph, which had been mistakenly included in HWb. Although it is barely possible that Mark Twain helped make such changes in proof, it is far more likely that Bliss took it upon himself to shorten "The Pioneers' Ball" to help him fit it on this short page. All of the revisions in SkNO are here attributed to Bliss. There are no textual notes.

The diagram of transmission is given below.

Emendations and Adopted Readings

369 *title*   The Pioneers' Ball (I-C) • The Pioneer Ball (P^1); "Mark Twain"—The Pioneers' Ball (P^2)

369.1–9   It . . . costumes. (P^2) • [*not in*] (P^1)

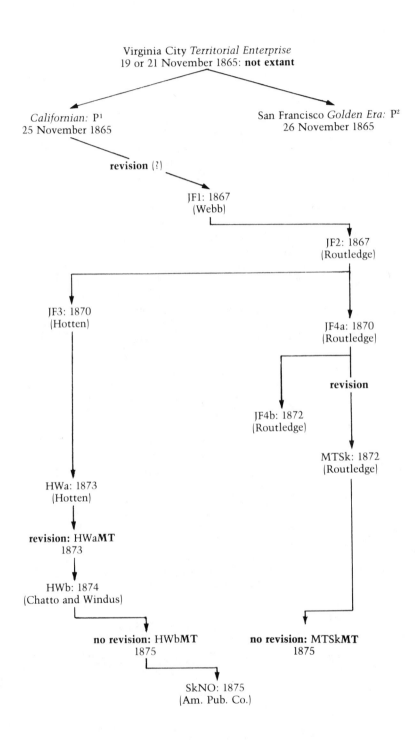

Virginia City *Territorial Enterprise*
19 or 21 November 1865: **not extant**

Californian: P¹
25 November 1865

San Francisco *Golden Era:* P²
26 November 1865

revision (?)

JF1: 1867
(Webb)

JF2: 1867
(Routledge)

JF3: 1870
(Hotten)

JF4a: 1870
(Routledge)

revision

JF4b: 1872
(Routledge)

MTSk: 1872
(Routledge)

HWa: 1873
(Hotten)

revision: HWaMT
1873

HWb: 1874
(Chatto and Windus)

no revision: HWbMT
1875

no revision: MTSkMT
1875

SkNO: 1875
(Am. Pub. Co.)

369.10   *foi gras* (P²) • *foigras* (P¹)
369.20   waterfall (P²) water-|fall (P¹)
369.23   R. (P¹) • B. (P²)
370.1   well-sustained (P²) • ~∧~ (P¹)
370.2   this (P²) • the (P¹)
370.4   sozodont-sweetened (P²) • ~∧~ (P¹)
370.7   dress (P²) • ~, (P¹)
370.22   permanently (P¹) • prematurely (P²)
370.27   knows (P¹) • knows that (P²)

Historical Collation

Texts collated:

P¹   "The Pioneer Ball," *Californian* 3 (25 November 1865): 12.
P²   " 'Mark Twain'—The Pioneers' Ball," San Francisco *Golden Era* 13 (26 November 1865): 5.

          [" 'After' *Jenkins*" in the following]

JF1   *Jumping Frog* (New York: Webb, 1867), pp. 85–88. Reprints P¹ with editorial and possibly authorial revisions.
JF2   *Jumping Frog* (London: Routledge, 1867), pp. 79–81. Reprints JF1 with one substantive error.
JF3   *Jumping Frog* (London: Hotten, 1870), pp. 82–83. Reprints JF2 without substantive error.
JF4   *Jumping Frog* (London: Routledge, 1870 and 1872), pp. 73–75. Reprints JF2 without substantive error.
MTSk   *Mark Twain's Sketches* (London: Routledge, 1872), pp. 99–101. Reprints JF4 with authorial revisions.
MTSkMT   Copy of MTSk revised by Mark Twain, who made no changes in this sketch.
HWa   *Choice Humorous Works* (London: Hotten, 1873), pp. 519–520. Reprints JF3 with few errors.
HWaMT   Sheets of HWa revised by Mark Twain, who made one deletion in this sketch.
HWb   *Choice Humorous Works* (London: Chatto and Windus, 1874), pp. 496–497. Reprints HWa with some of the authorial revisions from HWaMT.
HWbMT   Copy of HWb revised by Mark Twain, who left this sketch unrevised.
SkNO   *Sketches, New and Old* (Hartford: American Publishing Company, 1875), p. 256. Reprints HWb with editorial revisions imposed in proof.

Collation:

369 *title*   *The Pioneers' Ball* (I-C) • The Pioneer Ball (P¹); "Mark Twain"—The Pioneers' Ball (P²); "After" Jenkins (JF1+)

369.1-9   It . . . costumes. (P²) • [*not in*] (P¹); A grand affair of a ball—the Pioneers'—came off at the Occidental some time ago. The following notes of the costumes worn by the belles of the occasion may not be uninteresting to the general reader, and Jenkins may get an idea therefrom: (JF1+)

369.10   *pate de foi gras* (P²) • *pate de foigras* (P¹); *pâté de foie gras* (JF1+)

369.12   [¶] Miss (P¹⁻², JF1-MTSk, JF1-HWb) • [*no* ¶] Miss (SkNO)

369.14   [¶] Miss (P¹⁻², JF1-MTSk, JF1-HWb) • [*no* ¶] Mrs. (SkNO)

369.16   [¶] Mrs. (P¹⁻², JF1-MTSk, JF1-HWb) • [*no* ¶] Mrs. (SkNO)

369.23   R. (P¹, JF1+) • B. (P²)

370.2-6   The . . . multitude. (P¹⁻², JF1-MTSk, JF1-HWb) • [*not in*] (SkNO)

370.2   this (P²) • the (P¹, JF1-MTSk, JF1-HWb)

370.13-15   The . . . gay. (P¹⁻², JF1-MTSk, JF1-HWb) • [*not in*] (SkNO)

370.13   late . . . State, (P¹⁻²) • [*not in*] (JF1-MTSk, JF1-HWb)

370.14   good (P¹⁻², JF1) • great (JF2-MTSk, JF2-HWb)

370.16-20   Miss . . . it. (P¹⁻², JF1-MTSk, JF1-SkNO) • [*canceled*] (HWaMT)

370.21-32   Being . . . puzzle. (P¹⁻², JF1-MTSk, JF1-HWa) • [*canceled*] (HWaMT); [*not in*] (HWb-SkNO)

370.22   permanently (P¹, JF1-MTSk, JF1-HWa) • prematurely (P²)

370.23   slopping (P¹⁻², JF1-JF4, JF1-HWa) • prancing (MTSk)

370.27   fool (P¹⁻², JF1-JF4, JF1-HWa) • deceive (MTSk)

370.27   knows (P¹, JF1-MTSk, JF1-HWa) • knows that (P²)

370.32-36   There . . . howl. (P¹⁻², JF1-JF4, JF1-HWa) • [*not in*] (MTSk); [*canceled*] (HWaMT); [*not in*] (HWb-SkNO)

138. THE GUARD ON A BENDER

Textual Commentary

The first printing in the *Napa County Reporter* for 25 November 1865 (p. 2) is copy-text. Copy: PH from Bancroft.

Textual Notes

372.23   down street] A clearly authorial idiom: no emendation is required. Compare the same usage in "Jul'us Caesar" (no. 20) and "Fitz Smythe's Horse" (no. 132).

Emendations of the Copy-Text

372.4	drunker (I-C) • d[r]unker
372.5	got. They (I-C) • ~.— | ~
373.10	Market (I-C) • Markct
373.14	Kearny (I-C) • Kearney

139. *BENKERT COMETH!*

Textual Commentary

The first printing in the *Napa County Reporter* for 25 November 1865 (p.2) is copy-text. Copy: PH from Bancroft. There are no textual notes.

Emendations of the Copy-Text

375.10	music." And (I-C) • ~."— | ~

140. *UNCLE LIGE*

Textual Commentary

The first printing in the Virginia City *Territorial Enterprise*, probably sometime between 28 and 30 November 1865, is not extant. The only known contemporary reprinting of the *Enterprise*, the *Californian* 3 (2 December 1865): 12, is copy-text. Copies: Bancroft; PH from Yale. There are no textual notes.

Emendations of the Copy-Text

379.19	kind-hearted (I-C) • kind-|hearted
379.31	over-charged (I-C) • over-|charged

141. *WEBB'S BENEFIT*

Textual Commentary

The first printing in the *Napa County Reporter* for 2 December 1865 (p. 2) is copy-text. Copy: PH from Bancroft. There are no textual notes.

Emendations of the Copy-Text

383.3	Arrah-no-Poke (I-C) • Arrah-na-Poke
383.13	fine, (I-C) • ~[∧]

142. *A RICH EPIGRAM*

Textual Commentary

The first printing in the Virginia City *Territorial Enterprise,* probably sometime between 8 and 10 December 1865, is not extant. The poem survives in the only known contemporary reprinting of the *Enterprise,* the San Francisco *Daily American Flag* for 20 December 1865 (p. 1) (AF), which is copy-text. A clipping of AF is pasted in the Yale Scrapbook, and although Mark Twain did not revise the clipping, he did not cancel it either, indicating that he may have considered reprinting it in JF1. The sketch was not included there, and Mark Twain did not subsequently reprint it. Copies: California State Library, Sacramento; PH of the Yale Scrapbook, p. 38A.

Albert Bigelow Paine published the poem in *MTB* (1: 275–276) from an unidentified source. His text varies so markedly from the copy-text, and seems on balance so clearly an editorial modification of the original poem, that it has seemed unwise to conflate the two. Still, Paine may have had access to a more reliable text, or Mark Twain may have volunteered to revise Paine's text for him. We therefore provide a historical collation of AF and *MTB.* There are no textual notes.

Emendations of the Copy-Text

387.3	Macdougall (I-C) • McDougall
387.12	Macdougall (I-C) • McDougall
387.15	Vestvali (I-C) • [*indent*] Vestvali
387.18	Macdougall (I-C) • McDougall

Historical Collation

Texts collated: AF and *MTB* (see the commentary above).

Collation:

387.2	Torn with (AF) • Roused to (MTB)
387.4	Grabbed his throat (AF) • Tore his coat (MTB)
387.5	Tore his coat (AF) • Clutched his throat (MTB)
387.7	Shame! Oh, fie (AF) • For shame! oh, fie (MTB)
387.9	*Will* (AF) • Will (MTB)
387.10	bang and claw (AF) • curse and swear (MTB)
387.11	gouge and chaw (AF) • rip and tear (MTB)
387.12	unprepared (AF) • innocent (MTB)
387.14	See how you've left (AF) • Almost, you've left (MTB)
387.16	slashed (AF) • smashed (MTB)

143. *A GRACEFUL COMPLIMENT*

Textual Commentary

The first printing appeared in the Virginia City *Territorial Enterprise,* probably sometime between 10 and 31 December 1865. The only known copy of this printing, in a clipping in the Yale Scrapbook (p. 1A), is copytext. The clipping is damaged and therefore incomplete: the last eight words of the surviving text have of necessity been conjectured from fragments of missing letters and figures. How much more of the text is wholly lost remains unknown: the ellipsis at 392.8 is therefore editorial. Mark Twain slightly revised the clipping in early 1867 while preparing copy for JF1, and he listed the sketch as "Graceful Compliment" in the back of the scrapbook, along with six other sketches that did not "run average" (see the textual introduction, volume 1, pp. 538–539). The revised clipping remains in the scrapbook; the missing portion was probably lost through inadvertence, not from being removed for JF1 printer's copy. The sketch was not included in JF1, and Mark Twain did not subsequently reprint it. There are no textual notes.

Emendations of the Copy-Text

390.15	income (I-C) • i[n]come
391.6	Collector's (I-C) • Co[l]ector's
391.16	Soulé (I-C) • Soule
392.7–8	$1,200,000,000 . . . accumulated. . . .(I-C) • $1,200,[000,000] [*torn*] [the] int[erest] that has ac- [*torn*]

Alterations in the Yale Scrapbook

391.28	This . . . rough.] *canceled.*

144. *"CHRISTIAN SPECTATOR"*

Textual Commentary

The first printing appeared in the Virginia City *Territorial Enterprise,* probably sometime between 13 and 15 December 1865. The only known copy of this printing, in a clipping in the Yale Scrapbook (p. 52), is copytext. The copy-text remains the same for the quotations from the *Christian Spectator* because no file of the *Spectator* has been found. There are no textual notes.

Emendations of the Copy-Text

394.13	reflex (I-C) • reflax
394.24	Pierce; then (I-C) • Pierce; than

145. MORE ROMANCE

Textual Commentary

The first printing appeared in the Virginia City *Territorial Enterprise,* probably sometime between 13 and 15 December 1865. The only known copy of this printing, in a clipping in the Yale Scrapbook (p. 52), is copy-text. There are no textual notes.

Emendations of the Copy-Text

397.8   please (I-C) • blease
397.22   doubtless (I-C) • doubless

146. GRAND FETE-DAY AT THE CLIFF HOUSE

Textual Commentary

The first printing in the Virginia City *Territorial Enterprise,* probably sometime between 19 and 21 December 1865, is not extant. The sketch survives in the only known contemporary reprinting of the *Enterprise,* the San Francisco *Examiner* for 23 December 1865 (p. 3), which is copy-text. Copy: PH from Bancroft. There are no textual notes or emendations.

147. MACDOUGALL VS. MAGUIRE

Textual Commentary

The first printing appeared in the Virginia City *Territorial Enterprise,* probably on 22 or 23 December 1865. The only known copy of this printing, in a clipping in the Yale Scrapbook (p. 47), is copy-text. Clemens struck through the entire clipping, probably in January or February 1867. There are no textual notes.

Emendations of the Copy-Text

403.13   the (I-C) • [*not in*]

148. THE CHRISTMAS FIRESIDE

Textual Commentary

The first printing in the *Californian* 4 (23 December 1865): 4 is copy-text. Copies: Bancroft; PH from Yale.

Reprintings and Revisions. The sketch was reprinted in JF1, retitled "The Story of the Bad Little Boy Who Didn't Come to Grief," but not otherwise revised. The new title was derived from the subtitle of the

Californian printing, a clipping of which must have been taken from the Yale Scrapbook to serve as printer's copy. Although no sign of such a clipping or of authorial revisions and corrections (if there were any) now survives in the scrapbook, Mark Twain did list the sketch in the back of the scrapbook as "Children's Christmas Stories," indicating his intention to reprint it (see the textual introduction, volume 1, p. 538).

The reprinting of the JF1 text is described in the textual introduction. Routledge reprinted JF1 in 1867 (JF2), and Hotten in turn reprinted JF2 in 1870 (JF3). Routledge also reprinted JF2 in 1870 (JF4a) and, using the unaltered plates of JF4a, reissued the book in 1872 (JF4b). None of these texts was revised by the author, and the compositors made only one substantive change ("things" to "thing" at 409.26, made independently by JF3 and JF4). When Mark Twain prepared the printer's copy for MTSk in March or April 1872, he revised a copy of JF4a and presumably made four revisions in this sketch. He added "simply" (407.8), deleted "in" (408.25), changed "rock" to "brick" (408.30), and altered the phrase "she got over it" to "she hit back; and she never got sick at all" (410.11).

The previous year (1871), Hotten reprinted his JF3 text in Scrs. He shortened the title to "Story of the Bad Little Boy" and made one other substantive change, "nor" for "or" (407.19). In 1873, Hotten reprinted the Scrs text in HWa. When Mark Twain revised this book for Chatto and Windus in the fall of 1873 (HWaMT), he made no changes in this sketch, and it was reprinted in HWb from the unaltered plates of HWa in 1874.

When in 1875 Mark Twain prepared the printer's copy for SkNO, he revised this sketch in neither HWbMT nor MTSkMT. He entered the title "Story of the Bad Little Boy" as item 5 of the Doheny table of contents (see figure 23A in the textual introduction, volume 1, p. 624). The printers set the sketch from the unmarked copy of HWbMT, and Mark Twain made four revisions in proof: he changed "would" to "might" (407.12), "rock" to "brick" (408.30), omitted "to" (409.17), and changed the phrase "and look, and look through" to "and look, all through" (409.30).

Mark Twain had revised the JF1 printing of this sketch before making the revisions discussed above. Sometime in 1869 he made five changes in the Doheny copy of the *Jumping Frog*, JF1MT, one of which duplicates a change he made twice elsewhere ("brick" instead of "rock" at 408.30). One tantalizing but unexplained note appears at the beginning of the sketch: "Beecher—Holmes." All the latter revisions are reported in the historical collation.

There are no textual notes. The diagram of transmission is given below.

Emendations of the Copy-Text

407.16   good-night (I-C) • good-|night
408.11   didn't (I-C) • didn[∧]t

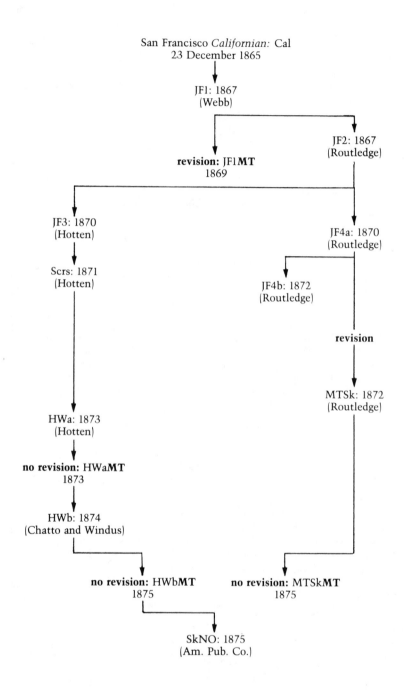

San Francisco *Californian:* Cal
23 December 1865

JF1: 1867
(Webb)

JF2: 1867
(Routledge)

revision: JF1MT
1869

JF3: 1870
(Hotten)

JF4a: 1870
(Routledge)

Scrs: 1871
(Hotten)

JF4b: 1872
(Routledge)

revision

MTSk: 1872
(Routledge)

HWa: 1873
(Hotten)

no revision: HWaMT
1873

HWb: 1874
(Chatto and Windus)

no revision: HWbMT
1875

no revision: MTSkMT
1875

SkNO: 1875
(Am. Pub. Co.)

409.17	household (I-C) • house-|hold
410.14	church-yard (I-C) • church-|yard
410.19	infernalest (JF1) • infernalist
410.22	Sunday-school (I-C) • Sunday-|school
410.24	life. (I-C) • life. | MARK TWAIN.

Historical Collation

Texts collated:

Cal   "The Christmas Fireside," *Californian* 4 (23 December 1865): 4.

[*"The Story of the Bad Little Boy Who Didn't Come to Grief" in the following*]

JF1   *Jumping Frog* (New York: Webb, 1867), pp. 60–66. Reprints Cal with a revised title only.

JF1**MT**   The copy of an 1869 impression of JF1 revised by Mark Twain. It was not used as printer's copy for any known reprinting.

JF2   *Jumping Frog* (London: Routledge, 1867), pp. 57–62. Reprints JF1 without error.

JF3   *Jumping Frog* (London: Hotten, 1870), pp. 53–56. Reprints JF2 with one error.

JF4   *Jumping Frog* (London: Routledge, 1870 and 1872), pp. 51–56. Reprints JF2 with one error.

[*"Story of the Bad Little Boy" in the following*]

Scrs   *Screamers* (London: Hotten, 1871), pp. 29–35. Reprints JF3 with one error.

MTSk   *Mark Twain's Sketches* (London: Routledge, 1872), pp. 40–44. Reprints JF4 with four authorial revisions.

MTSk**MT**   Copy of MTSk revised by Mark Twain, who made no changes in this sketch.

HWa   *Choice Humorous Works* (London: Hotten, 1873), pp. 541–543. Reprints Scrs without additional error.

HWa**MT**   Sheets of HWa revised by Mark Twain, who made no changes in this sketch.

HWb   *Choice Humorous Works* (London: Chatto and Windus, 1874), pp. 511–513. Reprints HWa from unaltered plates.

HWb**MT**   Copy of HWb revised by Mark Twain, who made no changes in this sketch.

SkNO   *Sketches, New and Old* (Hartford: American Publishing Company, 1875), pp. 51–55. Reprints HWb with four authorial revisions made in proof.

Collation:

407 *title*–4	*The* . . . THE STORY OF THE BAD LITTLE BOY THAT BORE A CHARMED LIFE (Cal) • The Story of the Bad Little Boy Who Didn't Come to Grief (JF1–MTSk, JF1–JF3); Story of the Bad Little Boy (Scrs–SkNO)
407.8	called (Cal–JF4, Cal–SkNO) • simply called (MTSk)
407.9–10	who was pious (Cal–MTSk, Cal–SkNO) • [*canceled*] (JF1**MT**)
407.12	would (Cal–MTSk, Cal–HWb) • might (SkNO)
407.19	or (Cal–MTSk, Cal–JF3) • nor (Scrs–SkNO)
408.3	she (Cal–MTSk, Cal–SkNO) • *she* (JF1**MT**)
408.16	books (Cal–MTSk, Cal–SkNO) • *books* (JF1**MT**)
408.19–20	get up and snort (Cal–MTSk, Cal–SkNO) • just rair & charge (JF1**MT**)
408.25	up in (Cal–JF4, Cal–SkNO) • up (MTSk)
408.28	Oh, (Cal) • ~! (JF1+)
408.30	rock (Cal–JF4, Cal–HWb) • brick (JF1**MT**, MTSk, SkNO)
409.17	to do (Cal–MTSk, Cal–HWb) • do (SkNO)
409.26	things (Cal–JF2) • thing (JF4–MTSk, JF3–SkNO)
409.30	and look, and look through (Cal–MTSk, Cal–HWb) • and look, all through (SkNO)
409.32	Oh, (Cal) • ~! (JF1–MTSk, JF1–Scrs); ~∧ (HWa–SkNO)
410.11	she got over it (Cal–JF4, Cal–SkNO) • she hit back; and she never got sick at all (MTSk)
410.15	Ah, (Cal) • ~! (JF1+)
410.24	life. (JF1+) • life.	MARK TWAIN. (Cal)

149. ENIGMA

Textual Commentary

The first printing in the *Californian* 4 (23 December 1865): 4 is copy-text. Copies: Bancroft; PH from Yale. The sketch was reprinted in the *Californian* 6 (12 January 1867): 7, evidently from a stereotype of the original printing. There are no textual notes.

Emendations of the Copy-Text

412.24	mad, (I-C) • ~.
412.25	relations. (I-C) • relations.	MARK TWAIN.

150. *ANOTHER ENTERPRISE*

Textual Commentary

The first printing appeared in the Virginia City *Territorial Enterprise*, probably on 26 or 27 December 1865. The only known copy of this printing, in a clipping in the Yale Scrapbook (pp. 55–56), is copy-text. There are no textual notes.

Emendations of the Copy-Text

414.1	Scoofy (I-C) • Schoofy
414.9	much. (I-C) • ~∧
415.12	his (I-C) • hif
415.12	by —— (I-C) • by——

151. *SPIRIT OF THE LOCAL PRESS*

Textual Commentary

The first printing appeared in the Virginia City *Territorial Enterprise*, probably on 26 or 27 December 1865. The only known copy of this printing, in a clipping in the Yale Scrapbook (pp. 55–56), is copy-text. There are no textual notes.

Emendations of the Copy-Text

417.9	condition (I-C) • contion
418.17	'Fourteener' (I-C) • "~"
418.24	city!—and (I-C) • ~!—|~

152. *CONVICTS*

Textual Commentary

The first printing appeared in the Virginia City *Territorial Enterprise* for 31 December 1865. The only known copy of this printing, preserved in photofacsimile by Richard E. Lingenfelter in *The Newspapers of Nevada: A History and Bibliography* (San Francisco: John Howell Books, 1964), following p. 4, is copy-text. There are no textual notes or emendations.

A1. *ANOTHER OF THEM*

Textual Commentary

The first printing in the San Francisco *Morning Call* for 23 June 1864 (p. 2) is copy-text. Copy: PH in MTP. There are no textual notes or emendations.

A2. *A TRIP TO THE CLIFF HOUSE*

Textual Commentary

The first printing in the San Francisco *Morning Call* for 25 June 1864 (p. 1) is copy-text. Copy: PH from Bancroft. There are no emendations.

Textual Notes

427.1   IF ONE TIRE] Possibly an error, but more likely an effort to use the subjunctive for heightened elegance: compare "ere the sea breeze sets in," another deliberate affectation.

A3. *MISSIONARIES WANTED FOR SAN FRANCISCO*

Textual Commentary

The first printing in the San Francisco *Morning Call* for 28 June 1864 (p. 2) is copy-text. Copy: PH from Bancroft. There are no textual notes.

Emendations of the Copy-Text

429.13–14   overbearing (I-C) • over-|bearing
429.16   concern (I-C) • conc[ ]rn

A4. *THE KAHN OF TARTARY*

Textual Commentary

The first printing in the San Francisco *Morning Call* for 29 June 1864 (p. 3) is copy-text. Copy: PH from Bancroft. There are no textual notes.

Emendations of the Copy-Text

430.1   Kahn of (I-C) • K[ ]hn of
430.5   Mr. (I-C) • ~[∧]
431.2   gentle (I-C) • gent[ ]e

A5. *HOUSE AT LARGE*

Textual Commentary

The first printing in the San Francisco *Morning Call* for 1 July 1864 (p. 1) is copy-text. Copy: PH from Bancroft. There are no textual notes.

Emendations of the Copy-Text

433.9   midnight (I-C) • mid-|night

A6. *CALABOOSE THEATRICALS*

Textual Commentary

The first printing in the San Francisco *Morning Call* for 14 July 1864 (p. 1) is copy-text. Copy: PH from Bancroft. There are no textual notes.

Emendations of the Copy-Text

434.5   Whee-heeping (I-C) • Whee-|heeping

A7. *THE "COMING MAN" HAS ARRIVED*

Textual Commentary

The first printing in the San Francisco *Morning Call* for 16 July 1864 (p. 1) is copy-text. Copy: PH from Bancroft. There are no textual notes.

Emendations of the Copy-Text

435.2   him. John (I-C) • ~.—~
435.13   about (I-C) • abou[t]
436.9   to-day • to-|day

A8. *THE COUNTY PRISON*

Textual Commentary

The first printing in the San Francisco *Morning Call* for 17 July 1864 (p. 3) is copy-text. Copy: PH from Bancroft. There are no textual notes.

Emendations of the Copy-Text

437.8   in (I-C) • [ ]n
437.16   whitewashed (I-C) • white-|washed
438.19   Prison-keeper (I-C) • Prison-|keeper

A9. *ASSAULT*

Textual Commentary

The first printing in the San Francisco *Morning Call* on 19 July 1864 (p. 1) is copy-text. Copy: PH from Bancroft. There are no textual notes.

Emendations of the Copy-Text

439.1   Mrs. (I-C) • ~$_\wedge$
439.21   Mr. (I-C) • ~[$_\wedge$]

A10. *THE BOSS EARTHQUAKE*

Textual Commentary

The first printing in the San Francisco *Morning Call* for 22 July 1864 (p. 1) is copy-text. Copy: PH from Bancroft. There are no textual notes.

Emendations of the Copy-Text

441.12   if (I-C) • i[f]

A11. *GOOD EFFECTS OF A HIGH TARIFF*

Textual Commentary

The first printing in the San Francisco *Morning Call* for 22 July 1864 (p. 1) is copy-text. Copy: PH from Bancroft. There are no textual notes or emendations.

A12. *A SCENE AT THE POLICE COURT*

Textual Commentary

The first printing in the San Francisco *Morning Call* for 22 July 1864 (p. 2) is copy-text. Copy: PH from Bancroft. There are no textual notes.

Emendations of the Copy-Text

443.4   larceners (I-C) • larcenors

A13. *ARREST OF A SECESH BISHOP*

Textual Commentary

The first printing in the San Francisco *Morning Call* for 22 July 1864, p. 3 (MC), is copy-text for all but the article quoted from the Stockton (Calif.) *Independent* for 20 July 1864, p. 2 (Ind), which is copy-text from the title through 444.14. Collation suggests that a clipping of Ind served as part of the printer's copy for the compositor of MC. One substantive alteration probably imposed by the compositor of MC ("time" instead of "weeks" at 444.3) has been rejected in favor of the Ind reading. Copies: clipping in Scrapbook 4, p. 8, MTP; PH from Bancroft. There are no textual notes.

Emendations of the Copy-Text

[*Copy-text from the title through 444.14 is Ind*]

444.1   Kavanaugh (MC) • Ravanaugh

[*Copy-text from 444.15 to the end is MC*]

445.26   would (I-C) • woul[d]

A14. *TROT HER ALONG*

Textual Commentary

The first printing in the San Francisco *Morning Call* for 30 July 1864 (p. 1) is copy-text. Copy: PH in MTP. There are no textual notes or emendations.

A15. *DISGUSTED AND GONE*

Textual Commentary

The first printing in the San Francisco *Morning Call* for 31 July 1864 (p. 1) is copy-text. There are no textual notes.

Emendations of the Copy-Text

447.7   to-day (I-C) • to-|day

A16. *ANOTHER LAZARUS*

Textual Commentary

The first printing in the San Francisco *Morning Call* for 31 July 1864 (p. 3) is copy-text. Copy: PH from Bancroft. There are no textual notes.

Emendations of the Copy-Text

448.17   repose, (I-C) • ~[.]

A17. *SOMBRE FESTIVITIES*

Textual Commentary

The first printing in the San Francisco *Morning Call* for 2 August 1864 (p. 1) is copy-text. Copy: PH from Bancroft. There are no textual notes.

Emendations of the Copy-Text

449.22   unctuous (I-C) • unctious

A18. *ATTEMPTED SUICIDE*

Textual Commentary

The first printing in the San Francisco *Morning Call* for 7 August 1864 (p. 1) is copy-text. Copy: PH from Bancroft. There are no textual notes or emendations.

A19. *MYSTERIOUS*

Textual Commentary

The first printing in the San Francisco *Morning Call* for 9 August 1864 (p. 2) is copy-text. Copy: PH from Bancroft. There are no textual notes.

Emendations of the Copy-Text

452.8   thoroughfare (I-C) • thorough-|fare

A20. *ASSAULT BY A HOUSE*

Textual Commentary

The first printing in the San Francisco *Morning Call* for 9 August 1864 (p. 2) is copy-text. Copy: PH from Bancroft. There are no textual notes or emendations.

A21. *WHAT GOES WITH THE MONEY?*

Textual Commentary

The first printing in the San Francisco *Morning Call* for 19 August 1864 (p. 2) is copy-text. Copy: PH from Bancroft. There are no textual notes.

Emendations of the Copy-Text

455.16   long-run (I-C) • long[-]run

A22. *IT IS THE DANIEL WEBSTER*

Textual Commentary

The first printing in the San Francisco *Morning Call* for 21 August 1864 (p. 2) is copy-text. Copies: clipping in Scrapbook 5, p. 58, MTP; PH from Bancroft. The article quoted from the San Francisco *Argus* for 20 August 1864 has not been found and may not be extant. That article in turn quotes from the previous appendix item, A21, however, and we have emended twice to correct the present copy-text's rendering of that article. There are no textual notes.

Emendations of the Copy-Text

456.6	company (I-C) • Company
456.8	company (I-C) • Company
457.19	chicken-coop (I-C) • chicken[-]coop

A23. *NO EARTHQUAKE*

Textual Commentary

The first printing in the San Francisco *Morning Call* for 23 August 1864 (p. 1) is copy-text. Copies: clipping in Scrapbook 5, p. 41, MTP; PH from Bancroft. There are no textual notes or emendations.

A24. *RAIN*

Textual Commentary

The first printing in the San Francisco *Morning Call* for 23 August 1864 (p. 2) is copy-text. Copies: clipping in Scrapbook 5, p. 41, MTP; PH from Bancroft. There are no textual notes or emendations.

A25. *A DARK TRANSACTION*

Textual Commentary

The first printing in the San Francisco *Morning Call* for 24 August 1864 (p. 3) is copy-text. Copy: PH in MTP. There are no textual notes.

Emendations of the Copy-Text

460.22	Esq. (I-C) • ~[∧]
460.26	stand; (I-C) • ~[;]

A26. *ENTHUSIASTIC HARD MONEY DEMONSTRATION*

Textual Commentary

The first printing in the San Francisco *Morning Call* for 30 August 1864 (p. 3) is copy-text. Copy: PH from Bancroft. There are no textual notes.

Emendations of the Copy-Text

461.6	adjourned (I-C) • a[ ]journed
461.7	Eolis (I-C) • E[o]lis

A27. "SHINER NO. 1"

Textual Commentary

The first printing in the San Francisco *Morning Call* for 31 August 1864 (p. 3) is copy-text. Copy: PH from Bancroft. There are no textual notes.

Emendations of the Copy-Text

462.3	swallow-tail (I-C) • swallow-	tail
462.8	jintlemen (I-C) • jintle-	men
462.9	widout (I-C) • wid-	out

A28. *THE COSMOPOLITAN HOTEL BESIEGED*

Textual Commentary

The first printing in the San Francisco *Morning Call* for 1 September 1864 (p. 1) is copy-text. Copy: PH from Bancroft. There are no textual notes.

Emendations of the Copy-Text

463.19	dining-room (I-C) • dining[-]room
463.19–20	gentlemen (I-C) • gentleme[s]

A29. *RINCON SCHOOL MILITIA*

Textual Commentary

The first printing in the San Francisco *Morning Call* for 1 September 1864 (p. 3) is copy-text. Copies: clipping in Scrapbook 4, p. 7, MTP; PH from Bancroft. There are no textual notes.

Emendations of the Copy-Text

465.28	unwarlike (I-C) • un-|warlike
465.28	patriots (I-C) • partriots
466.3	Principal's (I-C) • Principal

A30. *FINE PICTURE OF REV. MR. KING*

Textual Commentary

The first printing in the San Francisco *Morning Call* for 1 September 1864 (p. 3) is copy-text. Copies: clipping in Scrapbook 4, p. 7, MTP; PH from Bancroft. There are no textual notes.

Emendations of the Copy-Text

467.1–2	distressed-looking (I-C) • distressed[-]looking
467.13	over-fed (I-C) • over[-]fed
467.23	skill. (I-C) • ~[∧]

A31. *THE HURDLE-RACE YESTERDAY*

Textual Commentary

The first printing in the San Francisco *Morning Call* for 4 September 1864 (p. 1) is copy-text. Copy: PH from Bancroft. There are no textual notes or emendations.

A32. *A TERRIBLE MONSTER CAGED*

Textual Commentary

The first printing in the San Francisco *Morning Call* for 4 September 1864 (p. 1) is copy-text. Copy: PH from Bancroft. There are no textual notes.

Emendations of the Copy-Text

469.15	matter (I-C) • mat[ ]er
469.25	headed (I-C) • head[e]d

A33. *THE CALIFORNIAN*

Textual Commentary

The first printing in the San Francisco *Morning Call* for 4 September 1864 (p. 3) is copy-text. Copy: PH from Bancroft.

Textual Notes

470.6–7	Frank Brett Harte] Copy-text "Hart" is presumably an error. Harte's pseudonym, "Bret Harte," was a modification of his full name, "Francis Brett Harte."

Emendations of the Copy-Text

*470.7	Harte (I-C) • Hart
470.8	emanated (I-C) • em[ ]nated
470.9	take (I-C) • t[a]ke

A34. *A PROMISING ARTIST*

Textual Commentary

The first printing in the San Francisco *Morning Call* for 6 September 1864 (p. 1) is copy-text. Copy: PH from Bancroft. There are no textual notes.

Emendations of the Copy-Text

471.3   Mr. (I-C) • ~[∧]
471.13   away-at-home (I-C-) • away-at[∧]home

A35. *EARTHQUAKE*

Textual Commentary

The first printing in the San Francisco *Morning Call* for 8 September 1864 (p. 2) is copy-text. Copies: clipping in Scrapbook 4, p. 8, MTP; PH from Bancroft. There are no textual notes or emendations.

A36. *CROSS SWEARING*

Textual Commentary

The first printing in the San Francisco *Morning Call* for 9 September 1864 (p. 3) is copy-text. Copy: PH from Bancroft. There are no textual notes.

Emendations of the Copy-Text

473.17   corroborate (I-C) • corrobborate
473.22   it? (I-C) • ~.
473.23   punishment. (I-C) • ~[∧]
474.9   it, (I-C) • ~[.]

A37. *INTERESTING LITIGATION*

Textual Commentary

The first printing in the San Francisco *Morning Call* for 15 September 1864 (p. 1) is copy-text. Copy: PH from Bancroft. There are no textual notes.

Emendations of the Copy-Text

475.11   neighbor (I-C) • ne[ ]ghbor

475.12   Court, (I-C) • ~.
476.5   can't (I-C-) • can 't

A38. *A TERRIBLE WEAPON*

Textual Commentary

The first printing in the San Francisco *Morning Call* for 21 September 1864 (p. 1) is copy-text. Copy: PH from Bancroft. There are no textual notes.

Emendations of the Copy-Text

477.6   weapon (I-C) • w[ ]apon

A39. *ADVICE TO WITNESSES*

Textual Commentary

The first printing in the San Francisco *Morning Call* for 29 September 1864 (p. 1) is copy-text. Copy: PH from Bancroft. There are no textual notes or emendations.

Line numbers in the following apparatuses refer only to Mark Twain's text and do not include the editorial headnotes.

B1. *ATTENTION, FITZ SMYTHE!*

Textual Commentary

The first printing in the San Francisco *Dramatic Chronicle* for 26 October 1865 (p. 2) is copy-text. Copy: PH from Bancroft.

Textual Notes

482.2–3   "the *Colorado* . . . *hours.*"] Mark Twain deliberately altered both the wording and emphasis of Evans' original sentence, which read: "The Pacific Mail steamship *Colorado* arrived at this port from Panama on the morning of the 14th. after the quick passage of twelve days and twenty-four hours" ("Arrival of the 'Colorado,' " San Francisco *Alta California,* 25 October 1865, p. 1).

Emendations of the Copy-Text

482.13   Armand (I-C) • Armond

B2. *LISLE LESTER ON HER TRAVELS*

Textual Commentary

The first printing in the San Francisco *Dramatic Chronicle* for 30 October 1865 (p. 3) is copy-text. Copy: PH from Bancroft. Mark Twain quoted from three separate sentences in Lisle Lester's "Notes of the Insane," Marysville (Calif.) *Appeal*, 12 September 1865 (p. 1). In addition to capitalizing the first word of his quotations when necessary, he made three slight alterations in the emphasis to help his comic point: he italicized *"handed him to the sister"* and *"shut down"*; he also omitted the italics for "alone" (483.15–17). On the other hand, either he or the *Chronicle* compositor made two small errors in transcription that seem to have no comic purpose, and in this case we have emended to restore the reading of the *Appeal*, identified as A. There are no textual notes.

Emendations of the Copy-Text

483.15   women (A) • woman
483.16   *sister* (A) • ~,

B3. *MORE CALIFORNIA NOTABLES GONE*

Textual Commentary

The first printing in the San Francisco *Dramatic Chronicle* for 1 November 1865 (p. 2) is copy-text. Copy: PH from Bancroft.

Textual Notes

485.4–5   "left . . . nativity,"] Mark Twain quoted from "Banquet to a Departing Merchant," San Francisco *Alta California*, 30 October 1865 (p. 1). He deliberately, but very slightly, altered the original text, changing "leaves" to "left."

Emendations of the Copy-Text

485 *title*   Notables (I-C) • Notable

B4. *"CHRYSTAL" ON THEOLOGY*

Textual Commentary

The first printing in the San Francisco *Dramatic Chronicle* for 3 November 1865 (p. 3) is copy-text. Copy: PH from Bancroft. There are no textual notes.

Emendations of the Copy-Text

486.3   against (I-C) • agai[n]st

B5. *OH, YOU ROBINSON!*

Textual Commentary

The first printing in the San Francisco *Dramatic Chronicle* for 6 November 1865 (p. 2) is copy-text. Copy: PH from Bancroft. There are no textual notes.

Emendations of the Copy-Text

488.7 the business (I-C) • the the business

B6. *A WORD FROM LISLE LESTER*

Textual Commentary

The first printing in the San Francisco *Dramatic Chronicle* for 7 November 1865 (p. 2) is copy-text. Copy: PH from Bancroft. There are no textual notes or emendations.

B7. *EXPLANATION*

Textual Commentary

The first printing in the San Francisco *Dramatic Chronicle* for 7 November 1865 (p. 2) is copy-text. Copy: PH from Bancroft. Mark Twain quoted from "A Palpable Sell," San Francisco *Alta California*, 6 November 1865 (p. 1). He added two words ("He thought") to the quoted phrase. There are no textual notes or emendations.

B8. *"SURPLUSAGE"*

Textual Commentary

The first printing in the San Francisco *Dramatic Chronicle* for 8 November 1865 (p. 4) is copy-text. Copy: PH from Bancroft. Mark Twain quoted from "A Palpable Sell," San Francisco *Alta California*, 6 November 1865 (p. 1) (AC). We have emended one small error in the reprinted sentence. There are no textual notes.

Emendations of the Copy-Text

491.2 the (AC) • their

B9. *STAND BACK!*

Textual Commentary

The first printing in the San Francisco *Dramatic Chronicle* for 9 November 1865 (p. 3) is copy-text. Copy: PH from Bancroft. There are no textual notes.

Emendations of the Copy-Text

492.8   set (I-C) • sets

B10. *CHEERFUL MAGNIFICENCE*

Textual Commentary

The first printing in the San Francisco *Dramatic Chronicle* for 11 November 1865 (p. 3) is copy-text. Copy: PH from Bancroft. Mark Twain's quotations from Evans' "Magnificent Funeral Car," San Francisco *Alta California*, 10 November 1865, p. 1 (AC), are somewhat imprecise, but deliberately so. We have emended only once to restore the spelling of AC.

Textual Notes

494.6–9   He . . . America."] Evans wrote, in part: "excelling in elegance of design, beauty of finish, and costly material and workmanship, anything of the kind which has ever been produced in America." Mark Twain's quotations altered these words slightly, but with the intention of shortening rather than distorting the material. We have retained his version.

494.10   "the term, luxury of grief,] Evans actually wrote: "the term 'the luxury of grief.' " Although the deviation might be an error, it is at least as likely that Mark Twain deliberately altered the phrase to avoid repeating the definite article. We have retained his version.

Emendations of the Copy-Text

494.3   well-known (AC) • $\sim_\wedge\sim$

B11. *IN ECSTASIES*

Textual Commentary

The first printing in the San Francisco *Dramatic Chronicle* for 13 November 1865 (p. 4) is copy-text. Copy: PH from Bancroft. There are no textual notes.

Emendations of the Copy-Text

495.1   spasms (I-C) • spams

B12. *YE ANCIENT MYSTERY*

Textual Commentary

The first printing in the San Francisco *Dramatic Chronicle* for 16 November 1865 (p. 2) is copy-text. Copy: PH from Bancroft. Mark Twain's quotation from "Daring Hotel Robbery," San Francisco *Alta California*, 14 November 1865 (p. 1) is precise. There are no textual notes.

Emendations of the Copy-Text

497.9   'peculiar' (I-C) • "peculiar"

B13. *AMBIGUOUS*

Textual Commentary

The first printing in the San Francisco *Dramatic Chronicle* for 17 November 1865 (p. 2) is copy-text. Copy: PH from Bancroft. There are no textual notes or emendations.

B14. *IMPROVING*

Textual Commentary

The first printing in the San Francisco *Dramatic Chronicle* for 17 November 1865 (p. 3) is copy-text. Copy: PH from Bancroft. Clemens quotes from "Notes by the Way through Napa Valley," San Francisco *Alta California*, 11 November 1865 (p. 2) (AC). We make one emendation to preserve the otherwise perfect accuracy of his quotation.

Textual Notes

500.8–9   that leader was not half bad] The copy-text omits "not," but the sense of the passage makes it clear that a negative is required. Mark Twain may have written "wasn't," "was not," or he may himself have omitted the negative inadvertently. We have emended in accord with his customary practice.

Emendations of the Copy-Text

499.6   "Charlie's" (I-C) • "Charlies"
499.8   springtide (AC) • spring tide

*500.9   not (I-C) • [*not in*]
500.16   yet. (I-C) • ~∧

B15. *NO VERDICT*

Textual Commentary

The first printing in the San Francisco *Dramatic Chronicle* for 17 November 1865 (p. 3) is copy-text. Copy: PH from Bancroft. There are no textual notes or emendations.

B16. *BAD PRECEDENT*

Textual Commentary

The first printing in the San Francisco *Dramatic Chronicle* for 18 November 1865 (p. 4) is copy-text. Copy: PH from Bancroft. Mark Twain quotes from "Board of Education," San Francisco *Alta California*, 15 November 1865 (p. 1) (AC).

Textual Notes

502.2   Mrs. Stout] The *Alta* actually read "Mrs. C. H. Stout." Although the change might be an error, Mark Twain may have thought the omission improved his joke, and we have therefore not emended.

Emendations of the Copy-Text

502.1   ALTA (I-C) • *Alta*
502.3   Christmas (AC) • Cristmas

B17. *THE GOBLIN AGAIN!*

Textual Commentary

The first printing in the San Francisco *Dramatic Chronicle* for 20 November 1865 (p. 3) is copy-text. Copy: PH from Bancroft. There are no textual notes or emendations.

B18. *THE WHANGDOODLE MOURNETH*

Textual Commentary

The first printing in the San Francisco *Dramatic Chronicle* for 24 November 1865 (p. 3) is copy-text. Copy: PH from Bancroft. There are no textual notes.

Emendations of the Copy-Text

504.22–23 non-committalism (I-C) • non-commitalism

B19. *TOO TERSE*

Textual Commentary

The first printing in the San Francisco *Dramatic Chronicle* for 30 November 1865 (p. 2) is copy-text. Copy: PH from Bancroft. There are no textual notes or emendations.

B20. *SHAME!*

Textual Commentary

The first printing in the San Francisco *Dramatic Chronicle* for 30 November 1865 (p. 2) is copy-text. Copy: PH from Bancroft. There are no textual notes or emendations.

B21. *BRIBERY! CORRUPTION!*

Textual Commentary

The first printing in the San Francisco *Dramatic Chronicle* for 30 November 1865 (p. 2) is copy-text. Copy: PH from Bancroft. There are no textual notes or emendations.

B22. *DRUNK!*

Textual Commentary

The first printing in the San Francisco *Dramatic Chronicle* for 30 November 1865 (p. 3) is copy-text. Copy: PH from Bancroft. There are no textual notes or emendations.

B23. *HOW IS THAT?*

Textual Commentary

The first printing in the San Francisco *Dramatic Chronicle* for 1 December 1865 (p. 2) is copy-text. Copy: PH from Bancroft. Mark Twain quoted from Evans' "Human Remains Found," San Francisco *Alta California,* 30 November 1865 (p. 1), which is reproduced in full in the headnote. Clemens deviated slightly from precise quotation, but since his changes are clearly for comic effect, we have not emended. There are no textual notes.

Emendations of the Copy-Text

509.3   neck" (I-C) • ~∧
509.17   handkerchief (I-C) • handerchief

B24. *DELIGHTFUL ROMANCE*

Textual Commentary

The first printing in the San Francisco *Dramatic Chronicle* for 5 December 1865 (p. 4) is copy-text. Copy: PH from Bancroft. Mark Twain accurately quoted from "Lively Candy," San Francisco *Alta California,* 4 December 1865 (p. 1). There are no textual notes.

Emendations of the Copy-Text

510.5   naughty (I-C) • [ ]aughty

B25. *OUR ACTIVE POLICE*

Textual Commentary

The first printing in the San Francisco *Dramatic Chronicle* for 12 December 1865 (p. 2) is copy-text. Copy: PH from Bancroft. Mark Twain quoted accurately from "Shameful Attack on a Chinaman," San Francisco *Morning Call,* 10 December 1865 (p. 3). In his second quotation he omits the word "had" following "gentlemen"; we have not emended. There are no textual notes.

Emendations of the Copy-Text

511.1   CALL (I-C) • *Call*

B26. *HOW DARE YOU?*

Textual Commentary

The first printing in the San Francisco *Dramatic Chronicle* for 19 December 1865 (p. 4) is copy-text. Copy: PH from Bancroft. There are no textual notes or emendations.

C1. [*EXCURSION TO SACRAMENTO*]

Textual Commentary

The manuscript of this fragment, probably written in 1864 or 1865, survives in the Jean Webster McKinney Family Papers, Vassar. It is copy-text. The fragment is written in brown or black ink on three leaves measuring 9¼ by 7⁷/₁₆ inches. The leaves are numbered consecutively 16 through 18. The stationery is cream-colored laid paper with twenty-three blue horizontal rules, and the pages are embossed with the word "BANCROFT." This paper was used in letters as early as 25 May 1864 and as late as 1868. All three leaves are full, indicating that they are only part of a longer sketch, now lost. There are no textual notes.

Emendations of the Copy-Text

514.25   a (I-C) • [*not in*]

Alterations in the Manuscript

514.2   cheerful] 'h' *written over* 'o'.
514.25   think] *followed by canceled* 'that'.
515.5–7   don't . . . this?] *interlined with a caret.*
515.10   could] *follows canceled* 'understood'.

C2. [LETTER TO THE CALIFORNIAN]

Textual Commentary

The manuscript of this fragment, probably written between June and December 1865, survives in the Jean Webster McKinney Family Papers, Vassar. It is copy-text. The fragment is written in brown or black ink on one leaf measuring 11⅝ by 7¼ inches. The leaf is numbered 1. The stationery is cream-colored laid paper with thirty-two blue horizontal rules, and the page is embossed in the upper left corner with what appears to be a crown. The paper is identical with that used in three other sketches, also at Vassar: "Sarrozay Letter from 'the Unreliable' " (no. 86), "The Only Reliable Account of the Celebrated Jumping Frog of Calaveras County" (no. 117), and "Angel's Camp Constable" (no. 118). All but the first of these was written in late 1865. There are no textual notes or emendations.

Alterations in the Manuscript

516.6   THE CALIFORNIAN] *follows canceled* 'you lack'.
516.11   only] *interlined with a caret.*
516.13   Washington.] *added without a caret.*

WORD DIVISION IN THIS VOLUME

The following compound words that could be rendered either solid or with a hyphen are hyphenated at the end of a line in this volume. For purposes of quotation each is listed here as it appears in the copy-text or, when the copy-text is ambiguous, in the form chosen in the record of emendations.

15.3–4	arm-chair	221.22–23	blue-mass
26.38–27.1	horse-blankets	223.16–17	horse-type
29.12–13	red-hot	223.24–25	centre-piece
30.2–3	sun-rise	226.18–19	evergreen
46.11–12	council-room	227.32–33	time-worn
74.22–23	sunshine	230.25–26	non-fulfillment
75.27–28	sp-(ic!)-splennid	259.34–35	nutshell
84.37–38	to-morrow	261.7–8	midnight
88.24–89.1	vice-royalty	274.2–3	re-sketched
90.5–6	after-dinner	282.15–16	bald-headed
90.29–30	dead-walls	287.10–11	fore-paws
91.22–23	small-pox	287.35–36	front-yard
98.35–36	landlords	288.8–9	good-naturedly
114.21–22	Po-lice	292.8–9	tin-foil
139.1–2	fire-proof	296.2–3	earthquake
140.2–3	ruff-scruff	303.4–5	earthquake
140.10–11	sauer-kraut	303.24–304.1	north-west
155.38–156.1	window-pane	305.10–11	earthquake
166.35–36	steam-cars	306.33–34	earthquake
172.14–15	extempore	317.19–20	old-fashionedest
180.21–22	shingle-nail	319.3–4	side-whiskers
185.39–40	*quarter*less	327.18–19	handsprings
186.19–20	greenbacks	339.2–3	soothsayers
191.4–5	kings-*and*	361.2–3	Steamboat
191.7–8	home-trail	363.27–28	showman
195.2–3	Wat's-'is-name	364.33–34	showman
203.21–22	pile-driver	378.12–13	fair-haired
205.14–15	brasswork	378.15–16	saw-mill
213.12–13	death-bed	378.17–18	gravestones
215.22–23	*gewhilikins*	383.19–20	playwright
216.6–7	Gee-e-e-*whillikins*	383.24–384.1	oversize

395.22–23	policeman	438.16–17	whitewashing
415.2–3	Par-*riss*	455.21–22	scape-goat
415.3–4	Par-riss	460.20–21	Jewhilikens
421.13–14	light-fingered	464.9–10	wherewithal
429.13–14	overbearing	477.6–7	butcher-knife
434.5–6	honely	496.19–20	slung-shotted

INDEX

THE FOLLOWING ITEMS have not been indexed: place names unless the subject of an explanatory note; recipients of letters, when no pertinent statement is made about them; citations and "see" references; fictional characters; the guide to the apparatus and the individual textual commentaries. Works by Mark Twain are listed under their full titles; other works are listed only under their authors' names whenever feasible. The words "this volume" always refer to *Early Tales & Sketches, Volume 2.* When Mark Twain makes a literary allusion without mentioning the author or work, only the identifying explanatory note is indexed; the page-and-line cue of the note will lead to the allusion itself. Daily newspapers are listed under their city of origin, other periodicals under their titles. The abbreviations of book titles used in analyzed entries are explained in the description of texts (pp. 577–581).